The Perfect Shade of Whyte

Never rely on what you think you know, but ...

Proverbs 3:5

The Perfect Shade of Whyte

Although the Middle East is a large part of the story, this book does not claim to be complete of the full complexities of the conflict and should not be understood by the reader to be absolute or authoritative. There should be no judgement taken from this book as to the conduct, politically, militarily, and even personally, of the Jewish people or the Palestinians. In addition, no conjecture or judgement can be made from this story as to any true virtue or impiety of The Salvation Army or its members. In short, this is a Biblical view of the human condition.

This story is in keeping with the eleven **Articles of Faith of The Salvation Army**, but this book does not speak for The Salvation Army. The Salvation Army has not endorsed this book nor is critical of its publication. For information as to the work and beliefs of The Salvation Army, please visit the internet address,

 www.salvationarmy.org

Certain characters in this story are struck with cancer, but this story cannot convey the true enormity of this destructive and devastating disease, not only physically, but also emotionally and quality of life. To learn more of the need for research into the treatment of Brain Cancer, **which can happen at any age**, please refer to

 The Brain Tumour Charity at www.thebraintumourcharity.org,
 The National Brain Appeal at www.nationalbrainappeal.org
 and **Cancer Research UK** at www.cancerresearchuk.org.

Cover design based on Pexel.com

Typeset in Times New Roman

Other books by Neale Hambidge

 A Life Less Real, 2018
 Printed by CreateSpace ISBN 978-1-9164371-0-4

The Author

Neale Hambidge, having gained a degree in electronics from Queen Mary College, London, worked as an engineer testing the software development of the onboard Flight Control Computer System for the European Jet Fighter Plane, Typhoon. Writing as a hobby, he was able to publish his first novel, *The Inorganic,* in 2009.

In 2010, Neale was made redundant and decided to retrain to be now working as a surgical nurse in the NHS at the National Hospital of Neurology and Neurosurgery in London. It was during these years that Neale wrote his second novel, *The Perfect Shade of Whyte.*

In 2017, he rewrote his first book and renamed it *A Life Less Real,* and is now working on two more novels: *Million Miles a Minute,* being a coming-of-age story of two brothers and their motorbikes, with the dangers there are when we pursue our dreams to a reckless level, and *Mastery of Hate,* a crime and horror detective novel that characterises the end-time leader.

He grew up in the Salvation Army and is now happily married to Ilse. They first met in Jerusalem.

Foreword

There are so many romantic novels that I truly cannot compete. As such, I have not attempted. Instead, by adding different dimensions, this fictitious romantic story has many levels and intentions, making it all its own entity. On the surface, it is a story of romance with traces of *Wuthering Heights, Great Expectations, The Thorn Birds* and *An English Patient*; but submerging under you will find an undercurrent of Christian Doctrine, at least by having The Salvation Army as the story's setting. Sinking further in this 'evangelism by stealth,' are the true, complex, hidden drives of each character until reaching the seabed where the mixture of passions, fears, angers, indignations, motivations and ambitions are influenced by the explicit and subliminal logic they wish to believe; the embodiment of which reflecting in their actions and words at the water's calm or stormy surface.

There are two distinct reasons for the chosen title. When Henry Morton Stanley wrote *In Deepest Africa* in 1890, his writing spurred William Booth, Founder and first General of The Salvation Army, to choose the title of *In Deepest England and the Way Out* to publish his aspirations for the improvement of the destitute of England. As such, I am shameless in admitting that the title for my book has come as a derivative of *Fifty Shades of Grey,* being an antonym, so to speak. My original title was only to be '*The Perfect*' with the term used as a noun and not an adjective, and solely directed at a story theme of what we deem as perfect, the search for perfection, the perfect career, partner, life, and who God would deem as perfect. However, as writing continued, this theme became more and more dissolved with other aspects. In addition, having been influenced by John Bunyan's *The Pilgrim's Progress,* I created the main character to have the name 'Whyte', portraying purity and having a pondering nature with the hidden question. When *Fifty Shades of Grey* appeared in 2011 and knowing of *In Deepest England and the Way Out*, it became ideal to change the title to *The Perfect Shade of Whyte*, a singular perfect colour and written as though at the other end of the spectrum.

With an attempt to be alluringly evangelical without being fearful, forceful or disrespectful, an underlying aim of my writing is to spread the Christian faith to someone wondering about Christianity and to encourage any Christian in their faith. As such, my story is inspired by many of the books of the Bible, both Old and New Testament, and my subtle and overt intention is to artistically, rationally and imaginatively point to them. There is a mosaic of embedded Biblical stories, sayings and verses, and if you know of these accounts, then my writing will be amplified. However, my ultimate aim is to show the Bible as being credible, rational, inspirational and worthy of serious study for anyone who is hesitant.

That said, my story is also for anyone without a Biblical disposition. You may even have your own belief, as you do not need to agree with what each character says or does, but I hope it can be understood why they did what they did and thought what they thought, if anything, due only to psychology.

In terms of sociology, and the lack of unarguable proof in all things to an absolute unarguable standard, it should be legitimate to believe in what you wish, because ultimately you cannot be proven wrong, even if it is invisible fairies at the end of the garden. Whether it is reasonable to believe in such things or not is a different matter, but with no absolute proof, you are to have freedom to believe in what you deem reasonable, including the freedom to think other people are foolish. However, all things equal, people are to be free to believe in what they deem reasonable, including the freedom to think you are foolish. Again, with all these things equal, people are to be tolerant and live with kind consideration for each other, which follows the Law of Moses of respecting and loving others that all Abrahamic religions and any civil society should be upholding. In fact, anyone who has thoughtfully, intelligently, earnestly come to their beliefs through ardent searching, without having been indoctrinated by others, has lived far more than any adventurer who has been contained to the limits of this planet and is far greater than any eminent leader who has strayed from the principles and honour of serving others.

Character names in this book, being David, Esther, Jezebel, Jonathan and Haman, have been deliberately chosen to provide a link and metaphorical comparison to their Biblical namesake, although an absolute comparison must never be made. God is also a character in this book through Esther's dreams, which she writes about in her reflective writing. I have tried to ensure His persona is Biblically representative, as condensed as this is, but you must make your own verdict from the Bible itself. These 'visions' that Esther has should not in any way be viewed as anything but portraying Christian Doctrine at their centre and not adding anything detailed or new. The Bible's essence is to depict God's absolute care and sovereignty over all that He has created and I have not changed this message. Even though there is an element of 'the end times', this is not a detailed description of Biblical apocalyptic prophecy, but a way of presenting it as plausible and to elicit its warning, particularly when its fulfilment can happen within our generation.

If sounding virtuous, I do not wish you to believe this book includes no slander, assassination, terrorism or seduction. As scandalous as this may be for a book regarding itself as moral and Christian, these aspects are integral with the reason becoming clear as the story unfolds. With that, I hope my writing has achieved an intelligent, tactful standard and a means to elicit emotions to be a measure of your own character and judgement, even if this includes indifference.

Although attempting to explain some Christian Logic and give Christianity some credibility, I have dug underneath this logic to portray people with hidden agendas and secret motives, regardless to religious or antireligious beliefs, and to question what truly motivates someone to believe or not. Does a male want to believe because of the hope of gaining affection from an attractive female across the congregation? Does a female from a painful childhood believe solely for the emotional support? Do people believe because they want a formal belief in a personal Genie, use it like a magic charm? Do they use it as a subliminal means of perceiving to have the right to enter Heaven but behaving selfishly how they wish? Do people believe their religion because, knowingly or unknowingly, it makes them feel right and empowers them to gain a perceived self-righteousness by which to down-grade others and administer control and manipulation? Does the Atheist have indignation to believe in God because of arrogance to submit that runs counter to the way they want to live, or have fear of giving control to something unknowable? Is it legitimate to rebel against God when seeing so much suffering and evil in the world? Does God understand any of these faults and weaknesses? Can God use any of this for His glory?

People can find the logic they want to support their beliefs when there are deeper intentions, hidden motivations and secret wanting. Logical as Logic is, it is not always fact or truth. Logic can be redefined, manipulated or rationalised within our whims, desires and mind-games and still be viewed as logic, particularly when absolute proof in anything is never attainable. But that's psychology for you.

Not wanting myself to be judgemental, an open question is what would be my thinking and feeling if I were to have been born a Palestinian or an Israeli? How much of my mindset is conditioned by circumstances, history, the news, technology, science, religion, the society or era in which I am immersed? What would be my beliefs and character if I were to be suffering from cancer or employed in the justice system or be homeless or live in slavery? What would I believe or do if a mighty leader were to arise claiming to know all the right actions needed to create a better world that, under social conditioning, would pressure me to adjust my moral compass to conform?

This book is about each of us thinking we are perfect and deserving, or deeming we are worthy, above others, that we are always right and everyone else is wrong. As a consequence, this book is about judgement. It provokes judgment. Who is it who thinks they have the right to say what is perfect and what is punishable, and impose this on others? Who is it who thinks they can rule with absolute righteous sovereignty? Who is it that can put our judgement to shame? Who is it that has the highest judgement of all?

Intelligence and dexterity are needed by a surgeon to perform an operation, but most of all is boldness with modesty. It is this caring, modest boldness that I look for and respect, and wish one day to mirror in my Christian living. I write from my humble nature as someone searching for solid rock on which to build my life, so that when adversity comes in whatever form it will be, I can withstand the storm if God is at the helm.

I am slowly learning to have a faith of vulnerability in order to trust God, a bold faith to let go of the fear of what God could ask, and to have an intelligent faith in hope that He will enjoy sharing with me the time I have been given. In effect, this is my personal testimony to my faith in Jesus and a mirror reflection back at me as to how poorly I measure against God's standards on my own terms. In truth, I am continuously, consciously decoding life using the natural, organic circuitry within my own cranium, and I cannot find any hope of a solution unless Jesus is seriously considered the key. I believe that even though our Heavenly Father, at His infinite end, is so unknowable, He still makes Himself known to those who are searching with the right mindset.

It is my pondering on Christian Doctrine and applying it to difficult aspects of life, to ensure I understand my faith and to deepen it, my desire to write, and my scientific inspection of life and people, that has brought about the creation of *The Perfect Shade of Whyte*.   (1 Peter 3:15)

Acknowledgements

I am indebted to my parents and The Salvation Army of Gillingham Corps who accepted me from birth to be part of their family and where I learnt of God's standards, spurring me to ponder the meaning of this place where we breathe. From my youth to the age I am now, I am so extensively privileged to have had so many people, older and younger, past and present, to look up to; people who have built the person I am, as by their unknowing leadership.

This book is dedicated to my loving wife, Ilse.
I am fortunate to have married her.
Please forgive me for the many long years I spent writing.
Just be grateful you didn't marry Noah.

Elke dag bring die moontlikheid van 'n wonderwerk.

Contents

'Christians are not distinguished from others by country or language. They live in accordance and in such places as determined by their own circumstances and endeavours, following the customs of the natives in respect to clothing, food and of their ordinary culture, but within which displaying their deeper method of life. They dwell in their own countries simply as sojourners. As citizens, they share in all things with others and yet endure all things as foreigners. Every foreign land is to them as their native country and any land of their birth they inhabit as strangers. They pass their days on earth, but they are citizens of Heaven. They obey the prescribed laws of the country, but synonymously surpass these laws by their spiritual lives.'
Epistle to Diognetus

'Not pondering life, is a life not worth living.'
Socrates

Prelude : Influence the Future

Dying with Faith

My doctor encouraged me to write my feelings. I have been doing so since I arrived here at Halcyon. Find somewhere quiet and write, were his words. Now I have found myself alone and quiet, writing, even though I'm not really a writer. When I first started, feeling like it was long ago, I was despondent. I was anguished. My first page was full of misery and despair and shame. Everything was of the worthlessness and futility of life. You see, with my arrogance, I have destroyed all hope of peace in the Middle East and my family has been mercilessly killed. Reporters everywhere are relentlessly hunting me for entertainment in my plight and if all that is not enough, I have learnt of my terminal cancer. So much has been beaten from me. It was easier to be defeated against this mighty callousness and I did not want to continue living, except for the reason of David.

David, having kindly allowed me to stay here at Halcyon Manor, had left me not knowing of my illness. He left me alone with my jealousy for an attractive American actress who I thought would take him away, just at the time when I needed him for support, reconciliation, comfort and companionship. My guilt and love were crushing me. I was angry that I became foolish in having dreams for the future with him, knowing all along it would never be allowed.

But writing my feelings and thoughts, looking back over my life, pondering, even in pain and weakness, I am now confident of seeing life in context; not as a 'positive-thinking' mantra or an attitude that God is here to do my bidding, to solve life according to my will, but as one finely attuned to life, contrary to the dying I am doing. I am the dust and clay.

I feel old, yet I am young. My joints are fusing, my bones are cracking, my mouth is dry and my mind has fading memories and experiencing strange visions. I am weak. It is as much to lift this pen, than it is to write with weary thoughts. Each breath of mine becomes more laboured and more exhausting to take, and although my mind is consoled, my body is awash with fiery molten pain. I am fading, drifting, slowly shutting down, yet somehow my spirit is peacefully at rest and unharmed. I am dying, yet I am strangely at peace, somehow detached from my body, lying here on this bed. I already feel like my own ghost, haunting Halcyon Manor.

I drift in and out of sleep having had many vivid dreams that I thought was part of my medication: strange dreams, condemning dreams, uplifting dreams, each one driven by my feelings, my thoughts, my reading of the Bible. I had the same dream again last night, the one of the bright, abundant garden. Again, I was hiding within dark bushes and behind thick branches, ashamed for the many things I had done. I did not want to be found because of my wickedness, but beyond my poor refuge was the owner of this glorious garden, searching for me, yet He knew where I cowered. I became convinced that the brightness was not coming from the sky. It was coming from this redeemer. Then He called me by my name in a quality that soothed away my fears, and I crept from my hiding place, no longer afraid of being naked. I grasped His outstretched hand and He clothed me, and took me to a great mansion. My eyes were full of tears because who am I for Him to make a way back into His presence? From my darkness, He became my light. I am to respectfully, contently, peacefully enjoy His world and not fear it, because He has promised to be with me, to be with us. He created this world for us to enjoy, for us to rely on Him. But what have we done?

I can vouch for how undignified it is to be dying like this, and although I started writing with despondency all those months ago, I hope you, my new and unknown friend, understand why I am now so uplifted. I am being broken, but with it being renewed, remoulded, rebuilt with God leading me. I have never felt so much loving acceptance for one so lost.

You see, it is commonly said that you are born with nothing and you die with nothing. I believe that is so wrong, for I say, you are born with potential and you die with character. There is no other currency. Our character is the only thing we will ever own and even that is tentative. You learn who you are when you are desolate and drowning in despair, but so too do you give an account of what you stand for when you are at the top of success. I have learnt what I truly am: a mere woman who has experienced the sheer sovereignty of God's mighty authorship.

My pen is becoming worn, my hand is losing its feel, and I am rambling with a rambling mind. The colours I see are fading, time is fading, I am fading. Death is not dignifying, yet I am being drawn to it like a river now entering a magnificent ocean. I am longing to go home, to the mansion He has prepared. Who or what can now separate me from my loving, sovereign, heavenly Father. I pray that you come to know God, Abraham's God, and one day I will meet with you there. Even when you are at the last ounce of your faith, too weak to continue, God will remain faithful. He is not afraid to love you.

I look to the clouds. The light through the window is blindingly bright. It is as

And that became the last words that were written. The writer had stopped writing, and the reader had stopped reading, placing this last page back with the multitude of others.

The reader, a lone man of a retirement age but wearing a policeman's uniform, was sitting like a recluse in a quiet, secluded alcove of an arch within an old wall of an enchanting wild garden. He sat on a stone bench under a thatch-work of over-growing willow branches that maintained a natural roof, providing a means to prevent the recess from having become saturated by the earlier downpour. Fresh clean rainwater now dripped in the brightening day, beneath a sky that had been densely clouded and now making provision for a shining sun.

Then the quietness was broken by a call from afar from a younger male trying to find him: "Sarge?"

The entire estate garden was a vast mesh of interlacing gardens made from ruined, old mossy-green walls, choked in ivy, and deluged with bushes, trees and flowers. For decades, it had been unused, unknown and unkempt for the unmanaged manner of nature.

"Sergeant Richards!"

Grasses and flowers, herbs and hardy annuals grew abundantly, growing in a manner that showed coherence and harmony, as to say there was no need for a self-proclaimed gardener. Nature itself tailored the grounds far better than any conscious human thought or action.

"Hey! Sarge! Where are you? – Sarge? You here? – Oh, come on! – Hey! I'm going in five minutes! Five minutes! Hear me?"

The old man smiled contently to himself with being invisible.

"Sarge? There'll be trouble for you old man! Last day of yours an' all!"

Knowing he had been quiet long enough, he called out to his younger colleague: "Alright, I'm here!"

"That's not funny! The joke's supposed to be on you!" There then came the sound of splashing water and a few expletives given to the hidden pond that had tripped its prey. When a younger man appeared, the trousers to his police uniform were wet but he looked to be both relieved and annoyed with his older partner. "Why you hiding? What you doing?"

Quite relaxed and content, the amused older man, still sitting, looked up: "Hello my young constable Parker."

"Why you so cheerful? What you doing? You're in serious trouble."

"I'm reading. You should do it sometime."

Parker looked down at the large pile of paper on the Sergeant's lap, refusing to believe what he was seeing. "You're not bloody reading her suicide note, are ya? You know how forensics are! How many times have you had a go at me?"

"I think this time, it's different."

"Why should the law be different in her case?"

Richards stood up and came out into the open: "Trust my judgement. I need to make a decision about a particular page."

"What! I'm supposed to be getting you to the station for your farewell bloody retirement speeches."

"I think there's a lot at stake here. I'm worried that when this gets out, the media will cause a lot of damage."

"What damage? Her reputation? You can't get rid of evidence! You're a policeman! I can't believe this after all the things you've had a go at me about."

"It's my last day," replied the Sergeant, turning to make his way through the gardens. "What can they do?"

Parker was then following, still tense and argumentative with his superior: "You're not above the law!"

"Laws are there to do right, but what about when doing right means that these laws should be broken? Doesn't the law have a spirit? Some people legally bend the spirit of the law for their own gain, even though technically the law isn't broken. Well I want to do what is right in spite of the law."

"Is this your dementia talking?"

The Sergeant stopped, halting his junior, and looked up at the old abandoned manor house before him. Not addressing Parker and having other thoughts in mind, he said, "I think the reason this all happened starts in Africa, many, many years ago."

"Sarge, look, we need to sort out what happened to her."

"No, sit for a moment and at least peruse some of her writing."

"But Sarge, we don't have time."

"Just oblige me." The Sergeant proffered the main batch of pages to his younger partner, who took them bewildered. Taking a single page with him, he turned to leave.

"Where you going?"

"Just to wander and make that decision."

"What decision?"

"About this page I have. You just sit somewhere. I'll be back with my decision. Just read a bit. Start from the beginning."

Only God's Kingdom can Conquer

I am Esther Whyte and I have cancer.

There! I've now written it! What it is to see the word in my own hand on the paper. Through life's strange events, even though I know the Press is searching for me, I have now found myself a place that's remote, quiet, secret and restful, and using this solitude to write, just as the doctor ordered. But now, what else should start my writing? Every aspect of my life is disintegrating, weighing down on my thoughts and lungs. I have so much dejection, so much sadness, anguish, torment, that I don't know what to do with it. My heart, so broken, is now unknown to me.

And just when I need his complete support, David is going to America in the morning, visiting that Jezebel, the beautiful American film star and singer, who, I am certain, became famous from a pornographic past. I'm dreading his departure from me. I'm fearful of what may happen. I'm tempted to 'will' him to not go at all by the might of my own thoughts and hopes.

There is also my anguish with my arrogance, my arrogant attempt to bring peace to the Middle East. I am in horror as to what my words have caused. I wish for God to drop me down a deep, dark well and leave me there. What did I think I was doing? God's will, that was what I thought I was doing, but my actions have brought forward the final era of persecution, an eruption of world conflict, the time of the end. Please tell me I am exaggerating! I spoke like Job's friends, Eliphaz, Bildad, Zophar and Elihu, all of them heaped into one, preaching what I thought was God's mind. Now the roles have reversed, as they are now Eliphaz, Bildad, Zophar and Elihu, and I am Job, full of cancer!

I read the Psalms in the Bible and they are full of true feelings being poured out to God. I cry out to God my own true feelings of desolation, of how distraught I am, my anger for my condition, my suffering, my guilt for the death of my cherished family. My inner core has frozen over in shock. I no longer know what I feel, or even know what to feel.

Death is a morbid affair. It can strike at any time, at any one of us, good or bad, strong or weak, young or old. People walk down the street to shop and are shot by a madman seeking revenge on anyone, yet earlier that day everything had been normal. We feel so secure in what we think we know. One day they will cure cancer, but what then? What will be the next disease to cure? And then what? Are we to have faith that one day we will invent a cure for death itself? Are we that arrogant to believe we can win against death in our own efforts? There are people who think they can harm others, cause their demise, steal from their neighbours and feel it is their right to attack a civil society, but a society can hide behind its own bent rules that discriminate, that casts judgement, that can induce indoctrination. Human arrogance has shaped history and it sets the future. Each event being a part of the whole picture, like a mountain, a valley, all forming a map of time to view and decode what is to come.

The arrogant privileged have always protected themselves against the unprivileged, to keep the unprivileged – unprivileged. By way of wealth and class and social barriers, with laws and politics and manipulation, with segregation and repression and oppression, enforced resettlement and ethnic cleansing, massacres and genocide, people in power work hard to maintain power, until an uprising occurs, and a new set of privileged work hard to protect themselves against a new set of unprivileged. Eleven billion people are set to inhabit this planet by the end of the century: how will the world be? Even by my arrogance, I might have cut short history to start the time of the end. Who can now withhold or withstand what is to come?

A titanic ship, the largest that had been built, took to the seas in 1912 with all on board having the belief that it was majestically above the dangers of life; but their ill-founded faith was taken from them when the arrogant monstrosity sunk to the underworld in a horrendous, hideous laugh at man's claims. Did they die because they deserved to die? Was it because they sinned?

It got worse — 1914. A war was conjured from the fragile strands of political distrust, and invaded many nations. It was said to be the war to end all wars and it deceived everyone. Conflict now had a new nature: that men now fought with machines of immense metal and deathful power. When the futile war ended, society reeled at the discovery that the fight had had no honour and the true total of the many lost were affront to their way of a quiet life. The Many had been taken and made to live their last years in mud and filth, in dangerous, laboured, trenches, with provisions worse than prisoners, all for the waiting of orders to rush against the spite of guns and bullets that cut them down, tore into their limbs and left them for dead, discarded, worse than an animal. But the people still believed the final war had been fought, that nothing more dreadful could be invented and engineered for the furtherance of killing; that there was no longer the political will to fight again.

In a time less than that of forgetting, another war came: a global war. A war that erupted with insurmountable hatred, with more lethal armaments, a war that circumnavigated the world, where nation fought with nation and country fought with country. The armoury became more immense and more powerful and more accurate. The fighting became more desperate and more consuming, and each country was more destroyed than ever before. At the culmination, Man was the owner of knowledge to obliterate entire provinces with enormous energy and fire and brimstone, that millions can be seared to oblivion in a time less than a conscious thought. The war taught that even evil limits can always be furthered when given to those in power, to dispose of entire populations due only to their ancestry and up-bringing, to attempt the complete annihilation of a race due purely to ethnic origin. In the air of victory and the wash of relief through the survivors, it was hoped that no more depths of war was possible, that no more war was needed; but they were wrong.

There then came about a new war: a cold, invisible war, set against the new empires that arose from the ashes of the previous global conflict. The unquenchable quest of each empire to ensure mastery over the other escalated the need to develop and increase yet more inimical weaponry. Driven by the emotion of fear and with the intellect of suspicion, the empires manipulated smaller nations and fought each other in foreign lands. They strove to reach the moon before the other, driven by the fear of losing technical supremacy and under the leadership of influential men. Man created the age of technology and they worshipped this new god.

There are now wars and rumours of wars. Earthquakes abound, epidemics increase, and many mighty wars blight our world as never before: all signs of the era of sorrow to come and I am blessed that my life is cut short, never to experience the Horrors. God is patiently allowing us the freedom to administrate and govern ourselves, expecting fairness and compassion that are essential for the human race to become successful. But what chaos are we truly creating? What view of us must God have from His position? What would we see of our mindless administration if, beside Him, see what He sees of us, our history, our achievements? Read the Bible and see the news, stand back and know! Only God's Kingdom can conquer what we have done. Only God can wipe out evil. He even has the power to turn evil around and use it for His Kingdom, as He will do in the last days.

We might feel we have a right to be angry at God, but God has the right to be furious at us. Look around as you walk and know that we are on some stay of judgement, the calm before the storm. He will step in and take full command only when it has reached its worst and will eradicate all evil and suffering. He will do so because of His sheer enthusiasm for His creation and His love for those who see Him.

It is written that this commission, this governance, stewardship, the administration of this world, was commanded of us in the Garden of Eden, but 'they' say it all started in Africa. My story starts in Africa by the death of my heroine, Captain Evalynne Lovert, decades before me. Even now, thinking of her, my heart has started to tune in to the golden hope of God's goodness to come and of His final victory.

I remember Africa.

Come by here, Lord

Within an African forest, encased within miles of trees, was an empty road of orange and red dirt. One particular junction, turning onto a track of dirt, had by way of a humble wooden sign, a direction to a place called Kombaiar. Following this track with a river nearby, led to a homely settlement that had the traveller arriving at an open area where numerous vehicles could park and then welcomed by a large, central forecourt that was serving numerous buildings.

Many of the buildings, aligned in rows, were long wooden huts that stood upon a multitude of thick, solid stilts above the bare, dry ground, with stairways allowing access to a veranda balcony surrounding each dwelling. Most catered for many beds, with one structure, full of desks, being a school.

The first wooden building to the forecourt had a large wooden cross on its roof, and above the main door was a board with 'The Salvation Army' neatly painted. This door was kept wide open showing the wooden pews of the meeting hall within, with a small platform, lectern and a piano at the furthest end. Aligning the back wall were some Salvation Army flags, and to the side were a few unattended brass instruments and music stands, and songbooks stacked neatly in their shelves were at the front. It was to the front of this building in the forecourt that a tall pole held up, high above everything, a flag of blue and red with a central star of yellow.

One prominent, large building, being the hospital by way of the Red Cross painted on the front wall, was made of sturdier cement and blocks, and high enough to have a wide and open front porch entrance that was reached by ascending a few concrete steps.

In a wild, excited game, the forecourt teemed with eager children, all black-skinned, all of differing ages, all focused on a ball that showed signs of having been kicked far longer than it had been designed to achieve. They laughed and tackled and ran around as if Heaven was a simple football pitch.

It was watched by a white man, a forty-eight-year-old, standing on the veranda to the hospital building. He was too tired to laugh, but took in the happiness of the children and then turned to enter the hospital.

As bright as it was outside, the light in the ward was dulled by the limited number of windows and the air seemed to be in battle between a sick, ill smell and a sweet fragrance pervading from numerous dried plants that had been hung in certain places. The wooden beds, all of a battered standard, were in neat rows with children resting in a poor state. Some looked up to view the man with differing measures of interest, but most did not have the energy. There was not one bed vacant. Two female nurses, one of which was a young native, the other was white of a similar age to his own, did not stop in their caring of the children. The man quietly and slowly approached the white woman and stood by her as she nursed a severely ill young girl.

"She's still serious," the nurse told him, "but I think she'll pull through."

He sighed, partially from tiredness, but mostly from suffering his own compassion for the child. "Perhaps we're getting too old for this."

She wore a long, white dress, dirty and creased, with an apron showing a few splattered drops of blood. Her blonde hair was unkempt and initially she looked drained and weary. As soon as she turned to him, her whole appearance was transformed into a beautiful woman with a glorious, lovely smile and hair of gold. "Captain Lovert – Captain Joseph Lovert, I just know that tomorrow you'll be too absorbed again."

He did not change in his demeanour.

After a moment of looking into his eyes, she embraced him tightly.

As if breathing into her neck and hair, he whispered to her endearingly, "Oh Evalynne, you always know what to say."

"This girl would have died without your surgery." She smiled at him and that engendered a smile in return. "Go and get some rest."

Joseph nodded, but instead walked the length of the ward to the few rooms towards the end, entering one of them.

This room to the back had a very small window and prevented even less light than the main ward. Above the uncomfortable, wooden bench, which provided the means to support the patient, was a small light that construed to be the operating lamp, and to the side was a metal trolley that had on top certain small operating tools. Covering the trolley and many of the tools, was blood in differing colours from dark rouge to bright crimson.

Joseph started to clean.

The sun descended for an orange sunset. Everyone helped settle the children for sleep, and Kombaiar became quiet and dark. Only in the church hall was there any light from a few candles.

Kneeling and praying within this light, at a long wooden seat before the platform was Evalynne. In silence, Joseph crept into the room, knelt beside her and joined his wife in prayer. Half an hour later, they looked at each other.

"I can't perform any more operations," said Joseph, "until we have another proper air-delivery."

"We need to go to Amani tomorrow for a few things anyway, so I can arrange the next drop while we're there." Evalynne studied her husband and then said softly, "I'm proud to be your wife."

"Thank you," Joseph said, appreciatively. "And I've been praying that God does not correct you in the error of your ways."

Evalynne shook her head amused. "Silly," she replied simply.

"But wherever we are, that's our home – even if it's Heaven."

Tower of Siloam

On the forest road to the nearby town of Amani, with the sunshine of the next morning, was a procession of one lorry and two trucks. The lorry was large and green, and black smoke followed from the exhaust. It was completely dirty and deeply scratched, with certain parts having been scorched and some of the glass being cracked. The ill-maintained engine continued regardless, although on an un-healthy level. Covering the entire back like a tent was a sheet that was coloured in forest camouflage, and within, having a ride, was a large group of rowdy black men, smoking and laughing and drinking, and amused at the appalling jokes and stories they told each other. Be it a knife or pistol or rifle or even a machine gun, most of the men had a collection of weapons within an arm's reach. In convoy, the lorry followed the two trucks, both of the same level of maintenance, also carrying males, equally equipped, equally boisterous.

Not all of them were men. Almost half the group were children, some as young as seven, and two of them, at the back of the lorry, were being cajoled to take shots at designated targets in the surrounding jungle. Neither of the boys achieved hitting anything that was pointed at and they became the focus of ridicule, unable to retaliate.

Then the lorry passed a large stationary cart to the side of the road. A man stepped from the trees to watch them pass and, as pointed at by a soldier, became the next target. In anger of having been disgraced, both boys, determined to regain their honour, raised their rifles and fired.

The man lurched back and fell to the ground.

As the cart became smaller, they were all able to see a young boy run from the trees to the fallen man, crying and shouting. Both boys, now having their confidence return, took aim and fired again, but they were now too far away to know if they had struck the grieving child.

Little was known in Amani about what was coming. Ignorant of the danger, people continued in their humble trading and chores with everyone having awoken to an ordinary day. Joseph and Evalynne knew no better.

"Where have you been?" asked Evalynne, sitting on a large fallen tree log to the side of a busy market, guarding her shopping as Joseph approached. "Why that cheeky grin?" she added with her suspicion.

"Got everything?" Joseph, carrying a few boxes of produce and looking mischievous, motioned to leave with the nod of his head. Without a reply and expecting his wife to follow, he entered the busy market area again.

Evalynne caught up with her husband and, seeing his pleasant, knowing smirk, said, "I know that look. What is it you're after?"

"Nothing," he replied.

Reaching the other side, they left the market and followed a few quiet dirt streets to arrive at their jeep that was kept cool under a canopy of branches from the surrounding trees. The Land Rover series II had been white many years ago, but it was now battered, rickety, scratched and dirty, almost to the point where the words, 'The Salvation Army,' written as an emblem on each door could not be read. He opened the back and they offloaded their shopping.

"Well whatever it is," eventually said Evalynne, "we have everything now, so let's get back, I'm tired."

"Not quite."

"Oh? What have we forgotten?"

"We have another chore to do."

"What? Now?"

"Come on, come with me."

Joseph locked their vehicle and jovially motioned to follow him.

To Evalynne's surprise, she found herself eventually standing on a wooden porch that stretched the long length of a two-storey concrete building catering for many shops selling merchandise of all descriptions. They stood on the wooden walkway, off the dirt street, outside one particular shop front that displayed a multitude of rolls of fabric.

"I know you've wanted to make that dress for ages," he said, "so let's finally buy that material and get on with it."

Surprise and delight spread over Evalynne from such a single request. "Where did you get the money?"

"I sold some of my wood carvings and things I made. That's what I went off to do."

Evalynne embraced her husband in a manner that she could not have married anyone better. "You are a *good* man, Captain Lovert."

"Well let's not get carried away, it's only a few wooden things for a few lengths of textile."

"Yes, but I know how long it takes you to make something."

"Am I that bad a carpenter?"

They were almost laughing and playful as schoolchildren.

Then everything changed. A boy, breathless and wheezing, suddenly appeared along the road. He was exhausted and tearful. He tried to shout, but all he could do was gasp in mouthfuls of air. A man nearby spoke to him, and in a hurried conversation, the man instantly looked terrified and started shouting at everyone.

Everyone stopped and threw down their tools, and in an instant, the whole area became infected with despair. Some started to run in any direction, criss-crossing each other; some just stood stupefied with wide eyes; others dashed inside the nearest building that looked safe enough, avoiding the wooden shacks.

The English couple, alien to this reaction and still in the remains of their youthful embrace, watched spellbound from their wooden porch at the panic around them.

"What is this?" Evalynne asked with confusion.

"I don't know."

Not venturing far, they both approached an old woman who could not run and Evalynne spoke to her in the limited knowledge of the language, becoming more confused.

"Well?" asked Joseph.

"It doesn't make sense. Something called Godamna is coming here."

"What is that?"

"No idea but it's dangerous."

They heard the noise of vehicles approaching from afar, and turning the corner onto their road were two trucks and a lorry in the distance. They stopped hastily, and men and children jumped from them to start shooting people as quickly as their arrival. One moment of peace became a surreal place of terror: so fast, it was incomprehensible it was happening as people now lay on the streets losing precious blood.

Joseph, with help from Evalynne, almost picked up the old woman and they rushed into the nearest shop in the concrete building. The old woman whimpered and held onto Evalynne, talking to her with fearful gulps of air from her weak lungs.

"I know, I know, please hush, please hush," consoled Evalynne, forgetting that the woman had no comprehension of what she was saying.

They were alone in the dark front room, with only one window to the main street and a back door to rooms behind. Being another clothing shop, cloths and materials were around them in racks and tables, ready to be sold to customers.

Nearby, people screamed and begged for their lives. Gunshots and laughing would not stop, and screams were cut short.

A blaze of desultory gunfire battered their building and the walls became pitted by vicious holes. Joseph looked at Evalynne and pointed at the door behind them: "What's through the back?"

Crouching, Evalynne went to look and found a larger room with desks of sewing machines and shelves for storing material. A space for a small sleeping area was just to her side and in the far wall was a closed, wooden door that appeared to lead out onto the back street. At the far side was a dirty stairway to the above floor. She turned to answer, but could not speak when seeing how terrified the old woman, cowering next to her husband, had become.

After a few moments, the gunshots receded and sounded to move away, giving Joseph a modicum of courage to see what was happening outside.

"What is out there?" whispered Evalynne.

"Ssshhhhh!"

The soldiers were entering buildings, smashing things and grabbing what they thought worthy, bringing out their captured goods along with continuing to shoot anyone they found. Being dragged into the streets, bloodied victims pleaded for their lives with their terrified efforts being futile. Joseph, from the dark of his position, watched the horror, shocked that some soldiers were children who looked too young to hold the long cumbersome rifle they each carried and the pistols being large in their hands.

Joseph felt the old woman move. She too looked out with the same discreet manner, but her concentration was on a large, muscular, black man, wearing army fatigues and a black beret. He smoked a cigar and just stood in the middle of the road, performing his own vigil on the event. He held his rifle with the aim to the sky, and seemed to be both an entertained spectator and supervisory instigator.

"Godamna," she whispered.

Joseph looked at her confused, until she pointed to the man she watched.

"Godamna," she repeated.

Seeing a group of men who were coming nearer, intent on setting buildings alight, Joseph grabbed the woman and hauled her away from the window towards Evalynne, and saw the sudden look of fright in his wife's face. From behind his back, from the open front entrance, came the sound of guns being loaded. He turned and three angry children, alone and shouting, pushed them all aggressively into the workshop. In the commotion, Joseph tried to prevent the elderly woman from falling and being trampled underfoot, and was just able to let her fall onto a nearby rickety bed. With their bullying ways, the children were then separating them from her.

Both Evalynne and Joseph moved away, their hands in the air, as all three children, not seeing the older woman as much of a threat, held their aim on the two. They both stood, waiting to be shot as the children became quiet, overcome by a fierce, intense concentration of anger.

Then one of the children, without losing his aim, looked puzzled. His attitude became the attention of the other two and all three started to discuss something in a furious way. They spoke to question and answer each other, but one of them shouted out: "Kombaiar!" He shouted it a few times and turned to his neighbour, whom motioned him to leave, his footsteps becoming fainter with his departure.

Joseph and Evalynne remained standing, trying to be as calm as possible, their hearts pounding, staring at the children and guns. They waited as if on some stay of execution. The old woman, groaning from an ache, was ignored by everyone.

The sound of children wildly talking came to the front door of the shop, but their chatter stopped with the sudden series of heavy footsteps. Then entered Godamna. The look of terror spread over the old woman and she appeared to beg for something in her dread.

As if annoyed of her, Godamna took hold of his handgun and shot her dead, and all her pleading and anguish ceased as her blood gushed from her penetrated cranium. Her death had no visible affect on her murderer, who, without any more concern, turned to the two that remained alive and standing. With a cigar in his mouth, his stone-hard face was as unreadable as a book with blank pages. Only his pose could tell of his confident, arrogant attitude as he stood akimbo having returned his gun to its holster like a glamorous American cowboy.

The children were now quiet and waited for orders, never having removed their aim.

One child pointed at both Joseph and Evalynne and said again, "Kombaiar!"

Godamna suddenly looked pleased and started to nod at something that had not been uttered, taking the cigar from his mouth. "Salvation Army!" he eventually exclaimed very proudly as if to congratulate them in their way of life. "You two – you two – soldiers! Soldiers of God!" He then laughed and chuckled, turning into a hideous cackle and humiliating snigger. He started to walk about the room, looking around for something, and turned back to his captives: "You fight for God! Where is he?" He paused to allow their answer, but neither spoke. "Where is your God?" he continued. "I see him not! He is not – anywhere! You fight for nothing! Nothing! Soldiers, he will not protect you. He is not loyal to you." The evil man stared at Evalynne for a moment as if to weigh up how much pleasure he would get from her with the visions he allowed through his mind, and turned to Joseph to view him with distaste. Taking the cigar out of his mouth again and using it as an aid to address the two, he asked a question that appeared he had seriously been wondering about for a long while: "Blood and fire – . You have motto: blood and fire. What is meaning of this?"

Neither Joseph nor Evalynne had the courage to answer.

As if indignant of not receiving a reply, Godamna grew angry. "We have blood!" he shouted, pointing at the dead woman and the blood that had covered the wall and bed, "and here – is fire!" With a match, he set light to a small piece of cloth, allowed it to take hold and threw it into the room. "Blood and Fire! Blood and Fire! Hell for you!"

Godamna then left, angrily, giving commands to the children who obediently started wreaking both front and back rooms, setting light to more fabric as they disappeared.

Joseph and Evalynne ran to the closed back wooden door and opened it to find iron bars of a security gate that was locked shut and preventing their freedom to the deserted street.

"Help!" cried Evalynne through the grill, but Joseph grabbed her and pulled her away, closing her mouth.

"Sssshhhhh! There might be more! They might hear you!"

The room was becoming a blaze. They did not have long before the air became super-heated and the fragile ceiling to collapse.

Joseph grabbed the bars and shook the gate: it was held by what appeared to be weak bricks and mortar. He shook the bars again, feeling a chance of breaking the joints free from the wall, but the gate did not relent. He was grabbed by the shoulder and pulled away by Evalynne. She pointed to the stairs across the other side, but Joseph saw the fire and shook his head.

"We have no choice!" she shouted above the roaring flames.

They fled through the furnace, crouching and darting from one place to the other, trying to keep away from the major blazes and surges of super-heated air. Making them cough, smoke was billowing above them and was slowly descending having filled the ceiling. Rushing up the stairs, they had to beat the flames out from their clothes, but they managed to get to the upper level with the floor becoming warm from the torment beneath. Frightened by the danger, they both were unaware as to how burnt they had become.

Joseph shouted between his severe coughing, "The floor's going to collapse!"

Evalynne, coughing with her husband, pointed to a door that looked to open onto a rooftop veranda to the back street.

Joseph tried with the force of his shoulder to break it open, but it was too strong. He swung a chair at it, but the chair broke into its smaller parts. Still holding a wooden leg, he turned to the nearby window and attacked it, shattering it into shards. With his help, Evalynne clambered through to the flat rooftop the other side, cutting herself on the sharp glass.

By now, the stairway was a chimney, saturating the air with hot, thick, black smoke that filled Joseph's eyes, making them sting. Violently coughing and unable to see, he forced himself through the opening, ignoring the deep cuts he was getting.

Anguished and wounded, they quickly moved to the rooftop edge, unprotected from falling by the lack of any banister, and saw the stony, hardened, treacherous ground beneath them.

Smoke wafted across the district along with the smell of burning timber and flesh. From their vantage, they could see the results of mindless savagery, but the perpetrators were now missing.

Evalynne held Joseph: "We need to get back to Kombaiar!"

"We need to get off this roof!"

"We need to get to Kombaiar!"

"Why?"

"Because they're going there!"

"Why? How do you know?"

"Joseph, I know! I just know!"

"We need to get off this roof!" Joseph motioned for his wife to sit on the edge and held her as she slowly let herself over, holding onto the roof ledge. "Be careful when landing. I can see it's uneven."

Evalynne nodded and let go, rolling over in the dirt without harm when landing. She moved back to let Joseph some room to do the same, but the roof started to crack and cave inwards. Joseph lost his balance.

He fell awkwardly in an unprepared jump and crumbled to the hard ground. In that moment, his face winced and he gasped with sudden pain, lying in the dirt clutching his ankle, groaning softly under his breath.

"You okay?"

He clenched his teeth and hissed his words through an angered face: "I twisted my ankle – there, on that stone."

"Can you walk?"

"In a minute."

"Can you walk?"

"I said, in a minute, woman! I need a few moments."

"We've got to go! They're going to Kombaiar. I know it."

"You don't know that."

"They are! We've got to get there. Can you get up? We need to warn them!"

"Help me up then." It was clear that Joseph no longer had the healthy ability to walk without the aid of his wife holding him.

Evalynne was saturated with trepidation: "Can we get to the jeep?"

"Okay! Let's see! Let's go!"

Dirty, burnt and coughing from tainted lungs, Evalynne and Joseph, making their slow, painful progress through the streets, saw the absence of the lorry, the trucks and the violent men, but everything else was either alight or dead or walked in a stupor. Children were lost and parents frantically looked wherever they could. Buildings were collapsing. Fires billowed and raged out of control. The unhealthy smell of burning rubber was toxic in the air and smoke wafted as though an evil spirit. Bullet shells littered the ground. Bodies were lying in contorted positions, blood-sodden and mutilated, and the living wailed hysterically with their new, sorry plight. It was as if the air could carry no more noise and muffled every sound, and slow motion was all that could be discerned with tortured minds.

Through all this torment, Joseph and Evalynne wandered onwards, looking too shocked, not believing their senses, too numb to help any of the people in despair. They approached their jeep seeing it perforated with bullets.

"That's not going anywhere," winced Joseph from a distance.

"There's a chance. Look, only the doors are shot."

"Evalynne! See the ground! It's soaked with fuel!"

Evalynne refused to accept defeat until standing a few yards from a great dark patch that had been discharged from the vehicle's tank.

Joseph pulled his wife away. "I'm shocked they didn't set light to it."

"We can't leave it like this. We have a duty of care, a responsibility!"

"Evalynne, there's nothing we can do."

"We can run!"

"What?"

"Run, we can run. I can run. I can take the ridgeway pass, head up along the river and get there before they do. The roads aren't direct."

He shook his head: "Even if you get there, you can't get there with enough time. You can't give enough warning. It's too dangerous. Help me down." Joseph dropped to the floor, grabbing Evalynne, pulling her down with him to speak face to face: "I don't want you to go. We're both still alive. If you leave me, you could die. Think about the danger you'll be in." He looked into her face, seeing something that he feared.

Evalynne shook her head: "Only a fool will try to keep something he never had, and not gain what he cannot lose."

"But not now, not here! Look! How do they know about Kombaiar? How do they know how to get there? Why didn't we know about this Godamna before today? They can't be that local, they just can't. There's every chance they've gone elsewhere. Please, Evalynne, my wife, my proverbs-thirty-one wife, please don't go."

"Joseph, I know you understand! I need to go! I need to do this!" With that, she left him and ran in her haste to get away.

Joseph called after her: "Evalynne! Come back! Come back! I love you!"

"I need to put God first!" was the only thing she called out as she ran into the distance. She was then gone.

'... Echoes in Eternity'

Evalynne left the town running along one of the main roads into the outback. There, she diverted along a pathway into the trees that in a short while took her along a rocky track through a hilly region, rising higher to a summit. She stopped at a vantage point to view the land around, seeing trees and hills, but could not be sure how the cavalcade was progressing, if at all. Not wanting to risk any more time, she descended the rocks and started running again through the woodland, and came to the verge of another road that cut through the forest. Being careful, she approached the edge and looked in both directions, knowing the trees, rocks and turns could obscure any approaching traffic.

Not seeing or hearing anything, she started to become hopeful of the soulless murderers having lost interest and driven away, but her conscience could not let her rest. Crossing the road, she continued through the trees, but this time, with her energy sapped and waning, she dropped to the dusty floor and rested against some large rocks that secluded her from being seen. Her sharp breathing slowly improved, but her heart thumped in her chest as she felt each beat.

"Please, Lord, please," she whispered. As if becoming aware of distant voices from awakening from a muddled dream, she jumped when a door suddenly shut. "Oh no, please, Lord, no."

Looking over the rocky outcrop, she cautiously peered to see the vehicles had parked, and the men and boys were milling around as if resting. One was urinating with no regard for privacy or sanitation, while others sat bored on the grass side or manhandled their guns. A group was discussing an issue with an intense attitude, pointing in numerous directions, until they all started nodding in one direction. It was the direction to Kombaiar.

"Oh no, oh no. Lord, where are you?"

Evalynne did not wait any further and started on the last course of her run, running deeper into the trees, faintly hearing them gather themselves, slamming doors and starting engines. The track led her down to the river that would take her directly there. She ran and ran, and then she heard them trundling along the nearby road approaching her position. She threw herself down and hid in the tall grass and bushes to see them drive past.

Dejected with tiredness and affright with despair, she withdrew from the road and ran though the woodland, drawn to the estate by her fear of its impending destruction. She stopped only when near enough to the entrance to remain hidden, breathing fast with her emotions and fatigue.

The three large vehicles had already arrived and had parked, and the soldiers were accumulating with no rush. Some workers and children of Kombaiar were outside the main entrance, almost in a curious trance, uncertain why men of military means were gathering at their humble address. The soldiers started to stand back as though to be entertained and their young militia prepared their weapons as though to start entertaining. The people of Kombaiar remained transfixed and unsure of the visitors.

In that moment, without any thought, Evalynne leapt from her hiding place and ran out to them, running through the group. "In the name of Jesus, stop! In the name of Jesus, stop!" She cried almost breathless, with all her emotion, stopping at the entrance to Kombaiar and trying as much as possible to cover terrified children that were now hiding behind her. Her lungs were burnt from friction. Her heart ached with fear. Her head felt heavy and her legs felt weak. Her skin was wet. Her dress was torn. She was dirty from head to foot. "In Jesus' name, stop!"

Godamna, pulling in a lungful of cigar smoke, changed his smile to a serious, determined stare at the pitiful female. Exhaling only in order to take in another lungful, he showed no signs of what he was thinking. Within his next sharp intake of breath, he took immediate aim with his handgun and shot the pleading woman through her chest.

There was a sickening horror in the silence. Even his soldiers stood still.

Evalynne did not believe at first what had happened. It seemed so impossible not to feel any pain. All that she initially felt was an impression of something hard pressing strongly against her breast and the light was fading into an indistinct wash of colours. The world slowed down. Her mind swirled. The air became cold. The land rose up in slow motion as if to gently give rest to her delicate collapsing figure, but she never fully felt it. The beautiful sky was all that was there to focus her last thoughts, and her life ended. She died before she could bear witness to her torn heart, her punctured lung, her gushing blood. She never became aware of the blood-sodden ground on which her body now lay.

A chuckle developed to a laugh from Godamna as he re-holstered his gun and smoked his cigar with a satisfied grin, and then noticed all his child soldiers were just standing where they had stopped. His grin vanished and his anger returned, and with a violent motion of his arms and infuriation in his voice, he urged his militia youngsters to obey his commands. He stood in front of the bonnet of the lorry, using it as a rest as he leaned against it.

The children started to spread out further with the appearance of manoeuvring to prevent anyone from fleeing, but, discreetly, they looked around at each other with a growing sense of wrong. It was a transmission of feelings through their eyes that they all knew what was now collectively being thought. Some nodded and the message of action was understood and agreed.

To the soldiers, nothing appeared strange until they realised no one was being killed. Pausing in their smoking and casual laughing, they were stunned and struck silent by their junior faction turning their guns away from the petrified people of Kombaiar. This short moment of bewildered silence was followed by a furious and frenzied attack as the children started to slaughter their older males. When the few remaining men realised they had been too slow to retaliate and were now out-numbered, they started to flee into the bushes and trees. They were chased and after a short moment later, more gunfire could be heard, followed by the children returning.

Godamna, smiling as if admiring his own child soldiers, stood at the centre of many aimed rifles. Remaining before the lorry, he watched as they approached, as if placing him in a stranglehold, making it impossible for them to miss their target. There was a quick look of passiveness across his face, and then he laughed mockingly. In the moment it took for him to shoot a child, the others had simultaneously shot him as many times as there were rifles pointing at him. He leapt backwards, hitting the front of the lorry, and fell to the floor. No one then cared if he was dead or alive.

In the full gaze of the midday sun, Evalynne, in stillness where she had collapsed, now attracted people to come and congregate nearby. They all came from where they hid and from where they had run, and they all stood around her, crying. The young militia dropped their guns and became still around the fallen woman, tears streamed down their cheeks. A few had come from Kombaiar before being snatched, and they recognised their mother-figure.

Book One : Be part of the Story

Dead Gorgeous

It was far more than what it first would look to any unacquainted or lost traveller. The first appearance would be that of stumbling across a seemingly large, yet unlived abode, as large as a manor house, deep and forgotten within a vast forest, starved of much attention for many years. The walls were of thick stone, reminiscent of something coming through from the medieval era, and with just one look and a paused moment, it could conjure much history to the imagination. In pausing more, it became noticeable that it had been the only structure to survive something cataclysmal and that it was not as uninhabitable as it appeared.

As it was, many decades had passed since the last nomadic traveller had stumbled across it, as the whole estate, once having been a working hamlet and Abbey, was broken, obscured and missing on modern maps. History had weathered it with time, adding to the destruction of the small populace of many centuries earlier, and any memory of its existence was now lost to the thick forest. Mossy walls, built of rocks and stones that had cracked and crumbled, stood uneven like vast, jagged gravestones, just able to give evidence of once supporting roofs and availing windows and doors. Much of the stonework had totally disappeared, as if the inhabitancy at large had fled, taking the walls with them.

Most of the protection the ancient area possessed was afforded by the seclusion made by the surrounding enchanted forest, but like a mote, the immediate grounds had become an extensive natural garden. The old ruined walls, with ivy and climbers, some having archways, others having collapsed in parts, made a patchwork of many outside rooms of smaller gardens. Hidden statues and steps and verandas; natural flowers growing in harmony; small ponds looking lost within covering foliage; trees reaching high; bushes, brambles and wisteria, honeysuckle and lavender, all in abundance: it was clear that nature was the gardener.

Contrary to any dereliction, the building itself, stilled in its own time, held on to a life of its own and continued posing as a possible residency. It aired a beauty that emanated a perfect, tranquil life that was possible for any potential owner worthy of owning it. The walls were of stone and timber, with a form that gave an appealing shape. The tiled roof was twisted in places, showing the construction gave little consideration to building regulations, and cared nothing for symmetry and neatness that added to the charm. Ivy and wisteria grew abundantly to coat and colour the walls and windows, and although the dwelling was not a mansion, it was large enough to boast of five chimneys.

The front grand entrance was upon a few eminent steps up from a graceful entrance courtyard with a pathway leading through foliage to a wide track that encircled an old and stopped fountain statue of a woman with a vase. Then the route departed through an opening in the woodland. Above the large wooden front door, set within the stone masonry, was carved the word, 'Halcyon'.

For all its grace, something had left this dwelling. Someone no longer lived here as evident from the rooks and crows that squawked in the surrounding ghostly mist and violated the eerie silence. The silence was broken further by the sound of banging that attempted to summon the inhabitancy to reawaken from a deathful slumber.

A woman, wearing a thick coat to prevent the bite of the cold, stood before the front entrance looking apprehensive. With no sign of movement within, she knocked yet again with more force. Although her age could consider her to be ailing, she had in fact ridden her bicycle to reach the house and it now lay to the side as she anxiously thumped the thick wooden door. So at peace was the resident, the booming resonance awoke nothing.

She turned to the sound of a car. It drove along the forest track to park near the broken fountain, and she was relieved to see through the foliage two policemen then approach her: one young enough to be in some form of training, and the other to be of retirement age. She went to them crying out: "Where have you been? Where have you been?"

"Sorry, Madam," replied the elder police officer. "I'm Sergeant Richards and this is Constable Parker. I'm sorry, it was difficult finding you."

"We had to get Central to explain where this place is," followed the younger. "It weren't clear." An air of youthful arrogance came from the lad who had yet to be subjected to a harsh lesson from life. There was an air of too much confidence in modern technology and nothing else was worth knowing. "It's not on any GPS and – I mean, I've driven past many times not – "

"Okay, sonny, the lady doesn't need your confusion." Richards turned to the shivering woman showing care and concern for her in his manner and voice: "Are you okay? Can we get you warmed up in the car?"

"I only wanted to check whether she's still okay."

"And you can't get in?"

"No, she isn't answering. I feel something's wrong."

"Well let's get you in the car. It's warmer there and leave this to us, Madam."

"No! I can't have you trampling all over this. There's something wrong." She continued being anxious and agitated, now having the additional problem of explaining the strange situation to two ignorant males.

The younger of the two men started to look over the building as if the evidence of someone within would be shown in some form.

"We need to confirm you are the lady who called us," continued Richards.

"Yes, I'm Misses Manning. Last time I was here, she said a few things that made me worry."

"The owner?"

The woman shook her head, but it was not sure as to whether the answer was confirming a definite reply, one of ignorance of an answer, or not wanting to answer. Her movement was tainted with her agitation. So too was her voice: "It doesn't matter who owns what! We don't live long enough to own anything!" She then considered herself bad mannered and tried to be more patient: "She just needs her time. She was working hard, writing a lot. She had the tendency to stay inside and write all the time."

"Writing? She's an author?" asked the younger man, suddenly showing an interest in the old woman rather than the house. "Is she famous?"

"No! She's – . Look, you're not helping! She's not an author, but – you have got to keep this secret." She stopped and almost spoke to herself: "I shouldn't have called you. She's probably out for a walk."

The two men looked confused at each other while the woman shook her head unaware of the unvoiced communication between her new companions.

"Well, who is she then?" asked Richards, perplexed. "Why can't you tell us?"

Misses Manning tried to answer, but no words seemed able to come from her moving, open mouth. She was clearly troubled by not only the absence of the owner, but by her inability to answer. It seemed to be of a delicate matter and was as if the name was unutterable.

Sergeant Richards motioned to his henchman: "All right, lad, let's break in."

Parker looked at the door. It was old and wooden, with metal hinge brackets that reached across the expanse of the heavy panels. It appeared far from being weak with the apparent thickness that came with such an imposing strong frame. "Yep, need something serious here," he said after little consideration and returned from the car having retrieved a long, heavy metal weight, shaped in the form of a long piston with a handle. After a few weighty slams, it quickly became obvious that the entrance was going to remain unyielding. The two men looked at the problem, while the lady looked at them expectantly.

"Let's go around the house and see what we can find," ordered Richards.

"I've already done that."

"Let's just see what we can find, Misses Manning."

They all walked around the building, trying to look into windows and view pass the closed curtains, but the inner house was cast in darkness and void of movement. Continuing through the surrounding entrenched gardens, through broken archways and walls threaded with foliage, they eventually came to another door contained in a quiet, alcove garden that kept a table and chairs content in their genteel isolation. Again, with more battering, this new door also failed to break.

"We sure we want do this?" asked Parker doubtfully. "Looks too nice a place to go smashing up."

Misses Manning looked around her into the forest: "Shhhh!"

"What?"

"Listen!"

"To what? There's nothin'."

Richards heard what the old lady referred to: "That's what it is, laddy: nothing."

"Well that's not true, is it!" retorted Parker. "There's those awful crows and rooks, crowing and – rooking."

They all stood still, looking around the dying estate, now conscious of the screeching of large black demon birds perched in the trees. It was as if someone had died, and along with it, so too followed the estate, no longer able to preserve the freshness that slowly evaporated into the still air.

"There's something not right," voiced the younger, sounding as if he had to tailor his usual words for public approval.

"I'm sorry officers, but we are wasting valuable time."

Richards took the battering weight from Parker, huffed and swung it against the nearest window. He hit it again until enough of the glass had shattered from the frame and motioned to the younger to grab his hand.

Parker understood without asking, and in one heave, the young policeman was hoisting himself up the wall using the older man as support. He reached above into the high opening and pushed through into the interior.

After a thump as the young man landed, it was then silent. Both Richards and Misses Manning stood waiting for a reply from within.

"Parker?" shouted Richards. "Parker! – Laddy, what's going on?"

"Nothing! It's just a – a – an old place. It's old! Like you!"

"Don't go too far by yourself! We don't know what's happened so don't go trampling over evidence!" Richards turned to Misses Manning, trying to sound reassuring and appear comforting: "Sorry. Not that I believe something's happened, but – you never know."

Misses Manning, looking anxious, just nodded quickly.

Parker came back to the window and looked down: "This door's locked. I'll go to the front and let you in. Be there in a minute if I can find my way. There doesn't seem to be anyone around."

"You'll need the keys," announced Misses Manning. "You'll find them in a small, closed, secret compartment within the wall panelling to the left side of the main door. You'll have to knock on some of the panels. When you've come across a different sound, open the hatch and you'll see some of the keys to the house."

Parker acknowledged the instructions and was then gone.

Richards escorted the lady to the forecourt and waited. Eventually, his irritation provoked him to shout at his colleague: "Parker! Why are we waiting? It's cold out here!"

There was no reply.

"And today is my last day, remember? So be quick about it!" He turned to the woman: "I'm officially retired on Monday."

The front door finally opened, and Richards and Misses Manning were let into the hall to find the house was as cold inside, as the outside.

"What took you?" asked a disgruntled Richards.

"Well I had to find this door and then these keys in the wall, old man!"

Richards turned to Misses Manning, who had gone quiet. "Are you okay?"

She nodded nervously.

"Would you rather wait in the car for us to find – to find what we're to find?"

"No! I have to be here!" The woman then acted subdued and a look of pensive dread invaded her persona.

The three had entered a commodious entrance hall, wood panelled from floor to ceiling, with the ceiling being of large, strong, dark wooden beams spanning the expanse, and having a floor of stone paving that looked like a church setting. It was severely old, looking akin to centuries with the wood having been attacked by woodworm and temperature. Cobwebs were rampant. Dust was ubiquitous. There was a look of disintegration and lack of maintenance from numerous enamel pots positioned on the floor to collect rainwater.

Through an archway was an elaborate, imposing, impressive staircase to a landing high above.

"This way," motioned Misses Manning and the two men followed her up to the next floor. They all moved as if to silence their approach to something that should not be disturbed and in following the woman also included copying her pensive, demure attitude.

After reaching the landing, she took them along a wood-panelled corridor to a door beside which she suddenly stood and waited. She looked around at the two men and then nervously knocked. They waited in the eerie silence for a reply, but only the silence answered them. Misses Manning took a small breath, appeared to steady herself and then opened the door. Creaking, it opened into a darkened room and the light cast behind the three made their shadows enter while they waited for any response.

Misses Manning stepped within and was lost to the dark until she had opened the curtains to reveal a large window providing a view of the grey sky and a grey day. She turned and gasped, putting a hand to her mouth from what she saw. The men made a few steps further into the room and would have instantly calmed the shocked woman if it were not for seeing the same sight.

The room was a bedroom, cold and spacious, elegantly furnished from a past era, and previously occupied by a solitary figure in whose recognition became the reason why the house had an inauspicious aura. On the large, four-poster bed was a beautiful woman with flaxen hair, whitened cheeks, a slender figure, peacefully at rest.

All three stood in instant, respectful silence. Not one moved or spoke. It was as if they were in danger of damaging the fragile, reverent air.

There was of no doubt to the three of who she was. Without the need to have ever met her, or spoken to her, without having known her personally or through acquaintances, with no introductions or explanations, the two police officers understood the concern for being careful and respectful.

Misses Manning kept her hand to her mouth as if worried her own breath would damage the scene or the wrong word would be uttered. She tried to keep back the feelings of grief, but a tear pushed passed her lashes and trickled down her cheek. A stream of tears started to flow from her reddening eyes.

Richards stepped forward with a careful tread over the creaking wooden floorboards and reached the bedside. After a pause, he bent down, almost courteously, not even disturbing the bed sheets, and brought his cheek close to the woman's mouth. He could feel no passing air and no movement of the chest was visible. He saw her ashen skin and sunken, black eyes, and the smell of decay became noticeable. With a sigh, he stood up, felt her brow and turned to the other two, who remained where they had last stood appearing not able to venture nearer. They looked at him expectantly, but he shook his head. "She's cold," he simply said.

Misses Manning gasped. "She was waiting for him," she breathed. "She died waiting for him."

Parker, incredulous, turned to the woman: "You've known that she was here! All this time! All along! When everyone's been looking for her?"

She cleared her throat: "Both me and my husband, yes, we knew she was here. She wanted space – with David. She wanted time to – to mourn. We thought people were trying to assassinate her and we knew the papers would ruin everything."

Neither of the men returned any comment, realising she was right.

In almost a whisper, with tears welling in her eyes, Misses Manning continued: "He never came. She never got to know what happened to him. She died alone. She died not knowing." In this silence, she turned and made her way along the landing and down the stairs, being heard to cry unabated.

"You think we should take her in for a statement?" asked young Parker, his previous confidence now more sullen.

Richards shook his head. "Take her home and get her some comfort. Take a statement there."

Parker nodded and was about to go, but was interrupted by his superior.

"Don't let anyone know about this just yet. Misses Manning is right. This is something big, and we need to tread carefully. There could be something political behind this."

"Tread carefully? You're laughin', aren'cha? I wish I hadn't come out with ya."

"This will get into the News and we're now in the thick of it. So I don't want it going wrong. This young woman deserves more than that."

"But we're not following protocol. We could be – "

"There's nothing here that can follow protocol!"

Parker nodded again, but remained where he was with hesitancy.

"You okay?" asked Richards.

"I'm – I dun'no. What are we gon'na do? What are *you* gon'na do? This was supposed to be your last day, an' all. You're supposed to be retiring."

"Get Misses Manning home. Don't go to the station and don't get anyone else involved – yet. I'll stay here and decide what to do without getting any more people around for a while. We're going to have a deluge of media interest, so it's absolutely imperative we do what is right. Make sure Misses Manning understands."

"Forensics?"

"I think we need to prevent as many people as possible coming here for as long as possible."

"But this is serious if we don't – "

"It's my last day. What can they do to me?"

"It's what they can do to me, I'm worried about. Look at all this?"

Boxes that undoubtedly looked to contain strong medication was on top of a bedside cabinet and, all around, much of it littering the floor, was paper providing evidence of extensive writing.

After a moment of silent inspection, Richards then said sternly, "Don't say a word about this, to anyone, not even Misses Manning."

"You think she took her life? She didn't seem the type."

"Don't conclude anything with a first glance."

"But she took her own life. This is her suicide note that's everywhere."

"Parker, just get Misses Manning home. If I'm wrong, then let me be the one to get into trouble."

With a final nod, Parker left the Sergeant and descended the stairs, and Richards waited for the house to be empty with their departure. After hearing the resonant boom of the front door, Richards made one more look at the woman and saw, in the dim light, the bed sheet she was under. It was a heavy flag, a red flag, with a blue border and a yellow star in the middle with an emblazoned inscription: 'The Salvation Army – Blood and Fire'. It was old and it was large: large enough to cover completely the large bed.

There was evidence that the woman had been extensively writing by way of her paper scattered over the desk, across the top of one of the bedside cabinets and over the bed and floor. A pen was not far from her right hand. He peered nearer and saw the pretty handwriting, flowing over the pages. He then inspected the medication which looked to have had very little of it taken. He decided not to touch any of the vials and pills, but against his better judgment, he picked up a page and read the words:

I have waited long enough for you, David, to come back to me. My waiting has worn away my ability to believe I will still see you while I breathe. If you are ever able to read this, please forgive what I have done, for all the things I should have told you, and for all the things that I am. What gives me comfort are the last few days we gave each other, when life around us transpired to bring us down, like surviving our very own nuclear holocaust, the swipe of a devastating disease across the land, like surviving a worldwide persecution given our own safety, here at Halcyon.

My dying wish is for your return and I wait eagerly to tell you my life's complexities. I wish I could have told you the influence that your Grandmother made on me. I wish I had followed her example and become a Salvation Army Officer.

This is my one and only testimony. Whoever has truly read all my words, you have become my new friend and I thank you for listening to my purist and deepest songs of my heart and seeing my many colours of my mind, but I ask that you please take care of my writing and respect what you have read. I am Esther Whyte and I have cancer.

Richards could see the pages on the bed sheets and on the floor were written of a hand that must have moved with great difficulty or pain, and were of the later work. Without page numbers, he collected every sheet and started to place them in an order which he thought looked correct, starting at the first and neatest page.

From the windowpanes came the sound of rain, making Richards look out to see malign clouds gathering. It also made him settle himself at a very old wooden desk that overlooked the garden and he started to read.

Discipline and Discipleship

After months of long, dark, cold days, and then after months of long, wet and windy days, the new season started to adapt to a more sunnier climate and people ventured into the English Outside with a freedom that was almost felt with each fresh breath taken. Such was the quiet afternoon of a quaint English country village that was known as Havenly. Through the quiet streets of small houses of old, stone brickwork, of tiled roofs of olden ways, and windows that seem to paint a picture of a pleasant household within, was a young, pretty woman of university age, riding her bicycle, enjoying the long-awaited change in the weather and the chance to ride without the cumbersome feeling of her usual over-coat.

She finally arrived at an old building that had its front along the pavement like a shop without any shop window. To the side was a wide alley that took the visitor to a main door, above which had the bold title of, 'The Salvation Army'.

Without being deterred, the pretty girl of flaxen hair stepped off her bike, walked the few steps to the entrance and went inside as bold and brazen as any welcomed member. She placed her bike within the foyer, took up her satchel and went through to the main hall, being that of a large room full of wooden chairs, a wooden stage, a rostrum in the most central place and numerous flags in notable positions. The ceiling was also wooden, with original beams of the upturned 'V' providing a comfortable, soft echo. To one side, alone and silent, was an old black grand piano.

She seated herself on the wide piano stool, took out some music and placed the chosen manuscript above the keys to start playing. Then the hall became full of the melodies she was making until an imperfect note interrupted the sounds and she immediately stopped, annoyed with herself.

"Esther, I told you to practise passion," came a female voice from the back of the hall.

Esther turned round: "I'm passionate about not making mistakes."

A woman of older years, with wrinkles matching her gentle wisdom, but with a presence of strength that matched her young attitude, walked up to Esther, whom was still seated, and smiled at her pupil. "That's not what I meant." Her hair was white and even though the weather had turned for the better, she still wore a cardigan that appeared to be a favourite of hers. Her maturity shone in a quiet wisdom, and a young outlook on life seemed to come from her friendly smile and her content appearance. There was a respectful air she generated, as if any comment given would be logical, unarguable and correct, even though having no passion to press upon someone disagreeable that her views were perfect. So perfectly gentle was her persona that anyone loving would be compelled to embrace her in a tight hug, which would break the reverent protocol surrounding her. "You want intense perfection, Esther, but you can't get it being just technical. I've been pushing you to drop that mechanical performance that makes you sound like you're living life like a frantic, obsessed duty or with mindless instructions, and not a deep ocean of zeal, spirit and mystery."

"You told me to learn to play with passion. Those were your words."

The teacher sat down beside the pupil on the wide seat, crossed her arms for comfort and viewed the student with a pensive face for a short while. "Yes, I did – and that's interpreted as earnestness, imploring, longing, eagerness to know the beauty in life that everyone is so ignorant of, a longing to please God, a battle to express your deepest feelings that cannot be spoken or even understood."

"Actually, you told me to stop playing like a resolute, judgemental Nunn who says her prayers out of conscription," replied Esther factually. "The week before, you said not to play like I'm learning to drive a twenty tonne lorry."

"Actually, I said, 'articulated vehicle,' but take it that I was exaggerating the point." The teacher smiled as if her factual assessment should be of an encouraging step to improve even the elite. "Esther, you know the techniques. Your technical performance is laudable, astounding even, but your quality will be complete only if I can hear your longing, your emotional power, the depth of your feelings, as if you are so free with God Himself to express sincerely all your hopes, fears, passions and weaknesses and failures and strengths: an absolution for your very own life." After being gracious and fluent with her spontaneous description, she leant close to Esther's face and said with more familiarity: "You know, sometimes, God is more pleased when we are sincere and open with failings, than a closed robotic machine going through the motions, as efficiently or dutifully, or as perfect as that may be. Read the Psalms, Esther." Again, the old teacher smiled at her apprentice, leant even nearer as if to confide, and then added, "So was the way my teacher expressed it to me – and he was very handsome, or so I thought."

Esther smiled back, but shook her head: "That's not exactly me, Elly."

"Well, come on, try. It's been your homework for the last ten centuries. Let's at least hear that you've tried. What piece did you chose this time?"

"Beethoven."

"Beethoven? Moonlight?"

Esther nodded.

"Now let's hear some deep, un-expressible emotion that can only be let loose through the mystery of music. Did that sound an impressive way of saying it?"

Again, Esther nodded with a smile.

"Then go to it, girl." The gentle woman then stood and seated herself in the vacant congregation behind the resident pianist and waited.

Esther sighed away some troubling thoughts as if her worries would contaminate her production, then delicately rested her fingers on the piano keys, breathed in, and started to play.

The hall, that was as silent as a peaceful sky, now became a place that started to stir, to awaken into something that stillness was no longer appropriate. The deep starting notes resonated with a throbbing undertone of longing, with the air desiring to be complete, the building determined to praise God with such delicate, moving music coming from its soul. It was as if the music supported the building more than the walls, and trying to rise higher than the entrapping ceiling and imbue into the old wooden floor. The notes became rich and rose higher in loudness and power. Any pure ear capable of hearing this exquisite tapestry of sound was unable to stop the heart from beating more passionately, to stop the chest from moving more deeply, unable to take the mind's concentration away from the enchanting call. The notes then started to fall in depth, in pitch and sound until the last note was struck, and the hall returned to a mundane structure, void of anything other than the air, which still resonated with the passing moment.

In The Salvation Army, there is a tradition that when a piece of enriching music is played with such delicacy and emotion, that the ending is not met with any applause – that any applause would shatter the delicate scene almost to the extent that the belief God would suddenly whisper was very real. Such was this moment.

In the silence, Esther, considering the stillness too prolonged, turned and looked at the woman behind who remained unmoving, portraying a face that could not be read. "I did practise hard, all the time. Was it not right?"

The teacher, without any emotion, decided to sit beside her pupil again, with arms folded as before, and provided a concerned look. "Where did that come from?"

"I don't understand?"

"You were feeling something when you played that, something I have never heard from you before, and what was more, you were consciously emanating it. For the first time, you freely allowed your feelings to radiate out."

Esther just looked at the piano keys and then looked at the music without really seeing it.

The matter was pushed no further. Instead, the teacher softly gave her succinct and final evaluation: "You've taken a very large step. Well done. I'm pleased for you."

The young woman grew quiet, and then quietly said, "Elly? I'm – ." Then she ran out of words.

"That playing came from deep down – *deep* down, Esther. You've been carefully keeping it hidden, but this time you didn't hold back like you normally do."

Esther remained quiet.

Elly then spoke with a soft, comforting voice: "Come on, Esther, tell me. It's about time you open up."

"Elly?"

"Yes?"

"I can't stop remembering my mother – my true mother and – him."

The older wiser woman remained silent, being available to listen with intense concern and interest.

"Joyce and Norrie have taken me in and adopted me, brought me here, to The Salvation Army – and they love me like a true daughter, for years now, and I do feel cherished, really, but – I'm so alone."

"You are developing into a beautiful, golden person, Esther. Over the years, I have seen you become, little by little, more confident since that shy, frightened little girl, traumatised by her past, who had to relearn to trust people; who is still learning to trust."

"Thank you, Elly, for all your years of help."

"It has always been my pleasure, Esther, and one day, you'll be teaching the piano to others."

"That will be the day."

"Yes, it will, and so will the day be when you let down your guard and have a handsome boy kiss you and treat you well."

Esther just smiled, hesitant in what to say.

"They'll be queuing up for you, believe me. I hope you'll be ready for when it happens. Females can be swept along and end up in all sorts of troubled places because of it. Guard yourself well against those who want what they want for themselves, but don't over-guard your life and miss out on what truly can be most fulfilling."

Esther nodded tentatively.

"Don't let a bad past cause a bad future. And you certainly won't be alone when you get to university. Have you finally decided what to study?"

"Religion and Political History, a joint degree."

"You should be studying music."

"I want to work for the Foreign Office. I've always wanted to."

"Well, let's see if you can also meet someone who will break down more of your walls for you."

Esther sighed, resignedly.

"I know that's what you really want, and yet – ." Elly smiled with assurance: "Perhaps he's yet to come into God's Kingdom."

"Who?"

"Who you're waiting for. Perhaps it's up to you to fish for his soul."

"What, a beer-swilling, football-sad, self-centred atheist womaniser? No thank you."

"Well promise me one thing. Promise that you take everything to God in prayer, each day, whatever you feel – and let me know about the boys chasing you."

"That's two promises."

"Actually, it's only one; the second is just a friendly request."

An Epistle

Letters fell onto the doormat with yet another daily visit from the postman, who could be heard walking away with his heavy boots and humming to the tune in his head.

A mother, late for work, bent down to pick up her post and hurriedly placed them on the small table by the front door. She turned to look directly upstairs and called out to the landing above: "David? I'm going now! I'm late!" There was no reply. "David? You're late as well!"

An adolescent male, cleaning his teeth, came to the landing and leant over the banisters to look down. "Any post?" he mumbled.

"Some. Look, I've got to go. See you tonight. Have a good day at school. Oh! And stop all these girls ringing our number. If you're dating them then get on with it. If not then stop playing around."

"I'm not playing around. They're chasing me!"

"David! You date them and then you drop them. That's not a nice way to treat girls' feelings. Anyway, I'm late. And so are you." With that, the woman was gone and eventually unheard after the shutting of the front door and her diminishing footsteps.

David quickly finished packing his school bag and hurried down the stairs, picking up the letters and finding one addressed to him. The address was handwritten and he studied the elegant calligraphy as he went through to the kitchen, scrutinising the delicate nature of the letters that gave the image it had been written from an old-fashioned feather. It was so crafted that the wording was art, written by a hand with a graceful nature and dedication to what most would consider a mundane task. It was as if the letter had come to him from a bygone age, when letter-writing was in fashion from the absence of modern distractions. He had no idea as to the sender and intrigued, he opened the envelope, no longer rushing to get his football boots from the utility room.

As expected, inside was a letter, written in the same motion as the address, with 'Yours, Grandfather Joseph Lovert' at the end.

This was the Grandfather he never knew he had. This was the Grandfather no one would talk about. This was the Grandfather he had never seen, spoken to or even had the wish to. There was not even a photograph available and he could not picture the writer's face.

David turned back to the beginning, thinking the letter was addressed to the wrong person; but there was no mistaking his own name there as the intended addressee. He looked at the clock, knew he should be leaving, but was too intrigued to put the letter aside.

Dear David,

There are some letters that are a pleasure to write and there are some that are a requirement to write. This letter, sincerely, is both and in the two is a request. As a pleasure, I am writing to congratulate you for getting to your Eighteenth Birthday, which I am fully aware was a few weeks ago. The requirement is to explain why you did not receive this congratulation any earlier, and indeed any other correspondence over the past eighteen years. Through my means, I have known about your 'growing up', and encouraged by your progress. I am proud that you are soon to attend the privileged setting of university and I understand you are to read electronics. I myself am not of a modern technological disposition, but I admire anyone wishing to develop and contribute to this facet and world-changing subject. I look forward to knowing of your further development and your career in life.

As to the request of the letter, I feel a need – or even a calling, if you wish – for you to know me, and I wish to have the opportunity to explain my absence. There is so much to say, and with that, I would greatly be endeared to you if you should wish to visit me before the start of the next academic year. I suspect, for a young male of your age to receive a letter from a vacant, unknown, family member, that a visit is not as enticing as all the other plans you must have; but I would most earnestly welcome you to visit, stay as long or as short as you wish, and for you to get to know me.

I enclose further details of how to arrive if you come, and I kindly ask to respect these details and put them in your care. Arrive any time you wish. You do not need to inform me of your coming.

Love and kind regards, and placing you in God's keeping,
Yours, Grandfather Joseph Lovert.

There was an extra page that gave a detailed, crafted map, drawn using the same ink and pen as the first page. It was as if the paper was old and the contents should be under secret guard for the lost treasure it could identify; but the 'X' was present beside what he could understand to be the village Inn with a leading trail from the railway station to its door. At the bottom of the page were instructions to speak with the landlord or his wife who will provide a room. Things could not be any more confusing, yet any more intriguing. He left the letter on the kitchen table, collected his football boots and rushed to school, thinking no more of it.

That afternoon, his mother met him in the kitchen as he came into the house from the end of his school day. There were no words, there were no movements, but the message was clear across her stern face. "Over my dead body!" was all she eventually commanded. It was as if her mind was performing so many somersaults that it hindered her ability to form many words.

David, never having seen his mother trying to control her own rage as much as this, was afraid to ask what she meant.

"You're not to see this man or his wife! You're not to see either of them – ever!" She held the letter in the air in a manner that seemed to be a threatening weapon. With tears down her cheeks, she then threw the letter to the kitchen table and forcibly, as if the house had to move out of her way, ran upstairs, and slammed the door to his parents' bedroom. The house became silent.

David just stood, stupefied, having never said a word nor moved since entering the kitchen. Eventually he sat at the table to re-read the letter with his thoughts not on the words, but on the writing that seemed to have been written by such a kind, gentle hand. After some time, he crept to the small hallway and to the bottom step to listen above.

At that moment, there was the sound of a key in the door and in came his father, suited and flustered, dropping his briefcase to the floor. After a sigh stating his relief to get home, he looked at David, smiled and then very tersely said, "Hi."

David did not reply, nor did he express why he was found at the bottom of the stairs without venturing anywhere.

It was this odd behaviour that made his Dad produce an enquiring, confused look: "Something wrong? Why do you look like you're loitering in your own hallway?"

David raised his eyebrows, emitting his lack of any immediate reason.

"Well, if you're taking to waiting for me then look more welcoming," his Dad added. "Where's Mum?" he then asked as he went through to the kitchen. "Is she not home yet?"

"Dad, I think you need to read this." David handed the letter to his father and watched him trying to gather the situation. "Who is Joseph Lovert?"

His Dad did not answer. He did not listen. He just read the letter to the end and then turned to David directly: "Mum's read this?"

David nodded.

"Where is she? Upstairs?"

"She ran up there and been alone for almost quarter of an hour."

"Okay, leave this to me, but we'll give her some space a little while longer."

"Dad, who *is* this Granny?"

"He's your Mum's father. He left to work abroad – him and your Mum's Mum. She feels like they deserted her."

"Did they?"

"I don't really know. Your Mum doesn't talk about it."

"She was really angry. I could see she was worried about me actually going. Her eyes were red and blood-shot."

"Are you?"

"Am I?"

"Are you going to go?"

"Not if they hurt Mum, but I would like to know why they did it. She was really upset. What did they do so many years ago?"

"When your Mum went to university, they left for Africa and she felt they abandoned her."

"But, at least Mum was old enough to be independent."

"David, I don't know, but there might be something more. Perhaps she was deeply attached to them."

"Really? Mum's quite independent."

"Is she? She's intensely attached to you. She had a bad time when Andrew left to go to university and she'll be worse when you go."

His Dad started to make a cup of tea, motioning to David if he wanted one.

David shook his head. "What was there in Africa to go to? And there's nothing here about any wife."

"Perhaps that's the reason why you should go."

"But this map thing is strange. Does he own a Pub?"

"Let me speak to your Mum, see if I can get something more out of her. Possibly get her round to allowing you to make your own mind. How was the football?"

"Pretty decent: won five-two."

The evening meal was a sombre affair. No one spoke. David's Mum had come down to prepare the food, Dad had opened all the letters and made replies, and David had set the table after attempting some homework. All three went about their chores with pressure weighing down on them from an overcast air. The two males knew to sit at the table when the plates were available and the cooked food was placed in front of them with a discourteous manner that would have seen a waitress fired. They ate in silence: the males making connecting gestures, solely with their eyes, while the cook ate, not wanting to be concerned for the company. Even washing the dishes was performed without words.

The whole evening was strained; the air seemed stifled of something fresh to breathe; there was an unclean spirit in the house. It was a relief to David when going to bed earlier than usual, and he heard his parents also retire earlier than normal.

Not long after, David became aware of lowered voices from the next room. He strained his ears to hear more, but could not place the mumblings into anything coherent. His curiosity won his confidence to venture to the landing and then crept closer to their door.

With nothing more being said, David was about to return, when he suddenly heard his Mum's whispered response.

"I can't let him go, I just can't."

He could hear his father comforting her again: "Sssshhhh, it's okay. They're not going to take him away. David's not wanting to go because it's upsetting you. Okay? It's fine, it's okay."

"But you don't know. You don't know what can happen."

"But who does with anything? And the more you act like this, the more he's going to start questioning what the real reason why you're acting so emotional. This can't be natural. If you're reacting this much about something that happened so long ago, and you can't forgive and forget, then something is really, really wrong. Even I'm wanting to question why you're acting like this – and even I can't get it out of you. It's as if you need to go and see someone about it."

"A shrink!"

"Ssshhh! Well what do you expect? Come on, love, we're both concerned."

"I don't want him to go."

"To see his Grandfather, go to university, to leave at all?"

There was no audible answer.

"I know you're going to miss him when he's gone. You need to let go. Children grow up. That's what they do. And parents need to learn to let them live their lives, like we wanted our own lives from our parents."

"Now Andrew's gone, how often does he call?"

"Andrew's working hard studying his beloved Physics. Let him get on with it. Your Mum and Dad may have deserted you, but Andrew's gone to study and David's going to follow soon. You can't control people based on your insecurities – whatever they are."

"Then what do you suggest, oh clever one?"

"Let him go and see his Grandfather, if he decides."

David listened intensely, but there came no more whispering.

Creeping back to bed, his mind became absorbed with too many thoughts, and sleep came only after a long time. In the morning, he was given his answer.

The War Cry

The train stopped, the doors opened and travellers stepped from their journey onto the awaiting platform into a sunny, breezy evening. As the station was not for a major town, the travellers were few and the platform was almost bare for the sparseness of people. By the time David had observed the exit sign, he was alone. With the letter and map in his hand, and his backpack hung from his shoulder, he left the station and entered the quaint town of Hallow. Referring to the map, he gained his bearings and made his way, following the lines drawn for the streets, lanes and walkways, and eventually came to a small bridge that crossed a waterway to the other half of the town. While the descending evening sun cast its bright, warm radiance, David almost walked past his destination with enjoying getting away. He looked up and there above him was the sign of the Inn, 'The White Rose': a building of dark beams and white walls and old windows. David went inside having to lower his head on a few occasions for the beams and lowered ceiling.

People were quietly at tables talking with drinks in hand, some were at the bar, and a man and a woman were serving their customers. The barman, while pouring a beer for an immediate customer, looked at the young David and gave him a welcoming smile. "Good evening, my young sir. Come far?" he said, motioning to the bulging backpack.

"All day on the train."

The customer was served and the change was received, then the barman turned to David giving better attention. "So, what can I get you?"

"Can I have a coke, please?"

"Certainly!"

"And a place to stay tonight?"

"I think we can manage that." He motioned to the woman next to him, who had heard already and was opening a big visitor's book.

She thumbed through the pages and then said, "There's one room, but can you give us time to get it ready? What name?"

"David Kingsley."

"Thank you," she said as she wrote. "We can get you a meal in the meantime," she added when looking up at him.

David looked through the menu and chose his meal, paid and made himself at home at a window seat, having the table all to himself. The sun was now fading into a red sky over the rooftops of the buildings opposite and the warmth of the spring day started to fade with the diminishing light. After a little while, the woman came with his meal and keys, and told him his room was ready.

He ate, suddenly knowing the full extent of his hunger, and became aware of someone arriving behind him who was cheerfully welcomed by everyone, so much so that David turned to see the new-comer speaking warmly to the barman.

"May I use your premises for God's Business, once again, Mister Lanley?"

It was a man entering his older years, and, although appearing to have retired numerous years ago, he looked fit and well. His short white hair and his face of creases, made him quite distinguished and noble, seemingly making old age to be fashionable. He wore a long, dark coat, a dark suit within, and a cap upon his head; a cap that was dark with a red band around the edge above the black, shiny visor, with 'The Salvation Army' written across the front. If this was not enough to make him stand out from the crowd, he also carried newspapers and a collection tin, and gave out a genial smile.

In response, the barman smiled at his guest while drying a glass: "Once again, you may! Who am I to stop God's Business?"

The exchange was jovial and endearing, and seemed to be a happy, traditional routine. Both with smiles, the Salvation Army gentleman acknowledged the agreement, took off his cap and started to talk with customers, who also pleasantly welcomed him, being happy to donate some coins to the collection tin and appreciative of receiving a newspaper. As David watched, the distinguished man spent time with everyone, even those who were young, playing a game of pool to one side.

As everyone seemed to know everyone, there was no thought of the Salvation Army man would speak to him, being not a local, but, to David's sudden dread, the man looked in his direction. David then felt uncomfortable and looked away as the gentleman approached and sat at his table opposite to him, putting now a smaller pile of papers to the side.

"Hello there, young sir."

"Is that how everyone greets everyone here?" asked David while finishing off his meal. It was then that he noticed an 'S' broach on both lapels. To David, it looked as if the cheerful interrogator once or still did belong to the Nazi Secret Service. Without showing it, he was amused and scoffed at the thought.

There was no look of confusion, there was no abruptness to his manner, there was no awkwardness to his answer, except a friendly questioning appearance that made him seem at ease with the abrupt question posed to him. "Not that I'm aware. Why do you ask?"

"The barman called me that, that same thing, that's all."

"Jim? He gets it from me. I've not seen you here before. I hope your visit is for fortunate reasons."

"I'm here to visit my Grandfather."

"Oh, he lives here, does he?"

David was organising his luggage to leave and not fully aware of the conversation, other than to leave it as soon as possible. He was handling his backpack below the table, moving it to a position to take hold of the handle in an easier way. "Yes, I'm meeting him now," he said as he stood up, "so if you please, I must go."

David was suddenly drained of confidence when he realised he was not leaving, but going upstairs to his room. He resigned himself to the danger of being considered rude and should brace the situation if anything to be rid of the ridiculous costumed artefact. "In fact, I'm tired and I'll meet him tomorrow. I'm going upstairs to my over-night room."

Now also standing, the interfering Salvation Army man was not in the least offended. "Well, it is nice to have met you. I hope you'll meet him soon. Sounds like you're quite eager to meet if you've travelled as far as you look."

It was this remark that made David suddenly aware that he was actually eager to meet and know this unknown Grandfather with a mysterious past. He had been treating this adventure to get away from home, but the journey's end now seemed to be unfolding in a sudden quest in itself.

This must have produced a certain, pleasant look on David's face as he was then handed a Salvation Army Newspaper, which he took out of intrigue.

"This might give you something to think about." The last remark was given by a comforting, avuncular smile and a short but comforting grasp of the arm. The touch was not offensive or unnatural and in a way made David feel at home.

"Thank you," was David's reply and after turning his back, the old man was not seen again. He made his way through to a back corridor and up some stairs, and was then in a large, attractive converted attic with two doors, one of which had his room number on the front. Entering, he was glad to see a large welcoming bed and an inner room that had the en-suite facility. After having a shower, he was ready for sleep, but decided, before turning out the light, to have a look at the paper given to him. At the top, spread across the page, were the words, 'The War Cry'.

He smirked to himself and thought it ludicrous, but he entertained his curiosity by opening the paper and reading a few passages. Everything he read was religious and, to him, was dull and irrelevant. Yawning and with more care for his own tiredness, David gave no more thought to any possibility of any divine existence, and fell asleep.

Pilgrim's Progress

During the night, an envelope had been pushed under David's door and he awoke to read the same handwriting as the original letter.

David, I hope you have slept well. News has reached me that you have come to visit and I am so looking forward to seeing you. I apologise for this strange way of meeting, but it is hoped that when we do meet, you will understand and enjoy the experience. Please follow these instructions to the letter and we will meet later in the day.

What followed as a description was of a particular bus to catch and to get off at the last stop shortly after it left the town. He was then to use a public walkway around a field to reach woodland, and then walk along a certain country road, and to keep walking. David doubted what he was getting himself into, but the writing and the apparent sincerity seemed to be an opportunity.

When paying for the night's lodging, the barmaid waved her hand in a manner of being no bother: "Oh, there's no charge, young man, the amount has already been paid, thank you, along with breakfast."

"Breakfast?"

"Yes, breakfast – what would you like?"

After ordering, he ate, drank, and was then finding his bearings. Following the instructions with catching the appropriate bus, he found himself at the other side of Hallow, watching his bus follow on without him. Pulling on his backpack better, he was then walking through the sunny day.

With only the birds being his company, he eventually came across the intended countryside road, which was quiet and empty, and started to walk along its grass verge. So dense and knitted were the trees and bushes that they stood tall and over-arched the road to block much of the sunshine, and it was only in parts through the foliage that he could see an old high wall of stone and flint, covered in moss. Any passing car would not have much thought of what was beyond this barricade.

You will know the right place to stop when you come across a small clearing that caters for a furtive dirt lay-by from the road. On the furthest side of this is a tree with a cross scratched to one side that you can only see if you are walking. Under this sign, under some stones, dig into the soil and you will find a key. Beside this same tree, reach into the ivy and feel for a padlock. You may need a lot of patience, but search and you will find.

He came to an area beside the road that matched the description, easily being missed as dried mud and weeds by a car travelling past. Beside it was the tree with the cross, and a key in a tin box was found under some soil and stones. Reaching into the branches and strands of the ivy, David sought the buried lock by pulling back leaves and foliage and became aware of a small rusting bar within the profuse plant life. It was only when he shook what he could get his hands to hold did he gather where the lock was. He inserted and turned the key, pushed against the hold of the ivy, and the whole portion before him relented enough for him to enter the world beyond.

It was a hidden, healthy woodland that looked extensive enough to believe the furthest side would only be reached by a long trek, and before him was a track, wide enough for a car to travel. All around were the trees high above him, with golden rays of sunshine gleaming down and all manner of birdsong coming from the branches. The floor into the distance was covered with a carpet of flowers that could encourage any dispirited traveller.

Here, I leave you to follow the track through the forest and to enjoy the bluebells.
Welcome to Halcyon Manor.

There was no Manor in sight. The forest trail continued into the woodland without anything apparent that it was reaching for. With nothing else to do, he closed the gate, locked it and followed the track of dried mud and small stones further into the woods.

It mattered little that time was taking its toll as relaxed as he was in this natural, tranquil world. After some time of walking, he stopped and listened: it was impossible to hear anything that was of any human effort. As if suddenly appearing within the trees, dispersed and neglected, were stone structures of ancient walls with major sections having collapsed. The forest was reclaiming something that had been deserted.

The track finally ended, finishing in a large circle that had at its centre a statue of a woman beside a well with numerous large stone jars beside her, having the appearance of being a fountain or water feature, now ceased to run. All around the ridge of the well, the jars and her lower legs were stained with green mould. In the wall of the well was carved, 'Samaria'.

As intriguing as this was, his attention was drawn to a gap in the bushes that made a natural path. Walking through it, he was then amazed to stand within an abundant garden with a huge, elegant, old building confronting him. This ancient manor house, complete with ivy and climbers growing from their chosen places, and moss and algae from other crevices, was like a mystical apparition. He made his way through the overgrown garden to the front entrance set within its own courtyard. It was a wide, dark, thick wooden door, hinged by three long metal brackets, and above it, inscribed in the stone masonry, was the word, 'Halcyon'.

David knocked to gain attention.

No one came.

He felt confident enough to explore the grounds, finding himself entering and leaving small, segregated gardens made by mossy walls and plants. Then suddenly, astoundingly, he stepped into an open, natural, healthy pasture of long green grass, proliferated with flourishing flowers, decorated by shrubs in bloom and tall bushes maintaining a strong presence, all in stunning colour. He meandered to stand beside a quaint well, looked down it to see the water below, and looked up to be still for a moment to marvel the beautiful scene.

"Good morning!"

At first, David thought he had imagined the words, even starting to believe his brain was inventing a garden that could talk.

"Have you found who you are looking for?"

Sat within an alcove within the neighbouring wall, tucked within climbers, sitting on a wooden bench, was an old man with white hair marking his age, wearing a shirt and trousers that looked to be once part of a smart suit. The gentleman, smiling, kept quiet, eager to know the response of the younger visitor.

"You!" exclaimed David.

He nodded contentedly.

"You knew it was me!"

Again, the reply was a smile and a nod. It was the Salvation Army man from the night before, smiling quietly and confidently at him, and he stood to welcome David.

"How did you know it was me?"

The old man chuckled. "I knew it was you, because you looked like you. David, I am Joseph – Joseph Lovert – your Grandfather."

David was aghast: "I don't understand. Why didn't you say anything last night?"

"Well, one, and this is in no order, can't an old Granddad have fun with his Grandson. And two, I find it difficult to accept that you did not see any family resemblance. And three, I wanted to see you before you came here, because, four – this place is an entire secret, from everyone, including your parents, so I thought to judge your personality. And five: call it a probing if you like."

David just looked at the old man.

"Welcome, welcome to Halcyon." Joseph then motioned to the large manor house.

David turned and was at a loss for words as he studied the old, elegant building. "Secret? This place is secret?"

"Yes, secret. Can't believe it, can you? It has been totally concealed, secluded from everywhere for hundreds of years. There's no traffic, no over-head cables, no telephone, no incessant humming. There are no thugs, no unwanted guests, no troublesome neighbours. There's no post. The Police don't come here. The Council doesn't come here. This place, David, is away from the world, a piece of Heaven." Joseph then started to walk through the garden to the house. "The danger is it could all be lost."

David picked up his backpack and followed. "You live here?"

"There is no gas, no electricity, no tap-running water, no modern sewerage system: I don't think so. I come here whenever I want to get away. I'm only the – caretaker. This place is mine only in trust."

There was no more elaboration on what was meant, or who it was that truly owned the property and grounds, but David was so taken by the experience that he did not question any further.

"Only me and God comes here – and now you. Ordinarily, I live in a mediocre little terraced house in Hallow. If ever you write to me, use that address. I come here only like Lewis's Narnia. This is my secret, sweet place of communion. Want something to drink? I have a fire going in the kitchen for a nice pot of tea, and some bread that I've baked."

"I thought you said there's no running water."

"Well, people of the past had their means. Come on, I'll treat you to a medieval cup of tea and bread."

Together they approached another arch and went under it to enter a small, quaint, self-contained over-grown herb garden, with a central table and chairs, and having its own door to the Manor. When entering the building, they went through a small vestibule of stone-paved flooring and stone walls, went up a few steps, and entered the kitchen, which had a large window overlooking this genteel garden.

Time stopped. It had stopped in this room for hundreds of years, such was the affect on David. Around the walls were old, worn, wooden shelves and cupboards. Utensils hung from hooks, along with strange herb-like plants. A large table of wood, thick enough to believe it had survived many centuries, was placed central to the room, and, with much space afforded the hearth, was a large, scorched fireplace set within the stone wall. If that was not enough, there was an old, dusty, black, metal wood-burning Aga for three ovens and numerous hobs, of which one oven had been in use.

"I've been baking," Joseph said, pointing to the bread on the table. "It might still be warm."

"It's like going back in time," said David, still looking around.

"You do like tea, don't you? I forgot to ask. Blame the age, if you want." Joseph placed the heavy, black kettle on the hob and turned back to the bread, offering David a knife to cut it.

"Mmmmm!" David said with a mouthful. "What *is* in this bread? It's fantastic!"

"It is, isn't it?" replied the satisfied chef. "It took me years to discover how to get the right balance between the ingredients, the timing, the temperature, and repeating it. Still, practice makes perfect."

"So how old is this place?"

Joseph looked around, as if in search of the right answer. Not finding it, he turned to David, held up his bread before taking a bite, and then said, "Old."

"Old? How old?"

"Enough to say there was something here in the medieval days."

"That long?"

"Oh yes. I get no one else involved in my research: this place needs to be kept tranquil and secret."

"How can something like this be secret?"

"The same way most Christians keep Heaven secret from everyone else: a lack of concern for the most part." While pouring the tea, Joseph gesticulated in the directions he thought were correct: "There is a thick, high wall surrounding three directions of this forest – all of them are over-grown with ivy, and most people see it as a massive bush. When I have the furnaces at full steam, we are too far away for people to notice. On the other side to one wall is the lonesome road you walked along and on the other side to the other two is the English Heritage Trust. They don't know about this place and think someone else owns the land, but other people think all this belongs to English Heritage. The worry is that developers will start asking questions."

"And the fourth side?"

"It takes you to a large lake that submerges the edge of the forest for much of the year. No one ever comes by boat as there is nowhere to land. No one comes here: no one."

They finished the tea and bread while talking pleasantly about David's old school, the plans for the summer holiday, and his potential to spend three years in London studying electronics. In a small, strange, unexpected way, David suddenly felt very close to his Grandfather.

"Well then, let's show you your room," said Joseph, placing his cup down with a satisfied expression.

"I have a room here?"

"Of course. Grab your luggage and let me show you some of the house."

After regaining his backpack, David followed his guide from the kitchen and found himself further back in time in the corridor beyond. The wooden flooring was old and scratched, and worn smooth and shiny. The walls were solid stonework with wood panelling that in part had broken away. The ceiling was high and sturdy with dark beams, and stains of soot surrounded the mountings of each candleholder and candelabra.

They came to the entrance hall for the front door where an old, scratched oval table with a vase of flowers was central, and a wide, impressive wooden stairway within its own vestibule was beyond a wide, stone archway. He followed his host up the stairs, along old, dark, dusty corridors of stone brickwork, passing closed doors, amazed that this place existed and he was in it.

Joseph came to a door and stood by it: "This is yours."

The door was opened and David saw a spacious room that was very basic, very old, with walls that were not exactly square with each other. Light was in abundance, flooding in through four high-reaching windows which were only a single-pane thick, giving the room a medieval coldness. A large, stone fireplace, black and scorched, allowed a breeze to come down from the chimney, seemingly to defeat the reason for the fireplace. A ceramic bowl on top of an old, wooden cabinet with a water jug to its side, catered for the en-suite sink, and, central, upon the dark, wooden floorboards, was a large, wooden bed. The best feature of all was the feeling of freedom for the commodious size it was, in contrast to his small bedroom at home.

"If you explore the next room along," continued Joseph, "you may find a bath and use the toilet. You'll understand the protocol when you see it. It's quite without technology."

"This is mine, for as long as I wish?" said David, amazed.

"Yes, of course, for as long as you wish. You can come back and stay any time."

"This is just brilliant."

"I'll be out and about picking a few things from the garden for a meal this evening. Then we can get a good night's sleep for tomorrow."

"Why? What happens tomorrow?"

"I don't know, I'm not a prophet, but it saves on the candles." There came a pleasant smile and then there was an after-thought: "If you go exploring, don't go too far into the gardens: I may never see you again."

When the door had closed and his Grandfather had faded away, David stood alone, captivated in the middle of this room. He placed his bag to the side, fell on the bed and decided to rest his eyes. It was not long before he had fallen asleep.

A Fallen Eden

When David awoke, the sun was still glowing through his windows, and from his watch he realised he had slept for an hour. Time was now being wasted, he felt, when there was so much to discover. He left his room to look within the nearest door and found the bathroom, and soon understood the toilet system. He tried not to let it spoil his view of the place, and was ready to explore more.

Making his way carefully and quietly through the house, as if trying to burgle anything of value, he found some rooms were locked, but one unlocked room was in such a state of ruin that he suspected they were locked for reasons of safety. Moss and algae was spreading, the floorboards were buckling, and cracks down the walls were made large by plaster having fallen, along with a splintering ceiling. A permanent dampness made the air smell musty, although strangely fragrant. The windows, although not with any holes, were cracked and covered in grime and mould. Other rooms, being in better condition, still maintained cobwebs, dust and dirt, and, for the sunny day beyond, the rooms were cool. It was as if this perfect house had fallen from grace and no longer was what it had originally meant to be. It had been corrupted by time and neglect, and waited for the era to reclaim its former glory.

When reaching the other side of the Manor, David discovered his Grandfather's bedroom, seeing the four-poster bed, the bedside cabinets, the wardrobes, and the large desk under one of the large windows, all of dark wood and befitting a by-gone age. Seeing the water jug and bowl, and then discovering the next room possessing the same facilities as his own, David felt better that he was not missing out on a better means to wash.

Descending the main stairs, he entered the reception hall and opened the unlocked front door to peer out into the overgrown courtyard, with the statue of the woman and her vases just about visible beyond the immediate, pervasive shrubbery. He decided to continue searching the house and after turning the corner within a corridor, found a door that opened to the library of the estate for all the faded books that aligned the walls. In the middle was a threadbare carpet which did not entirely cover the stone paving, and two alcoves to the far side let in much light from extensive windows and looked out to the peaceful, unkempt gardens. A few old leather chairs with high backs looked at home and were available for a gentle read, but it was equally a music room with the presence of a scratched grand piano to while away the moments. He crept closer to the keys and played a few notes, surprising himself of the soft sounds he created, and then spent some moments studying the rows of worn book covers and titles giving a multitude of subjects and classics.

Leaving the room, he found himself eventually back in the kitchen where the ancient Aga was burning hot and something had been in the process of being prepared on the table. The chef was no longer present, but it was within a few moments while David marvelled at the room that Joseph returned with hands full of picked herbs.

"Ah!" said Joseph seeing David, "I'm cooking us a nice beef stew."

He started washing the plants in a basin and ripping off the leaves from the stalks. "Discovered much?"

David took the initiative and cut the vegetables. "I fell asleep for some time and then found something I wish I hadn't."

"Ah! You found the bathroom. You made sense of the system then?"

"I wouldn't bring any girlfriend here, if that's what you mean."

"You're too use to modern luxuries. As long as the system is clean and hygienic, then what's the bother? Cleanliness is next to Godliness, David."

"I found the library and music room."

"Now *that* has an air of romance, don't you think?" Taking a lid off a small metal tray, Joseph produced cut meat and started to fry them in a pan with some seasoning, and then everything went into a large pot of simmering sauces with the finely cut herbs and other strange additions.

"Thank you for being so welcoming to me," Joseph then said. "You've made me feel at ease, even though I've been so absent from your life."

"I wasn't last night."

"I couldn't decide whether you were shy, tired, or naturally charmless, but there was some change in you when we parted. No matter, you're here now."

"This is all very – weird – intriguing, but weird, surreal even."

"I know you have a lot of questions for me, but as for now, let's have a good hearty meal this evening and leave them for tomorrow."

Building on Sand

Still in Esther's bedroom sitting at the desk, Sergeant Richards looked up from his reading to watch the continuous rain running down the glass, and then turned to the four-poster bed where Esther, somehow looking serene, still lay under the flag of The Salvation Army.

Her life would soon be trampled upon once the services arrived, and there was a sense of regret with knowing that official men, performing their routine work, were to roam around, inspecting and ruining the peace and sacredness of the place and moment. There was a sense of sadness that her life will soon be poured out into the news and everyone will come to know her sad end.

He knew he should not be reading her writing. His junior was right, but he strangely felt people would understand his motivation if they were ever to know. There had been something between Esther and David, he was sure of it, but what had it been? Had Esther written about this in detail? How honest was she? Would it ruin her reputation? It was for this reason that Richards, feeling loyal, respect and even worry, felt compelled, as if a mission, to avert this damage before the men who trampled over things, did their trampling. Esther deserved more than the media treading on something that should not be theirs, whether she was honest or not, whether she was true or not.

Richards, picking up all her writing, decided to leave the room and give Esther some reverence. Coming to the landing, he descended the stairs, entered the lobby area and crept along an adjoining corridor, suddenly feeling the ghostly nature of his surroundings. He could easily conjure faint figures coming from the walls taking no notice of him. Opening a door, he became spellbound by what he saw beyond it, as the whole room could only be described as a quaint museum for the Victorian era. With a better look, Richards realised all the items, be it brass, textile, book or painting, were of The Salvation Army. Brass musical instruments of all sizes, flags in salute and a painting of an old man with a very long white fluffy beard, were as if on display. There were even two figurines used by tailors that hung an old male and female version of the uniform. In the middle of the room were two chairs, and Richards sat on one to continue reading Esther's writing.

People can be quick to judge. Someone deaf can be mistaken to be rude or dull. Someone disabled can be completely dismissed for lacking every faculty. Someone poor can be disregarded as worthless.

It is demeaning to be looked upon with indignation and lack of respect through no fault of your own: when people disparage your talents, belittle your ambitions, refuse to recognise your achievements, because they see and understand so little of you. They get a miniature impression based on their restricted understanding. There are lies perpetuated, and people judge you on these misrepresentations. People can be so appalling. They judge as if they know you completely. They judge on incomplete knowledge. Anyone who hasn't seen me in the full range of what I can do, and yet thinks they know me, would surely be annoying and even exasperating. Why should I allow someone who is blinkered to limit who I am?

But is this any different to how God may feel when we view and judge Him in our blinkered understanding? What senses and perception has God given us to truly know and understand all there is, and for us to be the judge in all things? No wonder He can be indignant or angry with us when we have this horrid, arrogant attitude, when we know so little and have achieved nothing in comparison to the universe. Who are we to judge God when we can't know everything? I look back on my life and realise how horrid I truly have been.

In my last days of breathing, I know God has been transforming my old understanding, here, at Halcyon. Even in my dreams, I seem to learn what I feel I should have learnt many years ago. The night David left, I dreamt so vividly that it is scorched into my memory. I was literally in an enormous cavernous, castle-like Cathedral, walking across a floor of large square paving and beside walls of hefty stone that only a mighty force could have erected. Powerful columns supported the lofty roof where intricate carvings were of vines and grapes. I was walking along a wide area as though a veranda or promenade, because to the side was a stone balcony that overlooked the main worship area far, far below. There were many high arches above and below me, and many floors and levels, with steps and stairs interlacing each stratum within this monumental edifice. In the distance before me, was a golden gate, waiting for my arrival to lead me into an unknown place.

Everywhere was flooded with an uncountable multitude of coloured windows that made light descend in a glittering cascade of beautiful colours and warmth. The whole place was bright and clean and white and decorated by roses.

I knew this symbolised what I had been building all my life, with my life, with each motion and each word and every thought, with what I thought I understood. This was my life. I marvelled at my own creation and efforts. There was singing, beautiful singing. It was the singing of my soul, but it was interrupted.

A dazzling brightness came from below me beyond the balcony that was not of my doing, and I realised someone else was here by the way it moved. Then, echoing throughout, was an immense voice. It sounded wondrous and loud and powerful, majestic and paternal. It made me feel I was intimately known and it cut and burnt to the core of me.

"Hadassah! Hadassah!"

His voice was like a rushing mighty wind, the full force of an almighty waterfall, the blast of an awesome missile.

I tried not to be seen as I looked over the balcony into the colossal hall below to see a lone figure looking up, looking as though a figurine in the vastness of the nave. He was dressed in a fiery cloak that glistened as if made of liquid gold with burning embers and volcanic radiance. His hair was radiant white, glowing with purity, and His eyes were as bright as sunshine. He was looking for me, but I felt He knew where I was. I did not understand why He did not directly address me.

He started to increase in stature, in greatness, in brilliance. He grew and grew, became mightier and mightier, reaching the height of the balcony, becoming more mightier. In a manner of power yet compassion, in a way that you would be a fool to dispute His words, He then cried out: "I am the questions! I am the answer! I am the start and I am the end! I cannot be contained!"

So firm were His words, I could have walked upon them as a path with no fear of falling.

Then He roared: "I will not be restricted! I will not be restrained! Hadassah, you cannot limit me! I will not be controlled!"

Everything shook with His words. The structure feared His might. It was as though His spirit scorched the stones and all shuddered and shook open large cracks. Debris fell from above. The walls were being dismembered. The floor was twisting and buckling and stone was crashing around me. His increasing presence broke through the hefty, thick walls.

My frail temple, this grand cathedral I had built, was collapsing. It was collapsing in a deathful, complaining wail, struck by a disease of weakness, but the far, distant gate, this strong, unyielding, golden, shining gate, remained open, beckoning my escape. I was too shocked to move, mesmerised by the obliteration of everything around me. I mourned for the loss of my creation, for what I understood, and longed for its comfort. I wanted foolishly to remain, but the gate was closing.

With the last ounce of strength I had, I ran to this gate, trying not to look back, as destruction, like the pull of clutching hands, grappled with me, trying to prevent my escape before this closing gate was completely, permanently sealed shut.

Then I was through it and I fell into a vast, glorious golden field of wheat under bright sunshine, and I awoke to a bright day flooding into this room from the breaks in the curtains.

I was blinkered and thought I could box the entirety of my God into a container of my own understanding, a tiny figurine, but He was patiently waiting for me to find Him, to open and learn and acknowledge He truly is worthy of more than my expectations. I thought I was building on solid rock, with each day passing, but I did not notice I was in fact, building on sand. I was not totally relying on God alone.

My view of life crashed when I first came to Halcyon, and I can now quite understand how David's adolescent view of life crashed when he first came to Halcyon. It is here where David first met his Grandfather, Captain Joseph Lovert. I can imagine the old Salvation Army costume here was the one he used when he mimicked William Booth preaching down Mile End Road in East End London. And here was the place that Captain Lovert must have sown the first seeds of credible Christian ideas to David. Little did David know what affect his Grandfather would have. Little would I know the affect I would have. Little did David know the affect he would have on me.

We never truly know the influence we have on each other — like an uncontrolled programming, a modulation, the transmission we have of disparagement or encouragement, disillusion or enthusiasm, and the dispersal of this through time that forms the events yet to come. When David and I met, it was as natural as a waterfall.

The Proof There Isn't

Within the morning sunshine of a new day, Joseph, relaxed and quiet, was settled on a wooden seat in a sheltered part of the garden, reading a book. He looked up to watch a white butterfly, daintily floating from one flower to another, but he was then aware of something crashing through the undergrowth. Someone was coming towards him through the bushes, and David abruptly appeared from the leaves and branches.

David, trying to not look embarrassed when seeing his grandfather looking at him, just shrugged, having loose leaves fall from his shoulders. "I did actually get lost."

"Are you okay?" asked Joseph, putting down his book.

"I fell over," David replied, sitting down beside Joseph, rubbing his knee. "I tripped, hitting my knee on a hard slab, and got lost."

"I should have said there's a graveyard hidden in the plants. This place was once a medieval Abbey."

"So this place really has its own graveyard?"

"Yes."

"Cool."

"I thought you might think so."

"It's just so peaceful here."

"Every worthy garden should strive to be like Eden, I say."

David nodded obligingly, observing Joseph's sentiments.

"Where God can enjoy walking with whom He decides to have beside Him."

David did not respond, rather imagining walking here with a pretty girl.

"I would so love this place to be Eden and be walking with such a loving, amazing Gardener, an awesome Creator. I expect you would want to walk here with a girlfriend – or two."

"That did just cross my mind."

"But do you think this garden is worth it?"

"Worth what? Bringing a girlfriend here?"

"All the effort for this garden to exist. Who or what thought it was worth creating in the first place?"

"I don't understand."

"I'm just an old man, studying the beliefs of his Grandson. I'm interested in what you think you know about life."

"Are you asking about my beliefs on Creation?"

"I'm interested in whether you have any religious beliefs."

David shook his head: "There's enough proof that everything came from a big bang and then atoms formed and developed into more complex compounds and molecules."

"Yes?"

"Then things developed into an organic pool, which life grew from, and evolved into plants and animals. Then from monkeys and apes over millions of years, came us."

"Are you sure?"

"I studied it at school."

"Ah! Must be true!"

David raised his eyebrows, not knowing what to say in reply, but he saw the teasing look of his Grandfather.

"Come on," urged Joseph, "I can tell you are someone with a romantic edge, but you sound more passionate in telling me this all came from no intention, no thought, no design, no logic, all random, all of chance, all of no purpose, all of no reason; suffering, evil, poverty have no consequences; no reason for law and order. It's hardly a romantic answer. I wouldn't score much with a girl of worth if I used any of that as a chat-up line."

"But that's what I believe."

"There is no God?"

David shook his head.

"Not even one?"

David chuckled and shook his head again: "Where's the evidence? I prefer Darwin."

"So! There is no evidence for God. There is no evidence of life after death. There's no absolute right or wrong. There's no ultimate meaning to life. Doesn't sound very positive, does it? Not something to say to someone dying or in severe pain. They might as well be struck on the head and eaten as nutrients. Can't see life as enriching." The old man looked over his garden looking forlorn: "Seems like this garden wasn't worth it after all."

"I'm just being honest. I just don't think there's a God."

"So tell me why you believe what you believe. Was it to pass school exams?"

"Okay, there was once an experiment that was able to prove the conditions of the Earth millions of years ago was able to produce organic life."

"You are talking about an experiment performed in 1953 by Stanley Miller."

"You know it?"

"He reconstructed the Earth's atmosphere in a container and he flashed electric sparks across it."

"Yes."

"And it created a red goo containing amino acids."

"Yes."

"Where did the electricity come from and how did the atmosphere come to be as it was back then?"

"The Big Bang?"

"You sound like someone with faith in the Big Bang conveniently explaining it all – like someone with religion. It's still a massive leap to have any electric sparks or any weather existing from nothing, let alone to have amino acids advance onto proteins by pure chance. Sounds more like a clever systematic process. Perhaps, my young Grandson, this is God's chemistry, and He's not experimenting – He's engineering. Us, everything – all engineered. Don't you think that sounds more riveting at least?"

"Don't you agree with everything made in six days, as in the Bible?"

"I think God wants to have things simplified so that we don't get distracted from what really is important."

"Look, I know what you're doing, but – "

"There is no agenda here, David. You are free to believe what you like. I will not see it a defeat if you want to believe what you wish. I will consider it time well spent with my Grandson speaking of interesting things, getting to know him."

"Okay, go on: convince me there's a God, because there's no evidence. Evolution is more logical."

"There's not much evidence for many things if you want to be pedantic, and what sounds like logic is not proof. What looks logical does not have to be the truth. The sun may look as if it turns around us, but it doesn't."

"But the Bible is just a silly old book that no one reads."

"I read it. Have you read it?"

David shook his head.

"How do you know it's silly? Have you read Darwin's *Origin of the Species*?"

Again, David shook his head.

"I rest my case, your honour," the old man produced a twinkle in his eye with the way he smirked. "Darwin was quite an incredible fellow, you know, with his creative thinking and piecing together his own thoughts. No doubt about that, but he was still a limited human. His work was based on observations and some leading logic; but his theory hinges on two things: finding a series of steps from apes to modern man and the unknown way the simple organic cell came together. That is of course neglecting the chances of atoms and molecules coming together in the first place with no planning or incentive."

"Well one day they'll discover the missing link. We just need more time."

"And perhaps there is God and He's waiting patiently before He does something spectacular like appearing and judging Mankind. It's still having faith in one thing or the other."

"They've discovered many skulls that when placed together you can see a change. Why should I believe you?"

"Science is not able to explain everything, and it's God's prerogative not to explain everything. I dare say that someone else can be convincing that all I've said is nonsense, but that's not the point. The point is what *are you* going to believe."

"In proven facts, in facts proven to be reliable."

"Well define reliable. Science normally results with yet more questions being unanswered. What's more, scientists are still performing their experiments, which means they still don't know what's going on. Ask them about the critical mass of the universe and dark matter and dark energy, and what it all means to everyday life. And with all their research and thinking, they then come up with a mathematical formula, which they think is brilliant and makes them clever, but then have no thought or recognition to the sheer brilliance of the one true God who made it all happen in the first place. And you can never disprove that miracles can happen. In fact, Existence is a miracle, even with God the Creator – even more so with Nothing creating it. So science can't be the absolute, irrefutable, indisputable be-all and end-all people place in it."

"So what do you believe?"

"Well!" Joseph stood up from his seat. "This is the exciting part."

David watched bewildered as the senile, old man picked up a small stone and held it up high as though to place the stone on an invisible ledge in the air.

"Now watch this. This is amazing. Truly it is. Watch and see, and it's not magic." All Joseph did was to let go. The stone fell, hit the pavement, bounced, and then became settled, as if having done what was required. "Did you see that? Riveting, eh?"

David nodded, not sure what he was agreeing to.

"Here! I'll do it again." With this, the stone was held again from the same height and dropped. "You see, it's repeatable. Now that to me is not nothing."

"Yes, great, wonderful."

"You just don't see it, do you? The trouble is there are so many people who have grown up and are no longer impressed or excited about this amazing reality. Look! The stone will just lie there until something moves it. Don't you understand how incredible that is? You can rely on that as many times as you wish. In fact, you cannot, not rely on it. Can you imagine a life when this feature keeps changing? The miracle is that this reality doesn't change its physics. Isn't this reliability astounding?"

David scratched his head, confused: "Granddad, I'm beginning to believe we're not related."

"Well I'm impressed with gravity," Joseph said, sitting down, "as I am of galaxies and molecules. I think science is showing us that this reality is just too robust to dismiss as anything but sheer, brilliant engineering, David. There's a robustness to the nature of atoms; a solid, reliability that keeps going, uninterrupted; a robustness that we rely on to keep going, uninterrupted. Gravity never fails; light never fails; time never fails. Don't you think that says a lot?"

"I just think I haven't been alive long enough to think about it as much as you."

"Well, there is that, but even in your short life, you must surely be able to see what I'm saying. Everywhere seems defined by physical, mathematical laws that contain precise numbers to work: any ounce out of tolerance and the universe doesn't work. This place, our Earth, seems to have been finely crafted to support life. Isn't that spooky? Isn't that suspicious? Who or what secretly set this up? It's as if each aspect and facet of our earthly world is set as accurately as it can be to allow us to live, to be alive. I see all this as astoundingly exciting. Doesn't all this strike you as odd to be just as it is, prepared in some way?"

"I think you're odd."

The older man smiled pleasingly and ruffled the hair of the younger man, who grinned back.

"Seriously," continued Joseph, "doesn't it strike you as odd that although light and sound travel, they travel fast enough for my perception to be instantaneous? Doesn't that sound remarkable? Doesn't that sound engineered? What if physics had got it wrong and we had to endure all this at vastly different speeds and that gravity was unreliable?"

"It would be quite a problem."

"And then there's the intellectual logic of chemistry that has been skilfully crafted: all the separate atomic materials that builds and binds the universe by an intricate, yet mighty way into such a dynamic, beautiful place. Anyone knowing of this complete, awesome picture of chemistry should not see this as mundane or dull. The sheer existence of the logic behind chemistry must truly be astounding to us all. We should truly be mesmerised."

"I'm mesmerised when my school experiments go wrong."

"I suppose cosmology and chemistry aren't truly my specialities either."

"No?"

"No, I was a medic – a long time ago, mind. My knowledge is in cell biology, in human anatomy and physiology and some psychology. So you see, I'm not quite the goon the Atheists make me out to be. Officially, I'm intelligent. I have the qualifications to prove it. Have you done much biology?"

"Define 'much'."

"Any cell biology?"

"A little."

"The biological cell, when you study it, is like looking at another galaxy of molecular machinery, of many miniscule parts, a molecular production line. It's fascinating: all these atomic molecules building proteins and performing functions to keep life alive, to keep life going. I just marvel at the miraculous machinery of the human form, and all the dynamic microscopic structures within structures, the coalescences of inner gears supporting higher mechanisms that achieve human abilities of existing."

"I suppose the biology teacher could make it more interesting."

"What about the philosophy teacher?"

"Mister Roberts, the Geography teacher, thinks he's one."

"What does the Chemistry teacher say?"

"Just goes on about important exams we need to get top marks in, otherwise we become unimportant and melt into some insignificant goo."

"Ah! Well! There's your problem!"

"Is it?"

"Yes, so what enticed all these molecules, all this dust to come together, and to merge and grow and evolve into something living? And what makes it living? Enough to take Chemistry exams."

"Evolution?"

"How can all these separate cogs and gears just spontaneously develop mutually into the ultimate system of a living cell if there's no initial need or drive or incentive for anything to develop? If there's no initial need, because there is nothing in the first place to need anything to be created, then why should anything come about?"

"Because there's nothing better to do?"

"Seriously, how did nothing know what to develop into if there is no defined, set objective, no goal, no target, no incentive, no purpose, unplanned, thoughtless? The empty force of pure evolution succeeding against the huge force of purposelessness – is a self-defeating conviction, or so I think. Where's the blueprint for nothing to aimlessly follow to achieve what it doesn't know is needed, against the natural force to decay away and become uniform? And when you look at the sperm cell, it looks like NASA invented it. Don't use that as a chat-up line."

"No, I won't, but anything is possible if left long enough."

"So it's possible for God to exist, then?"

"Well, I wouldn't quite say that."

"Really? Even for us to have the intelligence to perceive a purpose in life requires a creative ambition in the first place. Why would no purpose achieve all this? We need to be enticed to eat food in order to be alive, so it tastes good – so how can enticement, incentive, meaning, motivation, drive, all be created from no purpose, no reason, no intention? Is it really true that from absolute nothing naturally appeared a society of rational-thinking humans who can think about where they came from? What are the chances of that? What are the chances of nothing producing a species that wants to find meaning? How can mindless evolution result in creatures having imagination? What exactly is imagination? How do unliving atoms end up producing consciousness? There must be an energetic, enthusiastic, powerful, intentional, sublime, inspirational motive, reason, force, passion of someone that brings together the initial spark of the universe to the initial spark of consciousness. As far as I'm concerned, it's by far more probable that intelligence is behind all this, as it's a bigger leap of faith to believe in the improbable randomness of nothing achieving so much of this greatness. I say it is easier to see it from an engineering view than any other."

David smiled: "Good try. I'm still not fully convinced."

Joseph chuckled: "You are hard to please. That's fine. You have your rights, and your free will."

"Yes, I do."

"Where did that come from?"

"You don't give up, do you?"

"I will eventually." There was a moment when neither of them spoke, but Joseph then continued: "So what are you thinking now?"

"Perhaps there have been many universes and this one got it right."

"Oh yes, I forgot: the multi-verse idea, that infinite universes are churned out of a universe-making machine that came from somewhere – and there's all these super strings and wobbly things. There's no proof of this universe-making machine. Why should it be so wrong to believe in a God? Having a grand, ultimate person, who is creative enough, intelligent enough, excited enough, fits all the explanations as to why we are here. Why should it be wrong to believe?"

"Science demands proof, whereas faith doesn't."

"Do you see the beautiful flowers and colours?"

"Yes, it's hard not to."

"But where's your proof?"

"Proof is in my seeing."

"Prove to me that you see the exact same colours as I do. Prove that the biggest flower over there is red. What is colour?"

"An electromagnetic thing."

"Light is seen by the eye and decoded into different wavelengths by the brain. The brain attributes these wavelengths to something we call colour. So the flower in the real world, the one on the other side to my cornea, the one on the other side of the garden, looks nothing like what I see. Your senses are fooling you. Don't be a fool to your senses."

"But where's your proof?"

"There is no proof. I accept by faith. Where's the proof in science? How can science be reliable today when we know it's going to change tomorrow? In fact, would you trust a computer that has been manufactured with no thought, no design, no systematic production, to provide you with reliable results?"

"I'd take it back to the shop."

"Evolution of the entire universe: unplanned and random, without purpose and no design and no reason and no order. I just can't see it. It doesn't compute. It's worse than magic. It's not something that's romantic and gives a meaning to life making it all worth it. The universe is wasted, I say, if life was not to be created. If there is blind evolution, then what is truly meant by beauty? Why would something arbitrary, like a country scene, or mountain terrain, or rolling oceans, a waterfall, be seen as beautiful? I tell you: creation is just so extraordinary! It's magnificent! There is no doubt, in my mind, even without proof, that someone praise-worthy was over-whelmed by excitement to create us, and exhilarated to do so. What He has done is fantastic. Fantastic, I tell you. Something mundane, like someone going to the shops is akin to something incredible when you measure up everything. The stone I dropped was the focus, but there is also my hand, and arm, and mind and strength. Why be mesmerised by a stone, or this entire universe of galaxies, when the God who sculptured its creation is far more spectacular? Whoever made Creation deserves my praise, my admiration, my awe, my respect, my life. It's just incredible – incredible, I say."

"Yes, you say."

"And the whole human person, with all the complexities and optimum design, the sensory system, the motor control, the immunity, the self-discriminating ability to think, to feel, to act, to say, to make decisions – it just stretches my imagination too far to see everything from no thought. Why would anything be regarded as logical when nothing logical created it? No, David, something of non-intelligence could not have done all of this. This place is engineered for sure. What would a pilot think to a plane that assembled itself with no cleverness, no aim, no way of having any idea to know what to do, nothing that says what a plane should look like? Think of the invention of robots."

"Robots?"

"Is it enough to believe that with natural laws, robots will appear from natural selection, with no thought to their creation?"

"We create robots."

"Yes, I know that, I'm not that old, but would they be created if we weren't here to create them?"

"I can't say that I can imagine it."

"So why should the idea of someone creating us be so abhorrent? If we become able to one day build inorganic intelligent life, then doesn't that make it more likely that we've been engineered – natural, biological technology."

"I never said that it was abhorrent, just – I don't know what I said now."

"Say I want an apple."

"An apple?"

"All right, a banana, then. Let's say that there are potassium sensors in my body that detect I'm low on potassium – say – and that these sensors send this information to my thalamus, which then sends this to my conscious brain."

"Say."

"Which then makes me want to look for and eat a banana."

"Okay, let's say all that."

"Don't you think that the engineering feat to accomplish the creation of a system to do all that would be wildly incredible to achieve."

"Just to eat a banana?"

"Yes – would you be able to do it?"

"Can't say it would be easy for me to build in my bedroom."

"True! So there's us wanting to eat a banana, but what about the want to study neurology? I don't have neurology sensors around my body telling me that my neurology levels are low. There's the want to eat and sleep and do whatever, but where and how is it that generates the want to make the personal decisions I do, such as to find you and share this time together, and to drop the odd stone? Imagine creating, from first principles, a human that wants to be interested and can do all that." Joseph shook his head in wonder. "No, my young Grandson, God is the ultimate engineer and architect. We are the machines! We are the robots who have been created for a reason, a purpose, a reason that was worth it. We are intricate machines that are so sophisticated that the whole apparatus becomes a self-discriminating, discerning, conscious being with perception and abilities, and self-resolve. Can evolution ever be considered great enough, even after millions of years of nonsense action and purposeless-driven wandering, to devise a species of intellect that can write, decide, live, create, destroy, have passion, have ambition, feel guilt, feel punished, feel elated?"

"I'm no longer convinced I can be convinced of anything now."

"Admit it: you require more faith in believing there is no God, than to believe in God. Looking at evolution and dismissing Jesus is like being so focused on a computer game that you starve to death because you forgot to eat. A horrible death is to live with no purpose, David, but the worst death of all is to *believe* in no purpose. You need to judge life by far more than the stories of evolution. What does Jesus mean to you? That's the question I ask you, because that's the question that's more important. And many people dismiss the issue at their peril."

"So God wants total adoration, obedience and focus, and is destructive otherwise."

"God wants us to enjoy His creation, to enjoy life, to enjoy His company and enjoy each other. We just have to be wise about what is meant by enjoyment, because responsibility comes with it. Look at life in detail, but don't miss seeing a small bird on a branch. Listen to it singing and fall in love with it, as God is in love with it, enraptured even. Fall in love with people, everyone, not with soppiness, but in a mature, intelligent acceptance. Sometimes it's a case of sitting back, being still and being amazed at what God has done."

David made no reply, stunned by the old man's fervour and energy, tired by the weight of his Grandfather's conviction, with his own concentration now starting to wane.

"Well, I think it's time for a good spot of reading in the library this afternoon. What do you say?"

"I need to lie down. That's what I say."

"Regardless to any beginning of the universe, I know you have many questions about the past. Perhaps tomorrow I'll give you your answers, but I warn you, it may change the course of your life."

'The Girl with the Flaxen Hair'

The night was black and silent, and David slept deeply through it. When the sunlight reached the house, he woke to the birdsong, warm in his bed of thick blankets, with the room being as cold as it was the day before. He thought he heard music in a dreamy way, as if the air and dust itself held its own natural melodic resonance. Then it was gone.

Getting up, he pulled aside the weighty curtains and the room was awash of gleaming brightness, and after looking out at the garden and forest, he poured the water from the jug into the ceramic washbasin to the side and was instantly awake from his cold rinse.

Then, as strange as it felt, he thought he heard piano music, a melody that was peaceful and tranquil, enchanting and captivating. It was not rigorous, nor was it timid, but had authority to engineer peace and gentleness that required great skill. He opened the door and heard the notes floating through the air. Feeling how cold it was, he quickly dressed and sought the music as summoned.

He found it to come from a room on the ground floor he had not yet entered; a room that was brightly lit from large windows and containing books and manuscripts of old, faded colours. Shelves also held other items like Victorian hats and tambourines. Some shelves had small brass instruments, while larger brass instruments were left on the floor, standing upright on their bell. They were all possessing dents and scratches. To one side, hung from flagpoles, were three flags, all of the same colours of blue, red and yellow, and there were two dressmaker's dolls dressed in Victorian Salvation Army uniforms, one male and one female. On one wall, was a large painting of an old man with a long white snowy beard and white hair, wearing a uniform that looked only slightly older than the ones on display.

To the side on a dedicated little wooden table was an old record player, with a wind-up handle and a large funnel extended from its side. A large record slowly turned and the needle picked up the tracked sounds, along with blips and hissing and chips and cracks and a rusty noise sounding the age of the device and age of the recording.

The record came to an end and the music stopped.

David picked up the record sleeve and started to study the picture and the contents.

"Look for the title of the very last piece," came a voice from a chair that was contained within a window recess, looking out at the world of the sky and trees. The leather chair had such a high back, that David was quite unaware it was occupied, and the man remained seated and waited contentedly.

"'The Girl with the Flaxen Hair'," read David.

There was no response.

David went to the side of the chair and saw his Grandfather looking pensive.

"Debussy," was all Joseph said.

"What?"

"Debussy – I haven't heard this in a long while, a very long while."

"Am I interrupting something?"

"I'm just going back to my younger days – which you are reminding me of."

David sat down on a nearby chair. It seemed inappropriate to ask what was for breakfast. "Why haven't you heard this for a long while?"

There was a long time in answering, but the answer seemed to be a release of something withheld from everyone for many years. "It was the colour of my wife's hair. I heard this piece played in a Salvation Army Hall, by a Salvationist, a few nights before I met my wife-to-be. I fell in love with her, instantly, blindingly, bindingly – uncompromising as if there would be nothing I would not endeavour to give her, even if that was to stay away if she commanded it. I had transferred to her hospital. She was training to be a nurse, and I was training to be a doctor and surgeon. We discovered that we were both Salvationists, and a month later, we both learnt we had been at the same concert listening to this piece of music. I bought this record you now hold and played it again and again and again. She and this music were almost the same. A pretty girl is like a melody that haunts you night and day, year in, year out."

David, still holding the record album, did not look away, as if he unconsciously waited for invaluable gossip to come out in a thick steam.

"Sounds romantic?" Joseph continued. "That was how it was. We talked and talked, and walked and walked. We were both told off for taking so long about our rounds. Mind you, the patients didn't seem to mind. They quite welcomed us starting our romance among them. She had this gorgeous blonde, flaxen hair, and a figure that was just incredible, and a face as gleaming and sculptured as pure beauty itself. She was perfect. Oh, David, if only you could meet someone like that. Just don't use any of your evolutionary notions though. None of it is romantic." Joseph studied David for a moment, then said, "I expect you're quite popular with the girls."

"I have my – interestees."

"But you have never met – her – yet."

"Who?"

"The one you're waiting to meet."

"How do you know I'm waiting?"

"Just by the way you said interestees. What do you know about The Salvation Army?"

"What has that to do with females? Are you saying it's a dating agency?"

His comment was ignored as the old man continued to track his memories: "She could play the piano, Evalynne could. I never could, but she did it very well. I played the trombone."

David got from his seat and sat on the stone window ledge in front of him to hear more.

"We were married on a day like this, a sunny day, with pure blue skies and everything – perfect. We had a baby boy, and in a year of him, we had a baby girl. The boy we named Samuel and the girl we named Jennifer, your mother."

It was incredible, inconceivable, unbelievable: "I have an uncle?"

There was another pause and something painful was about to be heard: "He died when he was sixteen: a motorbike accident."

David was shocked.

"It was a long time ago. I'm actually not surprised she hasn't spoken to you about him."

"I never knew."

"We were a Salvation Army family, but Jennifer became bored by it all and when Samuel died, she became closed – not in a dysfunctional way, but just – any notion of a loving, protecting God became impossible to her, and she resented us still attending. She left. She never said much, but she certainly made us know her feelings by the way she acted."

"Acted?"

"Women can let you know you're in a bad category using an ability of not saying anything. How did she react to you coming here?"

"She didn't like it. She lost her temper."

Joseph had already picked up a photo album and was thumbing through the pages, pausing at some to be deep in thought. He found what he was looking for and turned the album to David. "We went to Africa – me and your Grandmother, Evalynne. We worked at a hospital, with a school aimed at orphans."

There, in black and white, were two figures, one instantly recognisable as his younger Grandfather, standing beside a young, attractive woman. Both of them were wearing a white suit, with the woman wearing a bonnet, and surrounded by cheerful children. Behind the whole assembly, almost obscured by the group, was a large wooden building, raised up on beams and stilts, too large to be contained within the one picture.

David smiled and looked pleased at finding a picture of his ancestry: "My Grandmother?"

"Evalynne, yes, the woman alongside me. Look at the children. See how happy they are. But they were all so full of tragedy. If you really wanted to be angry at God, then here was the place. If you wanted a reason to hate Him, then this was it. If you wanted some form of proof that He didn't exist, then here it was." Joseph shook his head with reminiscing. From another photo album, he found a picture of a happy family of four: a proud mother and a protective father, a growing healthy spirited son and a pretty, little naive daughter. He pointed to the young boy: "Your uncle: Samuel. We gave him to God and He took him."

David studied the picture, not saying a word. There were too many questions to start asking for answers. He became aware that, previous to that day, he would not have been interested in such strange, old memorabilia of a strange, old Victorian religion and the strange connection it all had with his family heritage.

"When Samuel died, Evalynne and I started to become closer with finding more faith to cover our grief. Within a few years, we were accepted to work for the Army in Africa and when Jennifer was old enough at university, we went. Jennifer was independent and going her own way, whether we liked it or not. For us to go to Africa, to use our medical experiences, it was like a spiritual calling, but, and we never admitted it to each other, Evalynne and I were also going because of our loss of Samuel. Jennifer couldn't see it. From then on, she, all except in name, divorced us. She never responded to any of our letters, or our telephone calls, and believe me, to ring was quite a task in those days."

"But you did desert her."

"She was living her life. We all had developed coping mechanisms to cover for Samuel. Some children would give anything to be rid of their parents' interference."

"So she's just forgotten you?"

"I don't receive birthday cards, you can say."

"Does she know you're back?"

Joseph shook his head.

"I don't understand. Why not? This is a perfect opportunity to make things right."

"You don't understand what you're asking."

"I can go home and talk to her. She'll understand. I know – "

"She doesn't know that her own mother is dead."

David did not reply, as shocked as he was.

"She died – and I left her there."

It was clear to David and the entire room that she had not been left there: she was here, brought back in his memories.

"So what do you know about The Salvation Army?" Joseph suddenly asked.

"They play nice carols in the streets at Christmas. Now I know why Mum walks past so quickly."

Joseph motioned towards the picture hanging on the wall before them of the old man with a long white fluffy beard: "Do you know who he is?"

"You're going to say he started it all."

"Yes, he did. He is William Booth, a man before his time."

David just nodded, not sure what to say, trying to look interested. His mind was still mulling over the previous discussion of his ancestry, and was trying to piece together the history with what he now understood.

"He was a Methodist Minister and started to work among the poor of the East End of London where there was vast crime, deep poverty, unemployment, overcrowding, disease – and ignorance of the Gospels: a dreadful place. And from this work, working with volunteers from all sorts of church denominations, rapidly formed quite naturally a movement that he found himself to have created. Within one hundred years, The Salvation Army was in eighty-two countries."

"Not bad for a band of happy clappers," was all David could think of saying, wondering what it would feel like to wear the uniform.

"We have, as well as places of Christian worship, hostels for the homeless, training homes and places for the unemployed. There are hospitals, general and maternity and leprosy – and institutes for the blind, and schools for the poor; residential homes for street children, elderly, disabled; addiction rehabilitation programs. We have emergency disaster response teams, services to the Armed services – and a missing-persons detection service. There's also now a vital service to take care of those who have been trafficked."

David, as if only partially interested in his Grandfather's talk, got up and stood by the display of the male uniform.

"And it all came from the inspiration of one man – and that's him." Pointing at the painting seemed to amplify Joseph's show of respect for the Founder. "All from a man who looks dated. But don't worry, they'll look at you in two hundred years' time and think you look rather catastrophic."

"I doubt if anyone will be looking at me in fifty years." David by now had taken the uniform off from the tailor's mannequin and had dressed himself in it. "What do you think?"

Joseph was instantly amused as David modelled a long, dark, thick tunic, and an old cap reminiscent of the Victorian era. "Seriously, it looks quite fetching on you, bearing in mind that what you are wearing is about one hundred and twenty years old."

David continued to model the costume. "I think it looks really cool." He saw the study Joseph gave him, as if weighing a decision.

"God will be looking at you, David. God sees you, all of you, your entire life, like us looking at that painting." Joseph looked up at the painting of William Booth again. "But you are the painter with the choices you make. Your choices generate the music that God hears of you. You can decide to make your life into a sweet melody or produce something grotesque. God can see it all like an entire picture, with all your colours of all your life, and like hearing the entire melody you are. Talking of music, David, just for the old, reminiscing man, put the record on again and play the last track just one more last time."

For the remainder of the few days David stayed at Halcyon, Joseph never more spoke in such ways.

Hidden Agendas

In not receiving many trains, the railway station that served the quiet rural town of Hallow, could afford the luxury of hanging baskets, blooming with decorative flowers, all now wet having had a recent watering from a caring train guard. The waiting room, attached to the ticket office, was clean and lacked the litter and vandalism propagating most urbane railway tracks. With a good coating of paint around the quiet room, a floor without dirt and dust, and wooden seating that was not broken, two males were quite content to wait for the next train in the cool air. Looking out of the window at the platform's clock was Joseph. David was sat on a bench with his luggage.

"I know I might have talked too much," said Joseph, turning from the window, "but I hope it hasn't put you off visiting again."

"No 'course not."

"It's just that I have much I feel I want to tell you."

"I enjoyed being here. Thank you for inviting me."

"I'm pleased you came. I'm proud you're going off to university and I want you to accept this." Joseph handed David a wrapped parcel and David took it, intrigued.

"Thank you."

"Just open it when you get home."

They both allowed the arrival of the train to draw alongside without any words and they collected themselves to say a final farewell on the otherwise empty, quiet platform. David opened the train door, but paused before boarding to give a small moment in which the two could shake hands.

"Goodbye Granddad. I'll come again," said David.

"Come back any time, but remember I'm usually at my home in Hallow. Just strive to have meaning in your life. Find an extraordinary young woman, and make her life meaningful too."

The guard blew his whistle with vigour and tapped his watch for the only two on the platform to prepare for the train's departure.

"In fact," continued Joseph, "strive to make the lives of everyone you meet meaningful."

"I'll try," answered David as he boarded.

"Indulge me by seeing how The Salvation Army is along Oxford Street these days. Write me a letter and let me know."

"I will."

Before the door closed shut, David heard his Grandfather's last words: "You're in my prayers."

Through the windows, they waved and then parted with the departure of the train. When David had settled on a seat, he opened the parcel and found an old, intricate wooden chess set. Putting it aside, he was conscious of the thought that his Grandfather had a secret agenda, and somehow he was implicated in whatever it was.

Book Two : Purpose-Driven Everything

'Strangers in the Night, Exchanging Glances ...'

It took more than a month into the start of his university life that David obliged his Grandfather, and walking along Oxford Street with the loose aim of visiting The Salvation Army was due only to his growing obligation, guilt and curiosity.

It was a dark Sunday evening. The autumn season was turning to winter and the approaching night lacked warmth from the shortening days. People were milling around, some with purpose and some just drifting. David, feeling cold, decided to stand to the side, watching people pass by, wondering about his resolve.

It was obscure and questionable as to whether he had heard music, but there had been the beat of a faint drum in the distance coming across the traffic, getting louder. The traffic seemed to stop and then came the sounds of a brass band.

As if stepping from another world, a large group of people, all wearing a dark uniform, marched straight past him. The men each wore a cap and most played a brass instrument. The ladies, some also playing within the band and some having a tambourine, all wore a dark Victorian bonnet that appeared befitting a museum.

With his hands in his coat pockets, with his face becoming cold, he watched the rally of people performing a task that seemed out of place and irrelevant. They all had the look of earnestness in something that was of little or no importance to anyone, playing a tune that was not in keeping with modern culture, as jovial as it was.

As the last of the assembly left him, he decided to follow, and it was not long before they came to a stop in a side street and settled to form a section for the band. Another group formed as if to sing and a few spare members either seemed to be preparing to speak out to the public or to just meander and make conversation to whomever they met.

The leader, when ready, signalled to the band conductor and the band started to play a cheerful tune that contradicted the feel of the hour.

"Good Evening!" shouted the leader. "We're here once again to bring to you the good news – news that needs to be announced to a world of bad news. We're here to claim that Jesus Christ has lifted us from sin, and He can do that for you if you wish to accept Him as Saviour and Lord – this very night. The first verse of the tune the band has played, says this ... "

David was no longer listening. He studied the people wondering what truly motivated them to be this passionate about a message most people would rather walk past. With that, he was struck with the number of men of his own age, holding their brass instruments, making ready for the next verse. He imagined his own Grandfather naturally fitting into this group and milling with people, talking with them as some were now.

One young male Salvationist, not much older than David, was speaking to the man beside him. There was nothing religious being said. They were two strangers just kindly talking pleasantly about simple things.

Not having followed what the leader had been shouting, David heard him announce, " ... And now we will listen to the Songsters." The group beside the band then started singing, but it was not what they sang that held his fascination: it was the attractive women who lined the front row. Some seemed almost enhanced by the bonnets they wore. His eyes then became transfixed on one attractive young female whom he started to picture wanting to meet. She sang like a professional, singing the words from memory and intent on watching the conductor. He watched her throughout the song, and continued to watch when they had stopped. He tried not to look too intensely, but the Salvation Army man, who had been speaking to others, now stood beside him looking amused.

"That would be Esther," the Salvation Army man said, leaning nearer to David to avoid others from hearing.

"Sorry?"

A cheerful, unassuming, teasing smile came from this stranger, who was also looking in her direction: "She is pretty, for a Sally Army lass, that is."

"Sorry? Who?"

"The one you were admiring. I was trying to ask how you are, but you were in a world of your own."

"Sorry, I wasn't listening."

"Don't worry, I've been ignored by far better people with far worse reasons. I was just saying her name and you can't stop saying sorry."

"No, sorry."

"I'm Jonathan. Pleased to meet you."

David smiled in return and took the invitation to shake hands.

"So what brings you here, on this cold night?"

"I just needed to get away from my desk."

"You studying? Where about?"

"Yep, electronics."

"Where?"

"Queen Mary."

"Oh yes, I know. In the East End, near to where The Salvation Army started."

David was uncertain what to say about it, so instead, he ignored the comment: "So what do you do?"

"Work for the Stock Exchange."

David looked at him, not quite knowing what to say again.

"I know: a religious fruitcake who's a finance yuppie as well." Jonathan paused and looked at David: "There again, electronics has its reputation."

They both then grinned at each other.

"Anyway, I'm just meeting and greeting people. I like making friends with complete strangers: I'm going to meet loads of good people in Heaven who I haven't met yet."

David just smiled with a lack of anything to say, but was taken by the friendliness of Jonathan.

"It would be great to see you in the evening meeting though, straight after this open-air service. Just follow the band back. That's how it's supposed to work. And her name's Esther."

David smiled again and watched Jonathan turn to a young lad who looked like he was living on the streets. Jonathan's attitude was then different as he listened to the homeless boy tell his story. Then he motioned to the boy to follow him, and they were both gone to talk to another Salvationist.

This left David alone among the spectators to continue being curious about Esther, and he walked through the crowd trying to get nearer without being too obvious. She stood on the end of the front row, almost beside a group of people just milling.

It was when David was standing near that Esther whispered to the colleague beside her and turned to leave as if to attend to something. To David's surprise, his heart jumped when the pretty girl almost walked into him as she jolted and stumbled. The only way to stop falling was for her to reach out and grab something. That something was David, who instinctively held her arm.

"Sorry," she said. Letting go of him, she tried to stand, but she wobbled so much that David grabbed her arm again. "Thanks," she said gratefully. Now continuing to use his shoulder to steady herself, she reached down and felt for her shoe, took it off, and held it up to see the stiletto had broken loose and hung from a fragile strand. "Another one gone."

David realised she was standing on her shoeless foot, making her other leg bent in a glamorous appealing pose, completely oblivious of her affect while she looked annoyed. Even the broken shoe was pleasingly alluring.

Esther turned to him and sighed. "Do you know how many of these I've bought over the last two months?" She held up the shoe again to show him.

David, again, lost for words, just shook his head.

"Two! And I'm a poor student! I keep buying these cheepies." She reached for the bonnet strap, undid a catch that loosened the hat and pulled it off to scratch her hair as if there had been an annoying itch, which had been the reason to step aside. "Good job I love shopping for shoes."

He watched as she smoothed her hair, and in the poor light, he was convinced her colour was blonde, flaxen even.

"We stopped wearing these things a few decades ago, and then someone decided to bring them back for a special memorabilia evening. We all had to go looking in attics and lofts and share some around." Esther referred to the bonnet as if to apologise for it.

"I think it's quite nice."

"Nice?"

"Yes."

"Are you trying to be polite? These things itch like the plague."

"No."

Esther handed the hat to him, which he took and handled with great care. "You must think we look stupid in these things."

"No."

"Now I know you're lying."

"I might not be in your troops, but I don't lie – not often, anyway." David was not fully aware of the conversation as he studied the bonnet and felt the black silky ribbon that made a large bow to one side. Across the front, like a fringe, was a crowning red ribbon with *The Salvation Army* written across it. The whole item felt fragile and awkward to wear. He handed it back, not aware that Esther was amused by his fascination, nor was he aware that she had started to look at him in a careful study of his face and his facial expressions as he studied her bonnet.

"It's made out of straw," she replied to his interest.

"Really? This hat?"

Esther nodded: "You can wear one if you're brave enough."

"I think it looks more attractive on you, than me." It was his own sincere conviction, that he did think the hat a pretty thing for a pretty girl to wear, that surprised him. His second feeling was of being anxious for having said it aloud. He watched with concern as Esther placed the bonnet back on her head, appearing not to have noticed his comment. "Did I say that out loud?" David muttered to himself.

"Now I'll have to walk back." Esther was focused on her broken shoe, thinking about a potential fix. "I can't march with the others with a broken shoe." She was suddenly gone to a companion Songster and was then back with him. "Are you coming to the evening meeting? Like to escort me?"

David, having thought earlier of walking away before he had seen the women, raised his eyebrows, shrugged and then nodded, feeling his curiosity grow in the unfolding events, especially with encountering someone who made his heart pound more and skip a few beats now and then.

"Oh, sorry, I don't mean to somehow pressure you. It's just that you looked as if you're coming. I might want to walk back with someone who knows I've got a shoe problem and I saw you with Jonathan earlier chatting away."

"It's okay, seriously."

"And come in?"

"I'll leave you in suspense until we get there."

"You don't give much away, do you?"

David did not respond as the band gathered to re-form into a marching format again, with the songsters assembling behind and all others positioning themselves at the end, while the flag-bearers, each holding up a tall and heavy flag, stood in a leading position. One Salvationist looked on and when all was ready, bravely walked out into the road, stopped the traffic like a policeman and beckoned the assembly to march out into Oxford Street. Everyone obeyed, including the traffic.

"I think I'll take the other one off," stated Esther as she reached down to remove the good shoe, and she naturally held onto David without having the need to ask. "Gosh, the pavement's freezing."

David instantly liked her instant natural manner she had with him.

They walked back along the sidewalk, following the band as it played another lengthy musical piece, until they came to the main entrance of The Salvation Army in Oxford Street where everyone entered. After a corridor, and a reception room, they were all in the main hall with a surrounding upper balcony and a large stage, with side doors appearing everywhere.

When in full light, David saw how flaxen Esther's hair really was. He realised he was becoming infatuated, charmed, bewitched even, and it was happening too quickly for him.

"Where do you want to sit?" asked Esther.

"I don't mind. Where do you want to sit?"

"I sit up there," Esther smirked, "on the stage to your left."

"Oh."

"I mean, you could sit with me, but – ."

"Ah – mmmm – I'll sit somewhere where the crowd sits."

"Want a Bible, a song book, a tambourine?"

"Arrh, no, I'm fine thanks."

"You do have some 'Salvation Army' thing about you."

"No, but my – "

Esther suddenly looked flustered when realising the time and interrupted: "Sorry, I've got to go and get ready and sort out my shoes. Well thanks for helping me, and perhaps see you again."

David watched her turn and walk away, seeing how she took off her long black coat, noticing the shape of her figure. Her voice had been soft and welcoming. She had held onto him, a complete stranger, with confidence and acceptance. He was hoping she had seen something in him as well. He had so wished to have told her his name.

As for the service, his attention was interrupted for looking over to her, but he did become aware of the weird congregational songs that everyone sang with gusto about being washed in the blood of the lamb, and he half caught hearing the sermon about Jesus in the last supper asking the disciples to drink His blood. He began to wonder if he had suddenly attended some form of sacrificing cult, but everyone seemed too polite and friendly.

That was all forgotten when the Songsters stood to give a song and Esther stood with them, standing in the front row for David to be drawn into her prettiness. Any blood-letting or blood-drinking was no longer an issue. He was taken aback also by the song, the melody, the words, the vigour and skill in which it was given: "I'm going to make my life into a melody, I'm going to ..."

He was shocked that he found himself enjoying the song, and to return next Sunday to a strange gang of strange, yet friendly, good-natured people, became strangely compelling, even though his mind had not been fully attentive to the sermon.

When the service had finished, everyone mingled and met each other warmly, and David, having sat by himself, was welcomed with kind interest by those who introduced themselves. He felt a need to keep a vigil on Esther between people speaking with him, as one of the handsome guys from the band had sidled up to her and they were talking with a mutual subliminal fondness. David, still seated, started to feel anxious from being imprisoned where he was by kind people and fettered by his politeness.

"That would be Mark."

"Mark?" David replied, turning to the voice behind him.

Jonathan leaned forward to rest on the chair's back beside David. "He's the up-and-coming principal euphonium player. He plays all the tricky pieces and does all the euphonium solos. He's training to work in the operating theatres in one of the London Hospitals. Most of the girls are in love with him. Quite the clever guy."

"Oh." Jonathan's description helped deepen David's growing dread. As he watched, both Esther and Mark appeared to smile at anything, and David could imagine, at any moment, one of them lightly touching the other in a subliminal need to touch.

"Looks like you have competition."

David sighed: "No, I'm not even a Christian. I'm just passing by. I don't even know why I'm here."

"All the guys like her, but she's a bit aloof, doesn't want any attention or commitments."

"Oh." This time, David was relieved.

"If you ask me, I think that under that bold exterior, she's afraid to get close."

"Bold?"

"Get into a debate with her, and you soon realise you need the cavalry, but try and make friends and she's wary, shy and delicate – although she wasn't with you – so I noticed. So! See you again next week, David?"

David raised his eyebrows in consideration.

"I'll be here! You into football?" Jonathan asked quickly.

"I use to play for the school league, why?"

"Want to join us lot play?"

"Play?"

"As a student youth group and whoever else. We get together on Wednesdays and kick a ball around in the local indoor club. In summer we do it in the park."

"Sounds like fun."

"You're welcome to come along."

David found himself seriously considering it and, with that thought, heard himself accepting, all for the possibility of a link with Esther.

"Great! There's not one this week, we couldn't get the time-slot booked, but there is one the week after. Bring your own kit, though."

Pheromones, Heartstrings and Perfection

I felt guilty when declining Mark's advances, although I did it politely. He was always kind when he spoke, but I could tell he would be nervous. It was not as if he was not good looking or even lacked talent. He just couldn't bring down my own barrier. As for Jonathan, I am still puzzled as to Jonathan's motives and I initially regretted agreeing to his invitation to come along to that particular midweek football social event. As it was, Jonathan had a skill that could persuade people to commit to things they would otherwise be shy of. I entered the sports complex having arrived alone and went upstairs to the viewing gallery. I found some of the other girls already seated, watching the hall below them, calling out to give encouragement and drinking soft drinks. I felt welcomed and without asking, a glass of coke was placed in front of me. They were all talking about the new handsome male who kicked the ball in arcs into the goal. They then in good spirit teased me as I blushed, a grown undergraduate, when they mentioned they had seen me talking with him.

It was a custom to be invited back to Jonathan's place afterwards. I declined as I was conscientious of my studies, but while waiting for the group to gather in the foyer, Mark sidled up to me. He kindly asked about my week and I had to apologise as I had turned him down on a date earlier for the reasons of my studying, but he understood that Jonathan had a way about him. I could tell he was secretly disappointed. Looking back, he must have been more disappointed when I unconsciously gave more attention to David when he came from the changing rooms, because when I looked, Mark was then gone. David had also politely declined Jonathan's invite almost making us both walk back to the Underground together. There was suddenly a moment of secret measuring between us when we both stood on the platform needing to go separate ways, trying to calculate each other's motives during a moment of silence, looking in each other's eyes, wondering what to say next. Then it was broken as we said our goodbyes and went our own way.

My feelings were driving my dreams at night and my thoughts would always turn to David during lessons, or just waiting for the trains and busses. My heart would quicken as his image entered my mind, this stranger who had stepped into my life. It was strange that I had been quite natural with him from the start, with my usual attitude of reserve, mistrust and shyness. I felt naturally close to him when we first met. It was like a fresh breeze. I was looking out for him the next Sunday, and to my quiet joy and relief, he returned. I felt I was on the brink of falling in love.

My piano teacher, Elly Chapple, rang me during my first term. I remember telling her about David. I must have made an impression because she was concerned I had suddenly dropped too much of my defences for someone I hardly knew. You can't know true love that quickly and perhaps it was more to do with the smell of the pheromones than the heartstrings of poetry, she said. She told me I should just enjoy getting to know him, but not to hold any hopes. Well, I did enjoy getting to know him, but I had too much hope.

You see, David suddenly and quietly asked me for a date! I instantly said yes! As if knowing of Mark's feelings and Jonathan's forward ways, we mutually agreed secretly, and agreed to meet at the National Gallery to be cultural.

I remember that day. I look back and realise what really was occurring under the openness: a strong mutual attraction making a male Atheist compelled to listen to Biblical things from a female Christian, with that female Christian captivated and enthused to be evangelical to this attentive and attractive Atheist.

I dared to fantasize about him falling in love with me, and I let go to dream big dreams about big weddings and big houses and the perfect marriage. Yes, I know: silly little girl.

As I look back, I see such a silly, inexperienced, little girl in a young woman's body, acting mature, covering over her nerves by acting sophisticated. In my psyche, marriage was principally for me to feel wanted and cherished, to live that perfect life in that perfect world.

When I inadvertently became a public figure with all the media attention, I knew I was being presented as someone perfect. When my downfall came, they realised I'm not, and my current disgrace is the greater for it. But they don't understand the true disgrace there is. Having this time to reflect, I now know I am so, so far from perfection, of God's principles, that what a scandal is to us, is nothing compared to the real scandal God sees. In the depths of our own media scandal, embroiled in shame across the world, David and I had discovered that anything can come at us from nowhere, yet made by our own choices. I truly see how far removed and minor this disgrace is from the true scandal within all of us.

Sergeant Richards was now convinced he was going to read something of Esther's life that will dishonour her good name and reputation. He was determined not to allow the public know of this potential shame. She did not deserve it.

The police officer got from his chair and left the room of Salvation Army antiques to walk along the corridors until he found a large room, a small hall almost. Arches spanning the walls, all of cut stone, supported the ceiling as if a crypt, and on the far side was a large hearth and fireplace. Central, as if in wait for important guests, was a long, old wooden table and chairs for dining, and in some areas along the walls were wooden pews. The stained-glass windows, depicting Biblical scenes, were large, narrow, high and numerous to provide enough light, even on a dreary day as this with the rain falling outside. He settled onto a pew, looked around the room as if for clues, but then resumed reading.

God of the Living

It was not a day to be outside unless there was a specific reason, and David waited outside patiently, looking up from under the large front stone canopy of the National Gallery to study the malign clouds and the tall tower of Nelson's column of Trafalgar Square. People passed him by in their quests, but his was to wait. Depressed as the weather was, he was feeling elated and anxious, bold and nervous, relaxed and worried. From all his previous girlfriends, this one seemed to be the one he most hoped to work, but his mind was in turmoil with the differences he saw they had. He was determined to make this last, even as a solid friendship, but again, something within him saw it should be all or nothing. It was the 'all' he could not imagine what it should be, and it was the 'nothing' he feared.

He was taken from his thoughts when seeing Esther walk across the square towards him, and she looked up as she approached to see him watching her. She smiled in return to his smile as she climbed the steps to meet him.

"You're early," said Esther.

"So are you."

Esther nodded at the entrance: "Thanks for this. I've been wanting an excuse to be cultural."

"I'm not sure what you're going to get from an engineer, though."

"Well, let's see. Want to go in?"

David just shrugged in a way that showed he was subservient to Esther wishes.

"You don't give much away, do you?"

David laughed and then shrugged again, and Esther laughed in reply.

They entered the large foyer, left their coats with one of the cloakroom attendants and started to meander from one room to the other, trying to look as cultured as they could. For a while, neither spoke as they looked at certain paintings, sometimes pointing out certain features of interest, but in silence, they both surreptitiously studied each other, becoming more and more enchanted with the curves, posture and demeanour the other had.

Gracefully, Esther became poised before each picture in a pose that David found glamorous, as natural as she was. Everything she wore was compelling to study, even her graceful shoes and elegant feet and shapely legs. Her golden hair was draped down her back in a healthy mane, shiny and lustrous. David had to shake his head to stop being so mesmerised and to break his gaze: 'What an idiot she must think I am'.

Esther observed his commanding stroll and stance, studying the contours of his muscular legs that compelled her to walk beside him. Whenever she approached, she was sure she could feel his warmth. She just wanted to pass her fingers through his silky hair and kiss his neck.

Esther shook her head to make the images fall from her thoughts, annoyed that it was distracting: 'What is wrong with me?'

They eventually stood in front of one large painting, side by side, and Esther leaned towards him. "Don't worry, you look the part of an art expert," she whispered in the quiet room, suddenly captivated by his natural odour.

So endearingly close was Esther that her soft voice seemed to envelope him like a relaxing, warm bath. "Let's see how many hours I can pull it off then," he whispered back.

They both found themselves looking up at the large picture: a scene of a young girl wearing a white dress, holding a white flower, in a crowd within a medieval church setting.

Then David started to explain the painting, mimicking one of the tour leaders he had overheard earlier. "You see how the artist has not only cleverly chosen the right colours, but he has also cleverly painted in a technique to make the materials look as if they have the right texture and shading: silk looks like silk and cloth looks like cloth. The girl has been painted with an expression to get you questioning her thoughts as she looks around: is she looking for someone; is she looking with longing, fright, worry?"

"Or does she just want to go shopping?"

"Possibly, but I think we can do better than that: is someone looking for her? Does the young man at the back, looking at her, know her or is he transfixed by her sudden appearance and beauty?"

"And all she can think of is shopping."

"You're not taking this seriously."

"I am! I'm being educated by an Engineer, that's all." Esther fluttered her eyelashes for a quick moment that was not lost on David.

"I can tell you're not taking this seriously. I'm trying, believe me. I think I'm doing all right."

"Okay, I admit you're doing a pretty good job."

There became a moment when neither knew what to do, other than to kiss each other, but neither wanted to take the risk not realising they both had the same idea.

Now feeling awkward, David motioned to move to the next painting. "Actually, Art can be a mystery to me," David eventually admitted in a hushed voice. "I can see the skill and patience and dedication – and wanting to express something, but – it's just a picture at the end of the day. Why did some artists decide on such strange themes?"

"Now here's the real Engineer talking."

"Come on, admit it. Look at this one – another vase. And some modern art is utter nonsense. Just bits and bobs added together in ways that look random, but you know the artist insanely spent ages aligning it all to look rubbish. My bedroom can look like art at times and I did nothing skilful."

Continually walking onwards, Esther then deliberately stopped at another painting and observed it for a while.

David also studied it beside her, wondering why she had a fascination for an old man and a young boy walking up a hill alongside each other. "You see, this painting: what's the point?"

"Perhaps there's something you're missing about what's behind the art."

"The back of the frame?"

"Take this one we're looking at: an old man with some wooden sticks and a youngster going up a hill."

"Okay, impress me."

"This picture is of the life and times of the man that can arguably be the one to have caused the fighting in the Middle East to this very day."

"Really?" David looked at it again with stunned curiosity. "Where do you get that?"

"Ask why is the man walking up the hill with some sticks and a boy?"

"Why is the man walking up – "

"I mean, what would he be doing?"

"Cook something? Get away from the women? Burn something incriminating?"

"This man is Abraham."

"Who's Abraham? Where does it say that? How do you know his name?"

"I know the scene."

"Oh."

Their eyes suddenly met in a prolonged examination of their colours and trying to fathom what each other was thinking.

"And he's walking up the hill with his son," Esther continued, breaking the stare.

"Yes – I see that."

"With his son, who he's going to kill as a sacrifice."

David paused, finding himself staring at the curves of her lips and thinking how kissable they were.

Esther saw his stare and thought he doubted he had heard correctly: "Yes – a sacrifice."

"Really? That's awful! Where's the art in that?"

"It's Biblical, it's in Genesis."

"That's awful! Who would want to believe in all this?"

"God is testing Abraham's faith in Him."

"What a – it's just, how – . Don't you think this is disgusting?"

"I'd be quite horrified if someone was to try this today, if that's what you mean."

"But – it's horrible at any time."

Esther shrugged: "How far would Abraham go in following what

God wanted Him to do?"

"You mean God wanted Abraham to kill this boy?"

"Isaac."

"His son, Isaac?"

"Not only that, Isaac was born after considerable number of decades waiting by both Abraham and his wife Sarah. This is a huge test on him."

"What sort of God would put a test like this on anyone?"

"When Abraham had built the altar, he put Isaac on it and was about to kill his very own dear son."

"What an awful God! What was going through this Abraham's head?"

"Ssshhhhh!" A female gallery attendant had approached the two for the increasing noise they both were generating: "Please lower your voices or find somewhere else to discuss the paintings."

"Sorry," David answered, immediately responding in a hushed tone.

"There's the café, if that's an idea," the attendant suggested, not wanting to be too authoritarian, viewing the two as a loving couple.

"Thanks," replied Esther as the woman walked away.

David came nearer to Esther and, with some humour in his tone, whispered in her ear, which both tickled and soothed her: "Sounds like this Abraham was a psychopath." He smelt her perfume and did not withdraw away as quickly as he would have done, if only to savour the scent for a fraction longer. He noticed the slender, elegant contour of her neck and cheek and jaw.

They both smirked and moved quietly onto another section.

"It's a shadow of Jesus Christ in the Old Testament," said Esther eventually as they ambled along a corridor. "That picture about Abraham: it's the reason why we sing about the 'Blood of the Lamb will set you free'."

"Yes, but – it's a bit gory, isn't it: sacrifices, are you washed in blood, will you drink my blood? It's grotesque. Don't you think it's grotesque? I think it's grotesque. Who can really be Christian with all this in the background?"

Esther stopped walking to consider his remark.

"Sorry, I didn't mean to criticise," said David, stopping with her. "I hope I haven't offended you."

"No, I'm not offended, and Abraham wasn't a psychopath."

"No?"

"No, and it wasn't really a test on him, otherwise the place would have been named, 'the place of testing'."

"So what was it called then?"

"Yahweh-Yireh."

"Oh, what does that mean?"

"The Lord will provide."

"Oh."

"Because suddenly there was a lamb nearby with its head stuck in a thorn bush and he was told to sacrifice the lamb instead, as a substitute."

"Wow."

"God provided an experience for Abraham to deepen his faith by obeying, you see, and God provided the lamb. And then, John the Baptist, thousands of years later, started proclaiming that Jesus was the Lamb of God to take away the sins of the world, and Jesus came to be that Lamb with a crown of thorns, nailed on the cross, and be the perfect sacrifice on behalf of every one of us. Well, for everyone who wants to believe, that is. This time God gave His own Son as the perfect sacrifice for – atonement."

"I do see some sort of logic in it." Then David crossed his arms showing an amount of defiance: "But if this were to happen today, this Abraham would be locked up under some mental incapacity act."

Esther noticed the contours of his arms again, with his shirt sleeves now rolled up. Also crossing her arms, she mimicked his stance, and then shrugged and turned to him with a small cheeky, innocent smile as if she had just had the last amount of chocolate in the house: "Good job God chooses His timing right."

David smiled back at her amused look, seeing the shine in her eyes and the soft curl of her cheeks around the ends of her appealing mouth, but said nothing. He noticed her golden hair flowing over her brow and wished he could tuck it behind her ear, just to feel its softness.

Esther wondered what sort of strange images were going through his mind.

"You do know," said David eventually, "that you were evangelical with me."

"Yes, how was I?"

"Not bad, not bad."

"You know, I would have felt awkward saying all this to anyone else."

"I'm glad you find me worthy of being evangelised. How 'bout I try some evangelising on you?"

"You? On me?"

"Everyone's redeemable."

"You're not even a Christian."

"I'll give it a go."

"Okay."

David stopped at the next painting of a portrait of no one in particular: "I believe that time can be seen as an object as clearly as we can see this picture."

Esther had to raise her eyebrows and pursed her lips in appreciation. "Go on."

"Einstein said there is time beyond our dimensions that can be studied like us looking at this painting. And each painting is a person's entire life. You can see all their colours and shapes and nuisances, all their thoughts and feelings, what they've done, doing and what they will do."

"I'm impressed."

"The Gallery owner can look and see all of us, beyond what we perceive of ourselves."

"God can see all of us in all our time."

"And we can't, and that's why we need faith."

"Because we can never know it all."

"We paint the picture of our own life by the decisions we make, by the thoughts we have, with – "

"With what we do with our lives in the situations we find ourselves. God sees our entire personality."

"Because physics allows it."

"Does it?"

David shrugged: "I don't know. I'm not God."

There was a sudden silence as they both found themselves in their growing attraction to each other, but too shy to respond.

Esther then continued: "God may have predestined us for something, but there's nothing in the Bible that says we're locked into this. We can thwart it and turn it sour if we wish to. God is not a dictator. Take the Garden of Eden. What do you think?"

David shrugged again: "I just think that all pictures are equal, but some are more – exquisite than others."

They both stood for a moment, not looking at a picture, but looking at each other.

"Do you think God speaks?" David asked. "How did this Abraham know to do the things God was asking? Does He speak to you?"

"Perhaps He has a lot of things stored up to tell me later."

"Perhaps He's speaking now."

Esther was speechless, wondering why an Atheist would be saying such things. "I think more to the point is why God is silent most of the time," she said. "Perhaps it's to allow us our decisions, to know what we may do."

"Does He not know what we'll do already?"

"Then – perhaps – it's for us to learn to trust Him. I suppose God tests us to show *us* who we truly are – and to teach us that we have a need of Him – because He already knows."

They both remained silent, respecting each other.

"You know," eventually spoke David, "we make a good evangelical team, don't you think?"

Esther tutted and shook her head with amusement: "You're not even a Christian."

"Well, just imagine how good I would be if I was."

Esther laughed again: "Come on, let's see more paintings."

The rest of the day was spent quietly meandering through the building appreciating the art together and enjoying the act of being like connoisseurs of the profession.

David noticed the many pictures that had been inspired by religion. Not one picture had been inspired by evolution. He smiled to himself with that thought and watched Esther whenever he could, unable to imagine someone like her having been assembled from a stagnant, primordial goo that could exert a force against entropy. Even by the way she walked, there was something divine that had created her with her angelic persona.

"What are you amused about?" Esther whispered.

"Just something my Granddad said. Would you like a meal out?"

"What's the time?" Esther looked at her watch and gasped: "Is that the time?"

"Yes. It's dark outside."

"Where did the time go?"

David shrugged: "That's what it does."

Esther was suddenly rushing her words: "What about tomorrow evening? For a meal out? Leicester Square?"

"Can't make tonight?"

Esther shook her head without giving any reason. "I need to go," she said quickly, now almost rushing away.

David, walking fast alongside her, wondered if there was a horse-drawn carriage parked somewhere in danger of turning into a pumpkin.

"You're smiling again."

"My Grandfather had it so right. Okay, tomorrow, Leicester Square."

"Great! See you tomorrow! Sorry, but I really, truly have to go! Bye!" Then she was rushing away with a fleeting wave.

David stood, watching her leave, knowing his heart was pounding to see her again.

Kiss me, for I am utterly lovesick

"That was a lovely meal, thank you," said Esther to David as they left a restaurant into the night-time brightness of Leicester Square's Christmas lights. People were milling around, queuing to enter the local cinemas or restaurants, or just bustling through the area from one destination to another.

"Was it? Your steak was dripping with blood and mine was incinerated."

"Well, they got it right eventually."

"The company was great."

Esther smiled.

"Did I say that out loud?"

Esther nodded.

They walked through the crowds, not having a direction.

"I feel like I'm truanting," Esther said. "I wanted to finish an assignment today."

"Yep, I know how you feel, but my microwave circuits can be tackled tomorrow with the same amount of difficulty."

"I suppose the French and Russian Revolutions can wait for tomorrow." Esther then became pensive. "You're very clever," was all she said eventually.

David laughed. "Thanks! Why?"

"I would love to understand something complex."

"Isn't politics complex?"

"Yes, but – "

"Well, religion is definitely complex."

"So is technology."

"Modern digital electronics is simple: it either is, or it isn't; it is either on, or it's not; it's true or false; wrong or right – simple. If only life can be so easy, but analogue electronics can be all over the place. I tell you something that's complex."

"Yes? What's that?"

"You."

"Me?"

"Yes, you're quite a mystery to me."

Esther was amused and chuckled: "Okay, what's the mystery?"

"You seem to be by yourself. It doesn't seem right."

"I have loads of friend."

"You seem to be aloof and working and busy."

"You don't know me well."

"You sure?"

Esther hesitated for a brief moment, deliberating: "Okay, I suppose I can be focused and driven, if that's what you mean. I can pass over people. Too focused and too driven, says my piano teacher."

"You play the piano?"

"Yes, not very well, though."

"I'm sure that's not true."

"I told you that you don't know me well."

"I look forward to hearing how bad you can prove you're not."

Again, Esther smiled: "All right, I'm okay at it. In fact, I've got myself a job playing the piano in a restaurant. That's why I had to suddenly leave yesterday."

"How was it?"

"My first time. It went well. They want me back, but I tell you something: you seem to be someone who passes on from one thing to another."

"How do you mean?"

"You seem to be someone who drifts."

"Drifts?"

"I expect you're quite popular with the girls, yet you don't have someone special."

"You decoding me? Who says I don't have someone special?"

"Because she would be hanging on your shoulder right now."

"Well, you're here with me."

Esther stopped and blushed, then, recovering cheekily said, "But I'm not on your shoulder."

"Well what really mystifies me is that there's no one by *your* shoulder – by now."

"I have a few admirers, I have you know. So what about your admirers?"

"If that's what they were, I left them all back at school. I'm not in touch with them anymore and Engineering doesn't attract many females."

"No wonder you look lost."

"I look lost? I suppose I am, I mean, look around: this life is a mystery. Why exist? What is life's function? What is life's purpose? What's beyond? Who or what set all this in place? What should we be really doing? Why exist?"

"Yes, indeed," Esther answered smiling.

"Don't you think life is weird?"

"Weird?"

"I had a really happy childhood until the science teacher got us to keep dividing marbles and jelly."

"Wow! That would really ruin things!"

"It did! When we got to one marble, the teacher asked whether we thought everything was like marbles or jelly. It turns out that everything is like marbles – only they discover that the marbles are made up of smaller marbles – but – hey hoe."

"So? What happened after that?"

"Ruined my happiness. I was blissfully unaware, playing football with my mates – then I had to look at everything strangely, trying to believe the science teacher. Then, when I'm adjusted to atoms, electromagnetism, and light and evolution – Granddad comes along and makes me wonder if *anything* is true. This place is weird, bizarre. Don't you think so?"

"I, errm, take things as they are."

"Everything, even science is weird enough to almost believe in the tooth fairy. No one can explain to me what time is really about – apart from someone explaining it as a picture or a piece of music. I mean, what is everything all about? Here I am, so what of it?"

"Some big questions."

"Yes."

"I've got some big questions."

"Like what?"

"Why are you interested in us?"

"Us?"

"The Salvation Army."

"My long, lost Granddad was one. Well, still is."

"Long, lost?"

"I didn't hear of him until last spring."

"Really? What happened?"

"I don't know, but I know it's a long story. Something happened in Africa. What about your family?"

"I'm adopted," Esther muttered under her breath, and then said, "Would you mind if we changed the subject?"

"Sure."

"So how many girlfriends are there in your past?"

David laughed: "Wow! Now who's prying? Only seven – okay, possibly ten, perhaps eleven – ."

"Quite a record." Esther knew she needed to stop getting to know any more, realising she was becoming disappointed in David and jealous of these girls. Then she was annoyed with herself, having these childish emotions.

To David, Esther had grown silent and he found it hard to understand why. He asked the next logical question: "Okay, what about you?"

"What about me?"

"Boyfriends?"

Esther did not want to admit anything.

"You haven't had any, have you?"

"I just don't want to date someone if I feel like I won't fall in love." Esther instantly regretted her answer. She continued to act as if nothing was unusual with her dating method.

David became quiet, surprised with her answer, not knowing what to say.

Esther had to fill the silence: "I've come from a family background that makes it hard to – to – ."

"Hard to?"

"Feel comfortable with getting close," Esther said rapidly, and then with some relief said, "There! I've said it."

Neither knew what to say in the strained moment.

"How did you get to be in The Salvation Army?" asked David eventually. "And not walking down the catwalk?"

"That's flattery."

"I can lower myself quite well."

"I was adopted when really young by – by a loving Salvation Army couple." That was all Esther wanted to say.

Although there was much nightlife, neither gave much thought to what surrounded them as they meandered. Eventually they reached Saint James' Park, being quieter but still with some Christmas cheer, and they walked alongside the lake.

After some time of being quiet, David then said, "You said earlier you wouldn't date someone if you felt like you weren't going to fall in love."

"I said that out loud, didn't I? That just slipped out. Sorry."

"Is this a date?"

Esther did not answer. She even looked in need of her own answer.

"Does that mean – ?" David stopped short of finishing his question. With that, he stopped walking and Esther stopped with him.

They both felt like they knew each other's thoughts, but neither knew the reasons for it, as incompatible as they were in outlook. David moved closer, but Esther instinctively moved back.

"I'm sorry," Esther breathed. "Please try that again."

David hesitated.

"Please."

He moved nearer and she accepted his closeness. Then they kissed like two young teenagers, innocently exploring the first pangs of attraction. It was the first time Esther had been kissed in such a romantic manner, and it was the first time David felt it was real. They read and knew their mutual attraction and they smiled with the acceptance that they had started something they both longed for.

"Thank you," finally said David, "for a great weekend."

"Thank you," replied Esther, "but there is Sunday tomorrow."

"Another?"

Esther smiled and she reached up to kiss a second time.

After their lips parted, David then added, "Actually, I meant would you like another date?"

"Oh! I thought you meant another kiss!"

Like a couple who would have laughed at anything incomprehensible to anyone else, they both giggled.

"Yes, another," finally agreed Esther.

They kissed with more passion and confidence and completeness, and then stopped to look into each other eyes.

"Actually, I also meant another date," replied Esther.

They laughed again.

"Does The Salvation Army count as another date?" asked Esther, hoping he would come.

"Tomorrow?"

"Yes, it's Sunday tomorrow."

"Well, technically, no."

"Yes, technically it is Sunday tomorrow."

"Well, technically it can't be a date: going to church should be an act of worship, not a place for speed dating."

"Are you sure?" Esther smiled back.

"Well I suppose," smirked David, "I could pass over such religious fanaticism to accommodate seeing you."

Esther laughed: "Yours or my fanaticism?"

"Okay, seriously, I'll see you tomorrow, but what about next Friday? Are you free to see me again – for a proper date?"

"Friday?"

"Yep, is that a problem?"

"I can be free Friday afternoon. How about meeting at Saint Paul's Cathedral – for a proper date?"

"Esther, that sounds great, sounds truly great."

When reaching the bus stop, they kissed for the final time that day before Esther got onto her bus and they waved goodbye.

Esther, not wanting him to escort her, watched David as he stood watching her leave. She knew she was now too enamoured to think of spending the rest of her life with anyone else, but she knew she would be ensnared in her own trap if David refused to come close to God.

David watched her go, knowing there were some defences still to melt away, even though her last smile had melted every one of his.

Neither knew it would be almost a few decades for them to kiss again.

Don't awaken love before it's ready

Esther handed in her assignment to the lecturer in a hurry, knowing time was rushing, and almost ran to the nearest Underground station. The trains seemed to be slower than normal, and her conscious-self willed the trains to speed up and not stay at any station longer than they should. She clutched a small, wrapped present on her lap and wondered if it was a step too far.

She arrived at last and rushed past a nearby flower stall. Not thinking, she impulsively bought a white rose, ran up the steps to the entrance and entered Saint Paul's Cathedral. Appearing as if lost, she slowly looked at people while she meandered, holding her flower in front of her chest like someone from a quaint nursery story.

Then she saw David. He was directly under the dome, staring straight up at it, not appearing to be the scruffy engineering student, but someone dressed almost in a dark suit, almost out of place, mesmerised by the structure he studied and oblivious to her entrance as far away as she was. She was just able to see the white rose he held, having had the same thought as her.

She realised that with her coat, she predominantly wore white. Taken by a sudden vision of marriage, her exhilaration made her heart pound and her breathing deeper. She was even at the end of the central aisle as though ready for the organ to start announcing the approach of the bride.

David, having studied the dome above him, moved his concentration down the walls and along to the front entrance, having his eyes then stop on an attractive woman who just gracefully came towards him along the central aisle, holding a flower to her chest that she twisted unconsciously.

When she was next to him, they faced each other, not saying anything.

David reached out his flower for her to take and she accepted it.

Having two roses, Esther then handed her rose to David, and he, likewise took it.

They both smiled, unaware that people were quietly looking and forming their own opinions as to what was happening.

"The flower stall outside made good business from us both," said David.

"He must have good market insight. And this is yours as well." Esther handed him the small wrapped present she carried.

"I feel a bit uneasy. I didn't get you anything."

"Just accept it."

"Do I open it now?"

Esther thought for a moment, but shook her head. "You seemed fixed on the dome. You want to go up?"

After climbing the stairs, they reached the landing of the dome's inner level and looked down, trying to regain their normal breathing.

"The ground looks a lot lower from up here, than it does up here as high from down there," mentioned David, in a lowered tone. "Did that sound right?"

"I think it's quite high, if that's what you're saying. Want to whisper something?" whispered Esther.

"Like what?" he whispered back.

"I meant against the wall. Just sit here at the wall with me and whisper something. Apparently you can hear it no matter how softly you speak."

David joined Esther sitting on the continuous stone seat at the wall, turning to face it. "Okay – you say something," he said.

"Like what?"

"I don't know."

They giggled and then tried to stop when two people passed by who looked reproving of them. When this stern couple had moved away, they giggled again.

"Okay, how about this?" David then moved his mouth and lips until Esther pushed him almost over.

"You're not saying anything! Listen to this – Look away, look away." Esther waved her hand vigorously at David.

"You said, look away."

"No, that's for you to do not to repeat."

"Oh."

When David was looking away, Esther then whispered: "'For God so loved the world that He gave His only Son, so that everyone who believes in Him will not perish, but have everlasting life'." Esther then looked at David, who had his ear close to the wall. "Did you hear? Apt in a Church, don't you think?"

"Yes, of course I heard. You had a voice like an elephant."

"Thanks."

"My turn," whispered David.

"Okay."

"Never awaken love before it's ready."

"Sorry?"

"Didn't you hear me?"

"You said something about not awakening love."

"It's Biblical."

"You've been reading Song of Songs?"

"Yep, certainly have." With a gleam to his look, David continued to whisper: "Your waist is like wheat and you walk over rocks like a deer and you have all your teeth, they are all even white. Did you hear? My darling, you are perfume between my breasts."

"Of course I hear you. You sound like a squawking crow."

"Your nose is like the mountains. Your thighs are works of art. Let's stroll through the fields; right at our doorstep, I have stored up for you all kinds of tasty fruit."

Esther started to giggle, trying to suppress a blush: "I don't think it's quite written like that."

"There's a lot of breasts being mentioned."

"She meets a shepherd boy and they plan to marry, but he disappears and she has bad dreams and becomes distraught. Then he reappears as the king."

"Hence the breasts?"

"Well, yes, I can see your clear interest in the book." Esther looked around wondering who else could be hearing their conversation. "But there's nothing wrong with the love between a man and a woman."

With David's increasing confidence, he started going further: "Your arms are graceful, your breasts are perfect as pears, your lips are succulent – "

"Shall we go?"

"I'm enjoying this."

"Yes, I can tell."

"Is it the breasts that's embarrassing? It is Biblical, you know."

"I think you're enjoying my embarrassment more."

"Yes, you do look sweet when you blush."

They descended from the dome, walked down the aisle and were then back outside, in the cold, on the steps of Saint Paul's, with David still amused and Esther relieved.

"Okay, where to now?" asked David.

"There's Tate Modern just over the river. You can tell me how rubbish it all looks."

"Tate Modern? Okay."

They left the Cathedral, walked the few streets towards the Millennium Bridge and were then passing a large building that seemed to be built of crystal.

"That's the headquarters for the International Salvation Army," announced Esther. "We can have a coffee in the basement café."

"Sounds like a good plan."

"But let's cross the bridge first and go to the weirdo art centre and see what's expensive for no reason."

David raised his eyebrows and pursed his lips in consideration. "You now sound like an engineer."

"Come on. It's a freezing day and it's a freezing bridge and you look like you haven't enough to keep you warm: perfect for testing your resolve to stay with me."

"Like Abraham sacrificing his son?"

"It won't be that bad. You won't have to go that far."

"You're sure? It's pretty cold. We'll have to name this place as 'David's Place of Resolve'."

"Well perhaps something might happen and we'll have to rename it as 'Esther's Place of Testing'."

Again, they both laughed, even though there was nothing funny enough to laugh about, and they walked across the bridge reaching the other side.

Just about to descend the steps, David was suddenly tapped on the shoulder and he turned to discover two girls having come from behind, their full attention on him, with Esther being ignored.

"David!" said one of them. "I thought it was you!" She turned to her friend: "I said it was him!"

David was in shock and looked awkward, saying nothing to the forming confrontation he felt coming.

"Yeah, you said," replied the other female, both never resetting their gaze anywhere else.

Recovering, David then responded: "Surprised to see you both – again – here – today."

"We're studying in London," said one of them.

"Oh, I didn't know."

"Well, you wouldn't. We've both moved on!"

"Yes, well, that's – "

Esther then felt intimidated by the forceful, mocking, nasty glare at her from the two demonic creatures, being a deliberate attempt to make her feel unwelcome.

"So who's the latest you've got going, David?"

David turned to Esther: "Sorry, this is Libby and Tanya: old schoolgirls."

"Well congratulations, girlie, on being the next one," sneered Libby at Esther. "Don't worry, he's an easy kiss, but he doesn't shag well."

Tanya also sneered at Esther: "He won't stay around long. He knows he's crap!"

"Actually, this one looks all wrong," added Libby, looking at Esther with indignation, but clearly talking to her friend. "Can't see anything in her."

"She's too prim and proper. It's disgusting!"

"They probably haven't shagged yet."

"I bet my knickers, he's stalking us."

"Okay, that's enough!" snapped David. He turned to Esther: "Let's go."

Libby was not finished: "Oh! Leaving so soon? Well at least we were together this time longer than we dated! Well, see you – not!" Then the two girls, with an exaggerated dominating strut, walked away as if trying to ensure that they were not the victims.

David turned to Esther, feeling her concerned look: "I'm sorry, Esther, they were at my previous school."

"Did you really – shag them?"

"Oh Esther, please don't ruin the day even more. They're just two little girls still living in the school playground."

Esther looked disappointed.

"Look, nothing happened."

"I'm surprised you had anything to do with them." Then she sighed and added, "And I shouldn't judge, I suppose."

"I'm sorry, Esther. Let's get back to enjoying the day. Here, I'll open your present and I'll treat you to whatever you like."

There was no time given for Esther to object as David tore away the wrapping, but her heart sank when she thought she saw disappointment in his face when he held up the Bible she was giving him.

To David, it was not what he had been expecting and the shock was showing through his manner and tone: "That's great, very thoughtful. We can have that big discussion sometime."

"I'm not wanting to force my views on you."

"Yes, I know."

"I hope you don't think that – because I bought you a Bible – that I'm – ."

"No it's fine."

"You don't sound it."

"Esther, really, it's fine, it's great. Let's just forget this art place that we're not going to enjoy, and go back to have a coffee or something and be somewhere warm." He did not want to admit that he had already bought himself a Bible and felt awkward for Esther's consideration of him. Instead, he motioned to cross the bridge again.

Esther nodded in a subdued manner and they were then outside the International Headquarters of The Salvation Army. They entered and turned to descend the stairs to a lower level where there was a café. Although in the basement, it was a pleasant place, with light projected down from the openness of the windows above at street level, and fashionable chairs and tables provided customers with relaxing places to sit and have their meal from the self-service to the far side.

"You want something to eat?" warmly invited David when seeing the food on offer. When Esther shook her head and became non-committal, it was a sign that David knew he was now losing. "I'll get some coffees and join you wherever you want to sit."

Esther nodded and turned to find a quiet table that seemed to be the furthest table possible. She then sat and looked pensive, as if considering her options.

When David joined her, Esther looked up and smiled weakly. She accepted the coffee without giving any appreciation, and drank without saying much.

David felt the silence to be straining and to recover he turned to the side, where, in certain racks and shelves, was a collection of books. He reached over and took one to discover it was about The Salvation Army.

"It's the almanac of the Army's last year," Esther explained. Now no longer sounding distant, she appeared to attempt to be more accepting of him. "It details all the funds gained, corps opening, what's going on in each country."

David continuously looked over the book and appeared to Esther as if he was now ignoring her with this fascination. She felt disappointed that he had not had the same reaction with her present.

"It looks interesting," he eventually said.

"It's free if you want to take it."

"I will." After a further study, David put the book down and tried to make conversation with the first thing that came to mind. "So what do you want to do with your life? You want to become a Salvation Army Vicar?"

Esther, now unleashed to break free from her disappointment, allowed him to see her anger: "I most certainly do not!"

"No?" David was taken aback, but something told him this indignation should have been expected.

"No, I don't! Do I look like someone to stand on a stage and preach?"

Trying to sound pacifying, David said, "Oh, sorry, I just thought you were religious."

"Does that mean anyone religious wants to be a vicar?"

"No, sorry, I'm – I mean, that – anyway."

"Well there's no way I can see you being a Salvation Army Officer!"

This was David's turn to show his indignation: "No?"

"No, certainly not!"

"I can become a Salvation Army Vicar! It looks like a worth-while cause."

"You're not even a Christian!"

"Well, I'm – it's just that – . Look! If I think I can become a Salvation Army Vicar, then what's to stop me? Your judgement?"

"As a minimum you should be a Christian to do the job!"

"Isn't that racist?"

Esther rolled her eyes to the ceiling.

"Well what *do* you want to do?"

"I want to work for the Foreign Office! I told you that already!"

"What foreign office? The Salvation Army's foreign office?"

"You're obsessed with me being in the Barmy Army – no! Thee Foreign Office!"

"What you? A Sally Ann lass? Will they have you?"

"Why not? What's wrong with working for the Government?"

"Because they're all crooked."

"That's subjective and stereotypical, and why shouldn't un-crooked people work in all sorts places, if anything to make a good influence?"

"In a brothel?"

Esther had to stop and resolve her growing judgement with an intake of air. Her eyes became piercing with the narrowness of her stare and her pursed lips seemed needed to prevent an uncontrollable outburst. She stood up with anger, lowering her voice to stop too many people from over hearing: "You have most certainly ruined what could have been a perfect day – and it's called an Officer – it's a Salvation Army Officer, not a vicar, you idiot!"

Both looked at each other for a moment, and then Esther turned sharply and left, walking in a staunched, resolute style up the steps from leaving her white rose on the table.

It was with ease that David, with his view not of the stairs, could imagine the disgruntled and indignant look he was having lasered onto the back of his head, and with difficulty, placing his head in his hands, had to contemplate the ruins of the moment and try to have some hope in resetting time. When he felt there was no longer an infuriated beautiful woman standing on the stairs, he finished his coffee and then left, taking with him the almanac, Esther's present, and his rose, leaving behind the rose that had been Esther's.

On the way home, David could not understand how something that looked so secure had become so destroyed. He decided he had seen a side to the girl that he did not like and concluded with all his experiences, that women were all the same: so digital; so on and off. He opened the Bible and realised Esther had written in the cover: 'Hope this may answer your questions and may you find who you are searching for. Love, Esther X'.

The next Sunday, Mark sat with the band, consciously aware that neither Esther nor David were present, nor did David attend the mid-week football social. Then it was Christmas.

A young woman wants wisdom

The house was a small terraced place, tucked shoulder to shoulder with other terrace houses along the long road. Esther, having walked, now stood outside its front door, shivering in the dark, frosty air, waiting to know her feelings before knocking. After a sigh to relieve her apprehension, she knocked and waited and the door then opened.
"Happy Christmas, Elly."
"Esther! Happy Christmas! Come in, you must be freezing."
"Thanks."
"Come, come, let me take your coat. – Now, let's see you. You're looking well! University going well?"
"Yes, it is, thanks, Elly."
"Well, go through to the sitting room and I'll make some good cups of coffee. How does that sound?"
Esther smiled and nodded, and settled on one of the old flowery chairs that was opposite the warm and glowing fireplace. An ornate clock on the mantelpiece slowly ticked in a paternal manner. Everywhere was all sorts of old Christmas decorations.
When Elly had returned, Esther was warmed through and she accepted Elly's coffee with a smile.
"Your Joyce and Norrie okay?"
"They're fine. They're getting Christmas ready and – well, too many cooks spoil the broth."
"When did you get back?"
"A few days ago."
"And studying? How's that going?"
"Tedious, meticulous, grinding, gnashing of teeth – but it's completely, completely fascinating."
"Keeping up the piano lessons?"
"I use the practice room twice a week for a couple of hours, and I've started playing at a restaurant when their piano player can't make it. I think they're planning on me taking over his position. I might look into

doing this a bit more – you know, around the hotels and restaurants as background music. So how are you?"

"Oh, very much a wonder to most people. Nothing different there. Still playing on Sundays and now I'm teaching little Christopher, bless him." Elly stopped, pondered a moment, looked at Esther, and decided there was more to this visit than the current small-talk. "So any news about 'the one' you told me about on the phone? I did almost ring a few times out of intrigue, but then I resisted being nosey. I thought I would get news from Joyce, but I gather she doesn't know."

Esther smiled: "Joyce is like a Mum to me – so I don't tell her things."

"So what happened?"

Esther's face changed. It became gloomy and Esther sighed. "It didn't work out."

"Oh, shame, but you see, you shouldn't get too carried away too quickly. Don't build something before you know what it will cost."

"'Don't awaken love before it's ready'. I read the Song of Songs. I thought I understood it until now."

"Perhaps one day you will find yourself in a humble, secluded bedroom, distraught by the disappearance of the young, handsome man you love, a young shepherd boy, and you wait and wait and wait, and he reappears as the king of the land, returning from across the horizon in a swathe of dust, a thunderous cloud roaring ever closer. Perhaps one day you will truly experience the pang of waiting for Jesus to return."

"Well, perhaps it's a start with my stupidity with David."

"So what did happen?"

"We had an argument."

"Yes? And? I was married to William for forty-three years, and you should have heard our arguments, some of them very comical when I look back, and I still argue with him about his choice of words on his grave. Esther, you can't go round life thinking that arguments are unavoidable. Grant you that you shouldn't go around thinking they're necessary either. – So what were you arguing about?"

"Well, this is where it gets confusing. He asked me if I wanted to become a Salvation Army missionary."

"Yes? And?"

"And then I became angry."

Elly was at first struck incomprehensible. "Angry? Why? What you?"

"Oh Elly, I'm so ruined! I don't know what got into me. There was a build-up of tension, and we met some of his past girlfriends who weren't nice. They made out he had slept with them, and he didn't like my present, and he was really embarrassing me at Saint Paul's and – I really ruined it. I blamed him, as if it was all his fault."

"Did you really show him your feelings?" Elly asked astounded.

Esther nodded with caution, as if she should not admit to it, but then said as confirmation, "I shouted at him because I thought he had ruined the day, and then I stormed off."

"Well perhaps he is the one if he was able to provoke something emotional from you, even if it was a tantrum."

"I don't like this black, miserable feeling of having made a mistake."

"Learn from it – for the sake of developing a better character in you. There is more reward in putting in the effort to resolve conflict and tension, than running away from it. The failure will be not doing anything for the rest of your life for fear of making another mistake. There's no such thing as a mistake-proof life."

"Yes, I know all that – "

"Well, knowing isn't enough. Just knowing the music isn't enough, you have to play it, and even that's not enough, as you have to feel it – and to get there takes time, dedication and persistence – and many, many mistakes – many. How do you think I got to be me?"

Esther said nothing and finished her coffee.

Elly, enjoying living a younger life through her young guest, thought to enquire more: "He was able to see your emotions?"

"I was volcanic and explosive."

"Really! What happened afterwards? How long ago was this?"

"Two weeks, one day and eleven hours – thereabout."

"Didn't you make up? Why leave it this long?"

Esther shook her head. "I decided that if he wanted to, he would have called me."

"I bet you regret it now, though."

"What shall I do?"

"And this is 'the one'?"

"You should have felt my feelings, Elly."

"And now?"

"I'm irritated that I keep thinking of him."

"You really *are* a teenager. Why didn't you ring him and apologised and got it out the way? That would have been the most grown up thing to do instead of hiding behind an improper excuse of not doing anything. If you have done some damage, then you need to fix it. Take responsibility, because it could be that one thing that destroys your future if left unfixed. If fixed, it could be that one thing that changes the future for untold measures of fortune."

Esther made no reply.

"Get in touch for Christmas. It's the perfect time for this sort of thing. Do you think he would have become a Christian?"

Esther sighed, shrugged and shook her head: "I don't know, perhaps."

Elly smiled, "What was he like?"

Esther, from nowhere suddenly brightened up: "Ah he was sweet and handsome, charming and funny, and good company and – good at kissing – "

"Really!"

"He was great at kissing. Well, I enjoyed it. He had this smell about him, a natural smell."

"Smell?"

"A burning, smouldering, – sweet, rich, – enticing – coffee, woodwork smell about him."

"Coffee? Woodwork?"

Esther nodded and then shrugged.

"Well, he sounds like a bit of a catch, but don't be unequally yoked though. You know what this means?"

Esther nodded.

"If your lifestyles don't match then something needs to give, but he deserves a 'sorry' by the sounds of it."

"But I feel he needs time to get in touch with me."

"What, for *you* to apologise? Shouldn't you get in touch with him? Don't go to worship God if there is something wrong. First sort it out before going."

"Perhaps I should let him have some time."

"For something so minor? Well, it's up to you, but I think you're running away, hiding behind feelings that you should be old enough to drop. Even a silly minor argument can fester and fester until it becomes something beyond all recognition. Forgiving people for major things is not enough: you have to forgive people for minor things as well. That's why people hate God. His standards are so high." Elly looked at Esther's worried face. "You will forgive him, won't you?"

Esther nodded.

"And forgive yourself?"

"It's such a minor, minor quarrel. Why is it so large to me? I think I'm more mortified at how I acted, than worried about how – I'm not sure I know what I'm saying."

"Esther, the impact you have on someone can totally revolutionise their life. The wrong word can transform them into something less than what they deserve. The kindest encouragement can energise someone to achieve great things. The repercussions can be so far-reaching that you may not even get to know it."

Esther nodded, pensively.

"Society is extremely interconnected and nonlinear, Esther. Two plus two will not always equal four. A small drop can cause the greatest waves; the largest momentum can dissipate to nothing. The smallest gossip can topple empires; an emperor can die achieving nothing. Life is a complexity that cannot be known in a reductionist way as everything is linked and connected and influencing everything. It is said that we are six people away from knowing the whole world. Whether that's true or not, I understand the sentiment. Life is a responsibility because of this intricate connectedness. Decide what influence you want to have on others and how you want to be influenced."

Esther nodded again.

"So what are you going to do next?"

"I thought I'd play the piano."

"Mmm, not what I was really asking, but it will do. Want to play here? Now?"

Esther nodded eagerly: "Yes please. If I play at some top restaurants and hotels, I could earn some money to get me through Uni. The Dorchester is willing to pay really well."

"That's very enterprising of you."

"You're not disappointed I'm going outside The Salvation Army?"

"No, not at all. I'm just an old woman investing in you becoming the woman you are meant to be, learning to be disciplined to make beautiful music with your life. My reward is to see your moral fibre in the decisions you make. And anyway, having the ability to play music can be both therapeutic and enterprising. I don't know why more people don't take it up."

"Thank you."

"If you place God first, play wherever you feel like you should. In fact, play to them some rendition on some Salvation Army music, and pray for the people who are listening, for whatever secret stress they may have. Remember, people are defenceless against prayer: they can't stop you doing it."

"And do you know how to preserve a rose?"

"Oh that's easy – why?"

"I've got a rose I would like preserved."

"Leave it with me." Elly got up and motioned to Esther to do the same: "Come and play the piano for me before you swamp my house with your maudlin tears about this Mister Darcy of yours. I assume that's what the rose is about. Promise me you will apologise – if anything for your own sake."

Esther nodded, but became daunted by the realisation of how hard it was going to be. Changing the subject, she then asked curiously, "So what does your husband have on his gravestone?"

"John eleven, verses twenty-five and twenty-six."

"Oh – sounds reassuring to me."

"Yes, but his interpretation is inscribed as, 'Wishing you were here with me'."

A young man wants wisdom

An old man, sitting at his humble dining table with old Christmas decorations and merry well-wishing cards surrounding him, dutifully read the book that he had open. With no one else present, his mind mulled over the passages.

Then the doorbell rang.

Wondering who it could be on such a dark, dreary day, he got up and went through to the hallway, and opened the door. "Well, bless my cotton socks! It's my long, lost Grandson! Come in! Come in! Warm your merry cockles!"

"Happy Christmas, Granddad."

"And to you! Let me take your coat. Drink? Something hot? Soup? I do a good tomato soup."

"Oh yes please."

"Please go through." Joseph motioned to the door of the living room that also catered for a small dining area the other side of an archway.

David sat himself down on a tiny sofa and looked over the place while waiting. Then his Grandfather came in with two bowls of soup and toast on a tray and placed them on the dining table, moving his Bible aside.

"Come and sit," he requested and David joined him. "How have you been? How's the electronics?"

"Fine, just fine, getting on with it, getting good marks."

"And, if you don't mind me asking, why are you here? Does your Mum know?"

David nodded.

"Is she okay?"

"She went nuclear when I told her I wanted to visit, and then I had to leave because it became too radioactive."

"So you effectively ran away."

"I suppose. Dad said he would get in touch when the fall-out subsided. My brother's now home so things might get better."

"You can't spend Christmas without Mum and Dad, not like this."

David gave a look to contradict the statement.

Joseph raised his eyebrows in minor despair. "Bread?"

David took some that Joseph offered. "You won't mind if I possibly stay here?"

"I'm concerned about being too much of a division between you and your Mum, but you're welcome to keep me company."

"I'm actually asking to stay at Halcyon."

"I don't think that's wise. It's very cold at this time of year: definitely not for the likes of someone old like me, or someone inexperienced like you."

"But people used to live there in these conditions."

"Yes, and they were experienced. That's how they lived, and they died young as well. Remember, you're closer there to nature than your modern ways and cosy life-style. It could even snow."

"They haven't predicted it."

"No, but it is cold enough."

"I need to think. I don't feel like I can do it anywhere else." David paused and then said, "I met someone."

"Good for you! What's she like?"

"She's in The Salvation Army."

Joseph looked up with surprise: "Really!"

"I was wandering along Oxford Street and along came The Salvation Army marching, playing brass instruments and beating a big drum and then I thought of you and followed."

"I'm flattered."

"Actually, I saw some of the girls were pretty."

Joseph bellowed with laughter: "Excellent! Excellent!"

"You don't think that was shallow of me, then?"

"Of course! Of course! Why ever not? Men *are* shallow. You should really see how God sees us. Then you'll know how shallow we all are." Then he started to laugh again at David's expense.

"I can tell you're happy about this."

"Cheer up, Grandson! You won't go to Hell because you fancy a few women. What matters is what you do about it."

"Well that's the problem. What do I do about it?"

"Be wise! Live with decency and dignity. God didn't make attractiveness to be smutty; everyone else made it smutty. Hebrew proverb: always take your water from the same, private well. One woman is enough, and the right woman is the best. That's the way of it."

"There was only one that – she was – so – so beautiful."

"Always do a random act of kindness, and don't treat her like she owes you anything. My marriage was based on giving without expecting, and it worked. Marriage, my lad, is hard, but the effort is worth the gain, and you can learn a lot about yourself and something about God's ways in a good marriage."

"This was only a first kiss and a few dates."

"My marriage became a shade of how it should be between God and me. I wanted to care for my wife in the same way I wanted God to care for me. It was possible to understand how God sees me at times, and do things out of kindness, not because I feel like I owe."

"You're not listening, are you?"

"And you're not even married yet."

"I'm not going to be at this rate."

"I don't talk for that long."

"I mean, we're no longer together."

"Good job God invested in your brain to find more than one woman attractive then. – You don't seem to find this amusing."

David shook his head.

"You're quite taken with this one, then?"

"I'm all broken up about her, if that's something to go by. We had an argument."

"Ah! Definitely love!"

"Granddad, I want to know about being a Christian. Not that I promise to become one, but I need to – to sort this out. That's why I've come – to get away and think. What should I do about her?"

"Well, it's not wise to be, what is called in the Bible, 'unequally yoked,' meaning do not marry someone with a totally different view of life, with different goals, directions, ambitions."

"Granddad, I'm not talking about getting married!"

"Oh yes you are! All this dating is all about finding that special someone, whether you are conscious of it or not. So don't go telling me that I don't understand you."

David became pensive and even dour.

"So what is she like?"

Instantly, David's attitude stood up from lowered shoulders, and downcast eyes looked up and became bright: "Oh Granddad, if you were to meet her, you, of all people would understand why it's her. Her hair is a perfect shade of gold, her face is just perfect, her legs are – her figure – . Well, you know."

Joseph replied with a smile. "So what happened?"

"That's the weird thing about it. We were discussing what we wanted to do in life and she objected to me asking whether she wanted to become a Salvation Army Officer."

"Really?"

"And then she went berserk when I said I could become one."

"You can only become one if you are in The Salvation Army."

"Yes, she said that."

"She has a point, don't you think? And you have to be a Christian to be in The Salvation Army, eager to help the lost and feed the hungry."

"I was just trying to say that it's a worthy cause."

"Would you really consider becoming an Army Officer, leading in the Salvation Army?"

"You haven't answered my question."

"What about?"

"Esther, the one I'm in fear of losing."

"I think it's answered already. I don't understand why this is a major thing over a small tiff. You have to decide whether you truly love her. If you truly love her, then you show this by not being selfish and not taking her at your whim. There is a difference between a man who admires the beauty there is in a woman, and a man who wants her for his idolatrous selfishness. You must let her be her, and you need to decide as to your own aspirations, beliefs and way of life, because if you expect her to drop everything to support any sort of whimsical fling, then you are a very bad person indeed."

"I think she would put me in my place, but – there's something fragile about her. I suppose that's why I feel like I want to protect her. It was as if she wasn't as confident as she made herself out to be at times. There was something in her past that she didn't want to talk about. Why is love so difficult?"

"David, it was a minor tiff."

"Yes, I know, but – ."

"Don't chase her for selfish reasons because it's doomed from the start. Make sure you do it to enhance her life with what you can give, not by what you can take. And, by the way, perhaps she feels the call to become an Army Officer and she's fighting against it. Your comment may have come at the wrong time."

"She's adamant about joining the Foreign Office."

"The Government? The British Foreign Office?"

David nodded.

"She's ambitious, then."

David nodded again.

"Sure you're up to her standards?"

David shrugged.

"Well don't forget, Christians can also have a rebellion against God in their way. Take a lesson from Jonah."

"Jonah?"

"Yes, why is it you never seem to know any Bible stories? Just read it."

"Jonah wasn't a Christian."

"No, I know, he was Jewish, but that's not my point."

"So you think Esther may give in and become a Salvation Army Officer?"

"And if she does, you will have to make further decisions. Take seriously becoming a Christian, but consider becoming a Christian, not for her sake, but yours."

"To be honest, I don't know where to start."

"First things first, David. Write down everything you have a question about: everything, leave nothing out, everything that confuses you." Joseph took from the side a few sheets of paper and a pen, and passed them to his Grandson. "Tomorrow I will not answer any of them."

"Sorry?"

"I'm not interested in just giving quick, cheap, theatrical clap-trap. I want you to show me how hungry you are to know the answers you want. Who are you for God to answer your questions when you haven't searched for Him earnestly? How would the God of everything see a mortal who just wants quick answers? An indolent man full of his own pride who doesn't deserve anything, that's how."

David did not reply.

"It's a bit like finding an exquisite pearl, and then doing all you can to keep it."

Again, David was at a loss for a response.

"When you are searching for Him, like you've misplaced all your life's savings or your life depended on it, He will answer, but He will answer with His timing and in His way. Read the Bible with the purpose of finding Him. In fact, try and see it from His point of view – how would you feel if someone was just not that interested? But ask your questions. God wants you to ask Him questions – even with deep emotions. But never ask out of rebellion, as that means you're not going to listen anyway."

"But what about Halcyon? Can I go tomorrow?"

"No."

"Why?"

"It will snow tomorrow."

"It's not forecast."

"The place will be frozen as it is. How long would you stay there?"

"Only a day or so. I need to get home for Christmas really to patch things up."

"You came all this way to get to Halcyon, just to think?"

"Yes."

"Even though it might snow?"

"It won't."

"You will be isolated. Mobile phones do not go that far."

"Let me go, Granddad. Let me be this someone who's trying to earnestly show he's searching."

"Mmmmm – well, the only way to find out what happens next is to let you go, if anything, because you remind me of someone."

"Really? Who?"

"Me. Was the soup not good?"

Narnia

It was now snowing heavily. The air was full of large snowflakes slowly falling from an overcast sky. Each tree was fast becoming hidden for all the snow each branch held and the ground was already buried under a deepening carpet of white. The forest was slowly disappearing.

Walking alone, isolated, in this total silence, with the cold air biting his exposed cheeks, David trekked through this captivating winter wonderland that no one else could experience, although the beauty was lost on him as he had no choice but to continuously study the ground to stop from tripping. He stopped and looked up to see Halcyon suddenly materializing, as if a few more steps would have caused him to hit against it.

The manor stood before him eerily appearing as though a ghost house, a magnanimous virtual monument. For a few moments, he just stood marvelling this apparition, as if it was coming through from a better world just for him.

Noticing the cold again, he trudged to the front door and was quickly inside, shaking off the snow in the large reception hall, but continued wearing his coat, scarf and big boots as there was no difference in the temperature. He took off his backpack and carried it with him to the kitchen where he placed it on the large wooden table and got from it some matches. Logs were already prepared in the large chimney and David with his numb fingers tried to light a match. They all fizzled out.

His hands and feet were aching for warmth, and he started to become impatient. After a few moments of being unsuccessful, he gave up and went back to his bag on the table. He took from it a flask and drank some hot coffee, although by now it was a weaker version of the original.

Rifling through his own bag again, he came across Esther's Bible and read again what she had written in the front cover. It was then that he so wished he had a photograph of her, and with this thought, he placed the Bible to one side.

Although peaceful and scenic, the biting cold of his fingers, the scorching feel of his cheeks, and the struggle of his lungs fighting the freezing air, turned the idyllic conditions into something quite bleak and lonely. There was little food, there was no company, and this isolation seemed to enforce and amplify his loss and yearning. Reality was now commandeering his thoughts, making him question the wisdom he had the day before. He started to ask why his Grandfather had not been more dissuasive.

He returned to the hearth, having found the blocks of firelighters, and eventually made small flames erupt with his next attempt. After a few minutes, the fire took hold and the growing warmth and glow started to change the kitchen's appearance.

He laid out the sleeping bag and blankets beside the fire, sat at the kitchen table, placed some eating provisions beside him, and took out the pen and paper his Grandfather had given him. Then he just sat there, wondering what to write until the pen fell from his hand, his thoughts fell from being meaningful, and his tiredness made him fall asleep as soon as he got into his sleeping bag. He had written absolutely nothing.

This weird place where we breathe

Providing enough light for David to wake, the sun was up, but the sky was grey making the outer covering of the atmosphere appear as ash. The fire of the kitchen's hearth had mellowed to grey matching the sky and he awoke feeling cold, stiff and uncomfortable from the hard floor. It was then that he felt extra blankets over him and started to question his sanity, as he had settled for the night without them.

To his sudden fright, a series of steps, made from the wet boots of someone's arrival, led to and from the door to the rest of the building. Someone was in the house with him, and whoever it was, they had seen him asleep. He got up, followed the trail through the silent house, but stopped and became convinced that beyond the door now facing him was the crackling of a fire. He hesitated before entering, was about to knock, when he called out in a soft, enquiring voice: "Joseph?"

The door opened quickly which made him yelp with the suddenness, and David was then confused with the appearance of a woman wearing a coat, holding the door ajar, looking at him with a pleasant smile.

"Good Morning!" she spritely announced. Her age was above his Mum, but much less than Joseph. She looked pleasant and pleased to see him. "I'm sorry to startle you, but I'm Elsie, Misses Manning, Joseph's house-keeper."

"Who?"

"Misses Manning, and you should be David, if Joseph has it right."

"Yes, I am."

"I came earlier, but you were still asleep."

"How do you know of this place? Joseph said only a few know this exists."

"I'm part of the few. Did he not tell you he had a cleaner? Well, it's more of a cup of tea and chat."

David shook his head, trying to wake up from an uncomfortable sleep, his thoughts ruffled by this unexpected visitor.

"I've set the fire going in the Chapel and I've set aside a chair for you to be near it at the table. Go and warm yourself and I'll be back."

Still in a daze, David peered inside and saw the room with its tall, narrow stained-glass windows, with its archways criss-crossing the ceiling and side pews. Within the large fireplace was a fire, softly providing light and warmth to a nearby long wooden table and matching wooden chairs. With more wood, the fire would have become blazing. The woman had vanished when he turned back to her, so he decided to stand just in front of the hearth, feeling the heat.

"Here you are," came her voice from the door as she entered, carrying a tray containing a cup, a teapot and some bread. She placed it on the table and motioned for David to sit.

"Thank you."

"I know it's not quite breakfast, but I'll do some soup later. I suppose you're wondering about me being here."

"I was expecting Joseph."

"Yes, but he's not agile enough to come in this weather. He asked my husband to come, but he's got important work. I think Joseph was concerned that it was a bad decision for you to be here, after all."

"I came here to think. I think he realised that."

"Oh, he did. That's why he comes here."

"And you come here?"

"I've only come here a few times. I've known Joseph for sometime though. When I saw he could do with some help around his house, he allowed me to be his cleaner. He would go away and be strange about where he would say he was going. Eventually he told me of this place, even though my husband already knew. He's the solicitor, you see. I don't think we can stay long. Joseph will start to worry about both of us, but he understood the reason why you wanted to be here, and I think he wanted to respect that."

David nodded.

"I wouldn't like to stay here more than this afternoon. There was a mighty snowfall overnight, and I wouldn't want it to snow anymore before we get back."

"No."

"You can stay in this hall and write for a while longer. It's more inspiring than the kitchen."

"Thank you."

"Here's your paper and pen," she said, handing over the items. "I'll be in the kitchen." With that, she left.

David sat at the table and when finished his drink, he reached over, learnt there was more in the teapot, poured another, placed the paper in front of him, and set to work thinking and capturing his thoughts. The task was initially more difficult than planned, but when starting to write, the words came naturally. When he finished, he looked at what he had written.

To my future self,

These are my big questions for you to have answers for your past self.

Why choose Christianity, when there are so many religions? Which one is right, if any?

What about all the suffering in the world? What about the earthquakes, volcanoes and extreme weather that disrupt and kill, even those who are innocent? What about the crashes that kill and maim people? What loving God would allow that? Why do good people have to suffer? Why do good people get punished and criminals go without? Why doesn't God intervene? Where is He? How and why does God allow evil? What is evil and is Satan real? Are demons and spirits and angels folklore or to be believed as existing? Where does the sense of good and evil come from? Why is 'good' good and 'bad' bad?

What about the other species of humans who were here on Earth? Who was Adam and Eve? How can someone be punished for eternity, just for a few moments of sinning? Why should I suffer because of what Adam and Eve did?

Why are there four gospel stories of Jesus in the Bible? Why are they different? Why did Jesus have to die the way he did? What was the point? What was there to gain? Why isn't just declaring forgiveness enough? Why this extreme? What about Judas? What if he had not acted the way he did? Would Jesus have not gone to the cross, and if so, would this have mattered? If it did matter, then surely Judas did the right thing.

How can you tell if God is speaking to you? What if you mistake it for satanic voices, or mental health problems? What will happen if you believe you are doing what God wants, when you find out you're not? What right has God to judge us if we have mental health problems making our decisions? Are we the product of our brain, powered by DNA, experience and culture, or does our brain mould to the thinking of our free-will, an engine we control, like an exercised muscle?

What if you don't get to hear about Jesus? Why are the Biblical laws so judgemental and why are the punishments so severe in the Old Testament? Why does God come across as supporting war in the Old Testament, when He seems passive in the New Testament? Why is the Bible so blood-thirsty and permits and exhorts the killing of innocent sheep and lambs and delights in the spilt blood of these poor animals as a sacrifice to atone? Why would God let a man believe it was right to place his son on an altar and almost allow him to murder? If that were to happen today, he would be imprisoned, considered insane, and the amount of mental disturbance the child would have, would require decades of counselling.

Why does the Bible seem to upgrade men and downgrade women?

Why did Jesus come at the time he did? Why not some centuries earlier or later, or even from the beginning? And God, Jesus and Holy Spirit? How does the trinity makes sense? How much faith should make sense before you start to believe in the ridiculous without knowing? When should faith over-rule wisdom, and when should wisdom over-rule faith? Can the two ever be the same?

Chance, fate, destiny, free-will, choice? Once saved as a Christian, can I lose this if I then act the same old way? In which case, was I ever saved? If God can see all of my life, but can also intervene at specific points in my life that changes things, does this not forfeit my future that he originally saw?

If God exists, how did he come about? What truly was before the Universe? Where did it come from, and what should it mean to me?

Why are animals savage? Are humans savage because they are animals? Why is the natural world so violent? The animals attack and eat each other. Even the insects are hostile.

What should I do about Esther?

David sighed with irritation, thinking he had troubled to come all this way to write something he now thought he could have done in his bedroom, and decided to take the tray back to the kitchen, feeling obliged to return it. When he arrived, a small portion of the kitchen fireplace had been relit and a pot was hung above it boiling something.

"Soup," Misses Manning explained, sitting at the kitchen table, still in her coat with her own cup of tea. "We have this soup, and then you can have some more time to finish and then we'll leave. We can walk through the forest until we get a signal and I can ring my husband. He'll pick us up."

Misses Manning went to stir the soup. She tasted it with the long spoon and satisfied herself that a few moments more were needed.

They were both then sitting at the table.

"How much do you know of my Grandfather?" David asked. "I know he went to Africa, but – what happened to my Grandmother?"

"They went there together to work in a Salvation Army Outpost that I think he and his wife helped set up. I'm reluctant to ask too many questions because he seems to not want to talk, but she's buried out there. In fact, before they went to Africa, Joseph had some legal business with my husband's father, and whatever Joseph said to him, made him a Christian and the reason his son, my husband, grew up in the Baptist Church. But whatever happened in Africa made him leave The Salvation Army for some time."

"He left?"

"Because she died." Misses Manning got from her seat, removed the pot from its hook using a long pole and placed the soup on top of a wooden block on the table. Getting two bowls from the side, she ladled the soup from the pot into them, talking at the same time. "He came back to England and I gather he worked as a refuse collector for some years. Then he worked at the local hospital as a cleaner, but then assisted in A&E. That's where I met him, on my Chaplaincy visits. I convinced him to come along to one of our services. Then he started attending The Salvation Army, but we keep in touch considering we live in the next street."

"When did he get this place?"

"I think he's had this place for decades. My husband would know."

"And he did nothing about it?"

"It's only entrusted to him in some sort of legal maintenance contract by – I don't know who. My husband would, but legally he probably couldn't tell you. You're asking questions that I'm really only guessing."

"You mean he had all this and he became a dustman?"

"Your Grandfather can be a closed book at times."

They both became silent as they ate for a while, and then David finished and decided to resume his questions: "Misses Manning – ?"

"Elsie."

"Elsie, can I ask you a personal question?"

"Yes, of course."

"What does Jesus mean to you?"

"Jesus means everything to me."

David was disappointed by her answer. It seemed not to answer anything at all except for showing her heartfelt endearment or delusion, but then Misses Manning continued.

"I am like a kitten, playing within His hand's reach, and I cuddle up and sleep on His lap. I am to Him, what a kitten is to me. I trust Him to look after me in ways I can never understand. If God loves me as much as I love my cats, then I am a happy woman."

David remained quiet for a while, and then said quite respectfully, "I can't see how anyone can know someone so personally who lived so many centuries ago. It's just too idyllic."

"If you continue seeking, you will find Him, because He will allow you to find Him. That's what He wants. But if your heart is hard, He will harden it more. If you want to walk away, He will allow it. If you want to lose Him, then He will lose you. Talk to Joseph. He has more of a male mind to all this. We females aren't into the why's of it. If the snow has disrupted your travel home then you'll have a bit more time with him to ask your questions."

"I think I've written all that I'm going to write here."

Searching for an authentic Bible

Misses Manning left Joseph's house after they all said goodbye, and David sat in the lounge, politely waiting for the front door to close. He heard the few last words of the two, the short footsteps taken by Misses Manning and then the door finally closing.

Joseph came into the room: "She only lives in the next street."

"Oh."

"And I spoke to your Dad on the phone."

"Are they worried?"

"I think I convinced him you were safe with me. I didn't tell him I had let you go all the way, alone to an old, empty manor house that has no services, with scant provisions – in the deepest snowfall for a few years. I had to pull out a few misleading remarks when your Dad wanted to speak with you."

"What did you say?"

"I just said you had gone out, and will be back. I think they're under the impression you're here in a huff not to speak to them. Perhaps you can ring them back and say all is forgiven – whatever the trouble is. By the way, here's your flower." Joseph handed David a small wooden press, bolted together, pressing layers of cardboard. "You left it here, so I thought to preserve it for you. Want some tea? Would you like to have a game of chess? Evalynne and I loved chess. Played it for hours."

"Tea would be great, thanks, and thanks again for the chess set you gave me. It looks very old."

"It is. It was the one we used in Africa. Let me get some tea going."

When he returned with a teapot, Joseph knew that David had been silent enough to tell that a difficult question was about to be asked.

"Why did Jesus have to die the way He did? Tortured and then left to die, nailed to a wooden cross?"

"I thought you were going to ask something else."

"I asked Misses Manning about what Jesus meant to her. Is she a bit of a loony?"

"I shouldn't think so. She taught mathematics at the local Higher Education College."

"Oh."

"Why? What did she say?"

"It's just that I don't think I could ever be a little kitten sitting on someone's lap."

"Ah, yes, she does like her cats. Makes sense to me, though."

"She talked as if she was under a strange delusion."

"Well, I expect you didn't give her long."

"I always thought that it was schizophrenia when you spoke to imaginary people or things, like praying, talking to someone invented in your head."

"I can understand someone with mental health issues to have problems, but not Elsie."

"But there's more to just being a cat on a lap."

"True."

"So who was Jesus? A good man? A good teacher?"

"Goodness gracious, David! Jesus was more than a good teacher! He openly declared Himself as the Messiah, the Christ, the one foretold in the Hebrew, Israelite Scriptures!"

"Did he?"

"Yes! Read the four Gospel stories, David! Jesus is almost saying it all the time! In fact, read John's Gospel! He even uses Scripture to compare Himself as being divine, being the same as God, and at times He was going to be stoned to death for blasphemy, which means people understood what He was saying, and Jesus never corrects them for any misunderstanding. Even at His trial, He deliberately announces Himself to be the one foretold by the prophecy of Daniel."

"Daniel?"

"Yes, Daniel wrote of the Son of Man coming, which everyone knew to mean someone divine – of being God in flesh, coming in the clouds of Heaven to conquer the world and make it His Kingdom. And the indignant reaction He got meant they knew what He was declaring. So indignant and repulsed, they crucified Him for it. In fact, if someone teaches that Jesus isn't one with God, then he is a false teacher – avoid them. Any true and complete Christian will have complete faith in Jesus being truly God living with us as a man, truly dying from an execution, and, three days after His crucifixion, returning truly alive – and – in fact – have an active hope in His dramatic return."

"So what does Jesus mean to you?"

"He's my rock, my saviour, my friend, my master, my architect. He goes beyond all the words I can ever use."

David sighed.

"That doesn't mean much to you, does it?"

David shook his head.

"Well this female of yours means a lot to you, but I haven't met her. All I can tell is what she means to you. That doesn't work either, does it?"

David just shrugged.

"All this can only be academic unless you start to believe and take it to heart, but, for me, Jesus does go beyond all the words I can ever use – like an inexpressible feeling, a devotion that can't be decoded by words. You're an engineer – you know that language is a code."

"Yes."

"But everything is a code: language is a code, music is a code, chemistry is a code, mathematics is a code; number theory, modern software, DNA – is all code. You can look at anything, look into anything, and you will find some reason or clockwork. You just have to decode it. Doctors, detectives, scientists, psychologists, children doing their homework – they all have this pursuit in common. And if you read the Bible, you will decode something running through the stories and words that many overlook, yet it's plain if you read it with interest."

"You make it sound like a conspiracy."

"No, it's all there as plain as daylight to those who read it. You just have to read and look, and sometimes these connections leap out at you. You can't understand the New Testament fully, unless you know the Old Testament."

"Perhaps people see connections that aren't really there."

"Two of Jesus' disciples were walking to Emmaus. Jesus had been crucified three days earlier, so when a total stranger joins them in their walk, all they do is talk about it. But as confused and dejected as these two were, this stranger tells them of things in the Jewish Scriptures, the Old Testament, that predicts Jesus as a sacrifice: the prophesies, the signs, the portrayals of Jesus in the Old Testament, hundreds to thousands of years before He came."

"Oh."

"This stranger then reveals Himself as Jesus and the two then rush back to Jerusalem to tell the others that Jesus is alive. It must have been impossible for them to believe what they saw, but they did, they did believe. They knew it was Him and they knew what He said was exciting and knew it made sense. You can read this in Luke."

"I don't really understand what you mean by this code."

"Stories, events, sayings, systems and – blatant prophesy – a code, a joined-up code throughout the Bible, a patchwork of a consistent message that validates Jesus as the saviour – of us all. Here, read this." Joseph got from his seat and returned with his Bible. He spent a little time searching the chapters until he found what he sought. Then he offered the book, with the page open for David. "Isaiah chapter fifty-two, verses thirteen to fifteen and chapter fifty-three, verses one to twelve."

David read it for a while and then looked up at Joseph.

"That was written at least four hundred years before Christ. You know the Easter story? Any resemblance?"

David did not like to agree, but there was little he could say to disagree.

"Jesus said that He has come to fulfil the Scriptures, and that He will come back to complete His work, and only He can complete His work because only He can fully judge and eradicate evil and suffering. So you will find that what is most important – the most, most important, is what you decide about Jesus. And even if you decide nothing about Him, He will still decide about *you*! So if creation took six days or billions of years, then it's inconsequential."

David gingerly nodded: "I guess."

"If you know the Scriptures inside out, then you see it clearly."

"Yes, I suppose," said David, not knowing what else to say.

"Well the Pharisees didn't – and they should have done. They were the ones who knew the Scriptures inside out, and they knew some of these passages related to the coming Messiah, but because they wanted a warrior to lead them to victory against the Romans – in their agenda, their expectation – they rejected Jesus, because Jesus wasn't against the Romans and He was upsetting their authority. He was more against the Pharisees because they used their knowledge of the Law of Moses and their self-empowerment to burden people. And these Pharisees thought they were the good guys by keeping the nation's identity and traditions going. In fact, these Pharisees are still with us today. Between you and me, I think God is bigger than those who tell people that He doesn't exist, but what gets God irate are those who tell God how He should do things better and act if they can do a better job of it."

"How many are there of these prophetic examples?"

"Loads, hundreds. You'll be surprised. Search with all your heart, David, explore His book and discover what there is to discover."

"Why? Why have all this prophecy?"

"If you perform the right scientific experiments, study the results, follow the logic and come to the right conclusions, you get to believe in atoms. Anyone who is searching and reads the Bible and follows its logic, can find the confidence to have faith and hope in Jesus. Many Old Testament predictions of Him are naturally impossible to force or to manipulate, and Jesus deliberately enacts some prophecy as if to personally endorse His fulfilment. In the garden of Gethsemane, just before His arrest, Jesus said He would have to endure what was needed to fulfil the Scriptures, and after His resurrection, He appears to the disciples and tells them how the Scriptures point to Him."

David made no reply.

"Look at the Bible, David, like looking at a water lily painting by Monet. Even if there are human fingerprints in the mix of the writing, you can still see the main thrust of the Bible, the bigger picture, and see it in context to world history and the current news. And even if there is total archaeological and historical evidence to uphold the Bible, its authenticity can only come from your belief that Jesus fulfils it. If the Bible is fully authentic, then its claims on you can be your total downfall – or your only hope."

"So why did He die? Why all this crucifixion?"

"To claim mankind back from Satan from the fall in Genesis. To pay back God our punishment that we owe. To show God is willing to prove His sincere love and commitment to us. To show He cares. To understand our life from our side and is willing to suffer with us. To earnestly make us want to change our ways without Him being an absolute dictator. To defeat death for us in His resurrection. To demonstrate that He does deserve to judge us."

"All that?"

"Yes."

"Oh."

"Yes."

"But – why not just forgive?"

"Well that's cheap – if you consider sin not that serious. It's because of the enormous amount of love and enthusiasm He has for us, and the enormous amount of loathing He has for the way we treat each other and our neglect and mutiny of Him, that He can't just sweep it aside."

"But how does a loving God judge people to go to hell?"

"How can a Holy God, a God radioactive with Holiness, allow

unclean people into Heaven? David, believe me, God finds our sin, our self-centredness, our rebellion disgusting. He will not touch it. It's unclean. It's like water and oil. Even our belief that we are good enough, perfect even, ideal, as we are, without a need for forgiveness, is a major arrogance. Many of our decisions made out of perceived goodness is causing major illnesses for the planet and stored-up problems for the future, but it would be wrong to think He has given up on us."

"Would it? I think I would have abandoned mankind a long time ago, with that description."

"Well, I think the way God looks at you, I don't think He can leave things as they are. That's why He came here, totally God and totally human as Jesus, taking our place for the penalty that our sin condemns us. That's how serious sin is, that's how serious God deems it, and it shows how far He goes to put things right. That's how much He loves us."

"So we – what? Just accept? Just accept it? It's that easy?"

"You cannot secure a place in Heaven by working perpetually hard to be holy by obeying rules. You cannot follow rules and traditions, and then claim to be righteous. To God, it's a standard that just drops down the toilet. You can never get right with God with whatever you think you can achieve. He achieved the Universe. What standard is that – that we can ever match it? Perfection is a condition that none of us can afford. Never become arrogant to think you can reach it with your own might – because that sets you up to be your own god. It makes you conceited, and God hates that. It breaks the first commandment. It means we think Jesus' crucifixion, His sacrifice on our behalf, is inadequate, is lacking, means nothing. Jesus has paid the full, total, absolute, unrefundable cost for us to be acceptable – on God's terms. Go to Him with a contrite heart. Believe first! With Jesus, the cost has been paid. I am forgiven. I am accepted. I walk with my Saviour. Now is that romantic or not? Beats evolution any day."

"So there's nothing we can do?"

"God will not water down the standards, David. God will not abide with sin. God takes the penalty in Jesus that we can't achieve. God is the uncreated; we are the created. We are His slaves with freedom. Anything we do to place mastery away from God is mutiny and punishable. We are to live as saved people because of what Jesus has done. We're to live free and clean, guiltless and joyous, in obedience to His teaching, to have faith in Him, to trust Him with our life, with our death, and live in a manner that demonstrates this faith, no matter how things look. We are to be forever grateful, to let go, to be still, and love others, and have a continual deep regard to the consequences of His justice and judgement, because we're not forgiven to continue sinning, or to do nothing. We're to live a clean life, but to be cleaned to perfection in God's sight is to accept Jesus' death on the cross. I tell you this: the Christian should never complain of their hard life while knowing that Christ suffered for them. This was what brought me back. But, you see, is He really a harsh God? What harsh God would create such beauty in the world for us to enjoy? Just read Genesis, the beginning, and think of what Heaven would be like."

David made no reply as he seriously and secretively considered the request.

"Examine the Bible, David, and come to your own conclusions. At least show you are searching. This is a Holy love. This is a love of justice and a love of forgiving mercy. It's a love that shapes us. It's not a pretty love or a cuddly love or a love of attractiveness or fairytale. It's far more than romance. There, say that to your girl. Now how about that game of chess? A game of decisions, of incomplete knowledge, of strategy, of influence, battling side by side as king and queen. Romantic, don't you think?"

Wuthering Heights

From the drizzle it once was, the rain now came down with force and might, splattering the tall, stained-glass panes of the small hall that made the glass awash from the blustery winds. The sound of dripping water was then heard hitting enamel pots from around the house in an array of frequencies.

Sergeant Richards stood up from his pew to stretch his legs. He turned to look at the table, walked over to it and placed Esther's writing there, suddenly wishing he could imagine monks of ages past eating in this abbey-like room, or chanting, or within their own reading. He sat beside them with this image, looked down to see the next page and, absorbed, picked it up to read. It was then that the full force of the rain came down from blackened clouds and a flash of lightning lit the room. A clap of thunder soon followed.

I have been reminiscing about the day I was fuming at David and marching off after a silly disagreement. I stormed off into the streets leaving him to his coffee, angry over the ruin of our romance. I walked with pace, my mind spiralling in confusion, frustration, dejection and disappointment with a day that could have been so perfect.

But it was me that had been so reckless, thinking he had slept with many girls. I felt guilty of my judgement and upset that I had acted so childishly. Even to this day, I am riddled with guilt for this memory. I am still not sure I have forgiven myself. I remember rushing back, but it was too late. He had gone. I knew the extent of my terrible mistake when seeing he had left my rose on the table. I was so childish, like a little princess, thinking the world owed me a fairytale life to live. I sat there for a while, looking at this solitary flower and then I took it and I left.

I know I was searching for perfection, but in the wrong place. I was searching for a perfect life, a perfect husband, a perfect profession, a perfect marriage, a perfect world, free from imperfections that I saw everywhere. When I saw David not attaining the perfection that my infatuation maintained that he should have, I should have seen more of my own failings. I saw perfection as something I wanted, on my terms, but perfection needs to be on God's terms. Who is it who can truly draw the perfect circle?

I cannot fully express how low and sullen I became over that Christmas vacation with thoughts of David too immeasurable, nor can I convey the depths of my feelings for him, unutterable in any language. It became annoying that he could not be forgotten. To Elly, this was seen in the depth of my musical passion. She would remark with each piece, even those I had not seen before, that my emotions were now coming through, and I think she knew why. She never asked of him, and respected my silence.

I turned to the New Year and returned to University with longing as never before. I allowed him his freedom to come to me, but only because I was not mature enough to go to him. I waited and waited. Each new Sunday would come with his absence. Each week drew on and passed without any notice of him, except through my mind and feelings. I finally believed I was now discounted in his view.

I relented to the patient attempts of Mark to seek my close friendship, as kind and gentle as he was. I went to Mark's hospital and waited for Mark to finish his shift to surprise him. It cheers me now remembering the brilliant happy face he had when seeing me, only then to offload telling me about being bullied and belittled.

But I could not forget David.

Medication from Friendship

Mark left the operating department and walked along hospital corridors with his mind still numb and considering quitting his student position. He left the building to see the clouded afternoon sky and to feel the cold, chilly breeze flow around him, reflecting what he felt. People went their ways, their coats wrapped tight around them to ward off the invasive bite to the air. None of them were aware of him as they travelled within their own worries and worlds, but he became just as unaware of them as he journeyed into his own cares and concerns. He was tired and felt demoralised. Then something told him to look up, only to become confused, dismayed and unsure of whom he saw coming towards him. There, in the obscure drift of people, was a beautiful young woman who had stopped and now stood almost in his way, smiling back at him. They both stood for a moment, the public and their buildings and roads and noise becoming vacant and extinct.

"Hello?" said the female.

Mark was confused as he looked at Esther, there, standing before him as he spoke: "Did I hit my head? Did we plan to meet?"

"No, I just hoped to meet you as you came out," she replied to his misunderstanding. "I thought it would be a nice surprise."

"It is! You are!" Mark was suddenly gushing with cheerfulness, seeing whom he could hardly believe to be seeing.

"Yes," she laughed. "I decided to come and see where you work. You really work here? Wow!"

Mark nodded eagerly with suddenly being proud that it had such a respectable affect on the pretty, blonde girl.

"Wow, this is quite impressive."

"Don't get to think I'm Doctor Amazing or something brilliant. I'm just a trainee nurse in the operating theatres."

"I'm sure to make a Hospital work, everyone's important."

"Not everyone thinks like that. Are you cold?" asked Mark, looking at her in her long white coat.

"Well it would be nice to have a coffee somewhere, or are you on your way – somewhere?"

"I'm definitely going – somewhere, and if there's a coffee there with you, then somewhere is looking good."

"Okay, but I did think to take you to the hospital café."

Mark shook his head with a broad smile: "Good thinking, but there's somewhere better. Have you been to the British Museum?"

Esther shook her head.

"I'll take you there. It's quite a few stops, but it's worth it."

Esther could see that Mark was deep within his thoughts as they travelled on the Underground, and she did not push for much conversation other than the odd question or two: "So why the British Museum?"

"Why the British Museum?"

"Why not anywhere else?"

"I like it there. I go there a few times and walk around. I just like it there."

"Oh," she replied, and then, after a pause, she became committed to ask a probing question: "You seem quiet. Is everything okay?"

"Yep," was all he said with a nod.

Leaving the Underground, they walked the few streets and corners until reaching the museum. They entered the large building and went into the massive inner central hall, brightly lit from the extensive windows above with the white stone masonry that appeared to enhance the lighting.

"You didn't look very happy earlier. Is everything all right?" asked Esther.

"I'm sorry, Esther. It's been a tiring day. I started at three this morning, but the whole week's been draining. The museum's café is over there."

"I really don't want to keep you if you're tired."

"Esther, please don't feel guilty. I've wanted something specifically like this, somewhere, specifically with you – for a long time. Sorry, I'm rambling. That's how tired I am. What do you want?" Mark motioned to the coffee choices and Esther gave a running commentary as to what drinks she liked and disliked and eventually told him her favourite. "Okay, that's the one then."

"Oh no, this is on me. You need to sit down and I'll get them."

Mark looked indignant that a girl was going to buy him something.

"I insist! You're too tired to argue, so put your compulsion to one side and let a little shy girl bring it to you."

"But – "

"No, no buts, this is on me."

Mark resigned himself to find a quiet table and sat down, watching Esther for a moment as she queued. Then she walked over to him and sheepishly asked him a question: "Which coffee did you want?"

"I was about to tell you, but you seemed to be making all the decisions."

Esther's guilt showed from her blushing: "Oh, sorry."

"That's fine. I'll have an Americano, black with a little sugar, thanks."

"Okay," she said, still with a hint of embarrassment, and once again joined the queue. She turned round, hoping to see him looking at her, but he had propped up his head by one hand with his elbow resting on the table. She was beginning to feel this had been a mistake. He looked tired and subdued. Something was on his mind. When she eventually received her drinks, she joined him.

He looked up as if he came back from his ensnaring thoughts and smiled at her.

"What were you thinking about?"

Mark shook his head as if she should dismiss his dour attitude.

Esther watched him as he added sugar and stirred the drink, not sure of what he was thinking. "I've already added sugar." Then she started to smile to herself with a new thought, which then produced a little chuckle that she tried to stifle.

"What's amusing you?" Mark started to smile curiously, aware of her amusement.

Esther, taking a sip, shook her head, as if he should dismiss her childish behaviour, but she smiled more.

"No, come on, what is it?"

"I can't see you wearing a nurse's outfit."

Mark unexpectedly laughed. "Well, the stockings always split and the stilettos are hell to walk on."

They were both now smiling contentedly with each other.

"How's your coffee?" asked Mark.

"I didn't go for my favourite."

"No, I see. I would have bought it for you, though."

"So how is it?"

"It's still too hot for me."

"No, sorry, your work."

"Oh! Well, I enjoy the college work, and the work itself is great. You will never believe what I have seen and been involved in. I've placed my hands in all sorts of – well, you don't want to know."

"Sounds amazing – what is it exactly you do?"

"I'm training to be an ODP."

"ODP? Sounds like a secret agent during the Second World War."

"That was an SOE – Secret Operations Executive, or something like that. ODP stands for Operating Department Practitioner, or theatre nurse in old money."

"How come you ended up doing this role? Do you see lots of blood and guts and things?"

"It's no longer the Medieval days, Esther."

"Well, yes, I suppose."

"Today, operations are quite systematic and controlled, but yes, I do get to see blood and guts and things."

"Don't you ever pass out?"

"Never felt like I wanted to."

"I'm impressed."

"Don't be."

"So what's weighing on your mind?"

"People just make life bad and dreary and tiresome. It's like a prison at times. I just want to escape because of too many prison guards in life, in general. They all think they're in charge and make people bend to their rules. I don't want to work in this prison with these people. Life is miserable as it is and they all get on the bandwagon and make it worse. I feel like they hold my head down the toilet and it's hard to stick up for myself when these people need to sign off my training. I can't believe that this caring profession has some of the most uncaring people. There's this anaesthetist who wants to be nasty to the nurses and deliberately makes them cry for his own sense of fun. He makes other people make mistakes so he can feel he's better."

Mark stopped as if to allow Esther to reply, but Esther was lacking any response, so struck with his sincerity and earnestness.

Not in the slightest concern for Esther's silence, Mark continued: "The thing is, it's easy to criticize and moan because life is not ideal, it's not perfect, we live with limitations and constraints. So people feel fulfilled to put others down because it's easy and makes them feel important. If life was perfect, we wouldn't need surgery."

Esther watched Mark as he freely let open his feelings like an open tap, admiring him for this openness and wondered if she could ever be this open.

Mark had no knowledge he was being viewed with this respect: "I'm so sorry, Esther."

"That's okay."

"I've set my sights on going home one day – really going home – to join the perfect team in Heaven. If you really want to know, I'm doing this to learn to be bold. Two years ago I would never have thought it possible for me to be bold enough to do this."

Esther nodded.

Mark looked around and then bent forward. "You see, I'm being bullied," was all he said in a faint voice. He sighed, and then added, "It's quite embarrassing really when, as a twenty-year-old male, you admit to being bullied by a sixty-six-year-old woman – who's fat and ugly, and who scowls at you across the room for no obvious reason. She's like the witch in Hansel and Gretel and just criticises you for everything you do. Do you know how many times I thought about jacking it in whenever she's spoken to me?"

Esther shook her head.

"I don't know either because I've lost count. The thing is she thinks she's this great teacher, but she doesn't realise how counter-productive it is. She puts me down in front of others so that she can feel superior. The others tell me to ignore it, but I'm a student."

"She'll be retiring soon won't she?"

Mark looked exasperated, "She'll be dead soon, and she'll leave behind her the awful influence she's had on me. I'll remember her as an awful, dreary, ugly person – because that's the way she wants to behave and so that's the way she wants to be remembered. And when she's dead, I won't have any sympathy. That's her legacy. I've already written what's on her grave with the way she's affected me." Mark sighed and they were both silent. "Not the politically-correct thing to say really."

Esther tried to think of the perfect reply, but became defeated.

Mark drank some coffee in a deep gulp and shook his head. "She uses her knowledge to weigh other people down. I'm tired and stressed trying to do the right thing with this evil dragon perched in the same room, ready to devour my soul, but I'm concentrating on my stress rather than what I'm supposed to be doing. It's like Oscar Wilde's quote: everyone is equal, but some are more equal than others. Whereas I think everyone is dying, but some people are more dead than others, spiritually dead, like walking corpses waiting for someone to find them a grave. I just want to serve out my sentence, give in a good report and eventually go home – to a place where the bad ones won't go. I expect you're wondering what you've done now."

"It's not Oscar Wilde. It's Animal Farm, by George Orwell."

"Is it?"

Esther nodded.

"I'm sorry, Esther, I'm just rambling. It's been a long week."

"That's okay." Esther began to feel that this had been at the wrong time.

As if knowing her thoughts, Mark responded: "I wouldn't have changed this for the world – meeting you like this."

"No?"

"Actually, I would. I would have been happier. I'm so sorry, Esther."

"Do you really want to do the work?"

"To see little Lisa get better? Of course: a little girl who had her broken arm put right today."

That seemed to say everything Mark needed to say, so much so, that the conversation came to an abrupt end. For a while, they both sat in silence taking a few more sips as Mark's simmering diminished and Esther's indecision in what to say became more pronounced.

"Why bother with people, is really the question to ask," said Mark. "Why bother? Because Jesus bothered, that's why and anyway, I think this is what God wants me to do. He's the boss, not them lot. It's to Him who I hand in my report."

Esther became so proud of Mark that she could not say anything.

"I've set my sights on working for Great Ormond Street. That would be my career highlight. Oh, Esther, I am so sorry for being so, so miserable at the moment."

"I don't mind. It's nice that you've been open with me."

"I struggle to stick up for myself." Mark then thought for a moment. "Would you like to see an operation?"

"You mean, you could get me in to see one?"

Mark shrugged, not giving a definite answer.

"I'm not sure I would cope – with the blood and guts and things."

"When you look at it like a form of engineering, it's just fantastic. It never stops being amazing when you look at the sheer brilliance of our own machinery. It's like engineering, natural biological technology that's truly amazing. So amazing that it all becomes a person. It's like the ultimate engineering. I sometimes think I would have done better if I had become an engineer."

Again, Esther could not think of any reply.

"I might be able to get you to see an operating theatre, if you wish. Consider it a special date as I can't do it just for anyone."

"That would be a very special date, Mark."

"Okay, I'll see what I can do – considering they're called theatres for a peculiar reason."

Weeds or Wheat?

The east Thames region of London was now a new city, one within London itself with a modern skyline of tall buildings and sophisticated streets and shops. David walked along the promenade of an affluent harbour within it, with the mooring of large, clean, sophisticated boats and small ships. With the air still being winter-like and the waters ruffled by the cold breeze, there were few people to hear the banging of the rigging against the masts. Not totally convinced he knew the direction, he turned the corner from a set of high-rise apartments and one harbour, to discover more high-rise apartments and an extended harbour with yet more expensive boats. Then the building he was looking for, as described by his host who had invited him, was there standing high in his sight: a tall apartment, reaching the overcast sky.

David walked up the wide steps to the commodious entrance foyer, entered the building and approached the concierge at a wide desk, giving him a greeting and an apartment number.

In reply, the concierge courteously phoned the apartment, received an answer and invited David to use the lift to the far side, which opened for him to enter. When the doors opened again, David looked out into a clean and spacious lounge with comfortable leather chairs, indoor plants and pictures. In the time it took David to step into this room, was all the time it took for Jonathan to appear with a welcoming smile and an outstretched hand.

"Good to see you again, David! Haven't seen you for a while. Haven't seen you since Christmas. Was it that long ago?"

"I think so."

"It's supposed to be Spring, but look at the weather."

"It's pretty cold out there."

"Anyway, come in, I'll show you my place."

David followed Jonathan across the room and, turning a corner, was then confronted by a door befitting an elegant mansion.

"Come in!" ushered Jonathan as he opened it and went through.

"I thought we were in your apartment already."

"That's just the foyer for everyone who lives on this floor. Come in, I've things on the go in the kitchen."

"It looks good enough to live in the foyer."

"Yes, I need to get to the kitchen because I'm cooking things. Make yourself at home."

David was amazed at what he saw. All around the spacious lounge was expensive furniture, luxury flooring, a gigantic home entertainment system looking small to one side, and an entire wall open to a window view of London. The sofas were big and cosy and surrounded by a few houseplants and coffee tables.

Jonathan called from within a few open doors: "You can come

through, if you want!"

David followed the voice that coincided with following delicious smells, and discovered a kitchen he could only imagine from a salesman's catalogue and large enough to have a dining table with eight chairs.

"You live in style!" expressed David.

"Thank you. This is where we sometimes meet together and let our hair down."

David looked round: "Who's we?"

"Us, the Sally Ann gang with fun midweek get-togethers or sometimes weekend sleep-overs."

"I thought you all did Bible study."

"We do, and sometimes it's here."

David watched Jonathan working with all sorts of modern equipment, appearing to make a meal to the standard of the apartment with no effort.

"You must be doing well to afford this place."

"Oh, yes, I work hard. My employers trust me. They know who I stand for. They know that if ever they're audited, everything will bear up to scrutiny, because everything is above board, and, above all, our clients trust me. I get a lot of reward for being loyal, hard working, putting others first in my dealing and proving that they can count on me. And I'm still creative with finances – legally. Sounds good? Plus I inherited a lot from my parents, but they lived for money."

"Oh, sorry to hear that."

"Well, these things happen." Jonathan sighed and with this expressed that he would politely prevent any more talk of them.

"I wasn't expecting a Salvationist to live like this. Not that I'm criticizing."

"Believe me, we get everywhere. The sun never sets on The Salvation Army. Anyway, I can easily afford my tithing. I know many people can't. I am extremely grateful for my circumstances. Want a drink? Nothing alcoholic in the house though."

"A coffee or tea?"

"That's fine – a coffee or tea coming up." As well as walking from one end of the kitchen to the other performing his complex cooking program, Jonathan was able to fit in making a coffee for them both from the percolator machine. After putting the lid on a saucepan, Jonathan was able to bring over the drinks to the table and sat down with David.

"So, what's your news? Haven't heard from you for a while. It's almost Easter."

"I've been busy. Thanks for getting in touch and inviting me."

"I try and keep in touch with as many people I meet."

"Must be difficult."

"Well, I try. So what are you planning for this Easter break?"

"I've got an undergraduate place with Carnadyne, a company developing future medical technology. I'll be involved in state-of-the-art electronic systems for advanced radiotherapy cancer treatment."

"Wow."

"I've a placement there over Easter and Summer. I may even get sponsorship. I may even get a job there when I finish my degree."

Jonathan went silent, feeling David struggling with the next thing to say.

"How's Esther?" David eventually asked.

"She's good, she seems to be getting on with her studies, but – well, what do I know. She keeps things to herself, so I don't get involved often."

Again, David went silent.

"I think you should know that she's getting friendly with someone."

Without comment, David slowly nodded.

"It's nice to see. She seems to be opening up and becoming more involved in our fellowship."

"Mark?"

"Yes. You okay?"

"I still love her. I don't know what to do."

"Well, I think, unless you do something now, she'll be gobbled up by all the other suitors – and you're not even a Christian. You're not even in The Salvation Army."

"Is she happy?"

"I think she's getting to be happier than what she looked over winter."

"She was sad?"

Jonathan nodded, "Appeared so."

"You think that was because of me?"

"Look! I'm not sure what happened between you and her. I stuck my head in a few times and got bitten, so I'm not going to get stuck in like that again. I just saw the looks you both gave each other and thought I'd do something nice to some fellow humans with a random act of kindness. The Stock Market is less stressful." Hearing the cooking required attention, Jonathan excused himself and attended to his pots and pans, and started to cut some leaves of herbs into a fine powder with David having joined him.

"I should be studying," said David, abstractedly, "but the more I study, the more I learn; the more I learn, the more I know; the more I know, the more I realise I don't know; the more I don't know, the more I need to study."

"And you know what that means?"

"I fail my exams?"

"It means you need faith. By not knowing everything, means we are forced to have faith to live – to have faith in something at least. We need faith in a working universe for one thing, and that should be telling us our true place in all this. Okay, almost done! You hungry?"

With the meal now over, they both entered the lounge and David stood beside a massive window to look out on London. "This is so impressive up here," he breathed to himself.

Jonathan had already sat down in a comfortable sofa and David sat down opposite Jonathan. There was then a silence between them.

David capitulated to the quiet and to the pressure of what he wanted to say. "Okay, it's true," was all he said.

"What is?"

"I've been thinking long and hard about – ."

"Yes?"

"About – faith, things, my beliefs. What are my beliefs? I feel like I need to sort out what I believe."

"Sounds like you're struggling."

"I'm trying to make a decision without Esther wrapped up in it."

"So what is the struggle?"

"That it all turns out to be schizophrenia with all this praying."

"Sorry?"

"I'm wondering whether you need to have a mental problem to be a Christian."

"Listen, okay, I may not be the bright spark around here, but I'm clever enough to hold meetings between important financial clients and get millions of pounds flowing through the system. I can't have many mental problems if I can achieve that. Not that I'm blowing my own trumpet, but I do have finance qualifications coming out of my ears and I'm still able to be a Christian."

"I'm just an Engineer trying to see all the facts to make a logical decision."

"Well, actually, I think you're too scared. I think God is waiting for you to make a decision first to test your courage."

"Scared?"

"I think you're scared – scared of losing your macho I-play-football-with-the-lads feeling, but really you're prevaricating."

"I'm what?"

"Trying to hedge your bets, deciding if it's worth being an Agnostic."

"Well, maybe."

"There are always hidden, secret games we all play. Agnostics think they can live how they want and then defend themselves against God by saying there wasn't enough evidence. Same with Atheists, but they think they can claim there was no evidence and probably have a distaste for submitting to anyone anyway, let alone God. But everyone submits to something, David. And Christians can have secret mind games as well:

believing in having a ticket into Heaven, but then not paying much attention to the way God wants them to live. They believe because of what they can get out of it: security, employment even. Some people only want to see the moral side to Christianity. They don't want to see a spiritual, supernatural side, but if the resurrection of Jesus really did happen, then Jesus' claims about Himself must be true – and so His claims on us must be true. You can't believe in Jesus Christ without changing your whole life. So people are reluctant to think about it because of the repercussions to their lifestyle."

"And you think that's me?"

"I'm not saying anything."

"So how do you become a Christian?"

"Do you want to be one?"

"If it's not right, then no."

"What's not right about it?"

"Is it correct?"

"Is it not correct?" Jonathan looked exasperated. "Look! You can play this game all your life. It's not provable, matey. Is there proof there are fairies at the end of the garden who come out when no one sees? Is there proof there are no fairies at the end of the garden? Those who believe one or the other can't prove any of it."

David did not reply.

"Does God exist? Does He not exist? Who created God? It's all nonsense debate. It's a question that a naive adolescent would ask, not a university graduate. There's no way a little finite brain like yours can know everything, but it's not based on knowledge, David. You shouldn't need a PhD to get into God's Kingdom, otherwise God's Kingdom would be only for some. Abraham didn't know about atoms and what causes gravity. It's not knowledge or intelligence; it's faith. At one time or another, you need to just make the decision out of faith."

"Perhaps it's best not to decide."

"Come on, David! Be a man! Make a decision! Don't you think that's a big part of showing who we are? Every day I need to make business decisions without having time to research everything to make it a perfect decision, because the moment is then gone. It's a risk, but God seems to want us to decide and believe first, trust in faith, and then grow; not collect as much theoretical evidence as possible and then we're killed off by a bus before we decide."

David did not respond.

"Start with a decision for Jesus, David, and then make a lifetime developing a deeper understanding and a closer connection. The closer you get, the more you realise the tiniest ounce of sin is actually many tonnes to God."

"Might as well give up from the start."

"But you then won't see the mighty universe of excitement God has for forgiving us when we want to come even nearer. Some become Christians and then give up on prayer and reading the Bible, and then they wonder why their life stagnates. Learning how to live in the kingdom of Heaven on Earth is a discipline that takes time. The disciples dropped everything to follow Jesus, but Jesus still had to teach them His way for at least three years."

"But no one should come to God unthinking. You still need to see some logic."

"Or have a need and the wisdom to realise no one else can meet that need." Jonathan gave a considered look at David and then added, "You want to know why I believe?"

David nodded with enthusiasm.

"I believe in Jesus because I want to."

With Jonathan giving nothing more away, left David only to say, "Wow, that's incredible."

"That's one reason I'm a Christian. There's nothing wrong in just wanting to be one. I just love the stories of Him in the Bible, His wisdom, His cleverness, the miracles He did, His courage to suffer and be crucified and – . His whole persona is just too attractive to just take lightly. I would so love to get to know Him and follow."

"Wow," repeated David.

"And I love reading the Bible, all of it. I am so taken by all the logic, the history, the laws, poetry, wisdom, that's so fulfilled in Jesus. That's another reason why I believe: the way it all fits together with Jesus being the key to understanding it all. I can't believe it all to be coincidental."

"But still – ."

"Okay, you're a physics person, so how about this? As incredible as the Universe existing, the Universe actually does exist."

"Yes, and?"

"If the Universe is possible, then God is possible. You must see some logic in that."

"Well, I – "

"If you can believe in the miracle of creation, in the incredible miracle that the Universe is here at all, then you have the right, the freedom and ability to believe anything you wish. And wouldn't you just love to get to know who made the Universe, because it's – truly, truly impressive, don't you think? It's beyond anything I could do, and anyone able to create any universe is worthy of my total admiration, and I'm not even a scientist. You're an engineer: this must be plucking some of your heartstrings. And then there's law and order, justice and mercy, care and compassion – nothing makes sense unless I do believe in God and how Jesus fulfils it all. More reasons why I believe."

David just nodded.

"David, look, just read the Bible, read the Gospels. They were written for people like you. Read Mark: he wrote deliberately to have an action view of Jesus. Matthew, the tax collector, wrote his version to speak to the Jews who wanted to know how Jesus fulfilled the Old Testament. Luke, who was a doctor and never met Jesus, wrote his account with careful research and was still convinced of all the miracles and sayings to be true and historical. And John wanted to assure people that Jesus was divine, both man and God. They all have a different audience."

"Oh."

"But read all of them."

"I'll see how far I get with just one."

"It's best to read them all and you get a rounded view. You see, the book called Romans is good because it explains the Christian faith. Thessalonians talks about working hard and honestly, no matter how humble the job, even if you're not in full time ministry. Corinthians: love sacrificially; love out of a decision to put others first, even the unloved. Galatians: following rules and laws won't make you achieve salvation, because your sin is the belief of your self-worthy good behaviour and achievements – and don't think when you accept, when you give in to Jesus' sacrifice on the cross, that it's a licence to carry on living badly."

"I still think I'll try with just one for a start."

"In fact, Hebrews would be a good one to read. It's about faith. It's like a Bible commentary on itself. It explains how Jesus is the sinless High Priest for us all, and how He fulfils all the priestly duties of the Old Testament Levite priests, once and for all, and that He is higher than anyone else. He is the highest. And then there's Ephesians – "

"Yep, I get the idea."

"My worry, David, is that you may read around, and you may even become interested, but then it will all fizzle out. Although you can't gain your own entry into God's presence, faith that does not result in working for God's Kingdom is not real faith – it is just no more than an intellectual idea, and I think God will look down on people who consider Him as only an intellectual idea. That's pretty much what you'll read in James. You are looking at me as if this is hard labour."

"The Bible is such a big book to read it all."

"Life is a big book, David. Try to pray, just earnestly search for Him. Praying is good for you, David. It's healthy. It's not a medical problem. People are mentally stressed because they don't pray. Seek Him openly and rationally, and He will allow you to find Him. Don't have an irrational belief that becomes unhealthy or is enslaving or puritanical, as that becomes just as enslaving as what people want to escape. And when you do find Him, tell others so they can find Him. You may wrestle a lot, but – try. As for me, if Jesus was to walk into the room right now and ask me to go with Him, here and now, then I would have no hesitation in just dropping everything and going, and leaving all this.

The question is, would you? If you are in a burning tower, the last few decisions you make could be the difference in living and dying, and you may not even know the tower is burning."

Wrestling with God

The telephone rang and Jonathan, in his kitchen, answered, getting ready for work and eating some toast, "Hello? Good Morning?"

"Jonathan!"

"David! How's you? This is early for a student."

"Thanks for the meal and talk the other week."

"That's okay. What can I do for you? It's very early."

"Can we meet today?"

"Does it have to be today?"

"I think so."

"You want to meet me at my office? I can let you in and we can have a quick lunch there. I won't have long though."

David was impressed with Jonathan's office. Tucked away among other offices, it was still more spacious than the average with a main desk and a discussions table.

"This is just the thinking room as I call it," said Jonathan. "There's the frantic wheeling and dealing floor over in the other building, and the obligatory boardrooms with – anyway. Want a sandwich? Homemade?"

David shook his head as they both sat down at the table. "I had a game of chess," was all he eventually said.

"Come again?"

"I had a game of chess – using the old set my Granddad gave me."

"Yes, you said."

"With God."

"You played God at chess? Well – that's nice. I didn't know you played chess."

"You don't believe me?"

"Yes – sounds – great."

"I did what you said: I've been praying."

"Good!"

"But one night, by myself in my room, I tried to pray, but after a few moments of trying, I had this urge to have a game of chess."

"Mmm-mmm."

"I was even trying to ignore the feeling. I was trying to pray – and – this feeling kept forcing me to have this – stupid game."

"So what did you do?"

"I got the chessboard out, set up the pieces and then waited."

"Waited?"

"Yes, waited, and then when nothing was happening I decided to be

White, and God, Mister Invisible, My-Mental-Problem, was Black. So I moved my piece and then grabbed a black piece and moved it as long as it was legal."

"Sounds like you're more strange than I thought."

"I'm trying to be serious. In my mind I had this idea I was playing chess with God."

"So who won?"

"Well in the end I thought it was pointless. I took His Queen, Jonathan. I was just thrashing Him. So I went back to trying to pray, but I felt blank. So I started trying to look for Psalms, flipping through the Bible until I just stopped at a random page." David suddenly went quiet.

"You okay? What happened?"

"It's just so staggering. It's unbelievable. It's just too unreal."

"What? What is? Come on! I'm on the edge of my seat!"

"The first three words I saw – and I mean the very first three words my eyes saw was a title to a Psalm – the very first three words."

"Yes, okay, I get it!"

"It said, 'God always wins'." It was then that David half chuckled, half cried, and half tried to stifle the emotions. "And then I said, 'No He doesn't'. I had His queen! His queen, Jonathan! I was wiping the floor with His Queen!"

"So what then?"

"Well I went to bed."

"Oh."

"Then got up the next morning and went off to lessons."

"Oh, okay. Want a sandwich now? I made twice the lot because of you."

"But there is – errm."

"There's more?"

"I came back after lessons, saw I had left the game as it was and decided to finish it – for fun. And – ."

"Yes, and?"

"It was – it was – I was just, you see – ."

Jonathan's face dropped. "You lost?"

"After a few moves, I realised my Queen could be taken. So, Black took my Queen, and then – you know, I just can't believe I'm hearing myself admit to this – I started to lose. Black suddenly made a few good moves. It got to a point when I realised that White could never win. I couldn't believe it. I just couldn't believe it. I had to go for a walk to really believe what had just happened. A chill went through me, like a magical wash of something flowing through me, my bones, my skin, like the hairs on my neck brisling, and goose pimples, and – . Technically, I lost to myself. I can't believe it! In fact, I feel better if I had lost to God. And then it suddenly happened. I don't know what precisely, but it suddenly happened. I knew, from then on, that I believe, I just believe.

I've become a Christian."

Jonathan smiled in a warm, brotherly manner, got up, and walked around the table to shake David's hand. With the situation dictating that David should stand, Jonathan then embraced David in a brotherly hug. "David! Welcome to God's family and Kingdom."

There was a sudden knock from the door, and, without any warning, a male colleague barged into the room: "Hey, Jon, I think we – ." He stopped as soon as he saw the two together in their unexpected pose and looked mystified and awkward. "It's okay, I'll come back later," he stuttered and left the room as briskly as he had entered.

"Who was that?"

"The boss."

"Will this raise any questions?"

Jonathan shook his head. "No, we all love each other round here."

"Can you do me a favour?"

"Yes of course."

"In fact, a couple."

"Sure."

"Can you not tell Esther?"

"Why not?"

"Because I seriously don't want her to know I've become a Christian, making her think I did it for her."

"That's for you to tell her in your own time."

"And secondly, make sure no one gets to know I played a game of chess by myself and lost."

"Sure! God's Promise."

"And don't hug me like that again."

"That's three things. I agreed only to two."

A date at the theatre

The morning rush had subsided, but the Underground platform on which Mark and Esther stood, still had many passengers patiently waiting for the next train. When it arrived, Mark politely allowed Esther to squeeze into the packed carriage and squeezed in beside her.

"Are you nervous?" Mark asked when settled.

Esther, not liking her personal space overcrowded, was worried her fear of being close was showing: "A bit, why? Does it show?"

"You're quite quiet, that's all. Don't worry. It'll be fine."

"So how are you able to get me into an operating room? Wouldn't I need to be scrubbed and clean and germ-free?"

"Something like that. You'll need to change into scrub clothes, which isn't flattering, but you might pull it off, and you need to take off jewellery, wear a hat, and wear special shoes."

"Oh, and that's okay for me to do that?"

"Oh yes. Don't worry, I'll be there?"

"What, in the Ladies?"

"Perhaps not quite there."

"And why are we taking this route? Isn't there an easier way to your hospital?"

"Yes, but I've found this is less congested."

"Oh," replied Esther, feeling embarrassed about her confusion with the carriage being packed with passengers.

"And we're in no rush."

"I thought you said we had a time and date?"

"Yes, but it's – variable."

"Oh," again replied Esther in the same manner as before.

They then travelled in silence, standing near to the doors in the compression.

"This is our stop!" suddenly exclaimed Mark.

"Is it?"

"Yes! Come on!"

Mark grabbed Esther, giving her no choice but to be pulled from the parked train.

"But this doesn't make any sense."

"Yes, it does, trust me. Guy's like to be trusted. Trust me on that."

"Okay," Esther smiled, now becoming more amused than concerned.

Mark led the way to the Underground exit and walked from the station in a manner of assurance. So fast was his stroll that Esther had to quicken her pace to keep with his speed.

"We're not going to your hospital, are we?"

Mark shook his head with a bemused smile.

"Where are we going, then?"

Mark stopped and pointed up: "You see that church tower?"

"Yes."

"We're going there."

Within a moment, they were standing beside a porch that inside had a winding stairway leading to the heights of the tower.

"It's a church, not a hospital," said Esther.

"It serves the sick doesn't it? A lot of hospitals have been founded by Christian compassion."

"Something about this isn't right."

Mark, smiling, pointed to the sign to the side that Esther had over-looked. "This is where Saint Thomas's hospital once was before moving to Lambert. It's now a surgical museum."

"We were never going to one of your operating theatres, were we?"

Still smiling, Mark shook his head.

They both went through the entrance and climbed the winding steps to an upper floor where a young girl sat behind a desk. Mark paid for two tickets and they entered the old wooden loft space of the adjoining building.

Being the only two there, Esther felt obliged to whisper in the silence: "I don't get to see blood and guts and things?"

"No."

"That's a relief."

"You get to see the old surgical tools they use to use, and that's worse."

They stood studying the entirety of the attic where tables and glass cabinets showed dried herbs and weighing scales that took the visitor back in time to a three-hundred-year-old pharmacy.

Still being the only two people there, they walked around the museum, quietly making their own study. When Esther sidled up to Mark, she saw the medical tools that had Mark fascinated.

"Anaesthetics has come such a long way," whispered Mark again. "Can you imagine the pain if it weren't for being knocked out? I would hate to live in any other era."

"What about the future? Won't there be better healthcare?"

"What about future unknown dangerous diseases we can't tackle?"

"Well, there is that. Why are we whispering?"

"I don't know, but come this way."

Following Mark, Esther was led to a side door and they both went through into a well-lit room from an over-head window in the high roof. Being the sole focus of the theatre, was an old, wooden operating table, surrounded by many wooden tiers from where spectators would stand to follow the operation. It was hard to see anything that was not of wood, except for the metal railings, which prevented the audience from fainting and falling forward, and some of the metal surgical instruments, there for the delight or education of the audience.

"A nineteenth century operating theatre," quietly spoke Mark, "and the only one that survives today."

For a while neither spoke, but Esther became aware of something turning Mark dour. "Are you okay?" she asked. Even then, he remained quiet and Esther doubted whether he had heard.

"Do you know about my father?"

"No, should I?"

Mark sighed, considered a moment as if to decide in telling a large secret, and then answered: "My Dad's dying."

For an instant, Esther was stunned into silence and became absent of what to say. "I'm so sorry," was all she could muster in a quiet, sympathetic tone. "What is he dying of?"

"A brain disease. It's not common. Not many people know of it. We didn't." Mark suddenly stopped and looked at Esther: "Please don't tell them I'm being bullied at work."

"No, of course not. Why should I? I'm sorry, who should I not tell?"

"My parents."

"No, of course."

"They've got too much on as it is."

"I wouldn't tell anyone."

"Dad suddenly started to act quite strange a few years ago. His jokes became offensive and they upset everyone. Only that he didn't know. He slowly became insensitive and it was quite unlike him. Both Mum and Dad are in The Salvation Army and have been all their lives, so it was odd that Dad was changing. When we told him about it, he wouldn't believe us. He started to develop habits, annoying habits that drove Mum up the wall. My Dad is the most caring person I know, quiet, unassuming, friendly, wanting to help – well, that was how he was. Now he's almost in his own little world. At least we know what it is."

"What is it?"

"It's called Pick's disease."

Esther shook her head.

"It affects the front of the brain, where we make all our conscious decisions, our planning on what to say, what to do, who we are. It slowly just disintegrates and changes our personality, our character. She still loves him, Esther. Mum hasn't changed."

Esther did not know how to reply as evident from the moment of silence.

"When the doctors found out, they advised Dad to become creative in something."

"Creative?"

Mark unexpectedly suddenly smiled. "Yeah! Can you believe it? A degenerating brain and they say to take up art. So he did. Over the years, he just paints and draws and sketches and – I don't know, but they become quite – tasteful, strangely. I'll take you to that weird national gallery, where all the weird artists make fortunes out of weird art, and then you'll see how good my Dad has become." He stopped again, looked in need and added, "I love my Dad. I don't want him to change. I want him back." His outlook changed again and he smiled with his own joke: "Makes me wonder if anybody who's an artist has a degenerating brain."

Esther smiled, trying to lighten the moment: "You're talking to a pianist, here."

"Definitely degenerate! And I play the euphonium." Mark looked at Esther for a considered moment, and then said, "You can meet him, if you like. You can't understand until you meet him – and see his art."

"That would be nice."

"How about over Easter?" Mark said with an element of polite challenge in his intonation.

Esther thought for a moment and with a smile, nodded and agreed.

"So what about you and your Mum and Dad? You never really say much about yourself."

"I'm actually adopted."

"Really? I didn't know."

"I don't tell anyone. I like to think my adoptive parents have always been my family. I have their surname, and through them I met Elly who tried me out on the piano. I loved it. It taught me to focus on something and – helped me to forget – ." Esther stopped talking.

Mark was silent.

"You're not asking why I was adopted."

"I didn't think I ought to."

"Why don't you ask?"

"Do you want me to?"

Esther sighed from a heavy lungful of air and then nodded: "Do it quickly before the moment's gone."

"Okay – why was you adopted?"

Esther paused for breath, exhaled loudly and looked uncomfortable.

"Esther, you don't have to answer."

In a quick short speech that almost popped from her inability to hold back the weight, she said rapidly, "My Dad abused me and my Mum committed suicide. There! I've said it!"

Again, Mark was silent.

"Please say something."

"I just, it's a bit, I wasn't – ." Mark shook his head: "I'm so sorry Esther. What can I say? Just – thank you for being brave enough to tell me."

"I don't know when it started, but he – abused me where – ."

"Esther, you don't have to tell me anything, but I'll listen if it will help."

"He was sent to gaol and my Mum was found dead – some months after – ."

"How are you now?"

"I'm just about getting over it. I sometimes have the shakes, as I call it."

"I'm so sorry, Esther. Where's he now?"

"I have no idea. There was this court injunction on him not to go near me when he was released. I never saw him again. He never even tried to get in touch."

"Would you have accepted any apology?"

"It doesn't matter. I'm slowly forgiving them; shaking off those bad, sunken feelings, otherwise you imprison yourself and continue suffering. Forgive and forget and move on, but it's taking a long time. I can almost let go, but I don't think I would have come to be in The Salvation Army if none of it had happened. I suppose in a strange, hideous, morbid way, I should be thankful, but my Mum had to die for me to have this new life. – Oh, Mark, I can't carry on this conversation."

Mark held her arm and stepped forward into Esther's space.

Esther stepped away instinctively, and then realised what she had done. "Sorry."

"What for? You don't feel right to receive a hug? That's fine."

"No, I stepped back out of habit. I want you to hold me."

"You sure? You're not too convincing."

"Mark! I need you to hold me – please."

Mark stepped forward again, and they embraced in the middle of an old operating theatre.

Great Expectations

Mark, my dear Mark – every girl's dream. His patient seeking of me, his respect and kindness, his gentle nature, yet having a musical talent as a brilliant euphonium soloist, totally humble without pretence, was an attraction that I had initially unobserved. I became aware of his golden character. His kind consideration to people and the respect he had for others just shone in his endeavours in becoming an operating theatre nurse. Why was David on my mind instead?

When David did arrive on a particular Sunday, it was too late. He, without doubt, must have seen across the hall how friendly Mark and I had become. I turned and saw him and saw the sad look in his eyes. He left without saying anything. He left with me feeling too weak and ashamed. I lacked confidence and I resented it. I even used my shyness as an excuse in not doing anything.

It was that Easter holiday I went with Mark to visit his family. I met Morris, Mark's Dad, and understood his degenerating mental illness and his compelling urge to paint pictures all the time, even to the extent that everyone was ignored. I was at one moment bombarded with his previous paintings as he handed them to me. Most were unrecognisable as anything, but some were so alluring that they would look appropriate hanging in an executive office or company lobby, a hotel foyer, or a connoisseur's lounge. They would mistakenly make someone with a lot of money part with it to own each one. As it was, I was welcomed by Mark's Mum, and I saw how they coped. I also started to feel confident in being with Mark.

However, my confidence surged in other ways when I received my exam results of that academic year, but most of all when I found an opportunity to work during the summer break. Even though I continuously checked with the Foreign Office for potential employment, I came across an advert to work there in a student magazine when I wasn't looking. They were particularly keen to have someone for an administration position only for a month or so to help while someone was on their maternity leave. I suppose to them, a student was an ideal choice. To me, it was too ideal, and I got the position because my keenness was natural and they saw my ambition to work there long term. I never got to know how many others applied. I had to go through pain-staking security checks, get references, assessments — all for a summer job. The person I was assigned had not interviewed me, and I met my summer boss on the first day I started.

The Office

The morning was full of promise with the summer sunshine. Esther, with the idea of this being the first working day of her life, with it being the Foreign Office, had got up early with eagerness to walk serenely along the streets enjoying the excitement and anticipation. It was as if London had turned from a city of rushed business and unrewarding chores, stifled travel and ill-fitting queues, to one befitting an elegant orchestra playing to the whole nation that culture, interest, and life itself burgeoned into something to make even breathing a pleasure. Wearing a white cotton dress and blouse, she felt relaxed, happy, confident, and she even felt beautiful.

Walking along Whitehall, passing the Cenotaph War Memorial and Downing Street, Esther then turned down King Charles Street, a road beyond three arches, dwarfed by the buildings either side and Saint James's Park at its furthest end.

She arrived at the entrance, labelled elegantly by a plaque of brass on the side of the wall, and showed her employment letter to the armed security guard. He motioned to enter the short, open passageway that took her to a side room before coming to a secured turnstile. A female guard further checked, searched and asked Esther to submit her mobile phone, and then told her to read and sign some documents.

"This is the Official Secrets Act you're signing," the female guard stated, although the form had the title in bold across the top.

There was a photograph taken of her and immediately Esther had an identity badge. Then she sat and waited for more arrangements while she attended to her fears of not knowing what was to happen next.

"Miss?" spoke the guard now standing before her, holding her documents and passport. "Here are all your belongings back. We've called Miss Russell to come and collect you. She won't be a moment."

"Thank you."

"No problem, Miss. Hope you enjoy the day."

True to her word, a young lady appeared. "Good morning, Esther, I'm Judy Russell," she said. The woman, wearing a smart office suit, her hair brushed back into a ponytail, had a presence that immediately shone of how pleasant she was. Her smile was reassuring and gentle, and her posture was confident. "But just call me Judy."

"Pleased to meet you."

They both greeted the other with a warm, friendly handshake, both pleasantly smiling and Esther followed her host through more turnstiles into a large, open, square courtyard, which was looked down upon by a multitude of grand windows set within the enclosing stately white stone building. Centrally were a few bench-chairs as if this was within a park.

"Let me show you some of the building. We're all passionate about its history. It's listed, you know," said Miss Russell.

"I can imagine."

"This way, I'll give you a quick tour."

Re-entering the building by a different doorway, Esther suddenly felt like she had walked into a mansion with the impressive stone staircase that confronted her.

"I wouldn't get too worked up about this one," her boss said, observing Esther's look. "I'll show you the ones you *should* get worked up about."

Like a tour guide, Miss Russell showed her visitor numerous elegant rooms and courts that would be befitting a Palace and symbolised the important discussions concerning world events and problems. Even the stone stairways proved inspiring with the grandeur of historical paintings, balustrades and columns, giving an almost romantic elegance.

"Impressed?" Judy asked, as Esther looked at the view from the stone balustrade.

"Totally! I'm dumbstruck! It's like a fairytale! I want to work here!"

"I thought you might say that. Let's get to the office now and start with a working coffee break."

Along a few more corridors, some of which contained old, tall, locked bookcases that contained a multitude of large, leather-bound books of historic parliamentary proceedings, they eventually arrived at a door.

"Here's where I work," said Judy as she invited Esther through.

Again, Esther had to look in wonder at the large room, its fashion and grand windows.

"Well, this *is* a listed building," Judy said. "And my office is through that door over there. Welcome to the Africa department – well, the hub of it. Most of us are away on business."

Three other women were already working behind their desks in a spacious arrangement within the room, with numerous computers and filing cabinets, desks and chairs surrounding them. They smiled at Esther, as if knowing of her beforehand.

"Everyone, this is Esther Goodwin here for six weeks to help with that copying job." Judy then introduced each of the three, and showed Esther to a desk further away, allowing Esther to settle while she made a call to arrange a computer account.

When done, Judy returned with two coffees and started to discuss Esther's task. "You'll be working for me, directly," Judy explained, "which, don't worry, won't be too bad." The two smiled at each other again and Judy motioned to some old boxes to the side on the floor: "Now, you see here these old, old boxes?"

"Yes."

"And you see these nice, new modern boxes over there?"

"Yes."

"Well what we need done, simply, is all of what is in the old, gets scanned into the system, catalogued and listed for searches, and then filed as originals in the nice, new boxes. Sounds easy?"

Esther looked at the ten large old, dusty, cardboard boxes and at the twenty smaller new plastic boxes, and at the computer system on her allocated desk. "So good, so far."

"Now don't get the idea this is going to be a quick fix, because you will have to skim read it all to fill in the computer bits, so that it can be electronically retrieved. That will take ages, so none of us are expecting you to get through this before you leave."

"So what about Data Protection?"

"Yes, now all this is from African Embassies collected over the last sixty years, thereabouts – or supposedly – so we're not expecting any British military secrets or sensitive material; but you are never to speak to anyone outside this office of anything you read, regardless how innocent it seems, even after working here."

"Perfectly clear."

"Good! Because that's what you signed a few moments ago. Now Claire, the one you're replacing, did a few to get started before she left, so have a look at her work. I will need to get a few of my things done, but then we'll go through a few together before you get too engrossed, if that's possible. Sounds good?"

Esther nodded and, being left alone, she opened a box and started to read with enthusiasm the first item she took.

Write your own Psalm

With the forest birds singing, a tranquil soft breeze, and his footsteps crunching and snapping twigs, the only way David could describe his feelings was of being welcomed home as he trekked along the quiet secret woodland track to Halcyon. It felt healthy to breath and the troubles of life were lulled away by the peacefulness. The day was full of gleaming sunshine, beaming down through the branches, and coming towards him was someone in the distance also enjoying the scene. Finally, they met and stood in each other's way. They smiled and embraced each other in a warm welcome.

"Hello, Grandson," said Joseph.

"It's good to see you again, Granddad," replied David.

"I thought I'd chance meeting you; thought I'd give you some company along the way."

"How have you been?"

They turned and started on their walk to the Manor, sharing a conversation.

"I'm starting to feel old now, but – well, that's aging for you."

"You look good to me."

"You're just biased. And you? How's you? End of the first year for you now?"

"Finished my last exam eight days ago."

"Well time to forget about it: can't add to your life worrying now. The forest doesn't worry, but it's all provided for. I did miss your letters, though. I supposed you were either working hard or chasing the girls or both. I was hoping to know what happened to the girl."

"Ohhhh, the game's over. I'm angry that she just dismisses me. I'm so confused. I feel awkward and that annoys me. She's with someone else now. Didn't take her long. Sometimes I just want her to drop down some hole, but she's grown more on me now than she ever has. Sometimes I want to drop down some hole." David then went quiet as they walked.

Joseph realised this was not the time to touch the subject: "So what happens to you this summer?"

"I got that summer job working for Carnadyne developing future electronic systems for cancer radiotherapy. They're also giving me sponsorship and a career there when I qualify."

"Very good, I'm happy for you. Sounds like quite a blessing."

"I can only stay here three or four days as I need to start fairly soon. I stayed with Mum and Dad before coming here. I think things aren't great. My brother Andrew doesn't go home now as Mum's getting tense and angry with things. I think it's rubbing off on Dad. And it doesn't help that I have news that Mum won't like."

"News?"

"It's this news I've come all this way to tell you."

Joseph nodded and waited.

"Aren't you going to ask?"

"Okay, what's your news?"

"I've become a Christian."

Joseph laughed and hugged his Grandson in a tight squeeze, ruffling his hair endearingly.

David smiled: "It's what you've been praying for?"

"Certainly has and it only took a year!" The older man became silent and then started to speak as if to discuss a matter: "That means, as for Halcyon – ." For all the trees, Halcyon Manor could not be seen, but Joseph pointed in its direction. "Well, there's plenty to talk about later," was all his Grandfather finished with saying.

The two continued in a comfortable silence until they reached the unlocked front door, entering the hall and closing the door behind them.

In the silence, Joseph stopped and looked at David: "Don't give up heart with Esther. At least she made you consider having faith, which, in the long run, may have saved your life on the day of judgement. That's quite something, don't you think?"

David followed Joseph as he wandered off into the corridors of the building.

"People can thwart the plans God has for them, but He allows that. Leave it with Him now and learn. Be cheerful that she influenced you to become a Christian. And with that, I think we should have a Halcyon-style feast tonight to celebrate. How about that?"

"Sounds great, Granddad."

A good night's sleep in his usual chambers allowed David to awake early and refreshed, and although the sunlight was already up before him, he awoke to the dreamy sound of music. It was beautiful singing, hauntingly beautiful, coming from the air, the walls, the windows, from under the door, but his initial thought was that it was coming from his own ears. When alert, he knew it to be floating through the corridors and David lay awake listening. It was like a monastic chant, with feeling and depth, of longing and acceptance.

It eventually stopped.

Wanting to hear more, he got up, had a quick wash from the cold water in the awaiting bowl, and dressed to find the trace of the faded sounds. He guessed the room to be the library and found his Grandfather, seated and reading, having the gramophone on the table to the side.

Joseph looked up from his reading and across at David, who stood not having ventured much into the room.

"What was that?" David asked.

"Good?"

"Yes, what was it?"

"Gregorio Allergri's 'Miserere'."

David was still no wiser.

"Here – sit down." Joseph waited for David to be comfortable and then passed him the record cover, the creased and cracked cardboard sleeve showing a picture of a choir singing with apparent large lungs and gusto. "Gregorio Allergri was a composer for the Sistine Chapel in the Vatican in Rome, a long time ago, and he wrote – that." The last word was emphasised by pointing to the cover David now studied.

"'The Misser – what is it? Misery?"

"'Miserere,' it means Mercy. It was sung only in the Sistine Chapel. The Pope of the day considered it so beautiful, he forbade it sung anywhere else. He even went so far to make it illegal for copies of the music. The effect was to create a mysterious quality to the song among the population at large – until, that is, Mozart heard it and copied a version from memory."

"What was done to him?"

"Mozart? Nothing, it turned out to be a huge success, and everyone came to hear it."

"So it's about mercy."

"It's Psalm fifty-one, word for word." Joseph offered David his Bible, opened at the Psalm. "You want to read it?"

David took the book and started to read.

Joseph studied David for a moment. "I can tell you're still sad. Here's an opportunity to write your own psalm. Your name-sake King David, he wrote Psalm fifty-one in repentance after he finally admitted his adultery with Bathsheba."

"Who?"

"A beautiful, married woman; got her pregnant, as well."

"Well, I didn't get that far with Esther, if that's what you're thinking."

"I didn't imagine you did, if her impression on me is correct."

"My heart feels like it's a lead weight. My lungs feel empty. My stomach is like a rock of hot tension. My head hurts with loss. My thoughts always turn back to her. I must seem idiotic to you."

"I know how you feel, but you need to see there are others who are in worse peril."

There was a long silence.

"What happened?" asked David. "What really happened to my Grandmother?"

"I've seen people bleed to death on the operating table, all sorts of afflictions, poverty and believe me, it affected me, but I regarded my work as doing His duty. Then Evalynne was taken from me and my life collapsed, and even God couldn't reconcile the way she died. She left me, ran off to do her – her duty. She didn't even kiss me goodbye. She was slaughtered and I became angered, disillusioned, lost. I wanted to be lost. I wanted to be depressed, because I knew no other way to cope. I left the Salvation Army Mission and I left The Salvation Army. I came back to England and – was like a lost soul, a zombie, caught in my own lack of zeal for life, angry, depressed, alone – like Frankenstein's monster, angry, wanting to chase his creator to question the reason for my creation, for the sour life He had given me. He had taken my children, taken away my career, and killed off my wife. I wanted to storm into God's inner throne room and with my rage demand why He allows so much evil and suffering; to shake Him into action by my – my strenuous, miserable imploring, and demand that He annihilate everything that is wrong. With the years of His silence, my life then became purposeless, like living in a perpetual prison and I accused God of injustice."

Joseph stood up and wandered over to the window to stand looking out into the garden, but then turned and looked at David. "I'm not the only one. Job in the Bible accused God of injustice – and then, when everything had been said in nauseating length and detail, God defended Himself. He defended Himself against Job, having waited for the proper time. He defended Himself against Jeremiah, and against Habakkuk. They all had the same dispare as I and accused God for it. I was living the predictions of doom in the book of Revelation, and not living in the hope of Jesus returning. The same theme comes out, again and again, that God will do something."

David said nothing in the pause.

"You have to understand that I had read the Bible dozens of times to know what was there, but it was a case of how deep was the soil in me? How far could my faith go? There are plenty of people in the Bible having gone through far worse than me. Take Joseph in Genesis, *my* namesake, but he didn't complain. Throughout my misery, all along, I still felt that God cares, and is angered and saddened for all the wrong there is. But, you see, He created everything – everything – so who am I? Just clay and dust – we all are. How can I possibly understand this world with the mind I have? How can I possibly judge the God who has done all this? I learnt that even in the depths of my sadness, God has still built an immense, mighty, awesome world that I am utterly incapable of praising Him to the standard of His worth. It is not I that built a universe. Who did I think I was that I know enough to judge God and to judge His ways? Because one day, He will defend Himself against all our accusations – and in a big way. Job got his answer and so will Mankind – and so will Satan.

"And that's the faith I needed to return to The Salvation Army. I committed my life back to Him and started to return to being the man Evalynne loved. Suffering and troubles can be toxic to faith for some people, but to others it can give faith a meaning, a new life. I just want to thank God for being patient with me while I spent so many years wandering around in my self-pity. I learnt that I truly needed a vulnerable faith to place my trust in Him, a bold faith to step out, an intelligent faith for God to enjoy being with me."

All the while, David realised he still never received an answer as to why his Grandmother died.

"I can see you are sad about Esther and the mistakes you think you've made. David, do not be afraid to make mistakes, but keep your vision on Him. Learn to take a wise risk in faith to learn what there is to learn, but be bold and willing to look foolish to others, because His ways are foolish in the eyes of the world. They will think you to be unintelligent – so be strong, my David, to be unintelligent, because He will return – in a big, big way. Do not be foolish and reckless in God's sight. Do not make mistakes out of careless thinking, being unwise in the ways of the world as there is much to trip the goodhearted. Beware of wanting to believe there is a loophole in His ways, as you are only fooling yourself. Beware of feelings that wallow in sin. Wanting to hurt God, to hurt other people is not a mistake. It is sin, and *that* is rebellion and *that* is lethal; lethal to your soul, and that will make God sad."

"I just feel like I've lost a lot."

"Why don't you write your own psalm, David? Write to God and tell Him how you truly feel with prose. Use it to understand what you're feeling. Even be angry, but never lose respect. Write it out, throw ash over yourself, wear sackcloth – and then move on from Esther. Look forward to your new summer job and feel blessed by the blossoming career you will have. Write your own psalm of praise to God about that – even if it is only within your heart. Make it personal."

The Past and the Future in one day

Esther was sure she was not making enough progress. Over that first week since she had begun the job, her work seemed to have stagnated, but she continued to read all the strange documents she came across and this interest made an impression on the others in the office as she worked diligently without discussing much. The staff was happy to talk of all sorts of things during the day, but Esther kept from their gossip and wanted to make more of an impression on her work.

Judy sidled up and gave Esther a coffee.

"Oh, thank you."

"You know, we're not expecting you to work this hard. You're not paid enough."

"Oh, that's fine, I'm enjoying being here."

"We have a number of books on Africa that you can just peruse, and if you like, I can provide some insightful papers on British protocols to help you understand what we do here."

"Yes, that would be great. Thank you."

"I hear you belong to The Salvation Army."

"Yes, I go to the one along Oxford Street."

"Do you play the piano, by any chance?"

"Yes, why?"

"We frequently entertain foreign dignitaries here with a posh meal and usually have a pianist for tranquil background music. I've been told all our usual piano players are unavailable. Would you be up for it? Don't worry if not, but I thought you might like to – give it a try. Just that one of our ministers noticed you playing recitals in the Dorchester recently and asked me to ask you."

"Really? Well, I'm, it's – not that I'm – it's just that – . Will important people be there?"

"Of course! People in the international News, famous ones."

"I'm not sure I'm good enough."

"That's not what this minister told me. Go on! Give it a try! Don't hide your talent under a bowl."

"Okay, why not? I can give it a try."

Judy smiled and they discussed the date and time of the meal.

When Judy had gone to her office, Esther started reading the next paper to catalogue, being a letter dated November 1967, of a complaint against the lack of rules regarding poaching. Speed-reading the article, she diligently scanned in the paper, filled in the required electronic details and chose the next article.

So it went for the rest of the day: analysing financial accounts, reading letters of Ambassadors, studying the minutes of meetings, being bored by the inventories of what each Embassy owned, and evaluating the documents of each Embassy who attempted to make sense of their respective national African Government. It approached mid-afternoon when Esther, starting to feel tired and less eager to read, came across an internal report of an incident involving The Salvation Army. Instantly she was revived and her interest was re-lit.

Ambassador,

This report is in regard to the disappearance of the men who, prior to their disappearance, had violently killed 133 men, women and children, maimed 109 people, raped 9 women and destroyed many buildings of Amani, on the 11th day of June, 1974. A full report of this incident is given in my previous letter, dated, June 22nd 1974.

To gather information on their disappearance, I have gained witness accounts that this band of savage men including, it is alleged, a number of boys under the age of ten, all under the leadership of Beruité Godamna, arrived at Amani on the above date and committed the above atrocities, and then furthered their destructive ambitions on the Christian provision of health and school ministries of The Salvation Army Fort at Kombaiar 2 miles north east of Amani.

It is at Kombaiar that the trail of these men becomes lost and they mysteriously vanish as further reports of their atrocities or sightings no longer occur. There are no records of these men or boys being seen again.

It is with sadness that I now write of the death of Captain Evalynne Lovert, Salvation Army Officer and chief medical director, who stood before these men to defend her Christian Fort. She died from one bullet to the heart.

As there is no damage to the site or more victims, it is regarded that the death of this courageous Salvation Army Officer had such an affect to halt the advance of Beruité Godamna and his men, and to disaffect their influence on the region. Her husband, Captain Joseph Lovert, was visibly affected and our sympathies extend to him for his tragic loss.

I cannot write with enough words to express how much in regard the local villages now view Kombaiar. The event of Captain Evalynne's death has brought about an increased admiration for the Mission, and I consider yourself as someone who knows of their work also. To follow up the local detective agency, Kombaiar shows no signs of involvement of the men's disappearance and the rumours of God striking dead the men are unfounded. I conclude, therefore, that Beruité Godamna is now in fear of the threat of an uprising of anger against him by the communities that he repressed, and so hides to keep from being killed along with his loyal band. It should be added that local villagers no longer seem to fear neither Godamna nor his militia, all due to the courage of Captain Evalynne Lovert.

In conclusion, I deem these men to be at large and advise that this group is still maintained on the 'wanted list'; but due to the lack of resources and other matters now more pressing, this investigation should be given less priority until further evidence comes forward.

Yours Faithfully,
Elias Merrish, Secretary of Public Order Directorate

In this innocuous letter of faded typing and old paper, creased and yellowing, with patches of dirt, dated fourteen years before she was born, seemed to tell an entire story with very few words. Esther became lost in her eagerness to know more of this courageous Christian woman who fearlessly defended her faith to her death.

She scanned in the letter and made sure she had entered the relevant details as usual. Then she tried to forget the story and move on to the next paper. It was not long after, seeing she was being unobserved, that Esther made a photocopy of the article of Captain Evalynne Lovert and secretly placed it in her pocket.

Mark walked along King James Street wondering where the entrance to the Foreign Office was within the imposing high, white, grand buildings when he almost passed it. He caught sight of the small brass plaque on the wall and assured himself he had arrived, but when seeing the armed security guard, whom naively was missing from his original plan, he started to doubt what to do.

With his indecision and loitering, the lone, hardened gunman approached him out of suspicion. Knowing how he must look, Mark instantly became nervous, but the guard, contrary to the large gun he carried, politely greeted Mark and asked if he needed any assistance.

"I'm not, I'm just, I really – I don't know," was Mark's hesitant reply.

"You're at the Foreign Office, sir. Is this where you want to be?"

"Thank you, yes, I know I'm at the Foreign Office, and yes, this is where I want to be, but – I'm sorry, I'm just wasting your time."

The guard smirked, looked around him at the vacancy and silence of the street, and said, "You're doing me a favour, mate. I've got no one else to talk to here and I've been saying nothing to nobody for a few hours now. So I wouldn't worry about wasting my time. How can I help? I'm presuming you're not here to cause me a security risk."

"No, I'm not, I just, you see – ." Mark then settled his thoughts, succumbing to how ridiculous he now appeared. "There's this girl, you see, and she's, well she's – the – she's the light of my life actually, and she – "

"Works in this building?"

"I was going to finish by saying she's – really pretty."

"I see sir," the guard replied, and stood still and quiet, cradling his gun, looking at Mark straight-faced as if to hear more.

"And, yes, she does work here, somewhere – in this building." Mark, so unsure of what impression he was giving, had to fill the silence made by the authority figure: "I'm a trainee surgical nurse, you see, not that you want to know that, but she surprised me with a visit – a visit to my hospital, so that she – surprised me at the end of my shift and she works here – you see, so, I thought I'd – surprise *her*." Mark stopped his rambling.

"I see sir," the guard repeated after a pause.

"I just didn't think of this security."

"Well there's a park along there, sir. You can meet her there."

"Yes, true, I can meet her there, but – I wanted it to be a surprise, like she did to me and she would have to know I'm in the park and where to find me in the park and that – wouldn't be a surprise."

"No sir." The guard went silent again, trying to suppress his smirk, but this time Mark was so unsure of what to say that the guard capitulated to his own silence: "So what's her name?"

"Esther, Esther Goodwin."

He looked at Mark for a moment as if to weigh up his choices, making a decision based on how Mark looked and the extent he wanted to believe his story. "A surprise?" he finally asked.

Mark nodded.

The guard raised his hand to speak to a microphone attached to his jacket collar, but looked at Mark again. "Pretty, you say?"

"Well I think she is." Mark was then astounded to listen to the conversation as the guard spoke to his hand and neck.

"Got a kid here with a sweet romantic story of wanting to surprise the love of his life: Esther Goodwin. – Yep, something like that. Anyway, I wondered if we could do him a favour and let him into the courtyard. He'll be visible enough and probably won't move if we tell him it's mined." He winked at Mark as he listened to the other end. "Yep, something like that. Sounds like he needs all the help he can get. –

Okay." Turning to Mark, he said, "They're checking up on her and want to know how pretty she is. We might be able to let you through and sit you in the courtyard beyond those turnstiles."

"That would be great, just great, thanks."

"You'll have to have some photographic identification and leave your mobile phone with us."

"That's fine."

"Hang on, sir." The guard, as if having been interrupted, returned to his microphone: "He assures me she's pretty. – Okay, letting him through." Turning back to Mark, he motioned with his head to walk through the passage: "Just pop your head into the room at the end and they'll sort you out, sir." With a friendly wink and a smile, the guard allowed Mark to walk along the short walkway to a room inset, before reaching some turnstiles. He started to chuckle to himself when Mark was beyond noticing.

Esther looked at her watch and realised that home time was soon. She sat back in her chair, mindful of how tired she was, but having the image of a woman shot dead for her beliefs made her mind over-active and unable to switch off from the day. The more Esther thought of her, the more beautiful the Salvation Army Officer became.

"Esther?"

"Yes?" Esther said sharply, having been startled.

"You looked as if you were in another world," said Judy, standing to the side, holding paper of her own.

"Sorry, I was."

"It's time to go." Judy then exchanged sentiments to the other office girls and turned back to Esther. "Come on! Home! Esther!"

Esther started to neaten her piles and boxes and noticed Judy remaining by her side.

"If you keep doing this without breaks, which, incidentally, I've noticed you're not taking, then all this becomes tiresome. I wouldn't be surprised if Claire got pregnant to avoid it."

"I do come across things that are interesting."

Judy smiled: "But most of it is just drab."

Esther smiled back and nodded.

"Welcome to the Foreign Office. What did you find interesting?"

"Oh – it's now lost in the system," answered Esther, switching off her computer.

Knowing this had been a polite way of the young girl to say she would rather leave work, Judy dismissed the issue: "Well have a good evening, Esther. The sun is still out so go and get some of it. And don't forget about that piano recital tomorrow."

Judy returned to her inner office and Esther left to make her way through the corridors and down some of the stone stairwells that she had come to love; but her mind was still on the letter of a mysterious and courageous Salvation Army Missionary. Crossing the courtyard to the exit, she failed to notice a young man sitting on one of the benches with her mind intense on the thought of how far would her faith take her and the complete admiration she was developing for a woman whom she had never met. So captivating was the thought that even when a man started calling out and chasing her, she was still resolute on her introspection.

"Esther! Esther, wait!"

Esther stopped just short of the turnstiles and was amazed to see Mark standing there. "Mark! What are you doing?"

"Well, I thought I'd come to see you at work. You did it for me, so I thought it would be fun to do it for you."

Clearly lost for words, Esther spluttered a reply: "It's, I, errmm, well, I'm just – wow." Then a thought struck her: "How did you get in?"

"Oh, I just made friends with the security guards. You look – errmm – somewhere else. Is something the matter?"

"No! Oh, no! Sorry, Mark, I'm just thinking of something. They've asked me to play the piano tomorrow."

"The piano?"

"For a meal."

"A meal?"

"Quiet meal-time music for foreign important people."

"Wow."

"Thanks for surprising me. I'm – surprised." She started to laugh as if embarrassed and flattered.

"I've got tickets for a Thames cruise. You interested? It goes in twenty minutes. It's just down by Westminster Bridge."

"That would be brilliant."

"Great! Come on then!" Mark looked at the iron bars as if they deflated his eagerness. "Oh, I need to sort my things out. They kept my mobile phone."

"Yes, they do that."

As Mark collected his items, Esther was unaware of the polite, knowing smiles from the guards that they gave him, and his thanks meant more than just the return of his phone. Then the two left the building, saying goodbye to the lone guard at the front, who gave a friendly salute. Leaving the Foreign Office behind, they walked along King James Street, but Mark was certain that, although Esther walked beside him, she was elsewhere.

"Are you okay?" asked Mark as they walked under the archway to Whitehall. "I wouldn't worry about tomorrow: you're great with the piano."

"Sorry, yes, I'm fine. I'll shake off the day in a minute. Thank you for just coming. It's a great surprise. Come on, let's go and drift along the river together." Esther suddenly put her arm through his and cheered herself.

"What's made you all happy?"

"I can't say: I've signed the Official Secrets Act," she said with a playful smile.

'It is well with my soul ...'

We all finished our exams for the first year and then entered the second. I continued to study. I continued to attend The Salvation Army. I continued to play the piano at restaurants and hotels for extra money. Mark continued to battle his feelings as a student in the operating theatres, and David was just background news with what Jonathan let slip a few times, with David going elsewhere. In no time, the second year was over. I returned to the Foreign Office for summer work in addition to my piano recitals, and then we were all into the final year of university. In time, David became less, and Mark became more. I gained employment with the Foreign Office, in the Africa Department, and David, I learnt, had a respectable career for many years at a company developing medical equipment until he became redundant. David didn't have much to say about this period and I'm not familiar with what happened, so long ago as it was. I have no notion of whether he dated, broke girl's hearts or whether his social connections were large or small.

Mark completed his training and became an ODP, and I came to admire and respect him more and more for what he did. He found it hard and he still complained of being bullied by some of the older nurses. I could give him no encouragement to tackle them, and at times he allowed them to get him down. There seemed very little to pick him up and his father deteriorated, making his life silent at times. He would sometimes mull over God's judgement for someone with mental health issues. Quite strangely, his father remained quite optimistic in his blissful ignorance of his own illness. Mark had problems seeing how God could allow people to suffer. I think sometimes he dwelt on the suffering he saw, more than those who got better because of what he did.

What amazed me was that Mark could pick himself up from these downfalls and doubts. He had an inner strength that set an example for me. To Mark, as important as tasks are, friendships were more important. I look back and see myself looking at tasks being more important, as if I could not be complete in myself if each task was not complete and perfect.

Sometimes it's a case of working for those directly close to you and achieving more, than to do little for the whole world. What did I think I could truly achieve with the Foreign Office, with the Middle East peace negotiations? I know I spent more time at work than I should have. No one on any deathbed says they wish they had spent more time at work. I can vouch for that. I wish Mark and I had been more of a praying couple.

But I achieved what I had set out to achieve: to gain a full-time professional status at the Foreign Office. It was within the Africa ministry that my career blossomed. People learnt that I could play the piano, and eventually I was asked to play tranquil background recitals for dignitaries during official governmental meals with these public figures discussing important policies that would affect world relations. I would play reflective classic piano music from the great composers, but I would also equally play some Salvation Army music. No one particularly minded. Many of these fine, worldwide public men and women in high office – leaders, presidents, prime ministers, some royalty even – would tell me how well I played and what beautiful music. Little did they know it was Christian. However, after a while, it became a recognized custom of mine to always end the evening with one hymn in particular, and they would all wait and stop and listen when I played it. Such as it was, this hymn became known as my signature tune. It surprised me that they even came to know the words as I played my moving, touching, poignant version of 'It is well with my soul'. Even the Islamists would kindly respect the moment and be endeared, enamoured even, with this hymn. It was amazing how many famous people I met through this developed talent of mine and many would always return for other official visits and ask as to my welfare and happiness – politics and religion put aside. I became aware of the joke that world peace was held back because important discussions were suspended to listen to my piano playing while they ate. Needless to say, I had no time to play in restaurants and hotels anymore, even though that paid; the Foreign Office, didn't.

I had my blossoming career at the Foreign Office, and my peers and leaders regarded me highly, but with Evalynne, I was starting to romance the idea of becoming a Salvation Army Officer. I would get so far with the thought and then backtrack, but nothing stopped me daydreaming of meeting her in Africa in her time. I wish I could have met Captain Evalynne Lovert.

Book Three : Don't Perpetuate Sorrow

An unburnt Burning Bush

It was as if all his years and all his moments, all his dreams and hopes, his security and fears, had been heading for standing on a bridge, spanning across a deep river, wondering which way to turn. David stood in the midst of London, between the north bank of the Thames and the south bank, staring at the still surface of the water flowing with an undercurrent that was not to be trusted, along with pollution and diseases. It was busy with people passing by, but he just stood and looked down from the pedestrian Millennium Bridge. To his north was Saint Paul's Cathedral. To his south was the Tate Modern art Gallery.

It was then that he turned to the north side and caught a glimpse of a familiar figure walking towards him. It was a short vision that made him wonder if it had been imagined, as the crowds had disfigured his line of sight, but, as if appearing from a mist, the person, well dressed, approached David with an encouraging smile.

They stood smiling and then both embraced each other.

"David! It's good to see you!" exclaimed Jonathan. "After all these years! How are you?"

"It's good to see you. Thanks for meeting like this."

"No problem. When did you arrive?"

"Came in by train, got through the Underground, meandered around a few places and arrived ten minutes ago. No problems except for getting up early, but as a workaholic Stock Broker who gets the early worm you should know all about that."

"I've changed jobs."

"What?"

"Yeah, crazy hey?"

"When did this happen?"

"Six months or so ago. You want a drink? IHQ is just there."

"Yes, I know, I came here with Esther once."

"Want a coffee?"

"I don't want to take you away from your work."

"No matter. Come on, I'm thirsty."

They walked towards Saint Paul's and entered the main doors of the glass building of the International Headquarters of The Salvation Army.

In the foyer, Jonathan asked what David considered a strange, forward question: "You want a look?"

"Look? What of?"

"This place."

"Why would we be allowed to look around?"

"Anyone can roam here."

"Okay but if we get into trouble, I'm blaming you."

"So Adam-like. Well, here goes."

David followed Jonathan to a room near enough the main entrance to be, at first, considered an executive cloakroom, but when Jonathan peered inside and ushered David to accompany him, the room became a boardroom.

"Important decisions are made here concerning the international on-goings of the movement. All sorts of important people arrive once a month to discuss matters. There's a video link connecting to wherever else."

The room was plush, clean and well equipped with the ways of modern technology, with soft, comfortable, empty chairs around a circular table, void of anything except for its own top. David stood amazed that he was able to be in such an important room without being challenged, but the two receptionists just to the side of the main foyer were not appearing to be in the least concerned.

"Want to see upstairs?" asked Jonathan.

"You're not getting us into trouble, are you? You always were forward."

"Who? Me? Does it look as if we're being chased as spies?"

David shrugged: "Lead the way."

They wandered to the lifts and David noticed Jonathan give one of the receptionists a friendly wink.

David stopped.

Jonathan paused with him, watching the growing amused smile cross David's lips. "Yes?" asked Jonathan.

"You work here! You work here, don't you!"

"Good grief, David, for a top engineer, you're a bit slow. Come on, I'll show you the General's office. He's out today, so we'll not bother him."

Using the lift, they ascended to the floor above and David saw the myriad of desks within rooms of glass walls and partitions. Jonathan motioned to follow and they were then within a foyer that contained a multitude of portraits, starting at one whom David recognised.

"General William Booth," announced David. "Can't mistake him." He looked at all the others and then turned to Jonathan: "All the other Generals since then?"

"All of them, and through there is the current General's office."

David looked through the glass to see the office space was unoccupied and unconsciously followed Jonathan as he wandered onwards to another room with pews and a table at the far end before a decorative window.

"This is a quiet chapel to come to ask for inspiration."

"I might be in the right place then."

"Why? What's happened?"

"I was made redundant two weeks ago."

"Oh, I'm sorry. I didn't know. You didn't say on the phone."

"No, I know."

"What are you going to do?"

David shook his head: "I've become too specialised. Everyone wants instant engineers in whatever field without allowing any time to learn a new system. I was getting despondent at Carnadyne anyway."

"Despondent?"

"I'm fed up with the people! I was doing really well on radiotherapy systems. Then they moved me to advanced MRI scanners, which I don't know much about. There was a frantic panic. Nothing worked. The principal engineers didn't agree with each other. I was so certain I had found mistakes in the principle mathematics, but no one wanted to know. I would go around asking what each thought and they all have different views, criticise everyone else, and then shoo me away still baffled. So I go back to my desk, try and fathom out what I think and all that takes time, which management think I'm wasting! I was doing well on radiotherapy systems. It was great knowing I was helping beat cancer. Well – maybe someone close to me will benefit from my work. But now look what's happened."

"You may never know the true reason why you were made redundant. Maybe it's a blessing – if God's in this somewhere."

"But I've nowhere to go. I need to be out of my rented place in a few months. It's a blessing I didn't renew the contract."

"Won't your parents have you?"

"They're getting a divorce. I was going to tell them about getting made redundant, but then this letter arrives from Dad. I think I need to give them space. I think *I* need space, somewhere to go and get my head fixed."

"Well let's follow tradition when there's a calamity."

"Pray?"

"Well, yes, there is that, but I initially thought of having a cup of something. I'll treat you to one in the café downstairs."

"What about your work?"

"This is my work."

They left the chapel, descended in the elevator and arrived at the basement where Jonathan joined the queue. David sat at a table not far from where he remembered that fateful day with Esther, but his thoughts were interrupted as Jonathan sat opposite to offer him a cup of tea and an eager ear to listen. Instead, Jonathan had more questions fired at him from David.

"So how come you work here, now?"

"I quit the Stock Market and now work in the finance department. I have a desk upstairs."

"You enjoy it?"

"I feel like I'm able to do a good job, know my way around the financial world, I have good connections and what I'm doing will enrich other people. Yeah, I enjoy it. A lot of my old colleagues respect what I'm doing on a majorly reduced wage. But what about you? I want to hear about you."

David stirred his tea for a while, then looked up at Jonathan and motioned over Jonathan's shoulder to a particular table: "We sat there, Esther and me, on the last date we had. Gosh, this place brings back memories."

"It wasn't that long ago."

"Six years? Coming on seven?"

"Well, perhaps it was that long ago."

"I still think of her – now and again. I wonder how she is."

"Is that a rhetorical question, or do you want me to answer?"

"You still see her?"

"Yes, of course."

"How is she?"

"She's well, enjoying life at the Foreign Office. She's doing really well."

"Good. – Good."

For a moment, neither spoke: David judging whether to ask yet more questions; and Jonathan guessing what was to come. They both played with their drinks, either by drinking, stirring, moving the cup around or just staring at it.

"Yes?" eventually asked Jonathan, pre-empting David's question.

"Is she – happy? I mean, is she – is she – with – ?"

"Esther and Mark were engaged almost a year ago."

David's face visibly turned ashen and he looked ill.

"You okay?"

"I didn't think, that, I, I mean, I'm, it's just that, I'm not upset."

"Really?"

"Yes, I am."

"You weren't aware you still loved Esther after all these years – were you?"

David shook his head: "What am I going to do? I feel sunk! I feel lost. I've lost my job, my parents are divorcing, Mum has always been strange about me since I admitted I had become a Christian, as if it was worse than being gay, and now I have no idea of my future. I could have continued working at Carnadyne for the rest of my life."

"I thought you said you were getting despondent there."

"Yes, but – I don't know. I can't believe Esther's now engaged. It's a bit hard to take in. It's like the Titanic fared better."

"She moved on with her life."

"I feel strange, numb, shocked – shocked and cold that she's now permanently lost to me."

"But you haven't spoken to her in years."

"I think my mind is now totally scrambled. It's like everything's hit me all at once. I can't believe I still have feelings for her."

Jonathan sat for a while in silence, not knowing what to say, and then a thought came to him: "I have an idea."

"Assassinate Mark?"

"No, but I could see someone for you."

"And they would assassinate Mark?"

"No, something else."

"Who? About what?"

"You want to go abroad, have an experience, an adventure? You said you wanted to refresh your head. Well, here's a chance. I heard about it only a few hours ago. It might not be available for long."

"What are you talking about? Please don't tease me with one of your fun jokes again."

"I can put in a good word for getting you a place at a Salvation Army posting – in Africa, in Rwanda."

"Africa? In Africa? Abroad?"

"Africa is abroad, yes. It might do you some good to get away, see another culture, see some people worse off than you and put things into perspective. Rwanda is a beautiful country."

"Yes, I know – but – Africa?"

"You should just see it, David: a lifetime chance to do something amazing."

"Yes, I know, but – Africa?"

"Don't worry, God is already there."

"Yes, but – ."

"Okay, it might be a long way from Esther, but she's now gone. She might as well be on another planet. So how about making yourself feel good by helping others. Put your faith into practice: a faith without action is a dead faith."

"Yes, I know, but we're talking about Africa. I don't know anything about Africa."

"It's the large continent south of Europe. Scientists believe the human race came from there; very hot and very much full of interesting insects."

"I can go with The Salvation Army?"

"There's a position going at a Rwandan Salvation Army School for a year or so."

"A year! An entire year!"

"With an extension for two – depending on what happens."

"Two years!"

"Yes! Don't get too excited! There've been three applicants, but two have withdrawn – don't know why – and the person who accepted the job has now broken a leg or two or something and can't go. If you want to, I can get you an interview and I'm sure you'll be going – if you want to."

"Africa?"

"Yes – come on, it's beautiful."

"Why don't you go?"

"Because it's full of horrible insects."

"Thanks! So it's all right for me, then."

"You're the one needing a challenge."

"You think? I thought I needed a job."

"Perhaps this is the chance to prove a few things. Is God worth following when trouble comes along? Can we trust Him when He's testing our faith?"

"You think going to Africa is going to test my faith?"

"Well you're not strictly the wild country type. And then there are those insects."

"Malaria?"

"You can get a few injections."

"I thought you have daily pills."

"You're not up to date, my young laddy."

David shook his head to himself: "I don't know, Jonathan."

"Well, what else do you have on the horizon? Is it worth passing this chance? It's only come about within the last few hours and they're re-advertising it – now. You may miss it."

"I don't want to go to Africa."

"Really?"

"No!"

"Okay, it's up to you. I just think it's a great opportunity. Many kids go exploring the world and it costs them a bomb or two. This one has free lodgings and food and – free insects."

"Yes – insects: I don't mind the insects. It's the lions and tigers that worry me."

"Look, when trouble comes we can blame Him, be angry about it, decide not to believe He exists, or just learn to get near to Him. Joseph, in Genesis, one of the twelve sons of Jacob, multicoloured coat and all that, the one sold into slavery, thrown into prison – he made the best of his lot in life. He got on with it. He didn't mope around like you being made redundant. Joseph believed he was part of God's bigger story despite how things looked. Don't you want to be part of a bigger story?"

"I'm not into stories."

"What about some peace, some introspection? Africa could be that chance to just – ."

"To just – what?"

"Have a desert experience. It'll be fun. Have an adventure."

"It's in a desert?"

"Well, not literally."

"So what's with the desert?"

"Nothing, but – don't worry about it. Just refresh your head."

"I don't understand this desert thing."

"Even great men have spent time out, having a desert experience."

"But you said, there's no desert."

"No, it's a jungle."

"So what about the wildlife?"

"Yes! Wow! What about the wildlife? Wouldn't that be fantastic?

And see more of the world."

"Why don't you go?"

"I told you, I'm not into insects. And I like my boring accounting job here."

"You're doing a really good salesman job for someone who doesn't believe in his product."

"I feel like I'm where I'm supposed to be right now; but you? You're the one at a crossroads, not me. Go on! Develop your character while you're young, and if you don't like it, come back."

"I don't know."

"Consider it an adventure holiday – with God – like life."

David did not reply other than to purse his lips and then he shrugged in a motion that looked like his reservations were slowly being broken.

"Did you say your Grandparents were there for some time? Whereabouts did they go?"

"I'm not sure. I didn't ask."

"I can go, right now, and get you an interview, or you can consider it a chance to ask more questions. I know the person to ask. He's at his desk now. I can make this happen for you."

"What about my parents and family? What about my belongings? I need to get out of my rented place."

"Look, I have plenty of room – for your belongings. I still have my penthouse flat that has space. I can even help retrieve them."

"Yes, but my parents are divorcing. They'll need me. How's Mum going to take it? How's she going to cope with me going away for a year?"

"Perhaps two."

"Precisely!"

"David, are they so incapable of getting through this without you? I think you think too lowly of them. I think you're making excuses. You said earlier they needed space. Well how much space is going to Africa going to be? I think you're being a real Moses about this. Just listen to the Burning Bush."

"I think *you* really want me to go. Will they speak English?"

"The Africans? No, they live up in the trees hunting woolly Mammoths and Sabre-toothed tigers, making grunting and snorting noises."

"Well, I'm not going if I think I'm not going to get a good enough bath now and again."

"Look, they're like us. Some speak English and some don't, and they're proud of getting clean and having clean clothes. I'm not sure how they do it, but they're pretty clean people. And you can help teach English. Look, just come upstairs and you can ask the right person."

"What about travel insurance?"

"Are you coming or not? You'll be able to write home and I'll be able to write to you, and we'll all be happy writing to each other – post takes seven months."

"Seven months!"

"Calm down! I'm kidding! Perhaps go and get an idea of what it might have been like for your grandparents. It's worth just enquiring while you're here."

After a long sigh and a long pause, David, almost bowing his head not wanting to hear his own voice, said, "Well, it won't hurt getting to know what it's about."

"Good! Let's go then!" Jonathan winked, stood and motioned to follow him.

The next moment David realised he was following, and his reservation was following after him.

Jonathan then stopped and turned, and finally said with a cheeky, warm grin, "And then you can use the Chapel to think things through. We've got it all here."

An Unlikely Missionary

The plane was not as packed as he thought it would be, and David was able to have three seats to himself to have as good a sleep that can be achieved on a long haul flight. There came an announcement of the flight's near end and David prepared his belongings to disembark when landed. The book he had been reading, an old book with black faded hard covers, dated 1890, was placed back in the wrapping from which it came after having read the title again: *In Darkest England and the Way Out, by William Booth*. He read the writing on the wrapping of the parcel that Jonathan had given him, which said, 'Make sure you open this before checking in'. Most of the time, David looked down at Africa from his window, studying the magnificent landscape, wondering what new life he was going to have. Then it was time to land.

Kigali airport was a surprise. David expected a basic enterprise, but the establishment was comparable to any westernised version of an airport. As passengers were few, David found himself at customs fairly quickly. He handed his passport to the attendant and waited for questions.

"English! You are English! I will practise my English. My English good?"

"Yes, very good."

"Business or pleasure?"

"I'm going to work with The Salvation Army here and places, but I hope to see a lot of your country."

"Ah! Very good! Very, very good. Your English is very good. How long your stay?"

"I'm not sure really, but about a year."

"You have papers?"

David showed the clerk a set of papers of invitation from The Salvation Army, which was scrutinised with an eager eye for signs of corruption, or out of boredom. Then the careful worker, with a creased brow, called out to his supervisor and an energetic discussion between the two became an act for David to watch. Their discussion was so alien that David had no impression as to whether his situation was good or bad. Then they both turned to him providing toothy smiles in unison.

The clerk got his stamp and stamped David's passport. "We allow stay for three years – you, for three years. Welcome, David Kingsy, and I – trust to do us great service through The Salvation Army."

He was then allowed into the country, and he entered the airport main terminal area noticing a black smiling man in a white uniform, with cap, undoubtedly waiting for him. By way of age, clothes and skin complexion, they both knew who the other was.

With a big, beaming, almost cheeky manner, the big, black man in his white Salvation Army uniform held out his hand to David and they both shook. "Welcome, my friend, welcome to Rwanda. A good flight?" he said in a loud, strong voice.

"Very good, thank you."

"I am Captain Benaiah, Elisha Benaiah. I am happy to meet with you."

"Yes, thank you."

Captain Benaiah, although having a barrelled chest and stomach, and was slightly shorter than David, would still have portrayed a larger than life persona if he had been of an even smaller stature. Smiling as if David's arrival was an answer to his earnest prayers, the large man picked up some of David's luggage and beckoned to follow. With David in tow, they left the airport to wander the car park in the dazzling blaze of the African sun.

"Do not worry about Rwanda," he announced while walking. "My country is a safe, safe place – and clean, everyone cleans. There is no one bit that has rubbish. I want to show you what good leadership can do to a country after our horrendous past, my young kiongozi. Where there is no vision, people perish."

David noticed something was adding to the Captain's mirth, and it was not until they had walked in a few different directions that it became clear the car's location had been forgotten. To anyone else, this would have caused consternation and embarrassment, but to Captain Benaiah, this seemed to brighten his day with his own amusement. "Ah!" he suddenly said, and then they were both at a car, loading it with David's luggage.

Nothing was said when leaving the car park and nothing about this seemed awkward by way of the big man's smile. It was not until they had driven a few roads away from the airport that the Captain said anything: "Now! Here at last! I will take you to our headquarters where you can rest for this night. And tomorrow, I will take you to Ekhaya, one of our orphanages, where you can settle, and tell what you want to do. Our city is busy, hey? It will be easier to walk."

David looked out into the streets of people, congested for all their business and traffic, noise and commotion, with trees and worn-out recreational areas, small side roads of markets and stalls, boys playing, men selling and women carrying babies across their backs and wares on their heads. Cars hooted and people shouted. Strange smells of herbs, spices and meats invaded the car from a nearby market, and David became aware of smells he had never experienced before. It did not occur to David that within this swarming maze of a population, he was the only white person in sight.

"Thank you for collecting me."

"That is my pleasure, kiongozi. There are many who want to meet with you. You will need your sleep."

"Will I?"

"You will see. Have you long known Jesus?"

"Not long; five, six years."

"Ah! That is not long at all!"

"How long have you known Jesus?"

"Not long either – about thirty-six years!"

The Captain laughed and laughed, and it was hard for David to keep from his face a growing smirk of amusement.

"Can you cook?" asked the Captain.

"No, not very well, but I do if I need to."

"Are you good at woodwork?"

"No."

"Are you good at plumbing?"

"No, nothing."

"Are you good at building walls?"

"No."

"Teaching eager young children?"

"Like what?"

"Children are little people who yet to become adults. I am sorry, I am teasing."

David laughed with the unexpected reply: "Teaching what subject?"

"Anything?"

"No."

"Preaching?"

"No."

"Excellent!" Captain exclaimed. "Here is an excellent place to learn!" He then leaned towards David as if to confide in a secret or concern. "Do you play an instrument in the band?"

"A brass instrument?"

"Yes."

"No."

"The children will not leave you alone until they have taught you to play. Don't say I didn't warn you."

They eventually arrived at the Headquarters, a tall, office-looking building, terraced to other buildings of other businesses along a quiet wide road. Within the front was an entrance for vehicles and Captain Benaiah opened the large gates and drove through into a back courtyard, not large enough to have any more room other than their car, a small coach, enough space to turn and numerous large waste disposal containers.

"This is our headquarters where some of us can sleep and live. There is our kitchen and dining for cooking and feeding the people during the week and our meeting hall for our Sunday services. I will take you to your room, my young kiongozi. Here, let me help you."

They both carried luggage through the back door into a corridor that took them to the large hall and modest stage. To the side was a set of chairs in an arrangement for a small absent band or choir, and below was seating for the absent congregation. Beckoning to follow, the Captain took David along the side aisle to the side door and there, from a foyer, was a wide stairway. Ascending a few floors, David was shown to his room, and after a few welcoming words, he was kindly left to settle. He slept for a while, wandered downstairs to receive a meal from those who cooked and then adjourned again, giving his apology for not being sociable. He sat on his bed and started to wonder what strange world he had now allowed Jonathan to get him into.

Ekhaya

Another sunny day and another busy city scene passed by as Captain and Misses Benaiah drove David from the Headquarters towards the more rural suburbs. From breakfast to driving through the streets, Captain Benaiah had been talking and saying so many funny things, that David failed not to smile. There then came a soft reproachful tone from Misses Benaiah who requested that David be allowed to watch the scenery without interruption and the Captain obliged only after complaining he had not yet talked about the animals.

"Do not worry about the tarantulas," continued the Captain. "They are quite funny furry creatures that we can train to perform tricks! We need to find some! They learn to jump through hoops!"

Misses Benaiah tutted and turned round to David from the front passenger seat: "Do not worry about the spiders. They do stay away from busy households and curious children – like my husband."

"Ah! Yes! That reminds me of the baboons!" It took only a certain look from his wife, that he became quiet.

Without much further talk, David was allowed to watch all there was to see on their journey as the scene suddenly changed from a built-up commotion to that of a quiet countryside and thick woodland with occasional village life. The roads changed from being tarmac, to cracked tarmac, to hard red soil and then dust.

Everywhere was rich in colour from a vast blue sky and a glorious orange sun, a deep green foliage and a rich red soil, the sculptured dark mountains to the patterned clothes people wore.

David, having spent the night in trepidation of the unknown, was now relaxed in the company of the two Army Officers and their country they were showing him. They must have sensed his troubled feelings at breakfast as they both, in a respectful way, independently assured him of the great experiences he was about to gain.

Misses Benaiah turned round to look at David again. "We are soon there," she said. "I believe they have your room ready to have your luggage, and we will be in time to show you around before having a meal. Are you hungry?"

"Actually, it doesn't feel that long since breakfast."

"It will be nice to know you well, David. We will be honoured if you consider us your family away from home."

"Thank you."

She smiled and added, "That is how we are with the children here. Remember that they have no family, they are orphans, so we want them to know God's family, and we can all be part of that."

They pulled off the road and drove up to a metal-gated entrance of a high-walled compound of white plaster, within which contained a housing complex of white buildings and red-tiled roofing. It did not appear to be run-down in any measure, and as they drove under the sign 'Ekhaya' above the entrance, nothing deterred from the first impression. One of the workers closed the gate and Captain Benaiah parked the car to one side.

Laughter and cheering of children came from further within the complex, and the three walked through a small alley between the buildings to stand to the side of an open area where a multitude of children played.

Some had already heard the car and knowing of the visit had rushed to greet the Officers, and without introduction or shyness, they started to hug David. Some tried their skills of English and instantly wanted to know about David's brothers and sisters and his school and his favourite hobbies and where was his wife and what brass instrument did he play and what games did he like. As soon as he mentioned football, they all grabbed his hands, pulling him to the worn-out grass playground and an impromptu football match began without knowing who was playing who. Having not played for some time, David tried to regain his youth and some tricks started to return. They all cheered when he scored and became amazed at some of his footwork, which some instantly tried to emulate.

Captain Benaiah called out to them all in their language to stop and it was then obvious that a prayer was being said, after which the children ran into one of the buildings to wash their hands, and a clattering of dishes and cutlery was heard.

"You see, I knew you were instantly to be great," said Captain Benaiah. "They will teach you to play a brass instrument. Yes, I think you are going to be well here. Let me show you around and we can discuss what we both want to achieve."

David was shown the dormitories, with communal washing facilities segregated for boys and girls, followed by a few classrooms and a hall in which services were held, along with music lessons and other activities. The Captain then took David further into other buildings to show more work was required to get the rooms fit for any activity, and within one was the start of a workshop.

"This one, excuse the mess, is where we want to start a shoe-repair business, with the children learning to be responsible workers. I plan to have them run the business."

David looked around the room, full of old, broken machines and wondered what pieces the Captain had been referring to when he spoke of a business.

"And here!" he continued when they had left the buildings and stood in an open area populated with surrounding trees and viewing mighty distant mountains, "is where I believe we can have a well."

"A well?"

"Yes, a well, here. I believe we can find water under here – and as well as a well here, we can have a shade just there for people to – feel well."

"Where do you get the idea that there's water?"

"This is Africa. If we do not find water, then we might find some other mineral." His seriousness suddenly changed, and David knew he was being teased. "But I do believe there to be water here. Call it intuition. Call it faith. Where do the trees get their water?" He motioned to an empty plot of land: "I would like here to have a small place for people to have quiet prayer."

"I take it you would like me to dig this well."

The Captain looked at David incredulously: "Of course not – I want you to be friends with the children, teach English, help with plumbing and woodwork, build this quiet place, have time to read and see places, play lots of football, learn music – yes." He then paused more and added, "As well as dig this well."

"That sounds fine to me. How deep would this well go?"

The Captain shrugged: "This is Africa."

When the day was over, David laid in bed thinking of his new setting. Being mobbed by the children at one point, who babbled in weak English in an excited way, he realised he had never laughed so much in a long time. The children even played a tune in their humble brass band in his honour that they had been practicing for his arrival.

Rwanda

My time in the Africa Department was where the full thrust of my career started and rocketed, fuelled by my enthusiasm. I flew everywhere, visiting embassies, municipal buildings, government assemblies, all over Africa. I even went into the office on some of my off-days to complete work or dig into some of the piling up of chores. There was one day, however, that changed my perception, a day that seemed pivotal in my career and personal development. It was a day that I did not visit the office, but walked in Saint James's park discussing Rwanda's history. I had got to know a woman called Monifa through my work. She was a Christian woman working for the UN and she kindly accepted to spend some time with me out of office hours to tell me her tale. She had lived through the genocide during the 90's as a young teenager. I was horrified at such a way an entire country can turn against itself to leave millions slaughtered and left unburied on the ground, discarded in the streets, driven by a rapid escalation of hate. I could not contemplate what these scenes would do to my faith, but Monifa convinced me that her faith grew and got her through these times, even though her entire family had been sliced horrifically apart. She grew on me and I believe I grew on her because she knew I wanted to know these things for personal understanding and not professional progress. We stayed in contact and she was with me when I received my devastating news at the United Nations in New York.

What was chilling was her insight into persecution, a pattern that escalates into genocide, and it could happen again, anywhere, and on a massive scale. Monifa saw the evil strategy, a secret, subliminal, calculating nature to every massacre. Persecution has a method. It starts with deep-routed tension between groups of society that has lingered, and no one has tried to solve fully. There is unresolved bitterness that goes undetected for much of the time, a necessity to forgive that no one ever does. It is not even mentioned, but a trend or event triggers these hate-filled feelings to rise and take hold, and an uprising starts against the unprotected. Lies are said to enforce hatred views, to make hate sound legitimate. Propaganda spreads as far as those who wish to believe. Identities become important, and people are certified with a specific marking, one way or another. A group is blamed for the hardships or the reason for problems and dehumanised. When they are classified as vermin, cockroaches, germs, or demonised and pronounced as evil, witches even, their value is considered less human, and in the heat of hate, extermination is easier and can commence. The survival of the fittest is used as a fact. Evolutionary theory is pronounced a reality. Murder is less murderous. Through fear, love of power, self-worth, suspicion, arrogance, people become willing to be brainwashed into believing that wrong is right, and the mentality of peers enforces evil. When these things are not challenged, this hate becomes accepted, normalised, and considered supported. Even good people are converted to this hate. Evil thrives when good men are lacking or do nothing, and genocide erupts, witch-hunts ferment and barbaric executions perpetuate, all led by the mindless and committed by the indoctrinated.

Hitler, Stalin, Pol Pot, Idi Amin, Gaddafi — Yugoslavia, Rwanda, Sudan, Syria, Yemen — the French Revolution, the Russian Revolution — Protestants and Catholics, Shiites and Sunni — it's all the same. It all comes from the unconscious, unknowing diseases called hate and power and they can get at anyone, grow in anyone, at any time, regardless of gender, intellect, wealth, health, age, colour, or even religion. Hate and arrogance can creep without a sound or word into any religious or nonreligious person and society, and then with deceiving thoughts and words can make even murder sound logical and even God's will. Hate does not discriminate who it uses. Hate can be politically engineered to be contagious throughout a seemingly rational society that reduces its ability to diagnose others as being human and equal. Could world problems lead to a worldwide persecution, led by someone who has convinced the world he has the solutions, and allowed by those who deliberately look the other way?

It was after first meeting Monifa that my career seemed to blossom, as if she had secretly prayed a powerful prayer for me. I became a respected senior analyst.

Jacob's Well

"What is it you are digging for?"

Her soft, attractive voice, clear and distinct with a pleasurable sound of command and comfort, was not capable of competing with the heat and brightness from the scorching sun, the sound of digging and the feel of sweat trickling down his back, his forehead, his arms, and the trousers that stuck to his legs. All of David's concentration was in deepening the level his feet were at, and his immersion in his thoughts had switched off his ears. It was as if the voice calling down could not reach his depth.

Suddenly a small stone fell from above and David looked up to see a woman, dressed in white, looking down appearing to be amused: "If you are trying to hide, then I have found you."

"Sorry, Misses Benaiah, I was miles away."

"The hole is not that deep, yet."

David beamed with enthusiasm: "There's no water, but I'm getting nearer."

"Yes, nearer to what, my dear kiongozi? They say it becomes molten the lower you go."

"They say a lot of things."

"Are you coming up, before I hear my echo?"

David, four metres within the ground, climbed out of his fissure using the ladder and then picked up his towel to wipe himself. "Sorry, I'm sweating buckets."

"You know, I have heard you work during the midday sun. It is not good for you. I know you have been told." Misses Benaiah handed David his bottle of water and he drank appreciatively from it. "How is your well?"

"I now need to start concreting the sides and make the surrounding safety wall before I dig much deeper."

"Remember: the aim is to find water – gold or diamonds will just bring trouble. They will bring you the wrong women, but your looks are worth more than gold or diamonds, and your heart is worth a lot more."

David was not sure how to react, but he need not have fretted as the lady officer turned to admire the nearby arbour, walking nearer to view it better.

"My, you have been busy." With commendable eyes, she inspected the wooden beamed structure, complete with bamboo leaves thatched into a roof.

"I just roped together all the beams around the place and some of the children helped with the roof. Then I organised these cushions."

Misses Benaiah entered its shade, clearly delighted, and sat down, placing a parcel beside her that she had carried. She was then peacefully looking out across the view of trees and mountain ridges far away and appeared relaxed and happy in the silence.

David used the second towel to dry himself again.

"I am sure my husband was not clear," Misses Benaiah said. "I wonder whether he has given you the wrong idea as to why you are here."

David came into the arbour and sat opposite. "I don't understand."

"It is not that we do not want a well, or have outdoor shade for reading and prayer, or a labourer to be handy – we also want you to develop and learn and grow and take time to contemplate."

"I appreciate you being concerned, but I really do like the challenge of getting things done, seeing the end result, and the feeling that it's helping people – especially the children."

"Yes, they have taken to you. They enjoy your English lessons and playing football."

"Well they're teaching me to play a cornet."

"What are you feeling – being here?"

"To tell you the truth, it's difficult for me to accept that *I am* here. It's so – surreal – but here I am. Yet, that's what life seems to be – surreal – like it's a strange waiting room, or – playground, classroom, or – I don't know. Does that make sense? It's as if everything, this entire world, is my observatory and I'm trying to make sense of this place where we breathe."

Misses Benaiah nodded with politeness and respectfully remained quiet.

"Okay, that does sound funny, but – I don't know."

The Salvation Army Officer saw David's Bible to the side and opened it, curious as to the protruding stalk. The page opened to reveal a dried white rose that maintained a few sharp thorns: "Now I understand. Your heart is cut and slow to heal."

There was a silence between the two for a while as they pondered the scenery, but it was Misses Benaiah, who, leaning towards David with a soft, slight touch on his knee, that continued the conversation: "But she was pretty, wasn't she?"

"Yes, she was."

She offered her parcel to David: "This is the other reason for me visiting you. It arrived at our offices for you the other day."

David, recognising the handwriting, opened it, and was then holding a collection of books, which made the woman curious. He handed them to her one by one as he read the titles: "*The Confidence Coach, How to be Inspiring, Purpose Driven Life, A Christmas Carol, Great* – oh that's so Jonathan, *Great Expectations,* and – *Frankenstein!*"

The Officer looked at the books quite commendably and looked at David, as if for an explanation.

"I wrote to Jonathan to send me something good to read from England. I think this is his sense of humour."

"He obviously wants to encourage you." Misses Benaiah stood up to go, handing David back his books: "Well, I must leave you to your new reading. Remember, God wants us to enjoy life." She looked at his Bible, took the white rose, smelt it and placed it back within the pages, closing it. "When you are ready to be healed in heart, destroy this rose and allow yourself to choose another."

"Misses Benaiah, what would it take for me to become a Salvation Army Soldier?"

"I will speak to Elisha and you can discuss the process with him, but for now, learn to be still. What was the surname of your Grandparents? They served here as Officers, did they not?"

"Lovert. Why?"

She shook her head as if it was of no importance. "Africa is a big place and a long time."

Within the month, David had become a full-time member of The Salvation Army.

Misses Whyte

And so I married Mark Whyte. It was the best day of my life. There became a problem with my wedding dress hours before. Then the car broke down and we needed a taxi to get to Oxford Street. It was still the best day of my life. The small brass ensemble played 'here comes the bride' and my adoptive father, Norrie Goodwin, gave me away. I walked up the aisle feeling like a full woman, someone special, someone worth it. I felt I had been adopted into God's family, and Mark was part of it.

The timing was right for love to be awoken. Side by side, with his lovely smile, he took my hand and we became husband and wife. I could not have married anyone as sweet, caring and loyal.

I remember Elly telling me what marriage is about. Marriage is a responsibility, and a good marriage is a working partnership in dealing with God's commandments with each other. I loved my husband, but to live the perfect happiness that so many young girls are taught through fairytales does not exist here on Earth. When you decide to marry, marry to gain respect from God in your actions and the way you deal with marriage. It is not like the films with perfect sex and happiness ever-after. There is reality to live: the washing up, the refuse, the ironing, the cooking, all the bills to pay, all the maintenance, all the parenting, and employment. It is through these mundane actions that we show how much we love each other, and the keeping-on loving each other, mind, heart and strength. This is the contract as it is in marriage and in faith. I was always faithful to Mark – but he didn't think so in ways that were not imaginable to me then.

I kept David's rose. I hid it in my draw with jumpers and then it vanished. I could not find it. I looked and looked and looked, and then it returned as if having never moved. I became convinced this disappearance had been in my mistaken mind.

Even David was a poor second to my drive to do as much good through the Foreign Office. My career blossomed, and I was sure it was God's approval. Africa was the turning point in many ways. I became a household name and almost admired as a glamour model. The danger was that I started to believe in me something that I'm not, and the public didn't see this. People saw me in newspapers and the television, and saw me as the perfect person with all the answers, but the glamour started to affect my judgement, and I was far from being this perfect Christian. God started to become lower in my awe and wonder, and although I sang the hymns and said my earnest prayers, I did not realise I was not really worshipping Him, because He was not first. My work was first. I was poisoning the deep, pure, intimate well I shared with Mark, as I was with the spiritual, revitalizing well that was meant to be between me and God. How ugly am I truly?

How did Hosea feel?

Mark walked along the routine streets from the Underground station and stopped outside his terraced door, finding the keys. He was finally home and was relieved. "Honey?" he called out.

There was no answer except for a flashing light from the answering machine, which he played: "Hey, it's Misses Lovable. Hope your day was okay. I need to spend a few more hours at work. A last-minute thing has cropped up and some of us are going over it for tomorrow's debate. I'm not sure how long I'll be, but hopefully – well anyway, just in case: there's something microwavable in the freezer, so don't wait for me to eat. Love you, Hubby Lovable, and see you later." The message ended with a certain long beep.

Mark sighed, threw the keys onto the kitchen worktop, made himself a coffee, looked inside the freezer for what was on offer, and then loaded the washing machine with clothes for the wash. Taking his drink to the small study desk to the side of the lounge, he started to go through some letters, but his thoughts turned to one addressed to Esther that had been opened a few days before. He read it again, wondering where this was taking their marriage.

To Mrs Whyte,

It is with great pleasure to promote you to the position of Principal Analyst within the Africa Department and may you continue to serve your country in this worthy manner. I have observed your request to transfer to the Middle East Department and your credentials, aptitude and passion support your application. When a position becomes available, you will be notified as a matter of primary consideration.

Thanking you in your continued loyalty,

Mr. I. Hammon, Foreign Secretary,
Her Majesty's Government

Getting tired of the letters and with the whole house being too quiet, Mark decided to practise some music and spent thirty minutes playing his euphonium, from which time his tiresome feeling of loneliness made him stop. There then came banging on the wall from the neighbours who wanted him to continue. Smiling and understanding the request, he played them a few tunes, which received another encore. Again, he obliged them with a final tune, and no more requests came.

Having heard the washing machine was too quiet, he spent a few moments getting the damp clothes out and taking them upstairs to discover the airing cupboard was already full from the wash of the other week. He took his time in sorting out what was for ironing and what could be placed back into draws and cupboards before filling the airing cupboard with the new batch.

He listened to the silence, praying for the door to be heard opening, but nothing happened.

Outside was by now dark and he closed the curtains, and continued folding clothes, returning some to their rightful place. It was one jumper of Esther's that made him open one of her draws – and then he stopped: a strange green stork appearing from under the clothes took his curiosity. He rummaged to find a clear, cellophane bag tucked under the pile having been placed there in a hidden manner that contained a preserved white rose.

He could not help but sit on the bed for quite some time, mulling over his thoughts. His heart started to race. It was impossible, inconceivable, incomprehensible for Esther to have even a notion of having an affair, but this rose was old and the only source must have been David. The troubling thought was that she was not letting go of the past, and this meant she still had lingering feelings for him.

"Oh, why are you not moving on, Esther?" said Mark aloud. He lay on the bed, looking at the ceiling with his fingers in his hair. "Lord, what do I do? What can I do?"

But there was no answer.

"Okay," continued Mark, as if God was listening, "I know I have faults. I know I don't love You as much as I should. Please forgive me."

Still, there was no answer.

"Help me to be more committed to You – for my sake – and help me to help Esther move on. What do You do when people don't love You as much as they can?"

A thought then came to Mark. Not wanting to provoke an argument, he dismissed the idea of confronting her with his discovery, being fearful of saying the wrong thing in the wrong manner. Instead, the idea was to test her feelings. How would she react to not having the rose? Mark decided to hide it somewhere and her reaction would tell him what she truly felt.

This was a test Mark hoped his wife would pass.

Thrown to the Lions

With richly adorned wood-panelled walls, a thick carpet, tall elegant windows and a high ceiling with stylish lighting, the small luxury room was befitting a mansion house or palace; but the function was only that of an office – a reception for an office, at that, with a desk serving the purpose for the secretary. The quiet woman looked up when an older man, with scraggy white hair and white stubble entered the room. Although he wore a smart suit, it was old and worn, and he appeared as if he had come from a garden allotment without having done much work on it.

"Is he in?" the man asked.

"Yes, he's expecting you, Mister Scabbards."

"Thank you."

Mister Scabbards knocked on the internal door that was almost disguised within the walls of wood, and absent-mindedly read the title in front of his eyes: 'Mr. I. Hammon: Foreign Secretary'. Without any acknowledgement from within, he entered the office abruptly.

In a large, imposing, grand room, a suited, distinguished-looking man with his stern appearance from his dark eyes and grey hair, was standing, arms folded, looking out of one of the windows. The television to the corner, with its sound off, showed the News reporting a long item on a severe famine in Africa.

Scabbards politely stood in front of the large wooden desk and waited for a comment or movement from the Foreign Secretary.

The only response was a question without any acknowledgement that someone had joined him: "Is it done?"

"It will be in the news tomorrow. Muggerage will no longer be a problem. He'll have to step down with what's going to be released."

"Good! – Good, good, good." The Foreign Secretary left the window and returned to his desk. "Sinbad has certainly earned his money this time," he said seating himself.

"He certainly has. I have no idea how he found all that dirt – on Muggerage of all people."

"It's best if we don't know. Next time we use Sinbad, let him know he has surpassed even his own standards."

"Of course. Is that all Mister Hammon?"

The Foreign Secretary started to watch the continued News report of the drought, watching pictures of entire arid plains of barren rock, bones of starved animals, ribs of skinny children, sunshine that scorched life with no mercy. Where lakes and rivers were meant to be, there was cracked land. Where crops were supposed to grow, the soil was nothing except sand. A multitude of withered people, reaching far into the distant view, distraught or too lacking in strength to make a commotion, sat with no shelter, no nutrition, and no hope.

Scabbards was about to leave when the Foreign Secretary then asked a question: "What do we know about Esther Whyte?"

"She's the Salvation Army girl, very pretty and works hard in the Africa Office."

"She's going up the ranks."

"Yes, sir, she is."

"The Prime Minister has learnt of it."

"She's the one playing the piano during our fancy meals. I think all these officials like coming purposely to hear her recitals. May I ask what the concern is? I assume there's a concern here."

"Can I ever have a conversation with you without implying there's a concern or threat or problem or scandal?"

"No sir, you can't: it's my job to make sure that everything runs smoothly."

"I've been asked to organise a long trip for representatives to travel to Africa and help in this drought. The UN camps are growing too large. One is almost half a million people. We need to send at least two of our staff to observe and learn whatever. Prime Minister's orders, I'm afraid. I'm not going, obviously: got better things to do."

"And you want to know about sending this Esther?"

"I've been told to consider her. I think people have an eye on her going up the ladder."

"Sounds very promising. As long as she doesn't run for office."

"You think she's a threat to me?"

"She does have a far better figure than you, sir, but you just keep telling the public what they want to hear. You have a convincing talent for it."

"Thank you for your vote. What is this Esther's background? What's her education?"

"Are you asking me to get in touch with Sinbad to dig for a scandal?"

Hammon shook his head: "Too early. We're far from that, for now. It's just that I'm going to detest working with this little goody-goody empty doll."

"Who says she's going to be working close to you?"

"Some sort of PM's long-term plan."

"She has a degree in Politics and Religious studies, to answer your question."

"Religion! Bloody Religion! Gets in the bloody way of everything: demented Muslim nutters forcing their hate on everyone with their self-power in themselves; sodding pervert vicars allowed to rape children; arrogant Israelis thinking they own everything and getting away with breaking UN resolutions; mamby pamby do-gooders trying to change Government policy to have yellow flowers tax free. If only they would all just shut up, grow up, and start thinking of dropping ridiculous beliefs in a God that has caused more wars, more killing, more harm than anyone else, setting up stupid, outdated customs that mean nothing!"

"To then believe what, sir?"

"Nothing! Nothing, Scabbards! Nothing is far better! There's nothing out there to believe in. Nothing, Scabbards, will solve a lot of problems. Survival of the fittest, I'd say. If I had been the Health Secretary, I would have abandoned the NHS long ago, saved a lot of money and spent it on people who are worth it – those who will pay their taxes, who will live and work long enough to make it worthwhile, and just dropping those who become a burden. Who is in their grave any better or worse than anyone else?"

Scabbards just looked on amused.

"There's nothing to live for, Scabbards, so let's just get the buggers who have even less to live for, don't care for them and make them not a problem."

"That's forgetting the fact that the health service employs countless people, who pay their taxes."

"Well, I just know the National Health Service is dear to the dreadful voters, so let's keep with the pretence shall we?"

"As for this Esther?"

"I'm going to request she be sent to this damned drought, considering she's supposed to be a high-rising employee, and then make sure she's spotted by a film crew out there."

"How will any of this benefit you?"

"See to it that some strange, embarrassing questions are asked that make her look ridiculous."

"I see, sir. I'll ask some contacts then."

The silent television then showed the creation of a makeshift settlement with large white tents being erected, and pits were being dug by large bulldozers to start some form of sanitation, looking too inadequate for the sheer scale of the disaster.

"Let the blighters starve anyway. It will decrease the surplus population."

"If only the public got to really know your views."

"Let the public know what's good for society to know, Scabbards, and let the important people know what's important to get things done, so that society can continue being naive. There's just too many problems if they truly got to know what it takes for them to have their deluded lifestyles. They think I'm great because I tell them what they want to hear."

Mister and Misses Whyte

The night had already arrived when Esther left the Foreign Office, but she paid no thought to the late hour, walking along the street with her mind still on her work and mulling on problems left for tomorrow. She was about to walk past a man leaning contentedly against a wall, when something told her to make more of an effort to recognise the lone person.

When he stood, he smiled and waited for her to come nearer: "Would you, pretty lady, be grateful for a modest escort to show you safely home."

"I would, but my husband needs to give permission."

"He does indeed."

They then both kissed.

"What are you doing here, Mark? It's late. I told you I would be late tonight."

"One of the operations had complications, so I stayed late as well. I thought it would be nice to go home with my wife. In fact, is it too late to have a meal somewhere?"

"I'm not hungry, but I would love a walk along the Thames."

"Sure."

They walked arm in arm in a comfortable silence, making their way to the river. When they reached the Thames, they stopped to look at it with the lights of London shining as though stars caught in the water.

"I'm really, really grateful that you allow me to do my job," finally said Esther.

"Who or what would I be if I didn't? In fact, I'm proud of you."

"And I'm proud of you, for the job *you* do."

"I suppose I do get a kick out of helping people. So do you."

"How do you mean?"

"Come on, Esther, the real reason you're doing your job is because you want the world to be perfect."

Esther was taken aback for a moment. "What a strange thing to say."

"It's true though."

"Of course I want the world to be perfect. There's too many things going wrong – "

"That you want to fix."

"I'm doing my best. You sound like there's an accusation against me."

Mark shook his head: "No, only admiration. I just want you to know that I love you. I can't believe you're my wife."

"But?"

"But?"

"There's a 'but'?"

"You need to know that we're married."

Esther laughed. "I know we're married."

"If everyone tries to fix the world and not – ." Mark just stopped.

"And not what?"

"If everyone tries to fix the world and forget those who are nearest, then they're not really fixing the world when it is so close to them."

"I see."

"I'm not saying – "

"Yes you are, you are so, so very saying. But before you point the finger, Mister Gleaming Whyte, may I remind you about the hours you work, fixing people."

"Esther, I don't want an argument. I just want to let you know, and I'm doing it badly, that I want you more in my life than what you are. I'm not saying I'm beyond reproach either. Esther, I love you, you are everything to me. Let us not argue. I wondered whether to just go home, but then I wondered if you would like to spend the night with me in a nice hotel nearby."

"Really? Oh – I feel awkward now."

"Why?"

"You know the drought in Sudan?"

"Yes, it's the main News."

"I've been ordered to go there."

"What! Why? What tonight?"

"No! Not tonight! They want to send some from our department and oversee the UK and UN logistics. They want us to learn how things can be done better for future disasters. Well, that's the brief."

"And they're sending you?"

"And Judy."

"This drought is massive, millions of people are starving and dying, and just you and Judy are going! There's a huge war there, a savage, brutal, horrific war!"

"Yes."

"To solve it all?"

"Oh come on Mark! I thought you said you loved me and proud of what I do. I need to do this."

"Because you have a nervous disposition to fix the world?"

"Stop exaggerating! I thought you didn't want an argument."

"When do you go and for how long?"

"I go next week and I could be there generally until it finishes, but I'll need to come back a few times, coming and going with the RAF. I can be home quite often."

Mark sighed, looked at the dark water and then back at his beautiful wife.

"I'm sorry Mark."

"How can I be upset with you?"

"I'm sorry."

"But I am, you know, upset. I was looking forward to spending more time with you. I want a close marriage, Esther. I don't think either of us are getting it."

Esther nodded.

They embraced and held each other tightly.

"I know you're right," she said after a while. "I'm not spending enough time with you."

"You just go," said Mark supportively. "Go to Africa, get it out of your system and come home to me, and I will be waiting for you, like the husband I want to be."

"Thank you, but in the meantime, what about that hotel you promised?"

"Look, misses, I've learnt to never promise anything."

They both smiled at each other and kissed.

"Except be the husband I promised you I'd be," Mark added. "Let's find a nice hotel and treat ourselves."

A Valley of Bones

I travelled to the Sudan famine with my boss, Judy, and UN officials, charity representatives and army personnel, all in an RAF Globemaster cargo plane that was gigantic. It felt like having been eaten by a whale, along with two helicopters and a mass of containers packed efficiently.

I took along a book to read for the journey, a book that I had wanted to read for a long time and the situation seemed to warrant reading it as it stemmed from inspiration from the missionary work in Africa, even though the book was not in fact connected with Africa. The book I read, of course, was 'In Darkest England', written by William Booth, and throughout my Africa experience, I read until completing it.

We landed in Sudan at a large makeshift airport and taxied to a large warehouse where the world's aid was being stored and organised. Judy and I were then transported along with UN staff to the relief encampment by helicopter.

Nothing could have prepared me for what I was about to see. Even from above, the true extent of the disaster could not be imagined as I looked down on a land that seemed diseased with darkness and infection, and only when approaching did this disease come to be seen as people too weak to do anything other than wait to die. The whole floor, for miles and miles, was littered with hopelessness. It was like a Valley of Dried Bones and Judgement Valley. Was it ever possible for this nation to breathe, to grow sinew and become alive again? What was it that I thought I could do to help?

We lowered with a great deal of dust some distance from the multitude, and had our identifications checked by those who manned the landing site. We were then escorted on a preliminary, orientation tour of the main area, being briefed as to the scale of the work. Hundreds of tents and shelter had been erected. Bulldozers were hard at work digging pits for sanitation, and in other areas, pits for mass burial. Dotted around the site were certain aid charities performing their invaluable tasks. Water tanks were being erected and filled.

The starving people were so dejected that most did not look up when we walked past. All around was either a deathful silence taken away by the eerie wind, or the saturation of weeping and moaning, a soulless ghoul-like groaning that buried itself into the marrow of all who heard. Human tissue and sinew on living people was all there was to see and the flies were relentless. This was Hell, and there was nothing I could see I could do to solve anything. It was Biblical. It was apocalyptic. It was as if the world was to end, as portent as the experience.

Then it was ruined. Just when I was growing in love with Mark and, now in Africa, desperate to be with my husband and burning with anguish to fix all I could see, my emotions were re-ignited when I stumbled upon David again. When I thought David was far away, he was there in Africa, sitting there. Was God reminding me of a thwarted plan of His? Was God reminding me of my failure to let go of what He had by now closed shut. My emotions were too complex and wide open. Not even I understood them. Hell became more than Hell. I just could not shake my feelings for him.

Where is God?

To most people, the sound of youngsters learning music can be a form of torture that warrants the instrument either banished from the home, or broken beyond repair. At the least, the youngster is forbidden to play within the confines of what can be heard and duty-bound to practise at school or someone else's home; but this was not the case for forty-nine youngsters of Ekhaya, who, as a small brass band in the main hall, played 'Jesus wants me for a sunbeam,' for the tenth time.

David liked the esteemed position the children had placed him. Not only playing a cornet of his own, he also conducted the blithe ensemble with his free hand, and he led the group for them to watch his timing, deliberately going faster and then slower, making some notes extra long and other notes next to nothing, making the tune so distorted that they were all giggling uncontrollably. As agreed beforehand, they intentionally played the last note as dreadfully as they could, but at least it was in time to David's conducting. Then none of them could continue for laughing.

From the entrance came Captain Benaiah, also in tears of mirth, clapping and crying out, "Bravo! Bravo! Encore!" He walked between the chairs towards the seated band, clapping in his own standing ovation. "Make a joyful noise unto the Lord! A joyful *noise* indeed!"

After a few more tunes, better played, the Officer asked to close the practice in prayer. They all bowed, and then started packing away the instruments when the prayer had finished.

"You have improved," stated Captain Benaiah admirably.

"I can only do simple tunes, but – so only can they," replied David.

"Well, you all enjoy it. What is the point otherwise? Make a joyful noise to the Lord."

"You want to see me?"

"Yes, there is an appalling calamity, David, appalling, dreadful."

"A calamity?"

"A famine, there is a catastrophic famine. The Salvation Army has received a request to help join the relief agencies. I thought of you."

"Of course! When do we go? How far away?"

"We'll go together with Uzwela and Kanzima. We'll go in the jeep tomorrow and it will take five days."

"Five days?"

"Yes, it is in Sudan. We need to avoid an area of much conflict and Africa is big, my great man, so be prepared to leave tomorrow, physically and mentally."

Their journey started in the bright morning sunshine. The children waved them off, and the Land Rover, with Captain driving, left Ekhaya. Uzwela and Kanzima sat in the back, David sat beside the Captain, and they were all within their own thoughts while they stared out of the windows. Their journey was through endless forest and was without much thought to conversation until the Captain started to sing jovial hymns that encouraged the others to sing. Before the sun started to set for the day, they parked within an alcove of trees, prepared and ate a meal, and slept through the night after having watched the orange setting of the sun. In the morning, they prayed for the multitude who were destitute, and then continued their journey. With passing through checkpoints to traverse borders, such became the following days until the savannah showed signs of the foreboding presence of death as one carcass was passed, and then another, and then another with more frequency.

They came to a summit where the view of the vast plain beyond became tainted with a large dark stain in the distance, almost like an oil slick, the remains of a savage war, the disfiguring presence of an enormous swarm of locus. A dusty mist obscured the sickening scene and merged the valley plain with the mountains at the vast horizon. Something terrible had happened. The land looked as though annihilated by evil.

Spellbound, all four watched the desolation from their high view as the Captain slowly drove down into this valley. Midway down, Captain Benaiah stopped to the side of the mountain having turned off the road onto a lay-by, the front window now directly looking out at the plight of a nation of homeless people. David got from his seat and stood in front, looking at the scene. One by one, the other three joined him.

"I never knew it was going to be so large," David breathed.

In the silence that followed, Uzwela, aghast, then asked, "How do we help so many people?"

"Never let the scale become bigger than your belief in God," said the Captain. "God is bigger than this; bigger, far, far bigger. We are travelling into an awful world where we will question what we are to do, what we are to think, and even where God is. We are not to have faith in our doubts. We are to do the best we can for our fellow people. We are here to serve. That is what we are to do."

Stunned by this prospect, it was a while before they returned to the jeep, breaths full of heavy emotions, hearts with sunken concerns, minds full of unsure conjecture.

Such was the vast distance, it took another hour of driving before they reached the outskirts and parked where directed by some soldiers, having checked their identities. After waiting half an hour, a man came to them and introduced himself as a form of UN coordinator, having a Spanish accent. "English? You speak English?"

They all nodded.

"Salvation Army?" he said, seeing the uniform and emblem.

"We were told we should help wherever there is the most need, not necessarily as The Salvation Army," replied the Captain.

"Yes, thank you, we need people to help put up more tents, but any of you able to drive machinery, trucks, bulldozers?"

They all shook their heads.

"Medical in any way?"

Captain Benaiah shook David's shoulder and spoke to the official: "This one can be."

Without allowing David to disagree, he replied with urgency, "We need people to help with vaccinations to prevent the spread of disease to the stronger ones. I will be glad of your help, thank you." Suddenly, the man was shouting at one of his soldiers in Spanish, whom approached them to accept the given orders, and then he returned to Captain Benaiah adding, "This man will take you to your site. Thank you."

The subservient soldier held onto the side of their vehicle and ushered to drive away. Without any manner of knowing, Captain Benaiah started to speak in French and the soldier replied in French, giving instructions and a direction.

They entered the site, driving along a track through the throng of people who were too weak to lift up their heads. In places, there were tents and makeshift shelters with aid workers doing their best, and then with more people, there came more shelters and more marquee centres for water provision, food distribution and health clinics. It was an instant small town that was rapidly becoming an instant city. Still in French, the soldier told the Captain where to park and pointed at a large, white tent with a Salvation Army flag to its side, and then he left them.

They entered the tent and were immediately befriending other Salvation Army personnel as if part of the same family, as if the multinational colours and languages of the members had no bearing with matters of Salvation Army unity. Before long, they were at a bed of choice, their small luggage dropped on a simple mattress and were within discussions about the depth of the crisis and the plan of action. It soon transpired that there were sites allocated to The Salvation Army to supply not only the starving, but also give relief to the workers, whatever their nationality or belief.

"David," said Captain Benaiah, "the soldier told me where you should go tomorrow. I will take you there."

"But I have no idea about vaccinations. Why did you think I would be of any help?"

"Because you are a good man. I will introduce you to Doctor Bailey, American, you will like him."

"How do you know?"

"Where is the proof that you will not like him?"

"So what now?"

"We have been travelling through five days. So get some rest."

For David, that was easier said than achieved.

The next morning, after a simple unsweetened porridge-type breakfast and a black coffee, David and Captain Benaiah left their tent and walked the distance through a multitude of withered people too desolated with hopelessness invading the very fabric of each and every soul. Some stood and milled, some sat, too dejected to look beyond the few metres of their small space, and some were laid across the ground, adults and children alike, watched by those who had no strength to support the dying. No one had a mouth that was not dry. No one had enough moisture to even cry. The decaying smell drenched everything, heightened by the blistering heat of the relentless sun and the total absence of water. With no food, no water, no hope, it was easier to die. It was a condition that most felt justified in shaking a fist at God and cursing Him with His own name; but no one did.

David stopped and looked around.

The Captain stopped with him: "David, we cannot cure this. We can do only what we can do, as little as it is. Come, I am taking you to Doctor Bailey and you can start healing."

On the fringe of a complex of large, white marquees, they came across one small tent with its front fully open to a large area that sheltered under a raised canvas. A crowd seemed to wait in a nebulous queue around three small tables, two of which were manned by two aid workers. Some workers, with translators, were busy explaining things to the people who patiently waited, and others were within the back of this tent sorting boxes and supplying items to those at the tables. All the aid workers were multinational and Captain Benaiah approached one who wore a doctor's white gown which was by now far from being clean. There was a fair exchange in a welcome and the doctor looked in David's direction. The doctor took what was said and approached David with an outstretched hand.

"David, I'm Doctor Bailey," he announced with an American accent. "I appreciate your help."

"I'm not a medic. I've never done this before."

"Yes, that's fine. We're building up the team. Until more come, we have to get it done with who and what we've got. Don't worry, it's easy. Whoever stands in front of your desk, you check the drugs with your colleague, tick the boxes, draw them up and inject them. We'll teach you. Don't worry about who gets vaccinated – that's my job."

David nodded pensively.

"Please don't look worried. By the end of the day, you'll get it, and then you can rotate with others, sorting the medication. We're concentrating on vaccinating those who look strong enough to survive here."

Doctor Bailey showed David to a seat behind the third table, introduced him to Gabrielle, a young French woman who had suddenly appeared to sit beside him, and left them to let the pretty female with good English, to explain the tasks in detail. After that, for the better part of the day, David organised the drugs, checked each label and the expiry dates, and the woman injected each waiting patient. Then David took over the task of injecting and started to gain in confidence.

All the while, the suffering continued to arrive. Most of them were taken through to one of the large marquees nearby, some carried in the arms, some lying on stretchers.

Gabrielle motioned to the large tent, seeing David's curiosity: "In there is where the worse ones are receiving intravenous saline to rehydrate them. It has to be done very carefully for people so weakened. You shouldn't go in if you don't want to be upset with all the children there."

With the demand, there was little opportunity to indulge in conversation, no matter how much David liked her accent, and they started to gain pace with a routine.

"You are doing well, David. We will get you soon to be a junior doctor, no?" softly spoke Gabrielle towards the dying end of the day.

"There's just so much to do."

"So you will be back tomorrow?"

"Is there a better place around here?"

With the setting sun starting to cast a dying glow, David, alone, slowly meandered, making his way through a sea of withered people. With no breeze, the air was saturated with a heavy silence. He was sure that some he passed by were already dead. He stopped to look at one woman who sat with vacant eyes as she cradled a bundle of cloths, having at one stage been trying to breastfeed her baby. Her eyes were deeply inset. Her face was gaunt. Her hair was matted. She wore hardly anything worthy of being called clothing. Her legs and arms were scrawny. Her ribs were showing. There was no strength left to feel for her dead baby.

Then her eyes moved and looked at David, but still there came no emotion from her. Shocked, he stepped backwards with awkward footing and walked away to encounter yet more, and more, and more dying people. When he arrived back at his dormitory tent, the dust and the red cheeks gave away his attempt to cover over his sorrow.

"Remember," Captain Benaiah said when seeing him, "We are not called to solve this. God is not asking us to cure all there is, David. The only work God has commanded is to toil, yes toil on our character. If we think we are to do more, then that is wrong, as that is then doing His job. He is asking us to respond and leave the rest to Him in His timing. Have faith."

David nodded.

"I know you do not feel hungry, but to help them, you need to look after yourself. Here, eat!"

David relented and ate a small amount of a tasteless stew. He then lay on his bed and was soon asleep.

Such was the manner of the next few weeks repeated.

Instant Fame

The smell was inescapable. The sound of weeping and crying was unrelenting. The brightness from the sky scorched the eyes and the heat sapped the energy from everyone. Flies flew from one victim to another and on those whom they rested made no resolve to remove their stay.

Esther, alone, making her way through the throng of dying people, their bones showing with barely enough strength to hold their young, had barely any strength of her own to continue. She could not remember how long she had been walking nor where she was meant to be going, and she finally become lost in the vast hopelessness of the famine that stretched as far as she could see.

She dropped to her knees, pulled to the hard, rocky ground by her sorrow, with tears no longer held back by false bravado, surrounded by starvation. Her nearest neighbour was a lone little girl of an age Esther could not guess. The child looked back at Esther with bewildered, sad eyes, appearing confused and dismayed with her plight. No one seemed to own her.

With a heavy heart and sunken feelings, Esther got to her feet in an unsteady fashion and eventually stood to her height. As if returning from a sudden daze, she became aware of someone speaking, a male voice that was asking her a series of questions.

"Sorry, I wasn't listening," she replied.

"I'm sorry, I didn't want to surprise you."

The dirt on Esther's face showed the traces of her tears she had tried to wipe away.

"I was saying that we're from BBC Panorama," continued the man, "and we would like to ask you a few questions, Misses Whyte. Misses Whyte, isn't it?"

There were two men standing beside her: one of them had a large TV camera, who remained quietly filming, and the other held a microphone, who did the talking.

"Sorry, how do you know me?" Esther asked absently.

"You were described and they said you were wearing a Salvation Army logo on your shirt."

"Oh, – oh yes. Why do you want to ask me whatever it is you want to ask me?"

"To investigate what's being learnt and done by the British Government."

"Well, now I'm found, I'm not sure what – "

"Is it usual for representatives of the British Government to come to these events?"

"Event? You think this is an event? You make it sound like a concert."

"Does the British Government routinely send staff to emergencies as this?"

"Sometimes, but we mainly read the reports of the agencies and take into account what the UN prescribes and the advice of NGOs. Why?"

"So what is the real reason why you are here this time, and not previous – emergencies?"

"Because there's a need to learn at first hand."

"But why now?"

"Because this is the only largest drought in the world at the moment, and I expect there will be more to come. So whatever needs to be learnt for future – events – then the opportunity to learn is now. Mistakes of the past are meaningless unless they are learnt from."

"So you think there were mistakes in the past?"

Esther stopped before giving her answer, looked piercingly into the man's eyes, saw he wanted to disparage her and changed her persona to be defiant and authoritative: "Well, I think the real mistake is talking to you as I feel all you're trying to do is mince my words. So it would be better for me to get back to helping these people and not aid you dig for things to make it worse."

The cameraman choked back a small, astounded chuckle.

"Would you try and remain professional, please?" asked the questioner.

"Would you try and be more constructive with your questions, please! Look around you!"

"I see *The Salvation Army* emblem on your shirt."

"Observant for a reporter."

"How can you see God in any of this?"

"In the way we should respond."

"But where is God? Why does he allow this suffering?"

"Why do you ask? Is this anything to do with the British Government? Are you making a comparison between the Prime Minister and the Creator of all things? Are you asking me as a representative of the Government or The Salvation Army?"

"I'm after *your* answer. Where is God in all of this? Why does he let this happen?"

"Normally, for legal reasons, I can't answer on behalf of someone else. So it's best if you ask Him."

The reporter rolled his eyes to the sky and huffed.

"Why don't you ask Him?" asked Esther.

"Because he doesn't answer."

"Do you think He owes you an explanation? You, of all people! Why should He when you're trying to misrepresent Him as you are trying to misrepresent me? Who do you think you are? Perhaps He's looking at you to do something. What *are* you doing? Why accuse God of not doing something when He's probably looking at you, at us, to do something to help our fellow men, using the wealth and wisdom we've been given."

"But why did he let this happen?"

"Why did He allow us to mismanage His Earth, you mean? Why did He allow us to be slow to the suffering of others? If we decide as a humanity and as individuals that our total needs are met without Him and we know a better way, then there are consequences, paid out by the natural dividends of our idolatrous habit to favour our capacity to think we know it all. That's breaking the first commandment, by the way."

"So if God is not going to do anything, what does the British Government or The Salvation Army think they can do?"

"You're not listening, are you? It is written – avoid all senseless arguments and debates. This is going nowhere with you!" Esther looked around her: "Look! I can't believe I'm here answering these ridiculous questions. I know what you're trying to do – trying to find fault. Well, look at the place! I'm not big enough, old enough, wise enough and uglier enough to know what you are truly asking. What I know is that this place needs help! And I'm here – to help! *If* we've all evolved from muck and slime, then what does any of this matter? *If* we've evolved, then let them die as not being fit for living."

The microphone remained outstretched as if to capture more, but it appeared that the interviewer had gone blank for a lack of any more questions.

Esther continued, her growing irritation affecting her intonation: "There is a purpose to these things, even though I won't live long enough to see them, and I am here because I believe I am meant to be here, to help as much as I can to rebuild a fallen world in the tiny capacity that I can! I don't have all the answers! I have faith that God knows the answers and I play my part in that!"

"So you believe you're doing God's work?"

"My huge efforts are mere gestures. I know the little I can do, I chose to do, and I give back my efforts for Him to use."

"But how can you be here and look at all this and wonder about God?"

"And perhaps you are rightly muck and slime."

"Well, reason this: if God were good, he would wish to have his creatures happy. If God were all-powerful, he would be able to do what he wishes. As people are not happy then God is either bad or powerless or indifferent or – does not exist."

"I see, well not even an all-powerful God can give me true freedom at the same time guarantee I use it wisely. If God is love, then God is not a dictator. If God is not a dictator, then people are allowed their freedom. If people have their freedom, then they can fail. If people fail – then what fault is that of God? How about this: if God is all-powerful to create the laws of science, then God has the biggest view of all. If people are part of that view, then they cannot see the full panoramic view that God sees. If the laws of science and people become incompatible, then who is at fault? With just His words He will blow our flesh from our bones and we will all see what we truly are and what we've done, because somehow, and I don't know how, you're not genuine, and one day it will be seen sky high to Heaven!"

The reporter tried to look in control.

"I don't know why God allows suffering, but I do know there is a need to help – and that's what I'm doing without getting into non-sense talk that gets nowhere. And! By the way! God *will* do something – but in His time when He has given us all a chance! Now excuse me!"

The two men, one still filming, the other still holding the microphone, watched as the beautiful woman picked up the lonesome little girl and walked away.

"Man, you are in for such a big fat firing," announced the cameraman as they both watched her leave. "Where did all that come from? Who's paying you a massive bribe for whatever that was?"

When David arrived back at his tent from the day's work, he saw a large group around a table with Captain Benaiah watching something small that was obscured. The thing was speaking and David was just able to get a view to see a small laptop screening the famine and an attractive female.

"Ah! David! Look at this. This is new tube."

"What?"

"I don't know, but watch this."

"You mean You Tube?"

"She is one feisty, feisty woman! I spoke with her. She was here not long ago, but now look! She is now around the world! Look! Come! Come nearer." He turned to someone and with eagerness urged to have the item repeated. They all crowded around again.

The screen turned to millions of starving people across a parched land and a young pretty woman stood up from among them clearly having been crying. Then they all listened to her feisty answers, all amazed at her forthrightness.

Captain Benaiah turned to David: "This is being seen all over the world! What a great invention, a great, great invention, David. What do you say? You are quiet, David, even for you." He turned to the one whose laptop it was: "How many have seen this?"

"Coming up to two million and it's still increasing fast."

"At ten minutes ago it was only half that."

After a moment, David, still looking at the paused image of Esther, could only simply and softly mutter to himself: "Of all the famines in all the world, she would have to walk into mine."

Of all the Famines in all the World

"David?" called out a male voice.

David looked up from his work to see Doctor Bailey approach: "What is it, Doctor?"

"I know you're not going to like this, but I need more people to cannulate. Are you up for this?"

"I hardly know what it is."

"You're going to be of more service setting up IV fluids. Don't worry, I'll call you over later and show you what to do. I'll make a medic of you yet, yes?"

David shrugged, but his gesture was not noticed as the doctor had vanished, and even if David objected, the doctor would blithely ignore his objection.

"You are quiet today, my handsome Junior, no?" asked Gabrielle as she arrived with a box of medicine.

David did not reply as he injected the arm of yet another waiting patient.

She tried a second time to provoke a response: "Even for you, you are quiet."

"I'm just getting tired."

"What did the great American want?"

"Get me to cannulate. I don't even know what that is."

"Well we won't be able to continue soon with this injecting. The medication is now very low."

"So is my patience. I can't stand this sun anymore."

"I wondered how long your motivation would last. Mine is also lacking, but I am going home tomorrow."

"It's like all my efforts are like worthless filthy rags."

"Filthy rags?"

"It's Biblical, like this place."

"Well, filthy rags are better than nothing."

"I think if your heart isn't in it, or your thoughts are elsewhere, then God would rather close up the Churches and nail the doors shut. That's also something Biblical."

The two suddenly looked up, surprised to see, not a poor, starving wretch, but a woman of a gorgeous figure and glorious flaxen hair staring profusely at David, standing among those queuing. In the moment of silence, David stood, both transfixed by each other. Their eyes told a hundred stories. Their breathing spoke of hidden, irrational emotions. Their faces showed a complexity of many thoughts.

It was Esther.

"What are you doing here?" was all that David could say, stunned, incredulous.

"What?" Esther said, as if she had not heard. "What are *you* doing here?"

"Trying out a different life."

"But – but you're not supposed to be here!"

"What?"

"Why are you here? Of all the famines and within millions of starving, I would find you!" Esther looked at the French woman beside him. "Are you with her now?" she said antagonistically.

"What?" replied David with increasing scorn.

"How many more have there been?"

"Look! I came all this way to just – just, get away from being haunted!"

"Haunted?"

Entwined in their words were the fused emotions of irritation, disappointment and anger that shared no rational basis.

"Yes! Haunted!" David shouted back.

"By who? Me? You think I'm scary?"

"I wouldn't doubt it."

"You imbecile! You idiot! Look what you've done!"

"Done! You did it!"

"I did?"

"You went all manic on me and stormed off!"

"Me? You ruined the day! It was supposed to be perfect!"

"Perfect?"

"Perfect!"

"What are you talking about? What did I ruin?"

"Just – just ruined it all! You ruined everything!"

"No! *You* did! You killed off any chance we had!"

"I did?"

"Well actually, no you didn't. You did absolutely nothing! You went off and did nothing!"

"Me? I did nothing? *You* did nothing! I waited and waited, and – nothing. And now I find I'm haunting you. I'm not even dead – yet!"

"You are to me!"

Esther visibly shook with a chill up her spine.

Then the two stopped arguing, and for a sudden moment, they just stared, trying to both betray and hide what was buried within.

"You're married, aren't you?" asked David, almost as an accusation.

Esther nodded: "I never – "

David sighed: "What are you doing here, Esther?"

Esther, angered again, shouted back: "My job! What are you doing here? Being a medic? Think you're a doctor? Trying to be a Salvation Army vicar?"

"Well I see you're here trying to fix the world!"

"Don't try and get smart with me! I know I can't fix this! I'm doing what I can!"

"No! You think you're so perfect that you think you can fix everything and everyone."

"Certainly not!"

"You do, even if you don't know it."

"I can't fix you!"

"I don't need your fixing! You fixed me well enough already!"

"You're just trying to prove to me your own worthiness. Well becoming a Christian is a cheap trick!"

"Don't flatter yourself. I became a Christian because I realised I love Jesus and He loves me!"

"Well! You have a funny way of showing it – in front of all these people!"

"Oh! Really! And who else is arguing?"

Again, they both stopped to stare at each other, breathing heavily.

"Hhggmm, hhggmm." Not trying to become part of the argument, Gabrielle, still sitting, tried to gain their attention. When they both looked at her, she motioned to two men who approached: one held a microphone; the other carried a large camera.

Esther and David returned to look at each other, as if now trying nervously to discuss a mutual plan using their eyes.

"They're coming towards us," Gabrielle whispered, trying not to make it obvious.

Esther looked fatigued. "Oh no," she whispered under her breath.

"Misses Whyte," called out the reporter as they came nearer. "Misses Whyte, we're from CNN and wonder if you would like to talk about what you said the other day. We can also include your husband."

The reporter looked at David for a split second, and then back to Esther.

So caught with their sudden appearance after the intense trail of fierce words, neither Esther nor David had noticed the mention of husband, until the reporter, looking perplexed as to why there was a lack of response, asked again, "You are married, aren't you?"

"Oh, yes," answered Esther.

There was then a picture taken of the two, just at the moment they looked at each other.

David was about to reply when his French colleague held his arm and led him away to the last remaining boxes of medication as the News crew started to set up their equipment. She shook her head, put a finger to her mouth and whispered forcibility into his ear: "Ssshhhh! You'll mess it up. Stay out of the way. Count some medicine."

Their attention on the ampoules and vials was not without surreptitiously watching Esther as the interview commenced and then concluded, being at a distance not to have heard what had been said. When the cameraman had lowered the camera, there was another discussion and all three retreated into the crowds, talking and debating with no more regard to David. He watched her distance herself and turned back to his work.

Esther, turning to look for David, saw him more concerned with looking down than to pay her any attention. The only one looking back at her was the pretty woman assistant, and when Esther noticed her gaze, she averted her stare and became obscured by people, tents and blaze of the sun.

"My! You English are so complicated!" blurted Gabrielle. "Give me a French love affair any day: kiss, kiss, bang, bang, done, done."

"I'm not into kissing and banging – and then being done."

"No, you look done without the kissing and banging." She shook her head: "Whatever mind games you play, you two are so, so damaging yourselves. It's cute and ridiculous, but mainly ridiculous."

"Thank you," replied David.

"My pleasure."

Out of Africa

If I had thought at the time, as I do now, I would have regarded myself as hypocritical to have treated David so badly, and then acted so righteously in front of the television crew, who, I was sure, had a strange agenda to belittle me for an unknown reason. We never spoke again in Africa, but I would secret the odd occasion to watch from afar and marvel on his abilities to administer skilful medical treatment. It reminded me of Mark. In fact, Mark wanted to be an engineer and David seemed to enjoy being medical.

When returning home, I needed to explain the confusion there was in a picture taken of both myself and David, and presented as man and wife in a few national newspapers. Although I was convinced that Mark already believed in my answer, I was also convinced that he tried to not show his hurt, especially when I explained I would have to journey to Africa a few more times, with each stay being of a lengthy duration.

It was during my third visit that Judy persuaded me to venture out, track down the events of forty years prior and see the grave of my heroine. It would have taken a journey of four days by indirect driving across terrain that two inexperienced ladies should never take, especially one that was 'with child,' but an unofficial courier service by helicopter could do this within one day, there and back. I shudder at this expense, but Judy had cajoled the pilot that the flight was worth taking due to delivering and fetching certain supplies that I now forget. Plus the pilot took a fancy to her. In landing, we walked into Kombaiar, now no longer a Salvation Army missionary. A hospital had been established on the same site, but it was now surrounded with schools, churches, everything of a healthy town. Streets, churches, schools, all had her name, and then following signposts, we came to her grave in a small, peaceful, serene alcove of trees off the main route, finding it a humble yet significant stone block, almost as a church font for holy water. I read the words on all four sides and memorised them.

We walked about the town and watched the community go about its business. The sun shone not in any scorching, vengeful judgement, but in pleasure of serving light. There was freshness in the air, and children walked home from school proud in their clean uniforms, smiling and playing on their way. I wanted to believe this peace was the result of Evalynne. I thought of her as we travelled back, and travelled home. It was almost a calling, a nagging that I was not doing what I should be doing, but I was so encouraged with my progress at the Foreign Office that I could not understand what this nagging was, and whether it was justified, considering I felt I was already in God's service and performing His duties to mankind.

Anyway, in the meantime, I inadvertently became a personality in the media with my treatment of the journalists and my unconventional answers that ran accord with a portion of the population and dismay with the rest. All told, I had a following, if anything only for my prettiness, as not long after Africa, I received endless requests from newspapers and magazines to be interviewed. I was unique and an enigma to everyone for working in the Foreign Office and being a Salvation Army soldier. The first dozen I declined, being shy and nervous, but then I gave in, considering my attitude as pious, and I was edited into all these many glossy magazines as I answered questions as to my life and views. In some, I was able to provide articles as to my personal witness to Jesus and the reasons for my Christian stance, and I became amazed they were published in such secular places. I cannot deny that the money helped. Companies even approached me to appear in commercials, particularly beauty products, but these I declined.

Besides, my pregnancy started to show, but even then, after a year, some magazines were still interested in me in an ad hoc basis. I did agree to be glamorously photographed for a respectable fashion magazine when they appealed to my kind nature a year or so later. I felt like a film star. When it was eventually published, I was aghast as to how beautiful I was. I was taken in by it, almost a fool to my own looks. They had altered my appearance: small blemishes were no longer there, my hair was even more golden, my cheeks had more shadow, the colours of my eyes were deepened. When I saw it, it was glorifying me. I was horrified. No one else saw any wrong in it. I was then under pressure to fit in with this faulty image. I looked too perfect. I never did another request as a glamour model. Charm can be false and beauty fades — it is only character that remains.

It was when reaching home after the second trip from Africa that I had the positive result of being pregnant. I was overjoyed, and so was Mark. I returned to Africa for a few more times, but on this third trip, I stood before Evalynne's grave somehow wanting this experience to bless my unborn baby who was not even showing.

Meredith was born in due course, and we called her Merry for the joy she brought.

Doctor Livingston, I presume

Doctor Bailey, with arms folded and a visible smile, watched from afar a good-looking young man on the other side of the large marquee, who, having had no medical experience a few months prior, was now walking about seeing to patients with drips and prescribing medication and treatment. After a few moments allowing his pride, Doctor Bailey approached David, placing a hand on his shoulder: "Can't get away with this back home. They would have fired me by now letting you do the things you're doing."

"Ah! Doctor, come here and – "

"So how do you feel about things now?"

"I'm getting on okay. The medication is always mainly the same."

"Well, quite, there is that, but you're more fluent and confident than you were. How does all this now make you feel?"

"Hope! Hopeful! It's impossible to believe that in all this hopelessness, there can be so much hope. Most of these people, especially the children, the withered, spindly children, would be dead by now – but they're not. You can see them, visibly, just growing back, coming back to us. It's so hard to believe the difference. It's just – awesome to see such a fantastic change, just because we gave them what they needed."

"And it's a good feeling? Knowing that your work is making this difference in the lives of others?"

"It's a great feeling. We're now saving many people."

"You would have made a fine medic. What's the matter?"

David had lost his interest in the conversation and was looking across the tent to watch a new person who had entered from the other side, looking lost and weary.

"Another bloody reporter," moaned Doctor Bailey.

"No, not this one."

"How do you know?"

"By the way he walks. He's not carrying any heavy cameras or microphones, making his gait even, and there's an air of not having much English writing skills about him. He looks more like a financial busybody with numbers and sums."

"Very incisive for an ex-engineer."

"But my phenomenal psychiatric skills are more based on already knowing him."

"You know him?"

"Oh yes. He's the guilty one who got me into this mess."

"Then I best congratulate him when I have a spare moment."

Even though David now approached the newcomer through the throng of beds, patients and workers, the target man did not notice until they were facing each other.

"Ah! Doctor Kingsley, I presume," Jonathan simply said. "Fancy meeting you in darkest Africa. I almost didn't recognise you."

The two looked at each other, smiled and shook hands. With the absurdity of the formality, they then gave the other a heartfelt hug and obligatory slaps on the back while laughing. The meeting was observed by others in the immediate vicinity, disjointed from the reality surrounding them.

David was elated: "Jonathan! What are you doing here?"

"Finding you! I don't want you to get all the glory."

"Thanks so much for coming. It's just so great to see you. I got the books you sent."

"You liked them?"

"I'm still reading them."

"I noticed you stopped writing letters."

"When and how did you get here?"

"I booked a surprise trip a few months ago, arrived at Ekhaya a few weeks ago, found out you weren't there, and drove here a few days ago. I was told you would be in here. So you're a Doctor now? What's going on?"

"Doing what I can with what I'm told to do. What are you doing?"

"Cooking duties – doing what I can with what I'm given."

They walked to an exit in the tent, shielded their eyes from the sun's piercing gaze, and surveyed the scene of defeated and dejected people. They were as voiceless as those they studied.

"This feels like the end of time to me," simply stated Jonathan after the pause. "Surely God's not going to let this continue."

"Well, in the meantime, it's up to us to make our response, whatever His reasons."

Jonathan turned to David: "You've been listening to Esther."

David nodded.

"She's got a lot more fame coming her way, even if she doesn't know it yet."

"Why?"

"Even the news that she's declining TV chat shows is news. Everyone's clamouring to interview her."

David did not respond.

"I've discovered something that will interest you."

"Something?"

"I'll tell you about it sometime, but in the meantime, I'm here for these two months."

"Lots of insects, Jonathan."

"All for God's glory, David, all for God's glory." With an endearing touch of David's shoulder, Jonathan left.

In the evening that followed, Jonathan did not tell of his discovery, nor within the next two months did he even allude to the subject. It was never mentioned and was lost in the routine of each day that consisted of serving food or medication, as to their allotted tasks. There was little time for talk, as fatigued and hot as they were. A small, humble meal, and a time for sleep was all the space could allow. Such was their last day on the site. With more aid workers arriving, those who had served were replaced.

Ecclesiastes 7:2

On the morning of their departure, David said goodbye to Captain Benaiah and Doctor Bailey, and met Jonathan at his jeep who was waiting. Loading his small luggage in the back, David saw the provision of food and drink ready for a long trek.

"Well we need to eat and drink, David," Jonathan said as they both got into the dusty vehicle. He started the engine and drove away.

"Are we going around the world? Are we leaving anything for those starving here? What are they going to eat?"

Jonathan gave David a confident, friendly smile: "Just trust me."

Eventually they were leaving the outskirts of the famine and after some formal checkpoints, they left the scene with their thoughts remaining behind. For a while, neither spoke. Even when rising up the mountainside and parking on a lay-by, they were voiceless as they viewed what they were deserting.

"I think I can let go of Esther now," said David eventually.

"At last! What a relief!"

"I'm being serious."

"Yeah! So am I!"

"Well, it's not her fault. She didn't ask me to fall in love with her. I just did. I just want some good come from all this. She's become so – bold."

"I never told you of this thing I've discovered – and you've never asked about it."

"I thought you'd tell me in your own good time."

"Well, it's now. I'm taking you there."

"Ekhaya?"

"By a different route, yes. I spoke to Misses Benaiah when I was there and she told me of this place. I spoke to Captain Benaiah and he's advised me on the best way to go. It will take us four day's drive and then five day's drive back to Ekhaya. So I've prepared for it, you see."

There was still no full explanation given by Jonathan of where they were going, other than the place was named Amani and was in a country beyond the borders of another, which had no bearing on David. As they travelled, they talked at times, they looked in silence at the world travelling by, they ate what they could and slept where they felt safe, some evenings in the jeep, others in a bedsit. They did not dwell in any particular place, but marvelled at the countryside they traversed, like nomads not owning anything.

In Amani, David was now at pains to understand the reason for their trip, even more so when being told that, even though Amani was a major hub of the area, it was not the intended final goal. After one more night's stay, they awoke early and drove onwards.

"Okay, let me put you out of misery," finally said Jonathan.

"Good! Where are we going?"

"A place called Kombaiar. It's grown over the last few decades, but there are a few things that remain." Jonathan fell silent as he felt the air turn a shade more golden.

"We're going to visit where my Grandfather was, aren't we?"

Jonathan nodded: "But there's more to it than that."

"There is?"

"Your Grandmother – we're going to witness what she left behind."

"Evalynne?"

"Misses Benaiah looked into it for you and told me all about it. Evalynne became a martyr."

The remainder of the trip was wordless until they arrived at Kombaiar, a bustling town, slowly outgrowing its own boundaries. As they drove through the streets, Jonathan announced their arrival and reason for arriving: "This, all this, is the result. You can say she made a lasting impression."

"I'm sure that's an exaggeration."

"Really? What about that street name?" Jonathan pointed to the sign of the road they were turning into. "And over there, you see that church? I wouldn't be surprised if it wasn't named after her. This was just a missionary outpost. Now look at it."

A few moments more they were parked beside a stall that served drinks and fruit, which they both indulged in for a while, standing by their dirty vehicle.

Jonathan, half-finishing his orange, looked at David's solemn appearance: "You okay?"

David nodded: "It's – just – just a bit – strange being here. I never knew that one day I would be here. I can't wait to tell Grandfather."

"There is more."

"More?"

"She was buried here." Without any allowance for a reply, Jonathan had asked the stall's attendant, who, without voicing an answer, just pointed in the direction down the street. "You see, he knew what I meant, even across different languages. Coming?"

Walking, they followed the signs and came to a road that was bordered by trees and bushes leading to a hospital complex at the furthest end. Within the trees was a quiet, meditative alcove, where seats provided rest and flowers grew. In a particular angle, not central or square to the space, there stood a carved, large, stone block of a coffin shape and size, aging with moss and a pooling of water on top. What then confronted David were the words that were to be found circling all four sides. He read them all, stood silently for a moment, and then read them again:

'The grave of Captain Evalynne Lovert
of The Salvation Army,
loving wife of Captain Joseph Lovert
who lived on earth with us between

June 9th 1926 and June 11th 1974.
Died defending God's Citadel.

It is better to attend a funeral than a feast,
as a funeral focuses your time.'

Jonathan, sitting on one of the benches in the solitude of the clearing, waited for David to join him on the seat.

"It's time to go back home," eventually announced David.

"Ekhaya?"

David shook his head: "No, home."

Book Four : Perpetuate Hope

Waiting with Habakkuk

Sergeant Richards now stood at the doorway to the kitchen and then ventured to the table to place all the pages there. Gone was the thunder and the lightning, the rain had stopped, the dark clouds were disappearing and the day was now getting brighter. Richards was not interested. Instead, as drawn by his detective work, he continued reading to discover the true source of Esther's guilt.

Each act and achievement of David made me jealous and drove me to do more, to out-do his achievements for God's Kingdom, and although I denounced David many times, secretly he spurred me on. Our decisions made, God had closed the door on us, but I had not. Even so, God, without me being worthy, allowed me to marry Mark, the perfect husband, to have the perfect daughter, Merry, and still I ruined it. And Mark persistently loved me, like a testament to God's love.

It was with these feelings of guilt and shame that I found myself dreaming the other night. I was in a sandy town of palm trees and stone buildings, deep within a desolate desert. I was in the central, market square, down on the ground, in the dirt, as if having been thrown there, almost naked in my sparse and thin clothing. A group of menacing men were above me, full of hate. They were about to stone me to death. I knew I had done something dreadful, and I deserved judgement, but these men disregarded their own evil deeds, their hands held high ready to throw their jagged rocks. Then someone to the side said something, and these men, disappointed, turned away.

I was instantly taken and I reappeared in a gigantic, mystical, bright, majestic hall, brought by a means that I did not understand. Everywhere was light and made of glorious crystal.

I knew it to be the room of His throne, the ceiling too high to view, the walls too distant. I had the feeling I had no right to be there, that my actions and thoughts were not of the standard to permit me to be present. It was not that I was being tolerated, even though the filth in and on me condemned me to an execution, but that I was being accepted by a grace that had no means to be understood by any human mind. All around this hall was delicious fruit of rich and ripe colours ready for eating, so much of it that it was scattered and heaped over the floor. God's own presence shone from a large, glorious figure sitting on the throne. Pervading through the air from magnificent chalices was smoke that smelt fragrant and glowed white with His justice.

I stood amazed, horrified, in awe, and He spoke to me in a language my ears had never heard before, a language that had been purified from human contamination, in a voice that was majestic, authoritative, unquestionable, truthful, loving, absolute, forthright, caring, booming yet soothing, compassionate yet unyielding. His own sense of justice and holiness would prevail. I stood spellbound, as if the strength of my own horror and shock suspended me from falling to the ground, too afraid to move, too afraid to fall, too afraid to answer His call. Although my ears had never heard this beautiful language before, I knew precisely, without a doubt, without any mistake, what was being said. He was calling my name and was welcoming me into His presence.

As if released, I did fall to the floor, trembling, weeping, mortified, petrified, that although His voice was magnificent and assuring, without any condemnation, I still saw the dire peril I was in and saw the precipice I was on. I wept inconsolably. My spirit was so low. I crumpled even lower. I saw my life there before me like a page and nowhere on it could I see God being the focus. My life had been all about me, even my hard work to do good. I had looked everywhere for perfection, in relationships, in love, in marriage, in my career, in my own bent selfish desire to see the world rid of suffering and sadness, only so that I could live without suffering and sadness around me. I only partially longed for perfection in my relationship with my God, Abraham's God. Now I saw the perfectness in what He is and has done. I wept bitterly as I felt the loss there was in a beautiful, perfect relationship that could have been with me and the God of all things. Everything paled to insignificance when compared to the potential of this loving and living covenant. I yearned to correct my failings and I managed to start crawling across the floor, avoiding His bright gaze as I could no longer bear look at the brightness and knowing my shame. If only I could reach Him, if He could only allow it, I could be cleansed and healed if I could just touch His feet, touch the hem of His cloak.

He allowed me to come closer and He allowed me to be there at His feet. I saw the wounds there and I cried for the suffering there had been for me. My tears streamed and fell from my cheeks, and I became aware I was making His feet wet. Like a foolish gesture, I tried to dry them with my hair.

Then He reached down to me, cupped my face in His large gentle hands. My eyes were closed. I could not look into His face. He spoke, but not knowing each word, I knew what He was saying by the way I felt them. He spoke directly to my feelings, incising my outer crust, into the fragile softness of my core.

"Do not fear! The people I treasure are the humble — they depend solely on me — and I will leave ninety-nine to bring home one who is lost. I will bring home my flock. My home with many rooms is prepared. Hadassah, seek me in good times and bad times. I will be found!"

Then, with magnificence, He stood. "Do you think I have become frail? Do you think I no longer care? Do you think I cannot see? Do you think I cannot hear? I created sight and I created sound! I can hear the sound of light! My thoughts are beyond your thoughts! My people, Israel, wandered in the wilderness! I disallowed Israel to enter the Promise Land because they did not trust me! So trust me! I will do something amazing, Hadassah. You will not believe it, even if I were to tell you! I will destroy what there is to destroy, I will build what there is to build, and I will never confuse the two. Keep on waiting — it will happen. My words do not return to me without doing everything I send them to do. I am the light and I push aside darkness. Now be still and know me."

I turned and saw what He now pointed at: the Earth as though across a vast chasm. There, on its surface and under it, were people accusing God for the injustice in their lives, complaining about the desert that Earth had become. They hated Him because He accused them of evil, because they could not reach His standards, because they did not care for His answers or His claim on their lives. They gloried in their own creativity that could not match God's. They looked to worship their own achievements, their own answers and blanked out the God of Always and Everything. They were in a spiritual famine and they did not know it, or they wished to ignore. Their kindness was a pretence. They were worshipping what wasn't God.

The Earth was damaged. It was damaged beyond repair. Open ulcers and sores, putrid and festering, all from Man's overwhelming desire to serve himself, had stained and ruptured the vast crust of land, and the sea was full of decaying carcasses, a harbour for sickness, a haven for pollution. Man had corrupted what God had created and gone against God's command to care for the environment. They had desecrated the land and killed the animals.

Then came a dreadful creature, ugly, unholy, ill-formed, something that was or was part of an unholy trinity trying to imitate God. It was trying to 'solve the world' with its own misrepresentation of good, believing itself to have the ability to do God's work as God Himself. It was diseased with its own appalling righteousness that turned truth to lies and lies to truth. People were amazed as it had the answers they thought they needed. The fruit surrounding me, as ripe as it was, was now becoming rotten. The age of the world was now ripe for judgement.

"Watch and see, Hadassah, that I will truly do something amazing. Be still and know that I Am!"

He then spoke with lightning. His voice was like the roaring oceans, the jet thrust of a mighty rocket, the surge of a million jet fighters, the horrendous clap of a thousand thunderous lightning bolts, the collapse of a colossal building. His words burnt, they were solid, irrefutable, unretractable, and they physically moved me, vibrated through my being like huge shock waves, boomed through the ribs of my chest. I remained fearful for what was being declared by this awesome God. He spoke with thunderous authority to the Earth, and all the Earth and all of Heaven shook from His might.

"I see you all! I see all of you! You treat my suffering children so cruelly! You were to serve and care and protect each other and my world! I told you everything you need to know and do, but look and know what you have done! You are all so sure of yourselves, with your knowledge and inventiveness! What is it do you think you know? Who are you to tell me I did not create you? Who are you to question my ability to judge? Who are you to question my right to judge? Who are you to command the times and seasons? Who can measure my wisdom? Who can build mountains, move oceans, crash planets together? Who fashioned the forces that sculpture such beauty? Can you hold the Earth in your palm? Can you build a star from nothing, set them all in place and motion? Has any galaxy formed from your drawing board? Does the universe obey your laws? Who of you can invent consciousness, or is it a fake imitation of what I have done? Can your knowledge exceed the universe! How many sparrows die and where is each buried?

"Your crayons are no match for my thoughts! I see colour where you can only see grey! I hear symphonies where you hear nothing! I experience the vast distances that you cannot contemplate comprehending! How long did it take you to learn all the un-important matters of life, and how long will it take you to learn of all the important matters there are? Can your mind ever contain all there is to know? Is everything that is, was and will be, within the grasp of your intellect? I am in ultimate control! I can take away all I have done within the time it took to create! What abhorrent lifeless statue will you believe will rescue you, what man-made god, what shallow idea or weak philosophy? What weapon can you bring against me? What leader of yours will win the battle? Who said I will not disown all those who will ruin my home? I will accept even your heart-felt anger if you will only come to me! Come to me! This cost has been paid in full! I am the true father of my children and they will call me their true father!"

Then God's smoke intensified and glowed and billowed so much that it reached Earth, and everyone, everywhere saw and knew. So horrified, they wanted the mountains to fall on them in fear and terror.

But He had chosen those who loved Him to come with Him, as they did what pleased Him. They understood Heaven because they believed in what Jesus taught. They were searching for Him with receptive hearts. They were His sheep. They had accepted the sacrifice of The Lamb for their iniquities, their impurity, their brokenness from Him. All the people not of The Lamb's spirit were sent away to a place I never saw nor comprehended; to a place that did not exist, but it did; to a place that existed, but it didn't. And His kingly mansion became full of joyous people praising God for what He had done. In joy, peace and harmony — and relief from the tyranny of evil — we all, more refreshed than the air of the countryside, the air of the ocean, began a great feast of a glorious wedding. There was a sense of relief and joy and jubilation that we had pleased our Heavenly Father. So compelled by our joy that we sang in fullness of our souls to praise Him with heartfelt goodness.

We had stood, stupefied, in wonder, in amazement, in horror, in shock, in almost disbelief, with fear standing beside us, with what we saw God do to annihilate evil and suffering. What God will do will be truly incredible. Evil is exterminated, suffering is eradicated, but completed on God's absolute terms, in His righteousness, in His image. We had watched the earth scorched to cinders and even the Heavens broke away and was dismembered. A new earth and a new Heaven were restored. All glory and honour goes to our God of Abraham! Who are we in comparison?

It is frightening to know that to God, this destruction will be amazing, righteous, warranted and holy. What can defeat evil and suffering? God's immense loving anger and patience. Wait and see.

Revelation, plain and clear

In Africa, David cherished the times when it rained. Now in England, walking along the paved streets of the country town of Hallow and under the deep grey clouds, he was longing for the bright sunshine. Row upon row of rigid terraced housing passed him by, but the rain seemed to be forestalled until he arrived at his Grandfather's house. It then suddenly poured and David had to laugh, now soaked in a manner that he had been yearning for a month ago. In Africa, he would have stripped to his underwear to dance in such a shower.

Knocking on the door provoked no response and the occasion now seemed an anti-climax. Remembering the way to Misses Manning, he walked the streets carrying his suitcase until he found her address and knocked, now sopping wet.

A man came to the door.

"Excuse me, does Misses Manning live here?"

"Yes, I'm her husband. Are you by any chance, David Kingsley?"

"Yes."

"You are just in time. Come in." With that, Mister Manning beckoned David inside and gave him a towel. "You want a change in clothes?"

David nodded and explained he had some in his luggage. In a few moments, he emerged from another room having put on something dry.

Mister Manning, grabbing a jacket and keys, beckoned David to follow and join him in his car on the road.

"Is something wrong?" asked David as he settled in the passenger seat.

"It's Joseph. We think he's ill and needs to get to a doctor or hospital, but he insists on staying."

"Staying? Staying where?"

"At Halcyon."

When arriving at the hidden entrance, with the road deserted and the rain continuous, David pushed back the metal gating, overgrown with foliage as it was, and Mister Manning drove onto the forest estate, into the mystical woodland. With David back in the car, they drove along the muddy lane until Halcyon Manor materialised suddenly from its camouflage.

Misses Manning came to the front door when her husband had knocked loud enough. She immediately saw David and could not believe herself: "My! How Heaven answers!"

"What's the matter?" asked David.

"Your Grandfather. Come in, come in."

"Is he any better?" asked her husband.

She shrugged: "He's not any worse."

"Perhaps with David, we'll just grab him and take him."

Elsie Manning turned to David: "You better just go up and see him. He's not himself. He's in his bedroom."

David nodded, concerned and curious, and went upstairs, noticing that the Mannings chose to stay in the entrance hall. After a silent moment, he quietly knocked on Joseph's door, knocking a second time to receive an answer to enter. When he did, he saw his Grandfather on the bed, propped up with large pillows, looking at the windows, looking extensively aged from when the last of David's memory could recall.

Joseph slowly turned and saw David at the door. He was instantly overjoyed, almost laughing, and beckoned David come nearer to the point that David questioned the diagnosis of the Mannings. "Ah! David! My, you look greatly expanded in faith!"

It was then that Joseph directly became visibly fatigued and with no doubt, David could see something was wrong. It was also obvious to David that the old man could read his thoughts as though looking at a mirror. David remained standing having only entered a few steps: "Why didn't you tell me?"

Joseph was forlorn and sighed. "I did mean to write, but I didn't want you coming home on my account. And I'm not ill, just weak. I think this is the last time I will be able to spend time here."

"Why didn't you tell me about Evalynne?"

"Evalynne, yes – Evalynne – I miss her, David, I miss her. I miss her so much." He then looked at David as if remembering the reason why Evalynne had been mentioned: "What happened?"

"I found her grave. I stood there and read her gravestone."

Joseph smiled and said nothing.

"I'm so proud she's my Grandmother. Why didn't you tell me about how she died?"

"I felt like I couldn't survive the story being relived. Besides, we wanted to protect the children from prosecution and persecution, so we kept the secret." Joseph started coughing, receiving a glass of water poured out by David to compose himself. "The Police wanted us to remain silent," he continued. "They wanted to hush it up from being public knowledge. It was because the Government were corrupt and were in quiet league with these violent groups. They would want revenge." Joseph sighed as if in need of relief from the memories, and then he continued when returning to David. "We all agreed that this was in the best interest and – and kept quiet."

"Kept quiet?"

"A mob of savage murderers, murdered Evalynne, but the young militia turned and murdered their own masters. There were those who would have gone after these children with revenge."

"But you don't understand. Do you know what has now happened?"

Joseph shook his head.

"Her name is everywhere – everywhere: school names, street names, a hospital, and Kombaiar is just rebuilt – rebuilt and redeveloped into something – incredible. There's even a Church called Saint Evalynne. Almost everyone goes to Church."

"If you had met her, then you wouldn't be so surprised."

"Thank you."

"For what?"

"For getting in touch with me, all those years ago with your first letter."

"It almost didn't happen. I was frozen for many years, but what would have been Evalynne's faith if I had been the one to die? I learnt to forgive God for conditioning Evalynne to do what she did, and to accept that it was her choice to run back. I learnt to forgive me – I should have been the one to lay down his life, not his wife. It should have been me. It was my Christian duty, like Christ for His church. Women should not be looked down upon just because they are to obey their husband. The husband is to be worthy of obedience, and to lay down his life for her." Joseph's voice became soft, "Which is something never mentioned on the Wedding day. As for me, why waste life in depression?"

David said nothing, not being sure what to say.

"Come here, nearer, sit on the bed."

David did.

"David, – listen – listen to what I have to say – before my breath is out. I have wanted to say this for a – a long time, and was never sure if I would be – given the moment." The old man looked lost in his own forlorn breathing and moments had to pass before the grand gentleman suddenly started speaking as though in need of psychiatric counselling: "God hasn't destroyed us yet, even though we deserve it." Joseph stopped again, as if out of breath, as if working out his muddled thinking, as if trying to gain back a speech he had been rehearsing.

As time passed, David became convinced that Joseph had forgotten his presence and unsure of why his Grandfather had started to talk so distractedly. "I don't understand."

"Be quiet, I'm trying to be understood. Listen! God is quiet, allowing us to be with our freedom. You may not feel – you, you may not – feel like He is there because He is quiet – but what should we be doing? God is Holy and does what is right; not what is entertaining or makes Him happy."

"Granddad, I know all this."

"God expects us to be mature enough to govern ourselves. He will only step in – when it gets to its worst; but – but if we were truly to understand God's Holiness and our sin, we would not understand why – why He has not destroyed us all by now. When – when He steps in, His final anger towards sin – will be unleashed and unstoppable. Satan will be annihilated along with all those investing in his administration."

"Granddad, you're not making sense. Mister and Misses Manning want to take you to hospital."

"Listen! As much as all the prophecies of Jesus that came true, all the others will. It means everything will get far worse before He comes again."

"No – I don't want to know. You need to get to a doctor."

"See here! See! Open your eyes! Know with your mind and heart! These things will happen – as real as they are already happening. The weather will give us more droughts, more floods, more hurricanes, famine. People will be swept to their deaths as naturally as each second. The ice is melting. The sea and air will become more polluted, more poisoned, more acrid. Technology will not be able to sustain the masses. They will build machines that will make vast people obsolete, redundant, unwanted, unused – and disillusioned and displaced. They – they will build machines that can think – think in different dimensions – different realms – unknown to us. Weapons will have minds of their own. Technology and man's desire to see perfection – in his own image – has locked us on this trend to destruction. The system is now locked. We cannot go back."

"Granddad, you need rest. Slow down." But David was waved off.

"Stop sleepwalking! The Earth will stop giving up what people take. They are building a false dream. This tower to the sky will fall." Joseph was gradually tiring but fuelled by his own adrenaline as if holding a heavy weight that needed to be held at the cost of his own health. "There will be catastrophic consequences to the decisions and actions we are making from ill-founded knowledge on things we think we know. We are designing a world we are not meant for. We are not designed for this. Countries will arise and will demand the same standards as us in the West. The Earth cannot supply it. Slums and poverty will be on the increase. Populations will outstrip the supply of water and fuel and food, and will increase such that a few nuclear wars will make no difference. Countries will expand and then expire when they realise there is not enough for three or four Americas on the planet. Never-ending growth is not sustainable, and events will overtake our ability to solve them." His voice was becoming hoarse and modulated with wheezing, at times being short of breath. A faint crackling could be heard deep within.

"You're tired. Please rest."

"Listen! Listen with your intelligence! Can't you see and know? Diseases will adapt to overwhelm our defences, our understanding, and they will flourish. The population of the world will be a disease. People will live longer, but with illnesses that are more chronic. The young will not accept the burden that the older generation will create for them. There will be a call for a human cull to sustain the human species. The cost of repairing too many disasters will be too great for the burdened world economy." Joseph, coughing for a while, had to suspend his talking until he settled again, but his voice was just as wheezing.

"Granddad – "

"It starts here – now – this is when everything starts to turn. Everything has been leading to this coming age, but people refuse to see it – they see it, but they refuse to see it. Everything rests on something so fragile, but they believe in their security. They believed the Titanic would not sink, but it did, that – that monumental monstrosity of man's ignorance and arrogance." Joseph then became angry: "What is wrong with the – the Church? Why is the Church not warning people?"

The old man stopped and rested, appearing to forget the younger man was with him. Then Joseph turned to him, directly looking into David's eyes: "Save as many as you can. They don't see or want to see what is coming. Everything is now locked in; a positive, escalation of trends that will bring us this future. We have hit the iceberg. The ship will sink. There are two lists: those who are lost, and those who are saved. Save as many as you can."

"How do I do that?"

"There have been many hospitals that have failed inspection and failed the public – because no one stood up to poor practice, and poor standards became the culture. Stand up, withstand the onslaught of decline and do not allow God's standards to be – to be ignored by Man's love of himself and love of decadence. Conspire against those with a wanton desire to disregard the rights of others, but allow them their response and let God be God. Strive to – to work with Heaven's principles, to work as if the standards of Heaven apply here on Earth. The New Earth and Heaven will need such people."

"I don't think I'm bold enough."

"Nor did Moses."

"I'm not Moses."

"He's an example of character – that's the only currency in life and – death – life and death."

"But God promised Noah He will never again wipe out mankind."

"No, He said He would never – never again wipe out mankind – with a flood."

"You need to rest! Look! You're exhausted. Just sleep, Granddad."

"I cannot be caught to be sleeping! Listen! The success of humanity – is – is not sustainable. Science provides our solutions, but – more people, more success is not sustainable. People will beg for solutions. International crime, world diseases, – governments and leaders will not be able to make decisions quickly enough, and so a world government will naturally form to attempt to turn the tide and try to make a perfect world."

When Joseph had gone quiet, David thought he had stopped, but he continued.

"There will be an unholy, ugly allegiance of three, an attempt to recreate the trinity by Satan, the antichrist and a false prophet. Truth will be turned to look like lies, and lies will look like the truth, propagated, perpetuated, consumed by the public. What is abhorrent will be made to appear wise and – rational. People will believe and be relieved by the lies. They will be amazed at what is performed before them. They will believe wrong will be right. Many good people will be fooled. People will turn against God with all the anger they have for all the turmoil in the world. They will know everything about you – and you won't know it. They will control you and you won't know it. They will demand conformance. They will insert electronics into the hands and heads of those who wish to conform and live by the system. Persecution will naturally commence, as – as everyone needs to conform. Those who – who know this con-, conformance as worship, those who will refuse to worship the system and the man imposing his hideous solutions on the world, will be a stain to be, to be eradicated, and will be slaughtered or – or cut out of the system – neglected – to starve to death. This man will strive for, for a – a better world, a perfect world, but on his terms, in his ideal, in his glory. He will even strive to supplant God Himself and the populace will not see this, as great as this man will be."

"You're tiring yourself out."

"With all that is going wrong, God will be blamed, whether they believe in Him or not. They will be angry and place the blame on Him. They will rebel against God's people. There will be persecution and this will be made to look – righteous – necessary – and normal." Joseph sighed. "Yes, I'm tired. I will tell you more in the morning. Have your Bible ready. There's more. Look to the skies, David, look to the clouds – look to the clouds."

"I don't understand. Look at the sky?"

By this time, Joseph was closing his eyes with the failing strength to keep them open. "Yes, yes, look to the – clouds. Never – never get – never be disheartened by – the details of – of the book of Revelation. The final solution can only be for God's very own inter- – intervention. Just know that Jesus – in the end – will win. He cannot, not win. The lion of Israel will return. His sheep – His joyful sheep will – will be separated and – saved. The harvest will be brought in and the weeds will be burnt. Stay true to Him and – and give Him the glory. Know that – victory is in Christ. Perpetuate this hope. It is devastating that many will live life without living in this hope. Never lose your first love when you realised your forgiveness: being offered perfect eternity is something not short of – not short of – spectacular."

"Yes, but for now get some rest. You need a doctor."

"There's nothing wrong with me – except for – for wearing out. Look over me as I sleep. I need to tell you more in the morning."

David nodded, but Joseph was not watching.

"Look to the clouds," was his fading breath and then the old man was far from being awake.

Shocked by what he had heard, David had to compose himself for a while, watching the old sleeping man. He then went downstairs to the hall and found the Mannings waiting for him.

"He's asleep now," said David, "but can I trouble you to take him to his doctor tomorrow?"

"Of course, we'll be here in the morning," answered Mister Manning. "Are you staying?"

David nodded. "I'll look after him for now."

After he had heard the car drive into the distance, David returned to Joseph's chamber, settled into the old, tall Victorian chair to the side and sat for a while trying to adjust to the disbelief of seeing his Grandfather in such a bad way and for all the disturbing talk he uttered. His own thinking eventually tired himself to sleep.

When morning came, David awoke with the start of the dawn, but Joseph did not stir. He looked peaceful and serene, and David did not trouble him. Then he became aware that something was different, something was missing, and it was not until he had withdrawn the curtains that he realised Joseph lacked any form of movement. Coming nearer to his Grandfather's cheek, there was no breath, and there was no warmth. Captain Joseph Lovert was stone cold. He had died.

Isaiah 55

A simple funeral service was held at the Salvation Army Hall. Many attended, from those of local churches and those who had met him while he worked at the hospital in the last few years of his working age. Some patients of that period came and gave informal testimony of Joseph's visits and the encouraging support he gave them. His neighbours came and even the landlords of some of the Public Houses Joseph had frequented selling of the *War Cry* papers attended and quietly listened to the man's life. Some people had been asked to speak prior and there were some who wanted to speak on the day, rising when offered a general invitation from the conducting Salvation Army Officer. Until that event, it had never been known how a simple refuse collector, with medical experience, had affected so many people. With his coffin central to the hall space, with all that was said, not even Joseph would have known what his living had left behind.

The small brass band played a few tunes, and with hymns sung and Bible passages read out, the service eventually came to an end with the prominent tune of, 'Take my life and let it be'. In the following quietness, they each spoke with each other, slowly departing until only a few remained. Most of them were unaware of Joseph's true burial site, assuming it was the Crematorium. Instead, the coffin was placed in the hearse and driven to another but unknown destination. Only a selected few knew the truth and they followed to attend the final service for Joseph.

With the recent rain and the bright sunshine now breaking free, the serene stillness of the ancient garden graveyard of Halcyon allowed the final burial service to be completed. Five people stood before a fresh, empty grave, and within the fragrant scent of the garden, Joseph's coffin was lowered into the depths of the soil, either side of him being graves that were hundreds of years old, some prior to King Henry VIII.

The Salvation Army Officer gave the final Bible reading and then finished with a final prayer, while Mister and Misses Manning and David stood silently listening, along with an unnamed older man that everyone accepted as important to attend. David, heavy for the day, did not have the heart to ask as to this stranger.

Each adding their own words of condolence and encouragement to David, they all departed and left him to stand alone for a while, before he, solely, at his own request, buried his Grandfather within the ground on a peaceful day. When the grave was full, David moved four large stone slabs on top, and stood and rested, reading the words engraved in the stone.

'Here lies Captain Joseph Lovert of The Salvation Army,
loving husband of Evalynne Lovert,
who lived with us between
March 19th 1926 and September 29th 2015.
Died to join his wife with Christ.

It is far better to attend a feast than a funeral
as a feast is to remind you of Heaven.'

An Unholy Belief

Within a small, opulently furnished office, more befitting a stately home, sat a sole receptionist typing at her computer. Lowering her glasses to the man whom stood above her, of white scraggy hair and stubble, and clasping a batch of newspapers to his chest, she addressed his question and then continued typing: "Good morning, Mister Scabbards, yes he is expecting you. Go right through."

"Thank you, I will."

"You only have half an hour with him," she called out to his back as Scabbards reached the internal door made invisible within the wooden panelling.

He knocked and then said, "This won't take long, Miss."

"It normally doesn't."

As always, Scabbards read the title of the door – *Mr. I. Hammon: Foreign Secretary* – and again wondered what the 'I' stood for. His thoughts were interrupted by the reply within and he entered the larger inner office, making no noise as he walked across the thick carpet. Without any consideration, Scabbards dropped his newspapers on the desk with a thump and sat on a chair with a self-satisfied grin that was not immediately explained.

Continuing to scrutinise a document, the Foreign Secretary, feeling the new, smug air, spoke up: "You appear satisfied in something."

"You don't need to worry about little miss pretty for long, sir. She's now only in two of the broadsheets and demoted to page five in one and page seven in the other. All that gives a total coverage of – two hundred and six centimetres squared."

Hammon huffed and stopped reading: "About bloody time."

"A few months, on and off, that's not bad for a little nobody woman. She's all over the internet, though."

There was no reply other than the look given to the day outside the tall windows, a rub of his chin and to attend to his own thoughts.

"You don't like her notoriety, do you? This woman, – this very attractive, intelligent, vibrant woman, perfect worker, perfect wife and now soon to be perfect mum."

"She's just a confused little girl."

"Perhaps your effort to make her look ridiculous has made her into what she's becoming. It actually didn't matter what she said. It was her spirit that appealed to people. Quite entertaining as well. Even the BBC is making news for her about firing the reporter."

"What about those magazines you were telling me about?"

"She was turning them down, but has started accepting some, according to my sources."

"She's just a confused little girl enjoying the limelight. I know how the papers work and what people want to believe. If they want a fairytale, they'll get one out of her. Even if her popularity wanes for now, it will come back."

"You sound very sure."

"I am sure. The PM has spoken about her. He's just devoted. He wants her career to blossom and he'll somehow make it happen."

"Do you want me to get Sinbad to look into her past?"

Hammon remained within his own scheming and gave no answer.

"What about a set-up," Scabbards continued. "I can get some of her co-workers to cajole her into pole-dancing or something. That would look spicy for a do-gooder Sally Ann lass."

Hammon shook his head: "What does her husband actually do?"

"He's a nurse."

"A nurse!"

"Yes, a nurse, he works in a hospital. I've seen that he's applied to work at Great Ormond street."

"A nurse?"

"Yes, a nurse! Male nurses do exist, you know. He works in the theatres, doing theatre things, I don't know what."

"The people will love that!"

"Well I did say to get Sinbad on the case – if you're really worried."

"He's too expensive."

"If you say so, sir."

"There will be something else, sometime. There always is. These religious people always fall on their face when the right tripwire comes along. What gets my blood so fired is that they believe in this religious non-sense, ancient, out-moded, defunct rubbish. How can anyone believe in a god when there's so much evidence against it? All of them: Jews, Christians, Muslims, the worship of cows and statues. They all think they're right, but it's all fictitious idealism in their own sorry estimation of things, which they can't even live by." Hammon shook his head in disdain. "They look ridiculous, Scabbards, ridiculous because they're too concerned for their own worries and fears and their own interests than they are about God's kingdom. And those who *are* concerned for his kingdom look even more ridiculous to be of any earthly use – just fatally ill-adjusted."

Scabbards just nodded in a disingenuous manner.

"If there is something, then which god is the right god? I tell you, religion has caused more death and hardship than anything else. And it's not getting better with all this fundamentalism. No wonder the Middle East is just a cesspit of hate. Where most of the World's religions have come from is where most of the World's hate comes from. They're all mentally unstable, Scabbard's, mentally unstable. How do they hear from God? In their head? In strange visions? All of which can be downplayed as tricks of the mind, constructs of thoughts assembling apparitions from what the senses are obscuring – windy sounds, unfocused images, all making the creative mind conjure what is really not there. What is dangerous is if they can get you to believe in the absurd, then they can get you to do the atrocious. All religions should be regarded as a mental illness, Scabbards."

"I don't think the health budget would cover the costs, sir."

"And they ask how can we know what is good and what is evil without God? Without God there will be mayhem, they say, but is it that if God is removed, would they then commit crime? If people are good because they know there is a reward and don't commit crime because they know there is a punishment, then you have to question their true motives."

"But we have laws in society with that same aim."

"We don't need religion! We can organise ourselves! Just eliminate those who are abominable."

"If you are referring to Islamic militancy, then the war can only be fought with a persuasive ideological counter attack, a change in mindset from a militant view to a compassionate view, a theological war of how we should view God. Does God really need and want suicide bombers in his name? Does this entertain him? We need religion to counter-argue this conditioning of young, bored, disaffected male Muslims and stop them seeking self-glory and virgins in heaven. For that, you need religion. You need some form of belief for society to conform and perform."

"If I ruled the world, I would make it illegal and eliminate any who practise any form of religion."

"Any?"

"Any!"

"Not appreciating religion is hardly going to go down well at any Middle East peace conference."

"Then we should design and prescribe a logical, comprehensive, down-right better world religion for everyone to follow, for a better working model to eliminate problems, for society to conform; a new, better religion than the old defunct religions. Have you read the Bible Scabbards?"

Scabbards shook his head in a manner that asked whether the read was necessary.

"It's the most unholy book ever written: rape, murder, war, crucifixion, deceit, violence, Satan worship, adultery, slaughter. Do you really know how the twelve tribes of Jacob came to be? Read it! They all then traipse around a no-place and get given these rules, loads of them, not just those ten commandments, and they're bizarre, just chronically weird and uncaring at the most of times. Any ailment and you're either shunned or at worst stoned to death. No wonder they all deserted God and preferred to worship other ones. Then God got jumpy and nasty and allowed empires to trash them. So much for, 'I will be their God and they will be my people'. I wouldn't get your children to read any of it. It's barbaric."

"If you say so, Minister, but people need meaning in their lives, a purpose, a reason. They need religion to give them hope, to cure their conscience, give them comfort, a drive, even power. Some people use religion to gain power and impose a control over others. We needed to invent God to solve law and order and have any purpose. If you ask me, if mankind is not God's greatest invention then God is man's greatest invention. As for me, I'm indifferent. I don't care. Let them have their beliefs."

"But what man would invent such a despicable being? God is an unjust, angry, capricious bully, ordering people around with his self-satisfying laws, killing those who had no right to be killed and allowing some to go unpunished, forgiving some, but not others, caring when he wants and shoving suffering on anyone and any nation he wishes at any time. He rewards those who don't deserve it, and it's all there in the Bible, Scabbards, it's all there. Jealous if other gods are worshipped, he's vacant, invisible. I tell you, if he's that jealous, why does he not just show up and then we'll get on believing and he won't have to be jealous any more, and we can all just get on with everything and not slosh around in the murk, annoying him in our lack of knowledge. Surely a God like this would do more to announce himself and explain his reasons. With so much pain and suffering and hatred in people, you would have thought a caring something would do something about it."

"Perhaps he has, sir, and you haven't noticed."

"I know you're deliberately being annoying."

Scabbards shrugged: "Look, you're just getting worked up about nothing. If God does not exist, then there's nothing to get worked up about. You're giving Atheism a bad name. Hardly anyone goes to church anymore, so don't trust what people say in polls and surveys; look at their commitment. People are just scared of dying, and they want this permission into Heaven by just believing in it. Then they can get on with their lives without any more worry. That's not really a belief in a god, sir; that's believing in a personal genie. The majority are Atheists and they just don't know it. They don't even care to be Agnostics. As to the Israelis: how many of them still follow the Levitical laws of Moses? As to this Esther Whyte, she's in the minority. People just like her good looks and she makes having a faith look like a fashion accessory. They don't really think much to her actual beliefs."

"As to this Esther Whyte: I don't trust her and her nasty God and her Salvation Army. And these religious buggers indoctrinate, program, brainwash their children. Now that I find cruel! Cruel, Scabbards, cruel!"

"Sounds like you've actually read the Bible."

"I did attend Sunday School. Can you believe that? I was told these children's stories and when I started asking difficult questions, they just couldn't answer and told me I needed faith. Then I read the Bible and became an Atheist. I was horrified at all the awful things that were there. And what if I die and he turned out to be Baal, then would he be jealous that I had worshipped Yahweh or would he not understand my lack of faith with the lack of evidence? And where did God come from anyway? You understand where I'm coming from?"

"Yes, sir."

"So if this Esther Whyte comes up the ranks then I will use her to make religion look foolish and the whole bloody mess is the result of everyone's mental illness and denial of it."

"But you've tried that."

"Next time, I will bring her down personally."

"I still think Sinbad will get the job done better."

"Let's just wait to see what plans the PM makes with this piano-playing doll, and I will then be able to have her come crashing down with greater drama and calamity. Wait and see, Scabbards, wait and see."

Who rolled the stone away?

Alone, David walked the High Street passing 'The White Rose,' the Public House where he and Joseph first met, and came across the address he sought: 'Mr Manning and Partners, Solicitors'. Through the window, he saw a young girl sitting behind a desk, typing, and she looked up at him as he entered her office.

"Mister Kingsley?" she asked politely.

"Yes."

"Good morning. Please take a seat."

As David sat, the secretary spoke into her desk phone, announcing David's arrival. Within seconds, an elderly man came from an internal door and introduced himself with a handshake.

"Good morning, Mister Kingsley. I'm Mister Manning." The gentleman obviously saw David's confusion and added, "I was at Joseph's grave with you. I'm sorry I didn't introduce myself, but you seemed to need some solitude."

"Yes, I'm sorry I ignored you."

"No need to apologise, but to clarify further: Elsie Manning is married to my son, Mister D. Manning. I'm Mister A. Manning. It's confusing at times, but actually I'm retired and my son now has this practice. I help him in a few matters from time to time – such as this." With this explanation, David was welcomed through to a back stairway and led to an office above the shop front.

It was well furnished, with books lining most of the walls and a large antique desk being the central feature. Everything looked as a legal room would look, but this one was old with many scratches exposing the years, as thick and enduring as the wood was.

"Please sit down, Mister Kingsley."

After both becoming settled, there was a moment of silence. David was not sure whether to start the conversation or not, but decided he was the one to listen and remained quiet.

"I am so glad to meet you, Mister Kingsley, really, although preferably under better circumstances."

David nodded.

"I've invited you here to explain something both legal and personal, and both will hopefully make you understand the full situation."

To David, still not having said a word from across the other side of the desk, Mister Manning appeared to have formulated a plan on what to say and how to say it, which left very little chance for a young, polite man to change the course of the conversation.

"I actually want to say a lot, although I thought I would not live long enough to say it all to you personally. Sorry, I'm not being very clear. You see, I am in debt to Mister Lovert – Captain Joseph Lovert – of The Salvation Army. I owe a personal gratitude to him for a long, long time."

Mister Manning smiled to himself and came back to air what he was remembering: "He came to me, as young as he was when he went to Africa with Evalynne. He wanted me to look at some legal issues for the expedition and I became curious about his reasons. When he explained that he was going as part of The Salvation Army, this started a conversation I will never forget. You see, I couldn't understand why anyone would want to give up everything in this manner for this cause, and he simply told me how much he loved Jesus and wanted to do what he believed Jesus wanted him to do. Normally no one admits to this, even if this is their true agenda. When he politely asked whether I believed in Jesus, I politely said no, I didn't, and had no reason to and that the Biblical stories of Jesus were just so ridiculous that none of them could be believed. I said this with respectful tact, I must have you know, but essentially, that's what I said. He then didn't say much, nor did it sound clever, but the little he said, changed my life. He told me that if I was serious in my conviction, then I should read the stories and analyse them, as I would a legal professional on any other witness testimony – because if what was written turned out to be true, then the consequences for me were to be extremely serious."

The solicitor paused in his talk if only to re-evaluate his own words.

"Well, quite frankly," he continued, "I don't think Joseph thought I would, but I decided this would be good practise on my lawyer skills. So I did. I read the gospels in an effort to find contradictions that would substantiate my reason to not believe." Mister Manning shook his head in wonder and disbelief. "You see, at first I thought this would be easy and I came across a few things that did seem at odds, but the more I looked and analysed it, the more my vehemence dissipated away. I finally became convinced that there is more evidence to convict Jesus of being who He said He was, and what happened, than what would be used to convict a criminal in today's trials."

Mister Manning stopped to look at David as if to see the response of his statement, but this pause was only to provoke a courteous nod and smile of acknowledgement from the young man. Then he looked out of the window, settled his thoughts and continued: "Someone who is nailed to a cross would ordinarily shout out, 'Okay, Okay, there is no God, you have it your way,' if they weren't genuine, but Jesus didn't. People don't die for a dishonourable lie – unless they are deluded or lack intelligence – but Jesus doesn't come across as either in the gospels. His immediate answers to questions and situations are nigh on perfect. No one else in politics, in history or even today, can answer so intelligently.

"And then there's His powerful affect on people. These disciples that Jesus chose were so diverse in their character and outlook that living together for three years must have been difficult, but they did – they did live together for three years. There must have been a lot of tension and annoyance and arguments that could have resulted in the group breaking apart, but suddenly, after Jesus' resurrection, they were changed from simple, confused people into strong men, united, utterly convinced of their beliefs, strong to evangelise what they can testify. This utter transformation doesn't happen from a lie.

"You see, a group of people don't die for a lie, unless *they are all* deluded – but why were there so many people who allowed their witness accounts to go unopposed as accurate? Except to say that many people couldn't oppose because they were true. All these miracles Jesus did and His teaching and His resurrection from death could not be refuted because so many people witnessed it.

"And not one disciple went to their death saying, 'by the way, we made it up'. They were all committed in the face of persecution. And serious evidence that Jesus had not risen would have been presented by the enemies and more attempt to denounce the gospel stories, but they didn't. Why not? Because they couldn't. If the disciples had stolen the body, then they knew it all to be lies. There would be no Christianity if the disciples had not been convinced that Jesus had risen from the dead. Why do all this, having acted like imbeciles not understanding the meaning of these events, and then have such a great change in boldness afterwards? Something of great significance had happened and not a lie. They even went on to perform miracles of their own in Jesus' name and taken to court over it; but the judges could not dispute the miracles because those who were healed were there with them. Instead, the judges told them to shut up about Jesus because it undermined their own authority.

"And then there's Paul and Peter in the New Testament. They suffered prison and torture for their utter commitment to Jesus and that must have come from something genuine. In their letters in the Bible, they give encouragement to fellow Christians about suffering and persecution for following Christ, to suffer as Jesus suffered, to use this to trust God, as they were being persecuted. If none of it is true, you would have thought that any compassion they would have had, would have made them write to say to give up and not to suffer. And as different as all these disciples were, they would all have given up within the first few decades anyway, because the momentum needed to tell the world, to tell the good news to everyone everywhere, was enormous. Anyone with less conviction would have given up. But they didn't. They died not knowing the effect of their faith over the next two thousand years. We must be thankful, David, for their faith and courage and commitment."

David politely nodded when Mister Manning looked at him as if for confirmation.

The gentleman continued: "There are discrepancies between the gospels, yes, but there are too many to prove they were not written in collusion, and too many consistencies to prove they were not made up. They were utterly convinced and they want you to believe what they say as if you are the sole judge in their court case. You can tell they were writing events from memory, for you to come to your own verdict.

"And Paul's conversion – how can someone so committed to wiping out the new growing Christian movement, come to be so changed? It doesn't make sense unless it's true. And why did the early church not abandon the weird, impossible to believe virgin birth if they wanted to be taken seriously? And Luke, who wrote, 'Luke', was a medic, and he didn't disclaim the virgin birth, even though he must have been under some pressure with his understanding. And then, analysing the Old Testament, you realise how all the prophesies come true in Jesus. None of it can be coincidence. Just can't."

David, now having an invitation to contribute, just nodded.

"So I became a Christian – because of Joseph. When Joseph returned from Africa, I learnt of his wife. He was a broken man. He had totally changed. I told him I had become a Christian because of his testimony, but he very circumspectly said it was God's work, not his. I felt it was my turn to help him. I helped the buying of his house here in Hallow, but that was all I felt I could do – until I had an answer to my prayer. It was not in the way I was expecting, but it did come. You see, I was also the Solicitor to Lord Sommerton, who took such a keen interest in The Salvation Army, a distant one though, but an interest at that. He had, many years prior, made a Will with my services, and he knew of Joseph's return and wanted to help. Lord Sommerton lived in the Grand Mansion. His wife died a few years before, and his children were greedy. He requested that I change his Will to give the Grand Mansion to the newly formed English Heritage, and Halcyon, the hidden building at the lake, beyond the high walls, including the vast woodland, was to be given to Joseph in secret, so as to avoid his children becoming aware. Lord Sommerton personally knew of Joseph's work in Africa, he even sponsored it, went to visit a few times as well. When Lord Sommerton died, Joseph inherited Halcyon."

"So the owner was Granddad?"

"Yes."

"All along?"

"Yes."

"I thought it was some trust thing. Why did he not tell me he owned it all?"

"Well in a certain way, Joseph did consider it a trust contract. He never considered it his own." Mister Manning then looked down on his desk at the single document between his hands: "This is Joseph's Will, David. In it, everything, the Halcyon estate, and everything that is on and in the estate, is yours including his house, here in the town."

If David had been silent until now, he was ever more now silent. When Mister Manning passed the paper across the desk, it was a while before David took it, but when he did he saw his Grandfather's writing and a sentence caught his attention: 'Much is expected from someone given much, Luke 12:48'. "It's just a shock," David said without reading more. "I mean, why me? Why not my older brother?"

"Why did God chose Jacob over his older brother Esau? Because God liked one above the other?"

"I get all of it?"

"Yes."

"To do what?"

"Lord Sommerton wanted to give Joseph the choice as to what to do with Halcyon. You now have this choice. He must have had a high regard for you. You're not convinced?"

"I'm – I don't know. So this was his secret agenda all along."

"Someone may not be dynamic and achieve much in their own estimation, but they could be that one person, who says that one thing, or does that one act at the right time that makes someone change their life, who does go on to do great things for God's Kingdom. Who's the greater? I think Lord Sommerton wanted to be that one person to Joseph with Halcyon – and I think this is what Joseph had in mind with this Will and his attempt to shape your life. You now have this inheritance to decide what to do. It's your decision. Joseph could have given it to The Salvation Army, but he didn't. Only he knows the full reason – like God having His reasons. You need to know, although this is yours by inheritance, that there have been a few devious things we have done to ensure this inheritance is genuine and also anonymous to outsiders."

"So this is not actually an – accurate inheritance?"

"Oh, no, this is truly yours in law, but – although the English Law is law, it has no spirit of its own. It's just dull, lifeless rules that try to appear out of logic and consideration to execute what is right to be done; but in truth, it can be perverted and corrupted, and guilty men can be acquitted."

"I'm not sure I know what you're saying."

"Let's just say I would rather have as few people look closely at the full set of papers to keep Halcyon secret and private for you, until you have figured out what to do with it. It's in this spirit that you have inherited Halcyon. I know I have spoken a lot. I must have tired you out by now."

"I need to let this sink in."

"Of course, what about something to drink? I haven't even offered you any coffee or tea. A solicitor of my age gets out of sequence at times. Would you like a drink?"

"No, I'm fine, thank you. I need to think about all this."

"Well, don't forget that a lot of exploring is to be done there. Spend some time enjoying discovering what there is. Have you got yourself any work yet?"

"Actually I've got myself a temporary part time job with The

Salvation Army working in a homeless hostel back in London. I'll do that for a while and stay with a friend. I won't be paid much, so Grandfather's house here will be a hindrance with upkeep, so – can I leave it with you to sell, after I've spent a little time here?"

"Of course, but remember this secrecy around Halcyon can only be put off for a while. Sooner rather than later, someone will be eager to develop there and seek out the true owner. That would be you, now."

"I think you'll find that God still owns it, as He does everything. All I have is a responsibility."

"Then I think Joseph has made a fine decision."

Norton

It was good to be back at Halcyon, thought David, although there was a spirit to the place that was missing. He stood near to the front courtyard, viewing the tarnished yet mighty building with a sense of wonder. Behind him was the statue of the woman collecting water at her soiled well. She looked as though looking into the forest, watching someone come towards her.

He walked to the huge front door and inserted the key, turning the large lock. Then a thought came to him: why was she not concentrating on the well itself?

Dropping his case, David returned to the well, looked in the same direction as her and noticed, disguised in the bushes, an overgrown fragile path, a small track heading further into the forest. In following it, it was not long when he came to an abandoned moderate building that was old by many decades, so choked with ivy that it was obvious why it had been secluded from being seen. As large as it was, David could not decide whether a small room was on an upper level for the peculiar shape of the roof.

He stood on what must at one time been a driveway to a wide double door that opened outwards, although now flooded with weeds and thistles, and secured shut by ivy. To one side, two large rusting oxyacetylene cylinder tanks, far larger than the ones he had seen in his metalwork lessons, were left abandoned, and some areas around the building had piles of scrap, rusting metal, lost in plant-life. Various windows were cracked, but all of them were smeared with dirt and dust, and none would allow any light to filter into the interior.

Fighting his way through the foliage, he came to a side door and felt for a handle within the leaves, finding something metallic and rusty. Testing the resolve to withstand a shake, David became convinced that with a little more effort, this door would relent to his pushing, but it proved him wrong. Using one oxyacetylene tank, heavy in his arms, he rammed it open and, feeling his intrigue gather pace, he entered through the broken door. In the lack of light, David could step forward only so far.

His first view was of a gloomy, dusty, black inner world of what appeared to be a discarded workshop of decades long past. Dust sprang up from his feet and he smelt the air of oil, preservatives, rotting wood and old metal. As his eyes adjusted, he realised how packed the enclosure was, with a narrow wooden, broken, untrustworthy set of stairs to the side reaching through the wooden boarding to the attic above. There were old workbenches littered with tools and boxes. Saws and hammers, strange iron bars, all sorts of devices hung from the walls in pre-designated slots and hooks.

Despite the treacherous ground being unseen, what beckoned David was a monstrous bulk that crossed the floor, as high as his waist, as wide as any good table, its length unknowable. When he reached it and touched it, he realised not only was it so dusty and dirty, but it had attracted this dust and dirt for all its stickiness, and within was a structure that was misshapen.

Determined to know, he took the risk of walking through the murk, working his way towards the large, main entrance, and, almost falling a few times, he eventually reached its inner side. Again being wood and being in a state of disrepair, David leant forward with his weight and pushed against the double door. With more weight and more force, both sides gently ripped apart, but prevented from fully doing so by the tight knitting of the ivy. Using a discarded iron bar to the side, he fought against the extensive natural stitching, and with more light now flooding the interior, he turned and was confronted with a thick, heavy, old tarpaulin concealing a strange contraption beneath it.

The tarpaulin turned out to be a compilation of many covers, all wrapped around and pulled tight with cord. Finding a blunt knife, he finally wore some cord away to allow a cover to be partially withdrawn. There before him, as strange as anything he had come across, but which made sense to what at first appeared, was one of many bikes.

Not just any bike, but a motorbike of a past racing era.

Not just any motorbike of a past racing era, but a racing bike from a past racing era in pristine condition. So oily was the cover and so oily was the bike itself, that the small amount of dirt that had succeeded in undermining the cover could be wiped off easily. He withheld touching any more in fear of damaging something that someone had tried so hard to protect and preserve.

It was with the cost of a full day that he was able to discover eleven racing motorbikes of a design which predated by decades his own birth and seven older versions which predated racing itself. He stood before them, spellbound by his discovery. Not only were they ancient, they were all Norton. There was not one of any other type. When tired in bed later that evening, David was kept awake trying to solve this significance.

There was no music echoing through the building when he awoke to the next morning. There was nothing softly filling the air with something sweet to hear, and he washed and shaved and got ready for the day, as anyone living a prior era would have done. In silence, he made breakfast; with the quiet, he ate what he prepared; alone, he relaxed in the kitchen, opening the door to the herb garden to see in the new day.

He felt like he was becoming a ghost with the estate, and he felt he was being accepted as one who belonged. It was even such that he felt Halcyon to be imperceptible to anyone else walking the woods, and his, and only his, spiritual essence was being embalmed into the stone and grass to allow his return, and to prevent trespassers ever to witness the place.

David entered the library where the grand piano stood, dusty and in want of a musician, and started to strike a few keys. Playing these notes and hearing the perfect pitch and charm of each strike of the hammer, he decided to reach for the old gramophone and placed a record on the turntable. Winding the handle, the record turned, the old funnel resonated, and music came to the air. He sat back in one of the comfortable leather high-backed chairs and listened to someone playing the piano. If only Esther could be here, he thought.

With his mind turned to Halcyon and his discovery of the garage, his only conclusion was not to rush his decisions, but to return to Jonathan and start his temporary job at the homeless hostel in London. He also decided to keep Halcyon secret from even his best friend.

It's who you know that matters

The Economy was falling fast. We, at the Foreign office, got wind of the rumours before it became public news and we worked hard to prevent its affect on our foreign aid, knowing the dangers we were risking if we relented: the increase of corrupt African Governments; reduction in lifesaving healthcare to so endangered people; diminishing food to those who were starving; more risk of people being trafficked; the harbouring of terrorism. I even gave an impassioned plea direct to the Prime Minister during a routine meeting to continue honouring our manifesto pledge. He was rather taken by my imploring, but I had no idea at the time of my affect on him until he announced the troubled news of the economy to the public and pledged to safeguard foreign aid, even though many saw this as counter-productive and severely criticised his stance. What was more was when I started to go further and pleaded for the welfare of the poor of the country, like Abraham pleading with God over Sodom and Gomorrah. I could see I had overstepped my limit, but I made my last stance of just recommending that he visit some homeless hostels. Again, little did I know he would act on this and visit one of The Salvation Army's hostels in London, the very one that David had started working at, ignorant as I was to what David was doing. Even when the Prime Minister spoke to me a week or so afterwards to thank me about the advice, I was still unknowing of the dynamic young man he spoke of. I even became envious of someone I didn't know, and then became envious of David when I did discover his identity. Imagine my shock as we met again. I was pregnant with Merry and about to give a piano lesson.

David had established an enthused group of homeless people to start making electronic gadgets in a basement. He was also encouraging some homeless youngsters to take up music, to which advert for music teachers I had applied through the Salvationist paper, ignorant he was pioneering the work. That was until he walked into a lesson of mine in the hostel's chapel to a young man called Drew, who had been suffering drug addiction. I remember starting the lesson. I was so full of my memories of Elly that poor Drew must have suffered listening to a soppy, sentimental girl. It was while I was playing the first tune which had come into my head that I sensed someone else was in the room. I turned, and there he was, David, standing there, just looking at me. I remember looking back, unsure if he could read my mind of shock at the thought that I longed to just hold him, but he just backed out of the room. This was within mere months of us arguing in Africa.

I gave Drew only a few more lessons there, as pregnant as I was, but Drew came to my house on and off for further practice. Even then, I saw to it that he had better teachers than me long term, but I was flattered when he continued to visit for more lessons with me. I hope that Drew's dedication was inspired by me, which helped him eventually become the famous pianist he is today.

As to how David's charitable homeless business with The Salvation Army became such a national success is something even now I know little about. Everything seemed triggered when David unexpectedly and astoundingly came into possession of many antique racing bikes in pristine condition from a donor who wished to remain anonymous. There were some that looked old enough to predate biking itself, and when auctioned the total came to a staggering amount that I can hardly believe to write it. It was big news for The Salvation Army, especially when learning that the designer, James Lansdowne Norton, was a Salvationist in Birmingham. I recall it was said his death was due to cancer in the 1920's.

Jonathan told me much about David when we met on the few occasions we did. He became the accountant to all of David's enterprises and growing kingdom, as it was then. Dear old Jonathan: always loyal, never getting much credit or reciprocal attention from either I or David. I suspect Jonathan had earned a fortune from his stoke-broker days and given it over to this seeming empire. There just seemed to be a lot of money that appeared. Celebrities came to respect the work, some to gain their own publicity.

David, unrecognisable to me, was able to instil motivation in others. I could not put a permanent stop to thinking about him, as David, over the years, came into our home almost on a regular basis with all the newspapers we bought or were delivered, and eventually the television. David came to be someone in the news and someone the public liked. He was also through the front door with the very thoughts I had. It was as if he was working with all his might to prove how wrong I was, how wrong I am with my judgement of him. Little did he know he spurred me to do more. The spark of inspiration can ignite powerful consequences.

A growing team of enthused teachers just appeared to teach these homeless people, and classes were given for English and Maths. Science was taught which supported the growing enterprise in electronics and funded the pioneering outreach. Now some of them have succeeded in attaining places at university. For others, a small orchestra formed from the young destitute. Some children were running away from home to purposely join which had to be tackled. With gaining professional help, the orchestra extended their tour to Europe. One homeless young girl actually became a successful author with encouragement from David and is now trying to get into film production. Other lessons were given based on more people willing to teach plumbing, plastering, and bricklaying – all because people saw the vision and wanted to help, giving up their time and using their talents and skills to be passed on to those who had become lost to unfortunate circumstances. This was achieved with David's own willingness and his motivational drive that instilled an enthusiastic following in others. People took notice and success became an unstoppable tidal wave. It then all changed.

Eventually, people began to criticise the use of the homeless as cheap labour – not that the homeless were complaining – but because certain businesses were becoming undercut, they spoke out. Industry, who had at the start welcomed David's efforts and helped in sponsorship, started to show reserve when they realised there was a threat to their own performance and tensions arose. Not that I can imagine how a team of homeless people could ever seriously take on these giants, but the perception of some marketing managers can start to make some board meetings worry over silly things. But the problems truly came when the products David championed were no longer wanted because of too much success. From this niche market and successful advertising, giving that feel-good factor of optimism that people *needed in a time of economic decline, the demand then reached a peak and it naturally declined without him adapting. There became a reduction in demand and novelty faded like an ephemeral memory. Like most sensations in fashions and trends, sometimes you need to know when to start another product or service, else money earned is only fictitious and unsupported and becomes fragile. Even the old civilisations had to know when to adapt to the changing weather in order to survive or be exterminated.*

I watched from a distance as God seemed to honour David's kingdom for the poor, but somehow, it became too successful for anything God could use. Success got in the way when David thought he was in control.

Remember Samson: a weakness can come from a strength that has gone too far.

There's more to clean

In a room, not too dissimilar to a cosy, reasonable hotel was a black teenager, sitting on his bed shaking his bedside radio. The device had finally given in to time and events, and such was his frantic shaking, that the brokenness reflected his own life and he dropped it on the bed beside him. Although his room was homely, it was still small enough to have the door open to the long corridor beyond, helping him feel his life was not a prison.

He became aware of the approach of a cleaner vacuuming the carpet, noticing the work was done fastidiously with the slow progress. Eventually a male cleaner, and a handsome one at that, was at the youngster's door working hard, unaware of being studied. This worker switched off the contraption, removed the full tank of dust and left, leaving behind the vacuum cleaner. A while after, the man returned to wrestle the unit back into its place.

The teenager could bear it no longer: "You haff to unclip the clip more – by ya finga."

"Thank you." The voice was friendly, with handsomeness in tone and a happy melody that was genuine.

"I wish someone can take my dir' away," said the young boy.

The cleaner looked up again, at poise to switch on the suction: "Sorry?"

"I wish someone could clean my life like tha'."

The cleaner was visibly, suddenly, at a loss for words, or at least hesitant to say anything, but then he asked quite simply, "You okay?"

He nodded.

The cleaner noticed the black radio on the bed and motioned to it from the door: "Something wrong?"

The boy did not reply.

"I heard you getting upset and shaking something. Want me to look at it?" Without any invitation, the cleaner came into the room. "Perhaps it just needs the batteries changed."

"I did tha'! I keep changin' them!"

"Oh."

"I've had it ages. Now it's fffuc- – it's busted."

"Oh."

"Someone threw it ou'. I didn't steal it! I pu' ba'eries init an' it worked."

"Here, let me have a look."

"Who are you? Einstein? It's broke!"

"Well I may just mop the floors around here, but I do have a degree in electronics."

"What! Man! What you doin' here mopping the fu-, the bleedin' floors, man?"

"Perhaps I can fix it. I expect something's dislodged or burnt, but I could solder it back if you want."

"You'd do that?"

"Yeah, sure, why not – be fun – if I can get the parts and tools and space to do it."

"You know, I'd really apprecia'e tha'."

"You here tomorrow?"

"Won' see me goin' nowhere."

It was the next day, and the cleaner did return as he said he would carrying a case. He knocked on the open door and surprised the black youngster: "Hi, I've come with some bits to fix your radio."

"Thanks, man. I can't stand the fffu-, this shh-, the silence, man."

The cleaner entered and went to the small table where the radio had been placed. "Okay, let's see what we can do. Can I use this table?"

"Yeah!"

The cleaner sat down on the solitary chair and rummaged through his case, and then produced his tools to start work.

"I'm Noah, Noah Kofee."

"Good to meet you, Noah."

Noah became quietly upset with the cleaner when not venturing his own name, as focused as he was on the wretched, broken radio.

"Okay, let's see what we can do."

With the radio case now off, Noah was eager to make conversation. "So wha' ya doin' here, man?"

Still persistent with the electronics, he mumbled a reply: "I've just got back from Africa – "

"Africa!"

"Yep. Spent two years there working on an orphanage with The Salvation Army."

"Really?"

"Really."

"So where's this electro know-how come from then?"

"London University."

"University?"

"Yep, I got a degree in electronics and then I worked for a medical company developing future surgical technology in cancer treatment for – I don't know – five years."

"Wow! Man! Impressive!"

"Not really: they made me redundant and squeezed out all my confidence – as well as my parents divorcing, and my big brother going AWOL."

"Sorry, mate."

"I had the chance to go to Africa to – ." He looked up from his work, turned to Noah and said, "I suppose, find myself."

"That's great, you know."

The cleaner switched on the soldering iron and wrestled loose a wire between his tweezers, then started on some of the burnt components. "I hope the fire alarm won't go off."

"You're some wiz. Wha' ya doin' with the likes of me, man?"

"Why not, Noah?"

"I'm a nobody, a nothin'. If I exist it's because I exist as a problem, nothin' more."

"Here's a burnt capacitor. I think this bit got wet for some reason."

"Because I'm homeless, you fffuc-, you idiot. I've lived on the streets. I ran away. I couldn't stand livin' at 'ome anymore. Dad drunk, Mum being bea'en, me being bea'en, shou'ed at, ignored, social service wan-, workers being arseholes, school being a bunch of ffffuc-, a bunch of – . So I ran away."

"Have you ever been back?"

"Nope, never goin' back."

"Perhaps things have changed."

"Perhaps Dad's dead. Perhaps Mum's dead."

"And here's a burnt resistor. I wonder what value it was." It was held up for Noah to see using the tweezers, and intrigued, Noah leant forward to view and eventually took it.

"Wish I'd have gone to a proppa school."

"You're still young, you still have a chance."

"You being funny, mate?"

"No."

"Man, you seriously crazy. You should be on stage. There's loads you can be doin' instead of 'ere." Noah went silent and then, as if compelled, went on to explain the reasons for his limited choices: "I was gettin' into street crime an' guns. My mates raped a puss-, a girl, and I ran away. They're looking for me 'cause no one runs, no one."

This time, the worker stopped and looked at Noah. He said nothing, but his concerned look said it all.

"It's all right mate, we all have a ssshi- , we all have trouble, mate."

"If you were able to get back into school, would you do it?"

"School? – Yeah, man, but who's gonna teach me? I don' have any fuc- , no brains."

"What about learning how to solder?"

"Solder?"

"Yeah, solder. Here, fix your own radio."

Noah swapped places with the expert. In the quarter of an hour it took to describe the electronic parts, Noah remained engrossed.

"There, how was that?"

Noah shook his head, "No clue, man, I was nowhere near ya."

"I can explain it better with some paper."

"Don' have any."

From the door came the voice of a young man, "Want some paper?"

Noah looked at him and nodded: "Drew! Yeah, man, have any?"

The young man was gone and returned a few moments later with some scrap pages and a pen.

"Thanks," replied Noah. "Want to have a lesson from the Teach here, Drew?"

"Yeah, why not?"

The two made room for Drew and the lesson commenced with diagrams of electronics and motions of the pen, pointing to the parts.

All three were there for some time with the lesson turning to the techniques of soldering, which Noah was conscientious and took his time to get right.

The next person at the door was a Salvation Army Officer: "I thought I'd smelt something burning."

The cleaner looked sheepish: "Sorry, Captain Purkiss."

"We're fixin' my radio," replied Noah, as if the building could burn in fair comment, but his radio was worthy of resuscitation.

"That's okay guys," replied the Captain, "but I need to frown on it as we should be as safe and sound as possible."

"Is there another, better place we can go?" Drew asked.

"The basement? But that'll need clearing out."

The three looked at each other as if to confer their thoughts, and then looked at Captain Purkiss.

"I'm sorry, guys, but there's all sorts of things down there."

Drew being optimistic then asked, "Can we have a look?"

The Captain unlocked the door, switched on the lights that hardly illuminated anything, and allowed the three to enter to see the basement. It was old, dingy and low, as they viewed it behind banisters from a small wooden landing. The stairs to the side leading down to the dusky room had the best of the lighting, but what could be seen were dented brass instruments that in part had started to corrode. Shelves of books and piles of paper manuscripts lined some of the walls, and battered tables and chairs of all sorts of designs were piled to one corner. It had not been used for many years, but that did not dissuade them from using the creaking stairs to have a better look.

"It's not very useable," said Captain Purkiss. "I wouldn't want anyone down here with this poor light."

"Wha' if we hav' betta light?" asked Noah, now seeing the room with a dreamlike potential.

Drew looked at some of the instruments. He picked up a battered cornet and made a note. The sound shocked him as to how bad it was.

The others in the room were shocked that he had made a note at all.

Drew made a few more notes, but then put the instrument back: "Think I prefer the piano."

"Can we at least see if we can fix this radio down here?" asked the cleaner. "It won't take much to make some room and use some of these tables and chairs. There's a socket over there which we can use, if we can get a lamp."

Captain Purkiss pondered for a while.

"I know there's health and safety, but we're not going to be here long."

"Okay, let me get you a lamp."

By the time the Captain returned, the basement had an area cleared for a table and three chairs and a cleaner discussing something technical with Noah and Drew. So involved, the Captain received little thanks when switching on the tall-standing lamp for them. It was the passing of an hour that Captain Purkiss returned to find the lesson was still enticing two young men to be electronic technicians. So attentive, they never noticed the Salvation Army Officer appear or leave.

"Okay Noah," said the teacher, "just solder the last component and we can see if it works."

With the last component now fitted but without a signal, they all left the basement to enter the lounge area, where others sat and talked among themselves.

Noah switched on the radio, turned up the volume, and a blast of music came from it. "Yeah, Man! You did it! You did it, boss!" shouted Noah with excitement.

"Noah, just call me David."

"Okay, boss!" Noah, clearly enthused, started changing the stations to hear the Prime Minister explaining the state of the economy from a previous question. When the station remained unchanged, everyone started to complain, but Noah continued to listen.

"This is going to be a tough few years," the Prime Minister was saying, "I'm not saying it won't be – ."

The interviewer interrupted: "But the facts say it will be decades, we're going into another recession, and Europe won't be there to pull us out as they have their own crisis. America is in a poor shape and China's productivity is going to fall. Tough is not the word for it, Prime Minister."

"It will be a struggle, yes, but this mess was caused by the last Government."

"But it's now your responsibility to correct it. You were voted in because you wanted the responsibility and you convinced the country you could do it, and nothing is getting better."

"I have vowed to get this country going again."

"With inspirational leadership? With inspirational Government? Isn't that the crux of these problems? There is no inspiring leadership from you. And you tell us of more cuts? Is that inspiring? You've already mentioned about the public sector, but we are going to have more deep cuts than that, surely. Where is all this money going to come from to get industry working again? Unemployment is going to increase. Are you going to tax the rich more?"

"We are all going to have to pull our weight, and those who are parasitical on the welfare state need to be assessed as to their legitimacy of being in receipt of people's hard-earned money – "

It was at this point that Noah turned off the radio: "Tha' means we're buggered."

Propelled by the jet fuel of Inspiration

David stood in front of nineteen teenagers in the cramped basement of the hostel, that was now tidy and arranged as though a poor electronics workshop. The chairs and desks, which the group used to settle themselves for David's speech, were ready for soldering and wiring, with soldering irons, a selection of voltmeters and coils of wire available. No one took much notice of the odd assortment of boxes to the side.

They all looked at David, who continued to stand as if to make an announcement, but he never seemed to want to start. Instead, he looked at them all with arms crossed, rolled-up sleeves and a pensive, almost commanding, confident stance. He then picked up a Bible from the side, turned to a page and read: "Two Kings, chapter seven verse one: 'four lepers sitting at the gate – 'why are we sitting here waiting to die?' said one'." Then David closed the book with a bang, making everyone jump. "I know your lives have been a struggle. I know each of your stories. I know life has been against you, and I know most of you have wanted to just sit life out – but, to what end? Just to die? We can either get better or we can get bitter."

In David's pause, nobody replied.

"I want to give you a chance to make something, make something work and create some self-esteem for each other. I have designed and can make radios and clocks and gadgets that we can sell and make into a business. There are companies who, if I can convince them your skills are good enough, will contract out some wiring and soldering work to us which could lead to fulltime employment. There's potential for us, if we really want it and work hard for it."

Still no one said anything.

"Because the question is, *are* we worth it? Are *you* worth it?"

"Where's all this money coming from?" asked one lad.

"I've found some collectable antiques that can be auctioned to get started and I'm working on some more ideas. I'm in the process of designing voice-activated snooze alarms. You'll have to have some faith in me."

Noah, who was standing to the side, then asked, "Are ya sure t'is gunna work? Cuz none of us haff done t'is before."

"So this may be new," continued David. "None of you feel up to it. None of you feel confident. All of you lack self-esteem. We can all be addicted to all sorts of wrong ways, distorted perceptions, that gets us down and holds us back and see our lives crumble apart. We magnify and see events out of proportion and predict the worse and give up before we begin – because we've allowed being beaten too many times in the past. We rate ourselves against those who are better and discredit what we can do. We focus on the negatives and discount the positives. And that's been my problem."

They all started to look around each other, measuring the common reaction; but the common reaction was to remain sceptical, pensive and lacking confidence.

"So?" said someone.

"So! What is a strength? Something that has hidden weaknesses. What is a weakness? Something that can be turned into a strength to overcome weakness. Weakness can present opportunity, development of skills and understanding. Most people never realise their potential because of feelings of inadequacy and low self-esteem or ignorance, but if we did all the things we are capable of doing, we would literally astound ourselves. Never mind what others do; do better than yourself, beat your own record from day to day and *you are* a success. Don't you have a drive to have better opportunities? You've all told me your woes."

They all continued to watch David with closed emotions.

David continued with his speech: "Success is impossible unless you are at least willing to start. I can train you all, and in turn, you can train others. Are you in? Are you in it for the long term? Short-term intensity can't replace long-term commitment."

One male became angry: "Who are you? Who are you to think you know us? That you can help us?"

"You know who I am. I've spent time listening and getting to know you all here. You know I have."

"Doesn't mean to say you know me."

One of the girls turned to him, also annoyed: "Shu' up, will ya!" She turned to David and motioned to continue.

The male pushed the chair he was sitting on as he got up, deliberately to make a disharmonious noise as he left the room. He was followed by the male sitting next to him, both looking dissatisfied and using foul language to say they had heard it all before.

"You all know I'm a Christian," continued David, not perturbed, "and I'm not wanting you to drop everything and see things my way, but I see God works best when I admit my weaknesses. Throughout the Bible, God turned nobodies into people with potential – because God is stronger than our problems if only we believe Him. God's gift to you is the potential in you – your gift back is to use that potential."

Another two males walked out, disgruntled, also using foul language.

"And anyway, God isn't fully interested in our confidence and achievements. He's more interested in our integrity, endurance, commitment and reputation. Use brokenness, depression even, as its own medicine to learn to rely on God. He loves the contrite, broken, humble heart of someone who is learning to rely on Him. To be broken is to have the hard ground of your life ploughed over with heavy industrial machinery to make the soil good and fruitful. From that, with the right learning and mindset, anything is possible to grow."

They all looked at him as if he was just an animated object to just watch.

"I want to take this further," he continued confidently, "and get funding for an education for you to learn and pass national exams, learn a trade, learn to play musical instruments – anything. With God, we can have big plans, and I don't want to sit around life, like a leper, waiting to die like there's no purpose to anything."

David paused to study the group, but in this sudden stop, they started to disassemble, noisily and frivolously, as if the class bell had been rung. They all started discussing something and laughing, and David was not sure if there was humour being made at his expense.

With this, three girls sidled up to him. "We'll give it a go," said one of them.

"You're really crazy," said the second one.

"And we like crazy," said the third.

"You will?"

They nodded and left him, saying they would be back tomorrow to start, even though David had not set a date. It was with this informal milling that all the others in an ad hoc fashion gave their appreciation and gave an interest to start. They all eventually disappeared and only David remained with Noah and Drew.

"Good speech," said Drew quietly.

"Thanks."

"Opportunities like this don't ever come along, not for an ex-drug addict, like me, but I'm never gonna be into all this electronics."

"Yep, I know, I gathered. I'm putting out feelers for anyone out there who could teach you to play the piano."

"You are?"

"You told me already you wanted to learn, so I put out an advert. Let's see what happens."

"Wow, thanks."

Then Noah slapped David on the shoulder: "I'm with you, boss. I'm in."

"Well, I'm banking on God being the boss. You want to be the supervisor though?"

"Sure thin' boss."

Amos against the Super-Rich

When designing and building circuits, they had to be as neat as they could for David's sense of pride and in general he felt it was good when things were clean and tidy. He considered it one of his better traits, although others could see it as an obsession, particularly for David's new fanaticism to clean the street just outside the hostel. He would get so far along the pavement, look back, see the lack of rubbish and be proud, and then pack up for the morning. Others thought he was strange, particularly when he would wander further away from the entrance, each following day. Little did they know it was also a strange opportunity for David to dwell on things and yet still feel he was being productive and accomplishing something.

Wearing his old, blue boiler suit, David was brushing the street when Noah came from behind looking bewildered.

"Wha' ya doin'?" Noah asked confused and almost disdainful.

David did not look up, but continued sweeping: "I'm cleaning the street. What I always do in the morning."

Noah was incredulous: "Wha', all of it?"

"Just around the area."

"But the 'ouse is down there, man! We need a taxi back!"

"Just want to do a good job."

Noah looked suspiciously at David: "Is t'is because the Prime-Minister guy is comin' today?"

David instantly stopped his work in shock: "What?"

"That Prime Minister, tryin' to get a good image."

"The Prime Minister? Here? At the hostel?"

"Yeah, why? Wha's the problem? Is this why the stree' gotta be clean? I wouldn't haff bovered, mate. In fact, he's not here, he's down there – at the 'ostel. Why's this bit need be clean?"

Leaving the rubbish bags, David gave Noah his broom and started rushing back to the hostel.

Noah, not knowing what to do, followed in pursuit, carrying the broom.

"When's he going to arrive?"

"He's 'ere, wen' in ten minutes ago. People are askin' where you got to."

"We can't let him know about the business."

"Wha'! You a crazy man? Tis the best thin' goin'."

Arriving at the entrance, David noticed the executive car parked to the side, a driver in wait, and a police escort to one side. He bounded up the front steps, through the entrance and marched towards the nearest corridor, heading to the basement.

"Wha's got you so messed up?" asked Noah trying to keep alongside.

"Because he might shut us down. I don't trust people with power and their secret scheming, these bureaucrats and Pharisees."

"What! No way, man! People be too pissed wiv' him if he does anything as ssshh-."

It was too late. The Prime Minister was suddenly at the other end of the corridor, politely being escorted by Captain Purkiss towards the lounge area. Now being exposed, Captain Purkiss motioned to David with a friendly greeting as he ushered the Premier into the lounge to meet more residence and was then out of view. It was this chance that David and Noah needed to reach the door to the basement and they entered at a rushed pace, closing the door behind them. There below him, were ten young men, soldering away. Becoming aware of his rushed appearance, they all looked up at the landing wondering what the concern was.

Descending the stairs, David came to stand in the middle with Noah to his side, and he confused them with his irrational tone: "Do you know who's here?"

"The Prime Minister?" answered one of them.

"Yes!" David looked at them, realising none of them understood his agitation.

"Don't get too excited," replied another, "None of us are bothered."

"You don't understand."

"Wha's there to understan'?" answered Noah. "Some suit comes to get his pictures in the news looking like he cares."

"We don't pay tax!"

"But we've only been going a few months," replied another.

"We're no' earning much to pay tax," Noah added.

David was full of concern. "I don't know how the system works. And I don't trust administrations and systems and bureaucracy, where they make people redundant, write people off; where people sit at desks and nonchalantly tick boxes against us; executives who talk in ideals and keep hidden their real plans or have no clue as to anything practical. Destructive things happen to people because of it and no one gets to truly know why."

"Oh," was Noah's reply, "because nonchalantly sounds real bad."

"So what do we do?" asked one of the workers.

"I don't know. Just be quiet."

"Does the Cap'in know no' ta show t'is place?"

"I don't know."

It was then that the door slowly creaked open and they all looked up to view whoever was about to discover their covert, illegitimate venture. Even when the Prime Minister materialised and looked at them all, they continued to look culpable within their otherwise blank looks. They were as statues with guilty faces, looking as though being caught masterminding an elaborate bank robbery.

With a pleasant air, the Prime Minister nodded with appreciation and acknowledgement: "Well you lot seem entrepreneurial."

"We haven't started this long," said Captain Purkiss from behind, "but they're all keen to learn new skills. It's more of a trial that's going well."

"May I have a look?" The Prime Minister descended the stairs and looked around the benches to see radios and clocks being made, nodding with approval. "Very good. How did this start?"

They all looked at David as if urging him to say something, but he appeared unsure, baffled, shy, and was reticent to say anything.

Captain Purkiss motioned at David to say something, but had to introduce him to provoke a reply: "This is David Kingsley, he studied electronics and just started this little project."

All David could do was to shrug. Then he began to splutter as if wishing to have been prepared and rehearsed: "I – we – just – it just happened because one of the guys had a radio that – well, it didn't work, so with – with some tools, got it working, and – and people got interested and started making some of our own – and things."

"Very good – started from nothing then," nodded the Prime Minister.

There was silence as the basement continued to look guilty.

The Prime Minister nodded again with not much else to say and felt awkward in his interruption that evidently had not been planned: "Well, I see you're all being industrious – very commendable everyone."

Still no one said anything, although people started to melt down their statue-stillness with restlessness.

"What are they?" he asked, looking at David.

"They're clock-radios," answered Noah.

"Oh, very good." The Prime Minister understood the nervousness of the youngsters and gave a small enigmatic smile. "Well, thank you very much, and a good day to you all. We all must crack on." With that, he climbed the stairs and was gone.

Noah looked at David, whom was confounded and lost, and wished he had seen something better from his leader. It was then that David, suddenly looking fierce and defiant, stormed up the steps with everyone becoming more puzzled, provoking them to follow.

They were all within moments in the front lobby when David stopped and spoke out to the back of the Prime Minister as he was about to leave: "Don't shut us down!"

It was at this abrupt comment that the Prime Minister turned and looked at David.

"Our enterprise," continued David, "don't shut us down."

The comment shocked everyone with David's earnest expression of both boldness and defiance, totally unlike he had been a few moments before.

The Prime Minister at first looked blank and unsure how to reply, but then smiled and said, "I don't intend to. What would possess me to?"

Noah saw the same smile as David: a smile that a politician could give but possibly not mean.

To the Prime Minister, he was trying to cover over his confusion.

"Your welfare reforms, your protection of those who earn millions, your preference to those who are privileged against those who are not, whether you're conscious of it or not."

It was David's expression and boldness that made Noah see how important this had become, allowing no chance of anything to hinder, stall or prevent this endeavour. With what followed, Noah became enamoured with this cleaner.

"I'm not for any particular preference," the Prime Minister continued.

"Your policies are, the culture of society is, the force of discrimination and disparagement, sustaining bias and prejudice, the indifference to the poor and destitute."

"I assure you – "

"And I assure you! You are wrong! You're wrong until you have spent time with the underprivileged. It's a mathematical proven economic principle that the economy improves when people work hard for themselves *and* for others – not when they work hard and keep the proceeds to themselves. What does it profit a man to live in a castle surrounded by poverty? You allow the super-rich to our wealth, but we all work hard and everyone has stresses and responsibilities."

"The previous Government – "

"No! You asked for this opportunity! You! Not previous Governments! Only with true, worthy leadership will this country be truly worthy of being great. People perish where there is no vision."

"I came here to understand and support."

"But you don't support – nor do you understand! The system works against these people!" David's fervent anger was propelling what was becoming a speech. He became more and more animated with his arms and hands as he spoke in his increasing forthrightness. "I listen to them, day in, day out. The system doesn't care! People don't care! Society doesn't care! Cheap labour is treated as if it were water from a leaky tap, valueless, over-looked, passed-over. They lose self-esteem, deteriorate mentally and physically, lose their will to care. We need to tackle their hopelessness, like the drive you have to tackle the national economic hopelessness. Gaining new skills is not just a means of getting homeless people into employment. It builds confidence, gives a sense of purpose and achievement, improves mental health and well-being. Investing in learning and skills for homeless people can have multiple benefits for public spending. I believe that anyone, given the opportunities, given the drive, the motivation, the encouragement to achieve, to win, in education, in business, in talent, in inventiveness, can become an expert – anyone of any background. Intelligence and skills are a process, not a thing; a verb, not a noun. Expertise is not hardwired at conception to be an innate aptitude – but a collection of developing skills driven by the interaction of drive and opportunity, but it needs inspiration, embracing failure and setbacks as a high-speed propellant to learn and do better; not be defeated.

"I know there is untapped talent in the people you have written off! I will not allow you to go against these people! There is massive potential within them to make this country great as much as any other citizen. Whether cleaning the streets or being Prime Minister – God sees both jobs as important and looks at the character! There is just as much pride in keeping a street clean, as there is keeping a country clean. See that justice is done! God wants oceans of justice and rivers of fairness, but our justice is veering off, ploughing the sea."

In all this while, no one interrupted, no one looked away, no one moved, as captivated as they were by David's anger and spontaneous eloquence and conviction. They still looked at him even after he had finished his strong, heartfelt speech and watched him looking at the Prime Minister who was not the principal member of the scene.

David said his one last comment in the silence that followed, now partially out of breath: "I just want as many people as possible to work to have Heaven on Earth as much as possible – in this fallen reality."

All the Prime Minister could do, knowing he could not produce such a response to counter the success of David's resounding, fluent speech, was to nod in acknowledgement and respect. Eventually, all he said was a short sentence: "I'm afraid you place too much emphasis in one man solving your observations, Mister Kingsley. All I can do is support you however I can."

A silence reappeared.

It was Noah who spoke up: "Sell you one?"

"How much?"

"We've a sale. Can let one go for a fiv-ah."

"Fiver it is."

With that, in front of them all, the Premier received his clock-radio that Noah had been holding, in exchange for the agreed cost, which Noah received.

"I do assure you: all the best for your future." The Prime Minister turned and left.

After having been mesmerised, the crowd in the lobby started cheering and clapping.

"That was truly incredible," exclaimed Captain Purkiss to David. "Where did that come from? I never knew you had that power in you."

"I don't know, but it was Noah who took the opportunity."

"No, I mean that speech."

"I'm not sure. Tell me, how many enquired about that piano teaching opportunity for Drew?"

"Just one. She said she can help out for a while, while she's pregnant. She seemed keen when we spoke on the phone. But you wanted someone more long-term."

"Well ask her to come in and let's get this teaching effort started. See if we can attract anyone who will teach anything."

"Sure. What about funds?"

"I don't know. I was hoping they would do it as a sense of challenge, free of charge, with the reward that someone else's life is made better as the result."

"Well, after that, anything's possible. You'd make a terrific Salvation Army Officer."

"And I think we'll need an accountant."

"I'll find one."

"Actually, I think I have someone in mind; someone who has big connections with the City and has a passion."

Elly's Fortune

Captain Purkiss, sitting behind the reception desk at the hostel, looked up to see a young, pregnant, blonde woman looking down at him with a welcoming smile. He was taken aback with how attractive she was, but he instantly covered it over with his own returned smile.

"Good morning," she said.

"Good morning! Esther Whyte?" he replied.

"Yes, that's right. I'm here for the piano teacher position you advertised in *The Salvationist*."

"Yes, of course, we spoke on the phone last week. Thank you for coming. You want to see the room and meet the young man?"

"Yes please."

"Well, follow me and I'll introduce you."

Esther followed Captain Purkiss along a corridor until arriving at a room that was a mixture of a lounge and an informal chapel with a side table having a collection of books, most of which were hymnbooks and Bibles in varying grades of newness or tatters. To the side was an upright battered piano.

"Make yourself at home and I'll go and get Drew."

"Drew?"

"That's the young man: Andrew Last. He prefers to be called Drew."

Now alone, Esther went to the piano, settled herself there and lifted the lid from the keys. Flexing her fingers, she was about to play when Captain Purkiss re-appeared with a thin young man with long, dark hair, worn jeans and a roll-neck jumper.

"Esther, this is Drew; Drew, this is Esther. She's agreed to start giving you a few lessons to see what you make of it."

Drew was inhibited and Esther saw his shyness, not expecting this initial reaction. "Pleased to meet you, Drew," she said and stood up to shake hands.

The Captain made to leave: "Well, I'll leave you both to it." With that, the two were alone.

At first, neither knew what to say.

Esther could see her pupil was nervous. In the silence, she placed a chair alongside the pianist's and ushered Drew to sit.

Drew politely sat on the adjacent chair.

"You can't learn the piano sitting there, Drew. Sit here."

Feeling like he had made a mistake, Drew sat at the piano and Esther sat beside him.

"I use to have lessons," said Esther, "so I know what it feels like."

Drew continued to look at her, his thoughts obscured by his lack of a response.

"Not much of a promising start for someone attempting to teach someone else."

"It's nice that someone can be bothered," was all Drew said.

"Well, let's get started."

"Aren't you the one on TV? From that Sudan famine?"

"Well, I – well, yes."

"Don't you work for the Government?"

"I work for the Foreign Office."

"But you're teaching me the piano?"

"Well, I'm trying to. We haven't got far." Esther smiled as to apologise for her poor lesson.

"What shall we do, then?"

"Just rest your fingers on the keys – as if to start a gentle recital. Imagine you are confident and comfortable and you've been doing this a long time. How would you sit? What would be your posture? What would you be feeling? Imagine you are this grand-piano maestro, who has played to large, packed audiences, and you've just found some time to be alone and just play for the pleasure."

Drew was at first unresponsive, continuing to look mesmerised by her. "Wow," he softly said. "A first lesson, an' all." He turned to the keys, placed his fingers lightly there, sat upright, adjusted his posture, realigned his fingers, drew in a fresh breath, and then did nothing, other than to turn back to Esther.

"How does it feel?" she asked, looking at his posture.

"Okay."

"You need your shoulders more relaxed. You look like they're hunched. You don't want to become the hunchback of Notre Dame. That's better. You look good now. Looks like you've been doing this for years with just sitting better. Now whatever keys your fingers are on, just play them as if you are contemplating writing a melody that's coming from your calm emotions."

There was a slight pause, and then Drew played his chord. The strangeness of the sound echoed around the room and faded away. He turned to Esther in the silence.

Neither knew what to say but it did not take long for Drew to start chuckling, and Esther started to laugh as well.

"So much for being a maestro," he said. "That sounded creepy." It was in that one note that Drew had suddenly appeared to be opened. His shyness evaporated and he became settled.

"Still music though. Compared to my first note, you're already a maestro." Esther took a few moments to explain the best way to be positioned on the chair, the manner of the hands and fingers, giving reasons behind the advice, and then started to explain the best way to be mentally prepared. In all this while, Drew was attentive, adjusted himself accordingly and copied Esther's example as she demonstrated what she was saying. Now having fingers positioned, Drew played a new chord, which sounded like he had in fact been doing this for years.

"I have to admit this is not my exact first lesson," said Drew.

"I thought there was something behind you."

"I did get some moments at school, before I ran away. Not that they were lessons."

In Drew's pause, Esther just nodded.

"My family life was – it was just – total – abuse and shouting and anger and being told-off for – for rubbish things – and – it was abuse and hell – and bullying. I found I could escape when playing the piano, when I could creep into the music room at school. I've always had a passion for it ever since – but you don't get many pianos on the street and – and I got involved in – things, my demons – which I'm still battling."

Again, Esther sympathetically nodded.

"I can't read music. I've tried to learn, but, well, other things were my battles."

"I'll bring along a good book, but until then, just practise feeling comfortable sitting there. If you're passionate about spending long hours in practice, it's an investment to learn to get comfortable earlier rather than later. Can you do that?"

"Sure!"

"Experiment with the keys, playing chords, playing them with all sorts of emotions that you can create. Don't do anything more. Eventually I'll teach you how to move your hands and fingers, along with reading the music."

There was a silence between them for a moment.

"How much is this going to cost?" finally asked Drew.

"Cost?"

"Cost."

"A lot of sweat and tears and hours and energy, a lot of passion, toil, a longing to get things perfect, to be happy making mistakes and a satisfying drive to correcting them, seeing failure as something to learn from, having self-motivation, aiming for the ultimate best – dedication, perseverance, devotion, to care for your developing skill as it grows."

"I meant you."

"Me?"

"Your charge?"

"You mean, payment? Nothing."

"Nothing?"

"Nothing – I was taught for free by my Salvation Army teacher and to honour that, I'll do the same for you. My piano playing was also for my own demons. She understood that more than me."

"Oh."

"Take it that you pay me back by practising and growing your expertise. Nothing will come of this if you're not prepared to put in the effort, or have the wrong attitude. You need to have a healthy, hard working determination, but don't become so compulsive or obsessive or addicted that it totally takes over your soul. Nothing is worth losing your sense of wholeness, or becoming imprisoned in being only able to do just one thing. You control it; it does not control you. Make sure all your time at the piano is purposeful and productive and always enjoyable and satisfying. There's nothing more infuriating than spending countless hours at the keys with aimless practice. See to it that every hour is improving your own standards. There's no such thing as pure natural talent. Those who succeed are those who don't quit. Even Mozart became who he became because of his circumstances and determination and hard work."

"Really?"

"Really, and that's everything Elly taught me when I was first starting."

"Wow," Drew said again softly. "Want to play something for me?"

"Why not? What can I remember?"

Nineteen males, sat at desks soldering under much-improved lighting in the basement, required a lot for them to be quiet, even when focused on their work. David, sitting among them was just the same, and they all were making pleasant fun of Drew and the faint yet tortured piano noises coming down to them. Then their attention was aimed at Noah, whom David was coaxing into being the supervisor of them all. Noah, initially being reluctant, became encouraged with everyone cajoling him, and he went to each desk discussing progress and making everyone laugh with his wit.

It was during a bout of laughing that David stood up abruptly from his desk, as if a spark had ignited him to do so, and he had to silence them all with his harsh admonishment. Everyone instantly became quiet, more to the effect of wanting to understand why the need to be hushed and to wonder the reason for his sudden, stern seriousness. They all looked at David as he tried to hear the air surrounding them.

Then they all heard it: an exquisite, tranquil, melody that floated serenely through the walls, into the ground, up into the air and commanded people to stop and listen, even to pay reverent respect.

"It's beautiful," breathed David.

"Wha' is it?" asked Noah.

"Debussy: 'The Girl with the Flaxen Hair'. I haven't heard it in years."

"Well Drew's improved, then," came someone which provoked laughter from the others.

David ignored them, bounding upstairs to follow the music. He got to the open door of the Chapel and stopped, spellbound by the attractive young woman with her back towards him.

Drew, sitting beside Esther, turned to David and then back at Esther, with her unaware.

Esther was within her music. After the last few final notes, she composed herself and turned to Drew for a comment, as if he had become the teacher.

With Drew being so quiet, Esther realised that someone else was near and she turned and saw David standing by the door.

When the shock had dissipated, Esther stood, picked up her handbag and, speechless, politely made her way to the door to stand in front of David, whose stance barred her exit.

Then, in concerted movement, David stepped to the side as Esther left the room, and a few moments later, he sauntered away.

The effect of each other, on each other, was evident. Drew, having seen a state of kindness and respect showing in their eyes, yet sadness in their demeanour and deportment, knew to keep this encounter to himself.

Missing a White Rose

"What are you looking for?" asked Mark from their bedroom door, watching Esther furiously fumble through her draw of jumpers. "You're making a bit of a noise."

"Oh, I'm just – looking – for my nicest jumper."

"It's not cold, is it?"

"No, I just wondered where it was."

"Well it's here, on the top."

"Oh, oh yes, of course."

"Are you okay?"

"I'm sure being pregnant gets my brain in a mess." Esther, very pregnant and very due, stood up carefully to straighten her back. She then saw Mark's thoughtful look at her. "What are you thinking?"

"I was going to do this on Saturday, but I'm too eager to show you now. Come with me."

"Why? Where?"

Mark grabbed her hand and led Esther to a closed door.

Standing there, Mark allowed the excitement to well up in Esther like a girl at Christmas.

"Have you finished?" she asked rapidly.

"You want to see it?"

"Have you really finished it?"

"Yep!"

"Show me then!"

"Not without your eyes closed."

"Okay, I've got my eyes closed."

"Can I trust you?"

"Come on, come on! You can trust me!"

"Can I really trust you?"

"Yes! Yes! Get on with it! Look, my eyes are closed. Can I trust you to lead me into a room with my eyes closed?"

"Well if it's a trust thing, then – ."

Mark held his hand over Esther's eyes, unlocked the door using a key gained from his pocket and led her into the room by being close behind. Being awkward but laughing, they shuffled forward, and when Mark took away his hand, Esther could not contain her surprise and awe. The room had been painted into a country scene, with the lower half being of golden fields and the other half being blue sky and waterfalls from hills. The ceiling had swirls of clouds and to the corner was an orange circle with a yellow ray surround. All round the room were cows, sheep, tractors, flowers, trees, birds, bees, hills and lakes. It was not to a great professional standard, but enough for a proud father-to-be to have taken six months to create.

Esther gasped: "I never knew you could paint. Did you get someone in?"

"Esther! Really! It's awful. My Dad paints far better. I tried to get some perspective, but it just looks like the cow is bigger than the tractor and some bees are bigger than some birds."

"It's amazing. It's great. What's that though?"

"The farmhouse."

"Oh – it looks more like the Temple Mount in Jerusalem."

Mark just shrugged.

Esther embraced her husband and kissed him: "I do love you."

"Really? Even though my cows are bigger than my tractors?"

All the while they giggled, the old disintegrating white rose Esther looked for was now somewhere hidden in their daughter's room. Mark knew that in some deep way, Esther did love him; but David and her work were higher, even though she consciously did not know it.

Years of being Merry

With the sunshine broadening its light across a sky of dissipating clouds, Sergeant Richards left the kitchen and, drying a garden chair, settled himself near to the kitchen door at a small, rusting, genteel table. His reading was now of immersion, like that of reading a riveting novel, with no longer any resolve to piece the writing in its correct order.

As with all parents, years become measured by the age of their children, and this was no different between me and Meredith. Mark gained his position at Great Ormond Street Hospital when Merry was about born, and when Merry was two, he was at the next level up in his rank and well respected. When she was born, I had completed my assessment of the disaster response for the Sudan famine. When she was one, I put myself forward to join the Middle East team again. I pushed to become involved in any peace talks that always seemed to occur and then disappear with increasing unrest, for another set of peace talks a few years later. I achieved this eventually when Merry was becoming four.

Merry came to be a little girl with a continuous cheerful attitude, always smiling, running, playing, drawing, colouring, always noisily cheerful, always excessively happy. We had a piano in the lounge and I would come home and clean off the day's work with playing some soothing music. It seems strange now, looking back, that neither Mark nor I thought to teach Merry to play an instrument at her age, but she naturally one day started banging the keys with a natural eagerness to learn. All this from a three-year-old.

But it became an upheaval when Merry started asking incessant questions about life, death and Heaven with just her increasing curiosity. Her questions and incessant tittle-tattle, which would only stop as long as she was running around or drawing and colouring, were a burden to us, as sweet as Merry was.

How do you explain things to a child that you yourself have no clear absolute definition? How far do you go to teach a youngster absorbing things at twice the rate of your answers? I forget who it was, but when this famous someone died and was announced in the news, the torrent of questions this provoked, especially at the time when certain pets had died, almost drowned both me and Mark. We buried the pets in the garden and they would always be a place for Merry to talk to those who she was sure were now in Heaven — the hamster, the stick insect, the goldfish. Her bedroom had to be redecorated with angels, and Mark tried his best.

Mark and I made a conscious decision between the two of us not to indoctrinate young Merry. We taught her good from wrong and we took her to The Salvation Army as part of our family 'culture'. We did speak of Jesus and God, and Heaven and angels, but we always knew that one day, she would have to make her own decisions. We made her aware that other people think and believe other things, as was their right to do so. This did not stop Merry telling us her right to tell us that they were silly, because where were the angels in their beliefs. Dear, young Merry, she sings in my soul and the thought of her rocks me to sleep. I miss her deeply. My heart yearns just to cuddle her again, to see her saying goodbye to Hambert, Sticky and Goldie. I would give anything to see her draw another picture or to have another question. Meredith, my little Merry, my feelings are like raw tatters of flesh that have been ripped open and left to burn in scorching pain.

I see myself as Merry and imagine the way God must look at me, deciding what to say to the little girl I am. What can be said to someone so new? When Midgin, our little ginger kitten, was run over, we had to take him to the vet. To ease its suffering we had to take him through this prolonged fear without being able to explain our reasons. I think sometimes we're like this little kitten, and God is doing something fearful to us that we don't understand. What truly can an infinite, all-knowing, all-understanding God of everything, tell a finite, limited female dying of cancer that she can truly understand? Even the size and complexity of the universe is beyond me.

Leaving

In a bright kitchen, looking out to an overgrown back garden of a terraced house, was a mother washing the breakfast dishes. Her little three-year-old daughter quietly amused herself with drawing over a large sheet of paper spread out across the kitchen table, with odd moments of singing. The telephone started ringing further into the house and a male voice answered. After a faint one-sided dialogue, the husband walked into the kitchen, held his wife by the waist and kissed her neck.

"That's work, Esther," he said. "They want me in earlier as there's been a change to the surgery."

"When do you need to go?"

"Like now."

"Merry? Did you hear that? Daddy's going to work now."

"That's okay, Mummy," answered Merry, not looking away from her drawing. "So can we have a little cattie?"

Both Mark and Esther had to laugh.

"Was you listening to what we were talking about last night?" accused Mark.

Continuing to draw, Merry said, "No."

"When you were supposed to be fast asleep?"

"No."

"Merry, we're not good with pets, have you not noticed?"

"But we can *learn* and have a little cattie."

"You mean you will look after it?"

"Yes."

"And you will feed it?"

"Yes."

"And take it to the vets when it's ill?"

"He will be a boy cattie, Daddy. Can we call him Midgin?"

"Merry, we can't call him anything if we don't have one."

"Then we better get a cattie, Daddy. I can't call a cat, Midgin, if there is no cat. So we have to have a cat."

Mark sighed and looked at Esther.

Esther just smiled and shrugged, and then nodded.

Mark turned to Merry, who had by now stopped drawing and wanted an answer, as if it was a delicate matter of World Peace: "Okay, you've been asking for a kitten for a while, so, coincidentally, I got to learn that someone at work has had kittens and there is a ginger one left." Mark then turned to Esther: "And Mummy got all sentimental last night when I just happen to mention it in conversation about nothing at all – and saw the look in Mummy's eyes." To finish, Mark sat next to his daughter, who was suppressing her response until she had heard the entire account. "And I can't bear your Mummy looking more hurt than you, and I can't go against two females in the house."

"What does that mean, Daddy?"

"It means yes, we can have a little ginger kitten."

Merry, now having her absolute answer, allowed herself to celebrate her victory and gave her Dad a hug: "Thank you Daddy!"

"And we can call it Midget."

"Midgin!"

"Why are you going to call it Midgin?"

"Why did you call me Merry?"

"Because we knew you were going to be very merry."

"Well, I know that Midgin is going to be very midgin."

"Oh." Mark then saw Merry's picture and gave a puzzled look at Esther, which received a puzzled look in return. "I need to go now, so sorry my little munch-kin. I was looking forward to our walk in the park."

"You go and make them better Daddy, and then you come back with Midgin and make me happy. Will you read story when I go sleepies?"

"No, sorry, I can't bring the cat back like that and I'm doing a late shift. Mummy will read you your favourite story. She'll take you for a play in the park this afternoon. Will you like that?"

Merry just nodded, pleasant and cheerful as it was, but her full concentration was now focused on the colouring.

Mark then kissed Merry on the head and went to get ready.

Esther, having finished her tidying, sat beside Merry, just as the picture appeared to be finishing.

Merry looked up at her and smiled, as if to ask for a comment.

"That's a very nice drawing. What's that?"

"Our house, Mummy."

"Of course, and who are these people flying in the air?"

"That's you and that's Daddy."

"Why are we in the air?"

"You're angels, silly."

"Oh – and are these graves?"

"Yes. That one is Hambert, that one is Sticky and this one is Gerble."

"Of course, but we need to go shopping now, Merry. Then we'll come back and go to the park."

"Yes Mummy. Oh! Not before goodbye to Hambert, Sticky and Gerble."

"Okay, let's get ready first and then we say goodbye, but we're not gone for long."

Mark, now having got ready, came into the kitchen to give his final farewell, "I'm going now ladies. Please look after Mummy, Merry, you know how dear and fragile she is to me."

"Yes, Daddy."

"And I won't be able to cope with you, without Mummy."

"What was that Daddy?"

"Never mind, Picasso." He turned to Esther and motioned to the newspaper to the side: "By the way, have you looked through that?"

Esther shook her head.

"Have a look. David's in there."

"David?"

"You know David, David Kingsley. We used to know him."

"Haven't seen him in years."

"Well he's in there – again – making news about The Salvation Army. It would be nice to meet up and see how he is."

Esther became quiet and Mark noticed her fleeting troubled look.

"Anyway," he said, kissing Esther on the forehead. "I'm off saving poor children."

"Goodbye Daddy!"

"Goodbye Peeps!"

When Mark had gone, Esther sat quietly with Merry who had started another drawing that appeared to be a disjointed piano. After a moment of mulling, Esther, now burnt with curiosity, opened the newspaper and searched each page looking for the article. Then she found it:

> David Kingsley of The Salvation Army introduced the youth orchestra of once homeless children from broken families to the packed hall of The Salvation Army along Oxford Street. Andrew Last, with his new album selling in the charts and who started to learn the piano four years ago with their teaching, was also in attendance and provided his own recitals. The Mayor and other dignitaries and household names along with the audience, enjoyed the charm created by these musicians and applauded in a final standing ovation.

She resented her own sudden indignation she had for not having been mentioned as the one who spurred Drew's talent, and she resented having the feelings she had for David, realising her heart had started to pound more. Closing the paper quickly, Esther deliberately changed her thoughts to that of Merry.

Just before leaving the house, Merry was too eager to visit the back garden, and Esther obliged her daughter in the usual ritual in saying goodbye to the previous hamster, stick insect and goldfish. When in the garden, Merry bent down and almost lay in the grass talking to painted wooden sticks in three crosses that were sunk into the flowerbed.

"Goodbye Hambert, goodbye Sticky, goodbye Gerble in Heaven," she said. "We are going to have Midgin soon and he is a little, little cat and so I might not have time to visit you all soon as Midgin will need looking after, and then I'm going to the park with Mummy, but it will be all right: I will look after Mummy." Merry looked up at Esther and asked, "Where is Heaven, Mummy? Can we walk there instead of the park?"

"I don't know, sweetheart. I will know when I go."

"Will Daddy go there?"

"I expect so, Merry, but not for some time."

"When will you go?"

"Well not right now, as we're going to the park. Come on, hurry up saying goodbye and then we'll go."

"Will I go there? Will I meet Sticky?"

"Of course, Merry, now let's finish – "

"Can Daddy take me there, Mummy?"

"Well let's visit the shops first and then visit the park, and we'll do many things for many years before any of us go to Heaven. Come on, Merry, we're running out of time."

"I thought you said we have many years."

Esther decided not to answer, trying to control her exasperation.

It was a little while later that the two females were eventually in the hallway getting ready to leave with putting on their shoes when the telephone rang.

"Hello?"

"Esther."

"Hello Mum."

"Esther, it's bad news."

"Why, what's happened?"

"It's Elly. She died this morning."

"Mummy?" asked Merry, tugging her mother's skirt, "Why are you crying?"

"It's my old piano teacher, dear. She died. Now be quiet, Merry, I'm trying to talk to Grandma."

"Is she in Heaven now? Do they have pianos there?"

Samada Helay

Esther and Mark, having left early, had to suffer the chitter-chatter of Merry strapped in the back seat of the car all the way of their journey to Esther's home town of Havenly.

"Couldn't you have got something from work to sedate or anaesthetise this little girl?" asked Esther.

"Well I thought starting early would still have her sleepy."

Esther turned to Merry: "Merry, listen, this is Mummy's town. This is where Mummy grew up."

"Were you my age here?"

"Well, actually no, I came from another place far away, but Havenly is where I did the most of my growing up: going to school, learning the piano, boyfriends."

"You had boyfriends?"

"Well, actually no. Your Daddy was my first boyfriend."

"I have many boyfriends, Mummy."

"You do?"

Merry nodded: "They all go to Sunday School."

"They're just friends, Merry."

"They're just boys, Mummy."

Finding a place to park, they walked along the cobbled streets to arrive at the Salvation Army hall with Esther reminiscing to her family of two. When they entered, they were shocked to realise they had arrived early. Except for some helpers arranging flowers, moving chairs and organising the order of the service, there was no one else present. Central, on a purple velvet cloth draped over an unseen table, was a varnished coffin.

"Mummy! What's that box there?"

"A coffin, sweetie."

"What's a coffin?"

Mark smiled: "You did say this would be an experience."

Coming from a door from the stage, entered a female Salvation Army Officer. She saw the visitors and introduced herself: "Good morning, I'm Major Albright."

"I'm Esther. This is my husband, Mark, and daughter, Merry."

"Merry, if you would like to call me Happy, we could be very good friends."

Merry smiled, not knowing what to say in reply for a change. Instead, she turned to the coffin and pointed at it: "What is that, Happy?"

"That's a coffin, Merry."

"What is it for?"

"It's for a dear friend of ours who has sadly passed away."

"Has passed what?"

"Life, has gone on – to other things."

"So is she in Heaven?"

"Yes, my dear, she is."

"Why is that sad? Why does she need a box?"

"Well she is in the coffin, Merry."

"But you said she is in Heaven."

Esther felt the need to interrupt: "I'm sorry, Major, Merry is very inquisitive. We thought it would answer some questions and allow us to get our lives back."

"Esther, it's so nice to have someone so young so inquisitive. Are you ready with something to say during the service?"

"Oh, yes, I've got a short something to say."

"And you did remember that you're to play?"

"What, the piano?"

"Sorry, did she not tell you? Elly wanted you to play at her funeral. She sounded to me as if this had been a long-term understanding."

"No, I mean, this is a bit of a shock as I haven't played in years."

"You play piano, Mummy, all the time."

Esther blushed and the moment became awkward for her: "Yes, Merry, so I do."

"Why would she want you to play, Mummy?"

"Elly was my teacher."

The Major motioned to the grand piano: "Well, you're quite welcome to have a little time to practise. The music is all ready for you. It is Elly's wish."

"Of course, it's the least I can do."

Major Albright smiled and excused herself to make her own final preparations.

Before reaching the piano, Esther stood beside the coffin and placed a hand on it, with Mark, carrying Merry, coming near to stand beside her. They both saw the tears forming from Esther and even Merry realised her incessant questions were no longer appropriate. Breaking away, Esther placed her eulogy on the rostrum, ready for her speech, then seated herself at the piano and, gently placing her fingers on the keys, started to play as people arrived for the service. When finally concluding her practice, the hall was full of people, and Mark and Merry were quietly settled into their lulled sense of intrigue and mystery of the pretty pianist. Sitting alongside them were her adoptive parents, Joyce and Norrie, and she immediately went to embrace them. Esther was then continuously welcomed by friendly members who had not forgotten her or her husband and daughter, with some giving kind admonishment for not coming often enough to visit.

The scene was very much unlike a secular funeral. It was not sad enough with being aware that Elly had not deceased to not exist. Many of the hymns were cheerful and no one cried. People nodded thoughtfully to the kindness and enthusiasm of speakers paying tributes, reminiscing about certain endearing traits that Elly had.

All the while, Elly rested central to her own funeral.

Then there was a moment of silence for Esther to make her way to the piano, with no announcement other than following the order of service. When her fingers were on the keys, feeling the smooth, silky texture, her memory went back to the time when only Elly was sat behind her, in this very hall. Before she knew it, she had already played a few bars. It was as if she had never become anyone except that teenager about to set off on her travels to university.

The whole hall was powerless to resist the emotions conducting through the air. They were trapped in their seats. They were imprisoned by their ears. Their own feelings became enhanced without their control.

When the last chords had been struck, the ebb of the music faded to that of pure silence, and it was possible to believe that even God had paused in His work. There was no applause, so delicate was the ending.

Esther then stood at the rostrum before the congregation, paused, and her heart momentarily stopped with fright when she could not see her written script. She froze and in a sudden daze, wondered what to do, as trying to find it would damage the reverence of the moment. With the suddenness of new thoughts and returned confidence, Esther, deciding to command her own emotions, started another speech, a speech from the heart: "Elly was my piano teacher – but she taught me far more than the music itself ever could. She taught me that life is music. She taught me to make my own music with my own sense of life."

She stopped and spent a moment watching the congregation listening to her attentively. "This is something that is not meant to be easy. It means practise, means study, means diligence, means dedication; means searching. It means knowing how to know yourself, to be connected to your very own feelings. It means to write your own Psalms – to God – to please Him with what you do, with what you create – for yourself and for those around you. It means to enhance life, to give depth, to give a structure to your voiceless confusion and hidden fear. Elly was my strength and she knew to draw me out of my young days of gloom. She never wanted any thanks, because her duty and wish was to please God in teaching me, not knowing where this will lead. Her life, the way she lived it, her influence, shaped me. When you live a life that enhances the lives of others for the better, then your life can be a humble, quiet masterpiece. I am the woman of today because of her – and I hope I can one day make her proud of her legacy in me – my piano teacher, Elly Chapple."

As Esther stepped from the rostrum and down the steps, there came a hearty applause and she sat beside Merry and Mark, who remained deeply voiceless as they looked at this woman whom they thought they knew.

"Where did that come from?" asked Mark bending nearer in a whisper. "You should speak more often."

Merry, mimicking her father in a whisper and leaning even closer, added, "Mummy, you were like an angel."

Esther wiped the forming tears from her eyes.

When the service finished, Esther took the initiative to play some genteel classical pieces in the background for people to make their way home. It was during this that she started to become tearful again, but fought through it to continue playing, trying to resurrect her piano teacher through her very notes and chords. When she finished, she wiped her wet cheeks.

After the service, a few of the people followed behind the hearse, while a few others made their own way to the Crematorium. It was agreed for Esther to go and for Mark, Joyce and Norrie to take Merry to the local gardens and play.

With only the few privileged being present, Esther sang the last hymn and watched Elly's coffin as it moved into the furnace. Then she made her way back to the gardens she had walked through as a teenager to get to school, finding her family there laughing, with Merry playing and being the centre of attention. She smiled with the happiness that Merry brought them all.

Merry, seeing her mother coming toward them, ran to her exclaiming and shouting with delight: "My Mummy's an angel! My Mummy's an angel!"

"Oh Merry, when will you stop?"

"Stop what Mummy?"

On the walk back to the cars, Joyce started to ask Esther of her work.

"I've got an interview next Wednesday," replied Esther, suddenly eager to announce her news.

"An interview?" asked Mark.

"Sorry, I didn't tell you."

Joyce cut short their discussion: "What interview is this?"

"Well, it's not quite an interview. It's more of an introductory chat for my new job."

Again, Mark was puzzled: "What new job?"

"Well, it's more of a new position. I've got a place in the new Middle East peace delegation. I'm going to have a meeting with the Foreign Secretary on Wednesday."

"The Foreign Secretary!" exclaimed Joyce.

"Isn't it unbelievable? I'm going to be his personal assistant."

"When was you going to get round to telling me?" was all Mark's confusion and quiet annoyance could ask.

"I just couldn't believe it was real. I thought if I told someone, then I would wake up and know it was all a dream. This is my childhood dream come true. I'm going to be working on the new peace talks."

"Well done, dear!" Joyce exclaimed.

Norrie kissed her on the forehead: "Well done."

"Mummy, can I play the piano like you one day?"

"Of course, Merry, just practise well."

Driving home, Esther and Merry fell asleep and Mark was pensive. He knew Esther had not told him because of a growing concern about childcare, and he knew her workload was going to increase. He knew she understood the increasing pressure they were all going to be under, but she went ahead anyway. He looked at her beside him, but all he could do was love her more. "I wish I could have been your childhood dream," he said as she slept, "as you were mine."

Inquisition

From Hammon's office door came a knock, and Hammon, sitting at his desk and not looking up from the document he was reading, called out: "Scabbards!"

Scabbards entered the room giving out an air of verve and enjoyment in something: "Morning sir! Is everything right with the world today?"

"No it isn't," the Foreign Secretary replied, still in study of the file. He continued to do so, not appearing to care for this arrival. "And you know why."

"The new applicant?" Scabbards sat and rubbed his hands with glee, with an eager grin across his face.

At this, the Minister looked up: "Stop putting on a show. I know you're enjoying it. And it isn't an application: the Prime Minister is almost ordering it. He believes it will make him look more moral to the voters if he placed her in a high position. It would look bad if I didn't accept her."

"This is the Sally Ann girl, would it be? Esther Whyte? The one who's reported as being the perfect mother, wife and worker – solving all the world's problems? The one everyone talks about."

"Not you as well."

"She's just good-looking, that's all. I'm just enjoying the affect this little woman has on you."

"Looking at her file, she's ideal: degree in Theology and Politics, an impeccable work record with Africa and an active member of The Salvation Army. Her 'sweeter than honey' attitude and the awe she gets from the media, just – well, makes me want to push her down some stairs somewhere."

"You mean, there's a danger she'll keep you in check."

"Scabbards! You are deliberately trying to be annoying. At times, you really do over-step the mark. And now I'm having to interview her."

"I thought it was an appointment."

"She might think it's an appointment, but I'm going to ask her some questions. With skill, I will undermine her answers for the folly of her beliefs and get that reason why she shouldn't work at this level. Shouldn't be too difficult."

"She'll have a secret cupboard somewhere. People always have hidden skeletons and the saintly ones are the worst. Just get Sinbad on the job."

"It will be quicker to ask her some technical questions and see how much she squirms. The chances of God existing are as remote as a mouse with an extra ear on its back. I have more faith in science than I do an ancient set of cobbled-together texts that are not consistent and wrapped up to make Israel have a place on the map."

"As to this Misses Whyte?" said Scabbards pointing to the clock.

"I suppose she's waited long enough." Hammon then spoke into his intercom: "Rosalynn, can you send in Esther Whyte please?"

"Of course, sir."

A knock came from the door.

Scabbards stood, crossed the floor and politely invited the smart, elegant, young blonde woman into the room.

"Thank you," she said to the doorman and then looked at the Foreign Secretary behind his desk, "Good morning, Minister."

"Misses Whyte," cheerfully welcomed Hammon. "Please sit down next to my man."

Both Esther and Scabbards sat in front of the desk as if to discuss a major loan.

Hammon continued: "I'm glad you came by. I'm just going through your file."

"Thank you. I've always wanted to work for the Middle East Office."

"You certainly have a following. There are many who have given you much praise in your personal appraisals, and the Prime Minister knows of your accomplishments."

"I don't want to sound pretentious, but I do pride myself in working hard, doing a good job and getting results."

"Yes, you come across as a tenacious young idealist."

"Idealist, but not to the extreme that when it's impractical, then I insanely pursue the impossible."

"Really! So let's test that idealism, shall we? Let me put you under some pressure to see how you cope. Let's treat this as a means to understand each other."

"If you wish."

"So would you ever lie?"

"Yes."

"Oh – that was resolute."

"If I said no, then that would be a lie."

"So, I see: a chink in your armour already. I was either expecting a politician's indistinct answer or an insincere religious one."

"If I were to be a paramedic and tending to a person near death, I would lie to give them hope, and not tell them how desperate it really is. I wouldn't hold up their severed arm and say there's just too much blood gushing everywhere so we might as well give up and leave them to it. Giving hope can give strength where none is expected and that can profoundly change everything."

"Is that what religion is? A lie to give people hope? What if I told you to tell a lie?"

"I would try to avoid it, but I would have to know the reason to lie. The actual commandment is not to lie under oath, in other words to fraudulently mislead people to gain something unjustly or to get yourself out of trouble or falsely accuse others to get them into trouble."

"And if it was to cover my back?"

"I wouldn't cover your back. I'm aware you have a good reputation. So I wouldn't need to."

At this Scabbards jovially laughed. "Good answer, my dear."

Esther continued: "If the untruth was for personal gain or to put others deliberately down, then I would be diplomatic and tell you my reasons for telling the truth."

Hammon nodded, almost respectfully. "Let's discuss Israel, shall we? Now, as you know, Israel is doing some naughty things to the Palestinians. In turn, the Palestinians are doing some naughty things to the Israelis – which, in turn means the Israelis return in kind, if not worse. And what is worse, the Arab League has an opinion and America has an opinion, and everyone has an opinion, stretching to a bigger storm brewing. What do you do about that? Tell them to just forgive and forget, and do the hokey cokey?"

"I don't really have the right to."

"No?"

"I don't know what the hokey cokey is all about and I'm not perfect enough to tell them to forgive and forget – but I know God who does know what it's all about and has the right."

At this, Hammon smiled like having the next move as checkmate: "Then why doesn't he?"

"He wants us to take responsibility for our own actions with the brains He has given us. If you read the first few pages of Genesis, it becomes clear."

"It might to you, but not to others. Explain yourself."

"You get this image that God wanted to create all this out of extreme enthusiasm and be excited to share it with who He created; not in a dictatorship, or passive role as in looking into a fish-tank, but as someone who wanted to share His own life in a loving, connected respected rapport."

"And we then upset him? From a social experiment on us all, he rejected us from the fruit of a well-laid trap?"

"So as to allow us to understand who He is and who we are."

"So, Esther, may I call you Esther? What are your religious beliefs? If we're to work together, and let me state that you will be my personal, closest secretary in this peace process, involved in preparing my opening speech, then I need to know what your ideas are." At the last moment, Hammon was able to stop saying 'illusions,' or 'delusions,' and substitute the word 'ideas'.

Esther made no signs she suspected anything: "I have no right to force my views on people. Jesus told His disciples to preach to all the nations and make disciples throughout the world, and any town that did not listen, they were to walk on through, brush the dust from their feet and leave judgement to God – that Sodom and Gomorrah will fare better. He didn't tell them to force people to believe, obliterate their culture, declare them heretics, and burn them at the stake."

"They did in the Medieval era."

"Well they were wrong. The Spanish Inquisition was the evil system the Church used to purge the Church of evil – which they used against anyone who they saw opposing their authority and status."

"Oh, I see."

"The second commandment is to love others. That means in all that we are and do, we are to put others above us, in our marriage, in our parenthood, in our childhood, in the work and service we do for others, and it's indiscriminate. It doesn't matter as to gender, race, colour, age, wealth, ability, looks, health. It doesn't even matter if they're Jewish, Sikh, Islamic, Hindu, Christian, Buddhist, Atheist. The second commandment is indiscriminate. We should have the strength of character to not allow culture to hardwire our brains to see other groups and populations as inferior – that can be the start of persecution and genocide."

"That's very interesting, Esther. I thought there were ten commandments."

"Actually they can all be summarised into two."

"Oh, that makes it so much easier."

The cynical tone told Esther the conversation had a hidden agenda, but she made no signs that this was her thought. "So if you're worried about my views, then by my own religious standards and ideals, I will not interfere with the beliefs of others. I can only tell them what I believe."

"What if their beliefs are wrong?"

"Well obviously I will consider their beliefs are wrong, but I can still respect their views and care for them. I have no right to be disparaging and I'm inclined to dislike anyone who is bitter about other people having different beliefs and views. God doesn't fully force His views on me, so what right do I have to force people to accept I'm right."

"Doesn't he? What about Heaven and Hell?"

"He did create everything, which gives Him plenty of rights, and He allows our lifetime to develop a need of Him."

Hammon became overwhelmed with the multitude of questions and issues now storming his mind and his irritation abruptly showed: "Have you read the Old Testament?"

"Yes, of course. I had to, to do my degree and out of personal searching."

At this point, Scabbards, who had sat happily silent, leant forward to Esther, smiling in an avuncular manner: "Mister Hammon has already told me his views of the Old Testament."

"Well, yes," interrupted Hammon, "I really want to keep this one way, if you don't mind, Esther, as this is an interview."

Scabbards turned to Hammon: "I thought this was an appointment."

"Isn't there something you should be doing?" replied Hammon.

"Am I to take that literally?"

Esther interjected: "I'm not saying I understand everything, but I want to search for Him. That's *my* decision. That's what makes life have consequences. With all of us having freedom to choose is what makes life complex and interactive."

"And that's why the Peace Process will be a toxic mix of treading carefully and trying to get people to see sense."

"That's what God will be judging. He sees our true agendas, our hidden, dark plans and thoughts."

"Well what's your judgement on Israel, being the baddy about Palestine? If God has let out all his creation to our responsibility, what would you do with what is being done here?"

"Primarily, don't go against Israel."

"Really?"

"Do not curse God's people."

"Why ever not?"

"If you read the Old Testament, God has been true to His word: He has kept Israel going. In every era, with empires big enough to crush them out of existence, they still remain. Even without a country, they've remained a nation. Now they're back in their land. Where are these empires now? You have no idea of the Biblical significance of their return." Esther paused. "Everyone who has gone against Israel has been wiped out or decimated. No one has succeeded in making Israel extinct. God has blessed them because of His promise to Abraham."

"Don't go against Israel? Even when they're violating UN sanctions? Perhaps, my dear, you are not one for the job."

"Everyone and every nation is under God's judgement and laws. That includes Israel, perhaps even more so. So for all the wrongs they have done, God will have justice, but He will also, in the end, protect them and make them righteous."

"That's quite presumptive."

"Well, that's what I believe."

"You have an example? Can you back that up?"

"Obadiah, the shortest book in the Bible, prophesied that the nation of Edom would be annihilated by God because of their enjoyment of Judah and Israel being ransacked by Babylon. Edom at the time was deep in the mountains and considered impregnable, but they were eventually annihilated and they now no longer exist. And Obadiah isn't the only one: read Amos, read Nahum, Jeremiah, Ezekiel, Isaiah, read – ."

"Yes, well, let's just stick to modern times, shall we?"

"Well, one day, Jerusalem will be the world centre where righteous government will come. That's prophesied as well, and that's what I believe. You can't go against Israel just because you hate them or they are in the way. That's God's promise to them against you."

"They certainly weren't blessed when faring under Hitler."

"No, but the Holocaust is evidence as to how far savage, abhorrent and evil people can become; even civil people, people who think they're not evil, but doing it with their muddled excuses, trying to change the world for the better in their own idea of what is right, but what is in fact selfish. And anyway, why is there all this hatred for the Jews throughout history? Is it because Jesus came from them? There's something demonic in that, don't you think? A form of evil that people don't regard as evil, that can erupt into something – bigger. In fact, why does evil relish in Jesus' name being used blasphemingly, when Moses and Muhammad doesn't quite get the same – evil – satisfaction?"

"Yes, well, as to the Holocaust – "

"It was this horror that finally became the flash-point for Israel to regain their former land. Can't you see how significant this is in world history? And I think someone even more hateful will come along who will strive to totally eradicate them – and this will become the flash-point for – well – the end."

Hammon, with all the issues that irritated him earlier, became annoyed with his sudden feeling of being inept.

To Esther, this looked like contemplation, but she was still aware there was a hidden agenda.

"Their God still allowed them to be persecuted by the Nazis." It was at this point that Hammon tried not to show his triumph over the little naive girl.

"Those who were determined to survive were the ones more often having a deep conviction, a strong belief in life having a purpose, a meaning, a reason for creation, something worthy, something beyond their immediate, dire situation, something perfect. Life meant something to them, whereas to others with no belief, no inner strength, had less chances of survival."

"Yes, very good, but they were still allowed to be persecuted by the Nazis. A bit cruel of their god, isn't it?"

Esther sat back, took in a deep breath to help her think, and then answered: "People make decisions. That's what they do. Some people make decisions for the good; others – don't. That's the science of the place. You can ask why God hasn't destroyed the entire world in judgement of all the wrong and evil there is and has been and will be. There's the many centuries of the Black African slave trade and the human trafficking of modern slavery. There's the genocide in Biblical, Roman times to the ethnic cleansing of native American Indians, to Rwanda, Uganda, Sudan, Cambodia, Yugoslavia. Invasion and subjugation of other lands is always a form of persecution. There's the bombings from Vietnam to Northern Ireland; the hell-bent destruction of mindless terrorism; the arrogance to think we can achieve peace on Earth without God's help; the – the indifference to suffering. Anyone, absolutely anyone, can become evil, taking it step by step in that direction, as individuals, as a community, as a civilisation. If we want God to intervene because of something evil being done, then at what point should God stop? Stop just short at the point of getting to me? Why should He not wipe me out for stealing some paper from the work's photocopier? Who defines what is ultimately right or wrong, good or bad, righteous or evil? Society, religion, politicians, dictators, managers?"

Scabbards tried not to allow his own smile of respect and satisfaction show as Hammon sat back.

Esther continued unremittingly: "Those who lived and died in the Holocaust saw the consequences of evil and witnessed what evil is capable of, but if there is no God, then there's no consequence and no such thing as evil. Why then should we be obliged to help others if they are in some way inferior and should be wiped out? We could execute fat people, disabled people, diseased people, jobless people, homeless people, old people, people who are ugly, people who are weak, or shy, but to most people, this would give a sense of wrong. Everyone seems to have a deep-routed sense of what is good and bad, moral and immoral. The question, is why? Where does this come from if we are just advanced slime and muck? Surely good and evil exist as something – celestial. Evil is in this world because God allows it only because He made us with brains that think independently. We have our laws and courts, but they're not perfect. Perhaps true, perfect justice, punishment, mercy – solving the human problem, can only come with what God will ultimately do and nothing we can achieve. And I think, if you truly wish to know what I think, is that one day He will do something mighty, magnificent – horrendous even, to solve the problem of evil and suffering. And that is something only He can solve. We are to do our part in making the world a better place, but we can't achieve peace to God's standards on our own. Anyone who thinks they can, will be like the Anti-Christ, imposing their own doctrine on everyone and everything. One day Jesus will return, and restore Israel to its promised land, properly, in full, but only when the time is righteous to do so. That's scriptural. Until then, my part, my humble part, is only to do what I can to bring peace to all those living there currently, if anything by the way I live with people."

So baffled with Esther's answer that Hammon was unable to reply. Her words were so beyond his reasoning that there was no immediate credulous response. Instead, he attempted to let her know that her lecturing was not annoying, even though it was: "You should be a Salvation Army preacher."

It was Esther's turn to be baffled and she became silent, trying to read behind his tone of praise.

Hammon wanted to get back to the subject: "So what of Israel?"

"Israel?"

The Perfect Shade of Whyte

"Yes, Israel – what line of attack should we have about them defying UN resolutions?"

"If you really want to attack Israel, you do it by getting them divisive against God."

"Sorry?"

"They were conquered by the great empires of the day because of the prophesies coming true when they abandoned Him and worshipped other Gods and were unfair to the poor. In fact, read Deuteronomy."

"I'm not asking for another sermon."

"I'm being historical."

"I'm looking to the future, Esther."

"The greatest evil can present the greatest opportunity to do the greatest good."

"I can't see how the Holocaust was an opportunity for the Jews."

Esther became hesitant, but ended by not replying.

"Well, I'm sorry to have sounded harsh on you, but I thought I would test your mettle, and this discussion can go on and on and on some other time. As for tomorrow, find your desk, settle in and start reading the papers that Rosalynn will show you."

"Yes, thank you. I've started already." Esther stood up to leave, but then said, "I'm not talking about the past either, Minister. I'm also talking about the future. I'm talking about what is to come. I believe Ezekiel's vision of a valley of dried bones coming together in flesh and spirit is Israel that hasn't happened yet. I believe God is yet to show us who He is."

In silence, Esther was politely shown to the door by Scabbards, with her departure creating a smile from him and a release of tension from Hammon.

"Didn't checkmate her, did you," said Scabbards as he returned to his seat, "but she totally shemozzled you."

"She's a ninny!"

"You have to hand it to her, whether you agreed with her answers or not, she's no dim-wit – for someone who's religious and believes in out-moded non-sense, that is."

Hammon shook his head: "I've got to work with that, Scabbards, that thing that has just walked out of my office."

"Well I'm sure she'll cope."

Hammon was not listening: "Does that prove my point about such people? She'll wreak the Peace Process. I'll have to tell the PM. Why can't people just use good judgement without needing a divine mental problem? If they pray and it comes true, then they believe God has answered, but if they pray and it doesn't happen, then they believe God is testing their character. What nonsense is that? Life – God's petridish. How distasteful."

"Haven't you realised what she's done?"

~ 268 ~

"What has she done?"

"Told you how to attack Israel. That's what you want, isn't it?"

"She has said nothing except get them divisive? That's as obvious as 'united we stand, divided we fall'."

"A bit like survival of the fittest is obvious: people who are ill have reduced chances than those who are well? Look, you can use her. You can use her to understand someone with a religious way of thinking, and have someone on the inside as she deals with those you are trying to bring down. She's quite pretty as well. We all like a pretty woman around. That could be useful, especially if you can manipulate her."

Hammon huffed with irritation: "Oh, Scabbards, it's like I'm talking to a talking donkey."

Success is impossible unless you start

Gone were the days of working in a cramped basement. The enterprise had outgrown the space, and David walked into the spacious, clean and modern workshop, with each desk having someone working with the air of soldering, chatter and occasionally laughter and humour. There were almost fifty people of differing ages, both female and male, working on circuit boards, wires, and tiny electronic components, happily soldering them together. Some were experts and some were training. Those who were training, Noah was kindly and expertly talking with them individually, moving from one to the other, each attentive to his instruction and friendliness. Others looked at electronic digits on equipment as they probed the intricacies of the inner workings of the circuit before them, and others more were assembling the casing and producing the final item.

Noah looked up at David, gave a quiet friendly acknowledgement and returned to his lesson, having received a nod in return as David sat at a desk and switched on his own soldering iron. Then the few around David started to be amused at his late start and some joked about allowing strangers to join their business. In their jovial fun, David enjoyed the banter and joined in the work.

When Noah had finished, he settled beside David, resting against the side of the bench with a toothy smile: "How's da boss, boss?"

"Sorry I'm late, Noah."

Noah smiled and shook his head: "You're da boss, boss."

"How's things?"

"Fine!"

"We've got a film crew coming in to do a news item on us."

"Another?"

"Yeah, sorry."

"Hey!" Noah called out, "Another TV lot to gawp at us. Everyone happy wiv it?"

There came an assortment of replies ranging from the enthusiastic to those who were indifferent.

"When?" asked Noah.

"About an hour's time. They may want to speak to you. You keen?"

"Okay boss, but you think an hour?"

"Yep, why?"

"Well, I think you're wrong, man."

With that, two men entered the room: one carried a briefcase who was followed by the other carrying a larger case.

"Mister Kingsley?" enquired the first man, speaking across a few desks.

David switched off his soldering iron and stood to address them: "Yes, welcome, come in. Put your stuff over there." He motioned to the side at an empty desk that was available and greeted them both.

"Nice to meet you. I'm Bill and this is Ben, the cameraman. I take it you know we're to do a short interview?"

"Yes, yes."

Without any greeting, Ben had unpacked his hefty camera, placed it on his shoulder and found an angle of the scene that made him satisfied as if no one had any choice in the matter. "We're rolling," he stated.

"By the way," said Bill to David, who was just to the side, "we're not live, but we're filming this as if we are, so at the end I will cut back to the studio. It will seem weird, but don't worry." Then Bill stood straight, adjusted his microphone and started to speak to the camera: "Yes, thank you, Sharon. Well we've come here today to see some work done by The Salvation Army, and it's getting more and more attention and interest from the public because of the growing success in this small manufacturing venture here in this workshop, because all these workers are or were once homeless. This venture may be novel for us, but for The Salvation Army, this isn't new. In the Victorian era, before any Government scheme, they trained unemployed people on farms and made reforms to health and safety in the match-making industry at the time when none existed. So what is The Salvation Army doing now? Well I've come to this place, a small street near to Saint Paul's Cathedral, where David Kingsley is going to talk to me about the work they're doing." The interviewer then turned to David, who had been out of the picture: "So, Mister Kingsley, tell us how this new venture started?"

"It started really with meeting one young lad at one of our sheltered accommodations who had a clock-radio that wasn't working and we both fixed it and thought this could start something – and this is now what you see. We had to move into this place because it outgrew the basement."

"And now you have become a successful business."

"It's really more of a training scheme, but we want to make products that people actually want to buy, not out of obligation. We developed radio-clocks and the newer ones have voice-activated snooze. We also have electronic companies who contract out to us some of their extensive soldering work. Some workers have found fulltime employment with these companies, which is really the main drive here."

"But the success is achieving other things as well with the street projects, classroom teaching and music."

"Yes, we're netting an income that's funding the premises, but also funding the teaching of English and Maths for national exams and even science to some who are eager. I must thank all the teachers for their enthusiasm. An orchestra's been formed, again thanks to supportive teachers, some who are in the London Philharmonic, and they go out on tour. We're also teaching skills such as plumbing, carpentry and electrics, leading to certificates for future employment. We're thinking of starting a catering school."

"And it is interesting to learn that a lot of this momentum came from the sale of a lot of old motorbikes."

"Yes, someone, who wishes to remain anonymous, donated a large collection of classic Norton motorbikes. We were able to have them sold at auction for a lot of money."

"And there are famous people who visit and get involved?"

"We have celebrities interested and sponsoring us, yes."

"I understand some celebrities even come here to help."

"That's right, we've had all sorts of sport and film stars come by. They've even done some soldering for us, after some training, that is."

"So someone out there might have something made by someone famous?"

"Oh yes, but the biggest impact is people willing to give time in teaching and giving their skills, and the homeless taking this opportunity. If you can just get people to see the vision, give enthusiasm, work hard and let God have His way, then something beyond dreaming can happen. But I have to mention that this is only a small proportion of the homeless, so there's plenty more outreach to do."

"And what do you say about the welfare benefit reforms?"

"I know a lot of people say they should get jobs, but it's not as simple as that for people who have gone through major life tragedies that see them onto the streets. Then it spirals and the spark just goes. That's what homelessness does to you. We can't change all of them, and that's not what we're about. It's about being here to help, give some encouragement to those who are ready to take that step and stay behind them as they build their lives again. I'm proud to be part of The Salvation Army giving the homeless a hands-up. I wonder what most people would do when under the same impoverished circumstances."

"So what great plans are there for the future?"

"We're looking into providing special healthcare to the homeless, but that's work in progress before it becomes real. Homelessness means loss, loss, loss. It's not just the loss of a home, or family, or income. It's the loss of confidence and self-esteem, the loss of opportunities. Long term, it will wear you down and you live given up. They become institutionalised to the open streets. There is a higher risk of mental and physical health deteriorating, loss of ability or will to care, an increased danger of abuse and violence, increased chance of entering the criminal justice system, increased chance of not getting out of it. I've learnt that with all sorts of twisted fate and ill-turned corners, poverty can come at anyone. And often, alcohol and drugs are the only things they think can help. All this puts a strain on healthcare, so that's why this service is being started. We've got a property ready for it, as donated from a wealthy businessman, and we have support from local hospitals and medics, particularly students and junior doctors. None of this would be possible otherwise. It's a sign of a healthy society to help those who have fallen on bad times."

"I understand you were in Sudan during one of their famines. What was that like?"

"It was dreadful, appalling. We should never let it happen again. It was hot and, – ." David shook his head, not knowing what else to say.

"That was also the time Esther Whyte was first seen on television."

"Yes, that's right."

"What do you think to your's and her's growing celebrity status?"

David was at a loss for words again: "Well, I – I'm not – it's not really about being – well, being a celebrity or even well known – . You know, I don't think we're that well known, but it's not about getting fame but doing God's will and helping others. You see, there's this inner excitable buzz and satisfaction when you treat people with kindness, which becomes a reward in itself, but it's a miracle when a youngster says no to drugs and yes to education. It's a miracle when an alcoholic realises they have a problem. It's a miracle when the homeless can come and learn skills. What's happening here is a miracle, but I'm not doing anything more than doing my small bit. I can't solve and cure everything. That's for God to do when the time comes, but He expects us to work towards Heaven being on Earth."

"And Esther Whyte?"

"And Esther?"

"Is she connected somehow with this work? Did you meet in Africa?"

"She's doing God's work in the Foreign Office, I'm sure, and doing a great job of it."

"Well, thank you, David Kingsley for your time and showing us this optimistic work. I hope it continues to grow." The interviewer turned once more to directly look into the camera and finally said, "And now back to you, Sharon."

"David's doing well. He's even reached the evening news."

Esther did not reply to Mark's comment as he reached over the kitchen table and switched off the small television. Withdrawn into her own feelings, she continued to watch the screen, now black and motionless. The kitchen became silent with Merry already in bed for the night.

"I wish I could have become an engineer," continued Mark. "It must be rewarding to think of things and designing them and building them, and getting it all to work." Mark turned to Esther as she turned to him. "Just think of the satisfaction."

Esther did not appear to be listening.

"You okay?"

"Let's go to bed." Esther got from her stool and started to leave.

"I love you," Mark said when Esther had reached the door.

Esther turned and was about to reply, when she hesitated.

"You know, it's okay not to be perfect."

She did not respond, seeing her husband's earnest look.

"I know how you feel."

"You do?"

"It was all over your face."

She shook her head, trying to persuade Mark that his belief was inaccurate, but turned to leave again.

Mark followed and stopped her going up the stairs. "I know there's some part of you that feels you need to be perfect; that you can't stand the sin in you; that you work hard to get as much sin out of yourself and the world, but, Esther, it's not possible. I love you, as you are – it's okay not to be perfect."

"I don't know what you're talking about."

"Yes you do." Mark embraced his wife.

Esther whispered to his neck, "I'm sorry, Mark."

"It's okay. I know you love me."

Esther smiled with relief.

"Trust me – I know. No matter what happens, no one else got to marry you."

With the day coming to a close and everyone now gone, the electronics assembly room became empty except for Noah who settled beside David, whom continued to solder. "You okay?" he asked, seeing David in thought with his work. "It's night, boss. I'm just abou' to switch them lights off."

"Yeah, I'm okay."

"Wha' you thinkin'?"

"Oh, nothing much, Noah."

"You know that Esther, then?"

"We haven't met for a long while."

"Why not? I though' she was doin' the piano thin' with Drew when he star'ed."

"Yeah, well – just the way things are around here, Noah."

Noah could see David was not enthusiastic about his attempt of a conversation. "Time to go, boss."

"I'll finish off here."

"Okay, boss."

"Noah! You're the boss around here. I just pop in now and again."

"Sure thing, boss. What abou' this?" Noah produced a glossy fashion magazine with Esther being on the front cover. He gave it to David who took it with keen interest. "Have a read, man, she's doin' good."

"Thanks, I will."

When David had turned silent, Noah felt it time to leave. "Well, see ya, boss."

"Yes, have a good evening, Noah."

David was then alone in the silence. He looked at the picture of her for a moment, and picked up the expensive magazine, feeling his heart thumping stronger. She had never looked so amazing, so alluring, and as he read, he was drawn into the interview and her personal testimony in such a prominent, prevalent, stylish manner.

Erupting, he stood up angrily and shouted what he had been burning to scream like the thrust of a jet engine, "God! I just wish Mark and Merry be out of the way!"

The intensity shocked him and he sat back down and put his head in his hands as if this outburst had drained his strength. Then he sighed. "Sorry, I just wanted to let You know how I feel. And it's stupid, I know. I know You know how I feel, and I know my feelings are stupid." David sighed again. "I'm just telling You, okay? I just feel suffocated. I feel alone. I don't know if I can keep going."

There was no response.

"Ah, fat lot of help You are!" He cleared his desk and was about to leave when his conscience struck him again. "I'm sorry, I didn't mean it, truly. Just – just help me forget her. Please don't answer my mad wish for Mark and Merry."

Book Five : Queen of Persia

Blessed are those who labour for Peace

A tale of two cities: that can be said of Jerusalem and Tel Aviv: one is thousands of years old, the other, very modern; one being more of a hill, the other more a resort and beach; one more the synagogue, the other, more business. In a country where some lakes in the world are larger, these two cities, as opposite of each other, are within a coach journey.

Tel Aviv, the Israeli coastal city, a central place for tourists to explore the nation, was this particular day as any other hot metropolis. People awoke to the new morning, ate their usual breakfast in their usual manner, and travelled to work, as was their custom. From the city's coach station, one coach, now full of passengers, was about to depart when, breathless, a young lad carrying a backpack along with a heavy satchel reached the closing door and pleaded to board with his smile of gratitude. Annoyed for leaving late as it was, the driver allowed this one last passenger to board, emanating scorn as the youngster climbed the steps, and then commenced the journey to Jerusalem not waiting for the late passenger to find a seat on the packed coach.

Tourists talked to their fellow travellers, but most passengers were in their own thoughts. People in suits sat on the coach to complete their commute, and soldiers, young enough to appear to be on a school outing, were holding their rifles and sat in their groups.

The newcomer, having received his due contempt without much affect, sat down midway along the long vehicle beside a young soldier after a polite request to use the seat. The lone soldier beside the window, holding onto his rifle, shrugged as if there was no bother and returned to looking at the view passing by, trying to ignore the teasing remarks of the other soldiers from behind as an ongoing account of fun at his expense. The newcomer, only a year or so older, poked his neighbour and shook his head: "Ignore them." He then cheerfully introduced himself: "Hi, I'm Uri. Pleased to meet you."

The genial lad was met by one who was defeated, forlorn and reserved. "I'm Shimon," the soldier replied and turned back to looking at the window.

Uri took some headphones from his backpack, now on his lap with the heavy satchel by his feet, settled to listen to his music and looked out the large front window along the aisle, seemingly relaxed in the journey.

The view from the windows was of the desert and trees, and the occasional burnt vehicle that no one paid much attention. As it was, people continued in their own thoughts, talking to others, or reading newspapers or books. Then Jerusalem was upon them and the coach weaved in and out of the streets on route to the central bus station.

Uri started to inspect the neighbourhood in a vigorous manner, seeing shop fronts opening, people resolutely or apathetically wandering the streets, children walking to school. Such was his interest in the district that his motions, akin to a tourist, seemed out of place for one that appeared to be as comfortable as any native. So unaware of his disturbing intrusion, Shimon had to tap Uri's shoulder and motion to remove the headphones.

"It's just around the corner," commented Shimon, confused that a fellow citizen would not know.

"What is?"

"The terminal. You'll know when to get off. It's obvious."

"But I think this would be a good place."

"To what?"

"To get off. This would be a good place to get off."

"But we don't stop here. We stop at the terminal."

"But I'm getting off here." With that, Uri stood up, grabbed a cord from his backpack and shouted with the maximum extension to his lungs: "In the name of Allah!"

There was no time to stop him. Except for a gasp of terror from those who instantly knew what was to come, there was no time for anything that anyone could have done. The coach exploded in a ferocious roar, ripping apart the windows. The roof ruptured with the sheer force as if like paper. The entire vehicle lifted and then collapsed into its own disintegrating chassis. The fuel tank was breached. It detonated with the bomb and an eruption of fire burst out at the street, turning everything it could reach into a blazing rage. Innocent people were hideously seared alive to instant cinders.

The shock wave punched down the road forcing the obliteration of as many shop windows it could attain, throwing as many people that could not withstand the blast, tearing limbs, smashing bones, sucking the air from their lungs. Buildings stood as though their inner organs were now open to the road with their outer ribcage in tatters. Those who had strayed unknowingly close, had their last moment, never more to buy that dress, never more to reach that café, never to reach work or school, never to return home.

The news was instant. Within seconds, footage was transmitted throughout the internet. Within minutes, broadcasters around the world were becoming aware of the tragedy. Within the hour, the whole world knew.

In the aftermath, a hollow silence surrounded the burnt coach with the street evacuated and the fires extinguished. All items, large or small, significant or insignificant, damaged or undamaged, lay as they were, as if the people had suddenly vanished.

The Prime Minister arrived and was allowed through the cordon, escorted by a police entourage who gave their report of the scene. At one moment he stopped to stand, and took a long, pensive study of where so many, unknowing of their demise that morning, were now dead and gone.

"This is an outrage!" the Prime Minister told reporters, who had patiently waited to the side for this chance. "We will not suffer this atrocity and will seek justice for all those who have died today. We will protect ourselves and oppose those who threaten us with abject violence. We will rise against this barbaric action and let justice take its rightful course. My heart and prayers are for all the families of those who have died today, and I give my humble respect to the emergency services for their professional swiftness and for those of the public who provided invaluable aid to the many injured in this time of despair. Thank you – that's all."

In a barrage of unrelenting questions, the Prime Minister made his way through the reporters with the help of his bodyguards, and eventually reached his chauffeur-driven car. The door was opened by an aide and he escaped the mass of people, but then saw who was already sat beside him on the back seat. "Baruch? Why are you here? I will see you later this week as scheduled."

"Prime Minister, this needs to be said now," spoke the man with urgency, "before you go and announce anything."

"Okay, what can't keep?" asked the Prime Minister as the car drove away from the cameras and reporters within a police convoy.

"Melech can't keep."

The Prime Minister was aghast: "You've found Melech? Who is he?"

"No one. Melech as a person doesn't exist. We were chasing a phantom. Melech is a code name for a plan, a military plan. If Melech does refer to a man, then that man is General Blitzer, sir."

"General Cole Blitzer?"

"Yes."

"But he is one of my most trusted military advisors. He leads the army with impeccable ability and gets results. He has total loyalty of the soldiers and Parliament. He is a friend of mine."

"Yes, I know, sir."

The Prime Minister, with a screen directly preventing the driver listening to the conversation, spoke into an intercom: "Amiri, don't take me to Parliament; take me home instead."

"Yes, sir," acknowledged the driver.

"I thought you were going to address Parliament about this atrocity," questioned Baruch.

"I need to know what you know about Melech."

"We still don't know the whole plan, but it is like a cascade of violent events, triggered by an assassination, culminating in a – New Jerusalem."

"To provoke the apocalypse? I didn't think Cole was that fanatical. How does all this cascade? How does an assassination trigger all this? Who's the target? Why do we find that our greatest enemy turns out to be us?"

"You have to understand the mindset of this man."

"And I don't?"

"No."

"How come I don't?"

"Because you haven't infiltrated his inner circle."

"You have an agent next to him?"

"Yes."

"You felt you had to sanction a covert operation on one of our own Generals?"

"Yes, sir."

The Prime Minister sighed with disappointment: "Go on, then."

"The next peace conference is the trigger."

"Well that's not long from now."

"I know. The United Nations has nominated Britain as chairing the talks."

"Yes? And? You think I don't know this?"

"That would be delegated to the British Foreign Minister."

"Yes? And?"

"His name is Hammon."

"I know."

"Are you going to say you don't know the relevance?"

"Hammon?"

"His name is a derivative of Haman."

"You're not going to say this has some relevance to him being the enemy of Israel in the Book of Esther."

"Yes."

"How does that nonsense relate to us?"

"No one knows Hammon's first name, other than having the initial 'I'. It's thought it stands for Ishmael."

"Now that's absurd."

"It's reported that he sides with the Palestinians."

"And that's supposition."

"It doesn't matter. He's the poor stupid sod who's unfortunate to have the same name as this character, real or fictional, in a book written in a past, different era."

"So I take it that Hammon is the target."

"Yes."

"How does his assassination trigger all this Armageddon?"

"It's political. It's symbolic. It's following the Book of Esther."

"What are you talking about?"

"Haman was able to trick the King of Persia to make it law to kill all the Jews on a set date. But Esther, the Queen of Persia, unknown to everyone that she is a Jew, reveals her secret identity to her husband, the King. With the King's passion and anger, Haman is then hanged on his own gallows."

"Assassinated being the resemblance here."

"If you like, but it goes further, because the King is not able to revoke his own law. So he sets a new law to allow the Jews to attack back. General Blitzer is using this understanding as a battle cry to activate events that in turn are calculated to trigger certain Nations into war against us in a domino effect."

"Against us?"

"To create the impression we are under attack."

"I'm still not following."

"If we are attacked by our enemies then General Blitzer will legitimately attack back under the guise of defence to imitate the Book of Esther."

"And it's not?"

"No, he's been planning it as an excuse for an offensive. He's not involving you, because he knows you will oppose it."

"I'm not buying any of this, Baruch."

The wide and quiet, long road, each side in salute from regular trees, traversed a large territory of luxurious and opulent residential homes in stunning garden settings that hid behind high walls, fencing and bushes. Passing occasional entrances to these homes, the car then drove to a particular high metal gate within a tall wall and bushes, and passed into the elegant estate as it opened. With efficient timing, the gate closed behind them.

"Nice gardens, today, sir. It's nice to see everything in bloom."

"Well I can't take any credit."

In moments, the car had parked outside an attractive modern building, architecturally stylish, and the Prime Minister was greeted by a guard who had appeared from the house to open the car door.

Baruch entered the house with the Prime Minister. They were stopped in the hall going any further by another security guard who looked hesitant.

"It's okay," encouraged Baruch as he offered his identity card.

The credentials were inspected and handed back with the guard giving his apologies already aware of the person's status.

"That's fine, check everyone, no matter who you think they are," enforced Baruch. "That includes me. And can I have my briefcase, please." The case was handed to him and he then led the way, followed by the Premier, to a large room softly furnished with an imposing desk.

Ignoring the desk, the Prime Minister sat on a leather sofa and obliged Baruch to sit on the opposite sofa with a large glass coffee table between them.

Baruch retrieved a collection of photographs from the case he carried, showing the General on holiday, visiting fields and monuments, sitting and standing in boats, walking and being lectured by tour guides. As he spoke, he leafed through each one, dropping them on the coffee table for the Premier to observe, but there was only a fleeting glance. "General Blitzer arrived at Masada to give his speech at the soldier's passing-out ceremony after having spent two months travelling Europe – France, Belgium, Turkey, Italy, Russia, Poland – visiting the old sites of the concentration camps but – but mainly visiting all the major battlefields: Cannae, Stalingrad, Arnhem, Ardennes, Gallipoli, the Somme, Kursk."

"It matters that he went there?"

"Yes."

"On holiday?" The Premier picked up some pictures and viewed them like any would a set of holiday photographs, until holding one of a small fishing boat with the General being aided aboard from a jetty of an attractive fishing harbour.

"This was his visit of Northern France, seeing the landing sights of D-Day. He was particularly keen to see Omaha beach."

"There's nothing wrong in my military leaders studying these battles. He told me about this holiday before he even went. I allowed him the time off. In fact, I know he has an obsessive fascination for all this."

"He knows all these battles inside out. He only went for inspiration as a prelude, but also he's been finalising his plans."

"This is not helping your case. I need to have evidence."

"I can't get it to you. Everything I have is wrapped up with my agent."

"So what is operation Melech?"

"General Blitzer is convinced that by triggering a certain event, there will be an escalation that will suck nations into turmoil and combat, for or against Israel."

"That's not possible."

"It is sir, I assure you. It's happened in the recent past."

"An assassination? Triggering a major war?"

"The First World War was started by an assassination. Didn't you do history at school? There was then a ripple, a wave, a shockwave – a cascade that sucked in broader, bigger nations, until Europe and beyond were fighting, all because of allegiances and treatises, fear and mistrust, attacks in the name of defence, pre-emptive action, propping up of borders, securing borders by aggressively invading – it goes on. General Blitzer knows all this."

"It can't happen again."

"It can. The global political air is fragile and Israel is the key."

The Prime Minister sighed yet again.

"Look, this can either go the way General Blitzer has planned, with Israel annihilating its enemies, probably destroying much in the process, or his plan dissolves into nothing more than a fanciful fizzle and dies out, or – ."

"Or?"

"There's more at stake in this age of bigger, better weapons. Destruction awaits us all if this escalates beyond Blitzer's planning."

"Is that really credible?"

"Hammon sides with the Palestinians – fact. Israel will be accused of his murder. When it is public knowledge that it was a Palestinian gunman, then the anger will be returned and with increased intensity – because the hate is already there and just needs to be fuelled. Cleverly suck in Syria and you suck in Iraq, Turkey, Russia and the United Nations. Iran will want to be sucked in as they want to wipe us off the map. General Blitzer has been in clandestine meetings with many important people, negotiating deals they think he will deliver. In truth, he's been manipulating these diplomats and politicians, fuelling hatred perceptions of others, inciting vengeance for those who secretly yearn for more power. He is quite convinced he has psychoanalysed the major countries and knows how they will react. My agent knows that everything is planned precisely, in a cascade, and it starts with Israel. It starts with the assassination of Hammon. It starts with the peace conference, a place and time that will achieve the greatest impact."

"No, this can't be."

"Yes it is sir. You still don't know the full extent of what Blitzer wants to achieve."

"Extent?"

"He wants to claim all the land that God promised Abraham and take it, all of it, going beyond King David, King Solomon, to take all of what is described Biblically."

"Claim? In defence? Really? We just march into Lebanon, Syria, Jordan, Egypt, Iraq, all the way to the Euphrates? All in defence? All from a book thousands of years old, fighting our way?"

"A complete military strike as part of operation Melech."

"He'll never get away with it. The world won't let it happen. I won't let it happen, and he would know this – unless I'm part of the plan where he gets me out of the way – in this cascade." The Prime Minister turned to the agent for an urgent answer: "What happens to me?"

"You will be assassinated. It will increase the hatred and Blitzer wants to set himself up as leader, king even."

The Premier stood and went to the window where he looked at his thoughts, appearing to study the outside. "It's not every day you get to hear about your own demise and death," he muttered.

"Again, by the same Palestinian sniper that they're manipulating and framing."

The Prime Minister did not reply. He returned to the couch in a heavy manner where he had sat before.

"The conquest of the Promised Land is not the full concern."

Bewildered, his reply could not suppress the tone of disbelief: "How can there be more?"

"The Dome of the Rock."

The Prime Minister raised his hand in astonishment and sarcasm: "Of course! Of course! The Dome of the Rock! Why didn't I think of that? Throw in the al-Aqsa Mosque!"

Baruch ignored the disdain: "They'll be destroyed and the Jewish Temple rebuilt."

"We'll be attacked from all sides!"

"That's how he wants it. The attack will level everything to rebuild."

"This is insane!"

"And the Holy Temple will be rebuilt as described in the Book of Ezekiel."

"Ezekiel's Temple! Of course! What else can it be?"

Baruch again ignored the sarcasm: "Ezekiel's Temple design was never built, but they'll build it now, precisely as to the plans given by Ezekiel."

"This is nonsense."

"It could be the way it becomes true. Even the Christian Bible in Revelation describes a new Jerusalem being built. In the General's plan, the Islamic Dome of the Rock will go, Ezekiel's Temple will be built in prophecy, and there will be a New Jerusalem – and a new world order."

"What evidence do we have? Truly have?"

"What our agent is telling us."

"And that's it? Anything written? Anything tangible? Anything substantial? Cole is my friend."

"Here's the transcript of the General's speech to the new soldiers at Masada. What it contains is illuminating." From the case to the aide's side, was a set of papers taken and proffered to the Premier.

"I've read the transcript: very good, very inspiring, very rousing."

"If you read it again, knowing what you know now, you might understand it differently. It's all there. It's like reading hidden code."

The Prime Minister huffed, took the pages and dropped them on the table: "Is this all we have? Is this all we have as proper evidence against one of my best Generals and friend?"

"And the testimony of my agent."

"What if you bring in this agent?"

"That will compromise him and we need him in position to get more intelligence on this Palestinian sniper."

"There's no way I can talk with him?"

Baruch shook his head resolutely.

"What if you bring Cole in for questioning?"

"That would look too strange before the conference and again compromise our agent."

"So your advice is to do nothing. That's what you're saying, isn't it?"

"Worse things have happened by barging in. I think it's best if we keep a low profile and run the usual security checks for the peace talks as we would of any political event. That wouldn't cause any suspicion. We have our usual professionals checking for every possible sniper position."

"Is there any chance that this is all mistaken and nothing like what you're conjecturing?"

Again, the aide shook his head resolutely: "In my professional opinion? Not a chance. Melech is a definite plan, and it is real, real enough to make even me sweat fear and dread. There is a great chance this will spiral wider than my conjecturing."

"And the British? Should we warn them of this threat?"

"If we alert them they might start to act suspiciously, which might make General Blitzer suspicious. We should keep this to ourselves."

The Prime Minister thought for a moment and then, as if his thoughts had been elsewhere, changed the subject: "It would be good to meet Hammon's Secretary again. Would she be coming?"

Baruch was at a loss and confused as to the relevance: "Sorry?"

"The aide! The female secretary! Would she be coming?"

"That would be Esther Whyte, and yes she is coming – and no, she's not a secretary."

"Very pretty, very – what can I say? Wholesome? I've heard her play the piano – very beautiful."

"She does have – well, her virtues look just as good as her curves."

"She would certainly bring freshness to the talks."

Baruch nodded hesitantly.

"As usual, secretaries don't make much impact or intervene, do they? They just provide in the background, un-thanked and unknown."

Baruch did not reply while the other man paused in thought. Then he watched his leader walk to the window to look out, pausing again in thought.

"Why don't we try a bit of faith?" said the Prime Minister, still looking out.

"Sorry?"

"Nothing – just – ." There was another long silence, and then he turned to look directly at Baruch. "I said, why don't we try a bit of faith?"

"Sir? I didn't know you were religious."

"I'm not, but a little faith could go a long way."

"I'm not following, sir."

The Prime Minister paced the room as he spoke: "Let's go with your reference to the Book of Esther. How hard would it be to get Esther a more prominent position in the talks?"

"Sir?"

"Let's see how far this resembles the Book of Esther. Get Esther a speaking part."

"Is that something I should really be arranging? If it goes wrong, then – . Sir, I don't think it's ethical."

"Do it all the same. No questions, no complaints, just oblige me. Just don't let the British know. Can it be done?"

"Sir, I don't think we should be medalling like this."

"Look! I have Israeli businesses wanting to trade and make links with the Palestinians because, 'they are our neighbours,' they claim, and 'strife is bad for business'. I get letters from Palestinian women, mothers, educated ladies who, quite imploringly, intelligently, tell me that they want peace with us and are willing to do what it takes to do this peacefully for the sake of their children. These are heart-wrenching letters of the soul that I can't get out of my head."

Baruch shook his head and shrugged with confusion.

The Prime Minister sat down again, opposite Baruch: "There is here a form of psychology that everyone is contaminated with: we are good, they are evil; we are worthy, they are vermin; we are right, they are wrong; we are victims, they are savages; them and us. Look at it this way: a bomb has just killed innocent people on a coach in Jerusalem today. Innocent! All of them! Minding their own business! Not one of them personally involved in any strife with anyone to justify dying the way they did. I am to find those responsible to get justice. Justice, yes, but would that be true justice or would that be revenge? Would that solve anything between us and the Palestinians or not? Can we really, truly say that every Palestinian is guilty of every crime? Say I make some speeches about the need for peace, to forgive and forget with the Palestinians: what then?"

"The country will be just as divided as it is now."

"Precisely! There will be uproar from some and praise from others! But! I could be assassinated by those who want peace, just as much as those who want war!"

"I'm sorry, sir, but all this is lost on me. I thought Blitzer's plan was complex until I started listening to you."

"Baruch – Baruch – you are my most senior security director, yet I treat you as a confidant in political matters."

"Yes, and I respect that, considering these political matters highly involve security."

"You see, no matter what I say or do, there will always be division. But! What if an impassioned, beautiful young woman were to make this imploring stance for peace?"

"She's a woman. Would people really listen?"

"No, you forget, she's a beautiful woman with integrity and a drive to do what is right. With virtue, respect, beauty, modesty, may I say innocence as well – I think people will be captured and taken in – charmed even. If done with integrity, then that's true power."

"You want me to get her to speak at the Peace Conference?"

"I want her to give an impassioned speech, an imploring speech, the grand opening speech, one that will govern the direction towards peace, that will gain momentum and take the pressure away from me, as impotent my position really is. You must admit my hands are tied and

I'm damned if I do and I'm damned if I don't, and nothing good will come from any of it. Sometimes we need a strange event to jog the needle from the groove and track."

"This is assuming that she is capable."

"Yes."

"And willing."

"Yes."

"And that she will give this impassioned speech."

"Yes."

"That everyone will be amazed."

"There is that chance."

"That's a lot of fanciful suppositions."

"Of course."

"Boy, do you politicians have big dreams."

"This is applying the Book of Esther to save her people. It's your fault: you're the one who gave me the idea. So? Can it be done?"

"We just have to get Hammon out of the way, and that would be easy considering there's a legitimate reason he could be assassinated. It would have to be done at the last moment though, and some coaxing and conditioning done on Esther Whyte."

"Will you arrange it?"

Baruch sighed with the weight of the request, then, suddenly looking tired, he just nodded resignedly: "You know me, sir. I can do all things, but I don't think we should be playing with fire like this."

"Baruch, this is the peace talks. This is playing with fire."

"In my view, no one listens to them much anyway."

"I think if Esther were to speak, they would."

Balaam

Under the bright sunshine of California, within the palatial garden grounds of a luxury estate, secluded within woodlands and impeccable flowerbeds and immaculate lawns, was a young man of Asian origin who walked the pathways looking handsome behind expensive sunglasses. He wore only a smart jacket and matching trousers, making the lack of any shirt display his tanned and sculptured chest.

He was resolute in reaching a long swimming pool within this garden setting, strolling towards the water that, at the far end, had a small group of tanned youngsters, male and female, looking miniscule in the distance. They played and laughed under the sun, under umbrellas, reclined on chairs sipping drinks, none taking notice of the man that walked the premises.

As unconcerned as they were of him, he was as unconcerned of them with his reason for arriving being to visit the lone woman swimming in her pool. He stopped at the edge and waited for her to finish her lap and reach the side. The closer she got, the more obvious it became that she was naked, tanned and healthy in her feminine figure.

Reaching the end and holding onto the stone side, she looked up at the man and smiled: "Pashhur! You always have perfect timing."

"Only for you, my Queen Jezebel."

"Oh shut up," replied the woman with flattery in her tone. The woman lifted herself up onto the edge and out of the pool, the water shimmering down her silky body and her gleaming golden hair draped down her back. She had no fear of being totally void of any clothing, and hid behind nothing.

Pashhur, following her to her own sun-lounger far from the playful group, watched the small crowd in the distance. He continued to do so as she towelled herself dry.

"So how are you, Pashhur?"

"I'm okay, my Queen."

"Just Jezebel will do."

"Oh absolutely, Queen Jez."

Jezebel grinned: "Of course, my slave." Having dried, she wrapped a dry towel around herself, picked up her sunglasses, put them on and motioned for him to follow as she headed towards the house.

"So who are the new guys?" asked Pashhur as they walked.

"Just people I got last night. You like my new entourage?"

"Look fine to me. Going to have sex with them?"

"Na, did that last night. I'm just waiting for them to go."

The two approached the modern luxury building that contained a solid window from floor to ceiling, for a major part of the wall. Sliding a doorway within this window, they entered a vast room that accommodated a vast dance floor with the far walls catering for mirrors. In a stylish design, the whole place had good access to the sunlight outside for all the large and wide windows there were. They crossed over to a drinks bar and the woman made herself a healthy, refreshing fruit drink without offering one to Pashhur. Then she walked towards the side of the dance floor where a multitude of large, heavy, yet comfortable cushions were arranged where she reclined. Motioning for him to do the same, Pashhur joined her.

"So, my little cute man, what is the news you bring me?"

"Your latest film didn't do any better than the one before and the last album is struggling to get past number five in the charts. Net income though: eighty-five million, six hundred and eleven thousand or so dollars since the beginning of the year, but that includes other ventures."

Still wearing the sunglasses, Jezebel took a sip of her drink, remained quiet and looked disappointed. "That's bad," she flatly replied.

"Yes."

"It's not good enough."

"It's just the trends are now going somewhere else, to younger models."

"That's not the thing to tell your Queen. It will be off with your head if you're not careful."

"I'm telling you the way it is. Fashions come and fashions go. Icon's come and icon's go. It all changes."

"But I make those changes. I'm the one who changes those fashions. I made them."

"But people just go along with another up-and-coming act after they get desensitised. There's only so many times you can make a remake."

"Look at me! Does it look like I've reached my peak?"

Pashhur shook his head: "Perhaps the public has."

"Well I've been thinking, as for a new game, another challenge to get popularity."

"Go on."

"A scandal."

"A scandal?"

"There is no such thing as bad publicity."

"Depends on how it's engineered."

"Well I'm the expert. I've been planning a scandal."

"The President?"

Jezebel shook her head: "Won't get the same effect."

"You have someone in mind?"

"This man." Jezebel took from a pile of newspapers one that she opened at a particular page and showed the predominant picture to the confused man. "Know of him?"

Pashhur shook his head: "No, who is he?"

"He's English."

"How does that help you here? America's the market, my dear, not a puny little stepping stone. Conquer America and you conquer the world."

"He's in The Salvation Army."

"But you're not interested in The Salvation Army. Are you going to convert? Is that the scandal?"

Jezebel gave a self-satisfied knowing smile above the glass she held to her lips. She downed the drink, thumped it down to the side and continued her girlish grin. "Think better," was all her reply. "I can't believe you didn't think of it first."

"I get it, you're going to sleep with this nobody guy."

"Don't look so disappointed in my plan. It's brilliant. I've done my research on him."

"He'll be easy. What's the point?"

"I don't think he will. He has this highly sophisticated defence mechanism and high walls to get over to reach his inner sanctum, his inner desires. I think he will come crashing down but only after some clever, unsuspecting covert seduction that is slow, rational and strategic."

"He must know of your pornographic work. How are you going to get around that?"

"By being friendly, acting like someone normal like the girl-next-door. I'll take him aside, use my sweet nature and slowly gain his confidence – and then screw him when the time is right."

The man looked askance.

"Oh, come on Pashhur, look as if you're with me on this. I think I'm going to enjoy the challenge."

"It won't be a challenge."

"I think it will. I think it will take some time to take him off-guard, but I know how to do it. I've been studying him."

"And then? Renounce him to the world? Forsake him and let the press devour him?"

Smiling as never before, Jezebel nodded. "Think about it. Religion is believed to be true by the majority; religion is believed to be fake by the minority; and religion is believed to be useful by the likes of me. The more that people look up to this man, and the harder he withholds then the bigger the news. And if he comes crashing down sooner? I can find that useful as well."

Pashhur thought for a moment and took the paper to look at the photograph.

"He's quite cute," continued Jezebel. "I'll make sure he gets to enjoy all the best positions and then I really have him at my mercy."

"What do you want me to do?"

"He has a charity role to the homeless in London. It's actually some sort of business with success. Celebrities get publicity when they go there and support it. I want to be one of those famous. I want to be the most famous to visit and sponsor his cause. Even if nothing happens, I will increase my appeal in England."

"They'll just think it weird that you do something out of character."

"Publicity, publicity."

"Well, if it pleases my Queen, then consider the arrangements already done by the next time we speak."

Where there is no vision, people perish

David, in his Salvation Army uniform, his jacket hung from the back of his old chair, sat on his old desk, with only one box beside him, and contemplated his empty office. Having stored so much paperwork and so many cabinets, it was now full of new desks and chairs with a white board on the wall, ready to commence lessons.

"You okay?" came a voice from the door.

David turned and saw Jonathan leaning against the frame. "Yep, I'm okay."

"You seem a little lost."

"Just – just leaving this place is strange. I've come up with all my ideas and designs here. Just below are the guys building everything. Everything seems connected here."

"You said it yourself – we need more room for classes. We still have this place below for the electronics business, up here we gain another classroom, and we now have another building to set up the medical centre you dreamed of."

"I know it makes sense."

"If we want the medical centre to work, we need our new office to be there. We're still only across London. Anyway, I need to get a chore or two done, so I'll meet you later. Yes?"

"Yep, see you later."

They both said farewell and David spent one more moment looking at his old office, and then put on his jacket, picked up the box of his last items from off the front desk and left, descending the stairs. He entered a large area where sat fifty or so of all ages at differing stages of assembling electronic circuit boards. There had been laughing before he had entered, but now there was hush, as if a stranger had walked into their saloon. Not one looked up, all appearing to be too busy.

David sensed the reaction and placed his box to the side to approach Noah, who was beside a younger lad giving him instructions. "Okay, I'm off now, Noah."

Noah just looked up at him.

"The new English teacher will start on Monday."

"I know," replied Noah.

"Is there anything wrong?"

Noah did not reply at first, but then decided to say his mind: "We don' feel it righ' you goin'."

"You don't?"

"Na, none of us."

"Why is that?"

"Cuz all the drive, all the energy, the focus, the mo'ivation – comes from you, man! And you're no' gunna be here no more!"

"I'm not a thousand miles away."

"But you're no' gunna be *here!* This work's gunna dry up cuz we ain't the focus no more."

David looked around the group and saw they all had stopped and were watching his reaction. "Is this what you all think?"

There came no response, which intimated a consensus with Noah.

Noah continued: "Even I know tha' we will need to diversify – make new thin's, have new thin's to make and sell. Wha' we make will one day sa'urate our marke' and will dry up, unless we make new thin's. You said it yourself – *boss*. Wiv us ou' of sigh', we're gunna be second bes' now. You're the drive, man: where there's no vision, people go 'omeless."

David turned to look at the group, as if to make an announcement: "Look, this is not supposed to be a long term business. I know we call it a business, but this is to teach you all a trade and move on. This is not supposed to be David Kingsley Plc. There were companies out there who wanted to take you on fulltime, but most of you didn't want to go. Now I'm setting up a medical outreach to the homeless. You should all understand why I'm doing it."

Not one responded and their silence spoke volumes of their disapproval. One by one, they returned to their wiring and assembling. Only Noah and the young lad beside him remained attentive to listen, but portrayed a form of disappointment.

Noah shook his head: "You work too 'ard. At least par'y a bit with the famous guys you now mee'."

"That's not what I'm about."

There was no reaction. It was in an air of silence that David picked up his box of belongings and left the building. He made his way to the nearest Underground station in his Salvation Army uniform, not necessarily paying much attention to other people who walked by. Occasionally he would have someone say hello as if they knew him and he would politely reply in kind, not knowing who they were.

After changing a few trains and traversing the tunnels and escalators, David arrived at South Kensington Station and entered the day above. Walking the streets, he came to his new place: the small sign across the top of the door saying, 'The Salvation Army Homeless Medical Aid'. It was an elegant terraced house of four storeys with an imposing front entrance behind two stone pillars.

The door was opened by a young woman soon after he had rung the bell. "Good afternoon, David," she said with a smile as she returned to her nearby receptionist desk to continue sorting her belongings into the draws.

"Hello – ?"

"Samantha."

"Samantha, yes, sorry, I'll one day remember your name."

"Jonathan is already here on the fourth floor sorting his office, but the General arrived a few moments ago."

"Okay, thanks."

David entered the foyer. To the side were rows of chairs, as though a waiting area, but a set of stairs seemed to be the prominent aspect such that all the floors above, with their landings and banisters, could be viewed from where he stood in this airy stairwell. He started to climb.

With an absence of builders, the large, open-planned second-floor was in a state of being rebuilt. The third floor was also turning into something akin to medical assessment rooms, although everyone was missing. Continuing to climb, he reached the spacious top floor landing, which was large enough to contain a few inner rooms. "Jonathan?"

"Yeah! In here!" came a call.

Still with his box in his arms, David went to the door from where the call came and saw Jonathan in an untidy and dirty room with scratched office furniture and boxes scattered on the floor, having stopped in mid-flow of a sentence. Standing beside him was the General of The Salvation Army.

"David!" exclaimed the General and they both shook hands after David placed his box down on the desk.

"Hello, General."

"I thought I'd come and see how things are."

"Yes, we're still setting things up."

There was then a ringing telephone calling from the other office.

"The phones work then," said Jonathan as he left the room. "Don't worry, it's for me."

"Well this is going to be Jonathan's office, General," continued David, "where he's going to do all the finances for – well everything. He's got all the business connections, you see, which is a great help because they're drawn to us with all the famous people we have visiting. The office next door is mine and somewhere up here is a kitchen and we'll make some space for a lounge and possibly a bed."

"Good, good, very good."

They both left the disarrayed room and onto the wide, open landing.

"This entire floor is ours to do the business planning and getting funding. All the floors below are going to be assessment bays and a minor injuries clinic, a dentist room, a waiting area and – whatever else, but there is still a lot of building work needed to pass the next audit."

"It certainly looks like it's coming along. Why did you choose this building?"

"We didn't. It was donated by a wealthy businessman. He wants to be anonymous. He visited us at the other site, looked around the space we had there, and was keen on our idea of this healthcare centre. He came back to us with this place, but we couldn't have started if it wasn't for all these great doctors and nurses volunteering."

"Get people to see the vision and great things will happen, David." The General looked around, seeing more work than just some painting required. "What about liability and safety of the staff?"

"We've got CCTV and a buzzer to one of the Police centres. They seemed quite keen as it takes the workload off A&E."

"It's certainly a nicer area of London. I wonder what the neighbours will think about their visitors."

"I think they're all expecting the occasional celebrity."

"I saw your television interview the other day – very good, very encouraging."

"Thank you."

"Remember that we're not here to advertise The Salvation Army, though. Our job is to reach for souls and go for the worst; not to have The Salvation Army glorified."

"I think we should make more of a name in the public awareness to show what we're doing. Ignorance may well kill us off if we're too quiet."

"Well, yes, there is that, but I want to make sure God comes first, not us, otherwise everything comes crashing down. Too much success can be a sign of great testing, just as too much defeat."

David was silent, unsure what was truly meant.

"I'm a bit concerned about an American actress who's keen to come over and visit."

"You're well informed."

"I was just having a friendly chat with Jonathan and he let slip."

"Are you worried? What are you concerned about?"

"Her intentions."

"She wants to drop in. I don't truly know, but she may want to get involved. She may want to give a donation."

"David, there are many out there in that world who we need to be – wise about."

"What can she do? If she gets publicity with us, then we get that as well, and any donation is better than no donation."

"But donations are not the main concern. Jesus' work is the main concern. This Jezebel is very – worldly, shall we say. I mean, let's face it: she has a horrid reputation."

"Everyone's redeemable."

"Yes." There then came a troubled sigh from the General.

"Well her agent has got in touch with us, but we haven't replied yet. If you don't want us to get involved, then me and Jonathan can make a polite excuse."

"What are your feelings?"

"Jesus didn't shun prostitutes. The first one on the scene on His resurrection was possibly a reformed prostitute. It's all about influence. Can we be a good influence on her?"

"That's a bit like converting Richard Dawkins."

"You don't think it's possible?"

"I just know what I'm feeling. But you are right. We shouldn't be too judgemental."

"You did say that our job is to reach for souls and go for the worst."

"I tell you this: if you can convince me that this is a good spiritual enterprise, led by the Spirit and God will be honoured, then who am I to stand in the way. If God is in this, then there is nothing I can do anyway."

"I won't let you down."

The General nodded and smiled. "Well, I'll leave you to carry on.

I'm sure it will come together with God's blessing." The General made his way to the stairs, with David following, and was about to leave when he turned on the top step: "I almost forgot. There is of course another matter."

"There is?"

"I've heard reports of someone dressing up as William Booth and walking down Mile End Road."

"Really?"

"Yes, really, long white hair and beard and all."

"Oh."

"False long white hair and beard, and wearing the proper, authentic Victorian style of the age, and he preached as William Booth and got a good crowd. You wouldn't have any idea who it was? He was about your age."

"No, not really."

"Really?"

"Yes, really."

"That's a shame. It's just that I know you like to study the Founder's speeches."

"Yes."

"The crowds donated a lot of cash. He came in and gave it all and disappeared quickly."

"Really?"

"Yes! Really! All without a licence!"

"Oh."

"Yes, oh!" The General then smiled, said farewell and descended the stairs to be heard saying farewell to Samantha, who was still arranging her desk.

"I told you, you needed to get permission," said Jonathan from his door.

"I didn't think they were going to almost empty their pockets and not allow me to refuse their money. Why are you looking at me like that for?"

"Didn't Jesus say that the one who serves others is the greater?"

"Yes, He did."

"Then I'll get you some coffee."

"No, you get on with your work. I'll get the coffee. Perhaps a sandwich?"

"No, you get on with your important work. I'll get the coffee. What about a meal? And I'll dust and clean your office."

"No, seriously, it's fine, you've got very important clever money business to do, so I'll get the coffee, make a roast meal, and dust and clean the building."

"Well, at this rate, we're not going to get anything done."

"Let's start with a coffee."

"Right! I'll get you some coffee then."

"All right, but I'm washing your feet later."

The Mind of a Fanatical Christian Woman

With the meeting now over, Hammon collected his papers, shook hands in farewell to other members and the gathering dispersed throughout the building. Hammon eventually descended to the entrance foyer, walked through it and entered New York. A long array of national flags aligned the path of the United Nations, from which he came.

He disliked New York: not many people knew how important he was. With no hindrance from anyone passing him, he walked with little haste along the sidewalk and eventually came to a large metal statue of a dragon being slain by a knight on a horse, surrounded by a large, recently landscaped and manicured garden. Numerous benches were available for those to enjoy the park and the sunny weather, and he casually chose an empty bench to approach and sat down.

Soon afterwards, a man with white scraggy hair and stubble sidled up and sat beside him as if also out for a stroll. It took a while, but eventually the newcomer spoke: "They made this statue out of decommissioned nuclear missiles, sir."

"Scabbards, your knowledge astounds me at times," Hammon replied.

"Thought I'd start the conversation. It's nice that they've redeveloped the area. It was quite boring before."

"So what news?"

"You want me to start with Esther?"

"What is it she's doing?"

"Diplomatic visits to Israel, meeting Palestinians and Israelis."

"And?"

"And preparing the opening speech to the peace conference for you. Exactly as you instructed."

"Good."

"Why do I have this feeling there's a scheming plan here?"

"There has been for a while."

"You know, whatever it is, nothing is as successful as getting Sinbad to find something."

"Sinbad is expensive."

"So am I."

"True. I need you to arrange something for me. I need Misses Pure-Whyte to give the speech."

"Esther?"

"Yes, the opening speech."

"The opening speech at the Middle East peace conference in Jerusalem?"

"Are you humouring me?"

"But why?"

"I've been studying her."

"Yes, quite the figure."

"I'm referring to her modus operandi, the manner of her Christian mindset, her very psychology. I've been projecting what she may do under certain circumstances."

"And you want to put your understanding of her to the test?"

"As a means to make religion look ridiculous, yes."

"Are you truly that in awe of her?"

"She just needs – "

"A push down some stairs, yes, you've told me before."

"Her speech, that she thinks I will give to open the talks, needs to be perfect. The way it is given will direct the ease or difficulty of the process. Saying the right thing in the wrong way can be worse than saying the wrong thing. It also needs to be learnt and delivered with conviction, with inspiration, with belief."

"Why aren't you writing it?"

"That's my conditioning of her. Call it Pavlov's dogs."

"This plan gets grander and grander. If people truly knew how their politicians truly planned things then no one would get voted for."

"I'm exceptional at telling people what they want to hear and believe. Now I need you to listen, because my plan not only needs the conditioning of her, but the setting up of a situation."

"A trap?"

"With an open chance to give her own speech, she would say something totally different and totally undiplomatic. She'll produce some grotesque sermon that will infuriate everyone, all with a sweet smile of her single-shade-of-white naivety. So yes, a trap. Her passion is her weakness. To them, she is a mere little British woman, coming from the last Empire that tried to carve up the Middle East. It will totally infuriate them."

"Are you mad? Is she that brave? What is this woman to you?"

"I thought I'd get this reaction." Hammon handed Scabbards an envelope.

Scabbards pulled out a solemn notice of payment exceeding all expectations of any task given, including pushing someone down the stairs. "Okay, I accept."

"Good."

"She may give a better speech than you."

"I doubt it. She'll forgo everything, be challenged by what she'll see as coming from the almighty himself and give the squabbling tribes of the Middle East something to really war about with her tactlessness."

"What do you want me to do?"

"Cause a diversion, something – get me out of giving the speech at the last minute so Esther has no time to mull things over."

"How should I do that?"

"I pay you to come up with these details, and it would appear better if I didn't know. Do you think it can be done? All of it?"

"I think so."

"If Esther rises to the moment of her life and implores to have a better world, then she plays into my trap: the Israelis and Palestinians become infuriated and belligerent as predictable, Esther becomes the blame, the peace talks break down, and Esther is denounced. The peace talks resume by necessity and I take over to clear up not only Esther's mess that's infuriated the world, but also the whole sodding cesspit of hate – all caused by insane religion."

"Perhaps it's not religion that's the cause. Perhaps the problem is with people having hidden objectives, twisting what's there for their own cause."

"Don't lecture me, Scabbards, and still expect that hefty salary. Just get the job done, like what you're paid for."

"Of course, sir."

"Make sure she doesn't have the script – so it has to come from her heart. That will get them angry to the extreme."

"With her figure, everyone will prefer listening to her than you anyway," Scabbards said as he stood to leave, "and if she plays the piano, she may even delay Armageddon. Good day to you, sir. Enjoy the garden and decommissioned missiles."

I Will Go! Send Me!

From above, Esther thought London looked beautiful with its bright lights against the night sky. She stood beside a large window, leaning against the glass looking down from a great height from a lavish dining room, having eaten a delicious meal cooked by her single host. "It's always so relaxing coming here," she said. "I remember so many fun Bible evenings we had all though years ago."

Jonathan remained at the table, reading her script. "Mmm?" he replied, not looking up.

Esther rejoined him at the table with the remains of their meal still around them. "Thank you for helping me. I don't think I could have finished this off at home with Merry asking constant questions or be relaxed enough at work."

"Esther, that's fine. I always bring work back home. Perhaps I'm not quite used to having an important world-peace-making speech being finished here, but it's very humbling. Are you sure I should be reading this?"

"It just needs polishing and a little more panache. Some things can be said with more impact in the way it's said and the right choice of words."

"You're talking like a politician."

"No I'm not."

"You would've been a great politician."

"No I wouldn't. I can't speak to people about difficult issues."

"Really? Remember Africa?"

"They caught me off guard."

"And what about this speech?"

"Hammon's going to give it."

"But what do you really think about this speech?"

"Technically it's correct."

"Technically? Is that all it is? Do you really think this will get things going?"

"It's something like what the Foreign Secretary wants."

"Yes? And? Is that it?"

Esther appeared agitated but remained silent.

"Come on, Esther, I see it in your eyes. It's only highlighting everything that everyone already knows. Is that really going to change things with just an on-going lip service of previous talks? Something may be technically accurate, but is that the right spirit to it? Where's the passion to really get to the heart of things? You, I know, would say things differently, wouldn't you? Remember: in all of this, Israel is the key. Israel has always been the key – throughout history. Just think about their Holy Scriptures with the profound and utter affect on the world's justice and thinking and culture. And to top it, Jesus was one."

"Hammon will give the address; not me."

"Beware the Israelis, Esther, they love to argue."

"Yes, I noticed."

"But, beware the English more. They love to argue behind your back."

Esther chuckled.

"I'm serious. I don't think things are as they seem."

"Why?"

"Why does Hammon want you to write the entire thing? You! You're not a speech-writer. A draft perhaps, but not the whole thing."

"I'm just getting on with it like having a responsibility from God Himself."

"Sorry, Esther, perhaps I'm just being stupid."

"So how's David?"

"Fine, doing well. I'm proud of him. This medical aid project is proving difficult, but he's pushing through with it with his determination."

"Good. – Good."

"Although I do have a worry he's veering off with his, I don't know, obsession I suppose, with getting donations."

"He's getting big publicity with some big celebrities."

"Yeah, he's becoming quite a character."

Esther went quiet as if wanting to get off the subject and then said, "I need to be getting back to Merry and Mark, now. Mark must be pulling his hair out if Merry is still up."

"Do you want me to escort you home?"

"No, you've been enough of a gentleman already, thank you."

Jonathan fetched Esther's coat and helped her into it, then accompanied her politely to the lift and descended the levels to see her to the main reception lobby on the ground floor.

Esther was about to say farewell, when she became silent and hesitant.

"What's wrong?"

"Nothing's wrong."

"Yes, there is. You get that quiet, worried look across your forehead."

"Nothing, there's nothing wrong. I must be going now, so, thanks for the restaurant-standard meal."

Jonathan leant forward and kissed Esther on the cheek: "I hope it all goes okay. I'll be praying for you."

"Thank you. You've been such a help."

"Esther, if something does happen, just be the woman of the moment. You're quite capable of it, believe me. Something wrong?"

"It's just some pain thing I'm getting."

"Wow! You're not pregnant, are you?"

"I don't think so."

"Oh."

"But I do have something that feels painful once in a while. I have done for some time. Perhaps it's the stress. Anyway, I need to go now. Mark normally texts me, so I wonder what's going on."

Esther arrived home and closed the front door: "Mark?"

There was no answer.

She wandered into the lounge and then into the kitchen, but Mark was nowhere to be seen. The house seemed empty and Esther looked for a note to explain his absence, but there was nothing. She finally found him sitting on the bed, head in hands, not even to look up as she entered.

"Mark?"

He gave no reply.

Esther sat beside him and placed her arm around his shoulder. "What happened? Another child died?"

"My Dad died today."

"I'm so sorry – my poor Mark."

"Mum rang a few hours ago," was all Mark said next. "And she told me."

"Does Merry know?" asked Esther.

"No, Merry's fast asleep. I kept my feelings hidden until she was in bed."

They both embraced and remained clutched in each other's arms.

"She told me Dad died," continued Mark. "She said he died fretting about his paintings. That was all he was worried about – his bloody stupid paintings. He was convinced people were plotting to disfigure them and change them from what they were supposed to be. Mum said he could not be calmed. He died soon after. I can tell Mum can't forgive herself for the last few words she said."

"Oh Mark, poor Mark."

Mark looked into Esther's eyes with a solemn gaze: "But my Dad's death is the least of my sadness."

Esther was taken aback: "You're sad? Why else are you sad?"

"You just don't get it, do you?" Mark, now tinged with resentment, did not elaborate on his answer.

"What? What don't I get?"

"Me. You just don't get me, what I've been going through. You just don't get what I do – everyday – and you just don't get who I am."

"But – what am I missing?" Esther's confusion showed through her disorientation.

"I see things you will never believe. You see skin; I see what lies beneath. I do things people would never understand. People come and go, with their illnesses and diseases, and we take them next to death to cut open and mutilate in the name of health. People come in from emergencies, near death, and we bring them back – sometimes we do, sometimes we don't: blood everywhere – everywhere; consoling distraught families. And in all this, people still demand their instant, immediate right to health. I've done this every day since leaving school, wondering if I'm making a difference. I see cancer as a regular consequence of the day – and I ask myself – why does God allow it? Who is He to allow such awful suffering on people whose only sin is to be born?"

"I didn't know you felt like this."

"I know! That's why I know you just don't get it! Children come in and they are so brave – so brave, Esther, so much courage, braver than either of us, and they are so friendly, and they want me to be their friend! I look at them, wondering what have they done to deserve their horrendous illness and all I can do is be their sodding friend!"

"You must be making a difference. Surely, these children would be far worse off if it weren't for you doing what you're doing. We shouldn't be anaesthetised to the suffering of others, Mark! I'm proud of you!"

"But I came to you! I came to you, Esther! I looked to you for that comfort, but you weren't here! My sadness gets worse! It's worse than what happens at work – because I come back home! I come back home to it. And you don't! I came to you, Esther, but you weren't here!"

"Yes, I was here – "

Mark shook his head: "We have never been together. You've always been married to saving Africa, saving the Middle East, saving the World. I have always been second. Even your own health you don't care for." Mark paused, and then added, "And there has always been David."

Esther was so stunned that she had to lean away, and then stood up: "What?"

"You heard me," Mark said softly.

"How can you say such a thing?"

"It was me that moved your rose."

"What rose?"

Mark stood to face his wife: "You know the one! Soon after you arrived back from Africa: that rose. The white one you kept hidden from me. I took it and hid it, and watched you for months secretly trying to find it again. And even when I put it back, you said nothing!"

Esther looked blank.

"When we married, I wanted to treat you the way I wanted God to treat me. I remained here to support you, give you care, loyalty, friendship, partnership through life, love and commitment – and all I've achieved is to live like Hosea and to know how God feels."

"Mark, it's not like that, I've never been unfaithful. Hosea married a prostitute."

"Well that's what you've been to me. You've put your work first. You've put David first. Me and Merry are a poor second. If that's faithful, then show me unfaithful."

"But I do love you, Mark. I love Meredith! I do! I love both of you."

"Prove it."

"What?"

"Prove it!"

"Okay! I will! I'll prove it!"

"Come with me to my father's funeral."

"Of course, Mark!"

"Really?"

"Why shouldn't I – ?" It was Mark's intonation that Esther realised her true position. "It's when the peace talks are on, isn't it?"

Mark nodded.

"I'm so sorry, Mark, but I can't come. There's been so much work towards it. There truly seems to be a break-through here. I've got to go."

"You can't come with your husband to his father's funeral?"

"I'm sorry, but I must be in Israel." Esther started to cry.

"I'm sure they can have someone just as important as you there. Why do you think you can change something that has never been changed since Abraham's time?"

"All my life has been building for this one moment, Mark. Please understand this. I'm so sorry. I'm so, so sorry. I can't come with you."

Mark looked at Esther, "If I died, would you come to my funeral?" He then left the room.

Assassination

The weather was overbearing. The sun was too bright, too hot and too intense, but within an air-conditioned hotel bedroom of an upper floor, a man in a cleaner's uniform, assembled a military-grade, long-range powerful rifle from an opened case on the bed. He was meticulous, methodical, diligent and calm as the obscure parts came together and became a fully functioning killing instrument. He fitted the large riflescope, made a setting, and viewed the distance out of the window through the lens. Satisfied with his progress, he turned to his cleaning trolley, manoeuvred it into position and locked the wheels. He was then able to create a level, stable platform from strong struts that were surreptitiously part of the trolley's frame, and on top he constructed a rigid, balanced mount to which the rifle was secured into its position. Through the lens, he viewed his intended target over a mile and a half away that happened not to be there.

Instead, the target site was an entrance to an enormous square building that had a large open area to its front, where cars would arrive and bring men in smart suits carrying important briefcases and ushered in by doormen and guards. As the sniper viewed the scene within his sight, he could see in clear detail that one of the guards had missed some of his chin to leave some stubble, yet another guard had a slight stain to his collar. This was his view of the Knesset building, Israel's Government House.

From a cigarette packet, he retrieved a hidden bullet and loaded the rifle, checking the riflescope view another time. Finally, he placed a headset over his head and connected this to the small laptop computer, which he obtained from a secret compartment of the trolley. "This is Wormwood," he said quietly to the tiny microphone at his mouth. "Screwtape? You there?"

"This is Screwtape, acknowledged Wormwood," came the voice in his ear.

"I'm ready."

"Wait for instructions, Wormwood."

There was then nothing to do. Wormwood made himself comfortable on the bed with reading a magazine and time passed for another hour when the voice spoke in his ears.

"Wormwood, target now moving. ETA fourteen minutes."

"Acknowledged, Screwtape."

His first action was to open the window ajar, and then rested behind the gun, viewing the sight, becoming aware of an accumulation of security and police patrolling the target area.

"Wormwood, convoy is now arriving."

"There's an increase in security. Am I compromised?"

"Convoy now arrived. Target the British ministerial car."

"Confirmed, British ministerial car now stationary. Am I compromised?"

"Negative, continue the mission. The target is the British Foreign Secretary, Hammon."

"Mmmm-mmm. There's a bodyguard and – and now one woman getting out, a pretty woman. Hammon now getting out."

In the crosshairs of the sight, the target was now available as Hammon stepped from the car, with the door being held open by an aide.

"Preparing to assassinate," Wormwood said as a whisper to himself. He diligently placed his finger on the trigger, controlled his breathing and heart rate, and made ready his shot.

At the precise moment he almost squeezed the trigger, the woman innocently stepped in the way and the line of sight was blocked. It was then impossible to regain a shot as within an instant the two were immersed in a circle of men and swiftly escorted into the building.

"No clear shot, Screwtape. Please advise."

"Remain in position and wait for instructions."

"Acknowledged. Wormwood now on standby."

As soon as they had arrived at the Israeli Parliament, Hammon and Esther were instantly aware of extra men surrounding them who swiftly and professionally swept them into the entrance hall without being disrespectful. With the minimum of words, these men in suits hurried the surprised newcomers to one side, diverting them from the main openness of the foyer. There was no explanation given.

"I didn't expect this," whispered Esther, but the Foreign Secretary had seen Scabbards approach him with additional Israeli men and did not reply.

"Scabbards, what is happening?" he asked.

"Come with us, sir," Scabbards replied. "There's been an alert. You need to leave."

"An alert?" asked Esther. "Leave?"

Scabbards nodded with apprehension and discretion all in one action. He then motioned to Hammon to follow.

"What about Esther?" asked Hammon.

"It's just you, sir."

Esther became anxious: "What about the meeting? You need to open the peace talks."

Hammon, for the first time that Esther experienced, spoke softly to her, respectfully and reverently: "You can give it."

"No I can't! I'm the secretary! I'm the dumb blonde! They're all going to ask who's this blonde bimbo! What's with the bimbo? You've got the panache, Mister Hammon. I can't do it."

Scabbards held Hammon's sleeve and tugged at it: "We need to go, sir, now, with these men."

Hammon suddenly became imploring, maintaining his tact and respect: "You know the speech inside out. You know it better than me."

"I'm not one for public speaking. I'm not one for the public. I'm not even one for speaking."

"Esther! You've been on the News plenty of times. Now, for such a time as this, go and be the woman of the moment."

With that, Hammon, Scabbards and the bodyguards were gone after turning into a side corridor.

"Misses Whyte?" asked the nearest man. "I'm Baruch Gendel. This way, please."

But Esther was more attentive to her worrying thoughts.

"Misses Whyte? This way, if you please."

Esther looked at the man who stood patiently waiting for her response: "Yes, of course." She then followed his lead.

"The Prime Minister is fondly waiting to greet you," said Baruch as if to make light conversation.

"The Prime Minister?"

"Yes, of Israel."

"We have met once before."

"Really?"

"Yes, I played the piano. Can I have some moments to compose myself?"

"Of course, we can accommodate anything you wish. Here we are, through this door."

The door they had arrived at was respectfully opened and they went through to find, in the middle of a room set aside for welcoming dignitaries, a genteel man who stood up to greet her with gracefulness: "Misses Whyte, I am so pleased to meet you again. If you can remember, I'm Ananiah Schuber, the Israeli Prime Minister. May I call you Esther? I am so much looking forward to hearing your opening speech to the assembly. I consider it a first, in fact."

"A first?"

"That a mere British woman be given this opportunity."

Esther was startled and looked dismayed.

"My dear, you look worried."

"I am. I only came as an aide to my Foreign Secretary."

"I am totally assured that you have the necessary temerity to see this through."

"I'm sorry, Prime Minister, but – speaking frankly, I feel that something is amiss."

"I think that a heart-felt, sincere imploring woman, someone who is respected by her country, someone eager to say how things are, someone eager to do what is right, even though in strained circumstances, may be the one thing this peace process needs. I have full confidence in you."

"Prime Minister, the trouble is I'm not – "

"The trouble is, someone with beauty is never around to use it to good effect. Instead, they either flaunt it unceremoniously in fashionable, glamorous poses that are far from the real world, or they flaunt it ceremoniously in a beauty pageant and talk pretentiously about world peace. You, my dear, are a rare breed of female because you are none of that."

"Yes, but – it's just that, I'm not, you see, the type of woman to just – "

"You do not have to tell me you are nervous. I can see that you are, but courage is not the absence of fear. Courage is letting yourself do what is needed to be done, in spite of your fears. Say what is on your heart, Esther. Be the woman of the moment. It may transpire that what you say will prevent worse things happening." He ended with a graceful smile.

Hammon and Scabbards were shown into a small room containing chairs around a conference table. They were told to wait and then left alone, having security men outside keep guard.

Grinning, Hammon shook his head in amazement as he sat down. "Scabbards, I have to hand it to you. This is truly remarkable how you pulled it off. It looks all too authentic. I wanted Esther manipulated to give the speech and here it is happening. I didn't think you could do it."

"This isn't me."

"It isn't?"

"No sir, there is something happening for real."

Hammon's face of confidence was broken by an ashen look of dismay: "I'm in danger for real?"

"Yes sir, but they're not giving me full details."

With this revelation, Hammon sat back heavily in his seat.

"My plan was something else," said Scabbards, still standing.

"At least Esther is going to give her speech."

"There's something telling me they want her to give it anyway. The only thing that's gone to plan is she doesn't have it."

"Where is it?"

"In my pocket. She will have to perform unscripted if she goes ahead."

"If she goes ahead."

Esther followed Baruch Gendel along a corridor, through some doors, passing security guards, to find a closed entrance attended by a doorman.

Baruch turned to Esther, appeared to measure her eminence with his quick inspection and then nodded to the attendant.

The large assembly hall beyond was opened to Esther, who paused, seeing how full and large it was. "I'm sorry, I was only expecting to see a small delegation – around a table, a small table – of Israelis and Palestinians, in a small, small room; not the whole Parliament," she said quietly to Baruch.

"Well, they're here to see you," he replied, motioning with a confident smile to the stage and the podium, and gently touched her arm as if to escort her.

But Esther, now wanting to portray courage, entered of her own accord as though built of bronze to withhold feelings of her own beheading. As she made her way up the steps, the men of the hall became silent as they settled themselves and watched her approach the rostrum. Her heartbeat was pounding. She felt like screaming. Baruch was no longer at her side. She was totally alone. Without remembering how, she had crossed the stage and now stood before them.

With all the world looking at her, patiently, expectantly, silently, she gazed at them from her position, speechless with inner fright in not seeing the script. The podium shelf was empty. The script was nowhere to be seen. Unknown to her, she continued to appear in quiet contemplation and command, as if studying each member of the assembly and able to penetrate their hidden thoughts, secret agendas, private plans, inner complexities, bringing a controlling influence over them from the lone, single female. If that was not enough, they were quietly and unknowing entranced by her alluring beauty.

To Esther, her scrutiny of the hall was not a conscious method of controlling the atmosphere, although that was how it was perceived. In her inner mind, her hidden fears were on the absent speech and the terrifying waves of doubt about what she truly believed. In that moment, the walls of her inner-self were about to crack and bring about a crashing catastrophe. All she could do was to give a prayer within the turmoil of her thoughts and, with desperation, she willed God to know her plight and pick her up. Her impassioned motivation to tell of her drive for world peace had deserted her, and she stood mesmerised by this surreal position in which she now found herself. She could not remember the speech that she had written, nor the one she had been assembling in her head as she lay in bed, night after night, sleepless, with her imagination constructing the script of what she really wanted to say.

Then, from the result of her earnest prayer, the words and passion came to her in a flood of adrenaline, and her answer flowed as a serene river that found an awesome sea.

With the words now constructing themselves from her chaotic thoughts, she gave one final speechless look at her audience and then obeyed the words that had arrived.

"There is trouble – in Africa!"

Now that she had started from this strange stance, she had to continue and connect her position with Africa. She stopped again, the next set of words was missing, and she stood speechless. The audience was tense to hear more, their attention now fully gained. Then she continued from the rising of more words within her.

"There is conflict – in Afghanistan! There is turmoil in Iraq – and tension – with Korea! The Ukraine can erupt. Egypt and Libya are in disarray. Syria is being ripped apart. Yemen is saturated with strife. Sudan is entrenched in many decades of genocide. Weapons are prevalent. Crime is rampant. Corruption is rife. Slavery is endemic."

No one questioned her assessment.

"With access to arms, individuals with grievances assassinate their fellow citizens on their killing sprees with their deranged vendettas. Everywhere there is theft and murder and deception, and no one is honest. Abusiveness, incrimination, and foul language are in every direction. Hate and selfishness and perceived self-importance has saturated everything."

By now the assembly had noticeably sat back with the authoritative intonation of her words and the command she had.

"But there is one place, on Earth, that has no excuse – and that place is here."

Again, she stopped and looked almost at each member, waiting for more words.

"From all the religious leaders, the miracles, the laws and history, the Holy Land is mandated to be at peace. If peace cannot come here, then there is no hope for the world."

Esther was now in control, but unknown to her, she was running the danger of saying too much in her rolling pride.

"Mankind has always been driven by power, possessions and self-glory, with the belief that he is entitled to everything he surveys; that he can possess and control; that he does have power; that there is absolute understanding and knowledge in all there is – just as it was when we were told the lie of the forbidden tree and its fruit. And this tribal strife, here in this diseased land, is about possession and power. But pick up some soil, some sand, hold it in your grasp and ask yourself – who truly owns it? Who can truly hold on to a handful of soil and claim to be its owner? Who can truly claim to be able to take it through death to judgement day and still say it is theirs?

"I ask this not just of Israelis, or Palestinians. Does America truly own America when having taken the land from the native Indians? Who truly owns Northern Ireland, the Falklands? Who has the rights to own anything?"

Esther went silent, and then answered her own question, "No one lives long enough."

With a deep breath, she continued in tempo. "Do you think Abraham, the father of your nation, thought he could own the land as much as God Himself? Even Abraham, living as a nomad, never thought he would own the Promised Land, even when God promised it to him – because Abraham knew he would never live to see it.

"But does this mean we are born to die, with nothing, leaving nothing? Of course not. It is the responsibility we own, a stewardship we have for each other, for the world. We are to learn the potential within us and to die with character."

There was the glowing feeling of completeness within Esther's heart, a satisfaction that she was creating a masterpiece in their presence. They were witnesses to her winning her race.

"It is written within your own Scripture – that foreigners must not be ill-treated, as you were once foreigners in Egypt. It is written – treat them as well as you treat citizens and love them as much as you love yourself. You were His chosen people and much was expected, but despite you, Jesus still came. God kept His promise with Abraham."

It was now evident that the assembly was becoming agitated and rustled like annoyed leaves in sporadic drafts, but Esther, so within her speech, was not aware of any growing tension.

"So stand beside God, see what He sees, understand the world how God wants it – a Kingdom of justice, a family of Heaven, with God as our king. Stand beside God, look over the edge and see what He sees, as Sodom and Gomorrah were surveyed. See the world for what we have made it, for what it has become. Do you see a place that is even worth negotiating a rescue?"

Esther shook her head.

"We have all fallen: no one deserves to own the land, no one deserves to live. Who am I to come here, today, to stand before you, a mere woman with her own plight and failings? I have no right to tell you these truths, when there is unrighteousness in my own life. No one has the right to tell an Israeli father to forgive the Palestinian who killed his child. No one has the right to tell a Palestinian mother to forgive the Israeli who killed her child."

Esther paused, suddenly aware of the words having stopped in her mind. She looked out at those listening to her. None of them were inattentive and her pause heightened their focus.

Then the words came flooding back to her: "But God has the right. In Jesus, He came here, to Jerusalem, and we assassinated Him, Jew and Gentile, in the cruellest of ways – a horrific way that left Him alone, rejected by His own creation, to endure the torture that we inflicted on Him. But He forgave us, because He sees us as worth rescuing, even up until the very last moment before tyranny overwhelms the world.

"No law, no government, no signed agreement, no sprite speaker – no one can solve the tribulation the world is in – except God, and our changed heart. He is the only one who has the right to tell someone to forgive. Let forgiveness be your weapon. Only then will previous treaties and agreements, so worthless and ignored, will be so surpassed. Have His Scripture written into your very core and not on fabric. Let this be your Levitical sacrifice, worth more than anything in the Law of Moses.

"Make peace for all our children, that we don't teach them the ways of hate, to make changes for good that transcends not only those around us, but for all those living beyond borders we all erect. The leadership of the Holy Land should not be considered a trophy or glamorous or self-seeking, but a dedication to righteous administration to all those living here and the world, as Heaven would have things done. Peace on Earth, as it is in Heaven. Let Israel walk into Palestinian land – and, side by side with Palestinians – rebuild Palestinian homes. Let Palestine, side by side with Israel, build Israeli homes. Let the children of Israel comfort the children of Gaza; and the children of Gaza, comfort the children of Israel – so they learn they are of the same in grief – to teach them that more strength of character is needed to work for peace, than to relent to the anger of vengeance that will only escalate in ever increasing vengeance and lead to the annihilation of us all – a senseless rage that will bring about the end of *everything* within the age of this generation.

"Let God's strength destroy all our earthly monuments, our religious temples and sacred sites of antiquity. May He rebuild in every one of us an impression of His own character. Have the active hope that all evil and suffering will be eradicated by what He does. Live righteously in Jesus' judgement. Let us live, as men and women and children, as families, as people – as people of God's community, here on Earth – as Citizens of Heaven. Prepare for the time when Jerusalem will be worthy of being the centre of righteous government for the world and for the return of the Son of David, the King and High Priest of Mankind."

Esther felt her words were coming to an end, and she stopped, as if short of something more, but nothing more came. Now speechless, she concentrated on the audience and for the first time suddenly felt that not all was as successful as her passion had led her to believe. Before her, she saw confrontation and contempt, a darkness of ill-judgement, a brooding pit of vipers in need of unleashing their venom. They were now agitated and spoke with anger and dismay to each other; anger and dismay directed at her.

"May God forgive me if I sounded self-righteous," Esther breathed to herself, unable to move, mesmerised with the ill-effect she had produced. With the sinking feeling within her stomach, she could only stand as if transfixed, held within the imprisonment of her self and unable to prevent becoming a target for their aggression.

"We fought for this land!" was one irate elderly outburst.

Like a ricochet around the hall, came more cries from the growing loudness of discontent.

"They didn't kill your son!"

"When was your house bombed?"

"Destroy our holy sites? Blasphemous! Blasphemous!"

"Never trust the arrogant British!"

"Who are you? We survived the Nazi Holocaust!"

"How dare you declare that the Messiah has already come!"

"We all know how the Christians love each other! Just go to the Holy Sepulchre!"

It was at this moment that Baruch Gendel was by her side, grabbing her arm and leading her off the stage. "Keep with me. We need to get you out of here," was all Baruch said in a polite and modest tone as they left the hall to escape the insurgent anger.

"I went too far, didn't I?" Esther breathed as a statement. "What have I done?"

He did not reply but dutifully took her through the building as people appeared. They marched with determination through the corridors as men started to accumulate with intimidation.

Such was the hatred electrically charged in the air, it was almost conclusive that a new horrific persecuting war between vast populations was to erupt; religious, political, ideological, financial, even nuclear in manner.

The sniper, rifle still ready, had paced the room for a while, but had now returned to his firing position to study the view through his scope out of intrigue rather than professionalism. He then had a sudden demon's voice in his earpiece.

"Wormwood? You online?"

"Online, Screwtape."

"Target will be at the front entrance in one minute."

"Acknowledged."

"New target." There was then a pause with nothing forthcoming.

"Say again?"

"Target the woman."

"The woman?"

"The target is the British woman. Do you comply?"

"The secretary? The blonde?" Wormwood asked confused and aghast.

"Yes, the woman; the woman who arrived with Haman."

"You want me to assassinate the blonde woman?"

"Yes, the woman!"

"But she's a woman. What importance is she?"

"Are you questioning the order?"

"No."

"Are you refusing the order?"

"She's – no I'm not refusing the order. She's just – beautiful."

"You are paid to directly carry out orders!"

"When have I ever not?"

Uncle Screwtape ignored the comment as he fermented in his own marinating anger: "Who is she to lecture us? How dare an arrogant British female lecture us on forgiveness! What has she been through?"

Wormwood was no longer listening, fully attentive on performing his orders to the precise letter, skilfully, surgically, clinically. His wait was at an end when the woman appeared. She looked upset as she waited in front of the building. He placed his finger on the trigger, controlled his breathing and heart, but by staring at the gorgeous female and taking delight in her feminine figure, his heart was harder to control than usual.

The shot was clear; the shot was easy; the shot would kill and the target was waiting.

"Preparing to assassinate," he breathed to himself.

But he could not fire.

"What are you waiting for? Shoot the woman!" urged the demon in his ears. "Shoot the woman! Do it!"

"She's beautiful," he whispered.

"It's an order!"

With more conviction, Wormwood reapplied his finger to the trigger: "Preparing to assassinate. Targeting her heart."

At the precise instant he almost signalled his finger to contract, the voice shouted at him: "Don't shoot! Stand down!"

"What?"

"Stand down, leave her, go offline, now."

"I almost shot her! I almost shot her tiny heart out! What the Devil are you playing at?"

"Just obey the command and disappear quietly. There is a better time and place to end Misses Whyte."

"Okay, this is Wormwood, going quietly and disappearing until you get your act together."

Delayed Judgement

You cannot know my entrenched feelings of guilt and remorse. I perpetually return in my thoughts to Israel and that speech which fills me with dread for having given it. One day, after much terror, Jerusalem will have a new landscape, but with my last visit to Israel, I almost made it possible this would occur within my own lifetime.

I am reading the Bible as an obsession and my dreams at night are intricately linked to my feelings and reading. These dreams are vivid and powerful. I am not one normally to remember my dreams, but now I recall the colours, and I can smell fragrances and almost feel I am touching what is before me.

I was in another dream, a golden dream, a dream with golden fields of wheat that were vast. Beyond were green and auburn trees, tremendous mountains and glorious waterfalls. Clouds of pure white reached overhead within the brilliant, wonderful sky, with the air feeling fresh and with the smell of honey, the warm sunshine on my face. As I walked through the fields, I became aware that my direction was taking me to a mighty stone platform, a high stage, a massive dais, with steps on all sides leading up to the top from where all else could be seen. At the base of these wide steps was a man I could only describe as an angel. He peacefully stood, content in my approach, but beckoned me to hurry.

When I reached him, he ushered me up with a sense of urgency and I arose to the top to see it as a mighty stone dais for a towering throne, its tall majestic back to me. I crept to the back of this throne and then along its side, and saw at the front a bright figure standing, powerful by appearance and to be feared. His back was to me as He listened to the reports of the angels before Him, whose concerned faces I could see. I stopped where I was, fearful of getting nearer, but the angel who had ushered me up to this height was now standing to my side, behind me. He stood as if to do duty, as if to protect me, as if to assure me by the way he stood.

"Do you know what is being decided?" my escort whispered to me.

I said no, but it felt wonderful yet dreadful.

"The angels are reporting what is happening on Earth."

I continued to watch, spellbound, as this almighty figure, His back still to me, listened to the last few reports. He turned from them to consider His decision as the sky turned dark and aggressive. I hid behind the throne for the sheer weight of fear that swelled within me, but my angel beckoned me to the side again and see the events unfolding with the cover of the throne's arm. I saw the Heavenly King of all, suddenly weep and crouch with the weight of His sorrow, and with stormy anger, He stood up, defiant, with cutting judgement now filling the air.

"What is your command, Lord?" the angels, with bowed heads, asked.

With a booming voice, still soaked in sorrow but drenched with fearsome anger, the King cried out with a thunderous voice that shook everything and reached the skies. Everyone felt the weight of the wind from His lungs and the fire of His fury. Such were His words that they boomed from a cavernous chest: "Tear apart gravity! Rip it open! Annihilate time before everything is ruined! Crush every galaxy! Take away the planets! Put out the stars! Let nothing escape! Smash every atom! Extinguish every breath! Castrate all of life! Obliterate this vile evil!" He stopped as if to give some respite, but then

He roared His final command: "Unleash Heaven!" The last word was lengthened with the sheer power of His anguish and disappointment, as if the air of His lungs became a roaring furnace.

There was a silence as the thunder melted away, as if in wait, as if there was a purpose, an unspoken reason beyond my knowledge.

I knew there were my loved-ones still on Earth and I feared for them. I feared for all of them, because they did not know what was coming, and I rushed out into the blinding light, hiding my eyes behind my hands and arms. "No!" I cried. "No! Please not yet, please!"

When I looked, I was within the crowd of angels who looked at me, protecting me.

"It has been commanded," said one of them. "It is within Scripture. Any more time given and all will become rotten."

"No! Please No!"

I was told to look to the golden fields of wheat, but what I saw was now a vast sea of worthless weeds and thorns and dead wood. It was a wasteland, trampled into mud, with forests chopped down and discarded. A terrible mist was unmoving and dirty pools were not able to provide any life. Like an infection, sin had reached everyone and nothing was golden any more. Everything was wrecked and far from what had been intended with the golden life I had witnessed at my arrival. The Earth, in fact the entire universe had become a ghetto, and all those within it walked within streams of worms and awful, horrid insects, but they could not see it. Bacteria had 'gone wrong' and everyone had become diseased, and yet they still didn't understand the reason for their misery. They couldn't see any of it, because they chose not to. They did not know what was being decided in Heaven because they cared not to search.

I begged for mercy, but the angels told me it was time for the sheep and goats to be separated, for the Harvest of wheat and weeds, for the weeds to be discarded and burnt, and the wheat to celebrate in the new life, the new Earth, the feast with the Heavenly King.

But I turned and tried to confront the God of all, earnestly petitioning to withhold judgement if a hundred worthy people could be found on Earth. There was silence as I sensed impending doom on myself from my sudden wild, impetuous boldness. Then, with all incredibility, after a moment of silence, I received my reply.

"I will delay my judgement if a hundred people can be found," was His mighty answer.

In the following silence, I found it expectant of me to say what was to be said next, like a script everyone knew, as despair was within me that no one–

hundred people would be found. I argued for fifty people, just fifty people on Earth to be found worthy, but I instantly knew this was a useless gesture.

"I will delay my judgement if fifty people can be found," again was the patient, commanding reply.

I fought to withhold my petition, but there came a sense of real danger and hopelessness, and my fear and anguish burst from me in sobbing despair: "Please delay judgement if ten can be found, please, just ten."

He paused even longer to consider my request: "I will delay judgement if ten can be found."

I knew that not even ten would be found worthy and I found it within my heart to whisper my last request. Looking down, gloomily I asked, "What if only one can be found?"

He pointed to one enormous bronze cauldron, large enough to reach my chest from the floor and too large for my embrace to reach even half the diameter. It had my name on it: Hadassah. I looked within, knowing that what I saw represented all the prayers I had made in my entire life. The cauldron was hardly used. As plentiful as my prayer life I felt I had, I became despondent that my life could have catered for more prayer. I fell to the floor with grief for all the causes to pray, and I had not done so. I even realised my most golden prayers were before I had become a Christian, when I was being abused, as young as I was. I saw throughout my life that I had not mustered the strength to put God first. David was first. I wept bitterly for the little I had considered God's holiness and the great cost made on my behalf to permit such closeness. I wept that I had not come as close to this most wonderful, loving God as I could have done and I felt the extreme loss and waste of my life. My dress was sodden in the blood of my sins. It was on my hands, down my face, my back, my legs. I could not wipe it off.

No one said anything. I wept like an adulterous woman about to be stoned to death.

I knew not even one person would be found by God to be worthy. Not one of us was worthy to open the book of life, and I wept because of it.

Being gentle and kind, generating a wonderful, fulfilling love that could be felt with every part of me, with all the dust that I am, this dazzling figure crouched down as a loving father would and spoke to me with a soft voice that could not be argued against: "Fear nothing, I command, my child. The Lamb can open the book of life, for this is no longer the blood of your sins. This is the blood of the Lamb, the Passover, and the cost has been paid. I am not afraid to love you. Enter through this one gate. Enter the feast of the Tabernacle and enjoy my company. The Lamb has opened the book of life, my Hadassah."

I stopped crying.

"These things will happen, even if you were not to believe. I will delay Judgement until the unrighteous man has arrived. See and know that I will make all things new. All will know my judgement is perfect."

My body burnt with rushing fire and when it stopped, I looked down and saw I had been cured. I was wearing a white beautiful gown and a new wondrous body. I was given a new and replenished me.

He pointed to the horizon, and the golden fields had returned. I felt a strong sense of calm and peacefulness. I could have stayed forever, standing there blissfully admiring what I saw, but one of the angels took my hand and led me to the front of this huge Temple Mount to show me more steps leading down. My time to remain at home was still to come. I had to return to the ghetto. Instead of weeping for my plight, I was weeping from sheer relief of this forgiveness.

Sinbad's Charter

"Well congratulations, sir," announced Scabbards, dropping a heap of newspapers on Hammon's desk. "Peace talks are a complete shambles – a complete shambles they say."

Hammon did not reply, nor did he look up from his vacant thinking.

"Sir? Aren't you happy? This is what you wanted. And Esther caused it all. I'm impressed you made it happen."

At this Hammon looked up: "I've just had the American President on the phone congratulating me."

"He's impressed you made it happen as well?"

"On the contrary, he said someone should have been bold enough to have said it years ago, and then said the bad reaction was a shame. He didn't even want to discuss how to clear up this bad reaction – just gave a whole lot of praise for Misses Whyte for not being diplomatic, for saying it as it is and giving a good show about it. Not that he wanted to go on record. I think he's fond of her playing the piano."

"Oh well, I'm sure the PM will have something to say."

"He did! He also said Esther should be secretly given a medal or honorary title."

"Was he joking?"

"Certainly not, and he was almost ridiculing me on the shambles of my departure." Hammon shook his head, bewildered. "Look! Just look at these papers. All of them reporting on the bad behaviour of the Israelis and Palestinians and the collapse of the peace talks, but look at this – Esther is the hero of it all – even though she caused it! I can't believe it! It all goes wrong, she's to blame, but gets great respect for it, whilst I, not to blame, gets ridiculed!"

"I think deep down, actually, really, deep down, *you* now respect Esther – and it's this respect that is actually infuriating you."

"Don't be absurd!"

"Come on, she's perfect. Say it. Even all the Atheists are saying these things should have been said a long time ago. This Christian woman even has Atheists supporting her. That's got to be an achievement that's getting up your nose."

"You're not helping, Scabbards."

Scabbards, having stood all the while, sat down in the chair across from the desk. "What do you want done?"

"I want to fire her, but we're called to the UN Security Council in New York for further discussions and she's been ordered to attend. She should be given some other sideways job, out of the way, as we normally do with embarrassing bodies who can't really be fired."

"And what's the problem with that?"

"She has too much support and popularity from everyone to stay where she is."

"You surely can't keep her on? Surely she's like a red blanket to a seething pack of raging bulls in the Middle East. And everyone else is really only taken in by her good looks and pretty piano-playing."

"For the first time, I don't know what to do."

"What if you were able to get something legitimate? I mean, really something legitimately dirty to dishonour and sack her. No one will look at you strange if she had to step down because of something scandalous was found. You then clear up the mess, you then get the credit, and you destroy her popularity as you increase yours."

"You are referring to Sinbad."

"Get Sinbad to look into her background, history, banking, everything and let the dirt do the talking. Sinbad always finds something. Sinbad has never failed you. Sinbad's the best there is."

Hammon gave no reply.

"I've said this all along, but you wanted this elaborate plan. Believe me, elaborate plans never work. If you plan for bananas, like an executive making remote, intricate, elaborate plans, you get monkeys. So let me get Sinbad on the case. It's much simpler."

"What if there is nothing?"

"There will be something. Perhaps something messy happened between her and David Kingsley."

"But what if there is nothing? Can Sinbad set something up?"

Scabbards shook his head: "I've never known Sinbad to do that. I think there's always something that there's no need for a set-up."

"Okay, get some dirt on her, but let Sinbad know I'm prepared to raise his usual payment."

Queen Jezebel

"This is a bad idea," muttered Jonathan with dejection standing beside David.

"We said we would meet her at the airport. So here we are."

Waiting at the Arrivals gate of Heathrow and knowing from the information board that the relevant flight from Los Angeles had landed, David and Jonathan continued to study the swarm of reporters and television crew.

"No, she asked *you* to be at the airport and you said *we* will."

"Well, let's be true to our word."

"If you ask me, this is a bad idea. At least we're not in uniform. You do know that once she comes through Arrivals you'll have to get in front of that lot."

"They'll not be concentrating on us."

The two stood quietly watching the group of reporters getting ready.

"Esther came through here earlier," Jonathan suddenly said, "from the collapse of the peace conference."

"Yes."

"Another hour earlier and you two would have met."

"Mmmm."

"What do you really think to her speech?"

David did not respond.

"You know, I would have thought you would have had something to say about her. I saw her as quite the Salvation Army Officer."

"All right, if you really want to know: I thought what she did was truly enormous, moving, impressive. I certainly wouldn't have had it in me."

"Why don't you tell her?"

"No chance."

"Instead we're here. I don't know what we're doing here."

"Getting Jezebel away from the reporters."

"You really think Jezebel wants that? Did you see all the reporters chasing after Esther this morning? I feel for her. Poor Mark had a job to get her away."

"She liked the attention in the past."

"Well she looked quite fearful this time, but this Jezebel definitely wants the attention, massive attention. She craves all this media hype, and she wants you drawn into it. That's all this is. Getting connected to you gains her more novelty."

"Don't be daft. How will I ever be a novelty?"

"Publicity, publicity," Jonathan muttered with annoyance.

"Well let's just make the best of the moment, then."

"Which I think is now."

Jezebel's arrival could not be set by the time of a clock, but it could be set by the reaction of the reporters, who all became animated. Security also became vigilant with the increase of activity and then a sudden flurry of men taking pictures erupted as she walked through their milling.

Enjoying the wide interest in her, Jezebel walked from the Arrivals exit, smiling and looking stunning. She even stopped to give answers in the flare of flashlights and questions.

David was frozen.

Jonathan nudged him: "This would be your cue."

Taking a breath for reassurance, David approached Jezebel through the rabble.

Immediately when seeing him, Jezebel beamed a radiant smile and, bringing him closer, naturally allowed him to be photographed with her, arm-in-arm, smiling like never before. It gave the impression they had already met and were more acquainted than truth would admit. Truth or no truth, the reporters found the encounter all the more stimulating.

"Why have you come to London, Jezebel?" asked one reporter.

"I've come to prepare for my new perfume range to be launched here later this year." Her answer was relaxed, cheerful and courteous, and tinged with fun. "But I'm going to spend a few days just sight-seeing and visiting The Salvation Army and see their work. And here's my handsome English escort." With a smile that seemed to pre-empt a kiss, she turned to him: "Right, ready to go?"

David just nodded and motioned the direction to walk.

As they made their way, the reporters surrounding them naturally withdrew and diminished in number to chase time getting their photographs published. Within moments, Jonathan had joined David and they were at the side of a limousine that someone had organised.

"Welcome to London," said David, opening the door.

"Thank you. It's great to be here and to meet you, Mister Kingsley, or may I call you David."

Jonathan interjected before David could answer: "Call him what you like, I do."

This brought a chuckle from Jezebel who stood by the open car door, not about to enter.

"This is Jonathan," introduced David, "who does all the work that keeps it all going. Probably why he calls me anything he likes – with limits."

Jonathan turned to Jezebel: "I would call him the boss, but really it would be me."

Amused, Jezebel beckoned them to follow as she got into the car: "Listen! You guys hitch a lift with me." She repeated it with more encouragement when sat on the back seat.

The two men, raising their eyebrows at each other, stepped into the car to find a seat directly opposite Jezebel. The driver, who had been waiting, closed the door and drove them away from the airport, with the whole scene having been captured on camera by a few photographers and travellers passing by.

When the car was on its way, Jezebel took off a hairpiece, and, looking just as stunning with her natural golden hair, scratched her head: "I'm glad that's off. These things itch like the plague."

"Are you travelling alone?" asked David.

"My entourage has already arrived and already at the hotel. Want a drink? Don't worry, it's not alcoholic. I don't drink alcohol. It's not good for you. But I do have a cocktail here of healthy juices: orange, kiwi, mandarin, mango and other stuff. I love mango. You love mango?" She helped herself to a drink and maintained the offer to the two gents.

"I love mango," replied David and a drink was passed to him.

Jonathan declined.

With enthusiasm depicting years younger, Jezebel generated an excitement and showed her eagerness: "I would really love to see your work for the homeless. Can we do that this afternoon?"

"Yep," responded David. "We can show you around the workshop and take it from there. My office is actually on top of a healthcare centre, but we can show you that as well."

"And I would like to hear the orchestra of yours, if that's possible."

"It doesn't exactly belong to me."

"Well, whatever."

Jonathan, although silent and appearing congenial, had a weak shell around him where his dislike to the construction of the plans was breaking through to any psychologist.

The conversation was civil and respectful, and David felt that her demeanour was not what he had expected. Instead of someone who he thought would be thoughtless, she was knowledgeable and conducted a conversation any Manor house would be proud of with the details she already knew about The Salvation Army, London and David himself.

"You've done your homework."

Jezebel shook her head: "Only what I read in the papers."

"I'm in the American papers?"

Jezebel shook her head again: "No, English. I sometimes read the English papers and I also read the *Salvationist* now and again."

The rest of the journey saw Jonathan becoming more and more quiet, David becoming more and more attentive, and Jezebel continuing to be the actress with her chatter and amusement.

"Ah! And here we are!" Jezebel exclaimed, looking out of the window to see they had now parked outside the Savoy. "And there's Pashhur! Sweet Pashhur. He's very hardworking, you know."

The door opened and in looked a young, handsome Asian, wearing a smart, stylish suit.

"Pashhur!" exclaimed Jezebel, and she embraced him at the same time leaving the car. "Here are the two Englishmen who are kind enough to show me London."

Pashhur held out his hand and within a moment, all the men had introduced themselves.

"Come inside," beckoned Jezebel as she walked through the front entrance.

David and Jonathan followed and stood in the richly adorned foyer, quiet as any mouse, not feeling they belonged.

While Pashhur attended to the receptionist, Jezebel stood with the two, chatting merrily away. "Listen, I just need to get freshened up," she said cheerfully when Pashhur had finished, "and then I'll be with you to see your work, yes? Would it be all right for you to wait? We can go in my car."

David agreed while Jonathan maintained his politeness.

"Good! Thank you, both. Won't be long."

Jezebel, disappearing up the stairs with Pashhur, left David and Jonathan to loiter in the foyer.

"So how long is long?" asked Jonathan.

"She said she won't be long."

"So how long is not long?"

"Not long is not longer than long."

"Is that more or less than a while?"

"A while is longer than long."

"You do know that she could be up there a while or so getting ready. You know what women are like at the best of times, let alone a woman famous the world-over for changing her looks every ten seconds. Will we recognise her when she comes out again?"

"If she can change within ten seconds, she'll be quick, then."

Jezebel walked beside Pashhur as they made their way to the room, and then Pashhur opened the door and offered Jezebel to enter. There, in the luxury apartment were four females unpacking and making ready to create Jezebel into someone new.

Pashhur pointed at a door across from the main room: "Your bedroom would be through there. I have the next apartment along the corridor."

After inspecting what the women were preparing, Jezebel walked through to her inner room, beckoning with her finger for Pashhur to join her. When they were alone, with the solid, sturdy doors closed, they could say whatever they wished.

"Do you think he likes you?" asked Pashhur.

"Oh, he likes me: his gestures, mannerisms, posture, what he says, the way he says it, the way his dark pupils become larger when he sees me. He wiggles his foot when I wiggle mine, crosses his legs, licks his teeth when I do. Oh he likes me, Pashhur. I think there is a part of him that is deeply hidden, that is deeply sensuous, that I can softly and tenderly dig for – and reach at the right moment."

"Not the challenge you hoped for then."

"Oh there is a challenge all right. There's his conscience to break, and I'm not sure if his friend can sense my intention. I'll have to ask if it could just be me and David for the rest of the time here."

"So what's the plan, my Queen Jez?"

"I said to show me his work, but I'm a bit tired now. I don't want to show a shred of what could look like boredom. So I think I'll let him know to cancel it this afternoon, make a big day of it tomorrow. I'll get some sleep for now."

"What about tonight? You going to get him tonight?"

"Certainly not! I'm going to take my time. Besides I want him to take me out."

"A meal?"

"Something I have always wanted to do. Can you pass me that note pad and pen by the telephone? And call a porter to get this to him." As Jezebel sat at her dressing table, she started to write.

All the while, David and Jonathan waited in the Savoy foyer.

"What really was that about?" said Jonathan eventually. "At the airport?"

"She came into London."

"She made sure you were in the photos. She treated you like a long lost pal, like you and her has some lovey bond-thing stitching you both together."

"No she didn't. She was cheerful. She was more cheerful than you."

"This Jezebel is not good, David."

"She was polite and courteous. You weren't."

"You've been caught up in her charm already."

"No I haven't. What do you mean?"

"The way you are, the happy, subtle melody in your voice. You unconsciously copied all her subconscious moves, and your mannerisms were more pronounced."

"More pronounced? What are you talking about?"

Quietly for the thick carpet, came a young porter from the stairs and stood beside David: "Sir, there's a personal letter for you." The lad then held out an envelope and David took it.

"Thank you." David opened it and read the single page as the porter went on with his duties.

Jonathan became impatient: "What does it say?"

"She wants a night out."

"A night out? What does that mean?"

"And there's a cheque – for The Salvation Army."

Jonathan looked over David's shoulder and whistled at the amount.

"What does she mean a night out?"

"A meal? I don't know. Her handwriting is not her best feature. Here, you read it."

"Well we can't exactly take her to Pizza Hut."

"Why not?"

"You are joking, aren't you?"

"Looks like she's written something about soup. Where are we going to take her?"

"We? We? Look, I'm doing all I can for you, but I'm not going that far."

The two were then silent in their own thoughts and confusion.

"Okay," eventually sounded Jonathan, "how about I get in touch with some of my old bosses. They'll be able to get a booking at the last minute at a plush place for you – and her. How about that?"

"Thanks."

"I'm not saying this will happen though."

"No."

"But I'll do my best."

"Thanks."

"Let's just get out of here."

Why does Satan get all the News?

"Breakfast," announced Mark as he walked into the bright-white bedroom carrying a tray with a glass of orange juice, coffee, and a bowl of cereal.

Esther was still in bed but awake enough to sit up, although wincing with pain from her aches. She received the tray from her husband and kindly thanked him.

Mark sat alongside her, leaned over and kissed his wife: "Morning sleepy."

"What is the time?"

"Early afternoon."

"I was out like a light when we got in. Thanks for getting me away from the airport – and those reporters."

"Let's not go through that again. They were like a pack of hounds. Did you see how desperate they were?"

"I'm trying to forget."

"David was on the News earlier."

"Mmm?"

"He picked up that American Jezebel at the same place we landed. If we had got there an hour later, we would have met." Mark then thought he saw the heavy weight of Esther's feelings that she tried to cover and knew to pass over the subject. He got up, turned to the window and partially parted the curtains to study the reporters: "There are more of them now. No wonder celebrities get annoyed."

"Mummy! Mummy!" cried Merry as she ran into the room. She jumped on the bed for a hug, carrying her teddy bear that was half tucked into her dressing gown.

"Mind, Merry! Mummy's got a hot drink here."

Merry was imploring: "Make them go!"

"Can't make them go, sweetie, the street is a free place."

Mark joined the two females on the bed and took another sip of his coffee: "Well something needs to be done."

"They'll be gone soon," said Esther.

"You think?"

"Mummy? What do they want?"

"To ask questions."

"Why?"

"Why do you ask questions?"

Merry paused and in a soft voice said, "I don't know."

"Because – because they want to know a story. They're reporters, Merry."

"Go and tell them a story, Mummy."

Mark turned to Merry and said with a commanding tone, "Merry, Mummy's not well. She needs her rest. She's too tired to speak to anyone."

"Shall I read them a story?"

"No Merry," replied Esther, "they're not interested in Pip and Chip and – "

"Can I tell them to go away?"

"No, Merry," said Mark, "go and play with some angels and leave Mummy and me to think."

"Please, Daddy, don't be cross. I'm only trying to help." With that, Merry spoke to her teddy to say about leaving and then she was gone.

Mark lowered his voice to a whisper: "I'm half expecting Merry to be getting her books ready to go out there."

A young girl's voice came from beyond the room: "What did you say, Daddy?"

"Nothing Jackanory!"

Mark looked at his wife who had become pensive: "You okay?"

"What have I done, Mark? What was I thinking?"

"You were trying to make peace."

"But what have I done? What were the names of Job's friends?"

"Job?"

"Yes! In the Bible! Job's friends!"

"Something like Elihu, Zophar, Bildad, and Eliphaz. Why?"

"I was like all of them, all in one, talking like I knew things that I don't, judging on what I thought I knew, thinking I know God's inner mind."

"Esther! You were talking with passion to change things! Working for peace!"

"Mark! These Israelis and Palestinians have violently lost people dear to them, and then I come along! What a stupid, ignorant, little girl! How arrogant! How sanctimonious! I even have a bitter taste in my mouth. I feel so awful!"

"You're being too hard on yourself."

"How would I react to someone bombing my home, my family, live under imposed restrictions, live in fear? People have the right to defend themselves and have justice, don't they? What shepherd won't defend their sheep against wolves?"

"Esther, people just can't retaliate, retaliate, retaliate all the time. That only prolongs the misery."

"But people need to protect their family. What would I be doing if we were being attacked? Would I give them flowers? Send some chocolate? Oh Mark, I was talking about things I know nothing about."

"But you visited and spoke to suffering Palestinians and Israelis before all this. They even personally showed you their bombed-out homes and family graves. You spoke to both sides, personally, heard their stories. You even befriended them, calling them good people. You even told me that if it wasn't for all this past, they all could be close friends. In fact, you fell in love with them all, didn't you?"

Esther quietly became tearful.

"Come here," he said and comforted her in his embrace as they lay back on the bed. "Ssshhh, just don't think about it now."

"I can't stop thinking about it. I only meant to destroy their religious sites metaphorically – to stop idolising these places higher than – . I didn't mean literally to – . That would be – . I can already hear the death threats."

"Ssshhh, we all know what you meant. You're being too hard on yourself. Do you really think all these great politicians truly ever know what they're talking about?"

"I had another bad, pompous speech prepared and aimed at the Palestinians, and they have lost so much, so, so much. I thank God I never gave it. The whole Middle East might have unified against me."

"How's your pain?" Mark asked, looking into her face. "I'm more worried about that."

"Still there." Esther went to sit up and growled with the ache in her chest and abdomen. She nodded to her husband with some sense of her own mockery: "It's still there."

"Okay, I'm going to book that doctor's appointment."

"No Mark, it's not that bad. It comes and goes. It's not debilitating. I'll be up in a minute and it will go."

"You've been complaining of it for too long now. This can't be right."

"Just give me some pills. It's just the shock from what's happened. I'm just stressed – and so are you."

"You had it long before all this. Perhaps you could do with some therapy thing."

"Are you saying that I'm cracking up? I'm okay. I don't need a doctor."

"I think if these reporter guys don't go, we'll both be cracking up. I've got to go to work tomorrow."

"They'll be gone by then, I said." Esther, gritting her teeth, got from the bed and looked from the window, shocked to see how many there were. "There's loads of them. Why does Satan get all the news?"

"I don't know how the neighbours are taking this."

Still standing beside the curtain, Esther turned and looked at Mark as he joined her: "I think I do need to see a doctor."

"I'll arrange it," was his soft reply.

He was about to leave when Esther interrupted: "Mark – I – ."

"Yes?"

"I'm going to do one more trip for the Office – and then that's it. I'll quit."

Mark remained quiet.

"It's for the best: best for me, best for you, best for us, best for work – best for bloody world peace. They'll be expecting me to resign anyway; fall on my sword. Is that – does that make you happy?"

Mark did not respond.

"You've wanted me to step down for a long time now. I'm doing just that before the world blows up. Just one more trip, though."

Mark continued not to reply.

"Mark, what are you thinking?"

He answered with sincerity: "If that's what you want to do."

"Mark! Let me make you happy for once!"

"Esther, I'll support you whatever you do. I know what I said before you left – "

"And you were right. I should have gone with you."

"Esther – "

"It was your father's funeral!"

"Everyone understood why you couldn't be there."

"But – "

"I know what you have lived for and what completes you. If you had not gone, you would have always been questioning about what would have been. I'm sorry I was so angry before you went – I am, truly."

"But you were right. You had a right to be angry and upset. I should have been by your side."

Mark did not reply.

"Would you like me to leave my job?" Esther was now in doubt, seeing her husband's face.

"I want you to know that I am proud, truly proud to have you as my wife. You have done something extraordinary, unbelievable."

"Oh, Mark, that's not helping. I can't measure up to you."

"Don't be silly. Listen, if you genuinely want to continue, then I feel I have no right to prevent you, now that I've seen the – the natural power of what you can say. Everyone listened, Esther. It was incredible, monumental. The whole world has watched it by now."

"Mark! I've almost caused the third world war!"

"No you haven't, stop exaggerating. Admittedly it's a challenge now to pick up the pieces."

"I can't go on. I want to be with you. I want to be a mother to Merry. I thought that was what you wanted."

"It is."

"Then let me give up. One more trip and I can walk away. I need to go to New York with Hammon for talks at the UN – I can't get out of that – and then I'll resign just before anyone gets the chance to push me down some stairs."

"Let's just take one day at a time, and with each day given, regard it as a blessing."

Mark was about to leave her side when Esther spoke again: "Mark, I should have gone with you to your father's funeral. You're my husband. We are married. I should have been with you."

"You just rest. Leave it all with God now. We should have prayed together about this before it all happened."

"Thank you for forgiving me so readily. I know how much I hurt you."

Mark nodded, kissed his wife, and then gently embraced her. "If we both truly love who we are with, then it doesn't matter how bad things get around us," he said and stood back. "And I'm going to book the doctor now. As for today, let's all just ignore the outside and have a family day in." Mark then shouted out as if to the air: "How does that sound?"

Merry came screaming into the room with joy and jumped onto the bed, from where Mark started to tickle his daughter and she laughed and laughed as all children should.

The doctor's appointment a week later was a routine question-and-answer session, and the deposit of a urine sample was as if providing a strange investment to a bank, but Doctor Franklin gave Esther a warning that there was the possibility of further tests. Although the subject of stress was aired, he gave assurance there was nothing to worry about, but something in his tone made her think he suspected something.

True to his word, there were more tests, with each visit performed as surreptitiously as possible to maintain her confidentiality, and Jonathan, having taken Esther on all these occasions, made discreet any means of

Night Out with the Famous

"No, I didn't want a meal," Jezebel said, sitting at her dressing table. "It's very sweet of you, but you can't afford this."

David looked perplexed, standing beside Jezebel in her Savoy apartment. He was not sure what eventually to say to Jonathan, knowing the expense and time Jonathan had spent trying to get a place at short notice. He was also intrigued that the two of them were alone as she fussed over her hair.

"I wanted to spend the night with the soup run, a Salvation Army soup run."

"Oh."

"Take me out on one?"

"I'm not sure if that would be a good idea."

"Why not?"

"You never know who you're going to meet. Anything can happen."

"David, I assure you they'll never know who I am. Go on, take me out. Anything that happens will be on my head."

"I need Major Clifford to agree."

"Yeah! Sure! Go ahead. Use my phone here."

After the short call, David was able to confirm the arrangement: "He said that would be fine, but not to draw attention to yourself."

"Sounds like my Dad. In the meantime, would you like something light to eat in the restaurant with me?"

It was not common for the Savoy Hotel to have a Salvation Army minibus drive to its entrance, but following due courtesy of the Hotel, the doorman dutifully pulled open the large side door and politely ushered Jezebel and David to step inside and join those already seated.

There was an air of naive excitement from the passengers to meet someone so famous, but as they drove, one by one they explained to their new member what they did and what to expect. Jezebel, relaxed and friendly, nodded with each comment and asked sensible questions that soon got the team treating her as one of their own. They soon stopped by an underpass of a bridge and the full extent of what people, dressed in dirty clothes, sleeping on cardboard, really looked and smelt like.

While they assembled, a van appeared and parked beside the minibus. It opened up its side and became an instant food and drinks service.

Major Clifford, who had been the driver of the van, came to Jezebel and introduced himself: "Good evening, I'm glad you're all wrapped up sensibly."

"I thought I'd come prepared," Jezebel answered.

"I'm Major Clifford. I'm the officer of The Salvation Army along Oxford Street."

"I'm Jezebel, and I'm pleased to meet you."

"Pleased to meet you."

"Thank you for accepting me as part of your team."

"That's fine. Just mingle and chat to them. They mainly like a chat, someone to listen and that's what we do most of the time. Some like to be alone and have their soup to themselves. You just have to judge if they would actually accept some company. We've got blankets, soup, bread, tea, coffee, socks and gloves, and we have some cards with addresses as to where they can go for further help. The rest is up to them. We try not to have them depend on us, but sometimes – what can you do?"

Jezebel, along with the Major, watched the members, some in uniform, some not, as they interacted with the homeless people who accepted a cup of hot soup with a polite chat, where they lay or sat, or assembled around the soup van.

"Don't be fooled by the way some look," continued the Major. "Some of these homeless are very clever people with an education. Some have been homeless for far too long, that they don't know any other way to live and this is the way they do live. Don't try and fix them, as if they are a problem. They have to want to change – just like everyone else. God can't force people to love Him; they have to want to. Even Jesus had to ask for consent before He cured anyone."

"Thank you, I would just love to mingle."

"Of course, most of them are pleasant and are regular with us."

Jezebel merged with the crowd and started to speak and listen to a scruffy young man. Then she naturally started to listen to another who joined the conversation, both drinking their soup. No one thought any more of her than one of the helpers.

David watched her with the corner of his eyes, becoming more impressed and charmed as to how sensitive and accepting Jezebel was to the needy. All through the night, from one place to the next, he saw how pleasantly she handed out tea, coffee, soup and rolls and conversed as easily as talking to friends. She was an ideal ambassador of goodness. What stunned David the most was that not once did any of them knew who she was. Not one of them knew they were talking to a world-famous singer and movie star, and if they did, they made no comment or reaction of it. It was also endearing that the rest of the team took to her as one of their own, and Jezebel became quite natural in this new life to her. She genuinely appeared to enjoy being one of the team.

As David counted the last of the socks and gloves in the minibus, Jezebel approached where he sat and reached for a blanket from a pile within. David stopped her: "We need to be careful when we hand this out. Sometimes they sell it on for money, drink or drugs."

"Well, this man needs it," she replied, "and I like to think that if I lose everything and I'm made homeless, which *can* happen to me, that someone will give me a blanket." She then took the blanket, walked over to the man on cardboard and gave it to him.

At the end of the work, the Salvationists with Jezebel among them, congregated around one particular street lamp, and the Major said a prayer and gave his thanks to everyone for helping. They all then got into the minibus or the soup van and drove away.

Feeling like it was wise, Major Clifford, now driving the minibus, took Jezebel back to the Savoy first and he parked outside, allowing the side door to open. David and Jezebel stepped onto the pavement and the Major rolled down his window from the driver's seat: "Miss Jezebel, would you like to come to a Salvation Army meeting?"

Looking cheerful and pleased to have been asked, she came closer to the window: "I would really love to."

"Well, The Salvation Army along Oxford Street is having a midweek evening service. The band will play, the songsters will sing, there will be hymns, I'll give a short sermon, but don't let that put you off, and I think there'll be a small drama sketch thing. They normally ask to put on a little drama. They practise quite hard; write their own material as well."

"That would be great, thank you, Mister Clifford, I would love to come and I've so much enjoyed tonight."

"Well, thank you for your help, Miss Jezebel." said Major Clifford, and then he started to wind up the window. "Good night and see you Wednesday evening."

"Good night," she replied, happily.

David motioned to escort her along the final steps to the hotel's entrance.

"It's okay, thank you, I can find my own way, and I've kept you up all night already. Can I ring you later in the morning as to what time I will be over? I didn't expect to get back this late – or early."

"Sure, get some sleep," replied David, getting back into the minibus.

"Once again, thank you for a good night out – if that's the right thing to say."

Instead of returning to her room, Jezebel knocked on Pashhur's door.

"Do you know what time it is?" asked Pashhur, bleary-eyed and opening the door as Jezebel came into his apartment.

"I've got to tell you. I've got to tell you now."

"Tell me what?"

"I had a great night!"

Pashhur yawned: "Really? So how was it? Sounds like you've gone and joined them."

"They all must know what I'm like."

"Who?"

"The group!"

"The soup run?"

"The Salvation Army – they all must know what I'm like, but they just accepted me, like anyone else."

"I don't understand: how else are they to be?"

"I'm a big sinner. I have exploited everything of me that I can ever exploit, but I felt I wasn't being judged by them. They must know what I'm like. They can't be that naive."

"Mmmm, want a drink?"

"No thanks."

"So how do you feel about that: going out on a soup run?"

"It felt good feeling accepted. No one made a fuss over who I was. No one judged my immorality. No one was judgemental. I was simply part of the team and it felt good, and it was so – wholesome – and easy just helping and making friends with the homeless. I felt at home."

"Wow, so what's next?"

"See his business and I've been invited to a Salvation Army service."

"What, you?"

"Of course – don't you think I'm worthy? Aren't I redeemable?"

"You'll be playing in the band and shaking a donation box soon."

If the Planets Rebel

Wednesday evening and the Salvation Army hall was packed. David secretly studied the congregation in search of Esther, but she could not be found. In a way he was relieved that she would not see him with Jezebel, but there was dejection that he would liked to have seen her anyway. Jezebel arrived without much attention, smiling and being friendly as people cordially welcomed her. Seeing David, they both found available seats together and David started to describe some of the culture. Jezebel was unexpectedly enthused to listen.

"Aren't the band looking great in their uniforms," she whispered into David's ear. "Some of them are shockingly handsome."

The band played a tune to start and Major Clifford then gave a welcome to all new people and visitors, and opened the service with a prayer. After a congregational hymn, Major Clifford opened his Bible and, as if proudly, announced the Bible reading: "This is from Isaiah chapter sixty-four, verse eight – 'You, Lord, are our Father and we are nothing but clay. You are the potter who moulded us.'" He then closed the book. "Doesn't the man who made a jar have the right to use that jar for his own reasons? Let Him be the potter of your life – even if you do get dizzy on that wheel."

"You okay?" David asked Jezebel.

Jezebel nodded with a smile, as of a little girl who had just been given a little puppy and had no time to answer in any other way for the fear of missing something.

"And now," continued the Major, "the drama group would like to present a sketch they've written, entitled, 'The influence of planets'. If the sun has a purpose, then, all the more, so have you."

Major Clifford made way for three people to walk onto the stage. All three were dressed as planets, with one wearing a cardboard cut-out that hung around the shoulders painted as though the Sun, while another, dressed the same, had that of a blue-green Earth and the last was of a grey moon. They all moved some chairs out of the way, and the Sun, choosing a sturdy chair, stood on it, central to the stage.

Earth and Moon stood to the side and all three paused for a moment as though asleep.

The hall was more silent than it would have been empty.

Then, without looking up from their sleep, Earth and Moon took a few steps that made Moon move around Earth, and Earth move around the Sun and then they stopped.

The Sun yawned, stretched out and spoke, putting on sunglasses: "Rise and shine, everyone!"

Earth and Moon yawned as they awoke, and Earth, sprite and eager for the day, said to Moon, "Another day, Moon! Another day!"

"I don't know because I'm supposed to come out only at night," Moon replied.

"Well you just rotate around me, Moon," replied Earth, "like I rotate around Sun. Keep spinning, mind you, otherwise gravity won't work!"

"Well, I don't know about you, but all this heavy mass and spinning makes me feel – makes me feel – ."

"Feel what?"

"Like I've over eaten and drunk too much."

"We're supposed to have mass, Moon, and we're supposed to have gravity and we're supposed to be spinning. You shouldn't complain: I'm the one who has all the water sloshing around."

"Yes, but I'm the one that feels so dry and parched. You're the one with all the water, you lucky you. Hang on: time to change!"

With that, Earth and Moon made a few more steps as though to be in their orbit, and then stood still.

"Earth, I wonder what all this spinning and rotating and space and time is all about. Why do we do this? All this rotating? We've done this spinning for a while now and look where it's got us: nowhere."

"We do this because if we don't, something drastic will happen."

"Drastic?"

"Catastrophic!"

"Oh – I'm still dizzy though."

The two then paused.

"Earth?" continued Moon. "We're just rocks, aren't we?"

"Yes, Moon."

"If we try, do you think we can become alive? It would be nice to breath, have feelings and make decisions for a change. Wow! What a great way to influence people."

"Moon?"

"Yes?"

"It would be better if you just did what you were made to do. Leave the people to get on with what they were made to do."

"But I don't have any people, Earth. I only had some for a few days and then they left me alone. I wish I could have as much influence as you, Earth. I wish I could be a planet."

"Well you can't be a planet, you're a – you're a – you're a moon, Moon."

"I'm a moon-moon? What's a moon-moon?"

"Just take it from me that you will never be a planet."

Moon sounded dejected and lowered their head: "Oh."

"But you do have an influence, Moon, an important one."

Moon perked up: "Really!"

"You should be proud with what you're for."

"I should?"

"Yes! My tides won't work unless it was for you."

"Really?"

"And if my tides won't work, the water will get smelly."

"Smelly?"

"Yes, smelly and stagnant, and you know what will happen if the water gets stagnant."

"We all have to close our noses?"

"It will affect everybody on my surface."

"Oh."

"And not in a good way. And then there's my tilt. If it weren't for my tilt, which you knocked me into, there would be no seasons and no harvest, and – " Earth then chuckled, which did not appear to be part of the script. "Moon? Do you think we should have moved by now?"

Moon laughed and the two made some more steps around each other. Unscripted and laughing, Moon then grabbed Earth and spun around as if doing the Waltz, making Earth burst out more with laughter, and then they got back into position, bringing a smile to the congregation.

"Oh – Oh," said Moon. "I really don't know my next line, Earth."

Someone to the side repeated the line to Moon.

"Oh!" said Moon, "It's a good job we have our drama leader in orbit, Earth. So – yes so, I'm really quite important, Earth, if I affect your tides and tilt and seasons and life."

"Moon! Without you and me, the humans would not have happened."

"Or without Sun."

"Or without Sun, or the other planets, or things we're made from."

"But why? Shall we ask Sun?"

"She never says anything. Look at her, with her sunglasses on."

"Earth? Shall we ask the other planets? What do you think, Venus?"

To the side of the stage were three other actors who had in the meantime stepped into position. They were also planets, dressed obviously to signify which one they were.

Venus answered irritably, "It's all going to collapse in millions and millions and millions of times Earth goes around Sun. So I don't have time. Prove that all this is real! I could be in another solar system for all I know and could wake up feeling better about it."

"Very helpful, Venus, thank you. Don't call us; we'll call you. What about you Mars?"

"I could have been a great Earth! Just look at me now! Stripped of it all! And all they do is send over stupid things that break down! Still, I do have impressive mountains and canyons, far superior than any on Earth!"

"Oh, very sorry about that, Mars, but I was more interested in whether anyone is interested in what's it all about. What about you Jupiter? Do you know?"

Wearing sunglasses, Jupiter was relaxed with a toothy grin and said in a calm, cool voice: "Don't care, man, just don't care. Just take a seat in the heat, place a *stoooolll* by the *poooooolll* and *chiiiilllllll* where you *weeiiiiiiiiiillllllll.*"

"Earth?" said Moon, "I don't think anyone is interested."

Suddenly Venus pointed and everyone looked at where he pointed: "Hey! Look everybody! I've discovered a new planet."

"Where?" they all replied in exact unison.

"Over there!"

"No, that's Pluto!" announced Earth.

"Oh," replied Venus, acting indignant. "I thought Pluto was a dog."

"No, he's a planet," replied Earth.

Then Moon chirped in: "Is he not a moon, then?"

"No! He's a planet!"

"How did he get to be a planet then and not a dog?"

"Pluto is not a dog or a moon, Moon."

"What *is* a moon-moon?"

"We do all this, because that is what He wants."

"You mean, the great Him?"

"Precisely, Moon, the great Creator. Isn't He wonderful? Isn't what He's done so, so magnificent?"

"I think so, but I wish He had made me into a planet."

"He wants you to be a better you, Moon."

"A better U-moon? What's a U-moon, Earth?"

Earth continued blithely ignoring Moon: "We are the things and He is the thing-maker, and you don't give Him glory by being something He did not want you to be. If the clay does not want to be made into what the Master Potter wants, then the clay is discarded, Moon. And someone has to be the moon, and that moon would be you, Moon."

"So what is a U-moon?"

"Sometimes with what you do, you never really know the true influence we have on others. Even a tiny asteroid can have a big impact."

"Really?"

"Like a tiny lie can change everything for everyone. It can change history."

"Like a little asteroid?"

"A little asteroid."

"And wipe out a lot of Dinosaurs, Earth."

"Yes, the Dinosaurs, Moon: just a little asteroid is all it took. Take it from me, you are essential and even though you think you are small, and grey, and – "

"And dry – "

"And parched – "

"And dizzy – "

"And full of mass that means nothing to you, He has made you to have this important role – to influence me with your gravity, which you don't think you have."

"Wow!"

"Moon, we both have a reason to be here and be a part of His solar system. We are to obey His laws and not rebel. We are His slaves with freedom, and anything we do to place mastery away from Him brings collapse."

"And if we rebel, Earth?"

"Then there will be something drastic."

"Catastrophic! But what if the humans decide not to follow His laws?"

"Just look at their history and you will discover their future."

"Look, Sun's going down!"

"That's it, Moon, for another day. Good night!"

"Good night, Earth."

"Remember to keep spinning!"

All the players, with clapping from the congregation and almost in embarrassment from the level of applause, bowed and then returned some chairs to their original position. Jezebel was actually standing and clapping faster than anyone else.

"David," said Jezebel. "Come to America. Come and visit me. Don't pay lip-service, I mean it."

The United Nation's Security Council

New York's traffic was at a standstill, and through the tinted windows of their executive car, Esther and Hammon from the back seat looked out at the chaos and listened to the sirens and car horns sounding. As it was, the chauffeur was unperturbed.

"Must have been an accident," mentioned Esther, still looking around.

Hammon huffed and spoke to the chauffeur: "Can't we get some jurisdiction here? We are important people."

"Can't do any more than what I'm doing, sir."

"This is ridiculous. We can't be late for the UN."

"I'm sure they'll understand," Esther replied. "We can't be the only ones late."

"Well I'm not them. Come on, let's walk."

"Walk?"

"Yes! Walk! It's only just round the corner."

The driver interposed: "It's just a fifteen-minute walk, sir."

Hammon, now on the street, bent down to look inside at Esther: "Coming? It's no good if I arrive without you."

Esther, not knowing what the harm can be, joined Hammon on the sidewalk and they started walking as pedestrians, neither of them wishing to discuss anything.

"Wormwood, are you in position?"

Wormwood was irritated with the voice in his ears from the headset and spoke to the small microphone across his mouth: "Screwtape, I'm in position for the seventh time of telling you. I – am – in – position! And for the seventh time, I have four rounds loaded. Don't get me to come and find you."

"Both targets are now walking and should pass target area in eight minutes."

"Good!"

From a darkened bedroom within a high-rise apartment block, the sniper had assembled his rifle and was now standing in wait, resting against the bedroom furniture. The window was ajar and his view was downwards on the street with pedestrians walking past his aim at a particular point.

Again, the voice spoke as if a demon in his head: "Target One is the female. Shoot target One first. Target only the head. Target Two is the male. Shoot target Two, first in the groin, then chest, then head. Four bullets, Wormwood, please acknowledge."

"I can add, Screwtape."

"Ensure target Two has enough time to react to killing target One."

"Boy, our client must detest them."

"Targets are approaching."

"I now have them in my scope. She's very pretty."

"Don't hesitate: you are being paid more than all the other contracts put together."

"Preparing to assassinate," Wormwood whispered to himself, lowering his breathing and heart rate. The female was clear in his sight. There was no chance of missing. He squeezed the trigger and saw her instantly shudder, and she fell like a rag doll. In his scope, he watched the man who, shocked in seeing the limp body and the blood spread on the pavement, screamed and dropped beside her, watching the blood washing over his hands as he then tried to hold her head together. Anguish and disbelief took over the man and he held the body to his chest.

With the groin and chest now no longer visible, the sniper estimated the target points and fired one shot through the female to hit the man in the stomach and then did the same for the chest. Finally, he shot the head, and both bodies were no longer moving. The pavement was steeped with blood, tissue and bone.

"Uncle Screwtape, they can now be crossed off your Christmas list."

Walking past the array of world flags, Hammon and Esther arrived at the UN and went through to the large foyer. They were met by an escort whom they politely followed through corridors to arrive at the vast chamber hall of the World's Security Council. With the large circular conference table, around which a throng of dignitaries were assembling, an important debate was in preparation.

Hammon and Esther became settled at their designated seats for Britain, retrieving documents from their cases and accommodating people who approached them both to pre-empt questions on the developing crisis in the Middle East.

Esther was able eventually to slip away through the crowd having recognised Monifa across the room, remembering her from years ago when they had last met to discuss Rwanda's past. They greeted each other as the best of friends, with family news exchanged as a matter of priority and interest. They continued their conversation until a secretary stood to Esther's side and announced politely that there was a telephone call for her.

"Sorry Monifa," said Esther as she returned to her desk and sat to receive the call.

Through the throng of chatter and preparation, Monifa watched Esther's visible distress that was showing through her unsteadiness and knew the call was personal and of bad news. She rushed to be at Esther's side when Esther slowly replaced the handset. "Esther?"

Esther, tears now streaming down her cheeks, stood up, bewildered and stunned. Her eyes rolled unhealthily to the ceiling and Monifa had to hold her steady when Esther became faint, helping the weakening woman back into the chair.

Other people nearby came to help, with one coming to the aid with a glass of water.

"Esther? What's happened?" asked Monifa.

At first, Esther could not answer and another wave of fainting almost took her again. Gasping for breath, she then tried to wave people away as though they were drowning her.

"Esther! Have some water, please," urged Monifa.

As asked, Esther sat up and had a sip, and was then looking into Monifa's eyes.

"What happened?" softly asked Monifa.

"Mark and Merry have been shot."

"What?"

"Mark and Merry have been shot. They shot them, Monifa. Mark was taking Merry to the dentist."

"I'm so sorry," breathed Monifa.

"They're dead, Monifa."

With the immense shock, Esther fainted and became unconscious.

Two Queens

Jonathan walked hurriedly along a busy London street and stopped at a street stall selling souvenirs and newspapers. Quickly paying for a paper, he continued walking, although at a reduced rate for the reading he did at the same time. Eventually, his rate reduced so much that he stopped for his total focus to be on the article. Without much concern to folding it neatly, he practically ruined the pages as he thought of the consequences of what he had read. As people passed him by, steeped in their own worries, Jonathan sighed with a complex mixture of sadness, irritation, anger and grievance.

A young woman about to walk past took notice of his vacant stare and stopped to enquire about him: "Are you okay?"

Jonathan looked up, nodded and half-smiled.

The woman was not convinced and stood for a moment more, wondering what to say.

As it was, Jonathan said the next thing as if to fill the silence: "Nothing makes any sense. We're here one moment, and then gone the next. It's like chasing the wind." He smiled again, but with one of gratitude that the kind lady had stopped.

Making light of it, she smiled back: "You must work in London then."

They both laughed and went their ways.

Jonathan reached the healthcare centre and greeted the receptionist as he walked past her. Climbing the four storeys to the top landing, he went straight to David's internal office to look inside.

David was sat at his desk. He turned his eyes to Jonathan and sighed, and leant back in his large, leather chair.

"I didn't know whether you wanted to read what they say," said Jonathan, coming forward and dropping his newspaper before David.

David leant forward and grabbed his own set: "I didn't know if *you* wanted to read what they say."

Jonathan sat down heavily in an available chair. For a moment, neither of them spoke, alone together on the top floor. Then Jonathan broke the silence: "You okay?"

David at first did not answer. He swallowed with difficulty and, with a drawn-out breath, gave a sorrowful reply: "I murdered them."

"Don't be stupid. What are you talking about?"

"I murdered them."

"You hired the gunman?"

"It was as if God answered my prayer."

"No He didn't! You're just in shock."

"I wanted them out of the way. I prayed this lunatic prayer to have them out of the way. It's like me wanting Uriah at the front lines to be killed so that I can cart off his wife Bathsheba."

"Look at me! You're being irrational! Would you really want little Merry dead? Are you that sadistic? Is God that sadistic?"

"Is God that sadistic? Have you read the Old Testament? They shot them, Jonathan! They shot two lovable people: a husband and a sweet little daughter just going about their lives! Why?" said David exasperated. "Why, why, why?"

"So that Esther is pushed to the limit of what she believes. She's going to have to forgive them to be true to her word. But they don't want her to forgive. They want her to fail. They want her as miserable as they are."

"What do you think she'll do?"

"I don't know: possibly spend time with her adoptive parents."

"I mean, *will* she forgive them?"

"You know, this could be a time for you and her to make up, bury the hatchet and make peace. Forget about world domination. You two making up is probably what she needs right now to have the strength to forgive them."

"I might cause more strife."

"Oh, come on, David!"

"I'm going away for a few days to think things through."

"Again? Where's it that you go every time?"

David shook his head: "Sorry Jonathan, but that's my little secret."

"A big secret if you ask me. This time leave your phone on."

David nodded but there was no conviction that he agreed with the request.

"Okay, what about this Jezebel?"

"What about her?"

"This world famous actress and singer wants to date you. Isn't that a bit weird?"

"Are you saying I'm not to her usual standard?"

"It's not funny. Something isn't right here and you know it. You choose not to know it."

"She doesn't want to date me. It's all for show. Look! She was fine and polite with me when she was here, no controversy. She's just not understood. She was perfect with the homeless and she was better than any ambassador when she looked around the business."

Jonathan gave David a disparaging look. "You look at life with different lenses to the rest of us lesser mortals."

"Look, everything is fine. I know she's using me for her publicity, but I can use her for our publicity."

"And what did the General say about that?"

"Okay, he didn't like it."

"But you're going ahead anyway. Listen! This feisty woman has invited you over to visit her. It's not as if all the other celebrities that come along do the same thing. Isn't there a trap here?"

"But Jesus is my role model. It may well be that she actually wants to renounce her past and – ."

"And what? Look! I've got enough with worrying about Esther than to worry about you!"

"I said it will be fine. I'm sure somewhere under that persona, a little girl is wanting the right direction. Listen to some of her songs. I want to be a good influence on her, and perhaps I can be."

"That's what you told the General the other day. I think he was just as unconvinced as me. Just don't go. She's someone to avoid."

"The flights are booked. It would be good for me to get away."

"And what about the business? Things don't look too good for us, you know. If anything, you need to stay here and put things right. You've gone off gallivanting around everywhere and taken your eye off the ball."

"I've brought in a lot of donations and that's what this trip to Jezebel is all about."

"I don't think the General is too concerned about the donations. It's about things being done righteously in Jesus' name."

"But look at what we've achieved."

"Because we placed it in God's hands from the start, that's why. I'm not sure if that's still the case."

"Jonathan, just be assured that all will be fine."

"And Esther?"

David sat back in the chair, suddenly deep in thought again.

"Oh don't go off and disappear again! And Esther? Perhaps a lot more will be done if you two just forgive and forget and let the other know about it. I still don't know what happened between you two." Jonathan was then spellbound when David got up, took his coat and left the room, and he had to rush to reach David on the landing. "What is it with you?"

"I've got to go. I've just got to clear my head, pray, think, mull, get my emotions right. I'm going to my retreat and spending time there, but I'm going to Jezebel after that, as planned."

"Then don't come back looking for Esther. I won't allow it. Either you deal with Esther and forget Jezebel, or you forget Esther and deal with Jezebel, because one will cause strife; the other will be full of greatness. One is Jeremiah's well; the other is Jacob's ladder. I don't think it takes much to know which one is which."

Reap what you sow

From across the morning skies of London and into the early signs of nightfall, the long day had been coated with a continuous downfall of torrential rain poured from malign grey clouds that at best would ease to provide a moment of reprieve and at worst burst forth with angry rumbling and unrelenting misery. Few, as such, walked the streets and were drenched for it, and in many areas there was desertion, as there was within one particular expanse of land, enclosed to prevent public access.

It was this disused land, closed off since 1983, that contained the bleak derelict of what once powered London's electrical demand. Four tall brick towers supported four white chimneys that had bellowed thick black smoke from the enormous coal-fired generators, now removed to leave a darkened carcass of the past. Girders were rusted and brought bare from collapsing brickwork. Pools lay stagnant and water dripped from lofty heights. Weeds of all sizes grew from the concrete floors and brick walls, and moss and algae flourished with little to abate their growth. Birds sought refuge within the seams of what remained of the broken ceiling that mainly had been brought down by nature and made safe by engineers. Within the confines of the four towers, a large game of football was possible, and surrounding the structure, like a castle with a defensive mote, there was an open expanse of neglected, wasted land that developers had moved into and left heavy industrial equipment. Trains passed by, rumbling on the tracks, metal screeches scorching the ears of those who heard, piercing the roar of the rain.

It was into this scene that a dark Mercedes with dark tinted windows drove through, passing under the beams and girders of the ruined walls to finally park within the boundary of the four tall brick towers, the darkened sky-reaching chimneys looking strong from such a state of ruin. There was no over-arching ceiling and there was no over-arching defence from the weather from where the car had parked.

From the driver's door stepped a man with white scraggy hair and stubble, who reached for an umbrella and opened it, and then opened the door behind as a chauffeur would.

Within the dark car came a disparaging voice: "The old, run-down Battersea Power Station: never thought I'd be brought here today, Scabbards."

"You may like to make use of this, sir," replied Scabbards, not being affected by the derogatory tone and handing the large and strong umbrella to the Foreign Secretary as he stepped from the car.

"Why are we meeting here, in the open?"

"This is at Sinbad's request: wants to meet you personally this time."

"Is this wise? Isn't it going to be causing a risk?"

"Don't know sir, but if you don't meet face to face, then you won't get to know what you want. Sinbad is being strict about it, says it's important, and if you don't meet now then the opportunity will be gone."

"Okay, so where do I meet him?"

"Her."

"Sinbad is female?"

"Yes, sir, always has been."

"My, after all these years. Where is she?"

"You'll find her standing over there, waiting by the south tower."

Hammon looked in the direction and noticed the solitary figure in the distance, in the open below the towering chimney, standing in the rain wearing a cheap, red, cover-all plastic raincoat. He nodded under the umbrella and walked alone to then stand before her.

With a hood covering her head and the length of the plastic coat that covered her figure, there was nothing for Hammon to aid remembering her except for wearing old trainers and dirty jogging trousers. Not even a wisp of her hair was visible. She wore no make-up and the rain made her face look as though another. She looked homeless. She was shivering with her hands always in the coat pockets, and the rain continuously poured off her as she continuously looked at the Foreign Secretary. She did not utter a word, allowing the man, in his dark, thick evening coat under his umbrella, to study her void features.

"Sinbad?" he eventually asked.

The woman nodded.

"So, what do you have?"

This time she shook her head.

"Sorry, I don't understand."

She shook her head again: "Nothing."

"Nothing?"

"I have nothing: no report, no findings, no anything," she said, sternly.

Hammon was astounded: "Come on, you've never let me down like this before. Do you want more pay? Is this what this is about?"

"No."

"You've been able to get a fleck of dirt from the deepest, whitest snow there's been. I can't accept you've found nothing on her."

"Well you should. I found nothing, absolutely nothing. I went through her past, checked all the records, everywhere, everyone – and there's nothing. Employ someone else if you don't believe me."

"I will!"

"You're wasting your money then. You've probably always paid me from tax-payers' money anyway."

"There's got to be something. Everyone has a sin in their cupboard – or at least a skeleton. Someone should be able to up-turn something on her. No one is perfect, no one. Even the truth can be twisted."

"Well they can try, whoever you ask, but let me warn you that I came recommended as being the best and I've proven it over too many years. I guarantee there is still no one as good as me. There is nothing on Esther."

Hammon looked unconvinced.

"But now you listen."

"Okay."

"I quit."

"You quit?"

"Totally! I resign. You can look for another spy to do your sewer work."

"I'll pay any fee you request."

"Too valuable, am I? Oh, yes, you've done very well out of me finding the political filth I've found. But you just stop me resigning. I'll churn out more muck I've got on you if you display me in public. You've got more to lose. Me? I don't mind what happens – I deserve it – and so do you."

"Why? Why resign?"

"Why! Why! She's perfect! Perfect! I can't find anything wrong with her, nothing! She is just an innocent angel who has the bad fortune to be here with the fowl likes as you and me."

"But what about him? David Kingsley?" he continued. "They're connected to each other somehow. Something happened. There must be something bad."

"Oh, yes, him! Do you really want to know the filth?"

Hammon nodded with uncertainty.

"They went on a date!"

"So there is something! They had an affair!"

"No, it didn't work out."

"They had a bust up?"

"The worst sin there is, is just a kiss."

"So there is seriously nothing to dig up?"

"If you do want something – then the only thing it can be is that they're perfect for each other and whatever went wrong, they're living the consequences. The only bad thing is they're not together. Does that make you happy? Don't you think she's gone through as much as anyone can take as it is, without you wanting to find a scandal to dishonour her? If I tell you about the abuse she received before being adopted into a Salvation Army family will only gain more public sympathy. You want to know about that?"

Hammon gave no reaction at all.

"You want to know the sick details? What sick bastard are you?"

"Where is she at the moment?"

"No idea."

"No idea? Or not telling?"

"I have no idea."

"What you? Even you don't know where she is?"

"I – have – no – idea! Get it? She is gone! Disappeared! No one knows where she is! That's why everyone is trying to find her for that big scoop of a story!"

Hammon, from under his shelter, looked at the woman in the pouring rain, and studied her: "I think you know more than what you're telling."

"Okay, to shut you up: the last time I saw her was when she visited the Doctors, a week ago, and then she vanished, got into a car driven by someone I don't care to know and drove off. I purposely didn't get the registration."

"This is your last payment, then." Hammon held out an envelope to Sinbad.

It was viewed as something diseased and was declined. "The meeting is over, Mister Hammon, and be very watchful in future, very, very watchful on your career and your precious false reputation. I will come at you when you least expect it, and you will resign, at my say-so in a cloud of speculation because of what I know. Beware the cameras and microphones: they are everywhere. But remember, God is even more everywhere, and He has a lot more on you than I have. You might not think anything will happen after a time, when you feel like my words are just empty, but I will, believe me, return to you like the Grim Reaper. You reap what you sow, Mister Hammon. You will be found out. You will be judged. You are not even worth the material value of your own skin."

Prognosis of Life

A solitary receptionist in a small but plush office was sitting reading a letter at her desk when a gentleman from further within the building stood at her open reception window. The two gave each other a courteous farewell and the man left.

The intercom then beeped.

"Yes, Doctor Franklin?" asked the woman, pushing down a button on the device.

"Kelly, has Mister Anders now gone?"

"Yes."

"We still have our hidden patient?"

"She's been in our staff room, away from everyone, for the last twenty minutes."

"Yes, can you tell her to come through now and start locking up?"

"Certainly." The receptionist left her seat and entered the staff restroom, its door being closed to others and separate from the proper waiting room.

The lone woman waiting there, quiet and pensive, looked up from her seat in expectation.

"Doctor Franklin will see you now, Misses Whyte."

"Thank you."

"Just down the corridor and turn – well, you know the way."

"Yes, I do, thank you."

"You're welcome."

Esther walked the route and found the door she wanted was already open and a gentleman inside his surgery waiting for her.

"Come in, Misses Whyte."

"Doctor Franklin, thank you for seeing me."

"Esther, it's fine, I know how important you are."

"Please, I'm no more important than anyone else."

"Yes, but I don't usually have patients who are involved in world peace negotiations."

"I'm not in them anymore."

"And then there's everyone wanting your story."

"Well, yes, trying to avoid the press is unbearable."

"I've called you here to tell you what we've found from your tests and scans."

"Yes, please don't worry about – being frank with me, Doctor."

"I'm sorry, it's not good news, Esther. I know this is the last thing you need to hear right now, but I need to say it. It's my duty to say it."

Esther nodded, pursed her lips and then opened her mouth to her thoughts: "It's cancerous, isn't it?"

"Yes, it is."

"Benign?"

He sadly shook his head: "Malignant."

Esther took a reflexive intake of air and exhaled slowly to pacify her thoughts.

"We can tell from the results that it has metastasised – spread – it's travelled around you, some in your brain."

Esther nodded slowly. "I left it too late, didn't I?"

"Well, it didn't help."

"I was more worried about my job than my health. How long do I have?"

"I can't be sure, but in my experience absolutely nothing more than six months in extreme cases."

"Wow – my – . What can I do?"

"The best thing for you is to get out of the limelight. Get away from the stress."

"Is that all that can be done?"

"There's surgery, but with what has happened around your system, the chances of getting on top of it by surgery alone is minimal. There is the combinative approach with radiotherapy and chemotherapy."

"But you said my best option is get out of the limelight," replied Esther, maintaining an air of politeness and a sense of being realistic. "I find it hard not to notice within your tone that my chances aren't great."

"Esther, I can't cure you. We will only be prolonging the eventual pain. I am truly sorry, truly."

"Inevitable – death is inevitable: that's simply what you're saying."

"I know you to be a woman of integrity and strength and courage, so I feel I can be blunt and honest. You see, Esther, the problem is, people come in here and they think I can solve it all, that there's a pill I can give or surgery that can be done. They think that science has the answer and technology is the solution."

"But there is no cure for death."

"No."

"I'm going to die with this?"

"Yes."

"But, we're all going to die."

"Yes. I'm sorry to be brutal."

"My husband once said that all we are doing in the healthcare service is tinkering."

"We can push for these options, Esther, don't get me wrong. We can fight this all the way. You're a fighter and I will be beside you every step, but if you take this route, you need to be warned that the likely prognosis of any given treatment is to prolong the pain. It's up to you. I know you have a bigger faith than most to see you through whatever option you feel best."

Esther exhaled with the pressure of her emotions exerting a force on her lungs. "Well, I suppose I did ask for you to be brutally honest with me."

"I can get you a supply of strong pain-killers. They'll make you have strange illusions and dreams, but they'll be strong."

"Will I definitely need them?"

"I think so, yes. I can, of course, get a second opinion."

"No, there's something telling me this is true, but how did I get this, I mean, why? I've never smoked, never taken drugs, and never had alcohol."

"Yes," replied the Doctor sombrely and then he hesitated. "I was wondering that as well. You see, I was able to get hold of your mother's medical record, and – I'm so sorry, Esther, but – your mother had cancer. She was your age."

"My mother – my mother – she – she had cancer?"

"Yes."

"She knew this before she died?"

"Yes."

"Before she committed suicide."

"I'm so sorry."

Esther remained silent in her shock and grief.

"When it sinks in you'll need counselling and a good circle of friends. Don't think you can do this all by yourself, Esther."

"No."

"There's the MacMillan Cancer Support."

"Yes."

"Would it help to hear about the five stages in predicted death? It might help you focus."

"Yes, fine, thank you."

"The first reaction is often denial and refusal, but when this sinks in, there is anger as death is viewed as undeserved and blame is placed on things or others, which then can lead into some sort of bargaining – the dying person tries to make some deal with God or fate to let them live longer. Depression often occurs with a sense of loss, and then acceptance, the final stage, a possible sense of relief after a time of reflecting and introspection."

Esther remained quiet.

"Don't think you can hand it all over solely to your God and it will be fine. People have no ability to give something like this over to God. You need someone's help, professional help to support you through this. I can nominate a few good people who will understand. They'll be discreet as well to avoid undue media attention."

"Can I think about this?"

"Of course, you will need to, but just don't think you're on your own. There are people to help you. I can organise that long term."

"Doctor, I don't think I have a long term."

"No, I'm sorry, that wasn't said properly."

"Life is never long term, no matter how long we live here. What happens after is for the long term."

He nodded, not knowing how else to respond, but then asked, "Is there anyone to go to tonight, so that you're not alone?"

"Yes, there is. I have a good friend. There isn't anyone else, not even my parents, because the press is everywhere."

"Are you okay?"

"Thank you for your time, Doctor Franklin." Esther stood up, hesitated and then said, "I feel too weakened to have any more fight for this. It's already knocked out of me. With what more can God crush me?"

The Doctor stood up and went to her, looking respectful of her words and her right to tell him her feelings. "You may want to use this time to finish loose ends. Death has a habit of changing our perspective on priorities."

"Yes, it does."

They shook hands and she was then given a medicinal prescription.

"Remember I'm still here for you."

Doctor Franklin politely opened the door to his office, but Esther stopped, suddenly turned pensive and to his surprise, a warm, endearing smile shone from her.

"I can say I have no denial with your news, Doctor, and I feel no sense of anger. Perhaps this is from a sense of shock or perhaps I'm already numb from other things, but I know I have no right to bargain with God, and I should have always acted in the knowledge I will not always be here." Esther paused and the patient doctor remained silent as he saw Esther thinking about what to say next. "But you have reminded me that there is something I should fix."

"If it helps, write it, all of it, your personal account. Pour out your feelings. It will help. Find somewhere quiet. Don't get too wrapped up in all this positive-feeling literature that's out there. It's taken to an extreme that makes it a crime to be true to your own feelings. Try and be positive, though, even about being negative. I know that sounds weird, but – . What's best is to write everything down, every feeling, and try and make some sense of it all. Writing is very therapeutic. People never quite realise this until they try. Even I do it, so I can vouch for it."

"Yes, I will." With that, Esther left his office and went past the receptionist with saying a polite goodbye.

For the small size of the enclosed and private parking area, Esther was immediately at a car, and having a driver waiting meant she only had to settle into the passenger's seat and passively driven from the Doctor's premises. At first she said nothing, not even providing any wish to be taken anywhere, and the driver thought it best not to interrupt her thoughts.

They drove through the London traffic in silence, and then Esther spoke: "Thanks for doing this, Jonathan."

"It's fine, it's a pleasure, but we're going back to my place. Everywhere else seems to have reporters. Is that okay?"

"That's fine."

"Is everything all right?"

"Do you know where David is?"

"I have no idea. He goes off to – only God knows where at times.

There's some hideaway place where he switches off his phone. He doesn't tell me anything – and I'm his best friend. Why?"

"I think we need to finally get together."

"Get together? In what way?" Jonathan looked at Esther and then back at the driving, and he shook his head when Esther remained silent. "You're not going to tell me, are you? What a couple of friends you two turned out to be."

Esther smiled endearingly at Jonathan.

"What am I to do with you both, ey?"

"Thank you."

"For what?"

"For making me smile. You haven't asked about my doctor's appointment."

"Didn't think it was my business. It's not in my nature to be nosey." He smiled at Esther, winked, and she smiled back.

"It's not anything serious, just emotional advice."

"You're not taking any stress pills, are you?"

"He did prescribe me something, yes, but I still need to decide to use them."

"Well, please lean on me. Let's just get to my place. By the way, I have a letter for you."

"Really, that's strange."

"Major Clifford wanted me to give you a letter. He thought I would be the only one to know where you are. It's on the breakfast bar – along with all the newspapers about you, which you may not want to read."

When they entered Jonathan's apartment, Esther picked up the envelope that had only her name penned on its front. There were no details of the sender, nor any address of any kind. Not recognising the handwriting, assuming it to be the Major's, she opened it to find another envelope inside with handwriting she did recognise. Ripping it open, she read the lengthy letter within, while Jonathan made coffee from the percolator.

In the time it took for the coffee to be made, poured and stirred, Esther had read the letter a few times with her hand to her mouth in contemplation, tears trickling down her cheeks.

"You okay?"

Esther nodded and through her tears, she smiled. "Yes – yes, I'm fine," she snivelled. "Everything is going to be fine."

Jonathan nodded, thought about his question, then asked, "It's David, isn't it?"

Esther nodded. "Can I stay here a few days to just lose some tension? Then I'll be gone."

"Will you go to him?"

Esther nodded again.

"Always look on me as always ready to help, no matter."

"Thank you – thank you, you sweet man."

Book Six : King of Israel

Esther in Wonderland

In a world of turmoil and confusion, where heartache is in us all, there can only be moments where the true nature of the initial intention can pour through. Such a moment was of a vast expanse of woodland that generated its own mystical aura and timeless beauty within sunshine that was glorifying to bask under. The olden trees brought shade and tranquillity, and a fresh breeze kept the warmth of the day from becoming uncomfortable. Bluebells decorated the forest floor in a magnificent carpet of nature's many wonders and birds sweetly sang of their hearts' earnest hymn of creation's praise and worship, as natural as their own creation. There was no tension to keep with time. There was no pollution, no litter, no foulness, no illness or poverty. Stress was a word that had no meaning. Nothing cried in sorrow. Nothing wept for events of the past.

It was within this secluded forest, following a trail that cut through the trunks and bushes, that a young man walked carrying a single white rose with thoughts only on the one he was going to meet. He then stopped and smiled, now seeing her approach in the distance carrying a small suitcase.

She wore a white cotton dress, as sweet as any country girl could wear in her younger years, and so too carried a white rose with her. She saw him, and he could see her smiling. Neither rushed as they both savoured the moment in becoming face to face, and they just smiled, looking into each other's eyes, in reach of touching each other. It was a while before either of them spoke.

"How did you find me?" she asked.

"I used The Salvation Army's missing person's network."

"I received your letter."

"Yes," was all David said.

Esther nodded in reply and saw what he had in his hand: "I see you brought a rose."

"I would have liked to have said it was the one you gave me, but it withered away and I had to let it go. I see you brought a rose."

"Yours also fell apart. So I brought this one – to make sure I stand out in the crowd."

They both smiled.

David saw she had grown more beautiful. Her fashion was more mature and sophisticated, with an enchanting mix of glamour and elegance; but he also saw the blackness surrounding her eyes for the worry she held back in her thoughts.

Esther noticed in David's aging, that he had lost his look of youth to the value of a man of rugged handsomeness, who also portrayed a wise and commanding quality of himself; but his hair was less silky and turning grey, and creases were at the ends of his eyes.

David held out his hand and took Esther's suitcase, and they walked in a comfortable silence as they enjoyed their scenery.

"It's beautiful here," Esther said after a while.

"Yes, I try and come here fairly often."

"I see why. You come alone?"

"Normally."

"I don't blame you."

"Everything you see, I've kept a secret as much as possible."

"Yes, the wrong people will spoil it – like they would spoil Heaven."

"You want to see something cute?" David asked.

"All right then."

"I'll show you. It's up ahead."

David took Esther off the track and they walked through the bluebells. In a few moments, David stopped and looked into the forest depths.

"What are we looking for?"

"Ssshh, we'll chase them away," David whispered and then he pointed. "They were there when I came this way."

Esther whispered back with some excitement: "What were they?"

"There they are."

In the midst of a layer of blue flowers, a group of furry animals suddenly appeared to be playing.

"They're rabbits," Esther whispered.

"They were here when I walked past. I thought I'd show you."

It was then that Esther looked further along the trail and became confused, her eyes narrowing to attempt a better focus: "What is that? Where are you taking me?"

"This is where I hang out."

Esther laughed: "Hang out! With your mates?"

"Just me and the ghosts of all the hundreds of years of this place."

"Is that a building? Or a ruin? Is it overgrown?"

"That's where we're staying."

As the enchanted mansion slowly materialised through the forest, David gave a running commentary as to the premises and the history, as much as he understood it. He was still imparting his story as they stood within the wild, front grounds to the main front door of Halcyon, both looking up at the building.

"It's beautiful."

"It's all mine."

Esther looked amazed and mesmerised: "I can't believe all this is yours."

"Well, only figuratively. God owns it really, as He does the universe. I'm quite poor in comparison. Some people work hard as if they could own the universe, but why waste your efforts on a false dream?"

"Even so, what a perfect place."

"I wouldn't get too carried away. There's no electricity, no running water and no sanitation you would recognise. There's no central heating, no TV, no access to telephones or in reach of receiving mobile calls. It's covered in cobwebs. In fact, it needs major repairs, let alone a good deep clean. There are rooms where the rain comes through, mould creeps around the place, and the place makes strange noises at night."

"No heated shower, no shampoo, no hairdryer?"

"I didn't say that. We can easily heat water and have a great bath here, although it is made of tin, and I've fixed up a shower contraption. I've gone and brought some shampoo and other things, but you'll have to sit in front of a great fireplace with a log-fire to dry your hair."

Esther smiled: "No doubt I can rise to the occasion."

David smiled in return. "There's a quaint deep well in the garden that's always full of water and there's a natural cold room in the basement. I've packed it with ice to keep things fresh, so we can be here for some time. I'll have to eventually go and get some milk though. I'm not bold enough to cope with farmstead animals."

They stood looking up at the building.

"Come on, then," urged David, and they entered the unlocked front hall.

There before them was the grand staircase at the other end.

Esther was spellbound and had a dreamlike quality to her persona.

"As you can see, there's a lot to be fixed," continued David, pointing at numerous old, chipped, enamel pots on the floor waiting for rainwater.

Esther shook her head: "It's wonderful as it is."

"I have to warn you that I can't stay here long."

"That's fine, I won't be here long either."

"No, what I'm saying is that I'll have to leave early tomorrow, but you can stay as long as you want. I have an important trip organised to America. You can just relax, be quiet, think things through – be away from people and the press. No reporter is going to find you here. I'll come back and, if you wish, share more time with you."

"Thank you," said Esther. "I didn't think you thought much of me to help me like this."

"Well, it is our Heavenly duty."

Esther nodded.

David respectfully took Esther's rose and placed both roses in a vase with other flowers picked and presented in the entrance hallway on the oval table. He turned back to her: "I'm sorry – for everything – for your loss, for Mark, for Merry."

Esther looked to the floor as if wanting David to stop, and then looked up: "I love my husband, David. I still love Merry. There is nothing and no one who is going to take that away, even if they are taken from me."

"It would be wrong if they tried. You want to see the old chapel? It's also now a dining room."

Esther nodded.

After a few doors and passageways, as Esther made a curious study of the walls and floor and ceiling, they entered the hall and again Esther marvelled at the sight: "This is truly all yours – metaphorically?"

"Yep, since returning from Africa. I inherited it from my Grandfather – metaphorically. He's buried in the graveyard. We had a quiet funeral here for him."

"You have a graveyard?"

"It's more like a garden, really peaceful – overgrown though."

"You have your very own graveyard?"

"Yes."

"That's quite impressive."

"It is?"

"Not everyone can claim to have a graveyard."

"Not everyone would want to have one."

Esther viewed David quietly and with some admiration: "Can you show me?"

"You really want to see the graveyard?"

"Well you did say it was like a garden. I want to experience how peaceful it is. I might want to be buried there."

"That's not funny."

"I'm enchanted all the same."

"Okay, I'll show you the gardens."

It took another hour in the slow show of the estate with the portion they covered, but eventually they were within the area of the graveyard.

"Some of these graves date back hundreds of years," announced David, as if giving a tour.

Esther looked around her, seeing the age and quiet beauty there was. It was so ancient that every gravestone had eroded to no longer have any engraving, and the quietness was so peaceful, it generated a reverent protection to those buried under the grandeur of it all. "They look old. Where's your Granddad's?"

"Over there," he replied, pointing in the direction, and then he followed Esther as she made her way through the over-grown grass. He stood beside her as she stood in front of the newest grave.

She read the inscription in the stone laid over the ground, and surprise crossed her face and emanated from her posture.

"Are you okay?"

"Captain Joseph Lovert?"

"Yes."

"Captain Joseph Lovert, husband of Evalynne Lovert?"

"Yes. Is something wrong?"

Esther sighed and shook her head: "How so young and foolish I was."

"Sorry, I don't understand. Are you okay?"

Esther did not respond.

"You've gone through some traumatic times, Esther. I'll show you your room. You must surely need some rest or sleep by now."

Esther just nodded.

In a comfortable silence, they made their way under archways within ruined walls, some dense with a canopy of flowering climbers, and through profuse, flourishing blossom and flowers.

"It's like Heaven here," gasped Esther when they had arrived at the back door.

"It's like a fallen Eden. It's like a monstrosity compared to what it could be."

Esther appeared pensive for a moment, but then David motioned for her to go through into the kitchen and heard her gasp again. She spent a while looking at everything, even walking around to touch and study what she saw.

David started to place more wood in the oven: "Are you hungry?"

Esther shook her head still marvelling at the ancient kitchen.

"I can quickly cook something. It's no bother. A hot drink, then?"

She was not listening. She stopped across the other side of the room and looked at him to make a statement: "I will feel a lot better if we could talk about our past and fix things, a lot of things. I think I need to explain myself."

David nodded.

"To be honest, I don't have long."

"Well how long?"

"I actually don't know." Esther saw David's enquiring, confused look. "Please, now is not the time. Where are you going in America?"

"Los Angles. I've actually got a date."

"A date? As in – a date? Who is she?"

"Well, she's not really a date. She's more of a business contact who might donate a lot of money to The Salvation Army."

"Who is she then? American? Is she single?"

David nodded: "It's Jezebel."

"What, the singer? Jezebel, the singer, the raunchy singer and film star who's into all these affairs?" Esther was astounded, her mouth wide open with the shock.

"Yes."

"The world-famous singer and film star?"

"Yes."

"There's more to you than meets the eye."

"Impressed?"

"Hasn't she done – indecent things?"

"I'm not going to judge. I might be a good influence on her."

"She might be a bad influence on you."

David smiled with confidence and shook his head.

"Jezebel's very attractive: can't say much for her personality, though."

"She's really pleasant. She's got this cute excitable girl about her at times."

"She's also an actress, so just be careful."

"Well, who am I to let her down."

"I'm serious, don't let her trick you."

"Well if Jesus was able to spend time with sinners – and He's my role model to follow, then – ."

"Yes but just remember that you're not as perfect. Just promise me you'll look after yourself. I need you back for that talk. I need it to clear my head and move on to – to the next part of my, my life."

"Esther, bereave all you can here, make the most of the place, and I'll come back unblemished. I promise."

Esther crossed the room to stand beside David: "Bereaving isn't that simple or easy, David. Sometimes I can't stop crying. Sometimes I can't start crying. Sometimes time stops. Sometimes it disregards what has happened and just continues."

"Why don't you just write about it? Let your feelings do the writing."

Esther nodded and wiped a tear away. "I've had that same advice from someone else."

"Perhaps meditate on Lamentations and Psalms. Actively bereave to burn it through your system." David could see Esther was disintegrating by the way she suddenly appeared tired. "I'll show you to your room and you can settle in."

David led Esther through the house to the grand stairs at the front, with Esther this time paying little notice to the enchanting, old decor. From there, David took Esther's suitcase and escorted her up the steps to the landing, along a few corridors and turnings, to arrive outside a room, his Grandfather's old room, but he refrained from saying as much.

To Esther, it was just an old, thick wooden door having no bearing on her. With the door politely held open by David, she entered the room, seeing the four-poster bed, the wood-panelled walls and the dilapidated ceiling. The air was cold, but there was a musty, fragrant smell. To the side on a table was a washbowl with a jug of water from which to wash, and a vase containing a mass of flowers. Numerous sets of draws and a wardrobe furnished the room, but the most intriguing item Esther saw was a wooden desk beside a window that over-looked the garden grounds. She stood for a moment studying the contents without comment while David studied her, placing the suitcase by the bed.

"I'll get you another blanket," David interrupted, "and I'll get you some matches to light the candles whenever you wish."

"Thank you."

"I'll bring you a hot drink. Would that help?"

"Yes, thank you."

When David returned, Esther was sitting at the desk. She was writing and looked engrossed in her work, and he made a conscious effort not to intrude. The thick red-and-blue cloth, which he carried, he left on the bed, the matches in his hand were placed on the bedside cabinet, and the hot drinking chocolate was placed beside her. Without permission, David then unfolded the large cloth over the bed, smoothing over the creases.

"Thank you," Esther said, putting down her pen. She picked up her drink and stood at the end of the bed, looking down with amazement as to what now covered it in entirety: an enormous flag of The Salvation Army, a yellow star in the dead centre, then a deep red and then a blue surround. She looked at David as if for an explanation.

"It does get cold here, even in summer, and I didn't think: I should have got some more blankets in. All the others are too old, so this flag will have to do."

"I quite like it," she said. "Thank you."

"That's all right."

"About letting me stay – and making me feel welcome."

"Just learn to be still here. A cup cannot be filled if it keeps moving around under the tap." He motioned to the Bible in Esther's hand: "What are you going to read?"

"I thought I'd take your advice and read Lamentations and find a few Psalms to consider."

"I'll be here in the morning to make sure you'll be all right by yourself."

Their eyes met in a pause of their thoughts, both contemplating what their hearts were saying about the fear and excitement, the apprehension and enchantment of seeing the eyes of the other for a prolonged moment.

"Yes, thank you," Esther said with neither of them looking away.

Graciously, David smiled and then disappeared to the corridor with the closing of her door. Listening to his footsteps, she wondered if he would return, but he never did. She wondered what would have been his cause to return, and what would she have done if he had.

What Job learnt

When Esther awoke, the daylight was shining through the gaps of the curtains, and she got up to withdraw them and see in the day. There below was the garden and above was a bounteous sky of blue with pure-white clouds. As uplifting the scene, it could not bring relief to her sunken heart and deep, slow breathing. Her chest felt under a weight and she felt weak and withdrawn.

It was at this moment that Esther heard someone approach. The floorboards beyond creaked, and there then came a knock. "Come in," she said without any thought.

The door opened and David entered carrying a tray of toast and coffee.

Esther saw the sudden, subliminal startled look across David's face as he took in the full view of her in a nightdress by the full shine of the illuminating window. Shocked at this impropriety, she was actually caught frozen and unknowing of what to do without causing any more attention.

"Would you like breakfast?" he asked.

"Yes, thank you."

"It's only toast at the moment. I didn't quite know what to do, so – . I should have asked last night."

"That's fine."

There was a moment of awkwardness as Esther became fully aware that her curves were in full view, but David being gracious placed the tray beside her on the desk, making no comment and being magnanimous about his increased overt heart rate.

He looked up and looked into her eyes. "Would you – would you – like – anything more?" he eventually said.

"No, I don't think so. I'm fine, thank you."

"I didn't know whether you wanted jam or marmalade with your toast."

"Jam."

"Oh. I brought both, anyway."

"Oh."

"So that's all?"

"Yes – yes it is – thank you."

They looked at each other, not knowing what else to say for a moment.

"I need to be going soon – within an hour or so," eventually said David. "I can't be late for my flight."

"I'll say goodbye before you go."

"Yes."

Again, neither knew what to say.

"Well, your toast and coffee is getting cold," eventually said David. "I'll be getting ready."

"Yes, thank you."

When he could be heard no more, Esther looked out over the garden again, and suddenly felt extremely at peace, now having, with ease, renewed her friendship. She started to contemplate what would happen if time would allow. Then her illness came to remind her of her plight.

From her suitcase, she brought out a few boxes and started placing pills in her mouth, one after the other of all different types and swallowing them each time with her coffee, trying not to think anything more of it.

She washed and changed from her nightdress, left her room and descended the stairs to find David in the front hall putting on his coat. Esther stopped before getting to the bottom steps, seeing him look up at her pensively. In return, she looked at him pensively, worried that he might have deserted her without saying anything. Then the smile they gave each other broke down any impending doubt.

"I'm going now," David announced.

"How long will you be away for?" she asked as she approached him.

"Six days taking into account travelling to and from London. I can get someone to look in after you, someone reliable."

"No, it's fine."

"You're sure you're going to be all right here?"

"Yes! I'm a grown woman."

"Yes I've noticed."

Although David was quite serious, this still made Esther chuckle.

"What so funny?" David replied innocently.

She shook her head, convinced that she would never be able to explain.

To David, someone whose husband and daughter were murdered and had death threats from fanatical, demented people, was not meant to laugh. "Okay, well, as long as you're happy," he finally said.

"I'll be fine. Everything is going to be fine. Don't worry. Worry about yourself. Don't let her gobble you up for her own breakfast."

David shook his head: "I am a grown man, you know."

"Yes, I expect that's what she has in mind."

"Don't be silly."

"Seriously, though. Look after yourself. 'A bad woman is worse than death. She is a trap to catch your body and soul, but if you obey the Lord, you can escape'."

"Proverbs?"

Esther shook her head: "Ecclesiastes."

"You think that's what this is? A trap?"

Esther shrugged: "I don't know."

"Jonathan thinks it is."

"More reason to take care. And you need to come back, because I have something serious to talk about. Just don't have an extended stay out there."

"No I won't."

"Because I may not be here for long."

"I told you, you can stay as long as you want," said David as he bent down to pick up his backpack and hand luggage.

"Is that all you are taking?"

"I promised I'm not going for long."

David stood by the front door, opened it, stepped outside and Esther followed him into the courtyard. They looked at each other not knowing what to say for another moment.

"Have a good trip," said Esther, breaking the silence. "Say hello to her from me."

"You are going to be okay, aren't you?"

"Sure!"

With both of them confused as to what the etiquette should be, David smiled and just quietly turned and walked towards the garden and forest. Just before entering the trees, he turned, waved pleasantly at her, and was gone.

Esther stood, knowing she was already feeling a loss with his separation. Venturing to the edge of the garden to look along the forest track, she watched him, hoping he would look back, but he continued walking away. When he was out of sight, she returned to the front door, to the entrance hallway, back to the kitchen and just stood there, not knowing what to do. Then she drifted through the quiet property, aware that she had never been alone like this before.

She stopped on the stairs thinking of David and suddenly realised the clear danger she was in, with falling in love again: "Oh, Esther! What game do I think I'm playing?" Her own voice echoed through the house for no one to hear, and it became eerie as the noise vanished to a strange silence, as if something from the air itself had left with him.

Esther wandered back to her room, but she could not settle for listening to the emptiness. Standing still, she felt the place changing to be what it truly was: desolate, isolated and cold. The peace felt less consoling and she started to well up with tears from all the complexities of her sadness. She was now alone, totally, in life, physically and emotionally. She had been banished from Eden.

Now free from any human intervention, free to let go of the handrails she clung to mentally, free from open judgement, Esther, holding onto a post of the bed as if to prevent herself from falling, hollered to the empty air in a long screech: "NOOOOOOOOOOOOOOO!"

She knew, hearing her voice echoing through the building, that it was a pointless gesture.

With a rush of panic, she fled the room in despair, running through the inner core of the mansion, running and running until she fell into the chapel. She fell onto the stone floor and wept with all the strength and surge of her desperate emotions. The rush of confusion tore her away from being rational, making her dizzy with all the enormity of her life's trials for someone so ordinary. She felt the uncontrollable urge to let go of her rational good sense that spitefully held her emotions in a form of controlled, lonely constriction. For the first time since it all happened, there came relief from the collapse of her stoic temperament, and the full ocean wave of these events threw her against the harsh rocks of realisation. It was only now that she felt she could cry, relentlessly, yielding to the liberation in letting go.

Having tried to control her anguish over her deplorable arrogance on show to the world from Jerusalem, she now was too numb to care. No bitter blow, no punch to the face or kick to the head, no crushing force on her bones could compete with the ache and pain there was in the death of her husband and sweet daughter, the return of the awful memories of her father and sadness for her mother, the desperate situation of her cancer. What made her more wretched was the lack of control she had for the returning love within her for the man who was on his way to the dangers of another woman. The bitter poison of being alive mocked her as to the worth of her very being, mocked the rights she thought she had, mocked even the reason why she should continue.

"Your testing is malicious!" she shouted to the air, lifting herself to kneel on the cold stone floor. "God? You there? How can You be this cruel?"

The house was cold and silent.

Then the full rush of her anger, the ignition of her lungs, the fury boiling in her heart, made the air break with her roar: "Are You ethical? Are You righteous? You test me by killing my husband – by killing my daughter, my innocent Merry, my mirth! You killed my mirth!"

She stopped to regain her breath. Her face was red. Her head was spinning. Her pulse could be felt in her neck, but her lungs were engulfed by the rush of anger still saturating her blood: "You are cruel! You expect people to love You when You crush them! And You do nothing! Nothing! You hear me? Cruel! You are Cruel! My father abused me! My father! Are You the same? Are You listening? Answer me!"

The tortured woman started to hit the hard floor violently, spittle visibly coming from her mouth, and then with rage, she looked up to the ceiling shouting her own psalm from the writing of her very core: "What do You want? What have I done? How much more will You take from me? Why are You persecuting me? I am merely a woman, a wretched woman, a wretched woman with hatred and suffering poured over her! Can't You see? Where are your eyes? Where are your ears? Where is your heart?"

The house was as noiseless as it would have been without her.

She stood up, shaking her fist at the stained-glass windows and the picture of Christ there within: "So this is the way of it, is it? Well do it! Do it! Break every bone! Tear every limb! Smear me into the ground! Crush me back to dust! Is that what You want? Will that please You? Do You need my permission to macerate me?"

There was no answer and the air was just as cold and empty.

"What permission from me do You need?" she howled with her unrelenting fury. "What permission? Know my soul! Know my soul! I will let You pour out all my dignity, mock my humility in front of all the bloody, worthless world! Bring it on! And I will earn the right to spend a day in Your Holy presence! You! Hear! Me! If You want me crushed, then do it! Do it! Do it now! And I will still follow! Give me Your worse! I will not praise You only when times are good! Don't You dare question my loyalty! I will not become weary! I will not lose heart!" Then she shouted at all the walls surrounding her, "Satan! Satan, know my conviction! Know with whom I stand!"

Esther tried to regain her breath, being dizzy and swaying as she stood, her anger exhausted, her energy spent. "Lord, just take me, take me now," she said quietly, and fell to the floor weak from her own exertions, too weak to stop the tears that now softly trickled. In time, she fell asleep.

Esther awoke without knowing how far time had drifted. She slowly, lethargically, roamed the ground floor for a while to stand eventually staring at a piano in a room full of books. At first, she just looked at it and then sat down on the wide stool. With dejection, she violently crashed her fingers on the keys, making angry the air, but when hearing the distorted notes mirroring her inner feelings, she decided to be settled by breathing better. After looking at the keys again in quiet contemplation, she started to play melodically, sweetly, deeply, emotionally with great art in her skill, putting all her emotion in the melodies of the songs that came instantaneously, free-flowing, of just playing her feelings. One moment her spirit was raging to and fro, swerving viciously side to side, like a dog angered with its jaw unable to crush what it was biting. Then her spirit was soaring high above the grounds, floating away with the relief there was in the sudden wash of numbness, but then passion swept in and took her high on the winds of abandonment.

When she finally stopped, the sun was diminishing, and she knew that all the while the music played, her full confusion had been saturated on her illness and how to tell David. If she told him, what would that do to their renewed friendship? Could she live with the depression it would cause in him? David being happy was what she now needed.

Perhaps David's happiness was to be found in another woman. Perhaps David was to meet more of his future than he bargained for on this trip into a lifetime.

"Please come back," Esther whispered, as she sat, alone, at the piano, and played one last tune: 'The Girl with the Flaxen Hair'.

Esther's Lamentation and Psalm

My God, my God, why have you abandoned me? Why are you so far away? Won't you listen to my crying and come and rescue me? I cry out day and night, but you never answer and I find no rest. All my bones are out of joint. My heart is like melted wax.

I have suffered much because God was angry. He chased me into a dark place, where no light could enter. I am the only one He punishes, over and over again: my skin and flesh to waste away; my bones to be crushed and strewn in the ash. He surrounded and attacked me with hardships and trouble. He forced me to sit in the dark like someone long dead. God built a great stone prison wall around me that I cannot climb over.

No one knows the full power of your furious anger, Lord, but it is as great as the fear that I owe You. Please don't turn me back to dust. Please hide me, God, deep in the ground and when You are angry no more, please, please, please remember to rescue me. Correct me as I deserve, but not in your anger — or I will be dead.

If God gave you everything, would you see that as your right for believing? If everything is taken from you, without knowing why, would you still praise God? Is it truly right to follow Him purely in the selfish belief of entering Heaven? Jesus miraculously fed fish and bread to a multitude and they followed Him for more, but when the message of suffering with Jesus was heard, they did not love enough to continue. Satan then laughs at God because people only praise Him for what they can get from it.

Can you still love God, even when you think He has become your very enemy? Would you still praise God knowing you have no true reason for it? Can you keep being faithful, even when everything turns against you? Is He really worth your commitment?

Will you learn to trust God's ways when going through troubled times? Will you call to Him to help while times are harsh? How are you to learn about Christ's suffering for you and others? Can you in anger, show Satan where your loyalties are?

I see this as a fallen place, crying out to be solved one day. It is as if something is not right with the world, and if, with all your soul, you earnestly petition for a full answer, you are always feeling destitute. But if you are tired running with people, how can you possibly run with horses? Why attempt to seek answers of complex matters, when there are more simple matters that are more relevant? Jesus did not give reasons, but He cured the blind and sick.

God owes us no explanation as to why things are as they are. Who are we to ask? Why should God answer? A gathering of people told Jesus of the news that Pontius Pilate, the Roman Governor, had some Galileans murdered and they asked if God approved because of the sin these Galileans must have had to deserve being murdered. Surely God was ultimately behind their horrific deaths because they had deeply disgraced Him. Jesus reminded them of the tower of Siloam that had fallen and killed eighteen people and He asked them whether God had pushed over the tower because of the sins of the eighteen? No one answered and nor does Jesus gives an answer. Instead, He tells them that anyone who does not repair their ways with God risks perishing when their untimely death comes.

You know who you are when you are taken to the lowest depths of life. You truly know your loyalties and absolute base beliefs when everything you know to have, has been stripped from you, like an insignificant atom shattered to pieces in a physics experiment to learn of its structure by the way it disintegrates. A man suffering poor health undeservedly, and still loves God, is far greater than anyone who is unthankfully healthy. A man living in poverty and still chooses to live righteously, is far greater than anyone living for their own wealth. Be warned that success can illuminate your intimate true character and be just as soul-destroying as utter failure. Do not waste your investment in building bigger barns to cater for your material wealth. Why is there so much toil to become the richest man in the cemetery? Look for solid rock on which to build your life to endure calamity when it comes.

A detailed, refined wooden carving has more cuts than a piece of wood that is barely scratched, yet the elaborate carving can be of great value for being so exquisite. A vast metal girder to support great weight is fashioned with great heat.

God is involved in my suffering. God is not removed from my anguish. Jesus was nailed to the cross. He has endured more than I ever will. I must never complain of my suffering again, knowing what Jesus has gone through. He has never said that life will be without storms, but He has promised to share the yoke, and plough and produce a harvest together. Great faith comes with great trials. Facing suffering can find closeness to Him. He knows who are His and who aren't.

I now breathe the Psalms. Never before have they become so powerful and alive, now that I read them in my current deplorable plight. So Lord, hear me! I am vulnerable in an endless weird, awful universe. I am not aware of the bigger picture. I cannot see all the sides of a statue in one view. You can't expect me to understand what goes on in Heaven. I just know that You work on a different timescale to what I can imagine, and Your ways are mysterious. I only ask that You are with me as I travel through endless valleys dark with death, and keep me unafraid and make me safe for your Heaven to come, for me to live with You, forever, in your ever-lasting home.

Death by Immorality

As with all arrival areas across the world in any airport, people arrive and people meet, and for this they wait for the moment. Pashhur was doing just that and stood, not to the fore, but in a position away from others, although prominent to see who arrived.

The display showed his particular flight had landed a little while ago, and he waited for his guest to appear. When he did, Pashhur smiled to himself and walked towards the lost English soul: "Mister Kingsley, welcome to Los Angles, the city of angels."

"Thank you, Pashhur."

"Well remembered. Can I call you David?"

"Of course."

"Wow, man! You travel light!"

They both looked at David's small, single suitcase and backpack.

"Best way to travel," was all that David replied.

"Jez says exactly the same, but does the exact opposite because I'm the one carrying it. That's women for you, David." Pashhur then winked as if David would know all about it. "Well, actually, I never carry it. I organise others to carry it."

Leaving the terminal, David walked with Pashhur, who seemed amused by walking around the parking lot. Thinking they were lost, David suddenly stopped when Pashhur stopped to admire a luxury car.

"What do you think, David?"

"Wow, looks great," answered David, with rising excitement.

"This is so, so Jez. Anyway, let's keep going." Pashhur walked away expecting David to follow.

Having thought they had found their car, David was perplexed to find Pashhur then standing at another luxury car.

"Here we are! What do you think to this one?"

"Looks great as well."

"Man, you have impeccable taste." Pashhur went to the door as if having its key, but suddenly turned to open the car beside it: an ordinary car, much unlike what David was expecting.

Pashhur could see what David thought: "Yeah, bit of a let-down, hey? Don't worry, we're experts in not drawing attention when we don't want it." Having placed the luggage in the trunk, Pashhur opened the door for his passenger, and David settled in the seat, deflated with not being in one of the other cars. With Pashhur amused with his little fun, they were then leaving the Airport.

"Just sit back and enjoy the ride," said Pashhur. "Jez said for me to take you to your hotel."

"Thanks. I've been on the go for longer than a day so I need a good shower and sleep."

"Well she's getting ready to meet you fairly soon."

"Oh, I'll just have a shower and be ready, then."

"That's a good decision."

Pashhur was cheerful to oblige taking his guest directly to the hotel, and David felt better after having a shower even though his watch told him it was his midday from the day before without having had much sleep.

Meeting again in the hotel's foyer, Pashhur took him back to the car and, for a partial tour across Beverley Hill, they drove onwards through Los Angeles as the evening darkened.

"I think Jez has some plans to show you California."

"Really? I don't have long. I need to be back in three days."

Pashhur waved this off as if to suggest it was irrelevant: "That's okay. Leave it with me. I can rearrange your flights." He turned to David and looked sincere: "Really, leave it all to me. Consider it done."

David paused in thought, but then he aired his question: "Won't she be followed by everyone? How does she get about without being mobbed?"

"Exceptional tactics and planning."

"Really?"

"Absolutely!" Pashhur beamed a sunny smile and laughed. "She can just remove her make-up and she's a different person. Sometimes in the winter, she goes round with padding to make her look bigger – don't tell her I told you that."

David shook his head.

"And the use of wigs or doing something different, dye, cut, style, and wearing glasses or sunglasses – it all adds up. You wouldn't believe where she's been and no one has known."

"That's quite – quite impressive really."

"She likes to meander about in museums and galleries by herself, and no one sees her."

"That takes me back."

"To?"

"Just some time ago when I liked to visit museums and galleries with an old friend."

"They're just great, aren't they?"

"Museums or old friends?"

Again Pashhur laughed with his bright smile: "Man! I like you! No wonder Jez is keen! I meant places, but as you say, people are great with it."

Nothing had prepared David for the estate he was just about to visit.

The high gate opened without any command, without any aid. Driving through the grounds, with lighting embedded in the road and paving, showed an extensive garden of an exceptional standard that David thought should be open to the public. All the lights were gleaming, almost of a blue tint to bring a stylish elegance and brilliance to the scene. Even Pashhur was surprised.

"Wow! She doesn't normally have everything on. She obviously wants you to be impressed."

The house was not immediately visible for all the trees and walls of the garden. Then turning into what appeared to be a secluded courtyard, Pashhur drove under an arch in a wall and there was the house.

It was not as high as David expected, being predominantly only a single storey, nor was it as big, but everything was immaculate and clean and in perfect design, modern, stylish and aglow with lights that made the building appear to be made of stones that were radioactive in parts.

David's comparison was with Halcyon, being larger, older and darker, being in a state of disrepair, of a design that had evolved from an accumulation of generations and styles, with ivy everywhere and probably preventing some of the building from collapse.

Pashhur noticed David becoming quiet: "You okay?"

"Yep."

"Well she's in there. She's waiting for you."

David's immediate thought took him back to Esther, but then he realised to whom Pashhur referred.

Pashhur did not move from the car, and instead studied David, who studied the house.

"You know," said Pashhur, "I think she has a thing for you."

"Me?"

"Yeah!"

"Me? What could she see in me with all those famous handsome actors around?"

Pashhur laughed and shrugged: "That's women for you. Perhaps it's the English accent or your gentle eyes, or your good looks, and open and trustworthy nature."

David had no idea how to reply, but he felt a surge of flattery raise his heart rate.

With this, Pashhur got out and approached the front, wide, welcoming door.

Now feeling stunned, David followed and was surprised to see Pashhur with a key to enter the front hallway, encouraging David to enter with him.

"Jez! You've got company!" called Pashhur. "Jez?"

No one came.

"Sorry David, I don't know where she is. Come through to the side lounge."

David entered a large, open but cosy room, complete with comfortable lounge chairs and a massive screen.

"Make yourself at home. I'll go and find her and then be around to take you back to your hotel. Want a drink? There's a drinks bar over there."

"I don't drink."

"Of course. Anyway, I'll be back with your hostess." Pashhur left the room and was gone, and all went quiet.

David, with tiredness now starting to make his mind go weak, sat on one of the large, cosy chairs and within moments his eyes were closed. The chair, so cushioned and soft, was almost more than a bed and could easily smother its occupant. Sleep wilfully swept over him.

Quiet, settled and relaxed, her blonde hair loose, leaning against the doorframe to the room, stood an attractive woman, watching the man in his settled doze. After a few moments, she ventured softly into the room making no sound from the thick carpet, and stood almost on top of him. Bending down, she came near to feel his breathing on her cheek and she smiled at her little game.

Then she looked up to the door she had just come from and saw who was now an intruder, standing almost the same way she had. Trying to be quiet, she frantically waved him away.

Pashhur, arms crossed, just winked.

She had no choice but to leave the room and she pushed Pashhur into the hall to close the door as quietly and quickly as she could. "What are you doing?" she whispered with irritation.

Pashhur whispered in reply, but with amusement, "My, you're quick, as soon as the man's delivered you're about to devour him."

Jezebel was annoyed with his judgement of her: "No, I wasn't!"

"Was."

"Wasn't."

"Was."

"Look, this is my house, please leave."

"I thought you wanted me to stay and take him back to his hotel."

The woman huffed: "Yes, I did. Stick around."

Pashhur pushed open the door again and they both looked at David, still fast asleep on the overgrown couch.

"What do you think?" whispered Pashhur. "You've got the perfect opportunity. I can just leave him here with you."

Jezebel sighed and shook her head: "No, it's not right. During or after our tour would be far better."

"You're the boss. What do you want done now?"

"Help make the place look less daunting for this lesser mortal."

"Sure, want a drink?"

"Yeah, why not? Did you get him one?"

"He said he doesn't drink."

"He doesn't drink alcohol, you dummy. He would have liked at least something to drink. Not all of us are winos like you. In fact, just go. Leave me alone with him for a bit."

"But I thought – "

"Just go around the block or two. Go! Get your drink somewhere else! Leave me alone with him."

"How long shall I be gone?"

Just a look of disapproval was all the answer given, but Pashhur smirked and winked as he left.

When certain she was alone, she entered the room again and stood behind the drinks bar, preparing fruit and herbs and cream and juices into a cocktail shaker and shaking it with a skill of someone adept to cocktails and bar work. Then she used the blender and the sound made David suddenly animated, which made her chuckle. "Hi, sleepy!"

He looked over at her with bleary eyes, a confused look and a lack of recognition of the female, and smiled as one would trying to be polite having committed a social misdemeanour.

"I'm Jezebel. Remember?" replied the attractive woman. "I know: this is me without make-up, without hair dye, without fashion, with my natural blonde hair. This is me as unmasked as I can get."

David was still sleepy as he replied: "It's a beautiful wake up call."

"You've not slept long." Jezebel was not wearing anything that was revealing or suggestive, nothing that would warrant anything other than a loveable girl who looked to be in want of pizza and a good movie to see. He almost did not recognise her other than for her voice.

"Want a drink? It's not alcoholic," she continued. "It's one of my refreshing health drinks that's a secret mixture of only I know what. Want some? There's plenty I've made."

Without David answering other than a suggestive shrug, Jezebel brought over two glasses of her drink and sat beside him.

"I'm so sorry," David said, embarrassed. "I fell asleep. I don't know what happened. You must think I'm really rude and I – I suppose I – I was a bit – strained to see you again." David could not stifle a yawn and looked sheepish.

"Strained?" Jezebel laughed: "What does that mean? I've never met someone who has been strained to see me."

David laughed as Jezebel handed him the drink and became as baffled as she was. "I don't know what I'm saying. I'm too tired to make any sense. This is so cosy. I could sleep here forever."

"Why don't you? You're on holiday with me."

He took a sip and almost sat upright as if in shock: "Gosh, this is amazing stuff! What is it? What's in this?"

"I said, my handsome English friend, it's a secret. Like it?"

"Very much!"

"Have some more. I don't usually make it for guests. Only for me."

"Well bottle it and you'll be worth a fortune." David then looked around him.

They both looked at each other and burst out laughing as if drunk. The laughing became so energetic that neither of them could stop it and both would be encouraging the other when trying to calm down, creating another bout of giggles. Trying to calm down just prolonged their fun with the other suddenly not containing their laughter to spill their mouthful into the air, causing the other to laugh more. It lasted to a point that neither of them could remember why they were laughing.

"Oh, I'm sorry," apologised David. "I'm just tired and silly."

"I've never laughed so much before," Jezebel said, a hand to her chest. Her drink had spilt down her front and lap. "I'm so wet!" she said as she looked down at herself still within the last of her laughter. "You are so much fun! I would love to show off my country to you. My next production is months away, so I've got nothing in my diary until then and I can cancel anything if it's there. Stay for a while. When do you go back?"

"A few days."

"Days!" Jezebel tutted. "You came all this way for a few days? Mister, you ain't never been to America before! You need to have your flight cancelled."

"I, errmm, I don't know, can that happen?"

"Pashhur will fix it. Consider it done."

David did not reply, as sleepy as he was.

"I can tell you're not with me yet."

David shook his head as if drunk: "I think I need to get back to my hotel and sleep. Pashhur said he'd take me."

"Why don't you sleep here?"

"Oh, I couldn't do that."

"You were just now. Come on, I've got a nice comfy bedroom in a nice secluded place to itself. You can wake up at any time. We'll then have breakfast, Pashhur can leave us alone and we can discuss where you would like to be taken. I'm serious! It's no bother for me to take a few weeks or even a few months showing you the whole place. It's fantastic. No one will bother us."

"Sleep is all I can think of. Is it fine for me to stay?"

"Come on, let me take you there before you're gone again."

Jezebel led the way through her house to the other side and showed David a large bedroom, immaculate in furnishings, lavish in decor, flawless in comfort.

"You've got your own en-suite over there and the – actually you just want the bed don't you?"

David smiled and nodded.

"Well there are night clothes in the drawers. You'll definitely find something to fit and spare tooth brushes and – anyway, I'll leave you alone. Please sleep for as long as you want."

"Thank you. I wasn't expecting this."

"Who does? Good night, David."

"Good night."

She turned and left, closing the door, and wandered the house to find herself eventually in the kitchen with her thoughts elsewhere.

There came some sniggering from the door and she turned.

Pashhur was again leaning against the doorframe, smiling at Jezebel: "Did you drug him? Tie him up?"

"He's in bed, sleeping off his jetlag."

"Cute."

They both gravitated towards the large kitchen breakfast bar and sat with each other, for a moment without anything to say.

"So, we can take a compromising picture of him right now," Pashhur suggested eventually.

"No, that's just tasteless."

"Jez! You're an open-all porn star!"

"Well, I want this done right, with panache, with style."

"Wow, that's got to be a first. He must be having an effect on you."

"Shut up! Have you been priming him well?" asked Jezebel as if asking about preparations for an exam.

"As planned. I've been impeccable about it."

"So? What do you think?"

"I quite like him. He makes me laugh."

"No! I meant my chances?"

"You're asking me about your chances? As if he's gonna turn you down?"

"You don't think he will?"

Pashhur then suddenly went quiet and pensive: "Actually, something's happening."

"You're making me worried."

"I don'no. It's been niggling me now you've come to ask."

"What's niggling? I don't like things that niggle. No niggly things."

"He went quiet when I said that you want to show him California, and he thought back at something about an old friend for a while."

"So?"

"I don'no."

"Don't tell me things that are irrelevant. I have no time for it."

"His mind was definitely elsewhere."

"Thinking of me?"

"No!" interjected Pashhur with his sudden realisation. "No man!"

"What? What is it?"

"You know, I think he does want to get back."

"What?"

"I think he really does want to get back – and soon. I think there's someone waiting for him. I think he's waiting for her. Man, I think you've got big competition and I don't think you've got much time."

"Really? You worked all that out? I didn't think you were that long with him."

"Just believe me."

"What should I do?"

"You're asking me? I don't believe it! Hallelujah! Praise the Lord! She asks me!"

"Don't be stupid. I feel like everything has to be sped up. I was gearing for a long romantic holiday and then dropping him once I've gained his affection."

"You're falling for him, aren't you? You are falling in love with him."

"I said! Don't be stupid!"

"Well whatever you do, you've only got a few days, not weeks with him. He's going back when his ticket says he's going back and neither of us can change that."

City of Angels

Clouds were scarce. The sun was too radiant; the sky was too blue; the heat was too controlling and the brightness too strong. It was as much to tackle this glory by hiding within shade while the grass became straw.

Within her extensive garden, under a broad, flower-drenched pergola, Jezebel, with wet hair and dressed in a thin, comfortable, white cotton beach gown, which was translucent enough to display her physic in a white bikini, looked up from her reading at the sound of someone approaching. She instantly smiled. Her mouth curled in anticipation of fun and her eyes gleamed under her sunhat with exuberance. "Ah! Here's the sleepy Englishman!"

David came to stand beside her under the cover of the pergola, wearing a thick, white dressing gown. "Good morning," he said cheerfully.

"Aren't you hot with that on?"

"Just improvising."

"I've swam a few lengths already. Like to join me for more?" With that, Jezebel took a sip from the straw in some juice.

David shook his head: "You're just too fit for me."

"Come and sit down, then. Have something refreshing. You're still recovering from jetlag. You want a drink?"

"Is it always this bad?" David asked, sitting next to her.

"You mean you've never had jetlag?"

"No."

"Well you need some more of my bottled secret remedy you had last night."

"How do you cope with it? You must be travelling all the time all over the world?"

"I go actress class."

"Oh," was his only reply. After taking a sip, and then taking some gulps realising his thirst, he placed the glass back down on the table, refreshed, all the while being watched by a beautiful woman who looked amused with a smile at watching him drink. "That will explain it. Gosh, this is a fantastic drink."

"It's a fantastic morning."

"Thanks for letting me stay over."

"You're welcome. It's great that you look so at home here."

"I suppose I am."

"So let's discuss what you want to do here."

"Well, I need to get to my hotel and get changed. Can I be taken back?"

"Pashhur's not around anymore. It's just us two. You can have some clothes from here, gent's clothes. They'll really suit you, by the way. Did you not go through some of the wardrobes?"

"I didn't think I should. As I said, I'm improvising."

"Just make yourself at home! Stay as long as you want! I can get Pashhur to organise a later date back to England."

"Actually I do need to go back soon. There's a lot to do – "

"And someone to see?"

"Well, yes. It would be nice to spend these few days just seeing Los Angeles, but I do truly need to go back – really – truly."

Jezebel showed her disbelief in her amused smirk.

"I didn't think you would have this time for me."

"I wanted to show you the Grand Canyon and Las Vegas and Yosemite and San Diego and San Francisco and – everything."

"What about just showing me Los Angeles?"

"Okay then, as you are my very special guest: Los Angeles, the city of Angels, it is. You want breakfast?"

"I'm famished, yes please."

David expected a servant to take the request, but Jezebel vanished and returned after a short while having prepared it herself. She placed a tray beside him that showed their breakfast was not going to be any more complex than fruit, muesli, some toast and marmalade, and expensive coffee.

"I never have anything else myself," Jezebel said, "but I know how you English like your jams and marmalades. Now as to visiting Los Angeles, I can take you anywhere and we can do what you want."

"Can we visit a museum?"

"Certainly, why?"

"Because I like them and it will take me back to my young days. It would test something that Pashhur said."

"I know exactly what you mean. Don't worry, no one will recognise me. Remember, what's on stage or film is made up. It's never me."

David nodded and smiled back.

"Ready for another swim?"

"I haven't had my first and I'm not wearing anything to swim in."

It was this answer that Jezebel raised her eyes suggestively.

"I'm not swimming naked!"

Jezebel was then up, throwing off her gown and running to the water, shouting as she went: "Don't worry, I never swim naked either!" She dived perfectly into the shimmering water and came to the surface to call out to him: "Come on, lazy bones! Get your shorts on!"

Los Angeles was all and more than what David expected, and Jezebel was true to her word that no one recognized her. Wherever they went and whatever they visited, Jezebel was always smiling and chatting, and so focused on David, that her confidence and general good humour was like camouflage to those surrounding them. Jezebel even felt comfortable enough with David to place her arm within his as they meandered around the Getty Centre, studying each picture of Van Gogh within the clean, elegant white building.

"You see?" she whispered, being close to him, looking at the other people. "They don't really know who it is walking with them. They're in their own worlds. Even if a gorilla was to come along, would they ever see it?"

"Being with someone like me makes it more unlikely to them for you to be you."

"Wow, that's deep. I hardly understood it, but it was deep. You are quite a deep guy. You go down and down and down the more I'm with you."

David shrugged.

"As to everyone else, I think you'll find it's all the girls looking at you, not me." Jezebel could see through his embarrassment he was deeply flattered.

"Well that's nonsense."

"And yet here we are walking around, with all these beautiful girls looking at you. I like to think they accept me for who I am."

"And what's that?"

"Just a fellow girlie." She smiled. "Had enough? Want to see a beach?"

"Is there a reason why I wouldn't?"

Standing on the metro platform, Jezebel leant nearer to him to whisper: "I just want you to observe the people and know why this place is called the City of Angels."

David nodded and they sat together on the train that had just stopped at their station.

"I love the metro in LA," she said. "You can get on one and just sit and listen to the couple beside you talking about anything as if long-standing friends. Then the train comes to a stop and one of them has to get off. It's only then you realise they only just met and chatted. You don't get that anywhere else. People here are angels no matter the skin colour." She moved closer to him, leaving no trace of a gap between them. "Look at her," she whispered, motioning to a young black girl.

She had a baby tucked within a sheet around her front, and she held a cup for collecting money and a piece of cardboard with writing that explained her plight. She spoke to people who would more often speak back in conversation, asking about her predicament after having given some change as a fellow person would. There was no shun, no indignation, no discomfort.

Jezebel smiled at her and gave some money.

The young girl smiled back, almost curtsied, and continued along the aisle until she got off at the next stop.

"That's why we're called the city of angels," said Jezebel. "We don't just give money to get rid of the homeless. People actually talk to them as people."

When at the beach, Jezebel reached for his hand to hold as they walked. "I had a yacht once," she said after a long pause. "I kept it down at San Diego. Spent a million or two, I don't know, but I hardly used it: twice, three times, I can't remember. I got Pashhur to sell it. Listen to me: I must sound like I'm in another world."

David just smiled.

"I know I have a – reputation, but really I – I'm – ." She deliberately left the sentence unfinished for him to devise the rest.

David remained politely silent.

"You know, you're very cute. You're very sweet, a very solid kind of guy."

"I am?"

"You don't even know it. You're quite – irresistible." Jezebel was charmed by the thump of her own heartbeat, as of a young girl on a first date with a loved one. She naturally kissed him on the cheek, and instantly started to doubt her plan of seduction for one of just falling in love. She then chuckled at her own indecision.

"What's so funny?" David asked, joining in her amusement with his own smile.

"I just kissed you and you're, you are just – I don't know." She chuckled again, almost to herself, content and happy within her own mirth.

David was not sure how to deal with the closeness, but felt captivated by her happy demeanour.

"This is where I was discovered," said Jezebel, moving on, "along this stretch of beach. I just sang and sang and sang, and that got me noticed, and that got me into acting, if you can call it acting."

"You know, your songs are always catchy and positive and enthusiastic and loving – but full of longing."

"I do my best."

"Nothing like your – errrmm."

"Reputation?"

"Yep."

"Perhaps it's time to change my reputation." Jezebel smiled pleasantly, as if she truly was filled with virtues. "Want a drive through Beverly Hills? I can show you where some of the stars live and tell you a few stories."

"Actually, it doesn't appeal."

"We can go door-to-door collecting money for The Salvation Army."

"Now you're making fun."

"I know. Beverly Hills is a place that's over-rated, frankly."

"I thought you lived there."

"Not a chance. What do you want to do?"

"What would you suggest?"

"We can do more galleries and go home for a good cooked meal. I can get a great chef I know to cook for us. Interested?"

"Sounds great."

"Good! I'll arrange it."

They arrived at Jezebel's estate later that evening with the whole building elegantly lit in the descending dusk and the front door was opened before they arrived on the steps.

"Pashhur!" exclaimed Jezebel when she saw who had let them into the hall.

Pashhur grinned at them both: "And how is the happy couple on this happy day?"

"Just great!" Jezebel kissed Pashhur on the cheek as a daughter would a wealthy father having given her a stable of ponies.

"Well, if Mister and Misses would like to walk through to the dining hall, I will start to serve the first course."

The table was set with lit candles casting an elegant air, and romantic music was already producing a soothing sound to the room.

Pashhur, being genteel, moved a chair to aid Jezebel to sit, while David, also being the gentleman, allowed her to be seated before he sat opposite. Then, in a comfortable silence, Pashhur served the starters and poured an orange drink.

"Wow, compliments to the chef," David said.

"Wait for the next course," he replied, visibly pleased, "and I'll now leave you two alone to enjoy the evening."

"It's been an incredible day, thank you," Jezebel said when Pashhur had gone.

"That's just what I was about to say."

Jezebel became silent and looked expectant of something. "Would you like to pray?" she eventually asked.

David was taken aback by the request, but smiled and closed his eyes. "Loving Heavenly Father, we come to You in shame in not being able to thank You enough for all that You do and for all that You are. Help us to be thankful and help us to search for You in all that there is. Instil in us Your excitement in life as we both share in Your Creation. In Jesus' name, we ask this. Amen." David then looked up and saw Jezebel's stunned expression. "You okay?"

"Yes – Yes! Thank You! I mean – Amen! That's quite a prayer."

"Just be free to say what you feel. Praying is good! It's healthy. People are stressed because they don't. God isn't the one who's damaged if we don't pray; we are. He just loves us drawing near. He wants us to search for Him like children yearning to find a good father – or at least for us to remain within His reach. For a start, think of all the good things there are and thank Him."

"My praying would be non-stop, then. I wouldn't have time for anything else."

"What would you thank Him for?"

"You being here is good," answered Jezebel with a sweet smile.

"Well, I feel sincerely very flattered, considering all those handsome film stars you must know."

"They can be just as shallow as most other guys. Looks aren't everything, David, nor is money."

David was so surprised by the comment that he said nothing.

"I suppose I'm looking for something – something – not definable. I suppose I'm deep down wondering what life is all about."

"So what do you think life is all about?"

"Really? Really about? I have no idea."

"What is life? Life is all about making it worth living – not just for yourself, but for others, for everyone, to make them feel worthy and to feel worthiness in doing so, to respect and enjoy God's creation."

Jezebel just stared at David for a moment. "Wow," she softly replied. "Can I live up to that? I wouldn't know where to start. I thought life was about living healthy and being good. I'm into health and energy and keeping fit and eating nutritious food and – . I hardly ever drink alcohol. I've never smoked. Never taken drugs, either, being quite the good girl I am." Jezebel then smirked. "It's true!" she said emphatically to enforce some belief in David.

"You are such a good example. I can't remember the last time I did anything active." David picked up a glass of the available soft drink, spent a moment absently thinking and then shrugged: "I wouldn't know where to start. Cheers!"

Jezebel smiled at his smile: "Here's to not knowing where to start."

They both clinked glasses and drank their fruit juice.

"The film industry is just a massive money-making machine, nothing more, you know," Jezebel said.

"What about you, though? You gain a lot from it," replied David, not conscious of his comment being offensive.

Jezebel was suddenly taken aback and looked injured. "Well what about you?" was her defence. "You're making money for The Salvation Army. In fact, that could be the only reason you're here, and not to see me at all!" There was a moment's pause and Jezebel moved her plate away from her as though offended. "What am I to you if all I am is someone to give you money for your charity?"

"I'm sorry, I didn't mean to upset you."

"Well you have." Jezebel sat as if undecided on what she wanted to do. Then she stood up. "If you please excuse me," she said sadly, "I'm – I'm ready for bed."

David stood as Jezebel started to leave the room. There was no doubt in him that he had hurt her.

She stopped at the door, turned and, as if losing her indignation, then asked curiously, "Why aren't you a Salvation Army Officer?"

He shook his head in confusion, curious as to why the question.

"I like you a lot, David," was all Jezebel said in a forlorn manner before she turned and disappeared, leaving him no room to reply. Deliberately aiming to make him feel guilty with her acting, she realised she truly was upset about his comment about her money.

Head on a Plate

"Can we not zoom around so much today?" David asked at breakfast, wearing a dressing gown.

"Someone's old!" replied Jezebel, also wearing a dressing gown. "We can chill here if you like. Here, have an apple."

"I'm sorry, really, about – about what I said last night about money," said David after a while.

"Ahhh, that was last night. It's too tiresome to remember it now. I'm no longer a juvenile, you know. What about a walk around my gardens this morning? I like my gardens, they're so pretty."

For the course of that day, they started with a gentle walk through the flawless garden grounds, talking pleasantly about all sorts of things of childhood fancies and ambitions, picking flowers and at moments Jezebel initiating to walk arm-in-arm. There was not another soul.

After a light meal that they made together, they both lounged around the pool.

"You see, even a super, mega, infamous film star can be just like the girl next door," Jezebel said as they lay on blankets on the grass. "All this just happened to an ordinary girl like me. Want more sun-block rubbed in?"

David, lying on his front feeling too comfortable to object, allowed Jezebel to massage his back. "You know," he said eventually through his mouth that was half smothered by his bicep, "I have concluded, with my phenomenal, precision engineering thinking, that – ." He was too relaxed to know what he was saying and sounded as though almost asleep.

"Yes?"

"That you are so much – so much – fun."

Jezebel laughed.

"And very – very – clever."

"And you sound too relaxed."

"It's true, but the trouble is most people think you're just a blonde bimbo. That's just not true."

"I know – awful, isn't it?" Jezebel laughed again. "What did you think before you met me?"

"I didn't know what to think. You can't judge anything unless you know it completely."

"Spoken like a true Agnostic. Can you do me?"

"Do you?"

"Rub my back." Jezebel then lay on her front beside him in anticipation, making it rude if he ignored her request.

Although David had been almost falling asleep, he awoke enough to start massaging her in return.

Jezebel deliberately remained quiet to ensure his concentration was for her unblemished skin. She unclasped the top of her bikini and waited to see what David would do.

After a slight, wordless hesitation, he continued without saying anything further.

When done, Jezebel, holding her bikini top to her chest, sat up and motioned to David to clasp it together. "Coming for a swim?" she said, eagerly.

David shook his head and fell back on the blanket to how he was dozing earlier, falling asleep even before Jezebel had dived into the pool.

It was after many lengths that Jezebel, holding onto the side, decided to gain his interest again and splashed water all over him. "I thought you were overheating!" she laughed. "No good getting me back! I'm wet! I'm wet through!"

Now having his attention, Jezebel got from the pool allowing him to see the way the water shimmered off her slender and perfect figure. She saw his look of admiration and she realised the right time would be quickly gone.

"You want to be entertained," Jezebel said factually, as she dried herself. "I can imagine this is getting to bore someone like you."

"No, I'm okay. I'm enjoying it here – wish I could stay longer."

"Please do!"

"Truly, I need to get back."

"Verily I say unto thee," Jezebel replied with a teasing grin, "if it were not so I would not have told thee, open thy ears if thy have any."

David smiled, closed his eyes and settled into a snooze as Jezebel sat beside him.

"I like The Salvation Army," she said as if like a little girl commenting on her favourite colour. "I enjoyed the gathering you took me to, along that famous street. I still think of that drama – about planets spinning around."

David mumbled with half his mouth smothered with his bicep again, with his head rested in his crossed arms: "It was Oxford Street." Then he sighed with being relaxed.

Jezebel, lying down on her side, leant on her elbow, head in her hand, looking at the lazy man: "They stand outside playing hymns and tunes and shaking their shakers and proclaiming. They look nice in their uniforms. Did you ever do much of that?"

David showed more interest in snoozing. "Open-air meetings they're called," he answered, half asleep. "They go into the streets to lead a service in public. If Mohammed doesn't come to the mountain, then bring the mountain to Mohammed."

"Do you do any?"

"What?"

"These outside meetings."

"I did a little. Come along to one."

"I may even turn up wearing the uniform."

"You'd look great."

"I would, wouldn't I?"

"Yes."

"They would never know, would they, if I were to just appear, wearing one?"

"They might, if they ask you for your testimony."

"They're very entertaining: the band guys – they're very talented with their brass instruments."

"It's supposed to be a bit more than entertaining. It's supposed to draw people and help them think of religious matters."

"Jesus, you mean?"

"Mmm." With the sun and quiet garden grounds, David was too restful to make conversation.

"Jesus must have been great. I mean, to have followed Him around like that, and to have been there must have been – something. What do you think?"

"Yep," mumbled David.

Jezebel sighed with lack of participation: "Hey! I'm trying to entertain you!"

"Don't worry, you are."

"You find me entertaining, do you? What if you let me show you a new dance routine I've been practicing?"

"That would be good."

"Go through to my studio and make yourself comfy on the floor cushions and wait for me to get ready. Then I'll come in and show you."

Having stepped from the garden into a large, luxurious room, David found the array of large, heavy, comfortable cushions before a large dance floor, and he sat down on them, relaxed and full of anticipation. Beside him was a large bowl of fruit, overfull of sumptuous grapes, apples, oranges, figs and mangoes and directly on the other side of the room were large, drawn curtains.

He thought he heard music. It was so quiet that he doubted his senses when he could not see any mechanism that could produce it. Not discovering the source, but accepting it was coming from all directions, he sat back and started to enjoy the growing beat. The music became louder, generating an energetic, exciting pulse that grew in power. The beat was strong, pounding, growing into an urge to dance.

Suddenly, in time to the music, the curtains across the room almost exploded into the air to float free, and before him, wearing a white top with a sash and a white skirt, tight at the waist and hips, and picture-perfect, was Jezebel.

She wore a cowboy hat and boots, and stood in a pose that fully complemented her figure with the music as a backdrop to the scene. Then in time, she started to move to the beat, skilfully, passionately, beautifully, becoming vigorous, vibrant, making sure her audience took full advantage of each captivating view and alluring motion. The dress became ripped to a shorter skirt with a tear to the side to free her movement, and the sash around her waist became untied to float away to leave her shapely mid-rift bare.

Every move was quick and swift, deftly in time to the beat, exacting the thrust of the music, a power that was too enthralling to think about turning away. There were moments of beautiful grace and elegance, but as the dance continued, it became more suggestive, more appealing, more compelling to see more, a torture of anticipation. Her expression would change from racy, to having fun, to being erotic and enticing.

The torn skirt then became loose and thrown as she danced in white lacy underwear. The top was quickly off and discarded, and a hand then used to keep her chest from being seen until baring her alluring breasts. The remaining lacy underwear was untied and teasingly held up with one hand and thrown away while her secret curves were hidden using the cowboy hat. Throwing her hair and passing her hands through it in a lustrous show, the hat then disappeared and Jezebel danced tantalisingly without allowing her total nakedness be seen with her turns and having a hand quickly covering her last remaining place.

The music reached fever-pitch and collapsed. Facing David, she instantly dropped with the music to her knees, legs apart and bent backwards, breathing heavily as if too exhausted to move. Her golden hair had swept the floor and now lay spread-bound. She was fully tanned, fully shaven, toned to perfection, without a blemish, without a tattoo, without any trace of imperfection, flawless.

There in front of David, was the world's most famous woman, threadbare, showing her exact form.

Then, alluringly, like a snake under a charm, Jezebel arose and slithered towards him. In her total nakedness, she was natural, fluent, sensual, with no awkwardness, no embarrassment, no emotional hindrance.

"The dance of Herodias's daughter," she said smoothly when reaching him, "for every man who sees it, be powerless to resist, and every woman be sick with envy – and only you have seen it." She was then upon him, caressing his muscles, her mouth delicately, sensuously kissing his lips.

There was a moment that David felt he could say no. Instead, he said nothing. He made no attempt to prevent her exploring him. He accommodated her every move and became just as naked.

"Be relaxed," she said tenderly. "Let it happen."

David, with sudden passion, kissed Jezebel and forcefully turned her over onto her back to be then on top of her.

"I know you want me," she breathed. "You want all of me. Please – take all of me."

Advanced Gossip

Landing at Heathrow Airport, David became aware of people staring at him while queuing for border control. Some whispered to others, some discreetly pointed at him, but there would always be the odd glance in his direction and aversion when he returned their glance.

The customs officer, still maintaining a professional aloofness, also gave an airing of suspicion, even though David answered the questions with all honesty and completeness, and there was no need to doubt his answers. His passport was handed back with an amount of contempt.

Walking through the Arrivals exit, David, aware of the large crowd, was at first unaware their presence was for him. As family members and friends became reunited with loved ones, his appearance started to create a commotion, like a ripple that grew exponentially. Pictures were being shot and large flashes from cameras became invasive, threatening and disorientating. The cacophony of interfering questions, the calling out, the noise from the shouting, and the rush to converge on him, made David confused, and he started to quicken his pace to leave the scene in shock of the increasing development.

The gathering horde, like integrated parasites, continued to surround him no matter his attempt or direction. They were shouting questions he could not understand. Such was the furore that airport security had to use their might to gain back control of the forceful crowd.

Trying to find an escape, David was suddenly grabbed by the arm. He tried to tear his arm away, but the hold was too strong and David was forced to find the one who was grabbing him tightly: so tight, his arm became numb.

It was Jonathan. Not being heard, he motioned for David to come with him with urgency.

It was in this movement and the apparition of one acting like a bodyguard, that made the reporters unconsciously step back to allow some separation, but they followed like a thick layer of flies as David and Jonathan were able to start walking amidst the assembly. David had no idea where Jonathan was leading him, but he followed in trust.

Then the questions started to become coherent.

"Did you really do it?"

"Mister Kingsley! Did you or didn't you?"

"Do you have something to hide?"

"How did it happen?"

"How good was she?"

"Is it an affair?"

David stopped when hearing the last question and realised he was truly in the thick of a scandal.

Jonathan, looking annoyed, took hold of him again, but this time, with the strength of David's resolve, David pulled back his arm and stood within his own thoughts.

With the sudden stillness of the culprit, the journalists quietened in anticipation of his answer.

The question was repeated: "Are you having an affair?"

"Be honest!" said someone else.

David, returning from his inner world, with shock across his face, nodded.

In that one moment, the flashes and cameras intensified the attack and became a danger to each and every retina in the vicinity. Everyone hushed again to hear more.

"Yes. I did. I am."

With anger, Jonathan grabbed David once more and tried to march him away from the new, increased turmoil, as the reporters returned with such ferocity with their incessant, unceasing questions, that they all blurred into a noise that was horrendous, comparable to squawks, squeals, chirps and roars that would be found in a zoo or from

Parliament. With so much commotion, airport security had no choice but to attempt to break it apart, which moved the focus away from David and Jonathan. So large was the crowd that security had difficulty in dealing with the magnitude, but their impact was enough to disperse them like an ice pack being cracked open and made to float free.

Aided by security men through hidden, staff corridors, Jonathan and David were eventually able to get to Jonathan's car without being chased, and they finally sat inside it, letting their breathing settle.

After a sigh, Jonathan then asked a forceful question that defied being in receipt of a lie: "Did you sleep with her?"

"It's not what you think."

Jonathan furiously shouted: "It's not what I think? It's not what I think? David! What planet are you on? If you think that this is some sort of idiotic, fantasy play with you, King David, and Bathsheba then you have truly lost it! Anything that belittles the horror of sin is like pouring acid down your own throat! Sin is so awful, can you imagine having to kill a bull, see its blood over your hands and burn it all? And do it again and again and again? That's what they had to do for the Law of Moses, before Jesus, and Jesus dying on the cross isn't exactly tame! Sin is sin, you can't romanticise it! I knew this would happen! I even warned you about it!"

"What happened?"

"What happened? Oh come on, David! You need some serious psychiatric counselling! What do you mean, what happened? You're the one to know! She admitted on television across the whole world – that you and her slept with each other! Do you know what's happening to your Company? It's crumbling! Your Company is breaking apart, and that was happening before all of this. Now, the whole thing is kaput! Do you know how much time and money and energy I've put into it, just to let your idiocy destroy everything! Everything David! Everyone's walking out!"

"Just take me to my car."

"No way! There are reporters crawling all over it!"

"I need to get away."

"You need to clear up this mess!" Jonathan then started the car and drove, and David did not question where he was being driven. It was a long while before either of them spoke.

"I need to see Esther," quietly replied David.

Deridingly, Jonathan detonated with his answer: "Oh yeah! Sure! She's really gonna love you now! You've ruined everything! Everything! Including her! Hasn't she been through enough! I told you not to go, but you thought you'd do the 'what would Jesus do' trick, and go and evangelise to the corrupted! Wow! What a trophy she would have been! Haven't you read the Scriptures? It also says to not be of this world, not be one of these people, to not get entangled in their dealings or wanton women!"

"She doesn't know."

"Who? Esther? She will now! Unless you lock her up and lie to her all her life! Don't think that all your mighty 'good works' will save you! I know the real hidden agenda was to look good in front of Esther, not God, and to make you feel happier from your own self-centred self-pity, even though others had worse dumped on them! I can't believe I was drawn in by it all. Even though I knew, even though I saw you both competing to out-better the other in so-called God's work, I just let myself be sucked in like a misfortunate bystander! How much of it was real, David? Just tell me how much of it was truly for God's glory?"

"I just need to see Esther," repeated David quietly.

"Well, I can take you there, if you want! But being the friend you are, you won't tell me where to find her, will you?"

David shook his head: "I'm sorry, I just can't answer yet, just like God keeps back His answers."

This only provoked a more angered retort: "Oh! That's just great! That's just great! The great man telling me his excuses are – are – the same as God's excuses! Well that just reaches the limit, doesn't it, David! How can I trust you? You've had an affair!"

Then they both became quiet.

"Thank you," softly spoke David, almost dejected.

"For what?" replied Jonathan, without his anger subsiding.

"For rescuing me, like that, back at the airport."

Jonathan sighed, his vehemence dissolving, and shook his head, bewildered: "Somehow, no matter how I think I understand things, I still want our friendship to be worth holding on to. Don't think it's going to be easy, because it won't, but – help me think you're worth it."

"Trust me, Jonathan, please. I'll explain it all one day, but for now, I need to see Esther."

"Okay, what do you want me to do?"

"Take me back to my car."

"You can't spend long with her. If you want to resurrect the Company, you'll have to come back quickly and explain all this mess, not only to me, but to everyone else – and then we may have a chance of turning things around."

"It will all work out. I'm sure of it. I'm slowly letting go, learning to leave it all with Him. I don't think He needs my help."

Jonathan sighed again: "Well, I wish I can learn that neat trick to get me out of things like this."

"It's not to get me out; it's to get me through. Remember what Abraham had to go through, relying on the little God told him, and *he* made plenty of mistakes."

"Well, let's get you back to your Sarah then."

"I'll be with her four or five days. Then I'll come and help you with the business. I promise."

Leviticus says a lot

Arriving at the medical centre, Jonathan expected at least some activity, but there was nothing. It was empty and silent except for the lone receptionist who was clearing the draws to her desk.

"You okay, Samantha?"

"Yes, fine, thank you," she said hurriedly and under her breath.

"What are you doing?"

"Sorry," was all she said. "Very sorry." She appeared flustered, distracted, guilty and quietly indignant, and with the last of her items in a box, she marched to the front door. Not wanting his help, she balanced her belongings on one arm as she opened the door, and then she was gone.

Jonathan said nothing as he watched her leave.

The building was now bleak and empty. He walked up the stairway to the floors above to see the modern patient bays, discussion rooms and monitoring equipment, having no one in attendance. When reaching the top floor and seeing David's office vacant, he entered his own office, allowed his computer to start and added the newspapers he carried to the pile to the side that was already large. He read the headline of one of them, sighed, and made a coffee in the kitchen area.

He sighed again when settled back at his desk and started to read more headlines and stories in the news. Then he stopped: someone was coming up the stairs. The footsteps slowed as they approached his room and he waited expectantly as to who it was.

"Morning."

Jonathan looked at David standing at the door as if late for work: "Oh! You're here now!"

"I said I'd be back after a week with Esther," replied David.

"You said a few days. Do you know the news? Are you aware of what's going on?"

David shook his head.

"How can you not know the news?"

David did not answer.

"Well, I'm not going to spell it out." There was anger woven into Jonathan's voice, an unhidden agitation that he made no attempt of covering over with polished acting.

David tried not to be undermined and did not show his disquiet. Instead, he made sure he sounded pragmatic and business-like: "I don't want to know what's going on out there." He left Jonathan's office and entered his own, seeing his desk full of documents and paper.

In a reversal of positions, Jonathan came to David's door: "Where were you?"

"With Esther."

"You both just disappeared! How? How can you both just do that?"

David sat down and moved some of the work to the side. "I was with Esther for the entire time, and, yes, away from it all, just us two, building much-needed bridges between us. She wanted to tell me something, but she – I don't know, seemed not wanting to. Does that sound strange? I think she just wanted to treat the time without any – worldly rubbish."

Now less angered, Jonathan nodded and then asked, "Want to tell me about what did happen?"

"I found an old, typed letter tucked in her Bible like a bookmark. It was about my Grandmother, how she died in Africa as a Salvation Army Officer. I have no idea how she got hold of it. I'm wondering if she wanted to talk about becoming Salvation Army Officers together, but felt it too soon to discuss it."

"What! You had an affair with that Jezebel! How can you become a Salvation Army Officer?"

David shook his head.

"What then?"

"Everyone is redeemable."

"Oh, David! I expect they'll throw you out of the Army!"

"Can we talk about this later? I told Esther I'll come and help you sort this out, and I'd be back with her in a week."

"A week?"

"Yes! So what's happening with the business?"

"I'm not sure you quite know what you've done! *I'm* not sure! I just know everything is just collapsing. If we have had shares, they would be plummeting below bottom. Everyone has left. You have no idea what it's like when everyone looks at you with disgust and walks away. Of course the disgust is for you, but I get the brunt of it. You're lucky I'm the only one left here for you. Look around: the building's deserted. Not even you're here for you, and all this is supposed to be yours."

"It's not mine, it never has been."

"That's what you like to think, but this thing, this responsibility is owned by you, whether you know it or not!"

"Well what's happening out there?"

"The news about you and Jezebel, you mean, or the dire news about you stealing from the charity, or the news that Esther has disappeared and everyone is trying to find her for the big news she is? Which you're implicated as well, by the way."

"They know about me and Esther?"

"No, don't get your knickers spoilt. They're really after Esther for her own big story with Israel and her murdered family."

"Thank you for staying, truly."

Jonathan's simmering visibly subsided.

"So they think I've been embezzling? What on earth made them think that?"

"It's just some rubbish, free-wheeling, news-making gossip machine trying to cash in on your downfall and make more money for themselves by piling it on. The police aren't taking it seriously – yet."

"Let's just get back to the business."

"Well, let's make you a coffee first."

While Jonathan was gone, David rummaged in his desk draws trying to find a particular old envelope, but could not locate it.

"So how's Esther?" asked Jonathan when he had returned and was sitting down. "Did you say hello for me?"

David smiled, almost to himself: "It was – like sitting on the perfect beach with her, with the perfect view, just lasting and lasting, but still not lasting long enough. Neither of us wanted to – but – well – ." Everything existing and imaginable, everything logical and mystical, could be doubted and counter-argued, but not the rich healthy blood coursing through an enriched heart, all powered by a love for a girl and energised by the electrical desire of his thoughts. "I don't know how to explain it."

"I don't think you have to. Did you tell her of what happened in America?"

David nodded.

"Really?" Jonathan asked incredulously "And she – what? Understood?"

"Yes, actually."

"And what happened?"

"I told her the truth."

"Oh David! Why did you have to do that? She's hurt enough without you trampling all over her!"

"You don't understand."

"Too right, I don't understand! You admitted to having an affair on live, public television! Anything to do with Jezebel is big news, even the small news! So how did Esther take it?"

"She understood."

Jonathan sighed and shook his head: "The mad woman! She's *more* than a saint! She's just perfection! She's nearer to God than I thought!" He shook his head again. "I can't believe she just accepted your affair. It's just so – disappointing: you going with Jezebel. You have no idea the amount of damage you've done to everything – and that was damaged enough. You know, I had great hopes on you and Esther, right from the very start when I saw you innocently eyeing her up."

"I wasn't eyeing her up."

"Yes you was! I almost had to put your bulging eyes back in their sockets! And I had never seen her relaxed with anyone until you came along. And you ruined it."

"I didn't have an affair with Jezebel."

"You didn't? What was all that on television about then? You admitted it to the world! I was there when you said it. The whole week has been about you and her and the sex scandal – that she just loves, by the way. The newspapers are just full of it. I thought people would just get bored as they normally do – as they would have if she had been a little less famous and you being a lot more less perfect."

"I said, I didn't have an affair with Jezebel."

"You admitted to an affair – ." Jonathan was stunned by a sudden thought, holding his coffee in mid-air in pause of drinking: "Oh David! What have you done?"

David did not answer.

Jonathan, exasperated and annoyed, looked at David sternly for a moment, and then said angrily: "I'm sorry, David, I'm all check-mated out. I'm just too tired to know how to solve any of this." He got up, taking his cup and was leaving.

"Where are you going?"

Jonathan turned back to David: "I've had enough for one day. Whatever we can discuss and repair, we can discuss and repair tomorrow, because I'm going home now."

Jonathan had vanished beyond the door when David suddenly asked a question that stopped Jonathan going any further: "How come you have never been with anyone?"

There was a pause before Jonathan came back to the open door, still holding his mug: "What do you mean: 'been'?"

"You've never had a girlfriend, no one arm-in-arm, not even talk of one or the wishful hope."

Jonathan was firm in his answer, neither angry nor inhibited: "No, no one."

"That's sad. You'd make a great husband. I can't believe no pretty girl hasn't snapped you up."

A strange, pensive quietness came across Jonathan that made him look as though contemplating a difficult decision.

"Are you okay?"

"It's because I'm gay," Jonathan said.

David thought he had misheard.

"It's because I'm gay," repeat Jonathan with more conviction. "Shocked?"

"Of course I'm shocked. I'm just a bit dazed by – well everything."

"I've looked at you as this perfect, handsome man that God has made come my way, but you've really been a lesson that truly no one is right in God's judgement." Then Jonathan leant forward, pointing to his own chest to measure who he was talking about: "I'm gay. I've spent years battling with it and my beliefs, trying to put it into perspective, make an understanding of it. It's been and still is a battle."

There was a moment David thought the situation was not real.

"Well that's not what the scandal is."

David still made no reaction, remaining seated behind his desk.

"You don't know how to respond, do you?" Jonathan eventually asked, now directly standing opposite David. "Are you too shocked? Do you think I should be stoned to death?"

David shook his head, revolted by the thought but confused by his own thinking.

"'Are you appalled? Am I diseased? Have I wrong eyes? Have I wrong hands, organs, dimensions, senses? Do I have no affections, passions? Do I not eat the same food, be hurt by the same weapons, subject to the same diseases, healed by the same means?'" Jonathan stopped to sigh and gain his breath. "'Am I not warmed and cooled by the same summer and winter as – as you?'"

"This is Shakespeare, isn't it?"

"'If you prick me, do I not bleed? If you poison me do I not die and if I am wronged – .'"

"Yes? If you are wronged?"

"Do I not have the right to decide my response?"

"I think the correct line is something about revenge."

"'Am I here to be laughed at by my losses? Am I here to be mocked at by my gains?' No! I'm here because I am created!" There was a great amount of passion and anger in Jonathan, and it spewed out into his words. "So what is life about? Well, it's about Him; not us! It's about the God who has the right, the ultimate right, to do anything He chooses! It's always been about Him!" Jonathan watched David's lack of response. "What's the right thing for me to do?"

David sighed, shook his head and shrugged.

"To carry on!" Jonathan shouted. "This is my cross! This is what I bear! This is part of my work, performing my duty – not to you – but to Him, my Heavenly Father! You still think I should be stoned to death? Wait! I'll get you all the rocks you need, sharp, jagged ones, and you can throw them at me."

"Oh Jonathan."

"I'm actually better for it!"

"How?"

"How? Because there can never *ever* be a time when I can claim perfection in my own efforts. I can never reach His standards of perfection and enter His presence in my own degraded righteousness."

David shook his head and gestured his confusion: "That's just too complex for me right now."

"We all fall short, David, all of us. That's what the Law of Moses really says, and Jesus comes along and even raises the standards. If you lust – "

"I don't want a theology lesson!"

"No! You just sit there and listen! Listen! Jesus says that if you lust, then you commit adultery! If you hate, then you murder! If you're jealous then you steal! When you live for yourself, then you don't worship the true Creator of all things and you break the greatest commandment! We all quibble about all the other commandments we don't achieve, but we don't see the most important one! At least I know I can't be perfect with my own efforts! Whereas you try to be perfect, putting yourself equal to God with your own achievements!"

"No I don't!"

"Oh you might not realise it, but it's there! And I know! I study you! – I know I am under God's grace with the humble prayer of an unworthy sinner against that of the prayer from a self-righteous Pharisee!"

"I'm the Pharisee here?"

"A man beaten and stranded by the roadside, in need of help, and someone on their way to Church sees him, but walks on past because they need to be on time to read out the Bible passage to the congregation. A homosexual walks by! Me! What should I do? What did Jesus say I should do? Be very careful when judging others, David, because it might be your last if God decides, and He has the highest judgement of all."

"I'm the one walking by, am I?"

"Some Christians arrogantly walk into His presence and arrogantly expect Him to accept them on their own terms. Me? I come in my shame and trepidation, knowing I'm not worthy in my own right! I am forgiven because of what Jesus has done and my belief in that! Beyond what I can truly understand, is on that cross to take my punishment. That's how serious sin is. That's how holy God is."

"You think I don't know this?"

"Really? When the Old Testament prophets were predicting that Israel was going to be judged and trampled and punished by vast empires, it ain't because of the gays. And you know what? To all those who wanted me stoned to death, I won't even ask why they didn't go to the vicar and have their penis examined when they had a discharge. I won't ask why they didn't ask every woman if she's menstruating so they wouldn't be defiled if touching them, or why they no longer burn sheep and bulls on an altar for a pleasing smell to the Lord. Who has the right to say what is perfect and what is punishable? You? Believe me, Leviticus says a lot of things!"

"I get what you're saying."

"Really! Really! Would you stone me to death if I worked on a Sabbath? Would you kill me if I collected sticks for a fire on a Sunday? Well I *should* be stoned to death! We *all* should! So who truly has the right in these days to carry out that judgement? You? Them? Let God do His own work! Let me face God's judgement, not yours!" Jonathan wandered over to the window, paused to think, and then turned and continued with less force, but still irritated: "God's holiness will never tolerate any defect! But even though the Law stated a standard, 'should' didn't mean they had to! They weren't to marry outside their nation, but Boaz, the son of Rahab who wasn't an Israeli and was even an ex-prostitute, married Ruth, who also wasn't an Israeli – and they were direct ancestors of Jesus! And Moses married Zipporah, a Midianite, and he even murders an Egyptian! Paul wanted to kill off all Christians in the name of religion; Sarah lied – she lied even to God's face; and King David had an affair!"

"Jonathan, I'm not – "

"Mary became pregnant outside of marriage, but, you know what – Joseph didn't stone her to death, as the Law dictates. He was secretly going to stop the engagement to not have her killed, or even to prevent her reputation ruined in public – and that was before an Angel told him the real reason. And there was the adulterous woman brought before Jesus about to be stoned to death, but Jesus said that anyone who is without sin can throw the first stone – and no one did, even though the Law of Moses condemned her. These people weren't stoned to death as should be the consequences of their sins; they were forgiven, as the consequences of God wanting to repair the damage."

"Why did you not tell me?"

"Did I need to? Am I under an obligation?"

"I wouldn't have thrown stones. I feel bad you didn't feel you could just let me know."

"I still have the right to not tell you my inner feelings. You don't tell me where you go off to – your secret little hiding place. You don't even tell me where Esther is. Well that's your prerogative. God never told Job why he was suffering. Well, that's God's prerogative. God is allowed to keep His reasoning to Himself."

David slowly nodded: "I understand."

"No! You don't! You think you do, but you don't! Otherwise you would have responded differently! Even though I should be stoned to death, and so too should you with your adultery, the key is in forgiveness. None of us can understand fully. If we were to truly see God's holiness, we would not understand why He keeps patient with us." Jonathan returned to the window and, looking out and losing his angered tone, then added, "I might be homosexual, but I'm not the sordid one here turning the world into Sodom or Gomorrah. To answer your question – I have never *been* with anyone."

"You're referring to me?"

"Your sin is not just in your adultery! It's more in your arrogance in doing your work, doing all this," and at this Jonathan waved his hands to the walls and ceiling, "all this work, thinking it was all for Him, when in fact it was all for your own self-esteem! Responsibility has brought you perceived power and all this has come crashing down because you no longer have Jesus first. In fact, the other great failure here is you and Esther working against each other, and the hideous judgement you both had."

"We never worked against each other."

"You were both trying to outperform the other for God's Kingdom in this 'take over the world in the name of Jesus,' distorted corruption that you both did."

David put his head in his hands.

"You know the truth. At one level you both loved each other, at another level you both hated each other, and at another level you were both jealous of what the other was achieving – even in Jesus' name, and at yet another level you were both inspirational to each other. Where does God come first in any of that? The sin is you've placed Esther where God should be." Jonathan looked at David and studied the effect of his words on him.

David remained silent, looking down at the desk.

"This Company flourished when God was in command, when we prayed about it. It plummeted when you first started thinking you can run it." Jonathan left the room and was heard to clear his desk and switch off electrical equipment. Then he reappeared at the door, sighing and becoming calm: "You okay?"

David nodded: "You okay?"

Jonathan nodded in the same manner and smiled weakly: "Sorry, I'm just, it's just that – well."

"I can see you've had a lot on your chest to come out. I'm glad you had the courage to tell me some home truths."

Again, Jonathan nodded: "I could have said it with more panache, though. I did have something better rehearsed."

"Sounded really good as it was."

Jonathan, about to leave again, then said, "Remember, Moses was a murderer, Abraham hid behind his wife, Sarah lied, Elijah ran away, and Job accused God of injustice. All the disciples deserted Jesus and Peter denied ever knowing Him. Paul was going to exterminate Christians, and Samson – Samson squandered God's strength, went with a prostitute, married outside Israel and look what happened to him with his wife, Delilah. Everyone's redeemable, David. Samson, in his sincere, repentant prayer before he died was able to accomplish more for God and God's people than at any other time of his life."

"I just hope God can do something with all this – poo I'm in now."

"Well, I'll see you tomorrow," said Jonathan. "Get some sleep."

"Actually, can you make it a week?"

"Okay, a week, but we need to tie up before you go back to Esther."

"Yep, but I need to go over things alone. Will anyone else come here?"

Jonathan shook his head: "They've all gone. If you want to be alone, then no one will bother you here. No one will even know you are here. There's enough food in the fridge and freezer, the sofa-bed is still comfy – so – well, anyway – . I'll come back in a week or when you phone."

They left the office area together, descended the stairs and reached the front door.

"Just remember what the true, real scandal is," said Jonathan. "The one that's fat in God's full face – the one everyone ignores."

David nodded.

Jonathan smiled and then left, and David was alone.

The door closing shut made a rumble through the building, and the whole building resonated with eerie silence. When David had returned to his desk, he suddenly felt unwell, giddy and unsettled, with a film of sweat from being hot. Disregarding his condition, he searched the draws again and eventually found what he looked for: a folded, battered, dirty, torn envelope. From that, he withdrew the long list of questions he had written years ago at Halcyon. He picked up his pen, re-read his questions and started writing with the weight of thoughts cascading through him.

For an entire week, the only sound came from a telephone calling for attention, which stopped when realising it was not going to be answered.

Oil in the Lamp

Jonathan continued to be worried as to the effect of his speech. Determined to allow David his time alone, he succumbed to his concern and rang the office. It was never answered.

He decided that a well-written letter would suffice instead, but no matter how much time he spent writing it, the words never seemed to be reaching anything adequate, let alone describe his concern. Finally realising the letter was never to be perfect, he considered it sufficiently finished. With the letter written, he walked past the medical centre, slipped the envelope through the letterbox, rang the doorbell, and continued walking.

A few days later, when the day came as agreed to join David, Jonathan returned to the building, opened the door and saw that his letter had not been opened. It had not even been touched as it lay on the floor by his feet. Picking it up, he carried it further into the foyer.

"David?" he called.

Only the empty building answered him.

Jonathan huffed at David's impatience to return to Esther and not keep his word by staying a week. He also felt the inconsideration there was in David not even sending any form of a message to say of his early departure. David must have left even before the delivery of his letter.

Climbing the stairs, he made himself smile at David acting the lovesick, naive, all-or-nothing teenager, but he also worried as to the poor limit that David's work would have achieved. Entering the office area and discovering David's door locked, confirmed his conviction that he was alone, and he started his computer feeling it strange that not even a note had been placed on the keyboard.

Jonathan began to feel indignant.

Even when looking through his list of computer messages, there was nothing from David. Shaking his head, he went to the kitchen and started to make a coffee, and shook his head even more when realising that hardly any of the food had been touched and the milk was going sour.

Using milk he had brought, he completed his coffee and then, returning to his desk, stopped outside David's office. Something was now telling his senses that the scene was not right. Following his instinct, looking through the keyhole, he found the door to be locked, not from the outside, but from the inside. David was still at his desk.

"David?"

There was no reply.

"David!"

Jonathan kicked the door, but it was thick and strong, and he kicked it again in the hope it had weakened. With a few more kicks, the door was still unyielding. After calling David's name frantically, Jonathan was at last committed to calling the services.

By the manner he lifted the phone to his ear, his line of sight fell on the fire extinguisher. Putting down the phone and grabbing the heavy cylinder, he bashed it against the lock as a battering ram. The door succumbed and opened with a violent whack on the wall within.

There, slumped on the desk, asleep as any dreamer, was David.

Jonathan did not enter at first.

The blinds were closed, but let in a dimmed glowing light making the room appear tinted as auburn. The smell of the air, stuffy and stagnant, told of some unusual decay. It felt possible to believe dust had settled in an exaggerated advance of what was considered normal, and the silence was profound as though an established, unattended mortuary had occurred in the room. Creeping nearer, Jonathan reached close enough to just look down and know that David was no longer alive. Across the desk was David's writing, with his pen having dropped short of completing a sentence. He had died before completing it.

Jonathan stood in silence for a long while, almost in reverent respect, saturated in shock, but his thoughts returned to being rational and he called the services.

With the arrival of the paramedics, David's death was declared and recorded, and with the matching arrival of the police, the office area was cordoned off as a scene of a crime. Jonathan, having given his statement, sat in the waiting area, head in hands, when a familiar voice spoke down to him.

"Are you okay?"

Jonathan looked up.

It was the General of The Salvation Army. "I've spoken to the Chief Inspector. He says they're doing routine checks as with all mysterious deaths."

"Yes, I know."

"Where's Esther?" the General asked, sitting down.

"I don't know."

"Have you read the newspapers? A lot of famous government and presidential people all over the world are commenting on her disappearance."

"I think she played the piano to them at work."

"Really? Well I never."

Jonathan nodded.

"I've asked the police not to make any announcement about David, but they warned me that when the reporters learn something has happened, they'll start to speculate if there's no news."

"What speculating can they do?"

"David committed suicide?"

"David wouldn't do that."

"Well we need to allow the Coroner to make their decision, but I want to delay this news being broadcast. Esther should hear it from us first, not from them."

"Yes, of course."

"It was obvious they had an attraction. We just need to act responsibly with wisdom and compassion, and not cover over anything if – anything is discovered."

"But what's it to them anyway? Just entertainment, that's what. There's just going to be a lot of irresponsible media coverage."

"Are you sure you have no idea where she is?"

"I can't even give a proper guess. I get Esther's letters sent to me from her Doctor. She must have used me as her postal address. I told them I don't know where she is and I saw their worry. So all this makes *me* worry."

"Well the Chief Inspector has given permission to withhold the news until after the Coroner's report, but we're running the risk of people gossiping."

"It's more important for Esther be told first. Let Job's friends carry on being Job's friends, and let God deal with them."

"Well we have a time limit to find her. What's that you've got?"

"The letter I wrote to David that he never read. I've shown the police and they're fine with me having it."

The General nodded and then held Jonathan reassuringly by the arm: "No matter how dire the situation, just share it with God, let Him know your feelings, and give it all over to Him."

"That's harder to do than say."

"We will have a talk later, but for now, go home and get some rest. You look as if you need it. We shouldn't be here. We should let the police go about their work."

Jonathan nodded, but remained seated, even when the General left him after a supportive, endearing touch on his shoulder. Alone, he held the envelope and took out the letter, he himself wrote.

David, I said some things which will be unbalanced unless I balance them. I realise I under-rated Esther's credibility to forgive you, putting me to shame with my expectancy in God to forgive me for all my sins. You know how short-sighted I can be without numbers and balance sheets.

I also told you there is nothing you can do to gain God's acceptance. That is true, but is not the full truth. Being saved, He does not expect you to sit still and do nothing. Being in His Kingdom is about duty and loyalty and responsibility to performing not only a life that attempts to resemble the living He wants of us, but to go out in faith and learn to trust His presence, to work for His Kingdom in this world as if building a community of His people.

Faith without action is a dead faith. You are saved to do worthy things; not do worthy things to be saved. Genuine faith calls for action, not just to continually think you believe. A healthy faith is tested and it grows in confidence.

I have watched you grow in this faith since I first met you. You have achieved incredible things. You inspired all this because of your loyalty to God's vision. You became a leader of influence, of vision, of purpose and impact, without really knowing it. Be proud of the encouragement you give to others and of the lives you have revolutionised. Now be strong enough to give the reigns back to Him to whom everything begins and everything ends. Know that He is in ultimate control and even evil and suffering can be turned to accomplish His purposes for His people. Forgive even yourself, as God forgives you for the many years of brokenness from Esther.

Babylon can be defeated

London, although fully laid out before him from the view of his window, was far from his mind's view as he stood and looked out of his apartment. His stare was of studying the Capital below, but his thoughts wrestled with his feelings of loss and a future gone badly wrong. Jonathan just continued to stand and look, devoid of witnessing that anything was there, even though London, as large as it was, had grown from a thousand years. It was as if it was hardly worth the effort.

He was uncertain as to how many times the doorbell had chimed, but became aware it had sounded for a little while. Rushing to the door, Jonathan opened it to a man standing in his Salvation Army uniform.

Carrying a briefcase that Jonathan took little notice of, the General stood at the opened door with a look that asked a thousand questions of concern and sympathy: "Sorry to call, Jonathan, but I thought perhaps you may want to talk."

Jonathan was about to say something, but he instantly forgot what it was.

"Can I come in? I actually have something you ought to read."

"Of course, where are my manners?"

The General walked into his apartment, not mentioning anything about the spaciousness, the fashion, the tidiness of the place, and stood politely until Jonathan showed him the way to the lounge.

"Please sit down. Would you like a tea or coffee?"

"I'll have one if you're having one."

Jonathan shook his head: "I'm not sleeping." He then sat on a soft chair opposite the one the General had sat, no longer thinking of providing any refreshment for the guest.

"How are you feeling?"

"Drained, shocked, numb, confused. Everything seems damaged and unrepairable. I can't see a future. Everything is just – broken: the work's destroyed, absolutely destroyed; Jezebel is sheer evil; the Middle East is in turmoil; and nothing we've done has achieved any good. Mark and Merry have been slaughtered: I can't think of anything that's so sickening." Jonathan expelled a large lungful of dejection. "Esther's missing and David's – gone," he finally said.

"The coroner's report is out. David died of sepsis."

"Infection?"

"Yes."

"Where did he catch that?"

"He may have ingested it: came from a cut in the gums."

Jonathan looked askance: "He had eaten it?"

The General nodded and then shrugged: "I'm not a medical man."

"Does this mean they're going to release this to the press?"

"Yes."

"What about Esther? We haven't found Esther. She'll get to know. She can't go through this again. It will be too much. How much can God lay on a person?"

"Are you sure you can't even guess where she could be?"

"No, David had a secret retreat. I think she's there wanting to have some peace away from this dreary, lunatic world."

"She'll get to learn of his death in the news then."

Jonathan sighed, but then asked, "Did you approve of David visiting Jezebel?"

"I allowed him his own decision, to take responsibility for his own choices and actions."

"Yes, but did you approve of it?"

"If it had been my decision, then – no, I wouldn't have allowed him to go; but I felt a leading in my spirit to allow him his choice."

"She destroyed him and his work – with her spitefulness. Everything is so damaged. How is any of it going to be repaired? It's like everything we've all touched is just gone to waste. Even God Himself has discarded it."

"Don't be so harsh on yourself. Remember that everything seemed ruined and irreparable when Jesus died. But He arose, came back from the dead, very alive, and the confused and fearful Disciples became transformed and revolutionised the world. Allow God to make His decisions, Jonathan. Give all this to Him and allow Him to use it – for His glory, even – even though it looks like a complete failure. In fact, it's when we are broken is when He works His best."

Jonathan nodded.

"David will have his funeral service in three days' time."

"I'll be there."

"I would like you to speak, if you feel you're up to it."

"Can I call you on that?"

"Of course. There is something else I came here for."

"There is?"

"The Police gave it to me. You see, David was writing before he died. I've brought it here for you to read, before it gets out into the open. I'll leave it with you."

"Have you read it?"

"Yes, but you read it and keep it for now."

"Thank you."

"This is why I think things aren't so irredeemable as you think." The General took out of his briefcase a large leather wallet, from which he produced a few sheets of paper that had handwriting coating them. He left them on the coffee table. "Are you okay?"

"It was because of me he became a Christian."

"You only laid down the street for him to use – but I think Esther had a greater impact on him."

Jonathan suddenly laughed with a hint of facetiousness: "You can say that again!"

There was a long pause while Jonathan remained silent, suddenly drawn into his own mind again and the sheets of paper before him. He became unaware of the General standing up, he did not hear the words of farewell, and he became oblivious that he was then alone as he started to read.

Grasp hold of the Wind

I will always be intrigued in this place, this wide universe: this place where we breathe, this toyshop, this playground, classroom, this stadium, this great cathedral, this bounteous garden, waiting room, race track, prison, slum, this cemetery for the living, this formidable maze, this place in which we find ourselves. We live in this fish tank having more beyond our senses, outstretching our perceptions, where there are dimensions beyond dimensions, existence beyond the oxygen we breathe. What is beyond this life-long room? What is through the door? What can be seen through any window? I have tried to fathom what this place is, but questions produce answers that produce questions. I set myself a list of questions when young and I have spent my life so far trying to provide answers.

There is worship in searching for Him and having these questions when with the right heart. If God wishes to walk in His garden with zombies then He would not have been so willing to create the magnificent engine we call a brain. So amazing the design that it becomes a self-determined person and to accept everything with blind faith is not compatible with having a natural questioning mind. No wonder those on the outside consider the Church bankrupt of having any intellectual bearing when teaching to accept things without thinking. God is the greatest intellectual there is and I think He wants us to be in possession of self-determination and motivation to provide a conversation with Him in return.

That said, I now look at my list of questions and see how unimportant they have become. The disciples never stumbled with these questions. These simple, unknowing, argumentative cowards, transformed by something momentous, became compelled by their conviction to tell people the Good News that Jesus Christ was crucified and has arisen to beat death for us all. As foolish as this news can sound, Jesus must have had an enormous affect on them.

But as to my questions, here are my answers.

Why does the Bible downgrade women and upgrade men? It doesn't. There's the small print that men always overlook. And why is God sympathetic in the New Testament and angry in the Old? Actually, He's both in both if you read them.

And is God good? God must be great for all the great breathtaking beauty I can recognise in the world: the great mountains, the mighty oceans, the gorgeous blue sky and rolling clouds, the glorious brilliant sun, the green fields and valley rivers. God must be a great God to create the beauty there is in the world. He deserves my praise. Why would beauty exist for a species evolved from chance?

As to suffering, and evil and persecution, I think much of it is due to us, not God. In His own nature, God needed to give us the ability to believe and decide what we should freely decide. And this can thwart the very thing He wants. We can rebel. We can ignore. We can do a lot of damage. And what if nature, doing its work, gets in our way? What if our surroundings conspire against us? Then whose fault is that? If something crashes, is that a divine solution or an act of misled maintenance, someone's negligence, someone's meddling? Some things do go wrong. I can't imagine God is in all of its initiation. The only ultimate lesson Jesus taught on suffering is to be prepared in your soul with whatever comes at you, whether it is divine or not.

When I look at life and those who live in it, there is much to over-load the sensitive heart. I have never admitted this, but I have always suffered from depression, like living in a deep, dark well, trying to look up and climb to the light above. I have always sought to eradicate this black, broken, confused, untrusting, frustrating feeling. My own bleakness coerces me to fill this void and my character is developed based on what I do to fill it. I can use my own depression as its own medication to search for my Saviour's existence, to have faith in His compassion, to do good in the world, to learn what I can.

I look at myself, my thoughts and feelings, and wonder if absolute nothing can ever build the mechanism of me with the sheer galaxy of emotions and the universe of thoughts I have, a fear of death and decline, the hopes and dreams for lighter days. A DNA machine can never match what I am; a genetic construct can never accomplish the wealth of human emotions; a mesh of neurons will never attain the ambitions we have. Neither chance nor nothing can ever produce a species that can ever be sophisticated enough to invent a spectacular God or produce the alarming rate of technological advances that we are achieving. How can nothing invent the longing to understand something that cannot be understood, the compassion to risk life at the peril of death, or even to volunteer one's own death for a cause or belief? How does complete void of thought end with someone with the drive to survive against the force of 'no purpose'?

There is logic in evolution, yes, but that is not to say it is true; and because Genesis is too much of an abstraction, doesn't mean it's false. But to focus purely on evolution and forget everything else, to dismiss the claims of the Bible, is like forgetting to eat. What is the purpose to bereaving if dying is not important, because living is not important, because there's nothing to live for?

Nothing is provable! There are no answers in anything that can satisfy the doubt there truly is in life. Why is that? Why don't we just ordinarily know everything as naturally as breathing? Why have we come to exist in this expansive, dangerous maze of so much that is unknown and unknowable? Why is it that even from birth we have to learn and discover what we can, but still always have the universe a mystery? It is like chasing the wind. So removed is my consciousness, my thoughts, my very perception, from all the atoms and molecules that constitute my physical being, it is as if there is a reason for this detachment. Why all this effort, just for me to decide to walk down the street or not? Is this lack of proof deliberate?

Why is there no proof in anything? Why? So that we have no choice but to have faith, that's why! This place forces us to have faith! This world forces us to make decisions on incomplete, suspect, obscure knowledge and logic to come to our own understanding. Everything seems as if it is designed and perfected for us to become ourselves based on incomplete evidence, in a world full of too many questions. We have to have faith that copes with making decisions without knowing all there is to know. Even the human brain has been designed to compute and evaluate incomplete knowledge. Its neurons systematically weigh up their decisions. As such, the brain is a personified faith engine when it is used with intelligent maturity. We are not to understand everything. We are to act in faith and wisdom.

God wants obedience, trust and fellowship through a wisdom-coloured faith more than gold or self-righteousness, or abject, blind unintelligent faith. Don't be too confident in what you think you know. Your perception may truly be nothing like what the real world is. Heaven and Hell may be the true reality.

So as to what religion is the right one, I choose Christianity. I choose Christianity because I am drawn to follow Jesus because of the sheer impact of His character on me from reading the New Testament. When considering Jesus' replies to questions, they are neigh on perfect. So compelling is Jesus that no one comes close, and places the logic of all other beliefs into disarray. I am convinced of His genuine authority, taken aback in awe and shock by his horrendous death. I am drawn to accept and follow Jesus Christ as Lord, as my life is transient, ephemeral, purposeless otherwise. It is my life, and if this goes against the logic and views of others, then so be it. I am honoured to believe, even if this is foolish to everyone. I cannot doubt what He says, but don't take my word for it — Jesus said of Himself that He is the way, the truth and the life, and no one can come to the Father except through Him. That's quite explicit. What is important is what you decide about Jesus, but ultimate wisdom is to know that one day, Jesus will decide about you.

The world will become more polarised, vehemently polarised, for or against God, when the troubles of the world become unmistakable. God knows who is patiently waiting in faith for Him to finish His work.

This gets me to the heart of my mess. With everything that Jesus means to me, I am not convinced I have convinced anyone to follow Jesus. It is as if I have kept God secret and kept Him to myself, as if no one else is worthy of knowing Him. I know I had a great chance with Jezebel to tell her my personal Christian witness. She even started talking about Jesus with interest, but I said nothing and now everything is in pieces. I should never have gone to America. What was I thinking in leaving Esther alone, a poor, suffering woman to mourn her loss? I should have been with her in her time of need and it took me that journey to learn what I already knew. I took to America my self-glorious pride, went in my own strength, in my own confidence. I saw my achievements, considered them all my own and, in my arrogance, thought I was spiritually invincible like Samson with his great physical strength, and look what happened to him. Now I am in this position, caught in the consequences of my own actions with Esther back in my life. I am still recovering from the shock of the death of her husband and daughter, as if I had killed them, sent them to the battlefront to certain death, just as King David did to gain Bathsheba. I am so broken with guilt.

But of all the large, nasty things I consider I have done, my largest committed crime is not to have placed God consistently supreme in all my entire life. I am so condemned by a God who is worthy of constant, intense, pure praise. How can I ever reconcile myself through any means I can achieve, to an awesome, mighty God, who has the enormity to create such an immense, magnificent universe, and deserves to be constantly supreme in my life? There is nothing any human can do, and if they think they can, then that belittles God and that belittles His creation. It makes an arrogant mockery of His grace and love for us. There is ultimately nothing we can do, absolutely nothing that can put ourselves right with God, but we should not live despondent, lazy or inactive in faith.

In Jesus' death, there is perfect sacrifice, perfect atonement and absolute redemption for us all. I am forgiven and I know it, beyond the complexities of my mind, and all is accredited to my God creator who knows all things. I know that even though I fail, God delights to pick me up when I, penitent, come to Him in fervent hope. I will trust the loving mercy of my Heavenly Father through Jesus my redeemer, my defender, my Saviour, my Lord and Master, Friend and King. Through Jesus, God has given me a clean heart and has renewed a right spirit deep inside. God is so worthy of praise for His sheer creation, but how far more is He worthy for making a way to become reconciled to Him through Jesus?

It is written that if God has bent something, then who is there that can unbend it, except for God Himself? Please Lord, my God and Saviour, unbend my failures, straighten my life. You accepted Samson's repentance; accept mine. If You were to take me now, failings and sins, with all the many decades I hardly pleased You, with all the corrupted dust that I am, I beg that You take it all and use all this chaos and confusion and just downright poo that I'm in, and use it for Your purposes, somehow, anyhow, beyond my understanding. I lay down my life's problems into Your care and I let go of control. I earnestly ask that You grant me another chance, even my life's shadow, to touch those I have been allowed to meet and give a measure of Your Kingdom to them all. As I forgive those who have come against me in hate and inconsideration, I pray that they forgive me and my greater crimes against them, as I know I am forgiven by You, a great God, Abraham's God, Adam's God. In Jesus' name, I can let go of the longing to justify myself in front of You. I don't come to You on my own terms; I come forgiven on Your terms. Even my own death can never atone for my own sins.

Everything can be doubted. Doubt there is a sun, doubt there are *rolling oceans, doubt that clouds come and go, even dare doubt the universe ever occurred; but never doubt that I loved Esther as soon as she first looked into my eyes. I try and count all the days we may have left together. My heart is pounding, erratic even, with the thought of returning to her. I have palpitations and getting hot with the attraction, shuddering with my current withdrawal symptoms. I even ache with the waiting and getting more dizzy with the urge to return to her, like a return to Eden to repair what we have done.*

Heavenly Father, allow me please to live out all the breath I have left with her, at Halcyon. How I wish to be with her. I long to go home. May God, the ultimate engineer, the definitive architect, my perfect lawyer, omniscient surveyor, solicitor and grand judge, medic and King, grant my request. Use my failures, Lord. Bring Esther and I closer together. Please, take me there even now. Who am I to this world, but just a visitor? May God be prai

Book Seven : Kingdom Come

No Longer Remembered

Sergeant Richards, rapt by the beauty of the horizon, stood on a discarded, hidden stone terrace that had at one time been a promenade to the nearby lake. Over much time, the lake had receded away and this was as near to it as he could get with all the ensnaring and exhausting amount of trees and thick bushes there were, but he was peaceful enough to remain where he was, watching the water's surface, the ripples and the starry glinting from the sun. His awe, though, was not for the water, but for the glorious rainbow in the distance, clear, distinct in its colours, a sign, a confession. Little had he known at the beginning of the day, being his last day as a police officer, that he would be the one to discover not only the unknown location of the most sought-after woman in the current national news, but also the cherished writing of her last days. He looked at the page in his hand, no longer reading the words, just contemplating the sheet as he held it. It was time to return, but it was hard to leave.

Walking back through the sweet fragrant smells, through thicket, bushes, flowers, honeysuckle and wisteria, he reached the ruined garden walls and eventually found his younger colleague sitting where he had been left.

Richards stood in the bright sunlight, waiting for the downcast junior to look up and make a comment, but the youngster just huffed and showed his annoyance with a wordless shrug. Still standing in front and above him, Richards tried to provoke a comment: "Well?"

"Well? What?" replied Parker. "So did they or didn't they?"

"Did they what?"

"Did they?" It was hard for Parker to understand why Richards was so confused. "Have sex! Shagged each other! That David and Esther! What is it with you? What else would I be asking about?"

"What's it to you?"

Parker did not answer, seeing the page still grasped by Richards: "You decided?"

"Yes."

The younger man tried to swipe the paper from the older hands, but the older man was too quick as he whisked it out of the way.

"Oh, come on Sarge! Did they or didn't they?" moaned Parker.

"Aren't you interested in learning some of the virtues this poor dying woman learnt in her last few weeks here on Earth?"

"Naaa! They did, didn't they?"

"This woman died without knowing that David Kingsley would never return to her. She died alone, in hope. Don't you feel for her? Her husband and daughter were shot because of something she said somewhere across the world to people who wanted to be appalling."

"Yeah, that's sad, but – did they?"

Richards sighed with frustration: "Might have done; might not have done."

"Oh, come on Sarge. Hey! Where you going?"

The Sergeant walked off with the last page through the garden and Parker had to follow in a temper. He then stood in front of a stone bird-table, waist height as if like an altar. "I'm burning this page," he stated as soon as Parker had caught up with him.

"What? You can't do that!"

"Why not?"

"It's evidence. You'll be screwed if they find out."

"It's only one un-numbered page."

"They'll know."

"Forensics aren't the problem. It's when the media gets any ounce of a rumour that it will all crash. That stupid, sobbing American actress has already admitted to the whole planet she lied."

"Well the truth always comes out, like us burning this – "

"Ssshhh."

They both stopped as though thieves about to be discovered.

"Was that a car?" asked Richards.

"Didn't hear a thing. Must be your squeaky ears."

"Did you tell anyone?"

"No!"

"Then who's here?"

"I don't know! I don't have your years of detective intuition!"

"Go and see who it is."

With a huff, Parker left to return a few moments after. "I don't know. They've parked out the front, but gone off somewhere."

"It's not a police car then?"

"No. So what are we going to do, chief? We have a dead body upstairs, we're about to burn evidence, and someone else is roaming this crime scene."

"We're not about to burn evidence."

"Yeah? Well what are we about to do?"

"Sshhhh."

"What?"

Richards lowered his voice to a whisper. "There's someone approaching."

A male voice called out across the walls and garden: "Hello?"

"Over here!" shouted Richards.

The two listened to the noise of moving branches and foliage as the person drew nearer. They stood silently as the man appeared and came to stand beside them.

"I'm Mister Manning, Elsie Manning's husband," he said.

"I'm Sergeant Richards and this, my junior, is Officer Parker."

"Why are we out here?"

"I take it you realise the seriousness of what we've discovered."

"I should think so: the death of Esther Whyte. My wife told me."

"Then you know why this matter is delicate."

"It's going to be big news, that's for sure. What's the matter? What are you discussing?"

"We're discussing burning evidence," announced Parker with indignation, motioning to his superior.

"I'm afraid you can't burn evidence," replied Mister Manning. "You shouldn't say things like that to me, being a lawyer."

"He is," nodded Parker at Richards for a second time.

"You're a lawyer?" asked Richards, as for final confirmation.

"Yes, that's right. So this is her suicide note?" Manning asked, looking at all the pages in the hands of Parker. "Quite a lot of it, isn't it? When my wife said she was writing, I didn't expect a book."

Richards shook his head: "It's more of a memoire, her intimate thoughts. It's just this one page I have could be construed as an affair. It will ruin or deflect any good that can come from any of this."

"So what were you contemplating? Burning it?"

"This is going to be big news and everyone will want to read what she wrote. It's just this one page could be – twisted and made sordid. Here, you give it a read. You know Esther and David better than us. You're the lawyer. Our intentions are honourable."

Both police officers watched the lawyer as he read and with eagerness waited for his reply.

Parker was annoyed that he had not been allowed to read what the other two had: "Well? Did they or didn't they?"

Mister Manning looked at the Sergeant, nodding: "I understand."

"And?" asked Parker.

The two older men looked at the younger as if in consideration.

"Burn it," said Manning with conviction, giving it back to Richards.

Richards, receiving the page, urged for confirmation: "You're positive?"

"As you said, I know the two better, and I can vouch for you acting with honourable intentions."

"Vouch?" sneered Parker: "If this is burnt then no one is to know about it for anyone to vouch."

"He's right," said Richards. "We need to burn this with no acknowledgement that this one page ever existed between us three."

"Agreed," replied Manning.

"Okay," Parker said dejectedly, "burn the page of erotic sex, but only after I've read it!"

"There's nothing here to say anything happened."

"Then why did that David say yes at the airport? Why do we need to burn anything?"

The Sergeant shook his head: "You didn't read everything did you?"

"Na, I just skimmed through it to get to the juice."

Mister Manning huffed: "That's why we shouldn't allow irresponsible media coverage glean any of this. People are just going to smear it all."

"I agree." The Sergeant held up the page. "These are two well-meaning youngsters who don't deserve to be trampled on by the likes of the media."

Parker was irritated: "Look! I thought you said there's nothing written to say anything happened?"

"Sonny, this is clever, intelligent, beautiful writing, but people will read into it what they want."

"But, but – the Bible has its people with, with – warts an' all – doesn't it? I did go to Sunday school, as well, you know!"

The two men were suddenly stumped.

Richards looked at Manning: "He's right."

"If God has forgiven their sins," answered Manning, "and God has the power to forget, then I see there be nothing wrong in burning this page."

"Okay!" shouted Parker, finally defeated, "burn them! Burn the pages! Burn all of them! See if I care what they'll do to you! They want us back at the office for your last speech 'n all, so get on with it!"

"Give me your cigarette lighter."

"I'm not being implicated in this. Find your own lighter."

"You're already implicated. Now give me the lighter."

There was an initial reluctance, but the Sergeant took it the moment it appeared.

"Let me burn it," asked the lawyer. "It would be better coming from me."

"But I'm the one retiring."

Angered, Parker shouted at the two: "Will someone just burn the bloody page!"

Richards set light to it and made certain it completely disintegrated, with the fabric of the ashes gingerly dropped on the stone bird-table to scatter as dust into the air.

The garden accepted the burnt offering, and the page was no more.

"Happy now?" snorted Parker. "Come on, we're late for your funeral." Parker then spoke to Mister Manning as if to explain: "It's his last day and I was supposed to get him back to the station for those speeches for him."

"You forget, we still have Esther upstairs," delicately stated Mister Manning.

Richards turned to Parker: "Get to the end of the drive, get a signal and inform the station."

"Great," muttered Parker. "I'll let you explain the delay." He gave all the paper to Mister Manning and left dejectedly, with a car heard departing soon after.

It was at last peaceful and the two men were alone, breathing in the air, pondering their actions.

"Come on, Sergeant," beckoned Mister Manning, "let's leave these ghosts to their peace."

"I just want one last moment alone before the news hits the public and ruin the quietness. I'll wait here for all the others to arrive, if you don't mind."

"I'll be at the front then." Mister Manning nodded in return, understood the sentiment and left.

The old policeman looked around one more time as if eager to see a ghost and then made his way from the garden grounds into the house, listening to the silent air of history and the fading moments of centuries as time imbued into this continuing tapestry of the story. He walked into the kitchen and in his mind's eye suddenly saw the kitchen staff preparing a great banquet, dressed as though living in the Victorian Era; but then they faded to leave the fireplace unlit and the table inactive. His view through the window into the wilderness beyond conjured up the image of monks tilling the soil and quietly paying homage to the servitude of their devoted duties. Then he thought the piano was being played from the music room; the fragrant melodies rich in the air, tranquil and soothing. The ghosts were content in their own time, having had their time and life.

With the arrival of the multitude of police, Richards was no longer able to dwell on the tranquillity, now that it was being trampled upon, and it became known that reporters were congregating at the gate as the news escaped. Through the next hour, discussions, investigations and photographs were being taken, as well as Mister Manning obligingly being questioned.

After a while, it became evident that Richards was no longer required, and Parker, seeing the moment, ushered to take his long-term partner away in their available police car.

"What truly did happen here?" muttered Richards, as Parker drove away through the woodland.

"You're now retired, so switch off," replied Parker. "Perhaps they'll both haunt the place."

Ghosts

THURSDAY

Jezebel, fully unclothed, lying on cushions, looked up at David, now on top of her, just as unclothed. "Be in me," she said under her breath. "All of me is burning for all of you."

So soft and tender her voice, David felt it was like sweet honey over his lips, but suddenly the words seemed incompatible. Looking down at her, he saw Jezebel for what she truly was: she was not Esther. "This is wrong, so wrong," he whispered.

"That's why it's so right."

"You may look beautiful, but – I should have seen you for what you really are."

Jezebel became instantly angry and grabbed David as he was about to move from her and kept him from leaving: "But I've worked hard to look perfect. Who are you to tell me I'm not?"

"I've been such a fool. I know the one who *is* perfect." David tore himself from Jezebel and was about to get up when Jezebel grabbed him a second time.

Jezebel, her face becoming red, shouted back: "Who? Who's perfect? God? We're both as naked as you can get so I'm in no position for a Sunday school lesson!"

David did not listen: "She's beautiful without and within. I've been in love with her for years, yet there's – I'm such a twit. I've left her alone when she needs me."

"Well you're more the fool!" she replied with anger, quickly rolling back on top of him. "You're letting the love-fantastic slip away!"

"You!" cried David, returning in anger. "The love-fantastic? You're far from it!" He then pushed her to the side.

"I'm not talking about me! I know who you're talking about. I'm talking about the same one as you! You met her and you lost her! At least I have never met my love to then lose him."

David got up from the cushions holding his clothes and turned to leave.

"Hey! I've never been refused! Never! You can't go!"

But David was leaving.

There was then a rush of fright through Jezebel: "No! Don't go!" She leapt up and ran after him, stopping him leave the large room with the force of her imploring hold: "Where are you going? What are you doing?"

David shook his head: "Jezebel, this is wrong."

"David! I've only wanted to be loved! That's all!"

"There's more to life than just wanting to be wanted!"

Jezebel was suddenly anxious and fearful of losing him: "I'm sorry, David, I'm so sorry. Please! Listen! I want to be a mother." There was sincere pleading in her eyes and an abrupt fragility to this beautiful woman.

"What?"

"I just want to – have a baby," she said softly, almost dejectedly.

With her weakening grip, David brushed her away from him: "Are you for real?"

"Please, I want to care!" she urged. "I want you to care! I want you to care for me!"

"There's something very wrong here Jezebel."

"I'm not Jezebel. I never have been Jezebel. Jezebel is something I've invented to step into. I'm so screwed up."

David did not react, unsure of how.

"My name's Meredith – Meredith Hope. That's my real name."

"I'm sorry Meredith, but you've made me realise there is only one for me. She's in my mind, she's in my consciousness, in my unconsciousness, she's in my dreams, my waking hours. There is nothing I can do to remove her. She saturated my thoughts the first time she was in my eyes, and she filled my heart the first time she touched me. She's part of my DNA. She's part of my essence. And right now I know she needs my help."

Both standing close together, Jezebel nodded slowly, tears trickling down her cheeks. "It's Esther, isn't it?" she asked softly.

David nodded.

"Esther Whyte: I can see it has always been her." Jezebel looked earnestly into his eyes. "Come back to me – if she – if she doesn't want you."

David kissed her on the cheek and was then gone the next moment.

Jezebel, still standing as she was when he deserted her, waited for the house to be empty, and, hearing him no longer, started to weep with bitterness, with emptiness. Then, growing from within, she started to cry with searing anger and contempt. She picked up a heavy cushion and in violent resentment, threw it at the large window. He had not even said goodbye.

But the cushion made no affect and it fell before reaching the glass, as heavy was the cushion and as far was the glass.

"Esssstheeeeeeeerrrrrrrrrrr!" she screamed. So forceful was the effort, that she felt her lungs were scorched. "No one denies me! No one refuses me!" Screaming to the sky, she bellowed her curse: "David! May all the gods in history strike me down dead if by this time tomorrow, I have not destroyed you!"

FRIDAY

David had no notion, no recall, no understanding as to how he arrived at Halcyon. He faintly remembered being pulled away from the reporters by Jonathan, he remembered getting into Jonathan's car, and that was all there was. His mind was then a blank sheet of absent memory until realising he was driving his own car and there was now an absence of daylight. His only attention throughout had been spent on Esther, and now, with the front door opening to him, he was finally with her.

"Don't you have the key?" asked Esther innocently. "You're back early."

David stepped through to the entrance hall.

"Are you okay? What happened to you? You look ill."

"I can hardly bear to tell you."

"I have a roaring fire going. Try and tell me there."

David followed her into the kitchen, heart pounding, and stood before her, looking at her anticipation of what he was about to say. "You don't know what happened, do you?"

"No, out here why would I?"

"I didn't have an affair."

"Sorry? I – "

"With Jezebel."

Esther, shocked at first and confused, then replied consolingly: "I know."

"I came so close."

"What happened?"

"We were both there, naked – we were naked, Esther. I was on top of her and then I was on the plane home. I cut short my trip. I was on the plane home and then – and then – . I can hardly believe I'm telling you."

"It's okay. Would you like something to drink?"

David shook his troubled head, irritated: "No! I need to get this out!"

Esther patiently waited and listened to David's confession.

"She must have made an announcement while I was flying, saying we had slept together. I knew something was wrong when we landed and I queued and there was a heap of reporters all wanting to know the story and Jonathan was there and he got me out, and – . It was so confusing. I

– I accidently admitted to it."

"What? You admitted to it? Why did you do that when it wasn't true? Why did you admit to you and her – having it away?"

"They didn't say her name. I didn't know who they were talking about."

"David, I don't understand. Who else is there?"

"You."

"Me!"

"Yes."

"But we haven't slept together. We haven't done anything. I don't understand."

"No."

"What are you talking about?"

"In my heart – in my heart – we have."

"What!"

"It happened in my heart, Esther. It happens in my heart. What is in my heart and mind, to God is just as real and solid as what my hand can hold."

"Oh, David – what have you done?" Tears started to trickle down Esther's cheeks.

"We were – . She was so close to me. I felt her warm breath on my neck and – and her kiss was sweet and silky and smooth and tender. We were – "

"David, I don't want to know. I don't need to know."

David paused.

"Okay! I need to know!"

"She was so, so – so kind and gentle, and she – just wanted to be loved and be a mother."

"A mother?"

"Can you believe it?"

"What! She wanted you to be the father?"

"It was then, with all the rush of feelings and passion and rich chemicals that I realised how wrong it was. I couldn't do it, because – because I didn't love her."

Esther did not react, other than with tears trickling down her cheeks.

"I couldn't do it. I couldn't do it – because she wasn't you."

"Oh David." Esther was now crying.

"It never happened. I left. I left her there, crying. She was crying like a sweet little girl, just wanting to be understood – but I had to leave and come here as soon as I could. Physics just wouldn't let me come any quicker. I had to be next to you. I just had to be next to you. So I came, and they interviewed me and – actually it was more of an assault and their questions were confusing and I could only think of you and what was truly in my heart and thinking and soul. I had to let it out. I had to be honest. I had to be honest for once in my life – to God's standards. It was with you, in my mind, that I answered. I need you to believe that nothing happened. Nothing happened, Esther, with me and her. Actually, it doesn't matter if you don't believe me. It's only God that needs to know." David then looked at Esther. "Actually, please, it does matter. I'm telling the truth."

Esther's cheeks were now wet with tears and she tried to wipe them away in a dignified manner.

"They didn't say her name. I didn't know who they were talking about. I had you in my mind all the journey home. I came back for you. I kept myself for you. It has always been you, always, only you. Not even God stopped me. It was the thought of you. And that's my sin – that I have placed you first, all my life. All my work was an influence of you."

They both stood before each other, the roaring fire in the chimney breast burnt brighter in the darkening room as nightfall settled and their shadows crept into place as though to make ghostly markings of themselves into the mansion.

David heaved a sorrowful sigh of relief, and tried to unburden the weight in the air with a little humour: "Well, that's me done. How's you? What's your news?"

"Let's just spend some time together. I need you more than you understand. You see, I have to be strong and forgive people who want me not to forgive. They want me as vengeful as they are. I need you to forgive me. I need to recover from Mark and Merry. Please stay. Please stay with me. Stay with me for however long we have. I won't recover otherwise. Time is so precious now."

"I told Jonathan I'll be here with you for a few days and then go and help the business back on its feet – if that's ever possible."

"And then afterwards you'll come back?"

"Yes, of course," he breathed.

"Spend this week with me. There's enough food, and Misses Manning came to visit."

"She did?"

"Yes, but she understands not to tell anyone about us being here."

"You look tired."

"Yes, I am. So do you."

"I'll take you to your room."

The house was now in darkness that was kept at bay from the furnace within the fireplace and the available candles that supported their flame. On the kitchen table, was a candelabra with seven candles, brightly lit, with David having no notion of where it had been found. He held it up by the stand as a watchman of a past era would do to see across the dark moors.

Continuing the genteel attitude, David simply held out his arm for her to take, and she smiled when placing her arm within his. She picked up her own candle and followed his lead from the kitchen and through the cold, darkened world surrounding them. The candlelight flickered and fluttered, making seething noises at times, casting shadows in pictorial arrays in the world beyond the light. They ascended the old, majestic staircase, torn, scratched, broken as it was, and reached the landing, all without saying a word. From a few turns, they then stood outside Esther's room and simply looked into each other's eyes in the cast of the candelabra David held. He politely held open the door and allowed Esther into her room.

Esther turned, still holding her own candle: "Thank you for coming back home."

"I'm sorry I ever left you."

"Goodnight, King David."

"Goodnight, Queen Esther."

With that, the door was being closed.

"Esther! Wait!"

The closing door was then halted and then slowly withdrawn. From behind it, Esther's face in the orange light looked out at David.

"I know this is not the proper time, but – "

"I'm still in bereavement, David. In my confused, tortured mind, I'm numb, frozen, quaking. Inside I'm in deep torment and trying to see my way through. I'm in mourning and my guilt of many things is crushing me. I may look calm, but I'm not."

"All I request is a simple kiss."

Esther's look was unreadable.

David, without permission, held the door more open: "For tomorrow may never come."

She made no attempt to stop him preventing the door being closed, nor made an attempt to stop him approach her even further to deliver a kiss to her forehead.

"Why stop at a kiss that's not even tender?" Esther's lips reached for his and they kissed with more passion.

When they had stopped, unspeakable thoughts were transmitted between them by way of their eyes, as magnified by the candlelight and pounding hearts.

"I'm sorry," breathed Esther. "We shouldn't have done that."

It was a moment that beckoned dismissal, expecting David to leave, but David just simply said, "You're the story of my life."

Esther's simple reply came with a soft, caring voice as she touched his cheek gently with a tender caress: "No wonder you've been so dour – because God should be your author. Good night, David." She slowly closed the door for it to be finally shut with a soft click.

After a few moments of seeing the door fully in its frame, David wandered the corridors to his room, casting the shadows of his thoughts along with him. When closing his own door, his hands went to his head in his mortifying thoughts of embarrassment with the realisation of what he had just said: "'The story of my life' – did I say that out loud? What was I thinking?"

The next morning, Esther awoke to beautiful music faintly wafting through the air. She sat up and listened: it was a grand piano. She wondered how David had learnt to play. Dressing quickly with a gown over her nightdress and rushing to neglect putting something on her feet, Esther hurried across the upper corridor, descended the stairs and followed the music to the library, the stone-cold floor bearing witness to her eagerness.

Pushing open the door, she saw what was in the room: old, leather, high-backed chairs; broken, scratched shelving, reaching the crumbling ceiling; old, eminent books; and a small wooden table bearing a heavy gramophone with its large, old snail-like funnel. In prime position of the room, though, was the grand piano, unplayed and unused. Instead, a record was turning round.

Seated and also wearing a thick gown, David simply said without turning to look, "Debussy."

"I know." Esther ventured more into the room and sat on another available chair: "'The Girl with the Flaxen Hair'."

It stopped.

"Play it again? Sam?"

"I think so." But Esther removed the needle from the record, sat at the piano and played the same tune herself. When she had finished, she turned to David, giving a smile. Then she started to play more melodies.

"Aren't you hungry?" asked David. "Want a coffee?"

"That would be nice," she replied without looking at him, immersed in her music.

David got up to leave, but then said, "Are you warm enough? You should have something on your feet."

Esther did not want to admit that any footwear would make her feel unfashionable and foolish, far from the alluring appeal she wanted to show. Instead, she just shrugged, with her focus on the piano.

Even when he had returned with toast and coffee, Esther perpetuated her melodies and ignored his breakfast, being so engrossed that her music naturally merged and flowed from one piece to another. All morning, no one spoke and no one moved from the room. David was content and finding peace in Esther's company.

When Esther finished, she sat still, looking at the keys. Even when David approached and sat beside her on the wide seat, she still did not look up from the piano.

"You play beautifully," he softly said.

"Thank you."

"Just – stupendous."

Esther laughed: "Stupendous! Haven't heard that word for a while."

"What about amazing, astounding, astonishing, immense, mesmerising."

"You're just going through the dictionary. Elly, my teacher, she would always say that I played like a juggernaut or an unemotional matron or a duty-bound warden just doing their chores."

"Really?"

"She died only a few years ago. I use to play in the background at certain banquets at the Foreign Office as we entertained foreign dignitaries, presidents, prime ministers, high civil servants, kings of this and queens of that."

"Wow! Then she should be proud of you. What were you playing just now?"

Esther replaced her fingers on the keys and answered as she started to play again with another melody. "Chopin, well, some of his great melodic ones, some Satie, Schumann, Bach, Mendelssohn, Beethoven, and some variations on some Salvation Army tunes."

Halcyon Manor chimed with quiet glory with the sweet sounds that were coming from the old piano. The music was absorbed by the walls, it resonated through the beams, sank into the floor, imbued into the timeless existence of all that was romantic about the mansion. Then Esther played her last piece and stopped and became quiet with her tears.

For a while, David listened, knowing the tune, but when she had finished, he then said the title: "It is well with my soul."

"I would always close my playing with it. Its words always seem to say everything."

"It's a good choice."

"I miss them," Esther breathed. "I ache just to hear Mark talk about work, and Merry incessantly going on about everything. I even miss how annoying she was at times when I had my urgent chores and she just wanted to – to just be content with me. If only I could hear her talk, to hear her sweet, little innocent voice, here, now; to hear her angel-talk; for her to say hello to all the dead pets we accumulated. We weren't too good with animals. Even the stick insect died."

"Oh."

"I miss Mark's grumbling about people he worked with. I miss him telling me how many times he had to do so much at work with a bursting bladder. I miss how he put his socks on, the way he would leave cupboard doors open, the way he would always let me know where he was, always interested in how I felt. I miss his music, his cooking, the way he played with Merry, his intense love for her. And they died because I wanted world peace. They died because I worked hard. They died because I wasn't there with them, both shot in broad daylight, just walking to the dentist. They killed them only because they want me to know how it feels. That's all they want – to perpetuate their hatred."

Esther looked deep into David's eyes in an attempt to gauge how much he truly comprehended her feelings. "They want me to fail to forgive them. They want me as dead in my life as they are in theirs. Well I have forgiven them, just as I forgave my parents for what they did to me." Esther stopped with a long, deep breath and sigh, and stared at the piano. "How dare they think I won't forgive."

David remained quiet, and was then lost by the allure of the elegant curvature of her neckline and cheek, and the sweet curve of her eyelashes.

Esther slowly looked up at him and moved nearer on the seat. She smelt his natural, smouldering aroma. It had not changed from when she had first experienced it as a teenager, and tentatively, she kissed him. They started kissing tenderly, and then passionately.

But the tears did not stop trickling down her cheeks.

Esther broke away and looked down in sorrow. "I'm sorry," she said as she got up. "I'm sorry, I'm sorry. I can't." She left the room, bitterly crying, and left David alone.

When Esther reappeared, hours had passed and the sun was starting to set. Her silent appearance in the corner of the kitchen so startled David that he almost dropped the dish he was using to prepare a large evening meal. Such was his focus on his cooking, that Esther gave no evidence as to how long she had been there.

"Streuth! I thought you were a ghost," he said, now calming down. "How are you?"

"I slept after a while," Esther eventually said, then looked at what David was making, the hearth strong in flames and the table in full flow of ingredients. "I'm sorry, I'm not hungry."

"You need to eat, Esther. I don't think you're well."

After a sigh, Esther nodded. "Can I help?"

"You can help cut those vegetables."

The meal came together without much needed to be said, both knowing each other's tasks and intentions, and both feeling the lack of talk comforting. Finally, with the darkening sky outside bringing in the night-time, Esther set alight some candles and completed setting the table, and David started to serve soup for the first course as Esther sat down.

"It's hot," warned David.

"I expected it to be."

There was a long pause in anything being said as Esther weighed up what she wanted to say.

David saw her starting to grin with thoughts that were not being aired and started to become self-conscious. "What?" he said innocently as he sat opposite.

"Nothing," she replied, starting to have her soup and not attempting to disguise the contrary to David's question.

Having started his soup, David put down his spoon when seeing her wanting to giggle. "There's a smirk across your face."

"Talking of being hot, I find it quite funny imagining you with Jezebel."

"I have you know that we got on really well."

Esther smiled with the absurdity: "I just can't imagine you making soup like this for her."

"Actually, she was quite homely."

"I can't see it: this Hollywood seductress beauty – and you making her soup." Esther then burst out giggling.

"Go on, laugh! You're just jealous that I almost pulled the hottest woman in the world."

This only made Esther laugh more hysterically: "I bet you would have made a lovely couple."

David, smiling, just shook his head: "I'm glad you approve. Have your soup, it's getting cold."

Esther could no longer control her laughing. It was as if her chest and lungs had gone into a convulsion. Yet each time she began calming down, she would look at David and burst out again. "And then – and then – you go and admit to – to the wrong woman!"

"Laugh, laugh! Go on laugh."

"What's so funny – is – is – the whole – the whole world believes it!" By now, tears were streaming down her cheeks and she could only speak with a squeaky, wispy voice: "That's so funny. That's so funny." It was at this moment that soup was being spilt. Even the spilt soup was seen as hilarious.

David could only be amused at her amusement and each time she looked at him, she would burst out laughing again.

"Come on, you've got to find this hilarious!" Esther eventually said. "Can you imagine her with a tambourine? Saying prayers?"

David started to laugh as well, with more from the strength of seeing Esther so uncontrollable in laughter.

Esther then calmed down and said with seriousness, "I think she was someone hard and controlling and manipulative."

"Well I think you're being judgemental. Let me tell you that I actually upset her. I got her crying, like a fragile girl."

"Upset her? What you?"

David nodded: "Well I once upset you."

"True."

"She became quite upset when we talked about her making money. She was genuinely hurt, like I had pulled her pigtails."

Esther at first showed no signs of amusement until she burst out laughing again, as if trying not to find it funny.

David was about to take a sip of his soup, but then muttered, "And then she wanted to have my babies."

There was a pause and they then simultaneously became uncontrollable with their laughing. Each time they looked at each other, one would provoke further outbreak until neither could remember why any of it was funny. It was after a while that they were calm again.

It was Esther who broke the silence: "And they all think that you and her – did it."

"You really believe we didn't?"

Esther nodded with no hesitation. "You may have fooled the world, but not me. Shows how arrogant they are to judge on what they think they know."

"But you did think that I had slept with those immature school girls – the ones you met on the bridge – on that – fateful day."

"I know. I'm sorry. I misjudged you on what I thought I knew. I was just as arrogant."

David started dishing the next course, silent in thought, and Esther became quiet as David served and passed it to her. Even when after he had served himself, Esther remained unmoving.

"But we're being judgemental now," David finally said, "against Jezebel."

"You fell in love with her, didn't you?"

David hesitated and then nodded. "I started to fall in love with the woman she was showing me; the image she wanted me to have of her."

"What will you do now?"

"Nothing."

"Nothing?"

"Nothing – she was cramping my style."

"Stop fooling around, I'm being serious now."

"Eat up, it's getting cold."

"I did say I wasn't hungry. What do you really think will happen now?"

"I really don't know and – really – at the moment, I don't care."

"Perhaps you should care – perhaps still be in touch with her."

"Like long, lost friends? Like on Facebook? She's done a real dirty piece of work on me. I'm not about to go and trust her again."

"Perhaps she needs someone like you."

"You're starting to change your tune."

"I'm trying not to be judgemental. Perhaps she was just a misunderstood girl, who needs someone to lead her. I thought that was what you were trying to say earlier."

"Jezebel? You're joking."

"Everyone's redeemable."

"Can we just drop the Jezebel theme here?"

"Certainly, Elisha!"

"Elisha?"

"It was Elisha, wasn't it? Or was it Elijah?"

"Elijah. Jezebel in the Bible wanted to have Elijah killed within twenty-four hours, after he utterly defeated her prophets of Baal – or at least scare him with the threat."

"And that made him run away. Can you believe it? He ran away even though he had performed one of the greatest miracles of the Old Testament. And he was still able to fret."

"And your point is?"

"You would have thought that Elijah would have felt emboldened, empowered, invincible, fearless – at least supported by God, and not feared her shallow threat. Perhaps God is in this somehow, David. Perhaps you're the one running away."

"Esther! Jezebel gets pushed off the battlements or something and dies splattered across the ground! She's even left there to die where she hit the floor!"

"Perhaps she needs someone like you to forgive her."

"I'm here with you, and that to me is what matters."

"Perhaps this is the place where God will whisper to you, as he did Elijah."

David stopped in thought. "You know, I haven't even prayed about it. That sounds awful."

"Well tomorrow is Sunday."

David nodded and took some dishes over to the sink.

Esther burst out chuckling: "I still can't see you and a Hollywood glamour star together."

"You're just jealous."

She could not stop chuckling as she came next to him, bringing more dishes.

"Come on, admit it," said David as he started to tickle her. "You're jealous!"

She shrieked with laughter as she furiously tried to shake David's hands off her: "All right! All right! I admit it! I'm jealous! I'm jealous!"

David, as natural as a loving husband, kissed Esther on her neck.

In response, Esther paused and turned to him, looking both shy and flattered, like a sweetheart teenage girl, kissed in the secret meadow by her dream boy, looking pleased and nervous, confident and fragile.

There was suddenly an air of quiet awkwardness.

David fumbled for words: "I'm sorry, I just – I just – I'm not wanting to – you see, I'm not – I don't know what I'm talking about. It just happened."

Esther became subdued and looked without a means to read her emotions, but then with tears running down her cheeks and a sudden and pleasant smile, it was able to see her complexity. "I'm sorry, David, sorry for all this food you've made, but – I need to sleep. I need to go and sleep now, really. I'm sorry." She crossed the room to leave, but then she turned. "I married the right man in the end, David. I didn't marry you because we weren't – I wasn't right at the time. And proper love has its timing." Esther looked forlorn and tired, but continued: "Perhaps the right time will come for you and Jezebel."

"What about between you and me?"

"Then we must talk about the future, but – but when I'm ready, and when I think you are ready."

Esther took the nearby heavy candle and, in its light, left without waiting for a reply. When she reached her room, she closed the door behind her and when settled at the desk in her candle light, she continued with her writing.

David could not fall asleep easily. His mind was full of twists and turns with every idea creating alternative ideas, with every plan creating alternative plans, every thought driving more thoughts. Sleep was driven far from being achievable, yet tiredness was never far away. In all that his mind looked at and analysed, Esther was always there. It was impossible to see life, the future, the New Earth, the New Heaven, without her.

He even started to fear the future would be taken away for reasons he could only conclude as ridiculous, but as tiredness invaded his senses, his very thoughts were becoming more confusing, and as a drunkard trying to get home, so was he trying to find sleep. Would God really be that spiteful to remove the very next day, detach the entire future from this moment when the prospect of hope was looming in his life? Would that be of amusement to the God who knew how to tear to shreds the path on which people walked? He had seen it in Africa. He had seen it in the night-time streets of London. He had seen it everywhere. It was possible for God to do anything He pleased. He could sweep Satan to oblivion with one simple whisper. He could take away the next day with one breath.

SUNDAY

When David awoke, the sun had not yet risen, but the morning was light enough to know it was imminent. He got up, made himself ready for the day, and quietly made his way to Esther's room.

The creaking floorboards were not sympathetic in his want to approach unannounced, but his quiet knocking at the closed door brought no attention. Opening it and standing at the threshold, he saw that Esther had already left for the day, leaving the room empty. As if this was a sign of their future, David became despondent as a senseless adolescent, as if this had been the moment to seize, but was seized from him. Then he saw the desk and the multitude of paper that showed extensive writing.

He crossed the room and stood looking at her handwriting,

meticulous, neat and artful, but knew he would not be proud of himself if he were to study her private work any further. There were also small boxes on the bedside cabinet, numerous different ones looking medicinal, and he decided he did not wish to treat Esther in this secret manner. Touching her pillows he could feel the moisture of her tears and felt anguished that he could not withdraw her pain.

Before leaving, David picked up her Bible, wondering what passage she was reading, and found the bookmark to be an old folded paper, worn and creased. His curiosity won over his guilt, and he opened it to expose a photocopy of a typed letter. He could not believe what he saw. It was incomprehensible how she had come across such an item. He sat down on the bed in shock, reading a letter about the death of his Grandmother. After a while sitting silently, David returned the letter, left her room and wandered the house hoping to find her.

In the kitchen was the remains of a simple breakfast with some water left in a glass and a plate of breadcrumbs. He did not need to look at the garden to know that looking for her there would be foolish, but he opened the kitchen door in the hope it would speed her return. It was then that he decided not to admit his discovery to prevent compromising his misdemeanour.

Over the long time it took to get a roaring fire, his hope of seeing Esther walking up the path started to wane. Perhaps something had happened. Perhaps God had taken away their future together. Perhaps God had a better place for Esther.

There was then an urgent, senseless desperation within him to search for her to console his own tortured mind, and he stepped outside, passed the herb garden and stood inspecting the scene like a detective for evidence of Esther's presence.

It was in that instant that Esther appeared through an arch in a broken wall. She walked as though a country girl walking dreamily in her own thoughts. She looked up and saw him and they both stood, looking at each other for a moment. Then Esther, without making any signs as to what she was thinking, drew near and finally stood in front of David, and they held each other in a close embrace.

"I will need you in a while," Esther said.

David nodded. "I'll be here."

"I still need to tell you something – when the timing is right."

David nodded again.

"But can we just have a quiet day? Just reading and being – reflective? Even if we don't say much, can we just spend the time together?"

"Well it is Sunday. It's supposed to be a day of rest. Too many people are too full of strain and pressure because society doesn't accept a day of rest, and psychological problems are on the rise. We should know our spiritual depth by knowing the value of a day of rest."

"Just a 'yes' will do."

"Yes, we can have a quiet day. I need to draw some water from our well, but let's say after that we have something to eat and then spend the rest of the day in the library?"

"That would be nice."

Neither spoke much while they ate, other than the practicalities of preparing and waiting on each other. Afterwards, they left the kitchen to freshen up and later came together in the library as agreed, settling into their chairs to relax and read. Except for the occasional smile, neither spoke as they concentrated on their personal study.

It was like this for over an hour when David noticed Esther looking at him surreptitiously from her reading. At first, he ignored it and appeared to be too engrossed in his own book. When he eventually looked up, she averted her gaze, and then looked at him to smile and give an innocent air. The same procedure was repeated, but when Esther did it a third time, she did not avert her gaze when he looked at her.

"As it's Sunday," she said, "I think we should have a Bible reading and sermon. What Bible passage are you reading?"

"I'm actually reading Genesis, the Creation."

"Go on then."

"Go on what?"

"Preach!"

"Preach?"

"Yes, preach!"

"Okay – this first Bible reading is taken from Genesis chapter one, starting at verse one and going on and on and on until I see you sleepy."

Esther laughed then asked him a serious question: "Do you think God really made everything in six days?"

"Why would God waste His breath telling us details that would probably dumbfound us? Whether Genesis is historical or not, I think the true lesson is that God wants us to respect and enjoy His creation, and to do so honours Him; being subservient, honours Him."

"A sermon in a nutshell."

"It's a pity that the history of creation ended up producing so many unthankful, mindless hooligans."

"Well hopefully, God has found a way to sieve them out."

"I hope God doesn't think I'm a mindless hooligan."

"God did throw Adam and Eve out of the garden for only eating the wrong fruit."

"They still disobeyed, as I still do on many matters."

"Well, let's hear what God has to say, then," Esther said, pointing to the Bible.

David read, giving great animation to his act. He read each day that was created, he read about the Garden of Eden, he read about Adam and Eve and he then reached reading of Eve's encounter with the serpent.

"And that's when I stepped in and ruined it all," interrupted Esther.

"Yes, but I was equally guilty. I just as much ruined it as well. At least you were persuaded by Satan. I was persuaded by you – and God punished me for being so inept."

"And then the human race began."

"And everything was then ruined."

They both remained quiet.

"I know, how about this," said David as he then turned many pages to start quoting from what he had found: "'You are a princess and your feet are graceful in their sandals'." Looking up at Esther, he saw her smile and blush. Then he continued, looking cheeky: "'Your thighs are works of art, each one a jewel. Your navel is a wine glass filled to overflowing. Your body is full and slender like a bundle of wheat bound together by lilies'."

"I know what you're doing!" exclaimed Esther. "It so happens I also have read the Song of Songs."

David ignored her and continued: "'Your breasts are like twins of a deer and – '." He received a pillow that hit his head from a laughing, blushing Esther, but he continued, all the while Esther was trying not to laugh and contain her embarrassment: "'You are beautiful, so very desirable. You are tall and slender like a palm tree, and your breasts are full. I will climb that tree and cling to its branches. I will discover that your breasts are clusters of grapes, and your breath is the aroma of apples. Kissing you is more delicious than drinking the finest wine.' Well that's no good – I don't drink wine."

They both looked at each other, wondering what the other was thinking, both with strange, innocent smirks.

Esther then said, reading from her own Bible: "'I stirred up your passions under the apple tree – the passion of love bursting into flame is more powerful than death, stronger than the grave – love cannot be drowned by oceans or floods. It cannot be bought, no matter what is offered. Never awaken love before it is ready'."

A silence came between them as they tried to study each other's eyes.

Then Esther broke the gaze and got up to sit at the piano: "Come! Let's have a few songs. You got a song book somewhere?" And she started to play a hymn.

David took one from the shelf and found the song Esther was playing.

"Come on then! Sing!"

When David sat beside her and placed the book before them, they both started singing the old Salvation Army songs, and the more Esther played, the more they sang with gusto and fun, happy in each other's company, nothing else on which to concentrate but each other, contrary to the direction each song was attempting to direct them.

After an hour of feeling refreshed with glowing lungs, David made a quick escape and came back in a short while wearing an old, long, black tunic and dark trousers, and carrying a battered cornet.

Esther looked aghast: "Wow! You look great!"

"It's an old Salvation Army uniform. What do you think?"

"Looks very original."

"It is. You know, I wore this along Mile End in London and stood outside the 'Three Blind Beggars', like William Booth, selling the *War Cry*. I even put on a beard to look like him."

"Really?"

"Yep, I raised quite a lot of money; not that I went to raise any, but I did get into some trouble with the General. You see I didn't exactly have permission and I didn't exactly have a licence."

"Oh."

"But people knew me through the beard and they enjoyed the fun of it. They even urged me to preach – particularly as William Booth's statue was nearby."

"You know, you do really look good in that. Is there one for me?"

"Of course."

"Are you going to play that?" she said, pointing to the brass instrument.

"Of course."

"I didn't know you could play."

"You don't know me well."

"Will you wait for me to change?"

"I'll try my hardest."

When Esther returned, David was spellbound. She paraded her Victorian long black dress, wearing a black bonnet, as though mocking the fashion of the catwalk.

"You look incredible, Esther, really," replied David.

"Well it's now your turn to impress me." She pointed to the cornet as she sat down on the pianist stool to be happily entertained. After he had started, Esther could only stop laughing when fatigued. "You sound like a cat being strangled!"

"I've been practicing very hard to sound like that."

But Esther continued to giggle.

"Wait a minute," said David. "I can do better. How about this?" He placed a record on the gramophone, one of his Grandfather's old records, and slow dance-hall music filled the room: "Would you care for a dance?"

"A bit naughty on a Sunday?"

Esther stood up beside David. They both held each other and started to gently sway to the music, each track taking them back to an era of the Second World War, when people would dance, cheek to cheek, unknowing if they were going to be alive tomorrow. The atmosphere changed. They changed. Those who had danced to this music, in their era, were no longer living.

They slowly danced further into the evening and they slowly danced further into the night, and then politely went to their separate rooms, without saying much about what was truly on each other's minds.

MONDAY

The next morning, David awoke from a gentle knock on his door: "Come in?"

Esther in her dressing gown entered and stood to one side, seeing David still in bed: "Can I come in?"

"Sure."

She came more into the room and sat beside him. "What book are you reading?" Esther asked, referring to the black old book on the bedside cabinet as if in search of a conversation.

"In Darkest England."

"Really?" Esther then held it and gasped: "It's an original: 'In Darkest England', by William Booth, Founder and first General of The Salvation Army."

"It's quite long, but it has a classical read to it."

"But I've read this as well – not an original, though."

"You have?"

"Yes!"

"Really?"

"Yes!"

"Who would read something like this?"

Esther was not listening: "I don't believe I'm touching an original."

"The owner of this place, before my Granddad, was Salvation-Army crazy and just collected anything that was about The Salvation Army. It's quite a heritage site." David watched Esther as she thumbed through the pages, recognising and reading some of the passages. "You know, I remember the argument we had about me becoming a Salvation Army Officer."

"Yes, I remember."

"I remember feeling that I could have become a Salvation Army officer."

Esther remained silent with her guilt.

"With you," David continued. "That was my vision at the time. I wasn't even a Christian then."

"And I ruined it."

"We both did. We both made decisions."

"I left you sitting there."

"But I didn't chase after you."

"I went back and got my rose and you had gone. I wanted the day to be perfect. It was spoilt because I felt that you didn't appreciate my present, and those girls came and ruined things and made you out to be just a big empty flirt. And there was me, walking down the aisle of Saint Paul's, to my groom, picturing the perfect life with you."

"You thought that?"

Esther huffed: "Yes – silly little girl I was. Quite the Jezebel."

"That's quite, well, I'm – I just –. Let's just let the past be the past. Let's earnestly place the future in His care."

"You have to forgive me, David."

"You have to forgive me as well."

"Why? What did you do?"

David tried not to answer, but his conscience took hold. Sullenly he replied: "I wanted Mark and Merry – out of the way."

"What!"

"I prayed for Mark and Merry to be out of the way."

They both looked at each other, breathing more heavily than usual.

"I'm sorry I ever prayed that prayer," continued David. "It was years ago."

Esther was growing angry: "You prayed? For Mark and Merry to be assassinated?"

"No, I never meant for it to come true."

"Well it has!" Esther shouted. "God answered your prayer! And I still love Mark and Merry!"

"Yes, I know you do."

"To you, they were just in the way?"

"It's not like that." David was becoming more and more dejected.

"To you, they *are still* in the way!"

David did not know what to answer.

"I need to be alone," was all Esther said, and she was quickly gone from the room.

Having got dressed, David searched the house, but Esther was nowhere to be found. Knowing she had to be in the gardens, he allowed Esther to roam and for her to return when she was ready. When time started to seep away into the afternoon, David felt the need to search and eventually found Esther in the graveyard, sitting on a broken wall nearby Joseph's grave.

As he approached, Esther made no acknowledgement of him, nor did she react defiantly against his approach.

"You okay?" David asked. "I'm sorry, please forgive me."

Preoccupied with her thoughts, Esther was not immediate with her reply. "We said earlier we need to forgive, and I need this place to be a place of healing." Esther looked up at him. "I need to dig out the weeds of bitterness before they take root in my garden. I need to stop wallowing in this mud of despondency. If I don't forgive – you, them, my parents – myself – then they win – those who want me to fail, win.

They want me to fail, they want me full of rage, and live in the same strife and hurt and hate as they do."

"But there is a need for justice, Esther, for defence, for law and punishment, for protection, to safeguard against cruelty."

"But what sort? What is true justice? What protection can be given against death itself?"

David had no answer.

"If only God could come here and finish it, before some self-obsessed, arrogant, evil, – social engineering, clever charmer thinks he can." They were both quiet for a while and then Esther continued with her new thoughts: "'Returning hate for hate multiplies hate. Darkness cannot drive out darkness, only light can do that.'"

"Is that a quote?"

"Martin Luther King – from the oppression of racism. 'Love is the only force that can transform an enemy into a friend – more powerful than any nuclear conflict.'"

"He was quite a man."

"Yes he was. 'The weak can never forgive. Forgiveness can only come from the strong'."

"Martin Luther King?"

"No, Mahatma Gandhi. You need to forgive me as well. I judged you wrongly and I held a gigantic grudge."

"It's all in the past now."

"You will need to forgive me in the future."

David was about to ask further, but Esther waved it off as to politely leave the future in the future. He then sat beside her saying nothing for a while until reading the words written across his Grandfather's stone: "'It is better to attend a feast than a funeral, as this is to remind you of what Heaven is'."

"'It is better to attend a funeral than a feast, as this focuses the mind'."

"That's on my Grandmother's grave in Africa." David scrutinised Esther's response to see if she would betray anything she already knew.

Esther just nodded, refusing to acknowledge she knew anything.

Not wanting to push the subject, David stood to leave. "Come on, let's not stay in this place of death, but make the day something to live for." He held out his hand for Esther and motioned in the direction of the Manor: "Time to go back?"

"What about going back a different route, a long, wide, wild route?"

"What about this way?" David then pointed in a certain direction through and beyond some trees and into the forest.

"Why that way?"

"Because it's a longer way round. I think we have to keep an eye on the weather. It might rain later."

"Well, let's risk it."

They walked through the garden, dreamily and aimlessly, not talking most of the time. They touched each other's hands in brief, endearing moments, along with gentle, sunlit smiles and subtle laughter caused by the thought that they were with each other. Eventually they had meandered into the forest, still neither of them saying much except with smiles.

It was Esther, having turned pensive for a while, who was the one to break the quiet between them: "If you want to know why I had doubts of becoming a Salvation Army Officer, it was because I was afraid."

"Afraid?"

"Of people. Afraid of not knowing the answers they really need, meeting the public, having to answer their questions, solve their problems. But I'm learning now that it's not about knowing the answers – it's all about what you do and believe when you don't know the answers. It's about the path you tread in life, where life itself is a mystery and so unknowable."

David nodded, understanding her sentiments: "I came to know God because I doubted the world. It's my doubting that makes me realise I need to have faith – because there's no proof in anything. You have to live each day in faith, because we can't know everything. No one knows all the answers. We're not supposed to."

"I wanted to help people, care for them, but I set my heart on joining the Foreign Office. I wanted to get involved in the peace talks – because I saw Israel as the key. How utterly important I saw myself – ridiculous really. What did I really expect to achieve? I wanted to stop the feeling that the world wasn't perfect, to clear out what my true father did to me and – and what my mother didn't do. All my drive to put the world right was because of their – this is, – I don't know what I'm saying. I just wanted everything to be perfect." Esther sighed, looked around her and then said, "It's so tranquil here. It's like another world, a secret, hidden, beautiful world. What did you think to my speech?"

"Your speech? In Jerusalem?"

Esther nodded.

"Well, apart from almost causing World War Three, it was quite all right really, quite a sparkle to it."

"You weren't even there!"

"Wish I had been. It must have been a great sermon, Esther. You could have been a great Salvation Army Officer."

"Really?"

"Really and truly. It's a pity about what the congregation did, that's all."

"I still wonder why all this happened to me?"

"You know, God didn't give a reason why Adam and Eve shouldn't eat from the forbidden tree, and they didn't question His authority. They accepted that was the way it was."

"I think it's going to rain," said Esther.

David looked at the sky and nodded: "I think we need to go back."

"I know I said to take the longest route, but can we now go back using the quickest?"

"We've done some sort of 'C' shape with our walk. I suppose we can go back in this direction. It will be shorter. Go this way?"

"You're the man, Adam. Take responsibility for me."

"Well, Eve, let's go this way – and I can blame you if it goes wrong."

Esther followed David through overgrown foliage and she used his wake with the parting of the plants, both becoming green with the stains they received. Esther's white cotton top and dress became visibly smeared. She stopped and looked up: "The weather's getting worse. It's going to rain any minute."

"Ouch!" David pulled his hand away from the bushes he was holding back.

"What?"

"I cut my finger on something." He looked at the blood over his fingers and saw, hidden in the branches, the broken fence and wiring his hand had grasped. "Look at that. It's barbed wire."

"You okay? You may need someone to look at that because the wire's rusty."

David nodded then looked up in the direction they were heading: "Wait!" His finger was forgotten as he studied the field beyond.

"What?"

Standing at the edge of an opening into a field of trees, David looked around him, trying to gauge his bearings with Esther close behind. "I've never been here before."

They had walked to the edge of a very large, overgrown apple orchard.

Esther was amazed: "You've never seen this?"

"No."

"Well, you've been missing out on a lot of apples."

They entered cautiously as if to trespass and then roamed through the deserted, abandoned orchard with increasing amazement. The branches were profuse with leaves and apples. Tall, unkempt grass surrounded them. There was no sound except for the soft breeze. It was as though no one had walked there for many decades.

"I'm hungry," said Esther. "Want an apple?"

David grabbed her hand just as she was about to pick one: "Let's not."

"It's only an apple. It's not the original, and the Bible doesn't actually say what fruit it was."

David smiled but looked cautious: "Let's just not."

Esther laughed: "It's an apple. What can it hurt, my Adam?"

"I'm not sure this field belongs to us and this apple could be infected with something. It's been growing without much attention. Anything could have happened."

"Don't be daft. This could be the tree of life. Here, just take a bite." With this, Esther reached out and picked one, holding it out to him.

Obligingly David took a bite, the juices spilling across his cheeks. He pulled away with disgust crossing his face and the bitten lump was spat out into the grass. "Oh, that's disgusting. It's very sharp. It's really, really bitter. Here, you take a bite."

"No thanks, not from your reaction."

"Aw! It even cut my mouth. The skin or something went between my front teeth and gums."

"Are you okay?"

"Ah, don't worry, I'll still be all right for kissing all the girls."

"Are you still all right for kissing me?"

"Try and stop me."

"All right," she said with laughter, and she ran off, looking behind with a playful girlish smile, enticing David to chase. "You'll have to catch me first!"

In his pursuit, he caught her, but with a sense of fun, Esther, becoming a weight, brought them both down to the wayward grass where they started to kiss, more and more impassioned.

Then the rain started, at first a drizzle, but not enough to stop them kissing. They continued as the rain started to get heavier, and it was only when the rain became torrential that, with laughing, they had to get up to run to the nearest tree that would shelter them: a large tree with a thick, mighty trunk having branches allowing nothing to grow underneath, such was its wide coverage. Only sticks, stones, moss, mud and dirt were under its reach. They looked out from the shadow of the tree's protection at the heavy pounding of rain, breathless with healthy lungs.

David stood as to see all of Esther, her white dress, smeared with grass, now grey with being drenched and portraying her figure as it clung tightly to her immaculate shape. Some of his dirty blood from his fingers was on her. "I need to go back to London tomorrow," he said, clearing his thoughts.

"Yes."

"I'll come back, trust me, and we'll be together. Everything will be different."

"I want everything to be the same. When you're back, I will need to tell you something."

"Tell me now."

"No, it's not right. Just come back and I will tell you."

David nodded.

"Don't be long though as none of us know how long we have."

"I won't be a lifetime away, not anymore."

It was at this precise moment that Esther almost opened her mouth to say her life was not far from ending, but she suddenly refused to see David cheerless and depressed, and hoped David would return sooner than planned; otherwise, she knew, she could be dead the next time she was to see him. She decided she would be happier to have David happy in order to make her cheerful, and that was what she needed. "My lover is an apple tree, the finest in the orchard," she eventually said, coming closer.

David thought for a moment: "Song of Songs?"

Esther nodded and continued: "I am seated in his shade and his fruit is delicious."

"Esther – ."

"Feed me, as I am utterly lovesick."

After a moment of looking at her eyes, David replied with his own quote, both knowing this was out of context, but continued anyway. "My bride, my very own, you are like a private garden, a clear fountain just for me. You are a beautiful orchard, bearing precious fruit and life."

It took a moment, but when they were finally in an embrace, they then kissed tenderly.

The rain stopped, the sun suddenly came through as though trying to catch their attention, but they continued to kiss and hold each other, the damp of their clothing not being of any care. They gently and gracefully lowered to the ground, kissing all the way down and did not stop until they fully realised what was happening between them and succumbed to the pressure of their attraction, the momentum of their desire.

One more last time

The Manor was empty. David was gone, returned to London to resurrect his work, but that had been many weeks ago and Esther's hope of seeing him again was starting to wane. She was now deteriorating visibly and physically in pain and stiffness. To get out of bed was now a chore she never thought she would ever have to experience at her age. An old face with bruised eyes would stare back at her from the mirror.

Esther sat at the desk in her bedroom, looking out of the window into a day of sunshine. She had just read her own writing of the past she had before becoming adopted, of her memories of the awful abuse from her father and her mother's willingness to not see it. The memories came back as though the pain had seared into her subconscious processes to lie dormant until now, but Esther saw plainly how this had driven her to turn events of life from bad to good, no matter the pain. Even at the subliminal levels of her inner-self, she could finally let go, steeped in the total forgiveness that her soul now attained.

Her Bible was open before her at a particular Psalm, and knowing the depth and richness of her emotions, her passion, her guilt, her ambitions, her demise, she picked up her pen and continued writing.

How much longer, Lord, will you forget me? Will it be forever? How long will you hide? How long must I be confused and miserable all day long? How long will my enemies keep beating me down? Please listen, Lord God, and answer my prayers. Make my eyes sparkle again, or else I will fall into the dark sleep. My enemies will say, "Now we've won!" They will be greatly pleased when I am defeated. But I trust your love, and I feel like celebrating because you will rescue me. You have been good to me, Lord, and I will sing about You. I will sing of your great mercy and saving grace. I will praise you for your forgiveness of the ruin I have made of my life. Psalm 13.

A group of powerful men angered by a lone female, whom asks to forgive each other, must surely be seen as weak if they do not have the power to forgive that lone female. Instead, they murder her husband and daughter through their childish, bullying antics, driven by their zombified infection of hate. Only those who do not wish to know God would not forgive. They have a soulless, death-directed vengeance coursing through their dead veins. But what worth am I to them to cause this retribution?

On one of my diplomatic visits, I once stood on top of rubble that had once been the home of a Palestinian. It had been destroyed by the Israeli Army, but he never once showed me any grief, even with his young daughter in his arms. 'Do your utmost to live without distorting what Jesus taught,' he told me. 'Never let hate master you.'

This is not one sided. While she wept, an Israeli mother told me of her forgiveness of the suicide bomber, and all the psychological conditioning behind it, that killed her beloved son. 'Survival of the fittest is for those who have the strength to forgive,' she said, 'otherwise the human race is doomed to extinction by way of revenge and bitterness. You need to forgive to stop the bitterness from eating away your health, but also to know what it means to God to forgive you.'

In all the hostility of the conflict, I met countless people, Jewish and Palestinian, who prayed and worked for peace. If only they could walk as a march, together, arm in arm, in demonstration to the world of their desire for freedom from strife.

We are commanded to forgive our enemies, even when we don't understand their motives, even when it takes us to the extreme of our spiritual endurance with our enemies regarded as being 'the others' or being 'them'. But the forgiveness of friends can be harder to achieve than to forgive enemies, as the harsh betrayal of a friend is more brutal and bitter. Judas was not the only disciple to betray Jesus; they all did. They all ran and left Jesus to be betrayed, tortured and killed.

We are all miniatures to Him, in this toy village He has lovingly put together, brought about by His fervour and zeal to create something magnificent and beautiful. But how would you feel if these miniatures thought nothing to your brilliant creation, judged you on their perceived ideas, even spat in your face? Even just plain ignored you, no recognition you exist?

We all have prevaricated, lied, gossiped, cheated, delighted in the scandals of others, been jealous, experienced hatefulness, judged with cruelty, but there is a far, far bigger scandal that we fail to recognise. It is a scandal invisible to virtually all of us, yet we are all infiltrated with it. It has many dark facets, yet it is the most singular greatest crime there is. It is the offence of not putting Him first. No matter how sinful other people are, you can never see yourself as beyond the need to be penitent.

You see, we offend Him with our self-sufficiency, of not relying on God, with the arrogance we know better. We wound Him with our worry and stress, when we believe God will not be there to rescue us, that Jesus will never calm the storm. We fill Him with sorrow when we are without a holy anger, a holy anger against suffering, when we work more for our own home than for God's Kingdom. We demonstrate our disrespect when not being thankful and not making time to be still and be joyful. We can even be lazy and tepid and not care for His creation or concerns, or be over busy, working without rest, thinking we can do better than Him, that He cannot cope without us. We can have the belief we place Him first, when our prayer life and Bible study is so lacking.

I now see the importance I placed in myself, as if God's kingdom would collapse if I were not to exist. God's kingdom will not be diminished or enhanced in any way by anything I think I can achieve. God is by far so greater than this and by far so greater than I. God commands us to be still and know the enormity of who He is. Never think you can do something to outcompete what God has done or is yet to complete. Leave God to do His own work, as He will do it far better. I was like a little girl so focused on a childish egg-and-spoon race. What does it gain a man if he inherits a castle but to see a view of despondency and ruin and poverty from his window? But what character does it truly show of a man who works hard to eliminate impoverishment, just to improve his own view from his window? My life should have been more of an apprenticeship to work on my character, my nature.

None of us has honoured God persistently, perpetually, unceasingly completely, from every second to every second, every year to every decade, throughout our entire life. That's the true great scandal in us all. We are all guilty as charged. Who are we to argue? What have we been able to achieve and compare to what He has accomplished?

So be still, do not fear and know that God will conquer, even has already conquered all things with His absolute love and justice. With all that you have gone through, all that you are going through, as wrong and fallible as you are, our Heavenly Father is not afraid to love you. He will even run to you if you turn to Him. His is the greatest forgiveness there is and He will even celebrate your return. But fear the largest offence — that of not searching for Him, not even to want to search, to have a willingness to live without Him, our Creator, with all that is happening and will happen. In all, there is the sin in not allowing God to be God.

I found comfort in David in the last days we had together. It was a time perfect for us to repair our damages as we took down our barriers and slowly forgave each other. I even went as far to deny my cancer and dreamed that God had planned a future for us both. That was when it went wrong.

I did not tell David of my illness. I was in denial, I missed my chance and I now accept I will not see David within the time I have left. I have no idea as to who is reading this, if anyone. I hope he can forgive me. We foolishly spent that week trying to open the doors that were closed shut from decisions made long ago. God only allowed us our absolution before I am to die. What a kind God for patiently allowing us this time. It was like one more last chance. But we transformed this time into a gradual sophisticated decline of our barriers; cheek with cheek, skin with skin, soul with soul; an innocent, young, almost beautiful breaking down of highly evolved, deeply complex defence mechanisms of two intelligent, rational, spiritual people. We were repeating the rebellion of the Garden of Eden in our microworld.

In a sacrificial sign of true love, Jesus horrifically and grotesquely suffered to an extreme that I even fear to contemplate. He died, taking my punishment, treating my sin, my brokenness from Him, as something abominable to His nature. He is seriously against me having sin, but He is serious in giving me absolution. This is no little, easy, insignificant gift to lightly dismiss. How arrogant would it be if I did, and how much I would truly be missing? He would far prefer a passionate, truly repentant person, even if they had sinned deeply, than a lukewarm Christian. Even though we all do spit in His face, He is eager to forgive.

To please God is to trust Him to use our strengths, our failures, and to trust

Him with all our unanswered questions, to keep being faithful, even when to give up appears logical. So to those who murdered my husband, Mark, and my beautiful daughter, Merry, do not rejoice against me, because I will rise again. I sit in darkness, but God will be my light and I wait for God to save me. I am doing my best to please my Lord, my Saviour, and to have Him pleased is my reward alone. I place my trust in His abilities to use what I have done and will do, to increase the world to a better place by not infecting it with hatred. I will not stoop low enough to cause harm to anyone, and if I have, I ask forgiveness, as I forgive with my deep commitment and truthfulness, those who have viciously killed my beloved family, and those who had been placed as my parents and were to care for me in my vulnerability. I can now have the strength to let go of all my hurts, pains, anguish, to forgive even myself for ruining God's Kingdom with my misdirected Christianity, and be grafted into God's family and seeing things His way. True love is a promise, an absolute commitment, covenantential, but know that no matter what God says, He does believe in divorce. He allows it because one day He will be rid of all those who need to be pruned from life and discarded, like an abusive husband from his long-suffering wife, like an unfaithful bride from a perfect groom.

Find an Israeli who has the strength, the boldness, the tenacity, the audacity to forgive horrendous depths of loss and bereavement, and learn from them. Find a Palestinian who has the strength, the boldness, the tenacity to forgive excruciating sadness, affliction and bereavement, and learn from them also. Bring the two together. Find more. Find more and more, and perpetuate this hope. Build an army of people with hope-filled character. Even the leaders must gain friendship with each other as equals. Peace cannot come from a business deal. That is how you break the conflict. That is how you solve the Middle East. Blessed are those found doing the work God has assigned to them when Jesus returns. Blessed are those who work tirelessly for peace, as they shall be God's very own children.

God will see things through, and He wants you to win. He wants you to win your race. God's universal plan is to bring together people who can forgive and live for peace, and to separate them from those who cannot. Endure and overcome to see your name in His book and to eat from the tree of everlasting life.

Abraham's Daughter

In the dark of night, in a plain, old car, as unimportant as many other cars, was the Israeli Prime Minister, Ananiah Schuber, seated as a passenger in the back with his chief security advisor, Baruch Gendel, driving. They eventually stopped at an entry barrier to a vast factory estate to have security guards check their identities, and continued onto the estate when allowed to do so. The immediate front courtyard divided into numerous driveways and alleys within the industrial complex, and the one they drove along took them to the side of a plain, old building that had its entrance secluded from any major view.

Having parked near to the door, Baruch looked into the mirror at his distinguished passenger and acknowledged they were where they were supposed to be at the correct time, just by simply saying, "Sir."

"Let's do this, Baruch." Ananiah turned to the parcel on the seat to his side and held onto it.

Both men got from the car and went through into the safe house, into the foyer where men in suits acted as security.

"This way, sir," ushered Baruch.

Following Baruch, the Prime Minister was taken to a door that was guarded, and again their identities were checked to be finally let inside the room beyond; an unclean room full of old, discarded furniture. The Prime Minister looked at Baruch with amusement: "He's in here?"

"Yes, sir. Welcome to Narnia." Baruch then pointed at an old, large wardrobe.

"I see."

Baruch opened the doors and reached within the hanging coats to unlatch a secret lock to the back revealing a dark stairwell descending to a basement. Both disappeared down these steps and entered a reception and surveillance room where two armed guards had been playing cards while computer screens showed views of a particular room. The guards checked the identities of the new arrivals and one guard took the parcel that the Prime Minister carried and un-wrapped it to discover two books. After a thorough inspection, there was nothing deemed inappropriate and the books were given back to the Prime Minister, without an apology.

They were allowed to enter the final foyer containing five prison cells, but only one cell was occupied, the occupier unknown for the thick, heavy, windowless door that contained him to this inner chamber. Standing before it, Baruch announced the name of the criminal: "Prime Minister, General Cole Blitzer."

Ananiah nodded and when the door had been unlocked and opened, he went through alone and locked within.

Lying on a simple bed within a commodious prison cell was General Blitzer. He stood up and became expectant of an appeasement from the new arrival.

"Sit down," flatly asked the Prime Minister.

The prisoner remained standing for a while longer, but, with a continued judgemental glare, he relented and sat at a table, angry for allowing the chance for reconciliation that was rejected.

Ignoring this quiet rage, Ananiah sat opposite, placing both books beside him. For a while, he just sat contemplating the captive.

"Ananiah, why am I here? Where is here?"

"You need not concern yourself as to where you are. Even I don't know where we are, except to say it's a MOSSAD safe house in a country that is not Israel or Palestine. It isn't even in the Middle East. Even the host country doesn't know we're here."

"Why am I here? We used to be perfect friends, Ananiah. What have you done?"

"No Cole, what have *you* done?"

"I was born to be the man I am: a General in the army of Israel, and I am proud of that, and I am proud to be an Israeli, a Jew, an Israelite, a Hebrew."

"Does that make you immune?"

"Immune?"

"You really think you're immune when we have a great secret service to protect us?"

"What lies have you been fed?"

"We had an insider, someone close beside you."

"Who?"

"What do you care? We know all about Operation Melech."

"I know nothing of what you are talking about."

"Stop lying! MOSSAD infiltrated your confidence. We know everything! We know you were planning to destabilise everything in order to gain glory."

The General stood up and shouted: "Glory for Israel! Glory for our God of Abraham!"

The Prime Minister shouted back: "No! Your glory! Your hidden self-glory masked by religion!"

"Two thousand, three thousand years ago, I would have been a hero."

"On your orders you had murdered two innocent people: a hard working husband who helped little children as they went for surgery, and a beautiful daughter who was mad about angels! But not only did you want them killed, you wanted to obliterate them with your hate and vengeance! You even used a Palestinian to do it! You gave orders to use starburst bullets – bullets that obliterate internal organs – on a dedicated surgical man and his beautiful daughter! How contemptible! How evil! Just because Esther Whyte said a few things you didn't like!"

The indignation was clear on the criminal's face. He sat down still in defiance: "And what are you to do? Allow our enemies to continually tear at our limbs, our heart?"

With harshness to his whispered voice, the Prime Minister gave his answer: "Secretly, in my inner core, I see this as wrong, all wrong. People are to fight and rebel when it is right, for the right cause, in the right way, but this isn't it, Cole, this isn't it."

"Have you gone timid? Are you weak? You are sickening! What leader are you? We had the perfect moment for our total victory, Anaiah! I tell you, my plan has not been abandoned just because I am in here. I have trained and motivated the entire Army. I have nurtured each soldier. They will complete my mission."

"Your mission?"

"We will grind *our* enemies like grain, smash them like a bull with iron horns and bronze hoofs, crush those nations and bring their wealth to *our* God of Jacob, Israel! There will be a glorious New Jerusalem! We will build *our* Temple to the God most high! All other nations will bow down to *us*! We will conquer our entire Promised Land! We will live in *our land*! Of honey and wine! As it should have been from the start! The sacrifices must recommence! It is written! It is *our* destiny! What man are you to understand the Law of Moses? You are deluded and you bring shame to our religion."

"You are the one who brings shame to our religion."

"Don't *you* use religion against me! You're not even religious!"

"Not when there are religious people like you." Ananiah held out the bigger of the two books: "Take it. It's our Scriptures."

The General was confused as he took it.

"Don't you think it strange that after Jesus came, the Temple was destroyed, block by block, until nothing was there, as predicted by Jesus; that the Levite Priesthood was obliterated; the Royal line from King David, severed? We believe our conquering Messiah will come from this ancestry, our Scriptures foretell it – but there is no ancestry any more. There is no Royal line. There is no longer the Levite system. It's shattered, broken, defunct. There have been no sacrifices for almost two thousand years since Jesus was crucified – even though our Law of Moses commands it."

The large book was pushed away by the General in a disparaging, disagreeable manner.

"Don't you think that odd?" continued Ananiah, not daunted. "The whole system collapsed soon after Jesus. No wonder the Christians think of Him as the King, the Priest, the ultimate sacrifice, the Saviour – the conquering Messiah – who will come next in the clouds. Even I see the logic. And won't God be insulted if we resume our defunct Old Testament sacrificing, making a statement that we don't deem Jesus' sacrifice as good enough?"

General Blitzer continued to look rebuffed, repulsed almost.

"Our Scripture – you will have plenty of time to study it. I'll even get you a New Testament."

The prisoner took the book again, viewing it with contempt as something to be considered as hard labour.

"You will find I have highlighted the Book of Esther."

"Who are you to lecture me on our sacred writings?"

"To save her people, Israel, from being massacred, Queen Esther, the Queen of Persia, an Israelite, had to decide to stand before her husband, the King, with the threat of death if he was not pleased. And Esther Whyte had to decide to stand before us. And look what we did!"

There was no reply accept simmering rage.

"Esther wins in the end, Cole; not you. She's the one who saves her people. Esther had to decide, and she chose courage. You have lost everything, because you chose 'self'."

"You have nothing on me. You know it. The trial will be a farce."

Ananiah was livid: "I will see to it that you are put on trial for sedition and attempting a coup – as a minimum! You could have initiated the next major world war. Esther Whyte made that speech that changed everything, disrupted everything, and she didn't even know it. She even thought she had destroyed the Peace Process!" The Prime Minister had to stop for a moment to sigh away his feelings into the air, shake his head, and then felt able to continue. "She had the courage to stand in front of all us men, and say, from the heart, things that were cutting and wounding, and true; words from whom she believed to be her God, the God of Abraham. And what did we do? We acted like a rabble, pelting her with rocks of our own anger and indignation, our own sordid righteousness and judgement, acting like little, arrogant children, cruel and spiteful – where she acted on the truth. Us, the chosen people, God's chosen people, God's supposed chosen people, and she was preaching to us our own Scripture! Do you realise that? Our own Scripture! I think you'll find that she acted more like a daughter of Abraham than any of us. She even uses Psalm thirteen against us – a Psalm your righteous, mighty King David of Israel wrote – and he couldn't even keep his penis in his pants! Read the Book of Esther; read Psalm thirteen; read it!"

"She has nothing to do with Abraham! She is nothing to do with our chosen race."

This time, the Prime Minister stood up and spoke down to the General in his resentment: "Don't limit God! Don't you think He's totally capable of doing things beyond your limiting ideas of Him? God can make descendants out of stones if He chooses to. He made the flesh and blood that we *all* are! So who are you? The Messiah Himself will rescue us and transform Jerusalem one day, but in His image and Kingdom; not yours!"

"This is absurd! This is an insult! You don't even believe!"

"And don't get the idea of revenge, because you will never be given the opportunity."

The prisoner stood defiantly to retaliate: "Revenge? I want justice! I want – "

"Revenge! That's all you are stewing about! All you want is revenge over Esther. Well you can't have it. You will never be able to have it.

Six weeks ago, Esther Whyte was discovered dead. She died of cancer, alone, in a dilapidated house, never knowing the true reason behind her suffering, and all of her writing, expressing her dying feelings until her last breath, has been rushed into publication. Everyone wants to read it." The Prime Minister then pointed to the second book on the table. "Read the enormity of her words as she forgives you, unknowing of who you really are. And you think she had no right to ask us to forgive? Read her childhood. Read how filthy and degraded she felt because of the abuse she received from her father. And she forgave him! And she had the excruciating, towering strength of character needed to forgive the worst of all people – you! But what is so endearing to so many people is that she felt worse about realising she could have lived with God more in her life. She did have the right to ask us to forgive – just as God has the right, not only because He is the highest there is and the creator of all, but because of Jesus and the cruelty He endured by us and His forgiveness. Self-righteousness will be the monumental evil that will destroy mankind's future!" Ananiah then pointed to the book again: "If I were to be in my right mind, I would have you eat it page by page. I hope her forgiveness tortures you, Chol Blitzer – you unholy warrior."

Blitzer was dumbfounded as he looked at the title: *The Perfect Shade of Whyte.* "I did not expect this," he mumbled with etched confusion and dismay.

"Perhaps you would have fared better if you had joined The Salvation Army. They fight their war without assassinating anyone and they allow people their freedom to choose. By the way, the peace talks are going ahead in spite of you, to spite you. Israelis and Palestinians are holding a march of peace."

"It won't last."

"Not with people like you in the world. But know this: a woman, dying on a bed, with only the power of her words, has totally annihilated your entire arsenal that would have jeopardised world peace, and she didn't even get to know it."

"And now she's dead! The punishment from God she deserves!"

"You are just sick."

"She was just too perfect. People wanted her shot because it annoyed them."

"Really! How rousing! How inspiring! Is that something a glorious leader would say?"

There was no response.

"Tell me! A great empowering, inspiring General would say something like that? Is that something Abraham would say? Moses? King David? Is that what Jesus would say? Mohammed?" Ananiah just looked at the quiet man opposite, disappointed. "No, you're just a simple school boy never having learnt to mature in character."

The internal feuding and bitterness within the imprisoned man stayed within him, being held back by his own anger blocking his words.

"I pray that God doesn't harden your heart." Ananiah Schuber then knocked on the door to be let out. The door was opened and the leader of Israel stepped from the chamber, giving consent to have the door locked.

The General remained standing for a long while, bewildered as to what just happened, manacled by his own stupefaction.

Whoever is without sin ...

The television studio was empty and dark early that particular morning; the stage and audience seating, silent; the room, void of furnishings; the equipment, unpowered.

But during the course of the morning, staff arrived to arrange items for the stage as for flowers and backdrop, and technicians fussed over cameras, lighting and sound. Cleaners did what they could around the thrum of activity, tidying the audience arena of three hundred seats. Central on the stage was comfortable seating for a relaxed style of an interview.

The presenter arrived and discussed issues with the producer while the finishing touches were being added, and it was then time for the audience to be allowed in as the small band of musicians set themselves to one side and practised.

With the chatter of the public finding seats and being ushered by attendants, a man appeared on the stage and waited for the command through an ear-piece to start. He ushered people to settle as soon as possible and started to explain the proceedings, while the large television cameras became manned. When ready, he then expertly encouraged and enthused the audience to clap and cheer and become lively, so that when he had vanished to the side, and an announcement made of the chat show host's imminent entrance, they all hollered in excitement.

"And so, ladies and gentleman, for your show tonight, here's Mike Milligan!"

Sprite and enthusiastic, a smartly dressed man came bounding from the backstage to effervesce his frivolity before the audience and cameras: "Well, here we are again! What a week the News has been! What's happening in the world today? Well let's forget all that as we bring to you my guests for tonight and get to know their latest news. Later on I'll be chatting to Mel Gibson and George Clooney!" It was with the bright manner of the interviewer that the audience showed their enthusiastic anticipation, but then they settled for the man to continue: "But first! Please! Everyone! Welcome our very own – Jezebel!"

It was with the same enthusiasm that the audience cheered as the attractive woman stepped elegantly from behind the backdrop curtains, happy to walk across the stage and be invited to sit as kindly welcomed by the host.

The room became silent and Mike Milligan, with both him and his guest now comfortable, smiled and greeted the female: "So, Jezebel, welcome."

"Thank you, thank you for inviting me. How are you?"

"Fine, thank you, but how are you? We really haven't seen or heard from you for quite some time and everyone wonders what happened to the great Jezebel."

"I'm still here. You'll see me again. I've been hidden away writing music and I have a new film that will be in the making in the New Year. So – "

"Well, glad to hear it! We boys were missing you!"

This provoked a few wolf-whistles and accolades from the males in the audience.

"Well, thank you," she replied when they had quietened, "but certain things have changed with me."

"You're referring to your name change, of course."

"Jezebel was my stage name. I wanted to be someone who I stepped into to become a star, and I would do anything, say anything, get into whatever bed to get it, to become that star I was driving myself to be."

"But, you were very poor as a child, very poor."

"Yes – yes, I was. Being in poverty is so – so awful – and I compromised myself to get out of it. But now I'm no longer going to be part of – those explicit films. I'm going to be in films that actually require skill in acting, and my next film, a British Dickens film, is something I'm going to sink my teeth into. So, yeah, I'm forging ahead. I'm dropping the name Jezebel, and going to be known by my real name: Meredith Hope. I learnt that the Biblical Jezebel has a – an unbecoming end because of her cruelty."

"Really? What happens?"

"She gets thrown off a high wall and left there."

"Well, I can see why the name may not appeal anymore."

"One way or another, all nasty people eventually get thrown off, even if it's just to be remembered after their death as someone not worth mourning."

"And that's not the only change, so I've been told."

"Well, yes, I'm going to become a soldier of The Salvation Army." As if proud of herself, Meredith smiled with a beaming grin.

"Absolutely fantastic – isn't she, ladies and gentlemen!"

There then came applause from the audience, which simmered down to hear more.

"A total transformation," continued the host, "but people are saying this is another publicity stunt. What do you say to such people?"

Meredith shook her head and shrugged. "I can no longer control what people think. I was foolish to think I could. Slowly, I'm learning there's more to life than me. But to answer them, yes, you can be dedicated at the start, and then your faith can wane. That can still happen to me. You can start on the road to salvation, but never finish it. So, as I have a reputation for changing my fashion a lot, if I've got through two or more years in The Salvation Army, then this is giving people an idea of my dedication. The proof my faith is real is in how it has changed my life. That's my answer to such people – and I'm hardly front-page news anymore. It's quite liberating."

Not having had the chance to interrupt, as was his custom, Mister Milligan sat almost taken by surprise by his guest's answer. He quickly recovered and with a jovial but mocking manner then said, "So you're going to wear the uniform and swing that tambourine, and sing hallelujah songs!"

Meredith was not deterred: "In two weeks' time, yes, I will become a soldier of The Salvation Army, in full uniform, and be part of the work for the homeless in California."

Milligan tried a second time to provoke a retort, as disguised in his cheekiness: "Is it not going to be hard to become a Sally Ann lass, with all the – well, quite frankly, all the porn you've done? I'm surprised they've allowed you to join."

Meredith paused and then, with maturity, gave her reply: "There will never be a day when I can ever be proud of what I've done, and, yes, it is going to be hard, but it's going to be worse on the day I will be truly judged. I'm not proud of what I was, but I'm trying to be the person God will be proud of."

"So what made you want to change? Is this going back to last year with your, well, quite public and moving apology for lying about David Kingsley?"

"I lied about him as a spiteful, self-centred, horrible little girl. I saw the person I was and I turned my life around, and if someone like me can do it, an ex-prostitute, anyone can. William Booth urged his congregation to reach out and save souls, and go for the worst. Well *I am* the worst. I'm still appalled of the pain I must have caused David, and it hurts that he died before he heard my confession."

"And yes it was a moving confession, but people were cynical to think it was your acting skills for another stunt."

"I'm going to die one day, so do I want to take people down into spiritual poverty and filth, or do I want to leave behind a better place because of what I did, with my life that's on loan? Like Rahab, the prostitute in the Book of Joshua who changed, I am changing."

"A lot of lads are – "

"People might see me as filthy, but, believe me, I have spent so much energy, all my life, to find love, good love, worthy love, true love, but it's so hard to find. Real love is so scarce. People saw me for what they could get out of me, and I saw people for what I could get out of them. But, you see, now knowing Christ, I know what it is to be loved and to love. Someone who is forgiven much – will love much."

"Well, I – "

"You see, I'm the adulterous woman. I am to be stoned to death. That's what I deserve, but Jesus stopped them, because no one is worthy of judging. Who really has the right to throw the first stone? Anyone who has built an entire, fully functional universe probably can. He understands me completely – but He showed me mercy."

"But really you – "

"So you see, Jesus has become everything to me. I know my life here on Earth will be remembered for all those photos and films, but none of it will be remembered by a great God and I can be free of my past to seek Him and know Him in my future, to know Him in my now. I will not allow a bad past cause a bad future."

She paused, but her host did not interrupt and remained quiet, now intrigued.

"I was setting myself up to be my own god, living in the disgusting glory of me, my own self-importance, as ignorant as I was. I became addicted to me. I was my own false god. And so sickening my rebellion, Jesus went through unthinkable torture, physical and social, and died, horrifically, on the cross – in my place, because I can't meet God's standards or purity in my own strength for God to call me His own. I want to be that woman who washes His feet with her tears and wipes them dry with her hair, to be forgiven, to wash His hair in oil, to act beautifully for Him, to love others sacrificially as Jesus loves. But! I will still be amazed and extremely relieved to find myself in Heaven, because it's not about what I decide and think about Jesus – it's all about what Jesus decides about me."

Again, in her pause, the host did not interrupt.

"I want to work on Earth as though for Heaven. I will live life as part of God's loving plan, to enjoy life, to enjoy His company, to enjoy people, to make them feel life is worth living. I want as my reward, my God to look into my heart and be pleased and not be ashamed, as I am not ashamed to say that Jesus is my redeemer. That is what I now say to people. Search for God like a child yearning for a good father. Wait patiently with an active hope for His return and for the eternal life that our Lord Jesus Christ is passionate to give you. Always stay within the boundary where God's love can reach you. Never rely on what you think you know, but trust Him with all your confusion, with all your hopes, with all your heart, as that is His biggest delight. In His timescale, He has conquered everything, so be joyful. He turns water into vintage wine for a great celebration. He will turn the greatest calamity into the greatest miracle. My Heavenly Father will get His glory. He is not afraid to love me. Wait and see."

Obituaries and Legacy

In a heart-felt interview soon after David Kingsley's death, **Jezebel** sobbed with all sincerity when she admitted on television that there had been no committed adultery and that she had lied about an affair in the belief it would boost her popularity. She soon reverted from using her stage name, Jezebel, and returned to being called her real name of **Meredith Hope.** She became a Salvation Army Soldier a year later. After two years of acting some of her best parts, writing some of her most moving songs and working for the homeless of California, she volunteered for full-time service in The Salvation Army and became an Officer. When she died, her funeral was attended by film stars and dignitaries, and equally those who had lived on the streets. As a Salvation Army Officer, she wrote many popular Christian songs for small young choirs, many of which are still sung today. On her grave is inscribed, 'My grace is sufficient for you, for my power is made perfect in weakness, 2 Corinthians 12:9'.

General Chol Blitzer was put on trial, found guilty on a charge of sedition of the first degree, and spent fifteen years in prison with his title being stripped from him. He then spent the final three years of his life under house arrest. He never gave up hope in someone following in his mission and resurrecting operation Melech, and his dying words were of the coming time of Israel's vanquish over all the world history for the persecution of the Jewish nation. His sons and daughter disowned him.

Isaac Hammon resigned his Cabinet position two years after the death of Esther Whyte and had to withdraw from politics under suspicious and controversial circumstances that were never fully explained to the public. After becoming divorced, he eventually became a recluse, old and frail. When he died twenty-four years later, people knew little of him and the news was of little significance. His grave is now discarded and is attended to by only the burgeoning depths of weeds and moss and litter.

When the news broke that **Esther Whyte** had died, personnel of the Foreign Office and all foreign dignitaries then present requested a pianist, and in commemoration sang Esther's theme tune, 'It is well with my soul'. Esther's funeral service was held at The Salvation Army Hall in her home village of Havenly and she was cremated in the local crematorium with a plaque of her name alongside that of her husband and daughter, having the inscription of, 'For such a time as this'. People still occasionally visit and lay flowers on a nearby table that had to be set there to cater for this simple, quiet homage. It is said even today at certain private functions at the Foreign Office that the piano is played and ended with Esther's hymn.

Jonathan Bishop passionately continued his work with the homeless and used his financial skills to better their lives. He counselled businesses to work more ethically and with more responsibility for the health of wider issues of society that profit and financial reward never satisfy, and eventually became a consultant to the Government to start constructing the framework of the now on-going 'Business Balance'. He also became a great advocate for the book of Leviticus and frequently made public speeches from the book, portraying God's rule should cover not only cleanliness of soul and mind in sacrificial living and its fulfilment in Jesus' death, but also be involved in the practicalities of society, and the reason and importance there is in fasting and feasting. Remaining a staunch Salvation Army Soldier until he died, he never relinquished his professional and personal position with The Salvation Army as his primary career. He died with cancer while working on the 'Business Balance' project. 'Investing in Jesus brought me eternal profit,' is inscribed on his grave.

Noah Kofee gained a managerial degree at Kings College, London, and with Jonathan Bishop's support and consultation, Noah resurrected David Kingsley's enterprise, becoming himself a renowned figure, building up the lives of those who had been struck with poverty. Not only did he successfully restore the electronics initiative along with the academic lessons for national exams, but also over many years, started and enhanced the catering school for cooking and waitering that was able to train to the standards expected by the most exclusive hotels and restaurants in London. Noah died peacefully in his old age, never having become a Salvation Army Soldier, but passionately attended meetings since the week that David Kingsley died. On his gravestone is written: 'Now gone to a Great Meeting'.

David Kingsley's funeral service was held at The Salvation Army Hall, Oxford Street, London, and special arrangements were made for his burial to be beside his Grandfather at Halcyon Manor. On his gravestone it is inscribed, 'For David served God's purposes in his generation'.

William Booth, born on the 10th of April 1829, made his last public speech at the Royal Albert Hall in May 1912 to thousands of Salvationists. He died soon after at home in Hadley Wood, London, 20th of August of the same year, having spent his life dedicated to serving others in aid of their dire needs without discrimination that created the Christian movement, The Salvation Army. His street preaching outside The Blind Beggar Public House, Whitechapel, London, of June 1865, attracted the attention of other preachers who invited him to preach at a

Christian outreach within a tent erected in Vallance Road Gardens. This event was eventually to launch The Salvation Army. His wife, Catherine, died of cancer on the 4th of October, 1890, dying in his arms at Crossley House, Clacton-on-sea. When William Booth died, twenty-two years later, his horse-drawn funeral procession stopped London with ten thousand Salvationists following and forty Salvation Army bands playing. He is buried with his wife at Abney Park Cemetery. By the time of his death, The Salvation Army movement had reached fifty-eight countries. His legacy is such that The Salvation Army is at work in one hundred and twenty-four countries, performing the same ideals of spiritual warfare as his fiery preaching inspired.

Mastery of Hate

A Novel, by Neale Hambidge

'What is life? Life is all about making it worth living – not just for yourself, but for others, for everyone, to make them feel worthy and to feel worthiness in doing so, to respect and enjoy God's creation.' *The Perfect Shade of Whyte*

But this is not complete.

What if as individuals, as communities, as nations, we decide to thwart this aim, to work in the direction of self, to reverse any worthiness, to live as though others are less important?

What if someone, a society or country imposes their power, their laws on others, who always takes, always damages, always disregards?

What true justice can there be? What punishment would be right?
How far do we go to protect those we love or are vulnerable?
How far should we go to preserve our safety, our way of life?

What should be done, ethically, to deal with such individuals, such communities, such nations? What can be morally done to prevent increasing disparagement, cruelty, violence, abuse, revenge, murder, genocide, evil?

The full force of forgiveness cannot be the full answer.

What if dealing with this evil produces an even worse evil?

What if righteousness becomes so twisted that no one realises it has become insane malevolence?

A British Asian young woman, a new Police Constable, is fast-tracked to become a Detective, but she knows she is not suited to the job. Despite her feelings, she becomes that one person who comes to know all the pieces needed to solve a horrific series of murders in the Medway Towns of Kent.

With it, she uncovers more than what she expected.

What she uncovers goes beyond the crime and deep into the psychology of us all, for what she finds is the study into the most evil man that will ever live.

She needs to have a Mastery of Hate to keep sane.

A Life Less Real
A Novel, by Neale Hambidge

From the end of WWII, grew Praxis, a pioneering British research establishment. Its work was to advance technology to benefit mankind.

In truth, there was a deeper secret mandate.

A sociology experiment is conducted on the student population of a London University College and establishes that technology is so advanced, it is indistinguishable with being human. A male student, his true nature unknown even to himself, falls in love with a beautiful girl.

Sean Heyward, an MI6 officer, uncovers a link this experiment has to the work of Praxis and discovers this secret formula to machine intelligence and agility has been leaked to an opposing foreign power.

Dr Liz Kating, a leading engineer, becomes fearful for the danger now posed to the public and the destructive impact on a civilisation that cannot keep pace with technology.

A power struggle erupts within Praxis and an attack is made to reclaim the machine during the annual Valentine's Ball. But discovering his true nature, he fights back to protect the one he has come to love.

Britain and America learn of the battle, and chase and fight across the English countryside to capture and own the fleeing machine, but he realises there is more at stake than his own survival.

Can a computer learn what mankind has miscalculated?

And what technology is mankind?

Million Miles a Minute
A Novel, by Neale Hambidge

Two brothers infatuated with motorbikes since they could stand...

A death of a woman in the dusk of a Sunday evening...

The end of a long school summer holiday...

This is the world on the first day of her new school, as Jessica finds there is strangely no bullying as ruled by two enigmatic brothers. No one is able to join their magnetic clique until they learn that Jessica has always had a fascination for motorbikes.

And then she is drawn into an emotional, deep attraction, torn between the two as she sees them tearing themselves apart for different ambitions. With rough and rugged handsomeness, the older endeavours to become the number one Superbike World Champion, and the young and more steady has honour in joining the transport police.

> As brothers they are inseparable,
> but torn by different aspirations.

Is it always right to pursue your dreams and happiness at the consequence of others? Is the cost worth travelling at a Million Miles a Minute?

Printed in Great Britain
by Amazon

33554185R00255